MW00998303

Major Ingredients

The Selected Short Stories of Eric Frank Russell

Edited by Rick Katze

The NESFA Press
Post Office Box 809
Framingham,MA 01701

FIRST EDITION
Second Printing-March 2003

International Standard Book Number:
1-886778-10-8

For H. Allan Katze,
a loving father who died
far too soon.

Acknowledgments

The Introduction by Jack L. Chalker is original to this volume.
The Afterword by Mike Resnick is original to this volume.
"Allamagoosa" *Astounding Science Fiction* May 1955.
"And Then There Were None" *Astounding Science Fiction* June 1951.
"The Army Comes to Venus" *Fantastic Universe Science Fiction* May 1959.
"Basic Right" *Astounding Science Fiction* April 1958.
"Dear Devil" *Other Worlds* May 1950.
"Diabologic" *Astounding Science Fiction* March 1955.
"Fast Falls the Eventide" *Astounding Science Fiction* May 1952
"Hobbyist" *Astounding Science Fiction* September 1947.
"Homo Saps" *Astounding Science Fiction* December 1941.
"I Am Nothing" *Astounding Science Fiction* July 1952.
"Into Your Tent I'll Creep" *Astounding Science Fiction* September 1957.
"Jay Score" *Astounding Science Fiction May 1941.*
"Last Blast" *Astounding Science Fiction* November 1952.
"Late Night Final" *Astounding Science Fiction December 1948.*
"A Little Oil" *Galaxy Science Fiction* October 1952.
"Meeting at Kangshan" *If, Worlds of Science Fiction* March 1965.
"Metamorphosite" *Astounding Science Fiction* December 1946.
"Minor Ingredient" *Astounding Science Fiction* March 1956.
"Now Inhale" *Astounding Science Fiction* April 1959.
"Nuisance Value" *Astounding Science Fiction* January 1957.
"Panic Button" *Astounding Science Fiction* November 1959.
"Plus X" *Astounding Science Fiction* June 1956.
"Study in Still Life" *Astounding Science Fiction* January 1959.
"Tieline" *Astounding Science Fiction* July 1955.
"The Timid Tiger" *Astounding Science Fiction* February 1947.
"Top Secret" *Astounding Science Fiction* August 1956.
"The Ultimate Invader" Ace Double D-44 1954("Design for Great-Day" *Planet Stories* January 1953).
"The Undecided" *Astounding Science Fiction* April 1949.
"U-Turn" *Astounding Science Fiction* April 1950.
"The Waitabits" *Astounding Science Fiction* July 1955.
The Editor's Introduction by Rick Katze is original to this volume.

Contents

Editor's Introduction 8
Introduction *by Jack L. Chalker* 9
Allamagoosa 13
And Then There Were None 24
The Army Comes to Venus 76
Basic Right 102
Dear Devil 124
Diabologic 152
Fast Falls the Eventide 168
Hobbyist 183
Homo Sap 206
I Am Nothing 214
Into Your Tent I'll Creep 230
Jay Score 237
Last Blast 250
Late Night Final 287
A Little Oil 314
Meeting at Kangshan 330
Metamorphosite 342
Minor Ingredient 386
Now Inhale 399
Nuisance Value 418
Panic Button 472
Plus X 488
Study in Still Life 529
Tieline 549
The Timid Tiger 555
Top Secret 571
The Ultimate Invader 584
The Undecided 633
U-Turn 656
The Waitabits 665
Afterword *by Mike Resnick* 698

Major Ingredients

The Selected Short Stories of Eric Frank Russell

EDITOR'S INTRODUCTION

Eric Frank Russell has always been one of my favorite authors.

His stories first appeared in the science fiction magazines of his day. They are disappearing as the paper oxidizes. A collector can read them but they are no longer truly available to the general public.

His stories have been reprinted many times in countless anthologies as well as appearing in his own collections. Unfortunately they are now out-of-print.

This is what motivated me to produce this volume with lots of help from lots of friends. This project has taken several years of my free time but I believe that it has been time well spent.

This book contains choices. I looked at every story that Eric Frank Russell wrote over his career. It was easy to exclude some of them at first glance. By the time I was down to 40, I was feeling some pain. The list was finally narrowed to 36 stories, all of which I truly wanted in the book. You will find thirty of them in this volume.

They are listed alphabetically instead of chronologically. Wanting to begin the volume with "Allamagoosa" which won the Hugo for best short story and ending the volume with "The Waitabits" which you will have to read to understand why it should appear last was one consideration. Whim was another.

Rather than talk about each story, I suggest that you read them. They speak for themselves and show the measure of the man.

Both Jack L Chalker in his introduction and Mike Resnick in his afterward talk much more succinctly about Eric Frank Russell.

Unfortunately his novels are also long out-of-print. They and those 6 stories should really be reprinted in a permanent form. But that is the subject of another book which does not exist . . . yet.

Rick Katze
Norwood Mass
July 2000

Eric Frank Russell

by Jack L. Chalker

Eric Frank Russell (1905-1978) stands as a unique figure in the history of twentieth century science fiction, a writer who wrote a unique brand of *genre* story, who had enormous popularity and influence on many later SF authors, yet was and continues to be reviled or dismissed by many of his contemporaries and more of his critics, who often accuse him of doing things he denied doing.

Born in Britain, he spent virtually his whole life there, rarely, if ever, coming to the United States, yet his style and markets were such that most, including British SF people growing up in the World War II years such as John Brunner, thought he was an American. He was the first British SF author to find great success in the larger U.S. market and attain major status as a writer, and this appears to have fostered a good deal of resentment amongst his peers who often had problems breaking into any market except the limited British one. His style was breezy and crisp, more Heinlein than Stapledon, and he deliberately sought not so much to write like Americans (he said in letters) as to avoid being specifically British because, as he once wrote this writer, "I wanted to be read by everyone and not pigeonholed."

His style and clever plotting caught the fancy of John W. Campbell, Jr., the legendary editor of *Astounding* (later *Analog*) from 1938 until his death in 1971, the man who basically "discovered" and developed Heinlein, Hubbard, van Vogt, H.L. Gold, Arthur C. Clarke, and many others now considered the monuments of SF. It is a mistake, though, to believe that Russell's basic style and outlook was pandering to Campbell; indeed, Russell had sold to *Astounding* before Campbell took over (starting with "The Saga of Pelican West," 1937) and his pre-Campbell and those stories not sold to Campbell over the years are no different than the ones he did. Charges that he pandered to Campbell's alleged "Earth chauvinism," in that the humans in his tales tended to be every bit as smart or smarter than the aliens, is questionable on several grounds. Without taking the time to go point by point, I think it's better to take Russell at his word that he and Campbell were simply very much like-minded people, although I point your eyes to "Dear Devil" if you think he's an Earth Chauvinist Pig for one quick example. Russell also noted that, like most science fiction writers, he was never really writing about aliens, but rather about various aspects of human society. In the main, the trouble some have with his aliens is that they're not aliens at all; they're *people.*

This is nowhere more evident than in his best-known work, the novel *Wasp*, in which Earth is at war with a vast Sirian interstellar empire that, well, is more or less just like us even if they look a bit different. Even their culture isn't any more different than, say, England and Japan's. Russell was too old for combat when World War II came along, but after a number of Army jobs in London he wound up somehow in the Ministry of Slick Tricks, as he often described it, trying to work out schemes for messing up the enemy. Russell, however, was assigned to the Far East desk, and none of his dirty tricks ever got to be played on Japan, so he played them after the war in *Wasp*, making the Japanese the Sirians and even going so far as to simply reverse the first and third syllables in the Japanese Secret Police to get the Sirian Secret Police.

What *does* emerge rather clearly from Russell's writing is a total contempt for bureaucracy and authority. Try "A Study in Still Life." His heroes, too, are often off-kilter themselves; they are social misfits whom their bosses are generally happy to be rid of, and they don't play by the rules. "Plus X" is the ultimate type of this sort of troublemaker, and he turns out to be *so* much of a pain that even the enemy can't stand or handle him. That story, by the way, was originally an 80,000 word novel called *Next of Kin* which Campbell couldn't take because he was full up on novels; he suggested a bare bones paring that became this gem of a novella. Later, the same novel was rejected by many U.S. publishers, but Ace said it would take a 40,000 word version as half an Ace Double and so there's a middle length version called *The Space Willies* around as well. Oddly, reading them separately, you can't figure out what's added or what's cut.

Often, even when Russell's heroes try to do the right thing strictly by the book, they get their clocks cleaned. Pity the poor Navy officers just trying to get their paperwork right and proper in the Hugo winning "Allamagoosa." Or, worse, the poor administrators on a remote world eyeball to eyeball with a real potential alien enemy who simply are trying to order supplies in the proper manner in "Top Secret."

Most of his adult life, Russell was a Fortean at one time even heading the Fortean Society, a still-existent group who try and chronicle all those unexplainable things that happen every day all over the Earth. Not just UFOs, but rains of frogs, nutty apparitions, ice cubes falling on a desert oasis, you name it. Russell himself admitted to the belief that we were somebody's property, or at least somebody's play toys. He doubted that this "somebody" was human because he didn't believe humans could possibly maintain an organization this disciplined and secret, although he admitted to the possibility that all the bizarre things Forteans chronicled might just be bureaucratic bumbling on a cosmic scale. *Sinister Barrier*, his first novel, is a strictly science fiction attempt at showing just how this Fortean view might work and what might well lie behind it sixty years before *The X Files*.

Russell is often called by some the father of libertarian science fiction as well. Many libertarians think of "And Then There Were None" as the best expression of the soul of their philosophy. Like many, Russell was more this bent in the abstract than in reality. I've seen letters where Russell on the one hand attacks the Foreign Office vociferously with lots of shots at Inland Revenue (the British version of the U.S.'s IRS), yet in another written in the same month launches an impassioned defense of the British National Health Service. Still, if you're not enamored of government, bureaucracies, or your own bosses, you'll find a kindred soul here.

Russell had a much wider range than he's usually given credit for, a range only hinted at in this excellent but more representative than authoritative collection, and an imagination that was an often the awe of contemporary writers. The work that I believe influenced much of *my* own work is certaintly his novel *Sentinels from Space*, an unappreciated *tour de force* that, in the guise of a typical Russell adventure story, throws more curves and twists than any other work of its length. Nothing at all is wasted; it's tight and lean as a Chandler mystery, yet it manages to address the problems of racism and other forms of prejudice in a futuristic society in which a percentage of people have various forms of ESP powers, and a knock your socks off double ending that is about as cosmic as you can get. If you've never read it and can get hold of a copy, you should read it.

This book brings you many of the clever, often hilarious, occasionally sentimental tales of Russell, including equal doses of the familiar and the undeservedly forgotten. What you will find is that none of these exist for their own sake; instead, each of them is built around a single, often clever and highly original central idea, and most of them don't go where you *think* they're going to go. Try "Metamorphosis" for a synthesis of the best of both—you won't figure *this* one out unless you've already read it, and even as you admire his twists and turns it'll startle you. And, too, it's certainly nice to see "Panic Button," a legendary tale never before collected to my knowledge, which is the quintessential Russell central idea type of story. If *you* were the alien commander, just what the heck would *you* do? And if Earth humans are the be-all and end-all as John Campbell decreed, then why the fate of the poor protagonist in "Into Your Tent I'll Creep"?

Russell was involved off and on in British SF fandom from the late Thirties until he pretty much quit writing in the field and devoted his remaining years to Fortean matters in the Sixties. As such, he came to British SF conventions and was always delighted to correspond with new and up-and-coming science fiction writers and give them some advice and much encouragement. The plot, the idea, the concept was vital to him. "Keep them reading and involved," he told young would-be's. "If nobody's awake for the sermon, you might as well not deliver it." A number of writers who came up in the late Sixties and early Seventies owe a lot to him, including obvious ones like Alan Dean Foster and yours truly. I once asked him if any young *British* SF writers asked him for advice and he wrote back, "Yes, but, you see, over here they can't *admit* it."

His letters show the same wry humor, sense of satire and skewed view of the universe he'd begun with forty years earlier. If he'd wanted, he could have continued to write more tales, and those of us who loved him and his work spent a lot of time and effort encouraging him to do so, but basically he'd simply lost interest in doing it any more.

His voice remains so different, his stories remain so readable, because, as Dickens noted a century plus earlier, if you write about real people they will transcend their dates and times. It is good to have his best short fiction now preserved in a quality edition. And this is by no means close to even half of what he wrote, much of which remains uncollected. Just as his novels occasionally resurface (and *Wasp* seems to have a regular life all its own) it would be wonderful if, eventually, all his worthwhile short fiction was preserved in this sort of collection. In the meantime, enjoy this one, which does contain much of his best. If you haven't read them in a long while, be prepared to relive the sheer *joy* of these tales so often missing in today's SF; if this is your first time through, you're in for quite a treat. He remains one of those rare authors I go back to now and then and reread, and he never disappoints me.

Allamagoosa

Astounding, May 1955

It was a long time since the *Bustler* had been so silent. She lay in the Sirian spaceport, her tubes cold, her shell particle-scarred, her air that of a long-distance runner exhausted at the end of a marathon. There was good reason for this: she had returned from a lengthy trip by no means devoid of troubles.

Now, in port, well-deserved rest had been gained if only temporarily. Peace, sweet peace. No more bothers, no more crises, no more major upsets, no more dire predicaments such as crop up in free flight at least twice a day. Just peace.

Hah!

Captain McNaught reposed in his cabin, feet up on desk, and enjoyed the relaxation to the utmost. The engines were dead, their hellish pounding absent for the first time in months. Out there in the big city four hundred of his crew were making whoopee under a brilliant sun. This evening, when First Officer Gregory returned to take charge, he was going to go into the fragrant twilight and make the rounds of neon-lit civilization.

That was the beauty of making landfall at long last. Men could give way to themselves, blow off surplus steam, each according to his fashion. No duties, no worries, no dangers, no responsibilities in spaceport. A haven of safety and comfort for tired rovers.

Again, hah!

Burman, the chief radio officer, entered the cabin. He was one of the half-dozen remaining on duty and bore the expression of a man who can think of twenty better things to do.

"Relayed signal just come in, sir." Handing the paper across, he waited for the other to look at it and perhaps dictate a reply.

Taking the sheet, McNaught removed the feet from his desk, sat erect and read the message aloud.

Terran Headquarters to Bustler. *Remain Siriport pending further orders. Rear Admiral Vane W. Cassidy due there seventeenth. Feldman. Navy Op. Command. Sirisec.*

He looked up, all happiness gone from his leathery features, and groaned.

"Something wrong?" asked Burman, vaguely alarmed.

McNaught pointed at three thin books on his desk. "The middle one. Page twenty."

Leafing through it, Burman found an item that said: *Vane W. Cassidy, R-Ad. Head Inspector Ships and Stores.*

Burman swallowed hard. "Does that mean—?"

"Yes, it does," said McNaught without pleasure. "Back to training-college and all its rigmarole. Paint and soap, spit and polish." He put on an officious expression, adopted a voice to match it. "Captain, you have only seven ninety-nine emergency rations. Your allocation is eight hundred. Nothing in your logbook accounts for the missing one. Where is it? What happened to it? How is it that one of the men's kits lacks an officially issued pair of suspenders? Did you report his loss?"

"Why does he pick on us?" asked Burman, appalled. "He's never chivvied us before."

"That's why," informed McNaught, scowling at the wall. "It's our turn to be stretched across the barrel." His gaze found the calendar. "We have three days—and we'll need 'em! Tell Second Officer Pike to come here at once."

Burman departed gloomily. In short time Pike entered. His face reaffirmed the old adage that bad news travels fast.

"Make out an indent," ordered McNaught, "for one hundred gallons of plastic paint, Navy-gray, approved quality. Make out another for thirty gallons of interior white enamel. Take them to spaceport stores right away. Tell them to deliver by six this evening along with our correct issue of brushes and sprayers. Grab up any cleaning material that's going for free."

"The men won't like this," remarked Pike, feebly.

"They're going to love it," McNaught asserted. "A bright and shiny ship, all spic and span, is good for morale. It says so in that book. Get moving and put those indents in. When you come back, find the stores and equipment sheets and bring them here. We've got to check stocks before Cassidy arrives. Once he's here we'll have no chance to make up shortages or smuggle out any extra items we happened to find in our hands."

"Very well, sir." Pike went out wearing the same expression as Burman's.

Lying back in his chair McNaught muttered to himself. There was a feeling in his bones that something was sure to cause a last-minute ruckus. A shortage of any item would be serious enough unless covered by a previous report. A surplus would be bad, very bad. The former implied carelessness or misfortune. The latter suggested barefaced theft of government property in circumstances condoned by the commander.

For instance, there was that recent case of Williams of the heavy cruiser *Swift*. He'd heard of it over the spacevine when out around Bootes. Williams had been found in unwitting command of eleven reels of electric-fence wire when his official issue was ten. It had taken a court-martial to decide that the extra reel—which had formidable barter-value on a certain planet—had not been stolen from space stores or, in sailor jargon, "teleportated aboard." But Williams had been reprimanded. And that did not help promotion.

He was still rumbling discontentedly when Pike returned bearing a folder of foolscap sheets.

"Going to start right away, sir?"

"We'll have to." He heaved himself erect, mentally bidding good-by to time off and a taste of the bright lights. "It'll take long enough to work right through from bow to tail. I'll leave the men's kit inspection to the last."

Marching out of the cabin, he set forth toward the bow, Pike following with broody reluctance.

As they passed the open main lock Peaslake observed them, bounded eagerly up the gangway and joined behind. A pukka member of the crew, he was a large dog whose ancestors had been more enthusiastic than selective. He wore with pride a big collar inscribed: *Peaslake—Property of S.S. Bustler.* His chief duties, ably performed, were to keep alien rodents off the ship and, on rare occasions, smell out dangers not visible to human eyes.

The three paraded forward, McNaught and Pike in the manner of men grimly sacrificing pleasure for the sake of duty, Peaslake with the panting willingness of one ready for any new game no matter what.

Reaching the bow-cabin, McNaught dumped himself in the pilot's seat, took the folder from the other. "You know this stuff better than me—the chart room is where I shine. So I'll read them out while you look them over." He opened the folder, started on the first page. "K1. Beam compass, type D, one of."

"Check," said Pike.

"K2. Distance and direction indicator, electronic, type JJ, one of."

"Check."

"K3. Port and starboard gravitic meters, Casini models, one pair."

"Check."

Peaslake planted his head in McNaught's lap, blinked soulfully and whined. He was beginning to get the others' viewpoint. This tedious itemizing and checking was a hell of a game. McNaught consolingly lowered a hand and played with Peaslake's ears while he plowed his way down the list.

"K187. Foam rubber cushions, pilot and co-pilot, one pair."

"Check."

By the time First Officer Gregory appeared they had reached the tiny intercom cubby and poked around it in semi-darkness. Peaslake had long departed in disgust.

"M24. Spare minispeakers, three inch, type T2, one set of six."

"Check."

Looking in, Gregory popped his eyes and said, "What the devil is going on?"

"Major inspection due soon." McNaught glanced at his watch. "Go see if stores has delivered a load and if not why not. Then you'd better give me a hand and let Pike take a few hours off."

"Does this mean land-leave is canceled?"

"You bet it does—until after Hizonner has been and gone." He glanced at Pike. "When you get into the city search around and send back any of the crew you can find. No arguments or excuses. It's an order."

Pike registered unhappiness. Gregory glowered at him, went away, came back and said, "Stores will have the stuff here in twenty minutes' time." With bad grace he watched Pike depart.

"M47. Intercom cable, woven-wire protected, three drums."

"Check," said Gregory, mentally kicking himself for returning at the wrong time.

The task continued until late in the evening, was resumed early next morning. By that time three-quarters of the men were hard at work inside and outside the vessel, doing their jobs as though sentenced to them for crimes contemplated but not yet committed.

Moving around the ship's corridors and catwalks had to be done crab-fashion, with a nervous sideways edging. Once again it was being demonstrated that the Terran lifeform suffers from ye fear of wette paynt. The first smearer would have ten years willed off his unfortunate life.

It was in these conditions, in midafternoon of the second day, that McNaught's bones proved their feelings had been prophetic. He recited the ninth page while Jean Blanchard confirmed the presence and actual existence of all items enumerated. Two-thirds of the way down they hit the rocks, metaphorically speaking, and commenced to sink fast.

McNaught said boredly, "V1097. Drinking-bowl, enamel, one of."

"Is zis," said Blanchard, tapping it.

"V1098. Offog, one."

"Quoi?" asked Blanchard, staring.

"V1098. Offog, one," repeated McNaught. "Well, why are you looking thunderstruck? This is the ship's galley. You're the head cook. You know what's supposed to be in the galley, don't you? Where's this offog?"

"Never hear of heem," stated Blanchard, flatly.

"You must have. It's on this equipment-sheet in plain, clear type. Offog, one, it says. It was here when we were fitted out four years ago. We checked it our-selves and signed for it."

"I signed for nossings called offog," Blanchard denied. "In the cuisine zere is no such sing."

"Look!" McNaught scowled and showed him the sheet.

Blanchard looked and sniffed disdainfully. "I have here zee electronic oven, one of. I have jacketed boilers, graduated capacities, one set. I have bain marie pans, seex of. But no offog. Never heard of heem. I do not know of heem." He spread his hands and shrugged. "No offog."

"There's got to be," McNaught insisted. "What's more, when Cassidy arrives there'll be hell to pay if there isn't."

"You find heem," Blanchard suggested.

"You got a certificate from the International Hotels School of Cookery. You got a certificate from the Cordon Bleu College of Cuisine. You got a certificate with three credits from the Space-Navy Feeding Center," McNaught pointed out. "All that—and you don't know what an offog is."

"Nom d'un chien!" ejaculated Blanchard, waving his arms around. "I tell you ten t'ousand time zere is no offog. Zere never was an offog. Escoffier heemself could not find zee offog of vich zere is none. Am I a magician perhaps?"

"It's part of the culinary equipment," McNaught maintained. "It must be because it's on page nine. And page nine means its proper home is in the galley, care of the head cook."

"Like hail it does," Blanchard retorted. He pointed at a metal box on the wall. "Intercom booster. Is zat mine?"

McNaught thought it over, conceded, "No, it's Burman's. His stuff rambles all over the ship."

"Zen ask heem for zis bloody offog," said Blanchard, triumphantly.

"I will. If it's not yours it must be his. Let's finish this checking first. If I'm not systematic and thorough Cassidy will jerk off my insignia." His eyes sought the list. "V1099. Inscribed collar, leather, brass studded, dog, for the use of. No need to look for that. I saw it myself five minutes ago." He ticked the item, continued, "V1100. Sleeping basket, woven reed, one of."

"Is zis," said Blanchard, kicking it into a corner.

"V1101. Cushion, foam rubber, to fit sleeping basket, one of."

"Half of," Blanchard contradicted. "In four years he has chewed away other half."

"Maybe Cassidy will let us indent for a new one. It doesn't matter. We're O.K. so long as we can produce the half we've got." McNaught stood up, closed the folder. "That's the lot for here, I'll go see Burman about this missing item."

The inventory party moved on.

Burman switched off a UHF receiver, removed his earplugs and raised a questioning eyebrow.

"In the galley we're short an offog," explained McNaught. "Where is it?"

"Why ask me? The galley is Blanchard's bailiwick."

"Not entirely. A lot of your cables run through it. You've two terminal boxes in there, also an automatic switch and an intercom booster. Where's the offog?"

"Never heard of it," said Burman, baffled.

McNaught shouted, "Don't tell me that! I'm already fed up hearing Blanchard saying it. Four years back we had an offog. It says so here. This is our copy of what we checked and signed for. It says we signed for an offog. Therefore we must have one. It's got to be found before Cassidy gets here."

"Sorry, sir," sympathized Burman. "I can't help you."

"You can think again," advised McNaught. "Up in the bow there's a direction and distance indicator. What do *you* call it?"

"A didin," said Burman, mystified.

"And," McNaught went on, pointing at the pulse transmitter, "what do you call *that?*"

"The opper-popper."

"Baby names, see? Didin and opper-popper. Now rack your brains and remember what you called an offog four years ago."

"Nothing," asserted Burman, "has ever been called an offog to my knowledge."

"Then," demanded McNaught, "why did we sign for one?"

"I didn't sign for anything. You did all the signing."

"While you and others did the checking. Four years ago, presumably in the galley, I said, 'Offog, one,' and either you or Blanchard pointed to it and said, 'Check.' I took somebody's word for it. I have to take other specialists' words for it. I am an expert navigator, familiar with all the latest navigational gadgets but not with other stuff. So I'm compelled to rely on people who know what an offog is—or ought to."

Burman had a bright thought. "All kinds of oddments were dumped in the main lock, the corridors and the galley when we were fitted out. We had to sort through a deal of stuff and stash it where it properly belonged, remember? This offog-thing might be anyplace today. It isn't necessarily my responsibility or Blanchard's."

"I'll see what the other officers say," agreed McNaught, conceding the point. "Gregory, Worth, Sanderson, or one of the others may be coddling the item. Wherever it is, it's got to be found."

He went out. Burman pulled a face, inserted his earplugs, resumed fiddling with his apparatus. An hour later McNaught came back wearing a scowl.

"Positively," he announced with ire, "there is no such thing on the ship. Nobody knows of it. Nobody can so much as guess at it."

"Cross it off and report it lost," Burman suggested.

"What, when we're hard aground? You know as well as I do that loss and damage must be signaled at time of occurrence. If I tell Cassidy the offog went west in space, he'll want to know when, where, how and why it wasn't signaled. There'll be a real ruckus if the contraption happens to be valued at half a million credits. I can't dismiss it with an airy wave of the hand."

"What's the answer then?" inquired Burman, innocently ambling straight into the trap.

"There's one and only one," McNaught announced. *"You* will manufacture an offog."

"Who? *Me?*" said Burman, twitching his scalp.

"You and no other. I'm fairly sure the thing is your pigeon, anyway."

"Why?"

"Because it's typical of the baby names used for your kind of stuff. I'll bet a month's pay that an offog is some sort of scientific allamagoosa. Something to do with fog, perhaps. Maybe a blind-approach gadget."

"The blind-approach transceiver is called 'the fumbly,' " Burman informed.

"There you are!" said McNaught as if that clinched it. "So you will make an offog. It will be completed by six tomorrow evening and ready for my inspection then. It had better be convincing, in fact pleasing. In fact its function will be convincing."

Burman stood up, let his hands dangle, and said in hoarse tones, "How the devil can I make an offog when I don't even know what it is?"

"Neither does Cassidy know," McNaught pointed out, leering at him. "He's more of a quantity surveyor than anything else. As such he counts things, looks at things, certifies that they exist, accepts advice on whether they are functionally satisfactory or worn out. All we need do is concoct an imposing allamagoosa and tell him it's the offog."

"Holy Moses!" said Burman, fervently.

"Let us not rely on the dubious assistance of Biblical characters," McNaught reproved. "Let us use the brains that God has given us. Get a grip on your soldering-iron and make a topnotch offog by six tomorrow evening. That's an order!"

He departed, satisfied with this solution. Behind him, Burman gloomed at the wall and licked his lips once, twice.

Rear Admiral Vane W. Cassidy arrived right on time. He was a short, paunchy character with a florid complexion and eyes like those of a long-dead fish. His gait was an important strut.

"Ah, captain, I trust that you have everything shipshape."

"Everything usually is," assured McNaught, glibly. "I see to that." He spoke with conviction.

"Good!" approved Cassidy. "I like a commander who takes his responsibilities seriously. Much as I regret saying so, there are a few who do not." He marched through the main lock, his cod-eyes taking note of the fresh white enamel. "Where do you prefer to start, bow or tail?"

"My equipment-sheets run from bow backward. We may as well deal with them the way they're set."

"Very well." He trotted officiously toward the nose, paused on the way to pat Peaslake and examine his collar. "Well cared for, I see. Has the animal proved useful?"

"He saved five lives on Mardia by barking a warning."

"The details have been entered in your log, I suppose?"

"Yes, sir. The log is in the chart room awaiting your inspection."

"We'll get to it in due time." Reaching the bow-cabin, Cassidy took a seat, accepted the folder from McNaught, started off at businesslike pace. "K1. Beam compass, type D, one of."

"This is it, sir," said McNaught, showing him.

"Still working properly?"

"Yes, sir."

They carried on, reached the intercom-cubby, the computor room, a succession of other places back to the galley. Here, Blanchard posed in freshly laundered white clothes and eyed the newcomer warily.

"V147. Electronic oven, one of."

"Is zis," said Blanchard, pointing with disdain.

"Satisfactory?" inquired Cassidy, giving him the fishy-eye.

"Not beeg enough," declared Blanchard. He encompassed the entire galley with an expressive gesture. "Nossings beeg enough. Place too small. Everysings too small. I am chef de cuisine an' she is a cuisine like an attic."

"This is a warship, not a luxury liner," Cassidy snapped. He frowned at the equipment-sheet. "V148. Timing device, electronic oven, attachment thereto, one of."

"Is zis," spat Blanchard, ready to sling it through the nearest port if Cassidy would first donate the two pins.

Working his way down the sheet, Cassidy got nearer and nearer while nervous tension built up. Then he reached the critical point and said, "V1098. Offog, one."

"Morbleau!" said Blanchard, shooting sparks from his eyes, "I have say before an' I say again, zere never was—"

"The offog is in the radio room, sir," McNaught chipped in hurriedly.

"Indeed?" Cassidy took another look at the sheet. "Then why is it recorded along with galley equipment?"

"It was placed in the galley at time of fitting out, sir. It's one of those portable instruments left to us to fix up where most suitable."

"Hm-m-m! Then it should have been transferred to the radio room list. Why didn't you transfer it?"

"I thought it better to wait for your authority to do so, sir."

The fish-eyes registered gratification. "Yes, that is quite proper of you, Captain. I will transfer it now." He crossed the item from sheet nine, initialed it, entered it on sheet sixteen, initialed that. "V1099. Inscribed collar, leather . . . oh, yes, I've seen that. The dog was wearing it."

He ticked it. An hour later he strutted into the radio room. Burman stood up, squared his shoulders but could not keep his feet or hands from fidgeting. His eyes protruded slightly and kept straying toward McNaught in silent appeal. He was like a man wearing a porcupine in his breeches.

"V1098. Offog, one," said Cassidy in his usual tone of brooking no nonsense.

Moving with the jerkiness of a slightly uncoordinated robot, Burman pawed a small box fronted with dials, switches and colored lights. It looked like a radio ham's idea of a fruit machine. He knocked down a couple of switches. The lights came on, played around in intriguing combinations.

"This is it, sir," he informed with difficulty.

"Ah!" Cassidy left his chair and moved across for a closer look. "I don't recall having seen this item before. But there are so many different models of the same things. Is it still operating efficiently?"

"Yes, sir."

"It's one of the most useful things in the ship," contributed McNaught, for good measure.

"What does it *do*?" inquired Cassidy, inviting Burman to cast a pearl of wisdom before him.

Burman paled.

Hastily, McNaught said, "A full explanation would be rather involved and technical but, to put it as simply as possible, it enables us to strike a balance between opposing gravitational fields. Variations in lights indicate the extent and degree of imbalance at any given time."

"It's a clever idea," added Burman, made suddenly reckless by this news, "based upon Finagle's Constant."

"I see," said Cassidy, not seeing at all. He resumed his seat, ticked the offog and carried on. "Z44. Switchboard, automatic, forty-line intercom, one of."

"Here it is, sir."

Cassidy glanced at it, returned his gaze to the sheet. The others used his momentary distraction to mop perspiration from their foreheads.

Victory had been gained.

All was well.

For the third time, hah!

Rear Admiral Vane W. Cassidy departed pleased and complimentary. Within one hour the crew bolted to town. McNaught took turns with Gregory at enjoying the gay lights. For the next five days all was peace and pleasure.

On the sixth day Burman brought in a signal, dumped it upon McNaught's desk and waited for the reaction. He had an air of gratification, the pleasure of one whose virtue is about to be rewarded.

Terran Headquarters to Bustler. *Return here immediately for overhaul and refitting. Improved power plant to be installed. Feldman. Navy Op. Command. Sirisec.*

"Back to Terra," commented McNaught, happily. "And an overhaul will mean at least one month's leave." He eyed Burman. "Tell all officers on duty to go to town at once and order the crew aboard. The men will come running when they know why."

"Yes, sir," said Burman, grinning.

Everyone was still grinning two weeks later, when the Siriport had receded far behind and Sol had grown to a vague speck in the sparkling mist of the bow starfield.Eleven weeks still to go, but it was worth it. Back to Terra. Hurrah!

In the captain's cabin the grins abruptly vanished one evening when Burman suddenly developed the willies. He marched in, chewed his bottom lip while waiting for McNaught to finish writing in the log.

Finally, McNaught pushed the book away, glanced up, frowned. "What's the matter with you? Got a bellyache or something?"

"No, sir. I've been thinking."

"Does it hurt that much?"

"I've been thinking," persisted Burman in funereal tones. "We're going back for overhaul. You know what that means. We'll walk off the ship and a horde of experts will walk onto it." He stared tragically at the other. "Experts, I said."

"Naturally they'll be experts," McNaught agreed. "Equipment cannot be tested and brought up to scratch by a bunch of dopes."

"It will require more than a mere expert to bring the offog up to scratch," Burman pointed out. "It'll need a genius."

McNaught rocked back, swapped expressions like changing masks. "Jumping Judas! I'd forgotten all about that thing. When we get to Terra we won't blind *those* boys with science."

"No, sir, we won't," endorsed Burman. He did not add "any more" but his face shouted aloud, "You got me into this. You get me out of it." He waited a time while McNaught did some intense thinking, then prompted, "What do you suggest, sir?"

Slowly the satisfied smile returned to McNaught's features as he answered, "Break up the contraption and feed it into the disintegrator."

"That doesn't solve the problem," said Burman. "We'll still be short an offog."

"No we won't. Because I'm going to signal its loss owing to the hazards of space service." He closed one eye in an emphatic wink. "We're in free flight right now." He reached for a message pad and scribbled on it while Burman stood by, vastly relieved.

Bustler *to Terran Headquarters. Item V1098, Offog, one, came apart under gravitational stress while passing through twin-sun field Hector Major-Minor. Material used as fuel. McNaught, Commander.* Bustler.

Burman took it to the radio room and beamed it Earthward. All was peace and progress for another two days. The next time he went to the captain's cabin he went running.

"General call, sir," he announced breathlessly and thrust the message into the other's hands.

Terran Headquarters for relay all sectors. Urgent and Important. All ships grounded forthwith. Vessels in flight under official orders will make for nearest spaceport pending further instructions. Welling. Alarm and Rescue Command. Terra.

"Something's gone bust," commented McNaught, undisturbed. He traipsed to the chart room, Burman following. Consulting the charts, he dialed the intercom phone, got Pike in the bow and ordered, "There's a panic. All ships grounded. We've got to make for Zaxtedport, about three days' run away. Change course at once. Starboard seventeen degrees, declination ten." Then he cut off, griped, "Bang goes that sweet month on Terra. I never did like Zaxted, either. It stinks. The crew will feel murderous about this and I don't blame them."

"What d'you think has happened, sir?" asked Burman. He looked both uneasy and annoyed.

"Heaven alone knows. The last general call was seven years ago, when the *Starider* exploded halfway along the Mars run. They grounded every ship in existence while they investigated the cause." He rubbed his chin, pondered, went on, "And the call before that one was when the entire crew of the *Blowgun* went nuts. Whatever it is this time, you can bet it's serious."

"It wouldn't be the start of a space war?"

"Against whom?" McNaught made a gesture of contempt. "Nobody has the ships with which to oppose us. No; it's something technical. We'll learn of it eventually. They'll tell us before we reach Zaxted or soon afterward."

They did tell him. Within six hours Burman rushed in with face full of horror.

"What's eating you now?" demanded McNaught, staring at him.

"The offog," stuttered Burman. He made motions as though brushing off invisible spiders.

"What of it?"

"It's a typographical error. In your copy it should read 'off. dog.' "

"Off. dog?" echoed McNaught, making it sound like foul language.

"See for yourself." Dumping the signal on the desk, Burman bolted out, left the door swinging. McNaught scowled after him, picked up the message.

Terran Headquarters to Bustler. *Your report V1098, ship's official dog Peaslake. Detail fully circumstances and manner in which animal came apart under gravitational stress. Cross-examine crew and signal all coincidental symptoms experienced by them. Urgent and Important. Welling. Alarm and Rescue Command. Terra.*

In the privacy of his cabin McNaught commenced to eat his nails. Every now and again he went a little cross-eyed as he examined them for nearness to the flesh.

And Then There Were None

Astounding, May 1951

The battleship was eight hundred feet in diameter and slightly more than one mile long. Mass like that takes up room and makes a dent. This one sprawled right across one field and halfway through the next. Its weight made a rut twenty feet deep which would be there for keeps.

On board were two thousand people divisible into three distinct types. The tall, lean, crinkly-eyed ones were the crew. The crop-haired, heavy-jowled ones were the troops. Finally, the expressionless, balding and myopic ones were the cargo of bureaucrats.

The first of these types viewed this world with the professional but aloof interest of people everlastingly giving a planet the swift once-over before chasing along to the next. The troops regarded it with a mixture of tough contempt and boredom. The bureaucrats peered at it with cold authority. Each according to his lights.

This lot were accustomed to new worlds, had dealt with them by the dozens and reduced the process to mere routine. The task before them would have been nothing more than repetition of well-used, smoothly operating technique but for one thing: the entire bunch were in a jam and did not know it.

Emergence from the ship was in strict order of precedence. First, the Imperial Ambassador. Second, the battleship's captain. Third, the officer commanding the ground forces. Fourth, the senior civil servant.

Then, of course, the next grade lower, in the same order: His Excellency's private secretary, the ship's second officer, the deputy commander of troops, the penultimate pen pusher.

Down another grade, then another, until there was left only His Excellency's barber, boot wiper and valet, crew members with the lowly status of O.S.—Ordinary Spaceman—the military nonentities in the ranks, and a few temporary inkpot fillers dreaming of the day when they would be made permanent and given a desk of their own. This last collection of unfortunates remained aboard to clean ship and refrain from smoking, by command.

Had this world been alien, hostile and well-armed, the order of exit would have been reversed, exemplifying the Biblical promise that the last shall be first and the first shall be last. But this planet, although officially new, unofficially was not new and certainly was not alien. In ledgers and dusty files some two hundred light-years away it was recorded as a cryptic number and classified as a ripe plum long overdue for picking. There had been considerable delay in the harvesting due to a superabundance of other still riper plums elsewhere.

According to the records, this planet was on the outermost fringe of a huge assortment of worlds which had been settled immediately following the Great Explosion. Every school child knew all about the Great Explosion, which was no more than the spectacular name given to the bursting outward of masses of humanity when the Blieder drive superseded atomic-powered rockets and practically handed them the cosmos on a platter.

At that time, between three and five hundred years ago, every family, group, cult or clique that imagined it could do better some place else had taken to the star trails. The restless, the ambitious, the malcontents, the eccentrics, the antisocial, the fidgety and the just plain curious, away they had roared by the dozens, the hundred, the thousands.

Some two hundred thousand had come to this particular world, the last of them arriving three centuries back. As usual, ninety per cent of the mainstream had consisted of friends, relatives or acquaintances of the first-comers, people persuaded to follow the bold example of Uncle Eddie or Good Old Joe.

If they had since doubled themselves six or seven times over, there now ought to be several millions of them. That they had increased far beyond their original strength had been evident during the approach, for while no great cities were visible there were many medium to smallish towns and a large number of villages.

His Excellency looked with approval at the turf under his feet, plucked a blade of it, grunting as he stooped. He was so constructed that this effort approximated to an athletic feat and gave him a crick in the belly.

"Earth-type grass. Notice that, captain? Is it just a coincidence, or did they bring seed with them?"

"Coincidence, probably," thought Captain Grayder. "I've come across four grassy worlds so far. No reason why there shouldn't be others."

"No, I suppose not." His Excellency gazed into the distance, doing it with pride of ownership. "Looks like there's someone plowing over there. He's using a little engine between a pair of fat wheels. They can't be so backward. Hm-m-m!" He rubbed a couple of chins. "Bring him here. We'll have a talk, find out where it's best to get started."

"Very well." Captain Grayder turned to Colonel Shelton, boss of the troops. "His Excellency wishes to speak to that farmer." He pointed to the faraway figure.

"The farmer," said Shelton to Major Hame. "His Excellency wants him at once."

"Bring that farmer here," Hame ordered Lieutenant Deacon. "Quickly!"

"Go get that farmer," Deacon told Sergeant major Bidworthy. "And hurry—His Excellency is waiting!"

The sergeant major, a big, purple-faced man, sought around for a lesser rank, remembered that they were all cleaning ship and not smoking. He, it seemed, was elected.

Tramping across four fields and coming within hailing distance of his objective, he performed a precise military halt and released a barracks-square bellow of, "Hi, you!" He waved urgently.

The farmer stopped, wiped his forehead, looked around. His manner suggested that the mountainous bulk of the battleship was a mirage such as are five a penny around these parts. Bidworthy waved again, making it an authoritative summons. The farmer calmly waved back, got on with his plowing.

Sergeant major Bidworthy employed an expletive which—when its flames had died out—meant, "Dear me!" and marched fifty paces nearer. He could now see that the other was bushy-browed and leather-faced.

"Hi!"

Stopping the plow again, the farmer leaned on a shaft, picked his teeth.

Struck by the notion that perhaps during the last three centuries the old Earth-language had been dropped in favor of some other lingo, Bidworthy asked, "Can you understand me?"

"Can any person understand another?" inquired the farmer, with clear diction. He turned to resume his task.

Bidworthy was afflicted with a moment of confusion. Recovering, he informed hurriedly, "His Excellency, the Earth Ambassador, wishes to speak with you at once."

"So?" The other eyed him speculatively. "How come that he is excellent?"

"He is a person of considerable importance," said Bidworthy, unable to decide whether the other was being funny at his expense or alternatively was what is known as a character. A good many of these isolated planet-scratchers liked to think of themselves as characters.

"Of considerable importance," echoed the farmer, narrowing his eyes at the horizon. He appeared to be trying to grasp an alien concept. After a while, he inquired, "What will happen to your home world when this person dies?"

"Nothing," Bidworthy admitted.

"It will roll on as usual?"

"Of course."

"Then," declared the farmer, flatly, "he cannot be important." With that, his little engine went *chuff-chuff* and the wheels rolled forward and the plow plowed.

Digging his nails into the palms of his hands, Bidworthy spent half a minute gathering oxygen before he said, in hoarse tones, "I cannot return without at least a message for His Excellency."

"Indeed?" The other was incredulous. "What is to stop you?" Then, noting the alarming increase in Bidworthy's color, he added with compassion, "Oh, well, you may tell him that I said"—he paused while he thought it over—"God bless you and good-by!"

Sergeant major Bidworthy was a powerful man who weighed two-twenty pounds, had hopped around the cosmos for twenty years, and feared nothing. He had never been known to permit the shiver of one hair—but he was trembling all over by the time he got back to the ship.

His Excellency fastened a cold eye upon him and demanded, "Well?"

"He won't come." Bidworthy's veins stood out on his forehead. "And, sir, if only I could have him in my field company for a few months I'd straighten him up and teach him to move at the double."

"I don't doubt that, sergeant major," soothed His Excellency. He continued in a whispered aside to Colonel Shelton. "He's a good fellow but no diplomat. Too abrupt and harsh voiced. Better go yourself and fetch that farmer. We can't sit here forever waiting to find out where to begin."

"Very well, your excellency." Colonel Shelton trudged across the fields, caught up with the plow. Smiling pleasantly, he said, "Good morning, my man!"

Stopping his plow, the farmer sighed as if it were another of those days one has sometimes. His eyes were dark-brown, almost black, as they looked at the other.

"What makes you think I'm *your* man?" he inquired.

"It is a figure of speech," explained Shelton. He could see what was wrong now. Bidworthy had fallen foul of an irascible type. Two dogs snarling at one another, Shelton went on, "I was only trying to be courteous."

"Well," meditated the farmer, "I reckon that's something worth trying for."

Pinking a little, Shelton continued with determination. "I am commanded to request the pleasure of your company at the ship."

"Think they'll get any pleasure out of my company?" asked the other, disconcertingly bland.

"I'm sure of it," said Shelton.

"You're a liar," said the farmer.

His color deepening, Colonel Shelton snapped, "I do not permit people to call me a liar."

"You've just permitted it," the other pointed out.

Letting it pass, Shelton insisted, "Are you coming to the ship or are you not?"

"I am not."

"Why not?"

"Myob!" said the farmer.

"What was that?"

"Myob!" he repeated. It smacked of a mild insult.

Colonel Shelton went back.

He told the ambassador, "That fellow is one of these too-clever types. All I could get out of him at the finish was 'myob,' whatever that means."

"Local slang," chipped in Captain Grayder. "An awful lot of it develops over three or four centuries. I've come across one or two worlds where there's been so much of it that one almost had to learn a new language."

"He understood your speech?" asked the ambassador, looking at Shelton.

"Yes, your excellency. And his own is quite good. But he won't come away from his plowing." He reflected briefly, then suggested, "If it were left to me, I'd bring him in by force, under an armed escort."

"That would encourage him to give essential information," commented the ambassador, with open sarcasm. He patted his stomach, smoothed his jacket, glanced down at his glossy shoes. "Nothing for it but to go speak to him myself."

Colonel Shelton was shocked. "Your excellency, you can't *do that!*"

"Why can't I?"

"It would be undignified."

"I am aware of it," said the ambassador, dryly. "Can you suggest an alternative?"

"We can send out a patrol to find someone more cooperative."

"Someone better informed, too," Captain Grayder offered. "At best we wouldn't get much out of one surly hayseed. I doubt whether he knows a quarter of what we require to learn."

"All right." His Excellency abandoned the notion of doing his own chores. "Organize a patrol and let's have some results."

"A patrol," said Colonel Shelton to Major Hame. "Nominate one immediately."

"Call out a patrol," Hame ordered Lieutenant Deacon. "At once."

"Parade a patrol forthwith, sergeant major," said Deacon.

Bidworthy went to the ship, climbed a ladder, stuck his head in the lock and bawled, "Sergeant Gleed, out with your squad, and make it snappy!" He gave a suspicious sniff and went farther into the lock. His voice gained several more decibels. "Who's been smoking? By the Black Sack, if I catch—"

Across the fields something quietly went *chuff-chuff* while balloon tires crawled along.

The patrol formed by the right in two ranks of eight men each, turned at a barked command, marched off noseward. Their boots thumped in unison, their accouterments clattered and the orange-colored sun made sparkles on their metal.

Sergeant Gleed did not have to take his men far. They had got one hundred yards beyond the battleship's nose when he noticed a man ambling across the field to his right. Treating the ship with utter indifference, the newcomer was making toward the farmer still plowing far over to the left.

"Patrol, right wheel!" yelled Gleed. Marching them straight past the wayfarer, he gave them a loud about-turn and followed it with the high-sign.

Speeding up its pace, the patrol opened its ranks, became a double file of men tramping at either side of the lone pedestrian. Ignoring his suddenly acquired escort, the latter continued to plod straight ahead like one long convinced that all is illusion.

"Left wheel!" Gleed roared, trying to bend the whole caboodle toward the waiting ambassador.

Swiftly obedient, the double file headed leftward, one, two, three, hup! It was neat, precise execution, beautiful to watch. Only one thing spoiled it: the man in the middle maintained his self-chosen orbit and ambled casually between numbers four and five of the right-hand file.

That upset Gleed, especially since the patrol continued to thump ambassadorwards for lack of a further order. His Excellency was being treated to the unmilitary spectacle of an escort dumbly boot-beating one way while its prisoner airily mooched another. Colonel Shelton would have plenty to say about it in due course, and anything he forgot Bidworthy would remember.

"Patrol!" hoarsed Gleed, pointing an outraged finger at the escapee, and momentarily dismissing all regulation commands from his mind. "Get that yimp!"

Breaking ranks, they moved at the double and surrounded the wanderer too closely to permit further progress. Perforce, he stopped.

Gleed came up, said somewhat breathlessly, "Look, the Earth Ambassador wants to speak to you—that's all."

The other said nothing, merely gazed at him with mild blue eyes. He was a funny looking bum, long overdue for a shave, with a fringe of ginger whiskers sticking out all around his pan. He resembled a sunflower.

"Are you going to talk with His Excellency?" Gleed persisted.

"Naw." The other nodded toward the farmer. "Going to talk with Zeke."

"The ambassador first," retorted Gleed, toughly. "He's a big noise."

"I don't doubt that," remarked the sunflower.

"Smartie Artie, eh?" said Gleed, pushing his face close and making it unpleasant. He gave his men a gesture. "All right—shove him along. We'll show him!"

Smartie Artie sat down. He did it sort of solidly, giving himself the aspect of a statue anchored for aeons. The ginger whiskers did nothing to lend grace to the situation. But Sergeant Gleed had handled sitters before, the only difference being that this one was cold sober.

"Pick him up," ordered Gleed, "and carry him."

They picked him up and carried him, feet first, whiskers last. He hung limp and unresisting in their hands, a dead weight. In this inauspicious manner he arrived in the presence of the Earth Ambassador where the escort plonked him on his feet.

Promptly he set out for Zeke.

"Hold him, darn you!" howled Gleed.

The patrol grabbed and clung tight. His Excellency eyed the whiskers with well-bred concealment of distaste, coughed delicately, and spoke.

"I am truly sorry that you had to come to me in this fashion."

"In that case," suggested the prisoner, "you could have saved yourself some mental anguish by not permitting it to happen."

"There was no other choice. We've got to make contact somehow."

"I don't see it," said Ginger Whiskers. "What's so special about this date?"

"The date?" His Excellency frowned in puzzlement. "Where does that come in?"

"That's what I'd like to know."

"The point eludes me." The ambassador turned to Colonel Shelton. "Do you get what he's aiming at?"

"I could hazard a guess, your excellency. I think he is suggesting that since we've left them without contact for more than three hundred years, there's no particular urgency about making it today." He looked at the sunflower for confirmation.

That worthy rallied to his support by remarking, "You're doing pretty well for a half-wit."

Regardless of Shelton's own reaction, this was too much for Bidworthy purpling nearby. His chest came up and his eyes caught fire. His voice was an authoritative rasp.

"Be more respectful while addressing high-ranking officers!"

The prisoner's mild blue eyes turned upon him in childish amazement, examined him slowly from feet to head and all the way down again. The eyes drifted back to the ambassador.

"Who is this preposterous person?"

Dismissing the question with an impatient wave of his hand, the ambassador said, "See here, it is not our purpose to bother you from sheer perversity, as you seem to think. Neither do we wish to detain you any longer than is necessary. All we—"

Pulling at his face-fringe as if to accentuate its offensiveness, the other interjected, "It being you, of course, who determines the length of the necessity?"

"On the contrary, you may decide that yourself," said the ambassador, displaying admirable self-control. "All you need do is tell—"

"Then I've decided it right now," the prisoner chipped in. He tried to heave himself free of his escort. "Let me go talk to Zeke."

"All you need do," the ambassador persisted, "is to tell us where we can find a local official who can put us in touch with your central government." His gaze was stern, commanding, as he added, "For instance, where is the nearest police post?"

"Myob!" said the other.

"The same to you," retorted the ambassador, his patience starting to evaporate.

"That's precisely what I'm trying to do," assured the prisoner, enigmatically. "Only you won't let me."

"If I may make a suggestion, your excellency," put in Colonel Shelton, "let me—"

"I require no suggestions and I won't let you," said the ambassador, rapidly becoming brusque. "I have had enough of all this tomfoolery. I think we've landed at random in an area reserved for imbeciles and it would be as well to recognize the fact and get out of it with no more delay."

"Now you're talking," approved Ginger Whiskers. "And the farther the better."

"I'm not thinking of leaving this planet if that's what is in your incomprehensible mind," asserted the ambassador, with much sarcasm. He stamped a proprietary foot on the turf. "This is part of the Earth Empire. As such, it is going to be recognized, charted and organized."

"Heah, heah!" put in the senior civil servant, who aspired to honors in elocution.

His Excellency threw a frown behind, went on, "We'll move the ship to some other section where brains are brighter." He signed to the escort. "Let him go. Doubtless he is in a hurry to borrow a razor."

They released their grips. Ginger Whiskers at once turned toward the still-plowing farmer, much as if he were a magnetized needle irresistibly drawn Zekeward. Without a word he set off at his original mooching pace. Disappointment and disgust showed on the faces of Gleed and Bidworthy as they watched him go.

"Have the vessel shifted at once," the ambassador instructed Captain Grayder. "Plant it near a suitable town—not out in the wilds where every hayseed views strangers as a bunch of gyps."

He marched importantly up the gangway. Captain Grayder followed, then Colonel Shelton, then the elocutionist. Next, their successors in due order of precedence. Lastly, Gleed and his men.

The gangway rolled inward. The lock closed. Despite its immense bulk, the ship shivered briefly from end to end and soared without deafening uproar or spectacular display of flame.

Indeed, there was silence save for the plow going *chuff-chuff* and the murmurings of the two men walking behind it. Neither bothered to turn his head to observe what was happening.

"Seven pounds of prime tobacco is a heck of a lot to give for one case of brandy," Ginger Whiskers was protesting.

"Not for my brandy," said Zeke. "It's stronger than a thousand Gands and smoother than an Earthman's downfall."

The great battleship's second touchdown was made on a wide flat one mile north of a town estimated to hold twelve to fifteen thousand people. Captain Grayder would have preferred to survey the place from low altitude before making his landing, but one cannot maneuver an immense space-going job as if it were an atmospheric tug. Only two things can be done so close to a planetary surface—the ship is taken up or brought down with no room for fiddling between times.

So Grayder bumped his ship in the best spot he could find when finding is a matter of split-second decisions. It made a rut only twelve feet deep, the ground being harder and on a rock bed. The gangway was shoved out; the procession descended in the same order as before.

His Excellency cast an anticipatory look toward the town, registered disappointment and remarked, "Something's badly out of kilter here. There's the town. Here's us in plain view, with a ship like a metal mountain. A thousand people at least must have seen us even if the rest are holding seances behind drawn curtains or playing pinochle in the cellars. Are they excited?"

"It doesn't seem so," admitted Colonel Shelton, pulling an eyelid for the sake of feeling it spring back.

"I wasn't asking you. I was telling you. They are not excited. They are not surprised. In fact, they are not even interested. One would almost think they've had a ship here before and it was full of smallpox, or sold them a load of gold bricks, or something like that. What is wrong with them?"

"Possibly they lack curiosity," Shelton offered.

"Either that or they're afraid. Or maybe the entire gang of them are crackers. A good many worlds were appropriated by woozy groups who wanted some place where their eccentricities could run loose. Nutty notions become conventional after three hundred years of undisturbed continuity. It's then considered normal and proper to nurse the bats out of your grandfather's attic. That, and generations of inbreeding, can create some queer types. But we'll cure 'em!"

"Yes, your excellency, most certainly we will."

"You don't look so balanced yourself, chasing that eye around your pan," reproved the ambassador. He pointed southeast as Shelton stuck the fidgety hand firmly into a pocket. "There's a road over there. Wide and well-built by the looks of it. Get that patrol across it. If they don't bring in a willing talker within reasonable time, we'll send a battalion into the town itself."

"A patrol," repeated Colonel Shelton to Major Hame.

"Call out the patrol," Hame ordered Lieutenant Deacon.

"That patrol again, sergeant major," said Deacon.

Bidworthy raked out Gleed and his men, indicated the road, barked a bit, shooed them on their way.

They marched, Gleed in the lead. Their objective was half a mile and angled slightly nearer the town. The left-hand file, who had a clear view of the nearest suburbs, eyed them wistfully, wished Gleed in warmer regions with Bidworthy stoking beneath him.

Hardly had they reached their goal than a customer appeared. He came from the town's outskirts, zooming along at fast pace on a contraption vaguely resembling a motorcycle. It ran on a pair of big rubber balls and was pulled by a caged fan. Gleed spread his men across the road.

The oncomer's machine suddenly gave forth a harsh, penetrating sound that vaguely reminded them of Bidworthy in the presence of dirty boots.

"Stay put," warned Gleed. "I'll skin the guy who gives way and leaves a gap."

Again the shrill metallic warning. Nobody moved. The machine slowed, came up to them at a crawl and stopped. Its fan continued to spin at low rate, the blades almost visible and giving out a steady hiss.

"What's the idea?" demanded the rider. He was lean-featured, in his middle thirties, wore a gold ring in his nose and had a pigtail four feet long.

Blinking incredulously at this get-up, Gleed managed to jerk an indicative thumb toward the iron mountain and say, "Earth ship."

"Well, what d'you expect me to do about it?"

"Co-operate," said Gleed, still bemused by the pigtail. He had never seen one before. It was in no way effeminate, he decided. Rather did it lend a touch of ferocity like that worn—according to the picture books—by certain North American aborigines of umpteen centuries ago.

"Co-operation," mused the rider. "Now there is a beautiful word. You know what it means, of course?"

"I ain't a dope."

"The precise degree of your idiocy is not under discussion at the moment," the rider pointed out. His nose-ring waggled a bit as he spoke. "We are talking about co-operation. I take it you do quite a lot of it yourself?"

"You bet I do," Gleed assured. "And so does everyone else who knows what's good for him."

"Let's keep to the subject, shall we? Let's not sidetrack and go rambling all over the map." He revved up his fan a little then let it slow down again. "You are given orders and you obey them?"

"Of course. I'd have a rough time if—"

"That is what you call co-operation?" put in the other. He shrugged his shoulders, indulged a resigned sigh. "Oh, well, it's nice to check the facts of history.

The books *could* be wrong." His fan flashed into a circle of light and the machine surged forward. "Pardon me."

The front rubber ball barged forcefully between two men, knocking them sidewise without injury. With a high whine, the machine shot down the road, its fan-blast making the rider's plaited hairdo point horizontally backward.

"You goofy glumps!" raged Gleed as his fallen pair got up and dusted themselves. "I ordered you to stand fast. What d'you mean, letting him run out on us like that?"

"Didn't have much choice about it, sarge," answered one, giving him a surly look.

"I want none of your back-chat. You could have busted a balloon if you'd had your weapons ready. That would have stopped him."

"You didn't tell us to have guns ready."

"Where was your own, anyway?" added a voice.

Gleed whirled round on the others and bawled, "Who said that?" His irate eyes raked a long row of blank, impassive faces. It was impossible to detect the culprit. "I'll shake you up with the next quota of fatigues," he promised. "I'll see to it—"

"The sergeant major's coming," one of them warned.

Bidworthy was four hundred yards away and making martial progress toward them. Arriving in due time, he cast a cold, contemptuous glance over the patrol.

"What happened?"

Giving a brief account of the incident, Gleed finished aggrievedly, "He looked like a Chickasaw with an oil well."

"What's a Chickasaw?" Bidworthy demanded.

"I read about them somewhere once when I was a kid," explained Gleed, happy to bestow a modicum of learning. "They had long haircuts, wore blankets and rode around in gold-plated automobiles."

"Sounds crazy to me," said Bidworthy. "I gave up all that magic-carpet stuff when I was seven. I was deep in ballistics before I was twelve and military logistics at fourteen." He sniffed loudly, gave the other a jaundiced eye. "Some guys suffer from arrested development."

"They actually existed," Gleed maintained. "They—"

"So did fairies," snapped Bidworthy. "My mother said so. My mother was a good woman. She didn't tell me a lot of tomfool lies—often." He spat on the road. "Be your age!" Then he scowled at the patrol. "All right, get out your guns, assuming that you've got them and know where they are and which hand to hold them in. Take orders from me. I'll deal personally with the next one along."

He sat on a large stone by the roadside and planted an expectant gaze on the town. Gleed posed near him, slightly pained. The patrol remained strung across the road, guns held ready. Half an hour crawled by without anything happening.

One of the men said, "Can we have a smoke, sergeant major?"

"No."

They fell into lugubrious silence, watching the town, licking their lips and thinking. They had plenty to think about. A town—any town of human occupation—

had desirable features not found elsewhere in the cosmos. Lights, company, freedom, laughter, all the makings of life. And one can go hungry too long.

Eventually a large coach came from the outskirts, hit the high road, came howling toward them. A long, shiny, streamlined job, it rolled on twenty balls in two rows of ten, gave forth a whine similar to but louder than that of its predecessor, but had no visible fans. It was loaded with people.

At a point two hundred yards from the road block a loud-speaker under the vehicle's bonnet blared an urgent, "Make way! Make way!"

"This is it," commented Bidworthy, with much satisfaction. "We've got a dollop of them. One of them is going to chat or I leave the service." He got off his rock, stood in readiness.

"Make way! Make way!"

"Bust his bags if he tries to bull his way through," Bidworthy ordered the men.

It wasn't necessary. The coach lost pace, stopped with its bonnet a yard from the waiting file. Its driver peered out the side of his cab. Other faces snooped farther back.

Composing himself and determined to try the effect of fraternal cordiality, Bidworthy went up to the driver and said, "Good morning."

"Your time-sense is shot to pot," observed the other. He had a blue jowl, a broken nose, cauliflower ears, looked the sort who usually drives with others in hot and vengeful pursuit. "Can't you afford a watch?"

"Huh?"

"It isn't morning. It's late afternoon."

"So it is," admitted Bidworthy, forcing a cracked smile. "Good afternoon."

"I'm not so sure about that," mused the driver, leaning on his wheel and moodily picking his teeth. "It's just another one nearer the grave."

"That may be," agreed Bidworthy, little taken with that ghoulish angle. "But I have other things to worry about, and—"

"Not much use worrying about anything, past or present," advised the driver. "Because there are lots bigger worries to come."

"Perhaps so," Bidworthy said, inwardly feeling that this was no time or place to contemplate the darker side of existence. "But I prefer to deal with my own troubles in my own time and my own way."

"Nobody's troubles are entirely their own, nor their time, nor their methods," remarked the tough looking oracle. "Are they now?"

"I don't know and I don't care," said Bidworthy, his composure thinning down as his blood pressure built up. He was conscious of Gleed and the patrol watching, listening, and probably grinning inside themselves. There was also the load of gaping passengers. "I think you are chewing the fat just to stall me. You might as well know now that it won't work. The Earth Ambassador is waiting—"

"So are we," remarked the driver pointedly.

"He wants to speak to you," Bidworthy went on, "and he's going to speak to you!"

"I'd be the last to prevent him. We've got free speech here. Let him step up and say his piece so's we can get on our way."

"You," Bidworthy informed, "are going to *him."* He signed to the rest of the coach. "And your load as well."

"Not me," denied a fat man, sticking his head out of a side window. He wore thick-lensed glasses that gave him eyes like poached eggs. Moreover, he was adorned with a high hat candy-striped in white and pink. "Not me," repeated this vision, with considerable firmness.

"Me, neither," endorsed the driver.

"All right." Bidworthy registered menace. "Move this birdcage an inch, forward or backward, and we'll shoot your pot-bellied tires to thin strips. Get out of that cab."

"Not me. I'm too comfortable. Try fetching me out."

Bidworthy beckoned to his nearest six men. "You heard him—take him up on that."

Tearing open the cab door, they grabbed. If they had expected the victim to put up a futile fight against heavy odds, they were disappointed. He made no attempt to resist. They got him, lugged together, and he yielded with good grace, his body leaning sidewise and coming halfway out of the door.

That was as far as they could get him.

"Come on," urged Bidworthy, displaying impatience. "Show him who's who, he isn't a fixture."

One of the men climbed over the body, poked around inside the cab, and said, "He is, you know."

"What d'you mean?"

"He's chained to the steering column."

"Eh? Let me see." He had a look, found that it was so. A chain and a small but heavy and complicated padlock linked the driver's leg to his coach. "Where's the key?"

"Search me," invited the driver, grinning.

They did just that. The frisk proved futile. No key.

"Who's got it?"

"Myob."

"Shove him back into his seat," ordered Bidworthy, looking savage. "We'll take the passengers. One yap's as good as another so far as I'm concerned." He strode to the doors, jerked then open. "Get out and make it snappy."

Nobody budged. They studied him silently and with varied expressions, not one of which did anything to help his ego. The fat man with the candy-striped hat mooned at him sardonically. Bidworthy decided that he did not like the fat man and that a stiff course of military calisthenics might thin him down a bit.

You can come out on your feet," he suggested to the passengers in general and the fat man in particular "or on your necks. Whichever you prefer. Make up your minds."

"If you can't use your head you can at least use your eyes," commented the fat man. He shifted in his seat to the accompaniment of metallic clanking noises.

Bidworthy did as suggested, leaning through the doors to have a gander. Then he got right into the vehicle, went its full length and studied each passenger. His florid features were two shades darker when he came out and spoke to Sergeant Gleed.

"They're all chained. Every one of them." He glared at the driver. "What's the big idea, manacling the lot?"

"Myob!" said the driver, airily.

"Who's got the keys?"

"Myob!"

Taking a deep breath, Bidworthy said to nobody in particular, "Every so often I hear of some guy running amok and laying 'em out by the dozens. I always wonder why—but now I know." He gnawed his knuckles, then added to Gleed, "We can't run this contraption to the ship with that dummy blocking the driver's seat. Either we must find the keys or get tools and cut them loose."

"Or you could wave us on our way and go take a pill," offered the driver.

"Shut up! If I'm stuck here another million years I'll see to it that—"

"The colonel's coming," muttered Gleed, giving him a nudge.

Colonel Shelton arrived, walked once slowly and officiously around the outside of the coach, examining its construction and its occupants. He flinched at the striped hat whose owner leered at him through the glass. Then he came over to the disgruntled group.

"What's the trouble this time, sergeant major?"

"They're as crazy as the others, sir. They give a lot of lip and say, 'Myob!' and couldn't care less about his excellency. They don't want to come out and we can't get them out because they're chained to their seats."

"Chained?" Shelton's eyebrows shot upward. "What for?"

"I don't know, sir. They're linked in like a load of lifers making for the pen, and—"

Shelton moved off without waiting to hear the rest. He had a look for himself, came back.

"You may have something there, sergeant major. But I don't think they are criminals."

"No, sir?"

"No." He threw a significant glance toward the colorful headgear and several other sartorial eccentricities, including a ginger-haired man's foot-wide polka-dotted bow. "It is more likely that they're a hunch of whacks being taken to a giggle emporium. I'll ask the driver." Going to the cab, he said, "Do you mind telling me your destination?"

"Yes," responded the other.

"Very well, where is it?"

"Look," said the driver, "are we talking the same language?"

"Huh?"

"You asked me if I minded and I said yes." He made a gesture. "I do mind."

"You refuse to tell?"

"Your aim's improving, sonny."

"Sonny?" put in Bidworthy, vibrant with outrage. "Do you realize you are speaking to a colonel?"

"Leave this to me," insisted Shelton, waving him down. His expression was cold as he returned his attention to the driver. "On your way. I'm sorry you've been detained."

"Think nothing of it," said the driver, with exaggerated politeness. "I'll do as much for you some day."

With that enigmatic remark, he let his machine roll forward. The patrol parted to make room. The coach built up its whine to top note, sped down the road, diminished into the distance.

"By the Black Sack!" swore Bidworthy, staring purple-faced after it. "This planet has got more punks in need of discipline than any this side of—"

"Calm yourself, sergeant major," advised Shelton. "I feel the same way as you—but I'm taking care of my arteries. Blowing them full of bumps like seaweed won't solve any problems."

"Maybe so, sir, but—"

"We're up against something mighty funny here," Shelton went on. "We've got to find out exactly what it is and how best to cope with it. That will probably mean new tactics. So far, the patrol has achieved nothing. It is wasting its time. We'll have to devise some other and more effective method of making contact with the powers-that-be. March the men back to the ship, sergeant major."

"Very well, sir." Bidworthy saluted swung around, clicked his heels, opened a cavernous mouth. "Patro-o-ol! . . . right form!"

The conference lasted well into the night and halfway through the following morning. During these argumentative hours various oddments of traffic, mostly vehicular, passed along the road, but nothing paused to view the monster spaceship, nobody approached for a friendly word with its crew. The strange inhabitants of this world seemed to be afflicted with a peculiar form of mental blindness, unable to see a thing until it was thrust into their faces and then surveying it squint-eyed.

One passer-by in midmorning was a truck whining on two dozen rubber balls and loaded with girls wearing colorful head-scarves. The girls were singing something about one little kiss before we part, dear. Half a dozen troops lounging near the gangway came eagerly to life, waved, whistled and yoo-hooed. The effort was wasted, for the singing continued without break or pause and nobody waved back.

To add to the discomfiture of the love-hungry, Bidworthy stuck his head out of the lock and rasped, "If you monkeys are bursting with surplus energy, I can find a few jobs for you to do—nice dirty ones." He seared them one at a time before he withdrew.

Inside, the top brass sat around a horseshoe table in the chartroom near the bow and debated the situation. Most of them were content to repeat with extra emphasis what they had said the previous evening, there being no new points to bring up.

"Are you certain," the Earth Ambassador asked Captain Grayder, "that this planet has not been visited since the last emigration transport dumped the final load three hundred years back?"

"Positive, your excellency. Any such visit would have been recorded."

"If made by an Earth ship. But what about others? I feel it in my bones that at sometime or other these people have fallen foul of one or more vessels calling unofficially and have been leery of spaceships ever since. Perhaps somebody got tough with them, tried to muscle in where he wasn't wanted. Or they've had to beat off a gang of pirates. Or they were swindled by some unscrupulous fleet of traders."

"Quite impossible, your excellency," declared Grayder. "Emigration was so scattered over so large a number of worlds that even today every one of them is underpopulated, only one-hundredth developed, and utterly unable to build spaceships of any kind, even rudimentary ones. Some may have the techniques but not the facilities, of which they need plenty."

"Yes, that's what I've always understood."

"All Blieder-drive vessels are built in the Sol system, registered as Earth ships and their whereabouts known. The only other ships in existence are eighty or ninety antiquated rocket jobs bought at scrap price by the Epsilon system for haulage work between their fourteen closely-planned planets. An old-fashioned rocket job couldn't reach this place in a hundred years."

"No, of course not."

"Unofficial boats capable of this range just don't exist," Grayder assured. "Neither do space buccaneers, for the same reason. A Blieder-job takes so much that a would-be pirate has to become a billionaire to become a pirate."

"Then," said the ambassador, heavily, "back we go to my original theory—that something peculiar to this world plus a lot of inbreeding has made them nutty."

"There's plenty to be said for that notion," put in Colonel Shelton. "You should have seen the coach load I looked over. There was a mortician wearing odd shoes, one brown, one yellow. And a moon-faced gump sporting a hat made from the skin of a barber's pole, all stripy. Only thing missing was his bubble pipe—and probably he'll be given that where he was going."

"Where was he going?"

"I don't know, your excellency. They refused to say."

Giving him a satirical look, the ambassador remarked, "Well, that is a valuable addition to the sum total of our knowledge. Our minds are now enriched by the thought that an anonymous individual may be presented with a futile object for an indefinable purpose when he reaches his unknown destination."

Shelton subsided, wishing that he had never seen the fat man or, for that matter, the fat man's cockeyed world.

"Somewhere they've got a capitol, a civic seat, a center of government wherein function the people who hold the strings," the ambassador asserted. "We've got to find that place before we can take over and reorganize on up-to-date lines whatever setup they've got. A capitol is big by the standards of its own administrative area. It's never an ordinary, nondescript place. It has certain physical features lending it importance above the average. It should be easily visible from the air. We must make a search for it—in fact, that's what we ought to have done in the first place. Other planets' capitol cities have been found without trouble. What's the hoodoo on this one?"

"See for yourself, your excellency." Captain Grayder poked a couple of photographs across the table. "There are the two hemispheres as recorded by us when coming in. They reveal nothing resembling a superior city. There isn't even a town conspicuously larger than its fellows or possessing outstanding features setting it apart from the others."

"I don't place great faith in pictures, particularly when taken at long distance. The naked eye sees more. We have got four lifeboats capable of scouring the place from pole to pole. Why not use them?"

"Because, your excellency, they were not designed for such a purpose."

"Does that matter so long as they get results?"

Grayder said, patiently, "They were designed to be launched in space and hitting forty thousand. They are ordinary, old-style rocket jobs, for emergencies only. You could not make efficient ground-survey at any speed in excess of four hundred miles per hour. Keep the boats down to that and you're trying to run them at landing-speed, muffling the tubes, balling up their efficiency, creating a terrible waste of fuel, and inviting a crash which you're likely to get before you're through."

"Then it's high time we had Blieder-drive lifeboats on Blieder-drive ships."

"I agree, your excellency. But the smallest Blieder engine has an Earth mass of more than three hundred tons—far too much for little boats." Picking up the photographs, Grayder slid them into a drawer. "What we need is an ancient, propeller-driven airplane. They could do something we can't do—they could go slow."

"You might as well yearn for a bicycle," scoffed the ambassador, feeling thwarted.

"We have a bicycle," Grayder informed. "Tenth Engineer Harrison owns one."

"And he has brought it with him?"

"It goes everywhere with him. There is a rumor that he sleeps with it."

"A spaceman toting a bicycle!" The ambassador blew his nose with a loud honk. "I take it that he is thrilled by the sense of immense velocity it gives him, an ecstatic feeling of rushing headlong through space?"

"I wouldn't know, your excellency."

"Hm-m-m! Bring this Harrison in to me. We'll set a nut to catch a nut."

Grayder blinked, went to the caller board, spoke over the ship's system. "Tenth Engineer Harrison wanted in the chartroom immediately."

Within ten minutes Harrison appeared. He had walked fast three-quarters of a mile from the Blieder room. He was thin and wiry, with dark, monkeylike eyes, and a pair of ears that cut out the pedaling with the wind behind him. The ambassador examined him curiously, much as a zoologist would inspect a pink giraffe.

"Mister, I understand that you possess a bicycle."

Becoming wary, Harrison said, "There's nothing against it in the regulations, sir, and therefore—"

"Darn the regulations!" The ambassador made an impatient gesture. "We're stalled in the middle of a crazy situation and we're turning to crazy methods to get moving."

"I see, sir."

"So I want you to do a job for me. Get out your bicycle, ride down to town, find the mayor, sheriff, grand panjandrum, supreme galootie, or whatever he's called, and tell him he's officially invited to evening dinner along with any other civic dignitaries he cares to bring and, of course, their wives."

"Very well, sir."

"Informal attire," added the ambassador.

Harrison jerked up one ear, drooped the other, and said, "Beg pardon, sir?"

"They can dress how they like."

"I get it. Do I go right now, sir?"

"At once. Return as quickly as you can and bring me the reply."

Saluting sloppily, Harrison went out. His excellency found an easy-chair, reposed in it at full length and ignored the others' stares.

"As easy as that!" He pulled out a long cigar, carefully bit off its end. "If we can't touch their minds, we'll appeal to their bellies." He cocked a knowing eye at Grayder. "Captain, see that there is plenty to drink. Strong stuff. Venusian cognac or something equally potent. Give them an hour at a well-filled table and they'll talk plenty. We won't be able to shut them up all night." He lit the cigar, puffed luxuriously. "That is the tried and trusted technique of diplomacy—the insidious seduction of the distended gut. It always works—you'll see."

Pedaling briskly down the road, Tenth Engineer Harrison reached the first street on either side of which were small detached houses with neat gardens front and back. A plump, amiable looking woman was clipping a hedge halfway along. He pulled up near to her, politely touched his cap.

" 'Scuse me, ma'am, I'm looking for the biggest man in town."

She half-turned, gave him no more than a casual glance, pointed her clipping-shears southward. "That'd be Jeff Baines. First on the right, second on the left. It's a small delicatessen."

"Thank you.

He moved on, hearing the *snip-snip* resume behind him. First on the right. He curved around a long, low, rubber-balled truck parked by the corner. Second on the left. Three children pointed at him and yelled shrill warnings that his back wheel was going round. He found the delicatessen, propped a pedal on the curb, gave his machine a reassuring pat before he went inside and had a look at Jeff.

There was plenty to see. Jeff had four chins, a twenty-two-inch neck, and a paunch that stuck out half a yard. An ordinary mortal could have got into either leg of his pants without taking off a diving suit. He weighed at least three hundred and undoubtedly *was* the biggest man in town.

"Wanting something?" inquired Jeff, lugging it up from far down.

"Not exactly." Tenth Engineer Harrison eyed the succulent food display, decided that anything unsold by nightfall was not given to the cats. "I'm looking for a certain person."

"Are you now? Usually I avoid that sort—but every man to his taste." He plucked at a fat lip while he mused a moment, then suggested, "Try Sid Wilcock over on Dane Avenue. He's the most certain man I know."

"I didn't mean it that way," said Harrison. "I meant I was searching for somebody particular."

"Then why the dub didn't you say so?" Jeff Baines worked over the new problem, finally offered, "Tod Green ought to fit that bill. You'll find him in the shoeshop end of this road. He's particular enough for anyone. He's downright finicky."

"You misunderstand me," Harrison explained. "I'm hunting a bigwig so's I can invite him to a feed."

Resting himself on a high stool which he overlapped by a foot all round, Jeff Baines eyed him peculiarly and said, "There's something lopsided about this. In the first place, you're going to use up a considerable slice of your life finding a guy who wears a wig, especially if you insist on a big one. And where's the point of dumping an ob on him just because he uses a bean-blanket?"

"Huh?"

"It's plain common sense to plant an ob where it will cancel an old one out, isn't it?"

"Is it?" Harrison let his mouth hang open while his mind moiled around the strange problem of how to plant an ob.

"So you don't know?" Jeff Baines massaged a plump chop and sighed. He pointed at the other's middle. "Is that a uniform you're wearing?"

"Yes."

"A genuine, pukka, dyed-in-the-wool uniform?"

"Of course."

"Ah!" said Jeff. "That's where you've fooled me—coming in by yourself, on your ownsome. If there had been a gang of you dressed identically the same, I'd have known at once it was a uniform. That's what uniform means—all alike. Doesn't it?"

"I suppose so," agreed Harrison, who had never given it a thought.

"So you're off that ship. I ought to have guessed it in the first place. I must be slow on the uptake today. But I didn't expect to see one, just one, messing around on a pedal contraption. It goes to show, doesn't it?"

"Yes," said Harrison, glancing around to make sure that no confederate had swiped his bicycle while he was detained in conversation. The machine was still there. "It goes to show."

"All right, let's have it—what have you come here for?"

"I've been trying to tell you all along. I've been sent to—"

"Been sent?" Jeff's eyes widened a little. "Mean to say you actually let yourself be *sent?*"

Harrison, gaped at him. "Of course. Why not?"

"Oh, I get it now," said Jeff Baines, his puzzled features suddenly clearing. "You confuse me with the queer way you talk. You mean you planted an ob on someone?"

Desperately, Harrison said, "What's an ob?"

"He doesn't know," commented Jeff Baines, looking prayerfully at the ceiling. "He doesn't even know that!" He gave out a resigned sigh. "You hungry by any chance?"

"Going on that way."

"O.K. I could tell you what an ob is, but I'll do something better—I'll show you." Heaving himself off the stool, he waddled to a door at back. "Don't know why I should bother to try educate a uniform. It's just that I'm bored. C'mon, follow me."

Obediently, Harrison went behind the counter, paused to give his bicycle a reassuring nod, trailed the other through a passage and into a yard.

Jeff Baines pointed to a stack of cases. "Canned goods." He indicated an adjacent store. "Bust 'em open and pile the stuff in there. Stack the empties outside. Please yourself whether you do it or not. That's freedom, isn't it?" He lumbered back into the shop.

Left by himself, Harrison scratched his ears and thought it over. Somewhere, he felt, there was an obscure sort of gag. A candidate named Harrison was being tempted to qualify for his sucker certificate. But if the play was beneficial to its organizer it might be worth learning because the trick could then be passed on. One must speculate in order to accumulate.

So he dealt with the cases as required. It took him twenty minutes of brisk work, after which he returned to the shop.

"Now," explained Baines, "you've done something for me. That means you've planted an ob on me. I don't thank you for what you've done. There's no need to. All I have to do is get rid of the ob."

"Ob?"

"Obligation. Why use a long word when a short one is good enough? An obligation is an ob. I shift it this way: Seth Warburton, next door but one, has got half a dozen of my obs saddled on him. So I get rid of mine to you and relieve him of one of his to me by sending you around for a meal." He scribbled briefly on a slip of paper. "Give him this."

Harrison stared at it. In casual scrawl, it read, "Feed this bum. Jeff Baines."

Slightly dazed, he wandered out, stood by the bicycle and again eyed the paper. Bum, it said. He could think of several on the ship who would have exploded with wrath over that. His attention drifted to the second shop farther along. It had a window crammed with comestibles and two big words on the sign-strip above: *Seth's Gulper.*

Coming to a decision which was encouraged by his innards, he went into Seth's still holding the paper as if it were a death warrant. Inside there was a long counter, some steam and a clatter of crockery. He chose a seat at a marble-topped table occupied by a gray-eyed brunette.

"Do you mind?" he inquired politely, as he lowered himself into a chair.

"Mind what?" She examined his ears as if they were curious phenomena. "Babies, dogs, aged relations or going out in the rain?"

"Do you mind me being here?"

"I can please myself whether or not I endure it. That's freedom, isn't it?"

"Yeah," said Harrison. "Sure it is." He fidgeted in his seat, feeling somehow that he'd made a move and promptly lost a pawn. He sought around for something else to say and at that point a thin-featured man in a white coat dumped before him a plate loaded with fried chicken and three kinds of unfamiliar vegetables.

The sight unnerved him. He couldn't remember how many years it was since he last saw fried chicken, nor how many months since he'd had vegetables in other than powder form.

"Well," said the waiter, mistaking his fascinated gaze upon the food. "Doesn't it suit you?"

"Yes." Harrison handed over the slip of paper. "You bet it does."

Glancing at the note, the other called to someone semivisible in the steam at one end of the counter, "You've killed another of Jeff's." He went away, tearing the slip into small pieces.

"That was a fast pass," commented the brunette, nodding at the loaded plate. "He dumps a feed-ob on you and you bounce it straight back, leaving all quits. I'll have to wash dishes to get rid of mine, or kill one Seth has got on somebody else."

"I stacked a load of canned stuff." Harrison picked up knife and fork, his mouth watering. There were no knives and forks on the ship. They weren't needed for powders and pills. "Don't give you any choice here, do they? You take what you get."

"Not if you've got an ob on Seth," she informed. "In that case, he's got to work it off best way he can. You should have put that to him instead of waiting for fate and complaining afterward."

"I'm not complaining."

"It's your right. That's freedom, isn't it?" She mused a bit, went on, "Isn't often I'm a plant ahead of Seth, but when I am I scream for iced pineapple and he comes running. When *he's* a plant ahead, I do the running." Her gray eyes narrowed in sudden suspicion, and she added, "You're listening like it's all new to you. Are you a stranger here?"

He nodded, his mouth full of chicken. A little later he managed, "I'm off that spaceship."

"Good grief!" She froze considerably. "An Antigand! I wouldn't have thought it. Why, you look almost human."

"I've long taken pride in that similarity," his wit rising along with his belly. He chewed, swallowed, looked around. The white-coated man came up. "What's to drink?" Harrison asked.

"Dith, double-dith, shemak or coffee."

"Coffee. Big and black."

"Shemak is better," advised the brunette as the waiter went away. "But why should I tell you?"

The coffee came in a pint-sized mug. Dumping it, the waiter said, "It's your choice seeing Seth's working one off. What'll you have for after—apple pie, yimpik delice, grated tarfelsoufers or canimelon in syrup?"

"Iced pineapple."

"Ugh!" The other blinked at Harrison, gave the brunette an accusing stare, went away and got it.

Harrison pushed it across. "Take the plunge and enjoy yourself."

"It's yours."

"Couldn't eat it if I tried." He dug up another load of chicken, stirred his coffee, began to feel at peace with the world. "Got as much as I can manage right here." He made an inviting motion with his fork. "G'wan, be greedy and to heck with the waistline."

"No." Firmly she pushed the pineapple back at him. "If I got through that, I'd be loaded with an ob."

"So what?"

"I don't let strangers plant obs on me."

"Quite right, too. Very proper of you," approved Harrison. "Strangers often have strange notions."

"You've been around," she agreed. "Only I don't know what's strange about the notions."

"Dish washer!"

"Eh?"

"Cynic," he translated. "One washes dishes in a cynic." The pineapple got another pass in her direction. "If you feel I'll be dumping an ob which you'll have to pay off, you can do it in seemly manner right here. All I want is some information. Just tell me where I can put my finger on the ripest cheese in the locality."

"That's an easy one. Go round to Alec Peters' place, middle of Tenth Street." With that, she dug into the dish.

"Thanks. I was beginning to think everyone was dumb or afflicted with the funnies."

He carried on with his own meal, finished it, lay back expansively. Unaccustomed nourishment got his brain working a bit more dexterously, for after a minute an expression of deep suspicion clouded his face and he inquired, "Does this Peters run a cheese warehouse?"

"Of course." Emitting a sigh of pleasure, she put aside her empty dish.

He groaned low down, then informed, "I'm chasing the mayor."

"What is that?"

"Number one. The big boss. The sheriff, pohanko, or whatever you call him."

"I'm no wiser," she said, genuinely puzzled.

"The man who runs this town. The leading citizen."

"Make it a little clearer," she suggested, trying hard to help him. "Who or what should this citizen be leading?"

"You and Seth and everyone else." He waved a hand to encompass the entire burg.

Frowning, she said, "Leading us *where?*"

"Wherever you're going."

She gave up, beaten, and signed the white-coated waiter to come to her assistance.

"Matt, are we going any place?"

"How should I know?"

"Well, ask Seth then."

He went away, came back with, "Seth says he's going home at six o'clock and what's it to you?"

"Anyone leading him there?" she inquired.

"Don't be daft," Matt advised. "He knows his own way and he's cold sober."

Harrison chipped in with, "Look, I don't see why there should be so much difficulty about this. Just tell me where I can find an official; any official—the police chief, the city treasurer, the mortuary keeper or even a mere justice of the peace.

"What's an official?" asked Matt, openly puzzled.

"What's a justice of the peace?" added the brunette.

His mind side-slipped and did a couple of spins. It took him quite a while to reassemble his thoughts and try another tack.

"Supposing," he said to Matt, "this joint catches fire. What would you do?"

"Fan it to keep it going," responded Matt, fed up and making no effort to conceal the fact. He returned to the counter with the air of one who has no time to waste on half-wits.

"He'd put it out," informed the brunette. "What else would you expect him to do?"

"Supposing he couldn't?"

"He'd call in others to help him."

"And would they?"

"Of course," she assured, surveying him with pity. "They'd jump at the chance. They'd be planting a nice crop of strong obs, wouldn't they?"

"Yes, I guess so." He began to feel stalled, but made a last shot at the problem. "What if the fire were too big and fast for passers-by to tackle?"

"Seth would summon the fire squad."

Defeat receded. A touch of triumph replaced it.

"Ah, so there is a fire squad! That's what I meant by something official. That's what I've been after all along. Quick, tell me where I can find the depot."

"Bottom end of Twelfth. You can't miss it."

"Thanks." He got up in a hurry. "See you again sometime." Going out fast, he grabbed his bicycle, shoved off from the curb.

The fire depot was a big place holding four telescopic ladders, a spray tower and two multiple pumps all motorized on the usual array of fat rubber balls. Inside, Harrison came face to face with a small man wearing immense plus fours.

"Looking for someone?" asked the small man.

"The fire chief," said Harrison.

"Who's he?"

By this time prepared for that sort of thing, Harrison spoke as one would to a child. "See here, mister, this is a fire-fighting outfit. Somebody bosses it. Somebody organizes the shebang, fills forms, presses buttons, recommends promotions, kicks the shiftless, takes all the credit, transfers all the blame and generally lords it around. He's the most important guy in the bunch and everybody knows it." His forefinger tapped the other's chest. "And he's the fella I'm going to talk to if it's the last thing I do."

"Nobody's any more important than anyone else. How can they be? I think you're crazy."

"You're welcome to think what you like, but I'm telling you that—"

A shrill bell clamored, cutting off the sentence. Twenty men appeared as if by magic, boarded a ladder and a multi-pump, roared into the street.

Squat, basin-shaped helmets were the crews' only item of common attire. Apart from these, they plumbed the depths of sartorial iniquity. The man with the plus fours, who had gained the pump in one bold leap, was whirled out standing between a fat firefighter wearing a rainbow-hued cummerbund and a thin one sporting a canary yellow kilt. A late-comer decorated with earrings shaped like little bells hotly pursued the pump, snatched at its tailboard, missed, disconsolately watched the outfit disappear from sight. He mooched back, swinging his helmet in one hand.

"Just my lousy luck," he informed the gaping Harrison. "The sweetest call of the year. A big brewery. The sooner they get there the bigger the obs they'll plant on it." He licked his lips at the thought, sat on a coil of canvas hose. "Oh, well, maybe it's all for the good of my health."

"Tell me something," Harrison insisted. "How do you get a living?"

"There's a heck of a question. You can see for yourself. I'm on the fire squad."

"I know. What I mean is, who pays you?"

"Pays me?"

"Gives you money for all this."

"You talk kind of peculiar. What is money?"

Harrison rubbed his cranium to assist the circulation of blood through the brain. What is money? Yeouw. He tried another angle.

"Supposing your wife needs a new coat, how does she get it?"

"Goes to a store saddled with fire-obs, of course. She kills one or two for them."

"But what if no clothing store has had a fire?"

"You're pretty ignorant, brother. Where in this world do you come from?" His ear bells swung as he studied the other a moment, then went on, "Almost all stores have fire-obs. If they've any sense, they allocate so many per month by way of insurance. They look ahead, just in case, see? They plant obs on us, in a way, so that when we rush to the rescue we've got to kill off a dollop of theirs before we can plant any new ones of our own. That stops us overdoing it and making hogs of ourselves. Sort of cuts down the stores' liabilities. It makes sense, doesn't it?"

"Maybe, but—"

"I get it now," interrupted the other, narrowing his eyes. "You're from that spaceship. You're an Antigand"

"I'm a Terran," said Harrison with suitable dignity. "What's more, all the folk who originally settled this planet were Terrans."

"You trying to teach me history?" He gave a harsh laugh. "You're wrong. There was a five per cent strain of Martian."

"Even the Martians are descended from Terran settlers," riposted Harrison.

"So what? That was a devil of a long time back. Things change, in case you haven't heard. We've no Terrans or Martians on this world—except for your crowd which has come in unasked. We're all Gands here. And you nosey pokes are Antigands."

"We aren't anti-anything that I know of. Where did you get that idea?"

"Myob!" said the other, suddenly determined to refuse further agreement. He tossed his helmet to one side, spat on the floor.

"Huh?"

"You heard me. Go trundle your scooter."

Harrison gave up and did just that. He pedaled gloomily back to the ship.

His Excellency pinned him with an authoritative optic. "So you're back at last, mister. How many are coming and at what time?"

"None, sir," said Harrison, feeling kind of feeble.

"None?" August eyebrows rose up." Do you mean that they have refused my invitation?"

"No, sir."

The ambassador waited a moment, then said, "Come out with it, mister. Don't stand there gawping as if your push-and-puff contraption has just given birth to a roller skate. You say they haven't refused my invitation—but nobody is coming. What am I to make of that?"

"I didn't ask anyone."

"So you didn't ask!" Turning, he said to Grayder, Shelton and the others, "He didn't ask!" His attention came back to Harrison. "You forgot all about it, I presume? Intoxicated by liberty and the power of man over machine, you flashed around the town at nothing less than eighteen miles per hour, creating consternation among the citizenry, tossing their traffic laws into the ash can, putting persons in peril of their lives, not even troubling to ring your bell or—"

"I haven't got a bell, sir," denied Harrison, inwardly resenting this list of enormities. "I have a whistle operated by rotation of the rear wheel."

"There!" said the ambassador, like one abandoning all hope. He sat down, smacked his forehead several times. "Somebody's going to get a bubble-pipe." He pointed a tragic finger. "And *he's* got a whistle."

"I designed it myself, sir," Harrison told him, very informatively.

"I'm sure you did. I can imagine it. I would expect it of you." The ambassador got a fresh grip on himself. "Look, mister, tell me something in strict confidence, just between you and me." He leaned forward, put the question in a whisper that ricocheted seven times around the room. "*Why* didn't you ask anyone?"

"Couldn't find anyone to ask, sir. I did my level best but they didn't seem to know what I was talking about. Or they pretended they didn't."

"Humph!" His Excellency glanced out of the nearest port, consulted his wrist watch. "The light is fading already. Night will be upon us pretty soon. It's getting too late for further action." An annoyed grunt. "Another day gone to pot. Two days here and we're still fiddling around." His eye was jaundiced as it rested on Harrison. "All right, mister, we're wasting time anyway so we might as well hear your story in full. Tell us what happened in complete detail. That way, we may be able to dig some sense out of it."

Harrison told it, finishing, "It seemed to me, sir, that I could go on for weeks trying to argue it out with people whose brains are oriented east-west while mine points north-south. You can talk with them from now to doomsday, even get real friendly and enjoy the conversation—without either side knowing what the other is jawing about."

"So it seems," commented the ambassador, dryly. He turned to Captain Grayder. "You've been around a lot and seen many new worlds in your time. What do you make of all this twaddle, if anything?"

"A problem in semantics," said Grayder, who had been compelled by circumstances to study that subject. "One comes across it on almost every world that has been long out of touch, though usually it has not developed far enough to get really tough." He paused reminiscently. "First guy we met on Basileus said, cordially and in what he fondly imagined was perfect English, 'Joy you unboot now!' "

"Yeah? What did that mean?"

"Come inside, put on your slippers and be happy. In other words, welcome! It wasn't difficult to get, your excellency, especially when you expect that sort of thing." Grayder cast a thoughtful glance at Harrison, went on, "Here, things appear to have developed to a greater extreme. The language remains fluent, retains enough surface similarities to conceal deeper changes, but meanings have been altered, concepts discarded, new ones substituted, thought-forms reangled—and, of course, there is the inevitable impact of locally developed slang."

"Such as 'myob,' " offered His Excellency. "Now there's a queer word without recognizable Earth root. I don't like the way they use it. Sounds downright insulting. Obviously it has some sort of connection with these obs they keep batting around. It means 'my obligation' or something like that, but the significance beats me."

"There is no connection, sir," Harrison contradicted. He hesitated, saw they were waiting for him, plunged boldly on. "Coming back I met the lady who directed me to Baines' place. She asked whether I'd found him and I said yes, thank you. We chatted a bit. I asked her what 'myob' meant. She said it was initial-slang." He stopped at that point.

"Keep going," advised the ambassador. "After some of the sulphurous comments I've heard coming out the Blieder-room ventilation-shaft, I can stomach anything. What does it mean?"

"M-y-o-b," informed Harrison, blinking. "Mind your own business."

"So!" His excellency gained color. "So that's what they've been telling me all along?"

"I'm afraid so, sir."

"Evidently they've a lot to learn." His neck swelled with sudden undiplomatic fury, he smacked a large hand on the table and said, loudly, "And they are going to learn it!"

"Yes, sir," agreed Harrison, becoming more uneasy and wanting out. "May I go now and attend to my bicycle?"

"Get out of my sight!" shouted the ambassador. He made a couple of meaningless gestures, turned a florid face on Captain Grayder. "Bicycle! Does anyone on this vessel own a slingshot?"

"I doubt it, your excellency, but I will make inquiries, if you wish."

"Don't be an imbecile," ordered His Excellency. "We have our full quota of hollow-heads already."

Postponed until early morning, the next conference was relatively short and sweet. His Excellency took a seat, harumphed, straightened his tie, frowned around the table.

"Let's have another look at what we've got. We know that this planet's mules call themselves Gands, don't take much interest in their Terran origin and insist on referring to us as Antigands. That implies an education and resultant outlook inimical to ourselves. They've been trained from childhood to take it for granted that whenever we appeared upon the scene we would prove to be against whatever they are for."

"And we haven't the remotest notion of what they're for," put in Colonel Shelton, quite unnecessarily. But it served to show that he was among those present and paying attention.

"I am grimly aware of our ignorance in that respect," indorsed the ambassador. "They are maintaining a conspiracy of silence about their prime motivation. We've got to break it somehow." He cleared his throat, continued, "They have a peculiar nonmonetary economic system which, in my opinion, manages to function only because of large surpluses. It won't stand a day when overpopulation brings serious shortages. This economic setup appears to be based on co-operative techniques, private enterprise, a kindergarten's honor system and plain unadorned gimme. That makes it a good deal crazier than that food-in-the-bank wackidoo they've got on the four outer planets of the Epsilon system."

"But it works," observed Grayder, pointedly.

"After a fashion. That flap-eared engineer's bicycle works—and so does he! A motorized job would save him a lot of sweat." Pleased with this analogy, the ambassador mused it a few seconds. "This local scheme of economics—if you can call it a scheme—almost certainly is the end result of the haphazard development of some hick eccentricity brought in by the original settlers. It is overdue for motorizing, so to speak. They know it but don't want it because mentally they're three hundred years behind the times. They're afraid of change, improvement, efficiency—like most backward peoples. Moreover, some of them have a vested interest in keeping things as they are." He sniffed loudly to express his contempt. "They are antagonistic toward us simply because they don't want to be disturbed."

His authoritative stare went round the table, daring one of them to remark that this might be as good a reason as any. They were too disciplined to fall into that trap. None offered comment, so he went on.

"In due time, after we've got a grip on affairs, we are going to have a long and tedious task on our hands. We'll have to overhaul their entire educational system with a view to eliminating anti-Terran prejudices and bringing them up to date on the facts of life. We've had to do that on several other planets, though not to anything like the same extent as will be necessary here."

"We'll cope," promised someone. Ignoring him, the ambassador finished, "However, all of that is in the future. We've a problem to solve in the present. It's in our laps right now, namely, where are the reins of power and who's holding them? We've got to solve that before we can make progress. How're we going to do it?" He leaned back in his chair, added, "Get your wits working and let me have some bright suggestions."

Captain Grayder stood up, a big, leather-bound book in his hands. "Your excellency, I don't think we need exercise our minds over new plans for making contact and gaining essential information. It looks as if the next move is going to be imposed upon us."

"How do you mean?"

"There are a good many old-timers in my crew. Space lawyers, every one of them." He tapped the book. "They know official Space Regulations as well as I do. Sometimes I think they know too much."

"And so—?"

Grayder opened the book. "Regulation 127 says that on a hostile world a crew serves on a war-footing until back in space. On a nonhostile world, they serve on a peace-footing."

"What of it?"

"Regulation 131A says that on a peace-footing, the crew—with the exception of a minimum number required to keep the vessel's essential services in trim—is entitled to land-leave immediately after unloading of cargo or within seventy-two Earth hours of arrival, whichever period is the shorter." He glanced up. "By midday the men will be all set for land-leave and itching to go. There will be ructions if they don't get it."

"Will there now?" said the ambassador, smiling lopsidedly. "What if I say this world is hostile? That'll pin their ears back, won't it?"

Impassively consulting his book, Grayder came back with, "Regulation 148 says that a hostile world is defined as any planet that systematically opposes Empire citizens by force." He turned the next page. "For the purpose of these regulations, force is defined as any course of action calculated to inflict physical injury, whether or not said action succeeds in its intent."

"I don't agree." The ambassador registered a deep frown. "A world can be psychologically hostile without resorting to force. We've an example right here. It isn't a friendly world."

"There are no friendly worlds within the meaning of Space Regulations," Grayder informed. "Every planet falls into one of two classifications: hostile or nonhostile." He tapped the hard leather cover. "It's all in the book."

"We would be prize fools to let a mere book boss us around or allow the crew to boss us, either. Throw it out of the port. Stick it into the disintegrator. Get rid of it any way you like—and forget it."

"Begging your pardon, your excellency, but I can't do that." Grayder opened the tome at the beginning. "Basic regulations lA, lB and lC include the following:

whether in space or on land, a vessel's personnel remain under direct command of its captain or his nominee who will be guided entirely by Space Regulations and will be responsible only to the Space Committee situated upon Terra. The same applies to all troops, officials and civilian passengers aboard a space-traversing vessel, whether in flight or grounded—regardless of rank or authority they are subordinate to the captain or his nominee. A nominee is defined as a ship's officer performing the duties of an immediate superior when the latter is incapacitated or absent."

"All that means you are king of your castle," said the ambassador, none too pleased. "If we don't like it, we must get off the ship."

"With the greatest respect to yourself, I must agree that that is the position. I cannot help it—regulations are regulations. And the men know it!" Grayder dumped the book, poked it away from him. "Ten to one the men will wait to midday, pressing their pants, creaming their hair and so forth. They will then make approach to me in proper manner to which I cannot object. They will request the first mate to submit their leave-roster for my approval." He gave a deep sigh. "The worst I could do would be to quibble about certain names on the roster and switch a few men around—but I couldn't refuse leave to a full quota."

"Liberty to paint the town red might be a good thing after all," suggested Colonel Shelton, not averse to doing some painting himself. "A dump like this wakes up when the fleet's in port. We ought to get contacts by the dozens. That's what we want, isn't it?"

"We want to pin down this planet's leaders," the ambassador pointed out. "I can't see them powdering their faces, putting on their best hats and rushing out to invite the yoohoo from a bunch of hungry sailors." His plump features quirked. "We have got to find the needles in this haystack. That job won't be done by a gang of ratings on the rampage."

Grayder put in, "I'm inclined to agree with you, your excellency, but we'll have to take a chance on it. If the men want to go out, the circumstances deprive me of power to prevent them. Only one thing can give me the power."

"And what is that?"

"Evidence enabling me to define this world as hostile within the meaning of Space Regulations."

"Well, can't we arrange that somehow?" Without waiting for a reply, the ambassador continued, "Every crew has its incurable trouble-maker. Find yours, give him a double shot of Venusian cognac, tell him he's being granted immediate leave—but you doubt whether he'll enjoy it because these Gands view us as reasons why people dig up the drains. Then push him out of the lock. When he comes back with a black eye and a boastful story about the other fellow's condition, declare this world hostile." He waved an expressive hand. "And there you are. Physical violence. All according to the book."

"Regulation 148A, emphasizing that opposition by force must be systematic, warns that individual brawls may not be construed as evidence of hostility."

The ambassador turned an irate face upon the senior civil servant: "When you get back to Terra—if ever you do get back—you can tell the appropriate department how the space service is balled up, hamstrung, semiparalyzed and generally handicapped by bureaucrats who write books."

Before the other could think up a reply complimentary to his kind without contradicting the ambassador, a knock came at the door. First Mate Morgan entered, saluted smartly, offered Captain Grayder a sheet of paper.

"First liberty roll, sir. Do you approve it?"

Four hundred twenty men hit the town in the early afternoon. They advanced upon it in the usual manner of men overdue for the bright lights, that is to say, eagerly, expectantly, in buddy-bunches of two, three, six or ten.

Gleed attached himself to Harrison. They were two odd rankers, Gleed being the only sergeant on leave, Harrison the only tenth engineer. They were also the only two fish out of water since both were in civilian clothes and Gleed missed his uniform while Harrison felt naked without his bicycle. These trifling features gave them enough in common to justify at least one day's companionship.

"This one's a honey," declared Gleed with immense enthusiasm. "I've been on a good many liberty jaunts in my time but this one's a honey. On all other trips the boys ran up against the same problem—what to use for money. They had to go forth like a battalion of Santa Clauses, loaded up with anything that might serve for barter. Almost always nine-tenths of it wasn't of any use and had to be carted back again."

"On Persephone," informed Harrison, "a long-shanked Milik offered me a twenty-karat, blue-tinted first-water diamond for my bike."

"Jeepers, didn't you take it?"

"What was the good? I'd have had to go back sixteen light-years for another one."

"You could do without a bike for a bit."

"I can do without a diamond. I can't ride around on a diamond."

"Neither can you sell a bicycle for the price of a sportster Moon-boat."

"Yes I can. I just told you this Milik offered me a rock like an egg."

"It's a crying shame. You'd have got two hundred to two fifty thousand credits for that blinder if it was flawless." Sergeant Gleed smacked his lips at the thought of so much moola stacked on the head of a barrel. "Credits and plenty of them—that's what I love. And that's what makes this trip a honey. Every other time we've gone out, Grayder has first lectured us about creating a favorable impression, behaving in a spacemanlike manner, and so forth. This time, he talks about credits."

"The ambassador put him up to that."

"I liked it, all the same," said Gleed. "Ten credits, a bottle of cognac and double liberty for every man who brings back to the ship an adult Gand, male or female, who is sociable and willing to talk."

"It won't be easily earned."

"One hundred credits to whoever gets the name and address of the town's chief civic dignitary. A thousand credits for the name and accurate location of the world's capitol city." He whistled happily, added, "Somebody's going to be in the dough and it won't be Bidworthy. He didn't come out of the hat. I know—I was holding it."

He ceased talking, turned to watch a tall, lithe blonde striding past. Harrison pulled at his arm.

"Here's Baines' place that I told you about. Let's go in."

"Oh, all right." Gleed followed with much reluctance, his gaze still down the street.

"Good afternoon," said Harrison, brightly.

"It ain't," contradicted Jeff Baines. "Trade's bad. There's a semifinal being played and it's taken half the town away. They'll think about their bellies after I've closed. Probably make a rush on me tomorrow and I won't be able to serve them fast enough."

"How can trade be bad if you don't take money even when it's good?" inquired Gleed, reasonably applying what information Harrison had given him.

Jeff's big moon eyes went over him slowly, then turned to Harrison. "So he's another bum off your boat. What's he talking about?"

"Money," said Harrison. "It's stuff we use to simplify trade. It's printed stuff, like documentary obs of various sizes."

"That tells me a lot," Jeff Baines observed. "It tells me a crowd that has to make a printed record of every ob isn't to be trusted—because they don't even trust each other." Waddling to his high stool, he squatted on it. His breathing was labored and wheezy. "And that confirms what our schools have always taught—that an Antigand would swindle his widowed mother."

"Your schools have got it wrong," assured Harrison.

"Maybe they have." Jeff saw no need to argue the point. "But we'll play safe until we know different." He looked them over. "What do you two want, anyway?"

"Some advice," shoved in Gleed, quickly. "We're out on the spree. Where's the best places to go for food and fun?"

"How long you got?"

"Until night fall tomorrow."

"No use." Jeff Baines shook his head sorrowfully. "It'd take you from now to then to plant enough obs to qualify for what's going. Besides, lots of folk wouldn't let any Antigand dump an ob on them. They're kind of particular, see?"

"Look," said Harrison. "Can't we get so much as a square meal?"

"Well, I dunno about that." Jeff thought it over, rubbing several chins. "You might manage so much—but I can't help you this time. There's nothing I want of you, so you can't use any obs I've got planted."

"Can you make any suggestions?"

"If you were local citizens, it'd be different. You could get all you want right now by taking on a load of obs to be killed sometime in the future as and when the chances come along. But I can't see anyone giving credit to Antigands who are here today and gone tomorrow."

"Not so much of the gone tomorrow talk," advised Gleed. "When an Imperial Ambassador is sent it means that Terrans will be here for keeps."

"Who says so?"

"The Empire says so. You're part of it, aren't you?"

"Nope," said Jeff. "We aren't part of anything and don't want to be, either. What's more, nobody's going to make us part of anything."

Gleed leaned on the counter and gazed absently at a large can of pork. "Seeing I'm out of uniform and not on parade, I sympathize with you though I still shouldn't say it. I wouldn't care to be taken over body and soul by other-world bureaucrats, myself. But you folk are going to have a tough time beating us off. That's the way it is."

"Not with what we've got," Jeff opined. He seemed mighty self-confident.

"You ain't got so much," scoffed Gleed, more in friendly criticism than open contempt. He turned to Harrison. "Have they?"

"It wouldn't appear so," ventured Harrison.

"Don't go by appearances," Jeff advised. "We've more than you'd care to guess at."

"Such as what?"

"Well, just for a start, we've got the mightiest weapon ever thought up by mind of man. We're Gands, see? So we don't need ships and guns and suchlike playthings. We've got something better. It's effective. There's no defense against it."

"I'd like to see it," Gleed challenged. Data on a new and exceptionally powerful weapon should be a good deal more valuable than the mayor's address. Grayder might be sufficiently overcome by the importance thereof to increase the take to five thousand credits. With a touch of sarcasm, he added, "But, of course, I can't expect you to give away secrets."

"There's nothing secret about it," said Jeff, very surprisingly. "You can have it for free any time you want. Any Gand would give it to you for the asking. Like to know why?"

"You bet."

"Because it works one way only. We can use it against you—but you can't use it against us."

"There's no such thing. There's no weapon inventable which the other guy can't employ once he gets his hands on it and knows how to operate it."

"You sure

"Positive," said Gleed, with no hesitation whatever. "I've been in the space-service troops for twenty years and you can't fiddle around that long without learning all about weapons from string bows to H-bombs. You're trying to kid me—and it won't work. A one-way weapon is impossible."

"Don't argue with him," Harrison suggested to Baines. "He'll never be convinced until he's shown."

"I can see that." Jeff Baines' face creased in a slow grin. "I told you that you could have our wonder-weapon for the asking. Why don't you ask?"

"All right, I'm asking." Gleed put it without much enthusiasm. A weapon that would be presented on request, without even the necessity of first planting a minor ob, couldn't he so mighty after all. His imaginary five thousand credits shrank to five, thence to none. "Hand it over and let me try it."

Swiveling heavily on his stool, Jeff reached to the wall, removed a small, shiny plaque from its hook, passed it across the counter.

"You may keep it," he informed. "And much good may it do you."

Gleed examined it, turning it over and over between his fingers. It was nothing more than an oblong strip of substance resembling ivory. One side was polished and bare. The other bore three letters deeply engraved in bold style:

F—I.W.

Glancing up, his features puzzled, he said, "Call this a weapon?"

"Certainly."

"Then I don't get it." He passed the plaque to Harrison. "Do you?"

"No." Harrison had a good look at it, spoke to Baines. "What does this F—I.W. mean?"

"Initial-slang," informed Baines. "Made correct by common usage. It has become a world-wide motto. You'll see it all over the place, if you haven't noticed it already."

"I have spotted it here and there but attached no importance to it and thought nothing of it. I remember now I've seen it inscribed in several places, including Seth's and the fire depot."

"It was on the sides of that bus we couldn't empty," added Gleed. "Didn't mean anything to me."

"It means plenty," said Jeff. *"Freedom—I Won't!"*

"That kills me," Gleed told him. "I'm stone dead already. I've dropped in my tracks." He watched Harrison thoughtfully pocketing the plaque. "A bit of abracadabra. What a weapon!"

"Ignorance is bliss," remarked Baines, strangely certain of himself. "Especially when you don't know that what you're playing with is the safety catch of something that goes bang."

"All right," challenged Gleed, taking him up on that. "Tell us how it works."

"I won't." The grin reappeared. Baines seemed highly satisfied about something.

"That's a fat lot of help." Gleed felt let down, especially over those momentarily hoped-for credits. "You boast about one-way weapon, toss across a slip of stuff with three letters on it and then go dumb. Any guy can talk out the back of his neck. How about backing up your talk?"

"I won't," said Baines, his grin becoming broader than ever. He favored the onlooking Harrison with a fat, significant wink.

It made something spark vividly inside Harrison's mind. His jaw dropped, he took the plaque from his pocket, stared at it as if seeing it for the first time.

"Give it me back," requested Baines, watching him.

Replacing it in his pocket, Harrison said very firmly, "I won't."

Baines chuckled. "Some folk catch on quicker than others."

Resenting that remark, Gleed held his hand out to Harrison. "Let's have another look at that thing."

"I won't," said Harrison, meeting him eye for eye.

"Hey, that's not the way—" Gleed's protesting voice died out. He stood there a moment, his optics slightly glassy while his brain performed several loops. Then, in hushed tones, he said, "Good grief!"

"Precisely," approved Baines. "Grief, and plenty of it. You were a bit slow on the uptake."

Overcome by the flood of insubordinate ideas now pouring upon him, Gleed said hoarsely to Harrison, "Come on, let's get out of here. I gotta think. I gotta think some place quiet."

There was a tiny park with seats and lawns and flowers and a little fountain around which a small bunch of children were playing. Choosing a place facing a colorful carpet of exotic un-Terran blooms, they sat and brooded a while.

In due course, Gleed commented, "For one solitary guy it would be martyrdom, but for a whole world—" His voice drifted off, came back. "I've been taking this about as far as I can make it go and the results give me the leaping fantods."

Harrison said nothing.

"F'rinstance," Gleed continued, "supposing when I go back to the ship that snorting rhinoceros Bidworthy gives me an order. I give him the frozen wolliker and say, 'I won't!' He either drops dead or throws me in the clink."

"That would do you a lot of good."

"Wait a bit—I ain't finished. I'm in the clink, but the job still needs doing. So Bidworthy picks on someone else. The victim, being a soul-mate of mine, also donates the icy optic and says, 'I won't!' In the clink he goes and I've got company. Bidworthy tries again. And again. There's more of us warming the jug. It'll only hold twenty. So they take over the engineer's mess."

"Leave our mess out of this," Harrison requested.

"They take the mess," Gleed insisted, thoroughly determined to penalize the engineers. "Pretty soon it's crammed to the roof with I-won'ters. Bidworthy's still raking 'em in as fast as he can go—if by that time he hasn't burst a dozen blood vessels. So they take over the Blieder dormitories."

"Why keep picking on my crowd?"

"And pile them with bodies ceiling-high," Gleed said, getting sadistic pleasure out of the notion. "Until in the end Bidworthy has to get buckets and brushes and go down on his knees and do his own deck-scrubbing while Grayder, Shelton and the rest act as clink guards. By that time, His Loftiness the ambassador is in the galley busily cooking for you and me, assisted by a disconcerted bunch of yessing penpushers." He had another somewhat awed look at the picture and finished, "Holy smoke!"

A colored ball rolled his way, he stooped, picked it up and held on to it. Promptly a boy of about seven ran up, eyed him gravely.

"Give me my ball, please."

"I won't," said Gleed, his fingers firmly around it.

There was no protest, no anger, no tears. The child merely registered disappointment, turned to go away.

"Here you are, sonny." He tossed the ball.

"Thanks." Grabbing it, the other ran off.

Harrison said, "What if every living being in the Empire, all the way from Prometheus to Kaldor Four, across eighteen hundred light-years of space, gets an income-tax demand, tears it up and says, 'I won't!'? What happens then?"

"We'd need a second universe for a pen and a third one to provide the guards."

"There would be chaos," Harrison went on. He nodded toward the fountain and the children playing around it. "But it doesn't look like chaos here. Not to my eyes. So that means they don't overdo this blank refusal business. They apply it judiciously on some mutually recognized basis. What that basis might be beats me completely."

"Me, too."

An elderly man stopped near them, surveyed them hesitantly, decided to pick on a passing youth.

"Can you tell me where I can find the roller for Martinstown?"

"Other end of Eighth," informed the youth. "One every hour. They'll fix your manacles before they start."

"Manacles?" The oldster raised white eyebrows. "Whatever for?"

"That route runs past the spaceship. The Antigands may try to drag you out."

"Oh, yes, of course." He ambled on, glanced again at Gleed and Harrison, remarked in passing, "These Antigands—such a nuisance."

"Definitely," indorsed Gleed. "We keep telling them to get out and they keep on saying, 'We won't.' "

The old gentleman missed a step, recovered, gave him a peculiar look, continued on his way.

"One or two seem to cotton on to our accents," Harrison remarked. "Though nobody noticed mine when I was having that feed in Seth's."

Gleed perked up with sudden interest. "Where you've had one feed you can get another. C'mon, let's try. What have we got to lose?"

"Our patience," said Harrison. He stood up. We'll pick on Seth. If he won't play, we'll have a try at someone else. And if nobody will play, we'll skin out fast before we starve to death."

'"Which appears to be exactly what they want us to do," Gleed pointed out. He scowled to himself. "They'll get their way over my dead body."

"That's how," agreed Harrison. "Over your dead body."

Matt came up with a cloth over one arm. "I'm serving no Antigands."

"You served me last time," Harrison told him.

"That's as maybe. I didn't know you were off that ship. But I know now!" He flicked the cloth across one corner of the table. "No Antigands served by me."

"Is there any other place where we might get a meal?"

"Not unless somebody will let you plant an ob on them. They won't do that if they're wise to you, but there's a chance they might make the same mistake I did." Another flick across the corner. "I don't make them twice."

"You're making another right now," said Gleed, his voice tough and authoritative. He nudged Harrison. "Watch this!" His hand came out of a side pocket holding a tiny blaster. Pointing it at Matt's middle, he continued, "Ordinarily, I could get into trouble for this, if those on the ship were in the mood to make trouble. But they aren't. They're soured up on you two-legged mules." He motioned the weapon. "Get walking and bring us two full plates."

"I won't,"' said Matt, firming his jaw and ignoring the gun.

Gleed thumbed the safety catch which moved with an audible click. "It's touchy now. It'd go off at a sneeze. Start moving."

"I won't," insisted Matt.

Gleed disgustedly shoved the weapon back into his pocket. "I was only kidding you. It isn't energized."

"Wouldn't have made the slightest difference if it had been," Matt assured. "I serve no Antigands, and that's that!"

"Suppose I'd gone haywire and blown you in half?"

"How could I have served you then?" he inquired. "A dead person is of no use to anyone. Time you Antigands learned a little logic."

With that parting shot he went away.

"He's got something there," observed Harrison, patently depressed. "What can you do with a waxie one? Nothing whatever! You'd have put him clean out of your own power."

"Don't know so much. A couple of stiffs lying around might sharpen the others. They'd get really eager."

"You're thinking of them in Terran terms," Harrison said. "It's a mistake. They're not Terrans, no matter where they came from originally. They're Gands." He mused a moment. "I've no notion of just what Gands are supposed to be but I reckon they're some kind of fanatics. Terra exported one-track-minders by the millions around the time of the Great Explosion. Look at that crazy crowd they've got on Hygeia."

"I was there once and I tried hard not to look," confessed Gleed, reminiscently. "Then I couldn't stop looking. Not so much as a fig leaf between the lot. They insisted that we were obscene because we wore clothes. So eventually we had to take them off. Know what I was wearing at the time we left?"

"A dignified poise," Harrison suggested.

"That and an identity disk, cupro-silver, official issue, spacemen, for the use of," Gleed informed. "Plus three wipes of grease-paint on my left arm to show I was a sergeant. I looked every inch a sergeant—like heck I did!"

"I know. I had a week in that place."

"We'd a rear admiral on board," Gleed went on. "As a fine physical specimen he resembled a pair of badly worn suspenders. He couldn't overawe anyone while in his birthday suit. Those Hygeians cited his deflation as proof that they'd got real democracy, as distinct from our fake version." He clucked his tongue. "I'm not so sure they're wrong."

"The creation of the Empire has created a queer proposition," Harrison meditated. "Namely, that Terra is always right while sixteen hundred and forty-two planets are invariably wrong."

"You're getting kind of seditious, aren't you?"

Harrison said nothing. Gleed glanced at him, found his attention elsewhere, followed his gaze to a brunette who had just entered.

"Nice," approved Gleed. "Not too young, not too old. Not too fat, not too thin. Just right."

"I know her." Harrison waved to attract her attention.

She tripped lightly across the room, sat at their table. Harrison made the introduction.

"Friend of mine. Sergeant Gleed."

"Arthur," corrected Gleed, eating her.

"Mine's Elissa," she told him. "What's a sergeant supposed to be?"

"A sort of over-above under-thing," Gleed informed. "I pass along the telling to the guys who do the doing."

Her eyes widened. "Do you mean that people really allow themselves to be told?"

"Of course. Why not?"

"It sounds crazy to me." Her gaze shifted to Harrison. "I'll be ignorant of *your* name forever, I suppose?"

He hastened to repair the omission, adding, "But I don't like James. I prefer Jim."

"Then we'll let it be Jim." She examined the place, looking over the counter, the other tables. "Has Matt been to you two?"

"Yes. He refuses to serve us."

She shrugged warm shoulders. "It's his right. Everyone has the right to refuse. That's freedom, isn't it?"

"We call it mutiny," said Gleed.

"Don't be so childish," she reproved. She stood up, moved away. "You wait here. I'll go see Seth."

"I don't get this," admitted Gleed, when she had passed out of earshot. "According to that fat fella in the delicatessen, their technique is to give us the cold shoulder until we run away in a huff. But this dame acts friendly. She's . . . she's—" He stopped while he sought for a suitable word, found it and said, "She's un-Gandian."

"Not so," Harrison contradicted. "They've the right to say, 'I won't.' She's practicing it."

"By gosh, yes! I hadn't thought of that. They can work it any way they like, and please themselves."

"Sure." He dropped his voice. "Here she comes."

Resuming her seat, she primped her hair, said, "Seth will serve us personally."

"Another traitor," remarked Gleed with a grin.

"On one condition," she went on. "You two must wait and have a talk with him before you leave."

"Cheap at the price," Harrison decided. A thought struck him and he asked, "Does this mean you'll have to kill several obs for all three of us?"

"Only one for myself."

"How come?"

"Seth's got ideas of his own. He doesn't feel happy about Antigands any more than does anyone else."

"And so?"

"But he's got the missionary instinct. He doesn't agree entirely with the idea of giving all Antigands the ghost-treatment. He thinks it should be reserved only for those too stubborn or stupid to be converted." She smiled at Gleed, making his top hairs quiver. "Seth thinks that any intelligent Antigand is a would-be Gand."

"What is a Gand anyway?" asked Harrison.

"An inhabitant of this world, of course."

"I mean, where did they dig up the name?"

"From Gandhi," she said.

Harrison frowned in puzzlement. "Who the deuce was he?"

"An ancient Terran. The one who invented The Weapon."

"Never heard of him."

"That doesn't surprise me," she remarked.

"Doesn't it?" He felt a little irritated. "Let me tell you that these days we Terrans get as good an education as—"

"Calm down, Jim." She made it more soothing by pronouncing it "Jeem." "All I mean is that ten to one he's been blanked out of your history books. He might have given you unwanted ideas, see? You couldn't be expected to know what you've been deprived of the chance to learn."

"If you mean that Terran history is censored, I don't believe it," he asserted.

"It's your right to refuse to believe. That's freedom, isn't it?"

"Up to a point. A man has duties. He's no right to refuse those."

"No?" She raised tantalizing eyebrows, delicately curved. "Who defines those duties—himself, or somebody else?"

"His superiors, most times."

"No man is superior to another. No man has the right to define another man's duties." She paused, eyeing him speculatively. "If anyone on Terra exercises such idiotic power, it is only because idiots permit him. They fear freedom. They prefer to be told. They like being ordered around. What men!"

"I shouldn't listen to you," protested Gleed, chipping in. His leathery face was flushed. "You're as naughty as you're pretty."

"Afraid of your own thoughts?" she jibed, pointedly ignoring his compliment.

He went redder. "Not on your life. But I—" His voice tailed off as Seth arrived with three loaded plates and dumped them on the table.

"See you afterward," reminded Seth. He was medium-sized, with thin features and sharp, quick-moving eyes. "Got something to say to you."

Seth joined them shortly after the end of the meal. Taking a chair, he wiped condensed-steam off his face, looked them over.

"How much do you two know?"

"Enough to argue about it," put in Elissa. "They are bothered about duties, who defines them, and who does them."

"With good reason," Harrison riposted. "You can't escape them yourselves."

"Meaning—?" asked Seth.

"This world runs on some strange system of swapping obligations. How will any person kill an ob unless he recognizes his duty to do so?"

"Duty has nothing to do with it," said Seth. "And if it did happen to be a matter of duty, every man would recognize it for himself. It would be outrageous impertinence for anyone else to remind him, unthinkable to anyone to order him."

"Some guys must make an easy living," interjected Gleed. "There's nothing to stop them that I can see." He studied Seth briefly before he continued, "How can you cope with a citizen who has no conscience?"

"Easy as pie."

Elissa suggested, "Tell them the story of Idle Jack."

"It's a kid's yarn," explained Seth. "All children here know it by heart. It's a classic fable like . . . like—" He screwed up his face. "I've lost track of the Terran tales the first comers brought with them."

"Red Riding Hood," offered Harrison.

"Yes." Seth seized on it gratefully. "Something like that one. A nursery story." He licked his lips, began, "This Idle Jack came from Terra as a baby, grew up in our new world, studied our economic system and thought he'd be mighty smart. He decided to become a scratcher."

"What's a scratcher?" inquired Gleed.

"One who lives by taking obs and does nothing about killing them or planting any of his own. One who accepts everything that's going and gives nothing in return."

"I get it. I've known one or two like that in my time."

"Up to age sixteen, Jack got away with it. He was a kid, see. All kids tend to scratch to a certain extent. We expect it and allow for it. After sixteen, he was soon in the soup."

"How?" urged Harrison, more interested than he was willing to show.

"He went around the town gathering obs by the armful. Meals, clothes and all sorts for the mere asking. It's not a big town. There are no big ones on this planet. They're just small enough for everyone to know everyone—and everyone does plenty of gabbing. Within three or four months the entire town knew Jack was a determined scratcher."

"Go on," said Harrison, getting impatient.

"Everything dried up," said Seth. "Wherever Jack went, people gave him the 'I won't.' That's freedom, isn't it? He got no meals, no clothes, no entertainment, no company, nothing! Soon he became terribly hungry, busted into someone's larder one night, gave himself the first square meal in a week."

"What did they do about that?"

"Nothing. Not a thing."

"That would encourage him some, wouldn't it?"

"How could it?" Seth asked, with a thin smile. "It did him no good. Next day his belly was empty again. He had to repeat the performance. And the next day. And the next. People became leery, locked up their stuff, kept watch on it. It became harder and harder. It became so unbearably hard that it was soon a lot easier to leave the town and try another. So Idle Jack went away."

"To do the same again," Harrison suggested.

"With the same results for the same reasons," retorted Seth. "On he went to a third town, a fourth, a fifth, a twentieth. He was stubborn enough to be witless."

"He was getting by," Harrison observed. "Taking all at the mere cost of moving around."

"No he wasn't. Our towns are small, like I said. And folk do plenty of visiting from one to another. In town number two Jack had to risk being seen and talked about by someone from town number one. As he went on it got a whole lot worse. In the twentieth he had to take a chance on gabby visitors from any of the previous nineteen." Seth leaned forward, said with emphasis, "He never got to town number twenty-eight."

"No?"

"He lasted two weeks in number twenty-five, eight days in twenty-six, one day in twenty-seven. That was almost the end."

"What did he do then?"

"Took to the open country, tried to live on roots and wild berries. Then he disappeared—until one day some walkers found him swinging from a tree. The body was emaciated and clad in rags. Loneliness and self-neglect had killed him. That was Idle Jack, the scratcher. He wasn't twenty years old."

"On Terra," informed Gleed, "we don't hang people merely for being lazy."

"Neither do we," said Seth. "We leave them free to go hang themselves." He eyed them shrewdly, went on, "But don't let it worry you. Nobody has been driven to such drastic measures in my lifetime, leastways, not that I've heard about. People honor their obs as a matter of economic necessity and not from any sense of duty. Nobody gives orders, nobody pushes anyone around, but there's a kind of compulsion built into the circumstances of this planet's way of living. People play square—or they suffer. Nobody enjoys suffering—not even a numb-skull."

"Yes, I suppose you're right," put in Harrison, much exercised in mind.

"You bet I'm dead right!" Seth assured. "But what I wanted to talk to you two about is something more important. It's this: What's your real ambition in life?"

Without hesitation, Gleed said, "To ride the spaceways while remaining in one piece."

"Same here," Harrison contributed.

"I guessed that much. You'd not be in the space service if it wasn't your choice. But you can't remain in it forever. All good things come to an end. What then?"

Harrison fidgeted uneasily. "I don't care to think of it."

"Some day, you'll have to," Seth pointed out. "How much longer have you got?"

"Four and a half Earth years."

Seth's gaze turned to Gleed.

"Three Earth years."

"Not long," Seth commented. "I didn't expect you would have much time left. It's a safe bet that any ship penetrating this deeply into space has a crew composed mostly of old-timers getting near the end of their terms. The practiced hands get picked for the awkward jobs. By the day your boat lands again on Terra it will be the end of the trail for many of them, won't it?"

"It will for me," Gleed admitted, none too happy at the thought.

"Time—the older you get the faster it goes. Yet when you leave the service you'll still be comparatively young." He registered a faint, taunting smile. "I suppose you'll then obtain a private space vessel and continue roaming the cosmos on your own?"

"Impossible," declared Gleed. "The best a rich man can afford is a Moon-boat. Puttering to and fro between a satellite and its primary is no fun when you're used to Blieder-zips across the galaxy. The smallest space-going craft is far beyond reach of the wealthiest. Only governments can afford them."

"By 'governments' you mean communities?"

"In a way."

"Well, then, what are you going to do when your space-roving days are over?"

"I'm not like Big Ears here." Gleed jerked an indicative thumb at Harrison. "I'm a trooper and not a technician. So my choice is limited by lack of qualifications." He rubbed his chin, looked wistful. "I was born and brought up on a farm. I still know a good deal about farming. So I'd like to get a small one of my own and settle down."

"Think you'll manage it?" asked Seth, watching him.

"On Falder or Hygeia or Norton's Pink Heaven or some other undeveloped planet. But not on Terra. My savings won't extend to that. I don't get half enough to meet Earth costs."

"Meaning you can't pile up enough obs?"

"I can't," agreed Gleed, lugubriously. "Not even if I saved until I'd got a white beard four feet long."

"So there's Terra's reward for a long spell of faithful service—forego your heart's desire or get out?"

"Shut up!"

"I won't," said Seth. He leaned nearer. "Why do you think two hundred thousand Gands came to this world, Doukhobors to Hygeia, Quakers to Centauri B., and all the others to their selected haunts? Because Terra's reward for good citizenship was the peremptory order to knuckle down or get out. So we got out."

"It was just as well, anyway," Elissa interjected. "According to our history books, Terra was badly overcrowded. We went away and relieved the pressure."

"That's beside the point," reproved Seth. He continued with Gleed. "You want a farm. It can't be on Terra much as you'd like it there. Terra says, 'No! Get out!' So it's got to be some place else." He waited for that to sink in, then, "Here, you can have one for the mere taking." He snapped his fingers. "Like that!"

"You can't kid me," said Gleed, wearing the expression of one eager to be kidded. "Where are the hidden strings?"

"On this planet, any plot of ground belongs to the person in possession, the one who is making use of it. Nobody disputes his claim so long as he continues to use it. All you need do is look around for a suitable piece of unused territory—of which there is plenty—and start using it. From that moment it's yours. Immediately you cease using it and walk out, it's anyone else's, for the taking."

"Zipping meteors!" Gleed was incredulous.

"Moreover, if you look around long enough and strike really lucky," Seth continued, "you might stake first claim to a farm someone else has abandoned because of death, illness, a desire to move elsewhere, a chance at something else he liked better, or any other excellent reason. In that case, you would walk into ground already part-prepared, with farmhouse, milking shed, barns and the rest. And it would be yours, all yours."

"What would I owe the previous occupant?" asked Gleed.

"Nothing. Not an ob. Why should you? If he isn't buried, he has got out for the sake of something else equally free. He can't have the benefit both ways, coming and going."

"It doesn't make sense to me. Somewhere there's a snag. Somewhere I've got to pour out hard cash or pile up obs."

"Of course you have. You start a farm. A handful of local folk help you build a house. They dump heavy obs on you. The carpenter wants farm produce for his family for the next couple of years. You give it, thus killing that ob. You continue giving it for a couple of extra years, thus planting an ob on *him.* First time you want fences mending, or some other suitable task doing, along he comes to kill *that* ob. And so with all the rest, including the people who supply your raw materials, your seeds and machinery, or do your trucking for you."

"They won't all want milk and potatoes," Gleed pointed out.

"Don't know what you mean by potatoes. Never heard of them."

"How can I square up with someone who may be getting all the farm produce he wants from elsewhere?"

"Easy," said Seth. "A tinsmith supplies you with several churns. He doesn't want food. He's getting all he needs from another source. His wife and three daughters are overweight and dieting. The mere thought of a load from your farm gives them the horrors."

"Well?"

"But this tinsmith's tailor, or his cobbler, have got obs on him which he hasn't had the chance to kill. So he transfers them to you. As soon as you're able, you give the tailor or cobbler what they need to satisfy the obs, thus doing the tinsmith's killing along with your own." He gave his usual half-smile, added, "And everyone is happy."

Gleed stewed it over, frowning while he did it. "You're tempting me. You shouldn't ought to. It's a criminal offense to try divert a spaceman from his allegiance. It's sedition. Terra is tough with sedition."

"Tough my eye!" said Seth, sniffing contemptuously. "We've Gand laws here."

"All you have to do," suggested Elissa, sweetly persuasive, "is say to yourself that you've got to go back to the ship, that it's your duty to go back, that neither the ship nor Terra can get along without you." She tucked a curl away. "Then be a free individual and say, 'I won't!' "

"They'd skin me alive. Bidworthy would preside over the operation in person."

"I don't think so," Seth offered. "This Bidworthy—whom I presume to be anything but a jovial character—stands with you and the rest of your crew at the same junction. The road before him splits two ways. He's got to take one or the other and there's no third alternative. Sooner or later he'll be hell-bent for home, eating his top lip as he goes, or else he'll be running around in a truck delivering your milk—because, deep inside himself, that's what he's always wanted to do."

"You don't know him like I do," mourned Gleed. "He uses a lump of old iron for a soul."

"Funny," remarked Harrison, "I always thought of *you* that way—until today."

"I'm off duty," said Gleed, as though that explained everything. "I can relax and let the ego zoom around outside of business hours." He stood up, formed his jaw. "But I'm going back on duty. Right now!"

"You're not due before sundown tomorrow," Harrison protested.

"Maybe I'm not. But I'm going back all the same."

Elissa opened her mouth, closed it as Seth nudged her. They sat in silence and watched Gleed march determinedly out.

"It's a good sign," commented Seth, strangely self-assured. "He's been handed a wallop right where he's weakest." He chuckled low down, turned to Harrison. "What's *your* ultimate ambition?"

"Thanks for the meal. It was a good one and I needed it." Harrison stood up, manifestly embarrassed. He gestured toward the door. "I'm going to catch him up. If he's returning to the ship, I think I'll do likewise."

Again Seth nudged Elissa. They said nothing as Harrison made his way out, carefully closing the door behind him.

"Sheep," decided Elissa, disappointed for no obvious reason. "One follows another. Just like sheep."

"Not so," Seth contradicted. "They're humans animated by the same thoughts, the same emotions, as were our forefathers who had nothing sheeplike about them." Twisting round in his chair, he beckoned to Matt. "Bring us two shemaks." Then to Elissa. "My guess is that it won't pay that ship to hang around too long."

The battleship's caller-system bawled imperatively, "Fanshaw, Folsom, Fuller, Garson, Gleed, Gregory, Haines, Harrison, Hope—" and down through the alphabet.

A trickle of men flowed along the passages, catwalks and alleyways toward the fore chartroom. They gathered outside it in small clusters, chattering in undertones and sending odd scraps of conversation echoing down the corridor.

"Wouldn't say anything to us but, 'Myob!' Got sick and tired of it after a while."

"You ought to have split up, like we did. That show place on the outskirts didn't know what a Terran looks like. I just walked in and took a seat."

"Hear about Meakin? He mended a leaky roof, chose a bottle of double dith in payment and mopped the lot. He was dead flat when we found him. Had to be carried back."

"Some guys have all the luck. We got the brush-off wherever we showed our faces. It gets you down."

"You should have separated, like I said."

"Half the mess must be still lying in the gutter. They haven't turned up yet."

"Grayder will be hopping mad. He'd have stopped this morning's second quota if he'd known in time."

Every now and again First Mate Morgan stuck his head out of the chartroom door and uttered a name already voiced on the caller. Frequently there was no response.

"Harrison!" he yelled.

With a puzzled expression, Harrison went inside. Captain Grayder was there, seated behind a desk and gazing moodily at a list lying before him. Colonel Shelton was stiff and erect to one side, with Major Hame slightly behind him. Both wore the pained expressions of those tolerating a bad smell while the plumber goes looking for the leak.

His Excellency was tramping steadily to and fro in front of the desk, muttering deep down in his chins. "Barely five days and already the rot has set in." He turned as Harrison entered, fired off sharply, "So it's you, mister. When did you return from leave?"

"The evening before last, sir."

"Ahead of time, eh? That's curious. Did you get a puncture or something?"

"No, sir. I didn't take my bicycle with me."

"Just as well," approved the ambassador. "If you had done so, you'd have been a thousand miles away by now and still pushing hard."

"Why, sir?"

"Why? He asks me why! That's precisely what I'd like to know—why?" He fumed a bit, then inquired, "Did you visit this town by yourself, or in company?"

"I went with Sergeant Gleed, sir."

"Call him," ordered the ambassador, looking at Morgan.

Opening the door, Morgan obediently shouted, "Gleed! Gleed!"

No answer.

He tried again, without result. They put it over the caller-system again. Sergeant Gleed refused to be among those present.

"Has he booked in?"

Grayder consulted his list. "In early. Twenty-four hours ahead of time. He may have sneaked out again with the second liberty quota this morning and omitted to book it."

"That's a double crime."

"If he's not on the ship, he's off the ship, crime or no crime."

"Yes, your excellency." Captain Grayder registered slight weariness.

"GLEED!" howled Morgan, outside the door. A moment later he poked his head inside, said, "Your excellency, one of the men says Sergeant Gleed is not on board because he saw him in town quite recently."

"Send him in." The ambassador made an impatient gesture at Harrison. "Stay where you are and keep those confounded ears from flapping. I've not finished with you yet."

A long, gangling grease-monkey came in, blinked around, a little awed by high brass.

What do you know about Sergeant Gleed?" demanded the ambassador.

The other licked his lips, seemed sorry that he had mentioned the missing man. "It's like this, your honor, I—"

"Call me 'sir.' "

"Yes, sir." More disconcerted blinking. "I went out with the second party early this morning, came back a couple of hours ago because my stomach was acting up. On the way, I saw Sergeant Gleed and spoke to him."

"Where? When?"

"In town, sir. He was sitting in one of those big long-distance coaches. I thought it a bit queer."

"Get down to the roots, man! What did he tell you, if anything?"

"Not much, sir. He seemed pretty chipper about something. Mentioned a young widow struggling to look after two hundred acres. Someone had told him about her and he thought he'd take a peek." He hesitated, backed away a couple of paces, added, "He also said I'd see him in irons or never."

"One of *your* men," said the ambassador to Colonel Shelton. "A trooper, allegedly well-disciplined. One with long service, three stripes, and a pension to lose." His attention returned to the informant "Did he say exactly where he was going?"

"No, sir. I asked him, but he just grinned and said, 'Myob!' So I came back to the ship."

"All right. You may go." His Excellency watched the other depart, then continued with Harrison. "You were with that first quota."

"Yes, sir."

"Let me tell you something, mister. Four hundred twenty men went out. Only two hundred have returned. Forty of those were in various stages of alcoholic turpitude. Ten of them are in the clink yelling, 'I won't!' in steady chorus. Doubtless they'll go on yelling until they've sobered up."

He stared at Harrison as if that worthy were personally responsible, then went on, "There's something paradoxical about this. I can understand the drunks. There are always a few individuals who blow their tops first day on land. But of the two hundred who have condescended to come back, about half returned before time, the same as you did. Their reasons were identical—the town was unfriendly, everyone treated them like ghosts until they'd had enough."

Harrison made no comment.

"So we have two diametrically opposed reactions," the ambassador complained. "One gang of men say the place stinks so much that they'd rather be back on the ship. Another gang finds it so hospitable that either they get filled to the gills on some stuff called double dith, or they stay sober and desert the service. I want an explanation. There's got to be one somewhere. You've been twice in this town. What can you tell us?"

Carefully, Harrison said, "It all depends on whether or not you're spotted as a Terran. Also on whether you meet Gands who'd rather convert you than give you the brush-off." He pondered a moment, finished, "Uniforms are a giveaway."

"You mean they're allergic to uniforms?"

"More or less, sir."

"Any idea why?"

"Couldn't say for certain, sir. I don't know enough about them yet. As a guess, I think they may have been taught to associate uniforms with the Terran regime from which their ancestors escaped."

"Escaped nothing!" scoffed the ambassador. "They grabbed the benefit of Terran inventions, Terran techniques and Terran manufacturing ability to go some place where they'd have more elbow room." He gave Harrison the sour eye. "Don't any of them wear uniforms?"

"Not that I could recognize as such. They seem to take pleasure in expressing their individual personalities by wearing anything they fancy, from pigtails to pink boots. Oddity in attire is the norm among the Gands. Uniformity is the real oddity—they think it's submissive and degrading."

"You refer to them as Gands. Where did they dig up that name?"

Harrison told him, thinking back to Elissa as she explained it. In his mind's eye he could see her now. And Seth's place with the tables set and steam rising behind the counter and mouth-watering smells oozing from the background. Now that he came to visualize the scene again, it appeared to embody an elusive but essential something that the ship had never possessed.

"And this person," he concluded, "invented what they call The Weapon."

"Hm-m-m! And they assert he was a Terran? What does he look like? Did you see a photograph or a statue?"

"They don't erect statues, sir. They say no person is more important than another."

"Bunkum!" snapped the ambassador, instinctively rejecting that viewpoint. "Did it occur to you to ask at what period in history this wonderful weapon was tried out?"

"No, sir," Harrison confessed. "I didn't think it important."

"You wouldn't. Some of you men are too slow to catch a Callistrian sloth wandering in its sleep. I don't criticize your abilities as spacemen, but as intelligence-agents you're a dead loss."

"I'm sorry, sir," said Harrison.

Sorry? You louse! whispered something deep within his own mind. *Why should you be sorry? He's only a pompous fat man who couldn't kill an ob if he tried. He's no better than you. Those raw boys prancing around on Hygeia would maintain that he's not as good as you because he's got a pot belly. Yet you keep looking at his pot belly and saying, "Sir," and, "I'm sorry." If he tried to ride your bike he'd fall off before he'd gone ten yards. Go spit in his eye and say, "I won't." You're not scared, are you?*

"No!" announced Harrison, loudly and firmly.

Captain Grayder glanced up. "If you're going to start answering questions before they've been asked, you'd better see the medic. Or have we a telepath on board?"

"I was thinking," Harrison explained.

"I approve of that," put in His Excellency. He lugged a couple of huge tomes out of the wall-shelves, began to thumb rapidly through them. "Do plenty of thinking whenever you've the chance and it will become a habit. It will get easier and easier as time rolls on. In fact, a day may come when it can be done without pain."

He shoved the books back, pulled out two more, spoke to Major Hame who happened to be at his elbow. "Don't pose there glassy-eyed like a relic propped up in a military museum. Give me a hand with this mountain of knowledge. I want Gandhi, anywhere from three hundred to a thousand Earth-years ago.

Hame came to life, started dragging out books. So did Colonel Shelton. Captain Grayder remained at his desk and continued to mourn the missing.

"Ah, here it is, four-seventy years back." His Excellency ran a plump finger along the printed lines. "Gandhi, sometimes called Bapu, or Father. Citizen of Hindi. Politico-philosopher. Opposed authority by means of an ingenious system called civic disobedience. Last remnants disappeared with the Great Explosion, but may still persist on some planet out of contact."

"Evidently it does," commented Grayder, his voice dry.

"Civil disobedience," repeated the ambassador, screwing up his eyes. He had the air of one trying to study something which was topsy-turvy. "They can't make that a social basis, It just won't work."

"It does work," asserted Harrison, forgetting to put in the "sir."

"Are you contradicting me, mister?"

"I'm stating a fact."

"Your excellency," Grayder began, "I suggest—"

"Leave this to me." His color deepening, the ambassador waved him off. His gaze remained angrily on Harrison. "You're very far from being an expert on socio-economic problems. Get that into your head, mister. Anyone of your caliber can be fooled by superficial appearances."

"It works," persisted Harrison, wondering where his own stubbornness was coming from.

"So does your tomfool bicycle. You've a bicycle mentality."

Something snapped, and a voice remarkably like his own said, "Nuts!" Astounded by this phenomenon, Harrison waggled his ears.

"What was that, mister?"

"Nuts!" he repeated, feeling that what has been done can't be undone.

Beating the purpling ambassador to the draw, Captain Grayder stood up and exercised his own authority.

"Regardless of further leave-quotas, if any, you are confined to the ship until further notice. Now get out!"

He went out, his mind in a whirl but his soul strangely satisfied. Outside, First Mate Morgan glowered at him.

"How long d'you think it's going to take me to work through this list of names when guys like you squat in there for a week?" He grunted with ire, cupped hands round his mouth and bellowed, "Hope! Hope!"

No reply.

"Hope's been abandoned," remarked a wit.

"That's funny," sneered Morgan. "Look at me shaking all over." He cupped again, tried the next name. "Hyland! Hyland!"

No response.

Four more days, long, tedious, dragging ones. That made nine in all since the battleship formed the rut in which it was still sitting.

There was trouble on board. The third and fourth leave-quotas, put off repeatedly, were becoming impatient, irritable.

"Morgan showed him the third roster again this morning. Same result. Grayder admitted this world can't be defined as hostile and that we're entitled to run free."

"Well, why the heck doesn't he keep to the book? The Space Commission could crucify him for disregarding it."

"Same excuse. He says he's not denying leave, he's merely postponing it. That's a crafty evasion, isn't it? He says he'll grant it immediately the missing men come back."

"That might be never. Darn him, he's using them as an excuse to gyp me out of my time."

It was a strong and legitimate complaint. Weeks, months, years of close confinement in a constantly trembling bottle, no matter how large, demands ultimate release if only for a comparatively brief period. Men need fresh air, the good earth, the broad, clear-cut horizon, bulk-food, femininity, new faces.

"He *would* ram home the stopper just when we've learned the best way to get around. Civilian clothes and act like Gands, that's the secret. Even the first-quota boys are ready for another try."

"Grayder daren't risk it. He's lost too many already. One more quota cut in half and he won't have enough crew to take off and get back. We'd be stuck here for keeps. How'd you like that?"

"I wouldn't grieve."

"He could train the bureaucrats. Time those guys did some honest work."

"It'd take three years. That's how long it took to train you, wasn't it?"

Harrison came along holding a small envelope. Three of them picked on him at sight.

"Look who sassed Hizonner and got confined to ship—same as us!"

"That's what I like about it," Harrison observed. "Better to get fastened down for something than for nothing."

"It won't be long, you'll see! We're not going to hang around bellyaching for ever. Mighty soon we'll *do* something."

"Such as what?"

"We're thinking it over," evaded the other, not liking to be taken up so fast. He noticed the envelope. "What have you got there? The day's mail?"

"Exactly that," Harrison agreed.

"Have it your own way. I wasn't being nosey. I thought maybe you'd got some more snafu. You engineers usually pick up that paper-stuff first."

"It *is* mail," said Harrison.

"G'wan, nobody has letters in this neck of the cosmos."

"I do."

"How did you get it?"

"Worrall brought it from town an hour back. Friend of mine gave him dinner, let him bring the letter to kill the ob." He pulled a large ear. "Influence, that's what you boys need."

Registering annoyance, one demanded, "What's Worrall doing off the boat? Is he privileged?"

"Sort of. He's married, with three kids."

"So what?"

"The ambassador figures that some people can be trusted more than others. They're not so likely to disappear, having too much to lose. So a few have been sorted out and sent into town to seek information about the missing men."

"They found out anything?"

"Not much. Worrall says it's a waste of time. He found a few of our men here and there, tried to persuade them to return, but each said, 'I won't.' The Gands all said, 'Myob!' And that's that."

"There must be something in it," decided one of them, thoughtfully. "I'd like to go see for myself."

"That's what Grayder's afraid of."

"We'll give him more than that to worry about if he doesn't become reasonable soon. Our patience is evaporating."

"Mutinous talk," Harrison reproved. He shook his head, looked sad. "You shock me."

He continued along the corridor, reached his own cabin, eyed the envelope. The writing inside might be feminine. He hoped so. He tore open and had a look. It wasn't.

Signed by Gleed, the missive read, "Never mind where I am or what I'm doing—this might get into the wrong hands. All I'll tell you is that I'll be fixed up topnotch providing I wait a decent interval to improve acquaintance. The rest of this concerns *you.*"

"Huh?" He leaned back on his bunk, held the letter nearer the light.

"I found a little fat guy running an empty shop. He just sits there waiting. Next, I learn that he's established possession by occupation. He's doing it on behalf of a factory that makes two-ball rollers—those fan-driven cycles. They want someone to operate the place as a roller sales and service depot. The little fat man has had four applications to date, but none with any engineering ability. The one who eventually gets this place will plant a functional-ob on the town, whatever that means. Anyway, this joint is yours for the taking. Don't be stupid. Jump in—the water's fine."

"Zipping meteors!" said Harrison. His eyes traveled on to the bottom.

"P.S. Seth will give you the address. P.P.S. This burg is your brunette's home town and she's thinking of coming back. She wants to live near her sister—and so do I. Said sister is a honey!"

He stirred restlessly, read it through a second time, got up and paced around his tiny cabin. There were twelve hundred occupied worlds within the scope of the Empire. He'd seen about one-tenth of them. No spaceman could live long enough to get a look at the lot. The service was divided into cosmic groups, each dealing with its own sector.

Except by hearsay, of which there was plenty and most of it highly colored, he would never know what heavens or pseudo-heavens existed in other sectors. In any case, it would be a blind gamble to pick an unfamiliar world for landbound life on someone else's recommendation. Not all think alike, or have the same tastes. One man's meat may be another man's poison.

The choice for retirement—which was the unlovely name for beginning another, different but vigorous life—was high-priced Terra or some more desirable planet in his own sector. There was the Epsilon group, fourteen of them, all attractive providing you could suffer the gravity and endure lumbering around like a tired elephant. There was Norton's Pink Heaven if, for the sake of getting by in peace, you could pander to Septimus Norton's rajah-complex and put up with his delusions of grandeur.

Up on the edge of the Milky Way was a matriarchy run by blonde Amazons, and a world of wizards, and a Pentecostal planet, and a globe where semisentient vegetables cultivated themselves under the direction of human masters; all scattered across forty light-years of space but readily accessible by Blieder-drive.

There were more than a hundred known to him by personal experience, though merely a tithe of the whole. All offered life and that company which is the essence of life. But this world, Gand, had something the others lacked. It had the quality of being present. It was part of the existing environment from which he drew data on which to build his decisions. The others were not. They lost virtue by being absent and faraway.

Unobtrusively, he made his way to the Blieder-room lockers, spent an hour cleaning and oiling his bicycle. Twilight was approaching when he returned. Taking a thin plaque from his pocket, he hung it on the wall, lay on his bunk and stared at it.

F—I.W.

The caller-system clicked, cleared its throat, announced, "All personnel will stand by for general instructions at eight hours tomorrow."

"I won't," said Harrison. He closed his eyes.

Seven-twenty in the morning, but nobody thought it early. There is little sense of earliness or lateness among space-roamers—to regain it they have to be landbound a month, watching a sun rise and set.

The chartroom was empty but there was much activity in the control cabin. Grayder was there with Shelton, Hame, Navigators Adamson, Werth and Yates and, of course, His Excellency.

"I never thought the day would come," groused the latter, frowning at the star map over which the navigators pored. "Less than a couple of weeks, and we get out, admitting defeat."

"With all respect, your excellency, it doesn't look that way to me," said Captain Grayder. "One can be defeated only by enemies. These people are not enemies. That's precisely where they've got us by the short hairs. They're not definable as hostile."

"That may be. I still say it's defeat. What else could you call it?"

"We've been outwitted by awkward relations. There's not much we can do about it. A man doesn't beat up his nieces and nephews merely because they won't speak to him."

"That's your viewpoint as a ship's commander. You're confronted by a situation that requires you to go back to base and report. It's routine. The whole service is hidebound with routine." The ambassador again eyed the star map as if he found it offensive. "My own status is different. If I get out, it's a diplomatic defeat, an insult to the dignity and prestige of Terra. I'm far from sure that I ought to go. It might be better if I stayed put—though that would give them the chance to offer further insults."

"I would not presume to advise you what to do for the best," Grayder said. "All I know is this: we carry troops and armaments for any policing or protective purposes that might be found necessary here. But I can't use them offensively against these Gands because they've provided no pretext and because, in any case, our full strength isn't enough to crush twelve millions of them. We need an armada for that. We'd be fighting at the extreme of our reach—and the reward of victory would be a useless world."

"Don't remind me. I've stewed it until I'm sick of it."

Grayder shrugged. He was a man of action so long as it was action in space. Planetary shenanigans were not properly his pigeon. Now that the decisive moment was drawing near, when he would be back in his own attenuated element, he was becoming phlegmatic. To him, Gand was a visit among a hundred such, with plenty more to come.

"Your excellency, if you're in serious doubt whether to remain or come with us, I'd be favored if you'd reach a decision fairly soon. Morgan has given me the tip that if I haven't approved the third leave-quota by ten o'clock the men are going to take matters into their own hands and walk off."

"That would get them into trouble of a really hot kind, wouldn't it?"

"Some," agreed Captain Grayder, "but not so hot. They intend to turn my own quibbling against me. Since I have not officially forbidden leave, a walk-out won't be mutiny. I've merely been postponing leave. They could plead before the Space Commission that I've deliberately ignored regulations. They might get away with it if the members were in the mood to assert their authority."

"The Commission ought to be taken on a few long flights," opined His Excellency. "They'd discover some things they'll never learn behind a desk." He eyed the other in mock hopefulness. "Any chance of accidentally dropping our cargo of bureaucrats overboard on the way back? A misfortune like that might benefit the spaceways, if not humanity."

"That idea strikes me as Gandish," observed Grayder.

"They wouldn't think of it. Their technique is to say no, no, a thousand times no. That's all—but judging by what has happened here, it is enough." The ambassador pondered his predicament, reached a decision. "I'm coming with you. It goes against the grain because it smacks of surrender. To stay would be a defiant gesture, but I've got to face the fact that it won't serve any useful purpose at the present stage."

"Very well, your excellency." Grayder went to a port, looked through it toward the town. "I'm down about four hundred men. Some of them have deserted, for keeps. The rest will come back if I wait long enough. They've struck lucky, got their legs under somebody's table and gone A.W.O.L. and they're likely to extend their time for as long as the fun lasts on the principle that they may as well be hung for sheep as lambs. I get that sort of trouble on every long trip. It's not so bad on short ones." A pause while moodily he surveyed a terrain bare of returning prodigals. "But we can't wait for them. Not here."

"No, I reckon not."

"If we hang around any longer; we're going to lose another hundred or two. There won't be enough skilled men to take the boat up. Only way I can beat them to the draw is to give the order to prepare for takeoff. They all come under flight-regulations from that moment." He registered a lopsided smile. "That will give the space lawyers something to think about!"

"As soon as you like," approved the ambassador. He joined the other at the port, studied the distant road, watched three Gand coaches whirl along it without stopping. He frowned, still upset by the type of mind which insists on pretending that a mountain isn't there. His attention shifted sidewise, toward tail-end. He stiffened and said, "What are those men doing outside?"

Shooting a swift glance in the same direction, Grayder grabbed the caller-mike and rapped, "All personnel will prepare for take-off at once!" Juggling a couple of switches, he changed lines, said, "Who is that? Sergeant major Bidworthy? Look, sergeant major, there are half a dozen men beyond the midship lock. Get them in immediately—we're lifting as soon as everything's ready."

The fore and aft gangways had been rolled into their stowage spaces long before. Some fast-thinking quartermaster prevented further escapes by operating the midship ladder-wind, thus trapping Bidworthy along with more would-be sinners.

Finding himself stalled, Bidworthy stood in the rim of the lock and glared at those outside. His mustache not only bristled, but quivered. Five of the offenders had been members of the first leave-quota. One them was a trooper. That got his rag out, a trooper. The sixth was Harrison, complete with bicycle polished and shining.

Searing the lot of them, the trooper in particular, Bidworthy rasped, "Get back on board. No arguments. No funny business. We're taking off."

"Hear that?" asked one, nudging the nearest. "Get back on board. If you can't jump thirty feet, you'd better flap your arms and fly."

"No sauce from you," roared Bidworthy. "I've got my orders."

"He takes orders," remarked the trooper. "At his age."

"Can't understand it," commented another, shaking a sorrowful head.

Bidworthy scrabbled the lock's smooth rim in vain search of something to grasp. A ridge, a knob, a projection of some sort was needed to take the strain.

"I warn you men that if you try me too—"

"Save your breath, Biddy," interjected the trooper. "From now on, I'm a Gand." With that, he turned and walked rapidly toward the road, four following.

Getting astride his bike, Harrison put a foot on a pedal. His back tire promptly sank with a loud *whee-e-e*.

"Come back!" howled Bidworthy at the retreating five. He made extravagant motions, tried to tear the ladder from its automatic grips. A siren keened thinly inside the vessel. That upped his agitation by several ergs.

"Hear that?" With vein-pulsing ire, he watched Harrison tighten the rear valve and apply his hand pump. "We're about to lift. For the last time—"

Again the siren, this time in a quick series of shrill toots. Bidworthy jumped backward as the seal came down. The lock closed. Harrison again mounted his machine, settled a foot on a pedal but remained watching.

The metal monster shivered from nose to tail then rose slowly and in utter silence. There was stately magnificence in the ascent of such enormous bulk. It increased its rate of climb gradually, went faster, faster, became a toy, a dot and finally disappeared.

For just a moment, Harrison felt a touch of doubt, a hint of regret. It soon passed away. He glanced toward the road.

The five self-elected Gands had thumbed a coach which was picking them up. That was co-operation apparently precipitated by the ship's disappearance. Quick on the uptake, these people. He saw it move off on huge rubber balls, bearing the five with it. A fan-cycle raced in the opposite direction, hummed into the distance.

"Your brunette," Gleed had described her. What gave him that idea? Had she made some remark which he'd construed as complimentary because it made no reference to outsize ears?

He had a last look around. The earth to his left bore a great curved rut one mile long by twelve feet deep. Two thousand Terrans had been there.

Then about eighteen hundred.

Then sixteen hundred.

Less five.

"One left—me!" he said to himself.

Giving a fatalistic shrug, he put the pressure on and rode to town.

And then there were none.

The Army Comes To Venus

Fantastic Universe, May 1959

In thick, cloying mist the ship moaned like a tormented ghost of monstrous size. It descended slowly, warily, feeling with invisible electronic fingers for a place in which to sit.

Those below stood gazing up into the fog, not sensing the probing ray, seeing nothing. A bunch of hard-bitten, bearded men in oiled slickers down which moisture trickled in thin streams.

After a little while the fog appeared to solidify into an enormous wet cylinder with a steaming end. The ship came down, touched, settled. A sluggish wave of damp earth hunched itself on either side of the curved hull.

Airlocks opened, duralumin gangways slid forth. The bearded ones clustered closer, avid for new faces. A shock-haired, red-whiskered man was the first to emerge, staggering under the weight of numerous bags and packs, carefully feeling his way down the metal steps.

Somebody at the back of the waiting audience let go a yell of welcome. "Old Firelip, as I live and breathe!"

Pausing halfway down the gangway, the newcomer screwed up rheumy eyes as he sought to identify the shouter. "Duckass, no less! What made the parole board let *you* out?"

Listeners grinned, immediately accepting the new arrival as one of themselves. He had the two best qualifications, namely, a ready tongue and a friend in the attending mob.

A fat man came next, waddling down and letting his bags go bump-bump-bump from step to step as he dragged them behind. He wore three chins and an expression of moony amiability.

"Lookie, lookie, lookie, here comes Cookie," invited a brawny roughneck.

The others chuckled. The fat man stopped, studied the other, spoke in high-pitched but undisturbed tones. "You must have second sight, chum. A cook is just what I am."

"Then my belly says you're two years overdue. The few gals we've got here can do everything but cook."

"Everything?" asked the fat man with pointed interest.

"You try 'em sometime."

"Maybe I will." He lumbered the rest of the way down, his kit still bumping. Anything breakable in his bags was having a run of hard luck.

A dozen nondescripts followed, all heavily burdened with everything, but the farmhouse roof. Pioneers bearing their tiny personal worlds on their backs.

Several ship's officers and a few of the crew came out for a gossip, a sniff of moist air, a stamp around on real, solid ground. After them followed a string of people who looked like nobody in particular and wanted to stay that way. A few had the air of still trying to thwart the systematic circulation of police photographs.

"Where's the molar mauler?" bawled an onlooker with a lopsided face.

"Me," responded a white-haired ancient, trying to lug four boxes at once.

Gumboil grabbed two of them. "Good thing you've come, Pop. You've got a customer right now. One more day and I'd be off my nut."

They moved toward the nearby shanty town. The rest of the crowd remained to watch the ship; they were bored by frontier solitude and thankful for a petty event.

A person who oozed officialdom showed himself at the airlock, stared out with cold authority. Characteristically, they bristled at the sight of him. He went inside and did not reappear. It wasn't six months since they had pulled a would-be tax collector to pieces.

Several sluggards emerged, one dragging a pack resembling a tightly wrapped haystack. Half a dozen witnesses helped get it down amid a shower of wisecracks concerning weak bladders and portable comfort stations. The owner registered acute embarrassment.

Two girls came from the airlock, suddenly silencing the wits. They were full-lipped, full-busted, had brilliant eyes and emphatic hips. Both were bottle-blondes. A distinct sigh of gratification ran through the audience. The girls put on knowing smirks, revealed white teeth. They tripped down the gangway with dainty steps and beckoning backsides. Four of the crew toted their bags, surrendered them to eager helpers.

"Annie's place?"

The girls nodded, giggled, weighed up the hungry clientele. Two barrel-chested men indulged in an acrimonious shoving match for the right to carry a bag on which both had laid hands simultaneously, They solved the problem by bearing it between it between them, giving alternate tugs to tear it from each other at every tenth step.

Came a pause while the cargo-hatch opened, a long-armed crane swung out, began to lower boxes and crates. A few of the crowd shifted position to get a better view of the unloading.

Another girl appeared, accompanied by a ship's officer. She was vastly different from her bosomy predecessors: small, slender, oval-faced and cool. Her black hair was natural, her equally black eyes not glassy, her expression slightly wistful, instead of hard and brassy. Carefully the officer helped her down the steps, shook hands with her at the bottom.

"G'wan, kiss her, you dummy," advised a hoarse voice.

"Sailors don't care," commented another.

"Love 'em and leave 'em," added a third.

For a moment the officer looked as if he would like to make something of it. He hesitated, glowered at the ribald crowd to their immense satisfaction. Then he whispered anxiously to the girl, apparently questioning the wisdom of her remaining alone on this world. She smiled at him, shook her head.

"Not tonight, Cuthbert," jeered an onlooking tough.

"You've had your share," urged another. "Don't be greedy."

"Give real men a chance," suggested somebody else.

Several chortled at that sally, their tones loud and coarse. One smacked his lips in exaggerated anticipation. The officer lingered awhile, reluctant to go, but finally mounted the gangway and went into the ship. His expression was worried.

Left to herself, the girl surveyed the hairy mob with calm self-possession. They returned the compliment, taking in her slender legs, narrow hips, dark hair. They undressed her with their eyes and liked what they saw.

"You doing anything tonight, Honey-babe?" inquired a bear disguised as a man.

"You wait your turn, Bulstrode," ordered a scar-faced neighbor. He spat on thick, callused fingers, combed his hair and straightened an invisible tie. "This one is for gentlemen only." He leered with undisguised appetite at the subject of his remarks. "Isn't that so, Luscious?"

"All men are gentlemen." She looked at Bulstrode with a kind of dark-eyed innocence. "When they wish to be."

Bulstrode's optics dulled and his huge fingers twitched while he digested this. It took him quite a time. When he spoke again it was with an apologetic rumble.

"I was only kidding, Ma'am. I sought of thought—"

"She isn't interested, you hairy ape," interjected Scarface. "So don't waste breath advertising your ignorance." He rubbed his bristly chin and gave another pull to the non-existent tie. "Can I carry your stuff to Annie's place, Lovebird?"

Shuffling slowly around on big, cumbersome feet, Bulstrode faced him and growled, "What makes you think she's heading for Annie's? Why, you slit-cheeked, ragged-cared louse!" Extending a spade-sized hand he spread it across the other's unhandsome features, curled his fingers and squeezed.

The victim gurgled convulsively behind the horny palm, made frantic pulls at the thick wrist, finally kicked him good and hard on the shin. It sounded like kicking a tree. Taking no notice, Bulstrode began to twist the face leftward, bending him sidewise.

"Stop that," ordered the girl.

Still holding on, Bulstrode turned a surprised face over a massive shoulder. "Hey?"

"Stop it," she repeated. "You wouldn't behave that way in your own home."

Bulstrode removed his grip and started examining his hand as if he had never seen it before. His opponent made snuffling noises, voiced a lurid oath and let go a haymaker. The angry fist caught the big man smack on the chin, rattling his teeth but not knocking him down.

Sweeping a columnar arm around in the manner of one brushing away a persistent fly, Bulstrode pleaded, "Look, lady, just you go take a nice, quiet walk while I slaughter this jerk."

"Don't be silly." Her dark eyes reproved the pair of them. "You're like a couple of overgrown children. You don't even know what you're squabbling about—do you?"

They stared at her dully, not answering.

"Do you?" she insisted.

A tall, gray-haired individual spoke from the front rank of the vastly entertained audience. "You're not on the home planet now. This is Venus and don't you forget it. Terra never comes nearer than thirty million miles."

"Home is as near as your memory says it is," she contradicted.

"You may be right, but some of us haven't got so darned much worth remembering." He paused. finished without bitterness, "That's why we're here."

"Speak for yourself, Marsden," chipped in a squat, swarthy man standing behind him. "I'm here to make money and make it fast."

"I'm here because I love the sunshine," yelled a satirical voice from the rear.

Some laughed, some didn't. All glanced upward at the fog which permitted visibility to no more than two hundred feet. Once in a while it lifted to two thousand. Often it descended in a thick, cloying mass to ground level. Moisture condensed on their slickers and ran down in tiny rivulets. The girl's black hair sparkled with diamonds of wetness.

"If you're not going to Annie's," continued Marsden, "you'll have to find someplace else." A contemptuous sweep of his hand indicated her choice of six or seven hundred wooden shacks. "Take a look at what's on offer."

"No place for a girl like you," informed Bulstrode, trying to ingratiate himself and eyeing her like an elephant hoping for a cracker.

"Thank you, but I knew what to expect. I was well-primed in advance," she smiled at them. "So I brought my own home with me."

Turning away, she tripped light-footed toward the ship's tail-end where cargo was piling up as the long-armed crane swung to and fro. Presently those on the ship dropped a ramp and rolled down it a small aluminum trailer with two wheels amidships.

"Oh, ye gods!" griped a snaggle-toothed onlooker. openly disappointed. "I'm the only guy on the planet with a pneumatic mattress. And what's it to her?"

"If they're going to start transporting them homes and all," complained another, "it'll be the beginning of the end. Before you know it, this town will become too big for its boots."

"Which town?" asked a third, gazing around and pretending to see nothing.

Marsden saw her at her door three days later. Leaning on one of the hardwood posts that somebody had driven in to mark the limits of her property, he let his calculating gaze rest on the trailer, decided that what hung behind the facing window were the first lace curtains he'd seen in many years.

"Getting settled down?"

"Yes, thank you. I've been very busy. Unpacking and sorting things out takes quite a time."

"I suppose so. Has nobody helped you?"

"I didn't need any help."

"You may want plenty before you're through." He tilted his hat backward, went on, "Anyone bothered you yet?"

"Dear me, no. Why should they?"

"This is a man's town."

Looking as if she hadn't the vaguest notion of what he meant, she said, "Then why don't they give it a name?"

"A name? What's the use of a name? It isn't enough of a dump to deserve one. Besides, it's the only settlement on Venus. There isn't any other—yet. Anyway names cause arguments and arguments start fights."

"If they'll quarrel over the mere question of what to call this town it's evident that they haven't enough to do."

"When they're in the mood to let off steam they'll fight over anything. What else do you expect on the frontier?"

She did not answer.

"And they've plenty to keep them busy," he continued with a touch of harshness. "They're gnawing into a mountain of white granite that contains thirty pounds of niobium to the ton. It's mighty useful for high tensile and stainless steels. Also they're building a narrow-gauge railroad eastward to a deposit of pitchblende that makes a Geiger-counter chatter like a machine gun." He rubbed his lips with a thick and slightly dirty forefinger. "Yes, they work hard, swear hard, drink hard and fight hard."

"There are other things as much worth fighting for."

"Such as what?"

"This town, for instance."

"A cluster of tumbledown shanties. A haphazard array of smelly cabins. You call it a town?"

"It will be a real one some day."

"I can imagine." Marsden displayed a knowing grin. "Exactly as the boys would like it. Complete with city hall, police stations and a high-walled jail." He spat in the dirt to show what he thought of this prospect. "A good many of them came here to get away from all that. Do you know that at least forty per cent of them have served prison sentences?"

"I don't see that it matters much."

"Don't you?" He was slightly surprised. "Why not?"

"Men who are really evil prefer to take things easy."

"Meaning—?"

"Those who've seen fit to come this far must have done so to make a fresh start with a clean sheet. They'd be stupid to make a mess of their lives a second time."

"Some people are made that way," he informed.

"And some make them that way," she retorted.

"Oh, God, a reformer." He showed disgust. "What's your name?"

"Miranda Dean."

"Well, it could be worse."

"What d'you mean?"

"It could be Dolly Doberhorst."

"Who on earth is *she*?"

"An obese charmer round at Annie's." He studied her figure. "Some fellows like 'em fat. And some don't."

"Really?" She seemed quite unconscious of his meaning or of the trace of appetite in his eyes. "I'd better carry on with more chores else they'll never be done. Pardon me, won't you?"

"Sure."

He watched her enter the trailer but did not continue on his way. He remained leaning on the post, picking his teeth with a thin stalk of grass and thinking that she'd be very much to his taste without her clothes. Yes, she'd be clean and wholesome, not painted and gross like the others. For a short time he continued to exercise his masculine privilege of pondering delightful possibilities until suddenly he became aware of a huge bulk looming at his side.

Bulstrode followed his gaze and challenged, "What's the idea, staring at her place like that? You thinking of busting in?"

"You wouldn't dream of it, of course?"

"No, I wouldn't."

"Don't give me that. Females are females. She's merely playing hard to get. And you're a liar, anyway."

"That's enough for me," said Bulstrode, speaking low in his chest. "Take off that coat so I can start mauling your meat."

"You'd better not get tough with me, Muscle-bound." Marsden protruded a pocket significantly. "Because."

"There now, you've got a gun. Isn't that nice?" Bulstrode shuffled around to face him. "Like to know something?"

"What?"

"I just don't give a damn."

With that he thrust out a hairy paw, arrested it halfway as Miranda Dean reappeared and came toward them. Lowering the paw, he tried to hide it in the manner of a kid caught fooling with a prohibited slingshot. Marsden relaxed, took his hand from his pocket.

Reaching them, she said brightly, "I thought you boys might appreciate these." Smiling at each in turn, she bestowed a couple of little black books and returned to her trailer.

Taking one look at what he'd got, Marsden groaned. "Holy Moses, a prayer-book."

"With hymns," confirmed Bulstrode on a note of complete incredulity.

"A religious nut," said Marsden. "I knew she'd have a flaw somewhere. Nobody's perfect."

"Hymns," repeated Bulstrode with the air of one whose idol has revealed feet of clay. His beefy features registered confusion.

"What a laugh," Marsden went on. "When Annie hears about this she'll roll all over the floor."

"It's no business of Annie's," asserted Bulstrode, feeling belligerent for no reason that he could understand.

Jerking an indicative thumb toward the trailer, Marsden opined, "It's going to be. Sooner or later she will make it Annie's business. I know that kind of crackpot. I've met 'em before. They can't leave well enough alone. Stick their noses into everyone's affairs, They think it's their ordained mission in life to improve everything and everybody."

"Maybe some of us could do with it," Bulstrode suggested.

"Speak for yourself," advised Marsden scornfully. "A shave, a haircut and a bath and you'd rise almost to subhuman level." His tones hardened "But this is a free world. Why should you wash or shave if you don't want to?"

"It's honest dirt," said Bulstrode, giving him a retaliatory stare. "Soap and water can take it off—which is more than it could do for your mind."

"Suffering saints, that holy tome must be working on you already. Throw it away before it takes hold."

He set the example by tossing his own book into a bank of tall weeds. Bulstrode promptly retrieved it.

"If we don't want them we ought to give them back to her. She may have paid good money for them."

"All right," said Marsden with malicious anticipation. "You go tell her to put them where the monkey put the nuts. I'll stay here and watch the fun."

"I'll keep them." Bulstrode crammed them into a hind pocket. "I'll hand them back to her some time when I'm passing."

Marsden smiled to himself as he let the other amble away. Then he favored the trailer with another speculative stare before he departed in the opposite direction.

The ship lifted in the late afternoon of the third day, groaned high in the dank, everlasting fog and was gone toward the mother planet that no man on Venus could see. A sister ship was due in about six weeks' time and another two months afterward. In the intervals between such visits those who remained were a primitive community vastly marooned beneath perpetual cloud.

Miranda went out for her first sight-seeing stroll that same evening. It was pleasant enough because the vaporous blanket came no lower with the night, the air was rich with oxygen which clung to the lower levels although absent from the upper strata. All around were strong plant-odors and the area held comforting warmth.

Here and there amid the sprawl of shacks gleamed many lights served by a small generating-station astride a rushing stream three miles away. Quite a blaze of illumination came from one building midway along the straggling and badly rutted main street.

She walked slowly into this slovenly town whose citizens thought it unworthy even of naming. She noted the rickety fence around somebody's clapboard, one-room hovel and, nearby, the pathetic remnants of a tiny garden soon started and as soon abandoned. One Earth-rose still battled for life amid an unruly mob of Venusian growths intent upon strangling the stranger from afar.

To her right a larger, three-roomed erection had a dilapidated shop-front with a wire screen in lieu of precious glass, a few rusting hammers, saws, chisels, pliers and other oddments exhibited behind. In the middle of this display stood a crudely lettered sign reading: *Haircut $1.00. Beard Trim 40¢.*What she had seen of the inhabitants made her wonder whether this sign had ever attracted a customer.

Farther along she came to the extraordinarily well-lit building from which came the noise of fifty or more raucous voices and occasional bursts of song. By local standards it was a large edifice, built mainly of peeled logs and noteworthy for having windows of real glass. Somebody must have paid a fancy price to import those transparent sheets.

Over the door hung a big board bearing neat, precise letters from which condensation dripped steadily.

ANNIE'S PLACE
Anna M. Jones, Prop.

A burly, rubber-booted man trudged along the street, paused outside the door, examined Miranda curiously. He was a complete stranger to her and she to him.

"What's wrong, Sweetie? Annie gone bad on you?"

She eyed him in calm silence.

"Not deaf, are you?"

"No," she said.

"Then why don't you answer a civil question?"

"I didn't consider it civil."

"So that's the way it is, eh?" He gave a thin scowl. "One of those finicky tarts. Like to pick and choose." He shrugged broad, damp shoulders. "You'll come to your senses eventually."

"So will you."

"You'll change before you're through with this life."

"Don't we all?" she offered sweetly.

"Not the way we want," he countered.

"The way God wants," she said.

"Jumping Joseph, don't give me *that* stuff!"

With a loud sniff of contempt he went inside. The noise from the place boosted and sank as the door opened and shut. A waft of air puffed forth loaded with strong tobacco, strong booze and sweat.

Under one of the windows lay an empty crate. Mounting it, Miranda raised herself on tiptoe and glanced inside. Not for long. Just for a brief moment but somewhat in the manner of a general studying the field of battle. It sufficed to show the expected scene of tables, chairs, bottles and eight or nine blowsy women. And even a piano.

Thirty million miles. Every pound, every ounce had to be hauled a minimum of thirty million miles and often much more. So they didn't have this and they didn't have that—but they did have brewing facilities and a piano.

Well, she couldn't blame them for it. All work and no play adds up to a miserable existence. This was a man's world and men needed an outlet. Annie was supplying the demand. Annie was giving them light and laughter plus girls to whom nothing was too hot or too heavy.

But sooner or later men would discover that they had other needs, if not today then tomorrow or the day after, or next month, or next year. It would be for Miranda rather than for Annie to supply those.

This was a world in the earliest pangs of birth. Astrophysics was the skilled midwife but the fidgeting father was Ordinary Humanity. The world was destined to grow up no matter how reluctant to escape its easy-going, irresponsible childhood.

And it would grow up, become big and civilized, truly a world in its own right. The test of civilization is its capacity for satisfying individual needs, all needs, sober or sodden, sensible or crazy, the need for darkness or light, noise or silence, joy or tears, heaven or hell, salvation or damnation. The adult world would have room for opposites of everything—including Annie and her ilk.

Hurriedly returning to her trailer Miranda extracted something from its small case, returned to Annie's place nursing the object in her hands. Except for the tinkling of its piano, the building was silent as she neared. Then suddenly a chorus of hoarse, powerful voices roared into catchy song that shook the door and rattled the windows.

Anna Maria, Anna Maria, Anna Maria Jones,
She's the queen of the tamborine, the banjo and the bones;
Rootitoot she plays the flute in a fascinating manner,
Pinkety-pong she runs along the keys of the grand pianner,
Rumpety-tum she bangs the drum with very superior tones,
Anna Maria, Anna Maria, Anna Maria Jones!

They howled the last three words at the very tops of their voices and followed with much hammering upon tables and stamping of feet. Then came an anticipatory quietness as they awaited a response from the subject of their song.

Outside the door Miranda promptly snatched this noiseless pause, stretched her little concertina, made it emit a drone of opening chords, and commenced to sing in a high, sweet voice. The tune was fully as catchy, in fact it had a definite boogey beat, but the words were different—something about Hallelujah, Christ the King.

Within the building a chair got knocked over, a glass was smashed. There sounded a mutter of many voices and several coarse oaths, A crimson-faced, touselhaired man jerked open the door and stared at Miranda.

"Jeez!" he said, blinking. "Jeez!"

Several more joined this dumbfounded onlooker, pressing around him or peering over his shoulders. They were too petrified with amazement to think up suitable remarks. Eventually they parted to make way for one of Annie's girls. a startlingly overdeveloped female with hennaed hair and a revealing frock.

Crinkling heavily penciled eyebrows at the singer, the newcomer said in hard, brittle tones, "Beat it, you fool!"

"Haw-haw!" chortled the tousel-haired man, willing to extract the most from this diversion. "What's the matter, Ivy? You afraid of competition?"

"From that?" Ivy let go a snort of disgust. "Don't talk crazy."

"Oh, I don't know," he said, slyly baiting her. "Annie could use a young and slender one, just for a pleasant change."

"Not a blasted hymn-howler, she couldn't," contradicted Ivy with much positiveness. "And neither could you. Get wise to yourself. You're no scented Adonis."

"Off your knees, Slade," advised one of the others, trying to add fuel to the flames. "Ivy's got you down and she's counting you out."

"Wouldn't be the first time," grinned Slade, giving Ivy a you-know-what-I-mean look.

"Shut up," snapped Ivy irritably. She glared at Miranda. "Are you going to quit yawping or not?"

Miranda sang on, apparently oblivious to everything.

Exhibiting a fat fist ornamented with six rings in which zircons did duty as diamonds, Ivy rasped, "Shuffle off before I hammer you in the teeth. I'm not telling you again."

Adding a couple more decibels to the volume, Miranda poured her hymn through the open door.

Ivy's ample bosom heaved, her face flushed, her eyes glinted. "All right, Misery, you've asked for it. If the fellows won't close your sanctimonious trap, I will!"

So saying she stepped forward, intent on mayhem. Slade grabbed at her and got her big arm, his badly gnawed fingers sinking into the puffy flesh.

"Now, now, Ivy, take it easy."

"Let go of me," ordered Ivy in dangerous tones.

Miranda continued blithely to sing. For good measure she laid it in the groove with a couple of hot licks on the concertina.

"Take your paw off my arm, you smelly tramp," bawled Ivy, crimson with fury.

"Be a lady," suggested Slade, hanging on to her. "Just for once."

That did it. Ivy's rage switched its aim forthwith.

"What d'you mean, just for once?" Swinging her free arm she walloped him over the ear. The blow was intended to knock his head off but he had seen it coming and rocked with it.

"Haw, haw, haw!" laughed a bearded onlooker, holding his belly.

"Come take the keys to the Kingdom," trilled Miranda. *"Hallelujah! Hallelujah!"*

Still employing her unhampered arm, Ivy now smacked the bearded laugher clean in the whiskers. He sat down suddenly and hard, still chortling fit to choke. Several more cackled with him. Ivy hauled furiously against Slade's grip and voiced vitriolic imprecations.

"Ivy!" called a sharp, authoritative voice from somewhere inside.

"Look, Annie," hollered Ivy. "there's a dizzy dame out here and—"

"What's it to me?" inquired the voice acidly. "For the love of Moses come in and shut that door—the fresh air is killing us."

Loud guffaws greeted that sally. Ivy forced herself to simmer down sufficiently to obey, throwing Miranda a look of sudden death before she went inside. The others followed, openly regretting this swift end to the fun. The door closed with a contemptuous bang.

Miranda finished her singing and commenced addressing a speech to thin air. After four minutes of this an old frontiersman came creakily along the street, paused to look her over, stopped to listen. A bit later he removed his hat and held it in one hand. He was a scrawny specimen with clear blue eyes set in a face resembling an aged and badly wrinkled apple. For reasons best known to himself he did not consider it at all strange that a young woman should take time off to preach to a non-existent congregation.

In fact when she reached the end he wheezed an underbreath, "Amen!" watched her tuck the concertina under one arm and head homeward. After she had gone he remained hat in hand for quite a time before he planted it on his head and mooched ruminatively on his way.

From that time onward Miranda's singing became a regular evening performance, Sometimes she took her stand at one end of the potholed main street, sometimes at the other, and every now and again it was squarely in front of Annie's place.

Gradually the oldster made it a habit to provide her with a one-man audience, standing not too near, not too far off, watching her with bright blue eyes and never uttering a word other than the final, "Amen!" It wasn't inborn piety coming out in later years, it wasn't sympathy with the spirit of rebellion, it wasn't his way of protesting against things that are as distinct from things that ought to be. It was nothing more than the urge to cheer on a little dog fighting a big one.

Passers-by treated Miranda in three different ways. Some stared blankly ahead and refused to acknowledge her existence. Some threw her the brief, pitying glance one bestows on a village imbecile. The majority grinned and made her the target of coarse witticisms, always malicious and often cruel, opining loudly that religious mania is the natural result of chronic virginity. She never changed color, never winced, never permitted a barb to sink in.

Once in a while the latter type had a go at heckling her speeches, taunting her with unseemly parodies, filling in her pauses with bawdy wisecracks or giving her the mock-support of mock-piety. Her one loyal listener resented these tactics but held his peace and remained content to pose nearby, hat in hand.

There came a night when a burly, blue-jowled drunk dreamed up the ultimate insult. He stood on the boardwalk swaying and blearing all through the sermon, wiping glazed, out-of-focus eyes with the back of a hairy hand and belching loudly whenever she ended a sentence. Then when she had finished he turned to the oldster and ostentatiously tossed a coin into his hat. With a violent burp and an airy wave of his hand he staggered into Annie's place followed by three or four appreciative witnesses.

Gazing angrily into his hat, his blue eyes burning, the old frontiersman said, "See that? The boozey bum flung us a nickel. What'll I do with it?"

"Give it to me." Miranda extended an eager palm.

He passed it over like one in a dream. "Mean to say you'll actually take money from a no-good sot?"

"I would accept it from the Devil himself." She stuck the coin in a pocket. "We can use it for God's work."

"We?" He misunderstood her use of the plural, thought it over, eventually mumbled, "Maybe you're right. Money is money no matter how you get it." Then he had another long think, screwing up his wizened features while he wrestled with a personal problem. Reaching a decision, he moved across, stood beside her shoulder to shoulder and held out his hat invitingly.

"Would you care to sing with me?" she asked, squeezing an opening chord.

"No, Ma'am. I've got a hell of a voice. Just let me be as I am."

"All right." She closed her eyes, opened her mouth and jazzed up a fast one about marching, marching until we come to the Golden Gates.

Ten minutes later a hurrying, self-conscious man reacted to the offer of the extended hat, threw a dime into it, cast a scared glance around and beat it from the scene of the crime.

She had been on Venus exactly eight weeks. Another ship had come and gone. By now the community glumly accepted that it had a harmless lunatic in its midst.

Digging the little plot outside her trailer early one day, she paused to rest, rubbed the blistered palm of her right hand, glanced up and found a plump, frowsy-looking girl surveying her speculatively.

"Good morning," greeted Miranda, smiling.

"Morning," responded the other shortly and after some hesitation.

"It's nice to meet another woman, Miranda went on. "There are so few of us and so many men around."

"Don't I know it!" gave back the plump girl with subtle meaning. She looked warily up and down the street, eyed the trailer, seemed undecided whether or not to linger.

"Would you care to come inside" Miranda invited. "There's coffee and cakes and I'm starving for a gossip and—"

"I'm Dolly," chipped in the other, saying it with the air of begging pardon for a skunk in her purse.

"How nice. My name is Miranda," Dumping the spade, she went to the trailer, opened its door.

"I work at Annie's," announced Dolly, making no move.

"That must be very interesting. I'd love you to tell me all about it."

Registering a fat scowl, Dolly demanded, "Are you making fun of me?"

"Good gracious, no."

"They make plenty of you."

"I'm used to it."

"I'm not," said Dolly. She had another uneasy look up and down the street, added, "Hell of a place."

"If you'd care to come in, please do."

"I guess I will." She advanced as if breasting an invisible tide, "I've gone past caring, see?" Entering, she flopped onto a pneumatic seat, studied her surroundings with frank curiosity. "Nice little joint you've got here."

"Thank you. I'm so glad you like it." Pumping her kerosene stove, Miranda lit it and adjusted the flame.

"Damnsight better than my flea-trap. Everyone says you're cracked. H'm! It sure looks like it. This holy biz must pay off."

"It does."

"So I see," said Dolly with a touch of malice. Her eyes narrowed. "Where's the catch?"

Miranda turned to look at her, coffee percolator in hand. "I'm afraid I don't understand."

"Nobody makes a bad cent without surrendering their heart's blood for it one way or another," informed Dolly. "You have got to give in order to receive. What's your sacrifice?"

"Nothing much. Only my life, such as it is." Capping the percolator, Miranda placed it on the stove, asked with deceptively casual interest, "What do *you* give?"

"Shut up!" snapped Dolly savagely. She rocked to and fro, nursing a cheap and clumsy purse on her lap and staring down at her big knees. She did this for quite a time. Then without warning she harshed, "I'm damn sick of it!" and burst into tears.

Taking no notice, Miranda continued to busy herself with various tasks in the tiny kitchen and left her visitor to howl it out. Dolly shook and sobbed, blindly feeling for a handkerchief. Finally she stood up, tear-stained and full of embarrassment.

"I'd better be going."

"Oh, not now, surely. The coffee is just about ready."

"I've made a prize fool of myself."

"Nonsense. A woman is entitled to a good cry once in a while." Taking little cakes from a cupboard, Miranda arranged them on a flowered plate. "Makes one feel lots better sometimes."

"How the blazes do you know?" Dolly sat down again, dabbed the corners of her eyes, stared at the cakes. "Bet you've never bawled bloody murder."

"I did the day my father died."

"Oh." She swallowed hard, examined thick, unmanicured fingers, said after a long pause, "I don't remember my old man."

"How sad." Miranda poured the coffee.

"And not so much of my mother either," continued Dolly morbidly reminiscent. "I ran away from her when I was fifteen. She didn't think I was cut out to be a great actress. But I knew better, see?"

"Yes. I see."

"So I pranced around in the chorus line of a crummy road-show and that's as far as I got. The years rolled on, I couldn't keep my hips down and slowly but surely I was shoved toward the breadline by younger kids as daft as I had been. So . . . so . . . a girl has to do *something,* hasn't she?"

"Most certainly," agreed Miranda. "Will you try one of these cakes. I made them myself last night."

"Thanks." Dolly took a large bite, choked with emotion, blew her nose and said, "I went the way of all flesh, if you know what I mean. I got pawed around and kicked about something awful. But at least I ate. Thank God my mother never knew about it—she'd have died of shame."

Miranda, wisely, offered no comment.

"I finished up here with Annie. Sort of wanted to get away from everything over there." Dolly used her piece of cake to point more or less Earthward. "Now I'd go back on the next ship if there was anything for me to make it worth the going. But there isn't. Not for me. I picked this lousy, godforsaken dump and I'm stuck with it for keeps."

"Well, there is plenty for a woman to do here," opined Miranda, sipping her coffee.

"You're dead right there is—and I'm fed up doing it. What else is there?"

"This town will want hundreds of things as time rolls on. It can't grow without them."

"Such as what?" Dolly persisted skeptically.

"Just for a start, a little laundry might be a good idea."

"A laundry?" Dolly was reluctant to believe her ears. "The few girls do their own washing. The men don't wash at all. Who the blazes wants a laundry?"

"The men," said Miranda. "Obviously."

"Who'd operate it?" challenged Dolly, changing her angle of attack.

"We two."

She dropped her piece of cake, fumbled around for it, retrieved it and stared wide-eyed at Miranda. "Mean to say you really think I'd get busy scrubbing clothes for a living?" She gave an unconvincing sniff. "I wouldn't sink so low."

"I would."

"Then why don't you?"

"I intend to," Miranda indicated a couple of large packing cases looming outside the window. "One plastic tent and one fully automatic washing-machine. All I need is power. They're fixing me up with an electricity supply tomorrow."

"You've got a nerve," said Dolly. "Christ, you've got a nerve!"

"Haven't *you*?"

Standing up, Dolly prowled restlessly around the small space, gazed a couple of times at the packing cases, scowled and muttered to herself, mooched to and fro. After a while she said, "Don't tempt me."

"Why not?"

"Annie would sling me out on my neck. Either I work for her or I don't. Besides, I'd have no place to sleep."

"This is a two-berth trailer."

"So what?" Dolly let her hands flap around as if she didn't know what to do with them. "You don't need a haybag like me."

"Everybody is needed by someone," said Miranda gently. "Everybody."

"You're only saying that."

"It's the truth, all the same. Don't you believe me?"

"I'd like to. It isn't easy."

"It should be," Miranda mused. "I've never found any difficulty in believing the things I want to believe."

Ignoring that remark, Dolly again ambled round and round the tiny floor-space. "By God!" she said. "By God!"

"Besides," added Miranda for good measure, "we'd be helped quite a piece."

"Oh, yes? By whom?"

"By God."

Dolly flinched and snapped back, "We'll be on the skids with anyone less than God Almighty."

"All that's required of us is courage. One can still have that when one has nothing else."

"You're the kind of loony yap who can talk your way into anything and talk your way out of it again," observed Dolly. She reached a reluctant decision, shrugged plump shoulders. "Looks like you are touched in the head and you've made me that way too. Anyway, you've got company. If you can get away with it why shouldn't I?"

"Like another coffee?" Miranda reached for the cup.

They were having a hopeless struggle with the tent next morning when Bulstrode came along, joined the fray, pitted his brute strength against unruly folds of plastic. Between the three of them they erected it, pegged its stays, fixed it good and tight.

"Anything more?" inquired Bulstrode, brushing his hands.

"I hardly like to trouble you," said Miranda, her gaze straying toward the other crate.

"Think nothing of it," he assured, secretly surprised to find himself enjoying this spell of gallantry. It lent him a special air of proprietorship. Breaking the crate open, he dragged the machine into the tent, looked it over, asked, "What's the use of this gadget with nothing to drive it?"

"We're having power laid on this afternoon and water tonight," Miranda explained. "Tomorrow you'll see, this will be the M and D Laundry."

"The whatta?"

"The Miranda and Dolly Laundry."

"I've been wondering what you were doing here," said Bulstrode, giving Dolly an incredulous once-over. "Don't tell me *you're* in this?"

"Any objections, Hamface?" demanded Doily aggressively.

"No business of mine," he said, backing away fast.

"Thank you so much," put in Miranda, "We could never have coped without your help."

"It was a pleasure." He glowered around in search of witnesses, truculently ready to prove his hardness to any who might accuse him of becoming soft. There were none in sight. He lumbered away and they heard him growl underbreath as he went, "A laundry—holy mackerel!"

Staring after the burly figure, Dolly said wonderingly, "What made that muscle-bound bum pitch in?"

"We needed him," said Miranda.

Dolly stewed it over, responded quietly, "I'm beginning to think you've got something."

"Do you feel it strongly enough to come out with me this evening?"

"Out with you?" She showed puzzlement swiftly followed by uneasiness. "Singing in the street?"

"Yes."

"Nothing doing." Dolly waved agitated hands. "Don't ask me *that*! I've given Annie the brush-off and come in with you on this crazy stunt but don't ask me *that!*"

"What's wrong with it?"

"There's nothing *wrong*, I suppose," admitted Dolly, her alarm increasing by leaps and bounds. "It's not the sort of thing I care to do."

"Afraid they'll laugh at you?"

"And how! They'll bellow until their buttons fly off."

"They don't do that to me," Miranda mentioned.

"That's because . . . because—"

"Because what?"

"You've been around quite a time. They know you're off your head and they're tired of making the most of it. A joke wears thin when it's used again and again and again. They've come to the point of accepting you as you are."

"That's true, Dolly. It always happens if you are sufficiently determined, if you stick it out long enough. And it can happen to you too."

"I'm in no mood to try." Her voice went up a couple of notes. "I've been the plaything of boozey apes too long to make myself the target of their cheap sneers now. Don't shove me further than I want to go. Enough is enough."

"All right. You don't mind me leaving you by yourself for a couple of hours?"

"Mind? Why should I? Nothing can happen to me that hasn't happened fifty times. Besides, I'm not a kid. You go do your holy serenading. I'll tidy the place and have supper ready for when you come back."

"Thank you. It will be nice to return to someone." Miranda smiled at her, added, "I'm glad to have you with me. I'm really glad."

"Oh, cut it out," said Dolly, deeply embarrassed.

And so that evening one remained in the trailer and absorbed the long-forgotten atmosphere of a home while the other took the concertina into town.

The wrinkled oldster was waiting as now he invariably did. By this time Miranda had learned his name: James Hanford. But that was all she knew of him.

"Good evening, Jimmy," she greeted.

"Good evening, Miss Dean," he responded solemnly.

Then he stood beside her at the curb and held out his tattered hat while she began to sing. The collection amounted to one quarter, one nickel and one worthless brass slug.

There sounded an imperative knock at the trailer door in the midafternoon of next day. Answering, Miranda found a tall, stately woman waiting outside. The visitor appeared to be in her late fifties, with white, regal-looking hair and intelligent but arrogant features.

"Good afternoon," said Miranda, a trifle primly.

"That depends on what one makes of it," answered the other in sharp, cynical tones. She subjected Miranda to a careful examination with dark gray eyes that had seen more than enough. "May I come in?"

"Please do."

"Thank you." Entering, the visitor glanced around with begrudging approval, announced, "Doubtless you have heard of me. I am Annie." Her cultured voice held sour humor as she added, "Once known as Anytime Annie. But that was long ago."

"How interesting," said Miranda. "Do sit down."

"I prefer to stand." Again she had a look over the trailer. "H'm! Quite domesticated. Where is Dolly?"

"Outside. Working in the tent."

"So she really is here?" said Annie, in the manner of one confirming a ridiculous rumor. "Why has she left me?"

"She's ambitious."

"A clever answer," Annie conceded. "I admire you for it. You must be smarter than they say."

"Thank you so much."

"In which direction do her ambitions lie?"

"We've started a laundry."

"A laundry?" Annie's well-plucked eyebrows lifted a fraction. "Do you think you're a couple of Chinks?"

"I presume you mean Chinese?"

"That's right."

"Do we look like Chinese?"

"Dolly is and always has been far too stupid to know what's good for her," went on Annie, evading the point.

"But you are *so* much wiser?"

"I ought to be, my dear. Much as I hate to admit it, I am old enough to be her mother. I have been around for quite a spell. One learns a lot of things through the passing years."

"I should hope so," Miranda gave back fervently. "It must be terrible to learn them all too late."

Annie winced, recovered. "You have a quick tongue." She waved a hand to indicate the surroundings. "I think *you* could do better for yourself than *this*."

"I'm quite happy."

"Of course you are. You have youth on your side. The days of disillusionment have yet to come. But they will, they will!"

"I doubt it," observed Miranda. "My line of business is vastly different from yours. I find it rather satisfying."

"Clothes scrubbing and hymn howling," scoffed Annie, displaying a wealth of contempt. "Any incurable cretin could do either." She brushed the subject aside. "But I have not come here to waste time on profitless argument. All I want is a word with Dolly."

"Very well." Sliding the window to one side, Miranda called toward the tent. "Dolly! Dolly!"

In short time Dolly arrived, scowled at the sight of who was waiting for her, demanded, "What do you want?"

"You!" informed Annie succinctly. "It's plenty hard enough to drag girls all the way here without them going temperamental on me afterwards. So collect your clothes and your scattered wits and come back where you belong."

"You can go to hell," said Dolly.

"Someday I shall—according to those peculiarly well-informed." Annie threw a brief, sardonic smile toward Miranda. "But that time is not yet. Meanwhile, you will continue to work for me."

"I'm not your slave. Why should I?"

"Because I picked you out of the gutter and that's where you're heading right now."

"That is a statement of opinion rather than of fact," Miranda put in.

"I'll thank you to keep out of this," Annie retorted. "You have meddled enough." She returned attention to Dolly. "Well, are you going to see reason or not?"

"I don't want to go back."

"You will, in your own good time. And then I won't take you. Not at any price. You could starve to death on my doorstep and I wouldn't bother to toss you a crumb. So it's now or never." She studied the other calculatingly. "Opportunity is knocking for the last time. You can return to me or stay here and rot."

"I'm staying."

"Very well. Someday you'll regret it. When that time comes you need not bring your troubles to me." Turning to the door, she spoke to Miranda with exaggerated courtesy. "Thank you for having me."

"You're most welcome," said Miranda. *"Anytime."*

"So kind of you," responded Annie, refusing to twitch. Outside, she added, "I know your kind. I've met them before. You'll keep on and keep on squalling until you've got all the dopes solidly behind you." Her smile was a warning. "But you'll never get *me*."

With that she departed. Miranda went indoors, sat down, stared at the subdued Dolly.

"What a strange person. I didn't expect her to be like that."

"Like what?" asked Dolly, little interested.

"She seems slightly aristocratic."

"Pah!" said Dolly. "A vaudeville artist busted on the boards. A theatrical floppo. She rose higher than I did, fell farther and landed harder. Still flaunts the grand manner. Still thinks she's really somebody. It's one of the things I hate about her—always acting so clever, so superior."

"One must learn not to hate."

"Why?"

"Because people are as life has made them."

"You can't alter people," declared Dolly flatly.

"But you can change life," said Miranda. "Why, you have just changed yours."

At the end of another six months the laundry was functioning regularly, at a modest profit, and had a small but steadily growing list of customers who were discovering that a clean shirt goes well with a shave and haircut.

The tent had been replaced by a peeled log cabin built by Bulstrode and a dozen cronies who'd concealed their inward pleasure beneath a stream of blasphemy. The aged Jimmy had appointed himself general handyman and Bulstrode had developed the habit of keeping an eye on things by calling in from time to time.

Most importantly of all, the community had now accepted the situation as one unalterable either by opposition or by pointed criticism. Indeed, it was impossible to think up an adequate reason for opposing. In everyone's eyes Dolly had become established as a genuine laundress while it was understood by one and all that Jimmy had some sort of stake in the business and that the bearlike Bulstrode was its unofficial protector.

The days of ridicule and venom had drifted by like fragments of an evil dream. The subject was exhausted of cruel humor and there was nothing derogatory left to be said. Sheer persistence had converted the formerly odd into a present-day convention; all that once had been resented was now taken for granted and recognized as an integral part of the Venusian scene.

Sheer persistence.

Subconsciously sensing this change in social atmosphere, Dolly found that it required no redoubtable effort of will to go out with Miranda one evening. Taking a tambourine from its box in the trailer, she was satisfied at first merely to beat time with the singing but after four nights her courage suddenly welled up. She joined in with a bellowing but not unpleasant contralto and the town accepted without comment that now two voices were crying in the Venusian wilderness. Jimmy still remained silent, content to hold the hat and lend the moral support of his presence.

But they were three. A daft virgin, an aged washout and an erstwhile whore.

More ships had solidified out of the everlasting mist and dissolved back into it, the last bringing a couple of families complete with children. Swiftly erected shacks lengthened the main street by half a mile and there was half-hearted, perfunctory talk of throwing up a ramshackle school for the moppets. The nameless town was growing slowly but surely—creeping toward its destiny of a someday city.

One morning Miranda left the laundry in the others' care, picked her way across four miles of rubble-strewn ground and reached the niobium extraction plant. It was a big. dirty place where hammer-mills set up a deafening clatter and grinders roared without cease; a place full of big-chested men smeared with mud formed of granite-dust and moisture. Finding the office, she handed in her card.

Somebody conducted her to an inner room where a wide-shouldered man with dark hair and fuzzy mustache stood behind his desk, the card in hand. A second man, red-haired and lean-faced, posed nearby and studied the visitor with frank curiosity.

"Please be seated," said the mustached one, indicating a chair. "My name is Langtree." He motioned toward his companion. "And this is Mr. McLeish."

"So glad to know you," responded Miranda.

Waiting for her to sit, Langtree resumed his own chair, had another look at the card. "Now what can we do for you . . . er . . . Lieutenant?"

McLeish gave a slight start of surprise, bent over to examine the card for himself.

"I understand that this company registers title to land," said Miranda.

"In that respect we are functioning on behalf of the Terran Government," Langtree told her. "It is a temporary expedient. Copies of claims are shipped to Earth and are not effective until approved and recorded there. We have no real legislative status of our own. We are merely deputed to act until such time as this planet can support a few bureaucrats."

"All the same, you can assign unclaimed land?"

"Providing that it has no known mineral deposits," he conceded. "Do you have something in mind?"

"Yes, Mr. Langtree. There's a nice, large vacant lot right in the middle of the main street. I can't imagine why nobody has taken it. But if it hasn't been claimed, I want it."

He gave a rueful smile. "That particular piece of estate has been reserved for this company's headquarters whenever we can get around to some real, solid building."

"I'm sorry. I didn't know."

"Don't let it worry you. Recently we have changed our minds and it's most unlikely that we'll use that plot."

"Why not?" Her oval face became hopeful.

"Originally we supposed that the town would remain centered exactly where it is right now and that we had grabbed ourselves a good, dominating position. But now it is obvious that things aren't going to work out that way. Geologists have discovered rich supplies of pitchblende in the east, a railroad will be constructed in that direction and the town's natural tendency will be to spread along the tracks." He pandered a moment, said, "You realize what that means?"

"No—what does it mean?"

"If this place ever becomes big—which I think it will—and if it has a slummy area—which unfortunately is very probable—the plot you want will be smack among the shacks and garbage dumps. It will be in a district anything but salubrious."

"So much the better."

He frowned at that, went on, "'Moreover it is directly opposite Annie's dump where all the rowdies tend to congregate."

"So much the better," she repeated.

"Have you ever lived in a big city?" put in McLeish.

"Yes."

"In parts that are . . . well . . . not nice?"

"Nowhere else."

"And did you *like* it?" he persisted.

"Of course. It was very convenient for me because my work lay right outside my door."

"Oh!" He subsided in defeat.

Langtree harumphed, pulled at his mustache, asked, "For what purpose do you require this land, lieutenant?"

"For a place of worship—eventually."

"That is what I thought." He played the mustache again. "You put me in a poor position to refuse."

"Do you *want* to refuse?" she inquired, open-eyed.

"Not exactly." He sought around for means of expressing himself, continued, "Naturally we approve your plan. In fact we support it most heartily. But we deplore the timing."

"Why?"

"You've managed to establish yourself in a small and tough community. So far you've got by. But don't let that fool you. It's going to be lots tougher before it becomes easier."

"You really think so?"

"I'm certain of it. Since the first ship made its landfall we've had eighteen murders and forty or more attempted ones. Not to mention plenty of lesser crimes. That's nothing, nothing at all. The real labor pains are yet to come."

He paused for comment from her but got none.

"Immediately the railroad is completed we'll have four shiploads of roughnecks here to operate the mines. Only yesterday we received prospectors' reports of large deposits of silver and osmiridium in the north and those will entice plenty more hard characters." Studying her thoughtfully, he assured, "You haven't seen anything yet."

"Neither has this town," she gave back, smiling.

"I don't doubt that. And I don't doubt that you intend to show it plenty. But I'd feel a lot happier if you'd put the brake on your ambitions until at least we've reached the dignity of having a small police force."

"Wouldn't it be much more satisfactory never to need one?" she asked.

Throwing up both hands in mock despair, Langtree said, "I should know better than to argue with the opposite sex."

"Then may I have this piece of land?" She leaned forward, her expression eager.

"You're hamstrung, manacled, pinned down and counted out," opined McLeish, grinning at Langtree. "You might as well quit."

"I surrender." Langtree heaved a sigh of resignation. "Go fetch the papers."

When they had been brought he read carefully through them, filled them in triplicate, showed her where to sign; gave her one copy. She departed, grateful and bright-eyed. Langtree flopped back in his seat and gazed absently at the wall.

After a while, he said, "I guess it was inevitable. It had to come sooner or later."

"Think so?"

"Yes. Ever noticed how big cities are boosted out of the dirt?"

"Sure," said McLeish. "They're raised by a horde of steel-erectors, bricklayers, masons and hod-carriers bossed by fellows who wander around consulting blueprints."

"*And* by the long sustained pressure of a thousand and one determined groups," declared Langtree with emphasis. "The Quakers forced Philadelphia out of the earth. The Mormons raised Salt Lake City from the desert. Earth is spattered with New Jerusalems built by pernickety dissenters and various gangs of one-track-minders. Stands to sense the same things will happen wherever humanity is located."

"Maybe you're right," McLeish admitted.

"I remember that when they concocted that new rocket-fuel they said that space was ours. It wasn't. They had to spend years designing combustion-chambers able to contain the pressures. So now we're squirted across the heavens by a blast that is somewhat terrific. And still it isn't enough. Now we must settle, exploit and build under psychological thrusts that can't and won't be contained."

"So it seems."

"It's only a matter of time before some fellow with a bee in his bonnet will try to prevent all building within a particular square mile of land because he thinks it ought to be reserved for a city park. He'll get like-minders behind him. They'll bellow and bawl and agitate until the area is officially protected and finally becomes a park. Another mob will compel all booze saloons to behave in a civilized manner. Another gang will push and shove and play merry hell until we've a hospital and a maternity home long before we can really afford either. Sustained pressure—it gets there in the end."

"It isn't easy to brush it aside," remarked McLeish.

"It's well-nigh impossible," Langtree asserted. "The pushful groups provide a development-factor that objective scientists rarely take into account. They can bring about the cumulative effect of a very large bomb, but slowly." He thought some more, added reminiscently, "When I was a kid a creeper thrust a thin tendril through a minute crack in the garden wall. My old man wanted to cut it but Mom wouldn't let him. Sixteen years later that wall was busted. You'd have thought a heavy howitzer had scored a direct hit on it. My old man had to pay fifty dollars for new brickwork."

"That girl is different," said McLeish. "She's a human being. She'd have to push until she'd grown old."

"Man, I've seen them do that too." Langtree threw an inquiring glance at the other. "Would *you*?"

"Not on your life!"

"She would. And it won't surprise me if she does."

"It's a shame," decided McLeish for no logical reason. "But perhaps it's a good thing for this or any other world."

"This or any other world *needs* a few good things," said Langtree.

The vacant lot still remained a vacant lot at the end of another year. Some fine day when enough money, hands and material were available it would hold a stone-built, glass-windowed flophouse that would also be a house of God. At times it seemed as if such a culmination was an impossibly long way off, that the temporarily homeless would have no place to sleep, the spiritually hungry no place to pray. But the lot was held in stubborn possession because everything comes to those who wait.

At the laundry there were now three washing-machines and Jimmy had become an energetic, full-time worker therein. Bulstrode was a frequent visitor with the frequency increasing as the weeks went by. Once or twice the big man had been frightened and horrified by a secret desire to turn the street parading trio into a quartet. He had stepped upon it firmly, crushing it down.

His strength was also his weakness in that he doubted his ability to counter a crude insult with anything less than a broken nose. And from occasional remarks let slip by Miranda he'd gathered that nose-busting was out, most definitely out. That made it awfully hard on a powerful man with furry arms. It meant that he would have to answer blood-heating jibes with a forgiving smile when it would be less trouble and infinitely more satisfying to break a neck.

Such was the situation when the sixteenth ship came out of the eternal mist beyond which gleamed a host of stars including a great green one called Terra. The ship unloaded a little aluminum trailer the exact copy of Miranda's. An elderly couple, gray-haired and wise-eyed, arrived with it, positioned it next door, had a few small crates dumped alongside.

A sedate celebration was held in the log laundry that afternoon. The newcomers greeted Miranda in the manner of oldtime friends, were introduced as Major and Captain Bennett. Miranda handed around pie, coffee and cakes, her face flushed and eyes alight with the pleasure of meeting.

In due time Bulstrode wandered outside, stood gazing at the crates and whistling idly to himself. Soon Major Bennett joined him.

"More washing contraptions?" Bulstrode asked.

"Dear me, no. Three should be sufficient for a while." He examined the nearest boxes. "These are musical instruments."

"Huh?" Bulstrode's heavy face livened with sudden interest. Want them emptied out?"

"There's no hurry. I'm sure we can manage."

"I'm doing nothing. And I like busting crates open."

"Then we may as well deal with them," said Major Bennett. "The job has to be done sometime." Finding a case-lever, he started prying up slats with the slow carefulness of the aged.

Scorning this method, Bulstrode hooked big, hard fingertips under the lid of another, bulged his arms and drew it up with nails squeaking. He peeped inside.

"Suffering cats!" he whispered.

"What's the matter?"

"A drum." He voiced it in low, reverent tones like one uttering a holy name. Sliding trembling hands into the crate, he fondled the contents, "As I live and breathe, a big bass drum!"

"Surely there is nothing remarkable about that?" said Bennett, mystified.

With a faraway look in his eyes, Bulstrode told him, "For more than ten years I carried the big bass drum in the hometown band."

"You did?"

"Yes, tiger-skin and all. It was a darned fine band."

Lowering his arms into the crate, Bulstrode gently drew forth the drum. He made another dip, brought out a pair of fat-knobbed sticks, also a broad leather sling complete with chest and belly hooks. He tightened the drum's vellum. Then slowly, like one in a dream, he donned the sling, fastened the drum upon his huge chest, looped the sticks on his wrists.

For about half a minute he posed like a statue dreaming wistfully of days long gone by. Something took possession of him. Fire leaped into his eyes. He twirled the drumsticks into twin discs of light, spun them sidewise, above, inward, outward and across, flashing them hither and thither while flicking the taut vellum with expert beat.

Boom. Boom. Bop-bop-boom went the big bass drum.

Drawn by the sound the others came out of the laundry and watched fascinated while the drumsticks whirled and the great drum sounded. Finally, he stopped.

"Jeez!" he said, flush-faced.

Without comment Major Bennett extracted a silver cornet from its case and handed it to his wife. Next he produced a trombone, fitted it together, checked its slide action with a tentative toot. He eyed Bulstrode shrewdly.

"By hokey!" said that individual. "It takes me back years." He looked around in a semi-daze, noticed Miranda socketing together a pole bearing a large flag. "Years!" he said.

Still watching him, Bennett offered no remark. He had the manner of an experienced cook who knows exactly when the joint will be done to perfection.

"This town could use a good band," asserted Bulstrode, eyeing the trombone and licking his lips.

"We have nobody to play the flute, the oboe and the tuba," said Bennett quietly. "Nobody to beat the drum. Someday we'll find them among those able to kneel and pray, able to fight for the things they believe to be right."

Unhooking the drum and discarding the sling, Bulstrode carefully placed them on the ground. Then he stared at his feet, fidgeted about, transferred the stare to the sky.

"Reckon I'd better be going," he announced. Starting to back away, he met Miranda's eyes and found his feet strangely frozen to the earth.

"Goodbye!" encouraged Dolly in a tone he did not like.

A slight perspiration broke out on his forehead. His thick lips worked around but no words came forth. He was in psychic agony, like a man paralyzed by sheer need to flee.

Putting down the trombone, Major Bennett took him by the arm, led him into the trailer and out of the others' sight.

"Let us speak to God," he said and sank upon his knees.

After considerable hesitation, Bulstrode made sure the door was shut and windows obscured before kneeling beside him. Putting an arm across his shoulders, Bennett held him while they spoke to God because that is the fashion of their kind. Other pressure-groups, other rigmaroles. This was theirs: to say what they wished to say side by side, shoulder to shoulder, before their Supreme Commander.

When they came out, soldiers both, Miranda had opened another box containing hats but no uniforms. Peaked caps and poke bonnets ornamented with red-lettered ribbons. Self-consciously fitting on a cap, Bulstrode strove to divert attention from himself by loudly admiring Dolly in her new bonnet.

"My, you look good in that," he enthused.

"Don't you pick on me," she snapped.

"But I mean it. You look kind of . . . uh . . . nice."

"I'm as fat as a hog and I know it."

"Plumpish," he corrected. "Just the way you ought to be."

"Nuts," she said. "A hat's a hat and makes no difference to what's under it."

"There is a difference. You're not the same person.

"Oh, go take a walk you big, clumsy lug!" With that, Dolly produced a handkerchief and started to snivel.

"Jeepers," said Bulstrode, aghast. "I didn't mean to—"

Miranda pulled gently at his sleeve and explained. "A woman often weeps when she's happy."

"That so?" He crinkled bushy eyebrows at her, mildly dumbfounded. "Mean to say she's enjoying herself?"

Dolly sobbed louder to confirm

"Good grief!" said Bulstrode, quite unconscious of the pun. He studied Dolly in frank amazement until eventually she composed herself, wiped her eyes and gave him an embarrassed smile.

Now he refitted the sling and took up the drum in the manner of one claiming his own after countless years. He hooked it onto his chest, stood holding it in proud possession. He twirled the sticks, again delighting in the feel of them.

"Christ Jesus," he said without blasphemy, "this town is going to take an awful licking!" A thought struck him and he looked hopefully at Miranda. "How soon are we going to give it to them hot and strong?"

She didn't answer. She seemed to be waiting for something. All of them stood there in caps and poke bonnets watching him and waiting for something. Momentarily it puzzled him, that and the electric suspense in the air. For whom or what were they waiting? Was there any good reason to wait at all?

It entered his mind that the big drum takes the lead and sets the pace.

Always.

Involuntarily his fingers tightened around the sticks, his leg muscles stiffened in readiness, his chest swelled, his eyes flamed and what was within him burst forth as a triumphant shout.

"Now!"

It galvanized them into activity. Human pressure was on the boost. Old Jimmy donned the pole-sling, braced the flag in his grip. The others closed the trailers, collected their instruments, formed in two ranks of three each.

For a few seconds they stood to attention like troops on parade. The pale, fog-ridden Venusian light sparkled on cornet and concertina, trombone and tambourine, while the big drum hung poised and the great flag flew above them fast and free.

Then Bulstrode swung a stick and struck one loud, imperative note.

Boom!

In exact step both ranks started off upon the left foot and advanced with military precision upon the waiting town.

Glory! Glory!

The Salvation Army was marching into battle for the Lord.

Basic Right

Astounding, April 1958

They came out of the starfield under the Earth, from the region of a brilliant sun called Sigma Octantis. Ten huge copper-colored ships. Nobody saw them land. They were astute enough to sit a while in the howling wastes of Antarctica, scout around and seize all twenty members of the International South Polar Expedition.

Even then the world did not take alarm. The newcomers, who titled themselves Radians, hazarded a guess that within a fortnight Earth would become curious about the fate of the captured. But it didn't work out like that at all; contrary to expectations the Terran prisoners proved *so* submissive and cooperative.

By signs and gestures the Raidans conveyed their cover-up order: "Send out reassuring messages."

The captives did it willingly, in straightforward manner, playing no tricks, well-nigh falling over themselves in eagerness to please. Routine signals from the polar expedition continued to be picked up by listening posts in Australia, New Zealand and Chile. Nobody found reason to suspect that anything out of the ordinary had occurred down there within the ice barrier where blizzards raged throughout the long-drawn night.

Within the next eleven weeks the invaders learned the Terran language, devoting all their time to picking it up as fast and fluently as possible. This chore could have been avoided by insisting that the prisoners learn to speak Raidan but the tactic would have involved loss of conversational privacy. The Raidans preferred to do the work and keep their talk strictly to themselves.

In the twelfth week Zalumar, commander of the fleet, summoned Lakin, his personal aide. "Lakin, there is no need for us to waste any more hours upon this animal gabble. We can now speak it well enough to make ourselves properly understood. It is time to get out of this frozen place and assert ourselves in conditions of comfort."

"Yes, sire," agreed Lakin, heartened by the thought of coming sunshine and warmth.

"The leader of these prisoners is named Gordon Fox. I wish to speak with him. Bring him to me."

"Yes, sire." Lakin hastened out, returned shortly with the captive.

He was a tall, lean Terran, lank-haired, his face adorned with a polar beard. His gray eyes examined Zalumar, noting the broad shoulders, the long, boneless arms, the yellow eyes, the curious green fuzz overlying the skin. Zalumar found himself enjoying this inspection because it was made with a curious mixture of servility and admiration.

"I have something to say to you, Fox."

"Yes, sire?"

"Doubtless you've been wondering why we are here, what our intentions are, what is going to happen in the near future, eh?" Without waiting for a reply, he went on, "The answer is brief and to the point: we are going to take over your world."

He watched the other's face, seeking fear, shock, anger, any of the emotions normally to be expected. But he detected none of them. On the contrary, Fox seemed gratified by the prospect. There was no rage, no defiance, nothing but amiable complacency. Maybe the fellow had failed to grasp precisely what was meant.

"We are going to assume ownership of Terra lock, stock and barrel," emphasized Zalumar, still watching him. "We are going to confiscate your world because the rewards of life belong to the most deserving. That is our opinion. We have the power to make it the only acceptable opinion. Do you understand me, Fox?"

"Yes, sire."

"The prospect does not annoy you?"

"No, sire."

"Why doesn't it?"

Fox shrugged philosophically. "Either you are cleverer than us or you aren't, one way or the other, and that is that. If you aren't, you won't be able to conquer this world no matter what you say or do."

"But if we are cleverer?"

"I guess we'll benefit from your rule. You can't govern us without teaching us things worth learning."

"This," declared Zalumar, with a touch of wonder, "is the first time in our history that we've encountered so reasonable an attitude. I hope all the other Terrans are like you. If so, this will prove the easiest conquest to date."

"They won't give you any bother," Fox assured.

"You must belong to an amazingly placid species," Zalumar offered.

"We have our own peculiar ways of looking at things, of doing things."

"They appear to be vastly different from everyone else's ways, so different as to seem almost contrary to nature." Zalumar put on a thin smile. "However, it is a matter of no importance. Very soon your people will look at everything in *our* way, do everything in *our* way. Alternatively, they will cease to exist."

"They're in no hurry to die," said Fox.

"Well, they're normal enough in that respect. I had you brought here to inform you of what we intend to do and, more importantly, to show you why your people had better let us do it without argument or opposition. I shall use you and your fellow captives as liaison officers, therefore it is necessary to convince you that your world's choice lies between unquestioning obedience or complete extermination. After that, it will be your duty to persuade Terran authorities to do exactly as we tell them. Lakin will take you to the projection room and show you some very interesting pictures."

"Pictures?"

"Yes, three-dimensional ones in full color. They will demonstrate what happened to Planet K14 whose people were stupid enough to think they could defy us and get away with it. We made an example of them, an object lesson to others. What we did to their world we can do to any planet including this one." He gave a careless wave of his hand. "Take him away and show him, Lakin."

After they'd gone he lay back in his seat and felt satisfied. Once again it was about to be demonstrated that lesser life-forms are handicapped by questions of ethics, of morals, of right and wrong. They just hadn't the brains to understand that greed, brutality and ruthlessness are nothing more than terms of abuse for efficiency.

Only the Raidans, it seemed, had the wisdom to learn and apply Nature's law that victory belongs to the sharp in tooth and swift in claw.

In the projection room Lakin turned a couple of switches, made a few minor adjustments to controls. Nearby a large grayish sphere bloomed to life. At its middle floated a tiny bead of intense light; near its inner surface swam a smaller, darker bead with one face silvered by the center illumination.

"Now watch!"

They studied the sphere. After a short while the dark outermost bead suddenly swelled and blazed into fire, almost but not quite rivaling the center one with the intensity of its light. Lakin reversed the switches. The two glowing beads disappeared, the big sphere resumed its dull grayness.

"That," said Lakin, having the grace not to smack his lips, "is the actual record of the expulsion from the stage of life of two thousand million fools. The cosmos will never miss them. They were born, they served their ordained purpose and they departed—forever. Would you like to know what that purpose was?"

"If you please," said Fox, very politely.

"They were created so that their wholesale slaughter might knock some sense into their sector of the cosmos."

"And did it?"

"Beyond all doubt." Lakin let go a cold laugh. "On every planet in the vicinity the inhabitants fought each other for the privilege of kissing our feet." He let his yellow eyes linger speculatively upon the other." We don't expect you to believe all this, not right now."

"Don't you?"

"Of course not. Anyone can fake a stereoscopic record of cosmic disaster. You'd be gullible indeed if you let us confiscate your world on the strength of nothing better than a three-dimensional picture, wouldn't you."

"Credulity has nothing to do with it," assured Fox. "You want to take us over. We're glad to be taken over. That's all there is to it."

"Look, we can back up our pictures with proof. We can show your own astronomers upon their own star maps exactly where a minor sun has become a binary. We can name and prove the date on which this change took place. If that doesn't satisfy them, we can convert to a ball of flaming gas any petty satellite within this system that they care to choose. We can show them what happens and demonstrate that we made it happen." He stared at Fox, his expression slightly baffled. "Do you really mean to say that such proof will not be required?"

"I don't think so. The great majority will accept your claims without argument. A few skeptics may quibble but they can be ignored."

Lakin frowned in evident dissatisfaction. "I don't understand this: One would almost think your kind was eager to be conquered. It is not a normal reaction."

"Normal by whose standards?" asked Fox. "We are aliens, aren't we? You must expect us to have alien mentalities, alien ways of looking at things."

"I need no lecture from you about alien mentalities," snapped Lakin, becoming irritated. "We Raidans have handled a large enough variety of them. We've mastered more life forms than your kind can imagine. And I still say that your attitude is not normal. If Terra reacts in the way you seem to think it will, without proof, without being given good reason to fear, then everyone here must be a natural-born slave."

"What's wrong with that?" Fox countered. "If Nature in her wisdom has designed your kind to be the master race, why shouldn't she have created my kind as slaves?"

"I don't like the way you gloat about your slavery," shouted Lakin. "If Terrans think they can outwit us, they've another think coming. Do you understand?"

"Most certainly, I understand," confirmed Fox, as soothingly as possible.

"Then return to your comrades and tell them what you have seen, what you've been told. If any of them wish for further evidence, bring them here immediately. I will answer their questions, provide any proof for which they may ask."

"Very well."

Sitting on the edge of the table, Lakin watched the other go out. He remained seated for ten tedious minutes. Then he fidgeted for five more, finally mooched several times around the room. Eventually Fox looked in.

"They are all willing to take my word for it."

"Nobody desires to learn more?" Lakin showed his incredulity.

"No."

"They accept everything without question?"

"Yes," said Fox. "I told you they probably would, didn't I?"

Lakin did not deign to answer that one. He made a curt gesture of dismissal, closed the projection room, went back to the main cabin. Zalumar was still there, talking to Heisham who was the fleet's chief engineer.

Breaking off the conversation, Zalumar said to Lakin, "What happened? Did the bearded low-life get the usual fit of hysterics?"

"No, sire. On the contrary, he appears to enjoy the prospect of his world being mastered."

"I am not at all surprised," commented Zalumar, "Those Terrans are philosophical to the point of idiocy." His sharp eyes noted the other's face. "Why do you look so sour?"

"I don't like the attitude of these aliens, sire."

"Why not? It makes things easy for us. Or do you prefer to get everything the hard way?"

Lakin said nothing.

"Let us congratulate ourselves upon our good fortune," encouraged Zalumar, oozing oily self-confidence. "Victory without battle comes far cheaper than one paid for in blood. A planet mastered is worth infinitely more than a world destroyed."

Speaking up with sudden resolve, Lakin said, "According to the books we've found here, and according to our own preliminary observations, these Terrans have a civilization only a couple of jumps behind our own. They have short-range spaceships on regular runs to their outer planets. They've even got that small colony we noticed on the system of their nearest star. All that has to be born of and supported by a technology that cannot be the creation of imbeciles."

"I agree," chipped in Heisham, with the enthusiasm of an engineer. "I've been studying the details of their ships. These Terrans are supposed to be about twenty thousand years younger than we—but technically they're nothing like as far behind. Therefore they must—"

"Quiet!" roared Zalumar. He paused to let ensuing silence sink in, then continued in lower tones. "All species are afflicted by what they consider to be virtues. We know that from our own firsthand experience, don't we? The disease of goodness varies as between one life form and another. This happens to be the first world we've discovered on which the prime virtue is obedience. They may have a modicum of brains but they've all been brought up to respect their betters." He threw his listener a sardonic glance. "And you, an experienced space-warrior, permit it to surprise you, allow it to worry you. What is the matter with you, eh?"

"It is only that their submissive attitude runs contrary to my every instinct."

"Naturally, my dear Lakin, naturally. *We* submit to nobody. But surely it is self-evident that Terrans are not Raidans, never have been, never will be."

"Quite right," approved Heisham.

Now under double-fire, Lakin subsided. But deep down within himself he wasn't satisfied. Within this peculiar situation was something sadly and badly out of kilter, his sixth sense told him that.

The move was made next day. Ten ships rose from the barren land bearing with them the twenty members of the I.S.P. Expedition. In due time they landed upon a great spaceport just beyond the environs of a sprawling city which, Fox had assured, was as good a place as any in which to tell the world of the fate that had come upon it from the stars.

Zalumar summoned Fox, said, "I do not go to native leaders. They come to me."

"Yes, sire."

"So you will fetch them. Take all your comrades with you so that if necessary they may confirm your story." He eyed the other, his face hard. "With what we've got we do not need hostages. Any treacherous attack upon us will immediately be answered a hundredfold without regard for age or sex. Do you understand?"

"Yes, sire."

"Then get going. And you won't take all day about it if you're wise."

He strolled to the rim of the flagship's air lock door and watched the twenty make off across the hot concrete hurrying toward the city. They were still hairy-faced and wearing full polar kit under the blazing sun. Four clean-shaven Terrans in neat, cool uniforms drove up and braked at the bottom of the ladder. One got out of the car, shaded his eyes as he looked upward at the alien figure framed in the lock.

With total lack of amazement, this newcomer called, "You sent no beam of warning. We've had to divert two ships to another port. Carelessness like that makes accidents. Where are you from?"

"Do you really expect me to know your language and be familiar with your rules and regulations?" asked Zalumar, interestedly.

"Yes, for the reason that you had twenty Terrans with you. They know the law even if you don't. Why didn't you beam a warning?"

Because," said Zalumar, enjoying himself, "we are above your laws. Henceforth they are abolished so far as we are concerned."

"Is that so?" gave back the other. "Well, you're going to learn different mighty soon."

"On the contrary," retorted Zalumar, "it is you who will learn, we who shall teach." With that he returned to his cabin, smiled to himself, fiddled around with a thick file of papers. Three hours later he was called to the lock door by a crewman. He went there, looked down upon the same uniformed quartet as before.

Their spokesman said, blankly and unemotionally, "I am ordered to apologize to you for questioning your right to land without warning. I am also instructed to inform you that certain persons whom you wish to see are now on their way here."

Acknowledging this with a sniff of disdain, Zalumar went back to his desk. A multijet plane screamed far overhead and he ignored it. Doubtless some of the crew were leaning out the locks and nervily watching lest something long, black and lethal drop upon them from the sky. But he couldn't be bothered himself. He had these Terrans weighed up—they just wouldn't dare. He was dead right, too. They didn't dare. The shrill sound died over the horizon and nothing happened.

Sometime later Fox appeared with two other I.S.P. members named McKenzie and Vitelli. They conducted a bunch of twelve civilians into the cabin. The dozen newcomers lined up against a wall, studied the Raidan commander with frank curiosity but no visible enmity.

Fox explained, "These, sire, are twelve of Terra's elected leaders. There are thirty more scattered around, some in far places. I regret that it is not possible to trace and bring them here today."

"No matter." Zalumar lay back in his chair and surveyed the dozen with suitable contempt. They did not fidget under his gaze nor show any signs of uneasiness. They merely gazed back steadily, eye for eye, like a group of impassive lizards. It occurred to him that it was well-nigh impossible to discern what they were thinking. Oh, well, the time-honored tactic was to start by kicking them right in the teeth.

"Let's get something straight," harshed Zalumar at the twelve. "So far as we are concerned, you are animals. Lower animals. Cows. *My* cows. When I order you to produce milk you will strain to produce it. When I order you to moo you will promptly moo, all together, in concert with the other thirty who are absent."

Nobody said anything, nobody got hot under the collar, nobody appeared to care a solitary damn.

"If any one of you fails to obey orders or shows lack of alacrity in doing so, he will be jerked out of mundane existence and replaced with a good, trustworthy and melodious mooer."

Silence.

"Any questions?" he invited, feeling a little irritated by their bland acceptance of racial inferiority. A scowl, just a frightened half-concealed scowl from any one of them would have given him much inward pleasure and enabled him to taste the full, fruity flavor of conquest. As it was, they made victory seem appallingly insipid; a triumph that was no triumph at all because there had been nothing to beat down.

They didn't so much as give him the satisfaction of meeting their queries with a few devastating retorts of crushing them with responses calculated to emphasize their individual and collective stupidity. Still in line against the wall, they posed silently, without questions, and waited for his next order. Looking at them, he got the weird feeling that if he'd suddenly bawled, "Moo!" they'd have all mooed together, at the tops of their voices—and in some mysterious, elusive way the laugh would be on him.

Snatching up the intercom phone, he called Captain Arnikoj and when that worthy arrived, said, "Take these twelve simpletons to the registry on Cruiser Seven. Have them thoroughly recorded from toenails to hair. Extract from them all the details you can get concerning thirty others who have yet to arrive. We shall want to know who the culprit is if one of them fails to turn up."

"As you order, sire," said Arnikoj.

"That's not all," continued Zalumar. "When you've finished I want you to select the least cretinous specimen and return him to this ship. He will be retained here. It will be his duty to summon the others whenever I require them."

"It shall be done, sire."

Zalumar now switched attention back to the twelve. "After you have been registered you may go back to your posts in the city. Your first act will be to declare this spaceport the sole and exclusive property of the Raidan fleet now occupying it. All Terran officials will be removed from the port, none will be allowed to enter except with my permission."

They received that in the same silence as before. He watched them go out, moving dully along one behind the other, following Arnikoj's lead. Great God in Heaven, what witless animals they were!

Zalumar now stared querulously at Fox, McKenzie and Vitelli. "Where are the other seventeen members of your expedition?"

"They remained in the city, sire," explained Fox.

"Remained? Who said they could remain? They are required here, *here!*" He slammed an angry fist upon the desk top. "They have not the slightest right to stay behind without an order to that effect. Who do they think they are? I shall swiftly show them how we deal with those who think they can do as they like. I shall—"

"Sire," chipped in Fox, cutting short the tirade, "they asked if they might stay a short while to clean up and change into more suitable clothing. I told them I felt sure you would approve of them looking more presentable. It didn't seem reasonable to suppose that you might resent their effort to please you."

A momentary confusion afflicted Zalumar's mind. If a trooper goes AWOL solely to fetch his commanding officer a gold medal, what does the latter do about it? For the first time he sensed a vague touch of the indefinable something that was troubling the uneasy Lakin. All was not quite as it should be. This Fox fellow, for instance, was twisting his arm in front of two witnesses and there was nothing much he could do about it

Determined to concoct a gripe, he growled, "All right, let us accept that their concern for my pleasure is praiseworthy and therefore excusable. Why have you and these other two not shown the same desire to gratify me? Why have you returned in those shapeless and filthy clothes, your faces still covered with bristles? Am you telling me that seventeen care but three do not?"

"No, sire," said Fox, busily polishing apples that might prove to be scoot-berries. "Someone had to come back. We hoped that when the seventeen return you might graciously permit us to go and get cleaned up in our turn."

"You had better do that," conceded Zalumar. "We can recognize animals with no trouble at all. Therefore it isn't necessary for you to look like them, smell like them."

He watched the other carefully, seeking a hint of hidden anger such as a slight narrowing of the eyes or a tightening of the jaw muscles. Fat lot of good it did him. Fox's features remained wooden behind his polar mask of hair. McKenzie acted like he was stone-deaf. Vitelli wore the same unctuous smile that never left his moonlike face.

"Get out," he ordered. "Report to Arnikoj. Tell him you have my permission to visit the city after the others have returned. Be back by nightfall."

"And after that, sire?"

"You will remain under Arnikoj's personal command. I will send for you whenever I want you."

When they had gone he strolled to the nearest port, gazed out at the great city. Slowly and with miserly lovingness he took in its towers, spires, skyways and bridges, Mine, he thought, all mine. A worthy prize for the worthy. The battle to the strong, the spoils to the bold and brave.

Lakin mooched in, said hesitantly, "I have been thinking, sire. We're sort of all bunched up together. Ten ships practically standing side by side. Might it not be better if we spread ourselves a little? Couldn't we keep, say, four ships here and place three each in two other spaceports?"

"Why?"

"We don't yet know what their best weapons are like—but we do know that one well-placed bomb could vaporize the lot of us."

"So could three bombs. So what have we to gain by splitting up?"

"Unless they dropped them simultaneously, the first blow would warn the rest. Some of us could escape and hit back."

"If they can summon up the nerve to drop any at all," said Zalumar, "you can bet your life they'll drop them together. It's all or nothing so far as they're concerned. Probably they would do their best to wipe us out if they thought for one moment that it would do them any good. They know it won't. They know it would bring retaliation from the Raidan Imperial Forces. We would be avenged,"

"Not yet we wouldn't," Lakin contradicted. "To date Raidan hasn't the faintest notion of where we are or what we're doing. I have just asked Shaipin whether he has yet beamed our official report. He hasn't. Until he does so, and receives Raidan's acknowledgment, we are just another task force lost in the mist of stars."

Zalumar gave a grim smile. "My dear Worryguts Lakin, only *we* know that we're out of contact. The Terrans *don't* know it. They're not going to take the risk of enticing a full-scale attack that will cremate the lot of them. Like everything else, they have a natural desire to survive. They value their skins, see?"

""I asked Shaipin why he hasn't yet signaled our whereabouts," Lakin persisted. "He said he's not yet received the order from you. Do you wish me to tell him to beam our report?"

"Certainly not." Turning his back upon him, Zalumar again absorbed the glorious vision of the city.

"Sire, regulations require us to report immediately we have overcome opposition and taken complete command."

Swinging round, Zalumar spat at him, "Do you think I, the commander, am ignorant of regulations? Shaipin will send the necessary signals when I say so, and not before. I am the sole judge of the proper moment."

"Yes, sire," agreed Lakin, taken aback.

"And the proper moment is not yet."

He said it as though it might never come.

Zalumar was quite a prophet.

Shaipin still had not been given the order a month later. Nor three months later, nor six. It never occurred to him to query the omission or, if it did, he preferred to keep his mouth shut. As for Lakin, he had tactfully refrained from mentioning the matter again. To his mind, Zalumar had staked his claim to full responsibility for everything done or not done—and he was welcome to stay stuck with it.

Through the many weeks events had shaped themselves beautifully. The Terrans cooperated one hundred per cent, displaying no visible enthusiasm but functioning with quiet efficiency.

Whenever Zalumar felt like larruping the leadership he ordered the entire snollygoster to parade before him and forty-two of them came on the run. His word was their command, his slightest whim had the status of a law. He did not doubt that if he'd been capable of sinking to such childishness he could have made them worship the ground on which he trod and kiss every footprint he left in the dirt. It was a wonderful exhibition of what can be done when the choice is the simple one of obey or burn.

One result of all this was that he, Zalumar, had fled the confines of a warship for the first time in more years than he'd care to count. He was no longer encased in metal, like a canned *rashim*. The tactic had been the easiest ever, requiring not even the chore of waving a magic wand. All he'd had to do was ask and it shall be given unto you. No, not ask, *tell*.

"You will confiscate and assign solely to me this world's most imposing palace. Whoever occupies it at present will be thrown out. All necessary repairs will be tended to without delay. The palace will be decorated and refurnish in sumptuous style suitable to my position as Planetary Governor. You will provide a full quota of trained servants. I'll inspect the place immediately when everything is ready—and for your own good you'd better make sure that it meets with my approval!"

They made sure all right. Even on Raidan nobody had it half so magnificent or a third as luxurious. He could think of many military contemporaries who'd grind their teeth with envy to see Nordis Zalumar, a mere ten-ship commander, making like a natural-born king. Nay, an emperor.

The palace was enormous. The center portion alone came close to being an international monument in its own right, without considering the vast expanse of east and west wings. Even the servants' quarters were about the size of a large hotel. The grounds around the palace numbered four thousand acres, all carefully landscaped, complete with a lake filled with multi-colored fish and ornamental water-fowl.

It was evident that the place had been prepared with lavishness that had no regard for cost. A world had been looted to gratify the one who could vaporize it from poles to core. Three thousand million animals had combined to pay the heavy premium on a fire-insurance policy.

Zalumar approved; even he could not dig up a lordly quibble. There was only one snag: the palace lay two thousand miles from the spaceport, the city, the seat of world government, There was only one solution: he ordered a new spaceport built on the fringe of his estate. This was done and his ten-ship fleet moved to the new location.

Next, he commanded the entire world leadership to set up home immediately outside his guarded gates. Nobody moaned, groaned, raised objections or so much as favored him with a disapproving frown. There was a rush of prefabricated buildings to the designated spot, a new township sprang into being complete with a huge web of telephone wires and a powerful radio station.

Meanwhile Zalumar had taken possession of his property. The transfer was made without ceremony; he merely stalked in at the front door as becomes one who literally owns the earth. His first move was to assign apartments in the west wing to his senior officers, inferior ones in the east wing to his twenty-one Terran stooges. This tactic helped populate a great emptiness, provided company, ensured a constant supply of adulation or, at least, dumb agreement.

"Aie!" he sighed with pleasure. "Is this not better than squatting in a hot can and being hammered day after day for the greater glory of others but never of ourselves?"

"Yes, sire," dutifully approved Heisham.

Lakin said nothing.

"We shall now reap the rewards of our virtues," continued Zalumar. "We shall live the life of . . . of—" He felt around in his jacket, produced a small pocket book and consulted it. "A character named Reilly."

"I have heard him mentioned by the Terrans," said Heisham. "And I imagine this is just the sort of place he'd have." He let admiring eyes survey the room, finished, "I wonder who did own it and what has happened to him."

"We can soon learn," Zalumar answered. "A Terran has just crossed the hall, Go get him and bring him here."

Heisham hastened out, came back with Vitelli.

"To whom did this place belong?" demanded Zalumar.

"To nobody." Vitelli favored him with his usual oily smile.

"Nobody?"

"No, sire. Previously this was the world's largest and latest international hospital."

"And just what is a hospital?"

The smile faded away, Vitelli blinked a couple of times and told him.

Zalumar listened incredulously, said, "An individual who is sick or injured is either capable or incapable of recovering. He can regain his efficiency or he is permanently useless. One thing or the other—there is no third alternative. That is logical, isn't it?"

"I suppose so," responded Vitelli, with reluctance.

"You don't suppose anything," Zalumar contradicted in louder tones. "You *know* for a fact that it is logical because I have *said* that it is. And say 'sire' when you answer me!"

"Yes, sire."

"If an individual can recover, he should be left to do it as best he can; he has every inducement to succeed, knowing the penalty of failure. If he cannot do it, he should be got rid of in the orthodox way; he should be gassed and cremated. It is sheer waste of time and effort for the fit to coddle the unfit."

He stared hard at Vitelli who offered no remark.

"It is contrary to natural law for the efficient to assist the inefficient who should be left to stew in their own juice. How many defective bodies were being pampered in this . . . uh . . . hospital?"

"About six thousand," informed Vitelli, again forgetting the "sire."

"Where are they now?"

"They were transferred to other hospitals. It has meant a little overcrowding in some places but I guess things will be straightened out in due time."

"So!" Zalumar thought a bit, looked as though about to voice something drastic, changed his mind and said, "You may go." After Vitelli had departed, Zalumar commented to the others, "I could order the prompt destruction of all this defective rubbish. But why should I bother? The chore of tending a horde of mental or physical cripples keeps Terran hands busy. Things remain orderly and peaceful when everyone is fully occupied. It is a world with time on its hands that makes itself a dangerous nuisance."

"Yes, sire," agreed Heisham, admiring him.

"Well, we now know something more," Zalumar went on. "In addition to being cowardly and stupid they are also soft. They are soft and yielding, like this stuff they call putty."

Lakin said in the manner of one meditating aloud, "How far does one get by plunging a sword into a barrel of putty? How much does one really cut, stab or destroy?"

Studying him blank-faced, Zalumar harshed, "Lakin, you will cease annoying me with senseless remarks."

Everything worked smoothly for another two years. In between regal jaunts around his planetary property. Zalumar lurked in his palace like a spider in the center of its web. Terra remained utterly and absolutely his to command, ran itself according to his directions. There had been no trouble other than that attributable to ordinary misunderstandings. In nobody's history had anyone sat more securely upon the throne than had the Emperor Nordis Zalumar.

At his command three groups of Raidan officers had gone on a tour of inspection of Terran colonies on Venus, Mars and Callisto. No crude frontiersman would risk cutting their throats; the home-world remained hostage for their safety. They were due back most anytime.

A fourth bunch had gone to look at a small settlement in the Centauri group, Earth's first foothold in another system. They'd not return for quite a piece. None of these groups had sailed in a Raidan warship; they'd all been taken in Terran space liners, traveling in utmost comfort as was proper for a higher form of life.

Of the sixteen hundred Raidans composing the original task force less than two hundred continued on military duty. A hundred formed the permanent palace guard. Eighty kept watch on the ships. All the rest were touring Terra, going where they pleased, at no cost whatsoever. Every man a prince and Zalumar the king of kings.

Yes, every man, a prince—that was no exaggeration. If any one of them saw something he fancied behind a shop window he walked inside, demanded it and it was handed over. An expensive camera, a diamond pendant, a racing motor-bike a streamlined Moon-boat, one had only to ask to be given.

Thus two junior navigators owned a subtropic island on which stood a magnificent mansion. They'd seen it from a confiscated amphibian, landed, marched in and said to the owners, "Get out." They'd said to the servants, "You stay." So the owners had gone posthaste and the servants had remained. Similarly, twenty grease monkeys were touring the world on a two thousand tons luxury yacht, having ambled aboard, ordered all passengers ashore and commanded the crew to raise anchor.

It seemed impossible that in such circumstances any Raidan could be discontented. Yet here again was that whining nuisance Lakin with a further batch of moans and groans. Some folk evidently would gripe even if given the cosmos on a platter.

"It can't go on forever," opined Lakin.

"It isn't intended to," Zalumar back. "We aren't immortal and more's the pity. But so long as it lasts our lifetimes we have every reason to be satisfied."

"Our lifetimes?" Lakin's expression showed that a deep suspicion been confirmed. "Do you mean that Raidan is to be left in ignorance of this conquest and that contact with our home forces is never to be made?"

Zalumar settled himself deeper in his chair which resembled a cunning compromise between a bed and a throne. He folded hands across an abdomen that was becoming a little more prominent, more paunchy with every passing month.

"My dear witless Lakin, an official report should have been sent more than two and a half years ago. If, like these Terran animals, we had been dumbly obedient and beamed that report where would we be now?"

"I haven't the slightest idea," admitted Lakin.

"Neither have I. But one thing is certain: we would not be *here*. By this time a consolidating expedition would have arrived and off-loaded the usual horde of desk-bound warriors, noncombatant officials, overseers, exploiters, slave drivers, form fillers and all the other parasites who squat all day and guzzle the spoils that space roamers have grabbed for them."

Lakin stayed silent, finding himself unable to contradict an unpleasant truth.

"As for us, we'd be summarily ordered back into our metal cans and told to go find yet another snatch. Right now we'd be somewhere out there in the sparkling dark, hunting around as we've been doing for years, taking risks, suffering continual discomfort, and knowing the nature of our ultimate reward." He pursed his lips and blew through them, making a thin slobbering sound. "The reward, my dear fatheaded Lakin, will be a row of medals that one can neither eat nor spend, a modest pension, a ceremonial mating, a shower of kids, old age, increasing feebleness and, finally, cremation."

"That may be so, sire, but—"

Waving him down, Zalumar continued, "I am of a mind to let the parasites seek their own prey and thus justify their own existence. Meanwhile we'll enjoy the prize we have gained for ourselves. If greed and ruthlessness are virtues in the many, they are equally virtues in the few. Since arriving on Terra I have become exceedingly virtuous and I advise you to do likewise. Remember, my dear bellyaching Lakin, that on our home-world they have an ancient saying." He paused, then quoted it with great relish. "Go thou and paint the long fence, Jayfat, for I am reclining within the hammock."

"Yes, sire, but—"

"And I am very comfortable," concluded Zalumar, hugging his middle.

"According to regulations, not to send a prompt report is treachery, punishable by death. They will gas and burn the lot of us."

"If they find us, *if* they ever find us." Zalumar closed his eyes and smiled sleepily. "With no report, no signal, no clue of any sort, it will take them at least a thousand years. Possibly two thousand. When they rediscover this planet, if ever they do, we shall be gone a long, long time. I am splendidly indifferent about how many officials go purple with fury several centuries after I am dead."

"The men think that a report to Raidan has been postponed for strategic reasons known to the senior officers," Lakin persisted. "If ever they learn the truth, they won't like it."

"Indeed? Why shouldn't they like it? Are they so crammed with patriotic zeal that they prefer to be bounced around on a tail of fire rather than stay here living the life they have earned and deserve?"

"It isn't that, sire."

"Then what is it?"

"A quarter of them are near the end of their term of service."

"They have reached it already," Zalumar pointed out. "*All* of us have reached it." He let go the sigh of one whose patience is being tried. "We are in retirement. We are enjoying the Terran pension which is on a scale far more lavish than anything Raidan offers to its conquering heroes."

"That may be—but I fear it won't prove enough."

"What more do they want?"

"Wives and children, homes of their own among their own kind."

"Pfah!"

"We can mate only with our own species," Lakin went on. "Men detained here beyond their term of service are going to be denied that right. It is no satisfactory substitute to have absolute claim on this world's treasures. Anyway, one soon loses appreciation of the value of something gained for nothing, one becomes bored by getting it for the mere asking."

"I don't," assured Zalumar. "I like it, I love it."

"Every day I see windows full of gold watches," said Lakin. "They tire me. I have a gold watch which I obtained by demanding it. I don't want fifty gold watches. I don't even want two of them. So what use are all the others to me?"

"Lakin, are you near the end of your term?"

"No, sire. I have another twelve years to serve."

"Then you are not yet entitled to be mated. As for those who soon may be entitled, that is their worry and not yours."

"It will be *our* worry, sire, if they cause trouble."

Zalumar's yellow eyes flared. "The first mutineers will be slaughtered as a warning to the rest. That is established space-discipline which I, as commander, am entitled to order. Be assured that I shall have no hesitation in ordering it should the need arise."

"Yes, sire, but—"

"But what?"

"I am wondering whether we can afford to take such action,"

"Speak plainly, Lakin, and cease to talk in riddles."

"Three years ago," responded Lakin, with a sort of gloomy desperation, "there were sixteen hundred of us. There are less today."

"Go on."

"Forty-two died in that epidemic of influenza to which they had no natural resistance. Eighteen killed themselves joyriding in a commandeered plane. Twenty-three have expired from sheer overeating and indolence. Two vanished while exploring under the seas. This morning three met death by reckless driving in a powerful sports car which the Terrans had built to their order. About forty more have come to their end in forty different ways. We're being thinned down slowly but surely If this goes on long enough, there'll be none of us left."

"My poor foolish Lakin, if life goes on long enough there will be none of us left no matter where we are, here or on Raidan."

"On Raidan, sire, our passing would not be tantamount to defeat for us and victory for these Terrans."

Zalumar favored him with an ugly grin. "In death there is neither victory nor defeat." He made a gesture of dismissal. "Go thou and paint the long fence . . . "

When the other had departed Zalumar summoned his chief signals officer. "Shaipin, I have just heard that some of our men are getting restless. Do you know anything of this?"

"Somebody is always ready to gripe, sire. Every military force has its minority of malcontents. It is best to ignore them."

"You have six beam-operators per ship, making sixty in all. Are any of these among the grouchers?"

"Not that I am aware of, sire."

"More than two years ago I ordered you to put all the beam-transmitters out of action just sufficiently to prevent them from being repaired and used in secret. Are they still immobilized? Have you checked them lately?"

"I examine them every seventh day, sire. They remain unworkable."

"You swear to that?"

"Yes," said Shaipin, positively.

"Good! Could any one of them be restored in less than seven days? Could it be made to function in between your regular checks?"

"No, sire. It would take at least a month to repair any one of them."

"All right. I continue to hold you personally responsible for seeing to it that nobody interferes with these transmitters. Anyone caught trying to operate one of them is to be killed on the spot. If you fail in this, you will answer for it with your head." The look he threw the other showed that he meant it. "Is Heisham around or is he vacationing some place?"

"He returned from a tour three or four days ago, sire. Probably he will be in his apartment in the west wing."

"Tell him I want to see him immediately. While you're at it, find Fox and send him here also."

Heisham and Fox arrived together, the former wearing a broad grin, the latter impassive as usual.

Zalumar said to Heisham, "You are in charge of the nominal roll. What is our present strength?"

"Fourteen hundred seventy, sire."

"So we're down one hundred thirty, eh?" observed Zalumar, watching Fox as he said it but getting no visible reaction.

"Yes, sire," agreed Heisham too well pleased with himself to be sobered by statistics.

"A self-satisfied smirk is at least a pleasant change from Lakin's miserable features," commented Zalumar. "What has made you so happy?"

"I have been awarded a Black Belt," informed Heisham, swelling with pride.

"You have been awarded it? By whom?"

"By the Terrans, sire."

Zalumar frowned. "There can be no worthwhile award on a world where anything may be confiscated."

"A Black Belt means nothing if merely grabbed," explained Heisham. "Its value lies in the fact that it must be won. I got mine at the risk of my neck."

"So we're down one-thirty and you've been trying to make it one thirty-one. No wonder the men get careless when senior officers set such a bad example. What is this thing you have won?"

"It's like this, sire," said Heisham. "Over a year ago I was telling a bunch of Terrans that we warriors are raised like warriors. We don't play silly games like chess, for instance. Our favorite sport is wrestling. We spend a lot of our childhood learning how to break the other fellow's arm. The natural result is that every Raidan is a first-class wrestler and hence an efficient fighting machine."

"So—?" prompted Zalumar.

"A medium-sized Terran showed great interest, asked what style of wrestling we used. I offered to show him. Well, when I recovered consciousness—"

"Eh?" ejaculated Zalumar.

"When I recovered consciousness," Heisham, persisted, "he was still there, leaning against the wall and looking at me. A lot of witnesses were hanging around, all of them Terrans, and in the circumstances there was nothing I could do about this fellow except kill him then and there."

"Quite right," approved Zalumar, nodding emphatically.

"So I snatched him in dead earnest and when they'd picked me off the floor again I asked—"

"Huh?"

I asked him to show me how he'd done it. He said it would need a series of lessons. So I made arrangements and took the lessons, every one of them. I passed tests and examinations and persisted until I was perfect." He stopped while he inflated his chest to suitable size. "And now I have won a Black Belt."

Zalumar switched attention to Fox. "Did you have any hand in this matter?"

"No, sire."

"It is just as well. Folly is reprehensible enough—I would not tolerate Terran encouragement of it." He turned back to Heisham. "Nobody has anything to teach us. But you, a senior officer, consent to take lessons from the conquered."

"I don't think it matters much, sire," offered Heisham, unabashed.

"Why doesn't it?"

"I learned their technique, mastered it and applied it better than they could themselves. To win my prize I had to overcome twenty of them one after the other. Therefore it can be said that I have taught them how to play their own game."

"Humph!" Zalumar was slightly mollified but still suspicious. "How do you know that they didn't *let* you throw them?"

"They didn't appear to do so, sire."

"Appearances aren't always what they seem," Zalumar said, dryly. He thought a bit, went on, "How did it happen that the medium-sized Terran mastered you in the first place?"

"I was caught napping by his extraordinary technique. This Terran wrestling is very peculiar."

"In what way?"

Heisham sought around for an easily explainable example said "If I were to push you it would be natural for you to oppose my push and to push back. But if you push a Terran he grabs your wrists and pulls the same way. He *helps* you. It is extremely difficult to fight a willing helper. It means that everything you try to do is immediately taken farther than you intended."

"The answer is easy," scoffed Zalumar. "You give up pushing. You pull him instead."

"If you change from pushing to pulling, he promptly switches from pulling to pushing," Heisham answered. "He's still with you, still helping. There's no effective way of controlling it except by adopting the same tactics."

"It sounds crazy to me. However, it is nothing unusual for aliens to have cockeyed ways of doing things. All right, Heisham, you may go away and coddle your hard-won prize. But don't encourage any of the others to follow your bad example. We are losing men too rapidly already."

He waited until Heisham had gone, then fixed attention on Fox.

"Fox, I have known you for quite a time. I have found you consistently obedient, frank and truthful. Therefore you stand as high in my esteem as any mere Terran can."

"Thank you, sire," said Fox, showing gratitude.

"It would be a pity to destroy that esteem and plunge yourself from the heights to the depths. I am relying upon you to give me candid answers to one or two questions. You have nothing to fear and nothing to lose by telling the absolute truth."

"What do you wish to know, sire?"

"Fox, I want you to tell me whether you are waiting, just waiting."

Puzzled, Fox said, "I don't understand."

"I want to know whether you Terrans are playing a waiting game, whether you are biding your time until we die out."

"Oh, no, not at all."

"What prevents you?" Zalumar inquired.

"Two things," Fox told him "Firstly, we suppose that other and probably stronger Raidan forces will replace you sometime. Obviously they won't leave you here to the end of your days."

Hah, won't they? thought Zalumar. He smiled within himself, said, "Secondly?"

"We're a Raidan colony, That means you're stuck with the full responsibilities of ownership. If anyone else attacks us, you Raidans must fight to keep us—or let go. That suits us quite well. Better the devil we know than the devil we don't."

It was glib and plausible, too glib and plausible. It might be the truth—but only a tiny fragment of it. For some reason he couldn't define Zalumar felt sure he wasn't being told the whole of it. Something vital was being held back. He could not imagine what it might be, neither could he devise an effective method of forcing it into the open. All that he did have was this vague uneasiness. Maybe it was the after-effect of a persistent morbidity. Damn Lakin, the prophet of gloom.

For lack of any better tactic he changed the subject. "I have an interesting report from one of our experts named Marjamian. He is an anthropologist or a sociologist or something. Anyway, he is a scientist, which means that he'd rather support an hypothesis than agree with an idea. I want your comments on what he has to say."

"It is about us Terrans?"

"Yes. He says your ancient history was murderous and that you came near to exterminating yourselves. In desperation you reached accord on the only item about which everyone could agree. You established permanent peace by mutually recognizing the basic right of every race and nation to live its own life in its own way." He glanced at his listener. "Is that correct?"

"More or less," said Fox, without enthusiasm.

"Later, when you got into free space, you anticipated a need to widen this understanding. So you agreed to recognize the basic right of every *species* to live its own life in its own way." Another glance. "Correct?"

"More or less," repeated Fox, looking bored.

"Finally, we arrived," continued Zalumar. "Our way of life is that of ruthless conquest. That must have put you in a mental and moral dilemma. All the same, you recognized our right even at great cost to yourselves."

"We didn't have much choice about it, considering the alternative," Fox pointed out. "Besides, the cost isn't killing us. We have been keeping a few hundred Raidans in luxury. There are three thousand millions of us. The expense works out at approximately two cents per head per annum."

Zalumar's eyebrows lifted in surprise. "That's one way of looking at it."

"For which price," added Fox, "the planet remains intact and we get protection."

"I see. So you regard the situation as mutually beneficial. We've got what we want and so have you." He yawned to show the interview was over. "Well, it takes all sorts to make a cosmos."

But he did not continue to yawn after Fox had gone. He sat and stared unseeingly at the ornamental drapes covering the distant door, narrowing his eyes occasionally and striving within his mind to locate an invisible Terran tomahawk that might or might not exist.

He had no real reason to suppose that a very sharp hatchet lay buried some place, waiting to be dug up. There was nothing to go on save a subtle instinct that stirred within him from time to time.

Plus unpleasant tinglings in the scalp.

Another three and a half years, making six in all. Suddenly the hatchet was exhumed.

Zalumar's first warning of the beginning of the end came in the form of a prolonged roar that started somewhere east of the palace and died away as a shrill whine high in the sky. He was abed and in deep sleep when it commenced. The noise jerked him awake, he sat up unsure whether he had dreamed it.

For a short time he remained gazing toward the bedroom's big windows and seeing only the star-spangled sky in between small patches of cloud. Outside there was now complete silence, as though a slumbering world had been shocked by this frantic bellowing in the night.

Then came a brilliant pink flash that lit up the undersides of the clouds. Another, another and another. Seconds later came a series of dull booms. The palace quivered, its windows rattled. Scrambling out of bed he went to the window, looked out, listened. Still he could see nothing but clearly through the dark came many metallic hammerings and the shouts of distant voices.

Bolting across the room he snatched up his bedside phone, rattled it impatiently while his eyes examined a nearby list of those on duty tonight. Ah, yes, Arnikoj was commander of the palace guard. He gave the phone another shake, cursed underbreath until a voice answered.

"Arnikoj, what's going on? What's happening?"

"I don't know, sire. There seems to be some sort of trouble at the spaceport."

"Find out what's the matter. You have got a line to the port, haven't you?"

"It is dead, sire. We cannot get a reply. I think it has been cut."

"Cut?" He fumed a bit. "Nonsense, man! It may be accidentally broken. Nobody would dare to cut it."

"Cut or broken," said Arnikoj, "it is out of action."

"You have radio communication as well. Call them at once on your transmitter. Have you lost your wits, Arnikoj?"

"We have tried, sire, and are still trying. There is no response."

"Rush an armed patrol there immediately. Send a portable transmitter with them. I must have accurate information without delay."

Dropping the phone, he threw on his clothes as swiftly as possible. A dozen voices yelled in the garden not a hundred yards from his windows. Something let go with a violent hammering. He made a jump for the door but the phone shrilled and called him back.

He grabbed it. "Yes?"

Arnikoj screamed at him, "It is too late, sire. They are already—" A loud *br-r-op-op* interrupted him, his voice changed to a horrid gurgling that receded and slowly ceased.

Zalumar raced out the room and along the outer passage. His mind seemed to be darting forty ways at once. "They," who are "they"? Another Raidan expedition that had discovered this hide-out of renegades? Unknown and unsuspected Terran allies at long last come to the rescue? Mutineers led by Lakin? *Who?*

He rounded a corner so fast that he gave himself no chance to escape three armed Terrans charging along the corridor. They grabbed him even as he skidded to a stop. This trio were big, brawny, tough-looking, wore steel helmets, were smothered in equipment and bore automatic guns.

"What is meant by this?" shouted Zalumar. "Do you realize—"

"Shut up!" ordered the largest of the three.

"Somebody will pay for—"

"I said to shut up!" He swung a big hand, slapped Zalumar with force that rattled his teeth and left him dazed. "See if he's clean, Milt."

One of the others ran expert hands over Zalumar's person. "Nothing on him, not even a loaded sock."

"O.K. Toss him in that small room. You stand guard, Milt. Beat his ears off if he gets uppish."

With that, two of them hustled around the corner, guns held ready. Twenty more similarly armed Terrans appeared and chased after the first two, none of them bothering to give the captive a glance in passing. Milt opened a door, shoved Zalumar's shoulder.

"Get inside."

"To whom do you think you're—"

Milt swung a heavy, steel-tipped boot at the other's tail and roared, "Get inside when you're told!"

Zalumar got in. The small room held a long, narrow table and eight chairs. He flopped into the nearest chair and glowered at Milt who leaned casually against the wall by the door. A minute later someone opened the door and slung Lakin through. Lakin had a badly discolored face and a thin trickle of blood along the jawline.

"Arnikoj is dead," said Lakin. "Also Dremith and Vasht and Marjamian and half the palace guard." He touched his features tenderly. "I suppose I'm lucky. They only beat me up."

"They will pay dearly for this," promised Zalumar. He studied the other curiously. "I suspected you of disloyalty to me. It seems that I was wrong."

"One can foresee trouble without having to take part in it. I've known for long enough that Heisham was brewing something. It was obvious that sooner or later—"

"Heisham?"

"Yes. His term of service ended two years ago—and he was still here. He is not the kind to sit around and do nothing about it. So he waited his chance."

"What chance?"

"We maintain a permanent ships' guard of eighty men. Everyone serves in rotation. Heisham needed only to bide his time until he and a bunch of sympathizers were selected for guard duty. The ships would then be his to do with as he pleased."

"That would be of no use. He couldn't take away ten cruisers with a mere eighty men."

"He could make off with two ships, each with a skeleton crew of forty," said Lakin.

"The fellow is stark, staring mad," declaimed Zalumar. "Immediately he shows his face on Raidan he and all those with him will have to undergo interrogation, with torture if necessary. And when they've given up every item of information they'll be executed as traitors."

"Heisham doesn't think so," Lakin responded. "He is going to put all the blame on you. He's going to tell them that you prohibited the sending of a report because you wanted all the spoils and the glory for yourself."

"They won't take his unsupported word for that."

"There are eighty men with him and they'll all say the same. They've got to—they're in the same jam. Besides, he has persuaded the Terrans to confirm his story. When a Raidan commission arrives to check up the Terrans will give evidence in Heisham's favor. He's quite confident that this tactic will not only save his life but also gain him honor."

"How do you know all this?" demanded Zalumar.

"He told me of his plans. He invited me to come in with him."

"Why didn't you?"

"I didn't share his optimism, Heisham always was too cocksure for my liking."

"Then why didn't you inform me of this plot?"

Lakin spread hands to indicate helplessness. "What was the use? You'd have taxed him with treachery and he'd have denied it, knowing full well that you were already tired of my warnings. Would you have believed me?"

Letting that awkward question pass unanswered, Zalumar buried himself in worried thought, eventually said, "The Terrans will not support his tale. They have nothing to gain by doing so. It is of total indifference to them whether Heisham's gang live or die."

"The Terrans have agreed to confirm everything he says—for a price."

Learning, forward, Zalumar asked in tones of suppressed fury, "What price?"

"The eight ships Heisham could not take."

"Intact and complete with the planet-busting equipment?"

"Yes," Lakin brooded a moment, added, "Even Heisham would have refused such payment had the Terrans any idea of where Raidan is located. But they don't know. They haven't the slightest notion."

Taking no notice, Zalumar sat breathing heavily while his features changed color. Then suddenly he shot to his feet and yelled at the guard.

"You piece of filth! You dirty lowdown animal!"

"Now, now!" said Milt, mildly amused. "Take it easy."

The door opened. Fox entered along with McKenzie and Vitelli. The latter bestowed on Zalumar the same unctuous smile that had not varied in six long years.

All three wore uniform and carried guns. Thus attired they looked much different; they'd acquired a hardness not noticed before. It wasn't quite like Raidan hardness, either. There was something else, a sort of patient craftiness.

Zalumar still had an ace up his sleeve; without giving them time to speak, he played it. "The ships won't do you any good. We shall never tell where Raidan is."

"There's no need to," said Fox, evenly. "We know."

"You're a liar. None of my men would give you that information, not even a self-seeking swine like Heisham."

"Nobody did tell us. We found out from what they did not tell."

"Don't give me that! I—"

"It was a long and tedious task but finally we made it," Fox chipped in. "All your wandering, sight-seeing tourists were willing to talk, being lonesome and far from home. We chatted with them at every opportunity. Not one would say just where he came from but every one of them readily admitted he did not come from some other place. We have analyzed records of eighty thousand conversations spread across six years. By simple process of elimination we've narrowed it down to the system of Sigma Octantis."

"You're wrong," asserted Zalumar, straining to hold himself in check "Dead wrong."

"Time will show. There won't be much of it, either. Maybe we could build a super-fleet by combining the virtues of your ships and ours. But we're not going to bother. It would take too long. We'll have learned how to operate your vessels before another day has passed."

"Eight ships against Raidan's thousands?" Zalumar indulged a harsh laugh. "You haven't a hope of victory."

"There will be no thousands from Raidan, We're going to send those ships hotfoot after Heisham. Even if they don't overtake him they'll arrive so close behind that the Raidan authorities will have had no time to react."

"And what then?"

"A new binary will be born."

There was a brief silence, then Zalumar rasped with all the sarcasm he could muster, "So much for your well-beloved basic right."

"You've got hold of the correct stick—but at the wrong end," said Fox. "The right we recognize is that of every species to *go to hell after its own fashion.*"

"Eh?"

"So when you arrived we were willing to help. It was a cinch. One naturally expects the greedy and ruthless to behave greedily and ruthlessly. You ran true to type." Taking his gun from its holster, Fox carefully laid it in the center of the table. "This is further assistance."

With that they went out, Fox, McKenzie, Vitelli and the guard named Milt. The door slammed shut. The lock clicked. Metal-shod boots commenced a monotonous patrolling outside.

Zalumar and Lakin sat unmoving throughout the rest of the night and the whole of next day, staring blindly at the table and saying nothing. Toward dusk a tremendous bellowing sounded from the spaceport, screamed into the sky. Another and another, eight in all.

As the sun called Sol sank blood-red into the horizon, Zalumar walked ashen-faced to the table and picked up the gun.

A little later the patrolling footsteps went away.

Dear Devil

Other Worlds, May 1950

The first Martian vessel descended upon Earth with the slow, stately fall of a grounding balloon. It did resemble a large balloon in that it was spherical and had a strange buoyancy out of keeping with its metallic construction. Beyond this superficial appearance all similarity to anything Terrestrial ceased.

There were no rockets, no crimson venturi-tubes, no external projections other than several solaradiant distorting grids which boosted the ship in any desired direction through the cosmic field. There were no observation-ports. All viewing was done through a transparent band running right around the fat belly of the sphere. The blue-skinned, somewhat nightmarish crew were assembled behind that band and surveying the world through great multi-faceted eyes.

They gazed through the viewing-strip in utter silence as they examined this world which was Terra. Even if they had been capable of speech they would have said nothing. But none among them had a talkative faculty in any sonic sense. At this quiet moment none needed it.

The scene outside was one of untrammeled desolation. Scraggy blue-green grass clung to tired ground all the way to a horizon scarred by ragged mountains. Dismal bushes struggled for life here and there, some with the pathetic air of striving to become trees as once their ancestors had been. To the right a long, straight scar through the grass betrayed a sterile lumpiness of rocks at odd places. Too rugged and too narrow ever to have been a road, it suggested no more than the desiccated remnants of a long-gone wall. And over all this loomed a ghastly sky.

Captain Skhiva eyed his crew, spoke to them with his sign-talking tentacle. The alternative was contact-telepathy which required physical touch.

"It is obvious that we are out of luck. We could have done no worse had we landed on the empty satellite. However, it is safe to go outside. Anyone who wishes to explore for a little while may do so."

One of them gesticulated back to him. "Captain, don't you wish to be the first to step upon this new world?"

"It is of no consequence. If anyone deems it an honor, he is welcome to it." He pulled the lever opening both airlock doors. Thicker, heavier air crowded in and pressure went up a few pounds. "Beware of overexertion," he warned as they went out.

Poet Fander touched him, tentacles tip to tip as he sent his thoughts racing through their nerve-ends. "This confirms what we could see on the approach. A stricken planet far gone in its death throes. What do you suppose might have caused it?"

"I have not the remotest idea. I would give a lot to know. If it has been smitten by natural forces what might they do to Mars someday?" His troubled mind sent a throb of worry up Fander's contacting tentacle. "A pity that this planet had not been farther out instead of closer in; we might then have observed the preceding, phenomena from the surface of our own world. It is so difficult to properly to view this one against the glare of the Sun."

"That applies still more to the next planet, the misty one," remarked Poet Fander.

"I know it and I am beginning to fear what we may find there. If it proves to be equally dead, then we are stalled until we can make the big jump outward."

"Which won't be in our lifetimes."

"I doubt it," agreed Captain Skhiva. "We could move fast with the help of able friends. We shall be slow—going it alone." He turned to watch his crew as they poked and probed around the grim landscape. "They find it good to be on firm ground. But what is a world without life and beauty? In short time they will become tired of it. They will be glad to leave."

Fander said thoughtfully, "Nevertheless, I would like to see more of it. May I take out the lifeboat?"

"You are a songbird and not a pilot," reproved Skhiva. "Your function is to maintain morale by entertaining us, not to go roaming around in a lifeboat."

"But I know how to control it. Every one of us has been trained to handle it. Let me take it that I may see more."

"Haven't we seen enough even before we landed? What else is there to see? Cracked and distorted roads about to dissolve into nothingness. Ages-old cities, torn and broken, crumbling into dust. Shattered mountains and charred forests and craters little smaller than those upon the Moon. No sign of any superior life-form still surviving. Only the grass, the shrubs and various small animals, two or four-legged, that flee at our approach. Why do you wish to see more?"

"There is poetry even in death," said Fander.

"Possibly so—but it remains repulsive." Skhiva gave a brief shiver. "All right, have your own way. Take the lifeboat. Who am I to question the weird workings of the nontechnical mind?"

"Thank you, Captain."

"It is nothing. See that you are back by dusk." Breaking contact, Skhiva went to the lock, curled himself snakishly on its outer rim and brooded, still without bothering to touch the strange new world. So much attempted, so much done—for so poor reward.

He was still pondering the futility of effort when the lifeboat broke free and soared. Expressionlessly his multi-faceted eyes watched the energized grids change angle as the boat swung into a curve and floated away like a little bubble. Skhiva was sensitive to futility.

The crew came in well before darkness. A few hours were enough. Just grass and shrubs and child-trees straining to grow up. One had discovered a grassless oblong that once might have been the site of a dwelling-place. He brought back a small piece of its foundation, a lump of perished concrete that Skhiva put away for later analysis.

Another had found a small, brown, six-legged insect, but his nerve-ends had heard it cry when he picked it up so hastily he had put it down and let it go free. Small, clumsily moving animals had been hopping in the distance but all had dived down holes in the ground before any Martian could get near. All the crew were agreed upon one thing: the silence and solemnity of a people's passing was unendurable.

Fander beat the sinking of the Sun by half a time-unit. His bubble drifted under a great black cloud, sank to ship-level and came in. The rain started a moment later, roaring down in a frenzied torrent while they stood behind the transparent band and marveled at so much water.

After a while Captain Skhiva told them, "We must accept what we find. We have drawn a blank. The cause of this world's condition is a mystery to be solved by others with more time and better equipment. We are explorers rather than investigators. It is for us to abandon this graveyard and push on to the misty planet. We'll take off early in the morning."

None commented. Fander followed him to his room, made contact with a tentacle-touch.

"One could live here, Captain."

"I am far from sure of that." Skhiva coiled on his couch, suspending his tentacles on its limb-rests. The blue sheen of him was reflected by the back wall. "In many places the rocks emit alpha-sparks. They are dangerous."

"I know, Captain. But I can sense them and avoid them."

"You?" The other stared up at him.

"Yes, Captain. I wish to be left here."

"What?—in this place of appalling dreariness?"

"It has an all-pervading air of ugliness and despair," admitted Poet Fander. "All destruction is ugly. But by accident I have found a little beauty. It heartens me. I would like to seek its source."

"To what beauty do you refer?" Skhiva demanded.

Fander tried to explain the alien in non-alien terms. It proved impossible.

"Draw it for me," ordered Skhiva.

Fander drew it carefully, gave him the picture and said, "There!"

Gazing at it for a long time, Skhiva handed it back, spoke along the other's nerves. "We are individuals with all the rights of individuals. As an individual I don't think that picture sufficiently beautiful to be worth the tail-tip of a domestic *aralan.* However, I will admit that it is not ugly, even that it is pleasing."

"But, Captain—"

"As an individual," Skhiva went on, "you have an equal right to your opinions strange though those may be. If you really wish to stay, I cannot refuse you. I am entitled only to think you a little crazy." He eyed Fander again. "When do you hope to he picked up?"

"This year, next year, sometime, never."

"It might well be never," Skhiva reminded. "Are you prepared to face that prospect?"

"One must always be prepared to face the natural consequences of his own actions," Fander pointed out.

"True." Skhiva was reluctant to surrender. "But have you given the matter serious thought?"

"I am a non-technical component. I am not guided by thought."

"Then by what?"

"By my desires, emotions, instincts. By my inward feelings."

Skhiva said fervently, "The twin moons preserve us!"

"Captain, sing me a song of home and play me the tinkling harp."

"Don't be silly. I have not the ability."

"Captain, if it required no more than careful thought you would be able to do it?"

"No doubt," agreed Skhiva, seeing the trap but unable to avoid it.

"There you are," said Fander pointedly.

"I give up. I cannot argue with someone who casts aside the accepted rules of logic and invents ones of his own. You are governed by lopsided notions that defeat me."

"It is not a matter of logic or illogic," Fander told him. "It is merely a matter of viewpoint. You see certain angles whereas I see others."

"For example?"

"You won't pin me down in that way. I can find examples. For instance, do you remember that formula for determining the phase of a series tuned circuit?"

"Of course I do."

"I felt you would. You are a technician. You have fixed it in your mind as a matter of technical utility." He paused, looked musingly at Skhiva. "I know that formula too. It was mentioned to me, casually, many years ago. It is of not the slightest use to me. Yet I have never forgotten it."

"Why?"

"Because it holds the beauty of rhythm. It is a poem."

Skhiva sighed and said, "That's news to me.

"One upon R into omega L minus one upon omega C," recited Fander, showing mild amusement. "A perfect hexameter."

After a while, Skhiva conceded, "It could be sung. One could dance to it."

"Now I have seen this." Fander exhibited his sketch. "It holds beauty of a strange and alien kind. Where there is beauty there once was talent—and for all we know there may still be talent. Where talent abides one may find the seeds of greatness. In the realms of greatness are or will be powerful friends. We *need* such friends."

"You win." Skhiva made a gesture of surrender. "In the morning we shall leave you to your self-chosen fate."

"Thank you, Captain."

That same streak of stubbornness which made Skhiva a worthy commander induced him to take one final crack at Fander shortly before departure. Summoning him to his room, he eyed the poet calculatingly.

"You are still of the same mind?"

"Yes, Captain."

"Then does it not occur to you as strange that I should be so content to abandon this planet if, as you suggest, it holds the remnants of greatness?"

"No."

"Why not?" Skhiva stiffened slightly.

"Captain, I think you are a little afraid because you suspect what I suspect."

"And what do you suspect?"

"That there was no natural disaster. That they did this themselves—to themselves."

"We have no proof of it," said Skhiva uneasily.

"No, Captain." Fander posed there without desire to add more.

"*If* this is their own sad handiwork," Skhiva commented at length, "what is our chance of finding friendship among people so much to be feared?"

"Poor," admitted Fander. "But that is the product of cold thought. As such, it means little to me. I am animated by warm hopes."

"There you go again, blatantly disregarding reason in favor of an idle dream. Hoping, hoping, hoping—to achieve the impossible."

Fander said, "The difficult can be done; the impossible takes longer."

"Your opinions make my orderly mind befuddled. Every remark of yours is a flat denial of something that makes sense." Skhiva transmitted the sensation of a lugubrious chuckle. "Oh, well, so be it!" He came forward, moving closer to the other. "All your supplies are assembled outside. Nothing remains save to bid you farewell."

They embraced in the Martian manner. Leaving the airlock, Poet Fonder watched the big sphere shiver and glide upward. It soared without a sound, shrinking steadily until it became a mere dot about to enter a cloud. A moment later it had gone.

He remained there looking at the cloud for a long, long time. Then he turned his attention to the load-sled holding his supplies. Climbing into its exposed front seat, he shifted the control that energized the floating-grids, let it rise a few feet. The higher the rise the greater the expenditure of power. He wished to conserve power as much as possible; there was no knowing how long he might need it. So at low altitude and gentle pace he let the sled glide in the general direction of the thing of beauty.

Later, he found a small, dry cave in the hill on which his objective stood. It took him two days of careful, cautious raying to enlarge it, square its walls, ceiling and floor, plus half a day with a powered fan driving out silicate dust. After that he stowed his supplies at the back, parked the sled at the front, set up a curtaining force-screen across the entrance. The hole in the hill was now home.

Slumber did not come easily that first night. He lay within the cave, a ropey, knotted thing of glowing blue with enormous bee-like eyes, and found himself listening for harps that played sixty million miles away. His tentacle-tips twitched in involuntary search of the telepathic-contact songs that would go with the harps, and they twitched in vain.

Darkness grew deep and all the world a monstrous stillness held. His hearing organs craved for the eventide flip-flop of sand-frogs but there were no frogs. He wanted the homely drone of night-beetles but none droned. Except for once when something faraway howled its heart at the sallow Moon, there was nothing, nothing.

In the morning he washed, ate, took out the sled and explored the site of a small town. He found little to satisfy his curiosity, no more than mounds of shapeless rubble on ragged, faintly oblong foundations. It was a graveyard of long-dead domiciles, rotting, weedy, rapidly degenerating into complete oblivion. A view from five hundred feet up gave him only one piece of information: the orderliness of the outlines showed that these people had been tidy and methodical.

But tidiness is not beauty in itself. He came back to the top of his hill and sought solace by contemplating the thing that did have beauty.

His explorations continued, not systematically as Skhiva would have conducted them, but in accordance with his own mercurial whims. At times he saw many animals, singly or in groups, none resembling any life-form seen on Mars. Some scattered at full gallop when his sled swooped over them. Some dived down holes in the ground, showing as they disappeared a brief flash of white, absurd tails. Others, four-footed, long-faced, sharp-toothed, hunted in gangs and bayed at him in concert with harsh, menacing voices.

On the seventieth day, in a deep, shadowed glade to the north, he spotted a small number of new shapes slinking along in single file. He recognized them at a glance, knew them so well that his searching eyes transmitted a thrill of triumph to his mind. They were ragged, dirty and only part-grown, but the thing of beauty had told him what they were.

Hugging the ground low, he swept around in a wide curve that brought him to the farther end of the glade. He could see them better now, even the dirt-streaked pink of their thin legs. The sled sloped slightly down into the drop as it entered the glade. They were moving away from him, showing fearful caution as they watched for enemies ahead. His silent swoop from behind gave them no warning.

The rearmost one of this stealthy file fooled him at the last moment. Fander was leaning over the side of the sled, long tentacles outstretched in readiness to snatch the end one with the wild mop of yellow hair when, responding to some sixth sense, the intended victim threw itself flat. His grasp shot past a couple of feet short and he got a glimpse of frightened gray eyes a second or so before a dexterous side-tilt of the sled enabled him to make good his loss by grabbing the less wary next in line.

This one was dark-haired, a bit bigger and sturdier. It fought madly at the holding limbs while the sled gained altitude. Then, suddenly becoming aware of the peculiar nature of its bonds, it writhed around and looked straight at Fander. The result was unexpected: it lost facial color and closed its eyes and went completely limp.

It was still limp when he bore it into the cave but its heart continued to beat and its lungs to draw. Laying it carefully on the softness of his bed, he moved to the cave's entrance and waited for it to recover. Eventually it stirred, sat up, gazed confusedly at the facing wall. Its black eyes moved slowly around, taking in the surroundings. Then they saw Fander limned in outer light. They widened and their owner began to make high-pitched, unpleasant noises as it tried to back away through the solid wall. It made so much noise in one rising throb after another that Fander slithered out of the cave, right out of sight, and sat in the cold wind until the sounds died away.

A couple of hours later he made cautious reappearance to offer food but the reaction was so swift, hysterical and heart-rending that he dropped his load and hid himself as if the fear were his own. The food remained untouched for two full days. On the third, a little was eaten. Fander ventured within.

Although the Martian did not go near to him, the boy cowered away murmuring, "Devil! Devil!" His eyes were red, with dark discoloration beneath them.

"Devil!" thought Fander, quite unable to repeat the alien word and wondering what it meant. He used his sign-talking tentacle in valiant effort to convey something reassuring. The attempt was wasted. The other watched its writhings half in fear, half with distaste, and showed complete lack of comprehension. He let the tentacle gently slither forward across the floor, hoping to make thought-contact. The other recoiled from it as if from a striking snake.

"Patience," he reminded himself. "The impossible takes longer."

Periodically he showed himself with food and water. Nighttimes he slept fitfully on coarse damp grass beneath lowering skies while the prisoner who was his guest enjoyed the comfort of the bed, the warmth of the cave, the security of the force-screen.

Time came when Fander displayed unpoetic shrewdness by using the other's belly to estimate the ripeness of the moment. When on the eighth day he noted that his food offerings were being taken regularly, he took a meal of his own at the edge of the cave, within plain sight, and observed that the other's appetite was not spoiled. That night he slept just within the cave, close to the force-screen and as far as possible from the boy. There was no unpleasant reaction. The boy stayed awake late watching him, intently watching him, but gave way to slumber in the small hours.

A fresh attempt at sign-talking brought results no better than before and the other still refused to touch his offered tentacle. All the same, he was making progress. His overtures still were rejected but with less revulsion. Gradually, ever so gradually, the Martian shape was becoming familiar, almost acceptable.

The sweet taste of success was Fander's in the middle of the next day. The boy had displayed several spells of emotional sickness during which he'd lain on his front with shaking body and emitted low noises while his eyes watered profusely. At such times the Martian felt strangely helpless and inadequate. On this occasion, during another attack, he took advantage of the sufferer's lack of attention and slid near enough to snatch away the box by his bed.

From the box he extracted his tiny electro-harp, plugged its connectors, switched it on, touched its strings with delicate affection. Slowly he began to play, singing an accompaniment inside himself for he had no voice with which to sing and only the harp could make sounds for him.

The boy ceased his quiverings and sat up, all his attention upon the dexterous play of the tentacles and the music they conjured forth. And when he judged that at last the listener's mind was captured, Fander ceased with easy, quietening strokes, gently offered him the harp. The boy showed interest and reluctance. Careful not to move nearer, not an inch nearer, Fander offered it at full tentacle length. The boy had to take four steps to get it. He took them.

That was the start. They played together day after day and sometimes a little into the night while almost imperceptibly the distance between them became reduced. Finally they sat side by side, and the boy had not yet learned to laugh but no longer did he show unease. He could now extract a simple tune from the instrument and was pleased with his own aptitude in a solemn sort of way.

One evening as darkness grew and the things that sometimes howled at the Moon were howling again, Fander offered his tentacle-tip for the hundredth time. Always the gesture had been unmistakable even if its motive had not been clear, yet always it had been rebuffed. But now, now, five fingers curled around it in shy desire to please.

With a fervent prayer that human nerves would function exactly like Martian ones, Fander poured his thoughts through, swiftly, lest the warm grip be loosened too soon.

"Do not fear me. I cannot help my shape any more than you can help yours. I am your friend, your father, your mother. I need you as much as you need me."

The boy let go of him, began quiet, half-stifled whimpering noises. Fander put a tentacle on his shoulder, made little patting motions that he imagined were wholly Martian. For some inexplicable reason this made matters worse. At his wit's end what to do for the best, what action to take that might be understandable in human terms, he gave up the problem, surrendered to his instinct, put a long, ropey limb around the boy and held him close until the noises ceased and slumber came. It was then that he realized that the child he had taken was much younger than he'd estimated. He nursed him through the night.

Much practice was necessary to make conversation. The boy had to learn to put mental drive behind his thoughts for it was beyond Fander's power to suck them out of him.

"What is your name?"

Fander got a picture of thin legs running rapidly. He returned it in question form. "Speedy?"

An affirmative.

"What name do you give to me?"

An unflattering montage of monsters.

"Devil?"

The picture whirled around, became confused. There was a trace of embarrassment.

"Devil will do," assured Fander, open-minded about the matter. He went on, "Where are your parents?"

More confusion.

"You must have had parents. Everyone has a father and mother, haven't they? Don't you remember yours?"

Muddled ghost-pictures. Grown-ups abandoning children. Grown-ups avoiding children as if they feared them.

"What is the first thing you remember?"

"Big man walking with me. Carried me a while. Walked again."

"What happened to him?"

"Went away. Said he was sick. Said he might make me sick too."

"Long ago?"

Confusion.

Fander changed his aim. "What about those other children—have they no parents either?"

"All got nobody."

"But you've got somebody now, haven't you, Speedy?"

Doubtfully, "Yes."

Fander pushed it farther. "Would you rather have me or those other children?" He let it rest a moment before he added, "Or both?"

"Both," said Speedy with no hesitation whatever. His fingers toyed with the harp.

"Would you like to help me look for them tomorrow and bring them here?"

"Yes."

"And if they are scared of me will you tell them not to be afraid?"

"Sure!" said Speedy, licking his lips and sticking his chest out.

"Then perhaps you'd like to go for a short jaunt with me today. You've been too long in this cave. A little exercise would do no harm. Will you come for a walk with me?"

"Yes."

Side by side they went out, one trotting rapidly along, the other slithering. The child's spirits perked up with this trip in the open; it was as if the sight of the sky, the feel of the wind and the smell of the grass made him realize that he was not exactly a prisoner. His formerly solemn features became animated, he made exclamations that Fander could not understand, and once he laughed at nothing for the sheer joy of it. On two occasions he grabbed a tentacle-tip in order to tell Fander something, performing the action as if it were in every way as natural as his own speech.

The next morning they got out the load-sled. Fander took the front seat and the controls; Speedy squatted behind with hands gripping the other's harness belt.

With a shallow soar they headed for the glade. Many small white-tailed animals bolted down holes as they passed over.

"Good for food," remarked Speedy, touching him and speaking through the contact-point.

Fander felt slightly sick. Meat-eaters! It was not until a queer feeling of shame and apology came back at him that he knew Speedy had sensed his revulsion. He wished he'd been quick to blanket that reaction before the boy could detect it—but he could not be blamed for the effect of so bald a statement taking him so completely unaware. However, it had produced another step forward in their mutual relationship; Speedy desired his good opinion.

Within fifteen minutes they struck lucky. At a point half a mile south of the glade Speedy let out a shrill yell and pointed downward. A small, golden-haired figure was standing there atop a slight rise and staring fascinatedly at the phenomenon in the sky. A second tiny shape with red but equally long hair was partway down the slope and gazing upward in a similar wonderment. Both came to their senses and turned to flee as the sled turned, tilted and plunged toward them.

Ignoring the yelps of excitement right behind him, and the violent pullings upon his belt, Fander swooped, got one and then the other. The double burden in his grip made it none too easy to right the sled and zoom for height. If the victims had fought he'd have had his work cut out to make it. They did not fight. They shrieked as he snatched them and then relaxed with closed eyes.

The sled climbed and glided a mile at five hundred feet. Fander's attention was divided between his limp prizes, the controls and the horizon when suddenly a thunderous rattling sounded on the underside of the sled, the entire framework shuddered, a strip of metal flew from its leading edge and things made whistling, whining sounds toward the clouds.

"Old Greypate!" bawled Speedy, jigging around but keeping away from the rim. "He's shooting at us!"

The spoken words meant nothing to the Martian and he could not spare a limb for the contact the other had forgotten to make. Grimly leveling the sled, he gave it full power. Whatever damage it had suffered had not affected its efficiency; it shot forward at a pace that set the red and golden hair of the captives streaming in the wind. Perforce his landing by the cave was a little clumsy. The sled bumped down and lurched across forty yards of grass.

First things first. Taking the quiet pair into the cave he made them comfortable upon the bed, came out and examined the sled. There were half a dozen deep dents in its metal base and two bright furrows angling across one rim. He made contact with Speedy.

"What were you trying to tell me?"

"Old Greypate shot at us."

The mind-picture burst upon him vividly and with electrifying effect, a vision of a tall, white-haired, stern-faced old man with a tubular weapon propped against his shoulder while it spat fire upward. A white-haired old man. An adult!

His grip was tight on Speedy's fingers. "What is this oldster to you?"

"Nothing much. He lives near us in the shelters."

Picture of a long, dusty concrete burrow, badly damaged, its ceiling marked with the scars of a lighting system long rotted away to nothing. The old man living hermitlike at one end, the children at the other. The old man was sour, taciturn, kept his distance from the children, spoke to them seldom but was quick to react whenever they were menaced. He had guns. Once he had killed many wild dogs that had eaten two children.

"People left us near shelters because Old Greypate was there and had guns," informed Speedy.

"But why doesn't he consort with the children? Doesn't he like them?"

"Don't know." He mused a moment. "Once he told us that old people could get very sick and make young ones sick too—and then we'd all die. Perhaps he's afraid of making us die." Speedy wasn't very sure about this.

So there was some much-feared disease going around, something highly contagious to which adults were peculiarly susceptible. Without hesitation they abandoned their young at the first onslaught, hoping that at least the children would survive. Sacrifice after sacrifice to keep the race alive. Heartbreak after heartbreak as elders chose death in solitude rather than death in company.

Yet Greypate himself was depicted as very old. Was this an exaggeration of the child-mind?

"I must meet Greypate."

"He will shoot," declared Speedy positively. "He knows by now that you took me away. He saw you take the others. He will wait for you and shoot you first chance he gets."

"We must find some way to avoid that."

"How?"

"When these two have become my friends, just as you have become my friend, I will take all three of you back to the shelters. You can find Greypate for me and tell him I am not as ugly as I look."

"I don't think you're ugly," denied Speedy.

The picture Fander got along with that remark gave him the weirdest sensation. It was of a vague, shadowy and considerably distorted body with a clear human face.

The new prisoners were female. Fander knew it without being told because they were daintier than Speedy and had the warm, sweet smell of females. That meant complications. Maybe they were mere children and maybe they did live together in the shelters, but he was permitting none of that while they remained in his charge. Fander might be outlandish by other standards but he had a certain primness. Forthwith he cut another and smaller cave for Speedy and himself.

Neither of the girls saw him for four days. Keeping well out of their sight he let Speedy take them food, talk to them, soothe them, prepare them for the shape of the thing to come. On the fifth day he presented himself for inspection at a distance. Despite forewarnings they went white, clung together but uttered no distressing sounds. He played his harp a while, withdrew, came back later and played for them again.

Encouraged by Speedy's constant and self-assured flow of propaganda, one of them grasped a tentacle-tip next day. What came along the nerves was not an intelligible picture so much as an ache, a desire, a childish yearning. Fander backed out of the cave, found wood, spent the whole night using the slumbering Speedy as a model and fashioned the wood into a tiny, jointed semblance of a human being. He was no sculptor but he did possess a natural delicacy of touch while the poet in him ran through his limbs and expressed itself in the model. Making a thorough job of it, he clothed it in what he conceived to be Terrestrial fashion, colored its face, fixed upon its features the pleasure-grimace that humans call a smile.

He gave her the doll the moment she awakened in the morning. She took it eagerly, hungrily, with wide, glad eyes. Hugging it to her unformed bosom she crooned over it—and he knew that the strange emptiness within her had gone.

Though Speedy was openly contemptuous of this manifest waste of effort, Fander set to and made a second manikin. It did not take quite as long. Practice on the first had made him swifter, more dexterous. He was able to present it to the other child by mid-afternoon. Her acceptance was made with shy grace; she clutched the doll close as if it meant more to her than the whole of her sorry world. In her thrilled concentration upon the gift she did not notice his nearness, his closeness, and when he offered a tentacle-tip she took it absentmindedly.

He said simply, "I love you."

Her mind was too untrained to drive a response but her great eyes warmed.

Fander sat on the grounded sled at a point a mile east of the glade and watched the three children walk hand in hand toward the hidden shelters. Speedy was the obvious leader, hurrying them onward, bossing them with the noisy assurance of one who has been around and considers himself sophisticated. In spite of this the girls paused at intervals to turn and wave to the ropey, bee-eyed thing they'd left behind. And Fander dutifully waved back, always using his signal-tentacle because it had not occurred to him that any tentacle would serve.

They sank from sight behind a rise of ground. He remained on the sled, his multi-faceted gaze going over his surroundings or studying the angry sky now threatening rain. The ground was a dull, dead gray-green all the way to the horizon. There was no relief from that drab color, not one shining patch of white, gold or crimson such as dotted the meadowlands of Mars. There was only the eternal gray-green and his own brilliant blueness.

Before long a sharp-faced, four-footed thing revealed itself in the grass, raised its head and howled at him. The sound was an eerily urgent wail that ran across the grasses and moaned into the distance. It brought others of its kind, two, ten, twenty. Their defiance increased with their numbers until there was a large band of them encouraging each other with yaps and snarls, slowly edging toward him with lips drawn back and fangs exposed. Then came a sudden and undetectable group-command which caused them to cease their slinking and spring forward like one, slavering as they came. They did it with the hungry, red-eyed frenzy of animals motivated by something akin to madness.

Revolting though it was, the sight of creatures craving for meat—even strange blue meat—did not alarm Fander. He slipped a control-lever one notch, the flotation-grids radiated, the sled soared twenty feet. So calm and easy an escape so casually performed infuriated the wild-dog pack beyond all measure. Arriving in a ferocious cluster beneath the sled, they made futile springs upward, fell back upon one another, leaped again and again. The pandemonium they set up was insane in the extreme. They exuded a pungent odor of dry hair and animal sweat.

Reclining upon the sled in a maddening pose of disdain, Fander let them rave below. They raced around in tight circles shrieking insults at him and biting each other. This went on for some time and ended with a spurt of ultra-rapid cracks from the direction of the glade. Eight dogs fell dead. Two flopped and struggled to crawl away. Ten yelped in agony and made off on three legs. The unharmed ones flashed away to some place where they could ambush and make a meal of the escaping limpers. Fander lowered the sled.

Speedy stood on the rise with Greypate. The latter restored his weapon to the crook of his arm, rubbed his chin thoughtfully, ambled forward.

Stopping five yards from the Martian, the old Earthman again rubbed his chin-bristles and said, "Doesn't look natural to me. I'd call him a bad dream."

"No use talking *at* him," Speedy advised. "You've got to hold an end of him, like I told you."

"I know, I know." Greypate waved him down with elderly impatience. "All in good time. I'll touch him when I'm ready." He stood there staring at Fander with eyes that were pale gray and very sharp. Once or twice he muttered something under his breath. Finally he said, "Oh, well, here goes," and offered a hand.

Fander placed a tentacle-tip in it.

"He's cool," commented Greypate, closing his grip. "Colder than a snake."

"He isn't a snake," Speedy contradicted fiercely.

"Be quiet—I didn't say he is."

"He doesn't feel like one either," persisted Speedy who had never felt a snake in his life and had no desire to.

Fander boosted a thought through. "I come from the fourth planet. Do you know what that means?"

"I'm not ignorant," snapped Greypate aloud.

"There is no need to reply vocally. I receive your thoughts exactly as you receive mine. Your responses are much stronger than the boy's and I can understand you easily."

"Humph!" said Greypate, unimpressed.

"I have been anxious to find and talk with an adult because the children cannot tell me enough. I would like to ask you some questions. Are you willing to answer them?"

"Depends," said Greypate, becoming leery.

"Never mind. Answer them if you wish. My only desire is to help you."

"Why?" asked Greypate, searching for a percentage.

"We need intelligent friends."

"Why?"

"Because our numbers are small and our resources poor. In visiting this world and the misty one we've come near to the limit of our ability. But with assistance we could go farther, we could reach the outer planets. I think that if we were to help you today, you could help us tomorrow."

Greypate pondered it cautiously, quite forgetting that the inward workings of his mind were wide open to the other. Chronic suspicion was the keynote of his thoughts, suspicion based on life experiences and recent history. But inward thoughts ran both ways and his own mind detected the sincerity in Fander's.

So he said, "Fair enough. Say more."

"What caused all this?" inquired Fander, waving a limb at the world.

"War," said Greypate sourly. "The last war we'll ever have. The entire planet went crazy."

"How did that come about?"

"You've got me there." Greypate gave the problem grave consideration. "I reckon it wasn't just any one thing. It was a multitude of things sort of piling themselves up."

"Such as."

"Differences in people. Some were colored differently in their bodies, others in their minds, and they couldn't get along. Some bred a damnsight faster than others, wanted more room, more food. There wasn't any more room or any more food. The world was full and nobody could shove in except by pushing another out. My old man told me plenty before he died and he always maintained that if folk had had the horse sense to keep their numbers down there might not—"

"Your old man?" interjected Fander. "You mean your parent, your father? Didn't all this occur in your own lifetime?"

"It did not. I saw none of it. I'm the son of the son of the son of a survivor."

"Let's go back to the cave," put in Speedy, bored with this silent contact-talk. "I want to show him our harp."

They took no notice and Fander went on, "Do you think there might be many others still living?"

"Hard to say." Greypate was moody about it. "There's no way of telling how many are wandering around on the other side of the globe, maybe still killing each other, or starving to death, or dying of the sickness."

"What sickness is this?"

"I don't remember what it's called." Greypate scratched his head confusedly. "My old man told me several times but I've long forgotten. Knowing the name wouldn't do me any good, see? He said his father told him it was part of the war, it got invented and was spread deliberately—and it's still with us."

"What are the symptoms?"

"You go hot and dizzy. You get black swellings in the armpits. In forty-eight hours you're thoroughly dead and nothing can be done to prevent it. Old ones usually catch it first. The kids then get it unless they're put out of reach of the victims pretty fast."

"It is nothing familiar to me," said Fander, unable to recognize cultured neo-bubonic plague. "In any case, I'm not a medical expert." He eyed Greypate. "But you seem to have avoided it."

"Sheer luck," opined Greypate. "Or perhaps I can't catch it. There was a story going around in the long ago that a few people are immune to it, darned if I know why. Could be that I'm one of the fireproof ones—but I don't care to count on it."

"So as much as possible you keep your distance from these children?"

"That's right." He glanced at Speedy. "I shouldn't really have come along with this kid. He's got a poor enough chance as it is without me increasing the odds."

"That is thoughtful of you," Fander put over softly. "Especially seeing that you must be lonely."

Greypate bristled and his thought-flow became aggressive. "I'm not grieving for company. I can look after myself like I have done ever since my old man went away to curl up and die. I'm on my own feet and so is everybody else."

"I believe you," said Fander. "You must pardon me. I am a stranger here. I judged you by my own feelings. Now and again I get lonely."

"How's that?" demanded Greypate, looking at him with surprise. "D'you mean they dumped you and left you on your own?"

"They did."

"Man!" exclaimed Greypate, fervently.

Man! It was a picture resembling Speedy's conception, a vision elusive in form but firm and human in face. The oldster was reacting to what he considered a predicament rather than a free choice and the reaction came on a wave of sympathy.

Fander struck promptly and hard. "You see the fix I'm in. The companionship of wild animals is nothing to me. I need someone intelligent enough to like my music and forget my looks, someone intelligent enough to—"

"I'm not so sure we're that smart," Greypate chipped in. He let his gaze swing morbidly around the landscape. "Not when I see this graveyard and think how it was said to look in my great-grandfather's days."

"Every flower blooms from the dust of former flowers," said Fander.

"What are flowers?"

It shocked the Martian. He had projected a mind-picture of a trumpet-lily, crimson and shining, and Greypate's brain had juggled it around in aimless manner, not recognizing it as fish, flesh or vegetable.

"Growths of this kind." Fander plucked a few blades of blue-green grass. "But bigger, full of color and sweet-scented." He transmitted the brilliant vision of a mile-square field of trumpet-lilies, red and glowing.

"Glory be!" said Greypate. "We've nothing like those."

"Not here," agreed Fander. "Not here." He gestured toward the horizon. "Elsewhere there may be plenty. If we got together we could be company for each other, we could learn things from each other. We could pool our efforts and our ideas and search for flowers far away—as well as for more people."

"Folk just won't get together in large bunches. They stick to each other in family groups until the plague breaks them up. Then they abandon the kids. The bigger the crowd the bigger the risk of someone contaminating the lot." He leaned on his gun, gazing steadily at the other, his thought-forms shaping themselves in dull solemnity. "When someone gets the sickness he crawls away and takes his last breath alone. His end is a personal contract between him and his God, with no witnesses. Death's a pretty private affair these days."

"What, after all these years? Don't you think that by this time the disease may have run its course and exhausted itself?"

"Nobody knows. And nobody's gambling on it."

"I would gamble."

"You can well afford to. You aren't like us. You're different. You might not be able to catch it."

"Or perhaps I might get it and die more slowly, more painfully."

"Maybe," admitted Greypate, doubtfully. "Anyway, you are looking at it from a personal angle. You've been marooned here on your ownsome. What have you got to lose?"

"My life," said Fander.

Greypate flinched as if from a light blow. "Well, yes, that's a gamble. A fellow can't bet any heavier. All right, I'll take you up on that. You come here and live with us." His grip on his gun tightened, his knuckles showing white. "On this understanding: the moment you go sick you get out fast and for keeps. If you don't, I'll knock you off and drag you away myself even if that makes me get it too. The kids come first, see?"

The shelters were far roomier than the cave. There were eighteen children living in them, all skinny with their prolonged diet of roots, edible herbs, and an occasional rabbit. The youngest and most sensitive of them ceased to be terrified of Fander after about ten days. Within four months his slithering shape of blue ropeyness had become a normal adjunct of their small, limited world.

Six of the youngsters were males older than Speedy, one of them much older but not yet adult. Fander beguiled them with his harp, teaching them to play and now and again giving them ten-minute rides on the load-sled as a special treat. He made dolls for the girls and queer, coneshaped little houses for the dolls and fan-backed chairs of woven grass for the houses. None of these toys were wholly Martian in design and none were Terrestrial. They represented a pathetic compromise within his imagination; the Martian notion of what Terrestrial models might have looked like had there been any in existence.

But surreptitiously, without seeming to give any lesser attention to the younger ones, he directed his main efforts upon the six older boys and Speedy. To his mind these were the hope of what was left of the world. At no time did he bother to ponder that the non-technical brain is not without its virtues or that there can be times and circumstances in which it is worth discarding the short view of what is remotely possible.

So as best he could he concentrated upon the older seven, educating them through the dragging months, stimulating their minds, encouraging their curiosity and continually impressing upon them the idea that fear of disease and death can become a folk-separating dogma unless they conquered it within their souls.

He taught them that death is death, a natural process to be accepted philosophically and met with dignity—and there were times when he suspected that he was teaching them nothing, he was merely reminding them, for deep in their growing minds was the ancestral strain of Terrestrialism which had mulled its way to the same conclusions ten or twenty thousand years before. Still, he was helping to remove this disease-block from the path of the stream and was driving child-logic more rapidly toward an adult outlook. In this respect he was satisfied. He could do little more. In time they organized group concerts, humming and making singing noises to the accompaniment of the harp, now and again improvising lines to suit Fander's tunes, arguing the respective merits of chosen words and phrases until by process of elimination they had a complete song. As songs grew to a repertoire and singing became more adept, more polished, Old Greypate displayed interest, came to one performance and then another until by custom he had established himself in the role of a one-man audience.

One day the oldest boy, who was named Redhead, came to Fander and grasped a tentacle-tip. "Devil, may I operate your food machine?"

"You mean you would like me to show you how to work it?"

"No, Devil, I know how to work it." The boy gazed self-assuredly into the other's great bee-eyes.

"Then how is it operated?"

"You fill its container with the tenderest blades of grass, being careful to exclude all roots. You are equally careful not to turn a switch before the container is full and its door completely closed. You then turn the red switch for a count of three hundred, reverse the container, turn the green switch for a count of sixty. You then close both switches, empty the container's warm pulp into the end molds and apply the press until the biscuits are firm and dry."

"How have you discovered all this?"

"I have watched you make biscuits for us many times. This morning, while you were busy, I tried it myself." He extended a hand. It held a biscuit. Taking it from him, Fander examined it carefully. Firm, crisp, well-shaped. He tasted it. Perfect.

Redhead became the first mechanic to operate and service a Martian lifeboat's emergency premasticator. Seven years later, long after the machine had ceased to function, he managed to repower it, weakly but effectively, with dust that gave forth alpha sparks. In another five years he had improved it, speeded it up. In twenty years he had duplicated it and had all the know-how needed to turn out premasticators on a large scale.

Fander could not have equaled this performance for as a non-technician he had no better idea than had the average Terrestrial of the principles upon which the machine worked, nor did he know what was meant by radiant digestion and protein enrichment. He could do no more than urge Redhead along and leave the rest to whatever inherent genius the boy possessed—which was plenty.

In similar manner Speedy and two youths named Blacky and Bigears took the load-sled out of his charge. On rare occasions, as a great privilege, Fander had permitted them to take up the sled for one-hour trips alone. This time they were gone from dawn to dusk. Greypate mooched restlessly around, loaded gun under one arm and a smaller one stuck in his belt, going frequently to the top of the rise and scanning the skies in all directions. The delinquents swooped in at sunset, bringing with them a strange boy.

Fander summoned them to him. They held hands so that his touch would give him simultaneous contact with all three.

"I am rather worried. The sled has only so much power. When it is used up there will be no more."

They eyed each other aghast.

"Unfortunately I have neither the knowledge nor the ability to energize the sled once its power is exhausted. I lack the technical wisdom of friends who left me here—and that is my shame." He paused, watching them dolefully, then went on, "All I do know is that its power does not leak away. If not used much the power-reserve will last for many years." Another pause. "And in a few years you will be full-grown men."

Blacky said, "But, Devil, by that time we'll be much heavier and the sled will use proportionately more energy."

"How do you know that?" Fander asked, sharply.

"More weight, more power needed to sustain it," opined Blacky with the air of one whose logic is incontrovertible. "It doesn't need thinking out. *It's obvious.*"

Slowly and softly Fander said, "You'll do."

"Do what, Devil?"

"Build a hundred sleds like this one or better—and explore the whole world."

From that time onward they confined their trips to one hour at a time, making them less frequently than of yore and doing a lot of poking and prying around the sled's insides.

Greypate changed character with the slow reluctance of the aged. Leastways, as two years and then three rolled past he gradually came out of his shell, was less taciturn, more willing to mix with those swiftly growing up to his own height. Without fully understanding what he was doing he joined forces with Fander, gave the children the remnants of Earthly wisdom passed down from his father's father's father. He taught the boys how to use the guns of which he had as many as eleven, some maintained mostly as a source of spares for others. He took them shell-hunting, digging deep beneath rotting foundations into stale, half-filled cellars in search of ammunition not too corroded for use.

"Guns are no use without shells and shells don't last forever."

Even less do buried shells. They found not one.

Of his own wisdom Greypate stubbornly withheld but a single item until the day when Speedy and Redhead and Blacky chivvied it out of him. Then like a father facing the hangman he told them the truth about babies. He made no comparative mention of bees because there were no bees, nor of flowers because there were no flowers. One cannot analogize the non-existent. Nevertheless he managed to explain the matter more or less to their satisfaction, after which he mopped his forehead and went to Fander.

"These youngsters are getting too darned nosey for my comfort. They've been asking me how children are brought along."

"Did you tell them?"

"Sure did!" He sat down, staring at the Martian, his pale gray eyes bothered. "I don't mind giving in to the boys when I can't beat 'em off any longer. But nobody's going to make me tell the girls, not ever. I draw the line at that."

Fander said, "I have been asked about this several times already. I could not tell much because I was by no means certain whether you breed precisely as we breed. But I did tell them how *we* breed."

"The girls too?"

"Of course."

"God!" Greypate mopped his forehead again. "How did they take it?"

"Just as if I'd told them why the sky is blue or why water is wet."

"Must've been something in the way you put it to them," opined Greypate.

"I told them it was poetry between persons."

Throughout the course of history, Martian, Venusian or Terrestrial, some years are more noteworthy than others. The twelfth one after Fander's marooning was outstanding for its series of events each of which was pitifully insignificant by cosmic standards but loomed enormously in this small community life.

To start with, on the basis of Redhead's improvements to the premasticator, the older seven—now bearded men—contrived to repower the exhausted load-sled and again took to the air for the first time in forty months. Experiments showed that the Martian contraption was now slower and could bear less weight but had far longer range. They used it to visit the ruins of distant cities in search of metallic junk suitable for the building of more sleds and by early summer they had constructed another one much bigger than the original, clumsy to the verge of dangerousness, but still a sled.

On several occasions they failed to find metal but did discover people, odd families living in subsurface shelters, clinging grimly to life and to passed-down scraps of knowledge. Since all these new contacts were upon a strictly human-to-human basis, with no weirdly tentacled shape to scare off the parties of the second part, and since many were finding the fear of plague more to be endured than their terrible loneliness, many families returned with the explorers, settled in the shelters, accepted Fander, added their surviving skills to the community's riches.

Thus local population swiftly grew to seventy adults and four hundred children, many of the latter being parentless. They compounded with their plague-fear by spreading through the shelters, digging through half-wrecked and formerly unused expanses and moving apart to form twenty or thirty lesser communities each one of which could be isolated from the others should death reappear.

Growing morale born of added strength and confidence in numbers soon resulted in four more sleds, still big and clumsy but a little less dangerous to handle. There also appeared the first rock house actually above ground, standing four-square and solidly under the surly skies, a defiant witness that mankind still considered itself several cuts above the rats and rabbits. The community presented the house to Blacky and Sweetvoice, who had announced their desire to associate. An elderly adult who claimed to know the conventional routine spoke solemn words over the happy couple before many witnesses, while Fander attended the groom as best Martian.

Towards summer's end Speedy returned from a solo trip of many days, bringing on his sled one old man, one boy and four girls, all of strange, outlandish countenance. They were yellow in complexion, had black hair, black, almond-shaped eyes, and spoke a language that none could understand. Until these newcomers had picked up the local speech, Fander had to act as interpreter, for his mind-pictures and theirs were independent of vocal sounds. The four girls were quiet, modest and very beautiful. Within a month Speedy had married the one whose name was a gentle clucking sound that meant Precious Jewel Ling.

After this wedding Fander sought Greypate, placed a tentacle-tip in his right hand. "There were differences between the man and the girl, distinctive features wider apart than any we know upon Mars. Are these the differences that caused your war?"

"I don't know. I've never seen one of these yellow folk before. They must live a mighty long way off." He rubbed his chin to help his thoughts along. "I only know what my old man told me and his old man told him. There were too many people of too many different kinds."

"They can't be all that different if they can fall in love."

"Maybe not," agreed Greypate.

"Supposing most of the people still in this world could assemble here, breed together and have less different children, and the children bred others still less different—wouldn't they eventually become all much the same, just Earth-people?"

"They might."

"All speaking the same language, sharing the same culture? If they then spread out slowly from this central source, remaining always in contact by load-sled, continually sharing the same knowledge, same progress, would there by any room for new differences to arise?"

"I don't know," said Greypate evasively. "I'm not as young as I used to be and I can't dream as far ahead as I used to do."

"It doesn't matter so long as the young ones can dream it." Fander mused a moment. "If you're beginning to think of yourself as a back number, you're in good company. Things are getting out of hand as far as I am concerned. The onlooker sees the most of the game and perhaps that's why I'm more sensitive than you to a certain peculiar feeling."

"To what feeling?" asked Greypate, eyeing him.

"That this planet is on the move once more. There are now many people where once there were few. A house has been built and more are to be erected. They talk of six more. After the six they will talk of sixty, then six hundred, then six thousand. Some are planning to haul up sunken conduits and use them to pipe water from the northward lake. Sleds are being built. Premasticators soon will be built and protective force-screens likewise. Children are being taught. Less and less is being heard of your much-feared plague and so far no more have died of it. I feel a dynamic surge of energy and ambition that may grow with appalling rapidity until it becomes a mighty flood. I feel that I, too, am a back number."

"Bunkum!" said Greypate. He spat on the ground. "If you dream often enough you're bound to have a bad one now and again."

"Perhaps it is because so many of my tasks have been taken over and done better than I had been doing them. I have failed to compensate by seeking new tasks. Were I a technician I'd have discovered a dozen jobs by now. Unfortunately I have no especial skills. I think this may be as good a time as any to turn to a personal task with which you can help me."

"What is that?"

"A long, long time ago I made a poem. It was for the thing of beauty that first persuaded me to stay here. I do not know exactly what its maker had in mind, nor whether my eyes see it as he wished it to be seen, but I have made a poem to express what I feel when I look upon his work."

"Humph!" said Greypate, not very interested.

"There is an outcrop of solid rock beneath its base which I can shave smooth and use as a plinth on which to inscribe my words. I would like to put them down twice: in the script of Mars and the script of Earth." Fander hesitated a moment and then went on, "I hope nobody will think this presumptuous of me. But it is many years since I wrote for all to read—and my chance may never come again."

Greypate said, "I get the idea. You want me to put down your notions in our writing so that you can copy it?"

"Yes."

"Give me your stylus and pad." Taking them, Greypate squatted on a nearby rock, lowering himself stiffly because he was feeling the weight of his years. Resting the pad on his knees, he held the writing instrument in one hand while the other continued to grasp a tentacle-tip. "All right—go ahead."

He started drawing thick, laborious marks as Fander's mind-pictures came through, enlarging the letters and keeping them well separated. When he had finished he handed over the pad.

"Asymmetrical," decided Fander, gazing at the queer angular letters and wishing for the first time that he had taken up the study of Earth-writing. "Can't you make that part balance with that and this with this?"

"It's what you said."

"It is your own translation of what I said. I would prefer more of a visual balance. Do you mind if we try again?"

They tried again. They made fourteen successive attempts before Fander was satisfied with the outward appearance of letters and words that he could not understand.

Taking the paper, he found his ray-gun, went to the base-block of the beautiful thing and sheared the whole front to a flat, even surface. Adjusting his beam to cut a V-shaped channel one inch deep, he inscribed his poem upon the rock in long, unpunctuated lines of neat Martian curlicues. With less confidence and much greater care he repeated the verse in Earth's awkward, angular hieroglyphics. The task took him quite a time and fifty people were watching when he reached the end. They said nothing. In utter silence they read the poem and looked at the beautiful thing and were still standing there brooding solemnly when he went away.

In ones and twos and little groups the rest of the community visited the site next day, coming and going with the air of pilgrims attending an ancient shrine. All stood there a long time looking, just looking, and all returned without comment. Nobody praised Fander's work, nobody damned it, nobody reproached him for alienizing something wholly Earth's. The only effect, too subtle to be noteworthy, was a greater and still growing grimness and determination that boosted the already swelling Earth dynamic.

In this respect, Fander had wrought far better than he knew.

A plague-scare came in the fourteenth year. Two sleds had brought back families from afar and within a week of their arrival the children sickened, became spotted.

Metal gongs sounded the alarm, all work ceased, the affected section of the shelters was cut off and guarded, the majority prepared to flee. It was a threatening reversal of all the things for which many had toiled so long; a destructive scattering of the tender roots of new civilization.

Fander found Greypate, Speedy and Blacky armed to the teeth, facing a drawn-faced and restless crowd.

There's most of a hundred people in that isolated section," Greypate was telling the mob. "Not all of them have got it. Maybe they won't get it. If they don't it's not so likely that you'll get it either. We ought to wait and see what happens. Let's stay put a while."

"Listen who's talking," invited a voice in the crowd. "If you weren't immune you'd have been planted fifty years ago."

"The same goes for most folk here," snapped Greypate. He glared around, his gun held in the crook of his arm, his pale eyes bellicose. "I'm a fat lot of good at speechifying so I'm just saying right out that nobody goes before we learn if this really is the plague." He brought his gun up to the ready. "Anyone fancy himself at beating a bullet?"

The heckler in the audience forced his way to the front. He was a swarthy man of muscular build and his dark eyes stared challengingly into Greypate's. "While there's life there's hope. If we get out of here we'll live to come back when it's safe to come back, if ever—and you know it. So I'm calling your bluff, see?" Squaring beefy shoulders he began to walk off.

Greypate's gun was already leveled when he felt Fander's touch upon his arm. For a few moments he stood in a fixed pose, as if listening. Then he lowered the weapon and called after the escapee.

"I'm going into that cut-off section and the Devil is going with me. We're running into things and not away from them. We'll never cope with anything by running away." Part of the audience fidgeted, murmured approval. "So we'll find out for ourselves just what's wrong. We mightn't be able to put it right but at least we'll learn what the trouble is."

The walker paused, turned, eyed him and Fander and said, "You can't do that."

"Why not?"

"You may catch it yourselves. Much use you'll be when you're dead and stinking."

"What, and me immune?" said Greypate.

"The Devil may get it," hedged the other.

"Who gives a damn about that?" invited Greypate.

It caught the other off-balance. He fumbled embarrassedly within his own mind, avoided looking at the Martian, said lamely, "I don't see any reason for anyone to take risks."

"He's taking them because he does give a damn," Greypate fired back. "I'm no creaking hero—I'm taking them because I'm too old and useless to care a hoot."

With that he stepped down and marched stubbornly toward the isolated section, Fander slithering at his side. The muscular one who wished to flee stayed put, gazing after them. The crowd shuffled uneasily, seemed in two minds whether to remain and accept the situation or to rush Greypate and Fander and drag them away. Speedy and Blacky made to follow the pair but were ordered off.

No adult sickened, nobody died. Children in the affected section went one after another through the same routine of liverishness, high temperature and spots until the epidemic of measles had died out. Not until a month after the last case had been cured by something within its own constitution did Greypate and Fander emerge.

The innocuous course and eventual disappearance of this suspected plague gave the pendulum of confidence a push, swinging it farther. Morale boosted itself almost to the verge of arrogance. More sleds came into being, more mechanics serviced them, more pilots rode them. More people flowed in and more oddments of past knowledge came with them.

Humanity now was off to a flying start with the salvaged seeds of past wisdom and the urge to do. The tormented ones of Earth were not primitive savages but surviving organisms of a greatness nine-tenths destroyed but still remembered, each contributing his mite of know-how to restore at least some of those things which had been boiled away in atomic fires.

When in the twentieth year Redhead duplicated the premasticator there were eight thousand stone houses standing around the hill. A community hall seventy times the size of a house, with a great green dome of copper, reared itself upon the eastward fringe. A dam held the lake to the north. A hospital was going up in the west. The nuances and energies and talents of fifty races had built this town and were still building it. Among them were ten Polynesians and four Icelanders and one lean, dusky child who was the last of the Seminoles.

Farms spread wide. One thousand heads of Indian corn rescued from a valley in the Andes had grown to ten thousand acres. Water buffaloes and goats had been brought from afar to serve in lieu of the horses and sheep that would never be seen again—and no man knew why one species had survived while another had died out. The horses had disappeared while the water buffaloes lived on. The canines hunted in ferocious packs while the felines had departed from existence. The small herbs, some timbers and a few seedy things could be and were reclaimed and cultivated for hungry bellies. But there were no flowers for hungry minds. Humanity carried on, making do with what was available. No more than that could be done.

Fander was a back number. He had nothing left for which to live save his songs and the affection of others. In everything but his harp and his songs the Earthlings were way ahead of him. He could do no more than give of his own affection in return for theirs and wait with the fatalistic patience of one whose work is done.

At the end of the year they buried Greypate. He died in his sleep, age unknown, passing away with the undramatic casualness of one who is not much use at speechifying.

They put him to rest on a knoll behind the community hall and Fander played his mourning song and Precious Jewel, who was Speedy's wife, planted the grave with sweet herbs.

In the spring of the following year Fander summoned Speedy and Blacky and Redhead. He was coiled on his couch, blue and shivering. They held hands so that through his touch he could speak to them simultaneously.

"I am about to undergo my *amafa*."

He had great difficulty in putting it over in understandable thought-forms, for this was something quite beyond their Earthly experience.

"It is an unavoidable change of age during which my kind must sleep undisturbed." They reacted as if the casual reference to "my kind" were a strange and startling revelation, a new aspect previously unthought-of. He continued, "I must be left alone until this hibernation has run its natural course."

"For how long, Devil?" asked Speedy with anxiety.

"It may stretch from four of your months to a full year, or—"

"Or what?" Speedy did not wait for a reassuring reply. His agile mind was swift to sense the spice of danger hidden far back in the Martian's thoughts. "Or it may never end?"

"It may never end," admitted Fander reluctantly. He shivered again, drew his tentacles around himself. The brilliance of his blueness was fading visibly. "The possibility is small but it is there."

Speedy's eyes widened as his mind strove to adjust itself to the idea that Fander might not be a fixture, established for all time. Blacky and Redhead were equally aghast.

"We Martians do not last for ever," Fander pointed out, gently. "All creatures are mortal, here and there. He who survives his *amafa* has many happy years to follow—but some do not survive. It is a trial that must be faced as everything from the beginning to the end must be faced."

"But—"

"Our numbers are not large," Fander went on. "We breed slowly and some of us die halfway through our normal span. By cosmic standards we are a weak and foolish people much in need of the support of the clever and the strong. You are clever and strong. Always remember that. Whenever my people visit you again, or any other much stranger people come, you must greet them with the confidence of the clever and the strong."

"We shall do that," assured Speedy. His gaze roamed around to take in the thousands of roofs, the copper dome, the thing of beauty on the hill. "We are strong."

A prolonged shudder went through the ropey, bee-eyed creature on the couch.

"I do not wish to be left here, an idle sleeper in the midst of life, posing like a bad example to the young. I would rather rest within the cave where first we made friends and grew to know and understand each other. Wall it up and fix a door for me. Forbid anyone to touch me or to let the light of day fall upon me until such time as I emerge of my own accord. Fander stirred sluggishly, his limbs uncoiling with noticeable lack of sinuousness. "I regret that I must ask you to carry me there. Please forgive. I have left it a little late and cannot . . . cannot . . . make it myself."

Their faces were pictures of alarm and their minds bells of sorrow. Running for poles, they made a stretcher, edged him onto it, bore him to the cave. A long, silent procession was following by the time they reached it. As they settled him comfortably and began to wall up the entrance, the crowd watched with the same grim solemnity with which it had looked upon his verse.

He was already a tightly rolled ball of dull blueness, with filmed eyes, when they fitted the door, closed and locked it, leaving him to darkness and a slumber that might be eternal. Next day a tiny, brown-skinned man, with eight children all hugging dolls, came to the door. While the youngsters looked on, he fixed upon the door a two-word name in shiny metal letters, taking great pains over his self-imposed task and making a neat job of it.

The Martian vessel came from the stratosphere with the slow, stately fall of a grounding balloon. Behind the transparent belly-band its bluish, nightmarish crew were assembled and looking with great, multi-faceted eyes at the upper surface of the clouds. The scene resembled a pink-tinged snowfield beneath which the planet remained concealed.

Captain Rdina could feel this as a tense, exciting moment even though his vessel had not the honor of being the first to make this approach. One Captain Skhiva, now long retired, had done it many, many years before. Nevertheless this second venture retained its own exploratory thrill.

Someone stationed a third of the way around the ship's midriff came writhing at top pace toward him as their drop brought them near to the pinkish clouds. The oncomer's signaling tentacle was jiggling at a seldom used rate.

"Captain, we have just seen an object swoop across the horizon."

"What sort of an object?"

"It looked like a gigantic load-sled."

"It couldn't have been."

"No, Captain, of course not—but that is exactly what it appeared to be."

"Where is it now?" demanded Rdina, gazing toward the side from which the other had come.

"It dived into the mists below."

"You must have been mistaken. Long-standing anticipation can encourage the strangest delusions." He stopped a moment as the observation-band became shrouded in the vapor of a cloud. Thoughtfully he watched the gray wall of fog slide upwards as his vessel continued its descent. "That old report says definitely that here is nothing but desolation and wild animals. There is no intelligent life except some fool of a minor poet whom Skhiva left behind. It's twelve to one that he's been dead for years. The animals, may have eaten him."

"Eaten him? Eaten *meat?"* exclaimed the other, thoroughly revolted.

"Anything is possible," assured Rdina, pleased with the extreme to which his imagination could be stretched. "Except a load-sled. That is plain silly."

At which point he had no choice but to let the subject drop for the simple and compelling reason that the ship emerged from the base of the cloud and the sled in question was floating alongside. It could be seen in complete detail and even their own instruments were responding to the powerful output of its numerous flotation-grids.

The twenty Martians aboard the sphere sat staring bee-eyed at this enormous thing which was half the size of their own vessel. And the forty humans on the, sled stared back with equal intentness. Ship and sled continued to descend side by side while both crews studied each other with dumb fascination that persisted until simultaneously they touched ground.

It was not until he felt the slight jolt of landing that Captain Rdina recovered sufficiently to look elsewhere, He saw the army of houses, the green-domed building, the thing of beauty poised upon its hill, the many hundreds of Earth-people streaming out of the town and toward his vessel.

He noted that none of these queer, two-legged life-forms betrayed the slightest sign of revulsion or fear. They came galloping to the tryst with a bumptious self-confidence such as he had never expected from anything of radically different shape or appearance.

It shook him slightly and he said to himself, "They're not scared—why should you be?"

He went out personally to meet the first of them, suppressing his own apprehensions and ignoring the fact that many of them were bearing what appeared to be weapons. The leading Earthman, a big-built, spade-bearded two-legger, grasped his tentacle-tip as to the manner born.

A picture of swiftly moving limbs. "My name is Speedy."

The ship emptied itself within minutes. No Martian would stay inside who was free to breathe his fill of fresh air. Their first visit, in a slithering bunch, was to the thing of beauty. Rdina stood quietly looking at it, his crew clustered in a half circle around him, the Earth-folk a silent audience behind.

It was a great rock statue of a female of Earth. She was broad-shouldered, full-bosomed, wide-hipped, and wore voluminous skirts that came right down to her heavy-soled shoes. Her back was a little bent, her head a little bowed and her face was hidden in her hands, deep in her toilworn hands. Rdina tried in vain to catch some glimpse of the tired, peasant features behind those concealing fingers. He looked at her a long while before his eyes lowered to read the script beneath, ignoring the Earth-lettering and running easily over the flowing Martian curlicues:

Weep, my country, for your sons asleep,
The ashes of your homes, your tottering towers.
Weep, my country, O, my country, weep!
For birds that cannot sing, for vanished flowers,
The end of everything,
The silenced hours.
Weep! my country.

There was no signature. Rdina mulled it through many minutes while the others remained passive. Then he turned to Speedy, pointed to the Martian script.

"Who wrote this?"

"One of your people. He is dead."

"Ah!" said Rdina. "That songbird of Skhiva's. I have forgotten his name. I doubt whether many remember it. He was only a very small poet. How did he die?"

"He ordered us to enclose him for some long and urgent sleep he had to have, and—"

"The *amafa,"* Rdina put in comprehendingly. "And then?"

"We did as he asked. He warned us that he might never come out." Speedy gazed at the sky, unconscious that Rdina was picking up his sorrowful thoughts. "He has been there more than two years and has not emerged." The eyes came down to Rdina. "I don't know if you understand what I mean, but he was one of us."

"I think I do understand." Rdina thought awhile and asked, "How long is this period you call more than two years?"

They managed to work it out between them, translating it from Terrestrial to Martian time-terms.

"It is long," pronounced Rdina. "Much longer than the usual *amafa.* But it is not unique. Occasionally, for no known reason, someone takes even longer. Besides, this is not Mars." He became swift, energetic as he addressed one of his crew.

"Physician Traith, we have a prolonged *amafa* case. Get your oils and essences and come with me." When the other had returned, he said to Speedy, "Take us to where he sleeps"

Reaching the door to the walled-up cave, Rdina paused to look at the two-word name fixed upon it in neat but incomprehensible letters. They read: DEAR DEVIL.

"I wonder what that means," said Physician Traith.

"Do not disturb," guessed Rdina carelessly. Opening the door, he let Traith enter first, closed it behind him to keep all the others outside.

They reappeared an hour later. The total population of the city seemed to have congregated outside the cave. Rdina was surprised that the crowd had not satisfied its curiosity with the ship and the crew. Surely there could not be much interest in the fate of one small poet. Thousands of eyes were upon them as they came into the sunlight, carefully closed and locked the cave's door.

Stretching himself in the light as if reaching toward the sun, Speedy bawled the news to the crowd. "He's alive, alive! He'll be out again within twenty days!"

At once a mild form of madness overcame the two-leggers. They made pleasure-grimaces and piercing mouth-noises and some went so far as to beat each other.

Twenty Martians felt like joining Fander that same night. The Martian constitution is peculiarly susceptible to mass emotion.

Diabologic

Astounding, March 1955

He made one circumnavigation to put the matter beyond doubt. That was standard space-scout technique; look once on the approach, look again all the way around. It often happened that second and closer impressions contradicted first and more distant ones. Some perverse factor in the probability sequence frequently caused the laugh to appear on the other side of a planetary face.

Not this time, though. What he'd observed coming in remained visible right around the belly. This world was occupied by intelligent life of a high order. The unmistakable markings were there in the form of dockyards, railroad marshaling grids, power stations, spaceports, quarries, factories, mines, housing projects, bridges, canals, and a hundred and one other signs of a life that spawns fast and vigorously.

The spaceports in particular were highly significant. He counted three of them. None held a flightworthy ship at the moment he flamed high above them, but in one was a tubeless vessel undergoing repair. A long, black, snouty thing about the size and shape of an Earth-Mars tramp. Certainly not as big and racy-looking as a Sol-Sirius liner.

As he gazed down through his tiny control-cabin's armor-glass, he knew that this was to be contact with a vengeance. During long, long centuries of human expansion, more than seven hundred inhabitable worlds had been found, charted, explored and, in some cases, exploited. All contained life. A minority held intelligent life. But up to this moment nobody had found one other lifeform sufficiently advanced to cavort among the stars.

Of course, such a discovery had been theorized. Human adventuring created an exploratory sphere that swelled into the cosmos. Sooner or later, it was assumed, that sphere must touch another one at some point within the heavenly host. What would happen then was anybody's guess. Perhaps they'd fuse, making a bigger, shinier biform bubble. Or perhaps both bubbles would burst. Anyway, by the looks of it the touching-time was now.

If he'd been within reach of a frontier listening-post, he'd have beamed a signal detailing this find. Even now it wasn't too late to drive back for seventeen weeks and get within receptive range. But that would mean seeking a refueling dump while he was at it. The ship just hadn't enough for such a double run plus the return trip home. Down there they had fuel. Maybe they'd give him some and maybe it would suit his engines. And just as possibly it would prove useless.

Right now he had adequate power reserves to land here and eventually get back to base. A bird in the hand is worth two in the bush. So he tilted the vessel and plunged into the alien atmosphere, heading for the largest spaceport of the three.

What might be awaiting him at ground level did not bother him at all. The Terrans of today were not the nervy, apprehensive Terrans of the earthbound and lurid past. They had become space-sophisticated. They had learned to lounge around with a carefree smile and let the other lifeforms do the worrying. It lent an air of authority and always worked. Nothing is more intimidating than an idiotic grin worn by a manifest non-idiot.

Quite a useful weapon in the diabological armory was the knowing smirk.

His landing created a most satisfactory sensation. The planet's point-nine Earth-mass permitted a little extra dexterity in handling the ship. He swooped it down, curved it up, dropped tail-first, stood straddle-legged on the tail-fins, cut the braking blast and would not have missed centering on a spread handkerchief by more than ten inches.

They seemed to spring out of the ground the way people do when cars collide on a deserted road. Dozens of them, hundreds. They were on the short side, the tallest not exceeding five feet. Otherwise they differed from his own pink faced, blue-eyed type no more than would a Chinese covered in fine gray fur.

Massing in a circle beyond range of his jet-rebound, they stared at the ship, gabbled, gesticulated, nudged each other, argued, and generally behaved in the manner of a curious mob that has discovered a deep, dark hole with strange noises issuing therefrom. The noteworthy feature about their behavior was that none were scared, none attempted to get out of reach, either openly or surreptitiously. The only thing about which they were wary was the chance of a sudden blast from the silent jets.

He did not emerge at once. That would have been an error—and blunderers are not chosen to pilot scout-vessels. Pre-exit rule number one is that air must be tested. What suited that crowd outside would not necessarily agree with him. Anyway, he'd have checked air even if his own mother had been smoking a cigar in the front row of the audience.

The Schrieber analyzer required four minutes in which to suck a sample through the Pitot tube, take it apart, sneer at the bits, make a bacteria count and say whether its lord and master could condescend to breathe the stuff.

He sat patiently while it made up its mind. Finally the needle on its half-red, half-white dial crawled reluctantly to mid-white. A fast shift would have pronounced the atmosphere socially acceptable. Slowness was the Schrieber's way of saying that his lungs were about to go slumming. The analyzer was and always had been a robotic snob that graded alien atmospheres on the caste system. The best and cleanest air was Brahman, pure Brahman. The worst was Untouchable.

Switching it off, he opened the inner and outer air-lock doors, sat in the rim with his feet dangling eighty yards above ground level. From this vantage-point he calmly surveyed the mob, his expression that of one who can spit but not be spat upon. The sixth diabological law states that the higher, the fewer. Proof: the sea gull's tactical advantage over man.

Being intelligent, those placed by unfortunate circumstances eighty yards deeper in the gravitational field soon appreciated their state of vertical disadvantage. Short of toppling the ship or climbing a polished surface, they were impotent to get at him. Not that any wanted to in any inimical way. But desire grows strongest when there is the least possibility of satisfaction. So they wanted him down there, face to face, merely because he was out of reach.

To make matters worse, he turned sidewise and lay within the rim, one leg hitched up and hands linked around the knee, then continued looking at them in obvious comfort. They had to stand. And they had to stare upward at the cost of a crick in the neck. Alternatively, they could adjust their heads and eyes to a crickless level and endure being looked at while not looking. Altogether, it was a hell of a situation.

The longer it lasted the less pleasing it became. Some of them shouted at him in squeaky voices. Upon those he bestowed a benign smile. Others gesticulated. He gestured back and the sharpest among them weren't happy about it. For some strange reason that no scientist had ever bothered to investigate, certain digital motions stimulate especial glands in any part of the cosmos. Basic diabological training included a course in what was known as signal-deflation, whereby the yolk could be removed from an alien ego with one wave of the hand.

For a while the crowd surged restlessly around, nibbling the gray fur on the backs of their fingers, muttering to each other, and occasionally throwing sour looks upward. They still kept clear of the danger zone, apparently assuming that the specimen reclining in the lock-rim might have a companion at the controls. Next, they became moody, content to do no more than scowl futilely at the tail-fins.

That state of affairs lasted until a convoy of heavy vehicles arrived and unloaded troops. The newcomers bore riot sticks and handguns, and wore uniforms the color of the stuff hogs roll in. Forming themselves into three ranks, they turned right at a barked command, marched forward. The crowd opened to make way.

Expertly, they stationed themselves in an armed circle separating the ship from the horde of onlookers. A trio of officers paraded around and examined the tail-fins without going nearer than was necessary. Then they backed off, stared up at the air-lock rim. The subject of their attention gazed back with academic interest.

The senior of the three officers patted his chest where his heart was located, bent and patted the ground, forced pacific innocence into his face as again he stared at the arrival high above. The tilt of his head made his hat fall off, and in turning to pick it up he trod on it.

This petty incident seemed to gratify the one eighty yards higher because he chuckled, let go the leg he was nursing, leaned out for a better look at the victim. Red-faced under his furry complexion, the officer once more performed the belly and ground massage. The other understood this time. He gave a nod of gracious assent, disappeared into the lock. A few seconds later a nylon ladder snaked down the ship's side and the invader descended with monkey-like agility.

Three things struck the troops and the audience immediately he stood before them, namely, the nakedness of his face and hands, his greater size and weight, and the fact that he carried no visible weapons. Strangeness of shape and form was to be expected. After all, they had done some space-roaming themselves and knew of lifeforms more outlandish. But what sort of creature has the brains to build a ship and not the sense to carry means of defense?

They were essentially a logical people.

The poor saps.

The officers made no attempt to converse with this specimen from the great unknown. They were not telepathic, and space-experience had taught them that mere mouth-noises are useless until one side or the other has learned the meanings thereof. So by signs they conveyed to him their wish to take him to town where he would meet others of their kind more competent to establish contact. They were pretty good at explaining with their hands, as was natural for the only other lifeform that had found new worlds.

He agreed to this with the same air of a lord consorting with the lower orders that had been apparent from the start. Perhaps he had been unduly influenced by the Schrieber. Again the crowd made way while the guard conducted him to the trucks. He passed through under a thousand eyes, favored them with deflatory gesture number seventeen, this being a nod that acknowledged their existence and tolerated their vulgar interest in him.

The trucks trundled away leaving the ship with air-lock open, ladder dangling and the rest of the troops still standing guard around the fins. Nobody failed to notice that touch, either. He hadn't bothered to prevent access to the vessel. There was nothing to prevent experts looking through it and stealing ideas from another space-going race.

Nobody of that caliber could be so criminally careless. Therefore, it would not be carelessness. Pure logic said the ship's designs were not worth protecting from the stranger's viewpoint because they were long out of date. Or else they were unstealable because they were beyond the comprehension of a lesser people. Who the heck did he think they were? By the Black World of Khas, they'd show him!

A junior officer climbed the ladder, explored the ship's interior, came down, reported no more aliens within, not even a pet *lansim,* not a pretzel. The stranger had come alone. This item of information circulated through the crowd. They didn't care for it too much. A visit by a fleet of battleships bearing ten thousand they could understand. It would be a show of force worthy of their stature. But the casual arrival of one, and only one, smacked somewhat of the dumping of a missionary among the heathens of the twin worlds of Morantia.

Meanwhile, the trucks rolled clear of the spaceport, speeded up through twenty miles of country, entered a city. Here, the leading vehicle parted company from the rest, made for the western suburbs, arrived at a fortress surrounded by huge walls. The stranger dismounted and promptly got tossed into the clink.

The result of that was odd, too. He should have resented incarceration, seeing that nobody had yet explained the purpose of it. But he didn't. Treating the well-clothed bed in his cell as if it were a luxury provided as recognition of his rights, he sprawled on it full length, boots and all, gave a sigh of deep satisfaction and went to sleep. His watch hung close by his ear and compensated for the constant ticking of the auto-pilot, without which slumber in space was never complete.

During the next few hours guards came frequently to look at him and make sure that he wasn't finagling the locks or disintegrating the bars by means of some alien technique. They had not searched him and accordingly were cautious. But he snored on, dead to the world, oblivious to the ripples of alarm spread through a spatial empire.

He was still asleep when Parmith arrived bearing a load of picture books. Parmith, elderly and myopic, sat by the bedside and waited until his own eyes became heavy in sympathy and he found himself considering the comfort of the carpet. At that point he decided he must either get to work or lie flat. He prodded the other into wakefulness.

They started on the books. *Ah* is for *ahmud* that plays in the grass. *Ay* is for *aysid* that's kept under glass. *Oom* is for *oom-tuck* that's found in the moon. *Uhm* is for *uhmlak,* a clown or buffoon. And so on.

Stopping only for meals, they were at it the full day and progress was fast. Parmith was a first-class tutor, the other an excellent pupil able to learn with remarkable speed. At the end of the first long session they were able to indulge in a brief and simple conversation.

"I am called Parmith. What are you called?"

"Wayne Hillder."

"Two callings?"

"Yes."

"What are many of you called?"

"Terrans."

"We are called Vards."

Talk ceased for lack of enough words and Parmith left. Within nine hours he was back accompanied by Gerka, a younger specimen who specialized in reciting words and phrases again and again until the listener could echo them to perfection. They carried on for another four days, working into late evening.

"You are not a prisoner."

"I know," said Wayne Hillder, blandly self-assured.

Parmith looked uncertain. "How do you know?"

"You would not dare to make me one."

"Why not?"

"You do not know enough. Therefore you seek common speech. You must learn from me—and quickly."

This being too obvious to contradict, Parmith let it go by and said, "I estimated it would take about ninety days to make you fluent. It looks as if twenty will be sufficient."

"I wouldn't be here if my kind weren't smart," Hillder pointed out.

Gerka registered uneasiness; Parmith was disconcerted.

"No Vard is being taught by us," he added for good measure. "Not having got to us yet."

Parmith said hurriedly, "We must get on with this task. An important commission is waiting to interview you as soon as you can converse with ease and clarity. We'll try again this *fth*-prefix that you haven't got quite right. Here's a tongue-twister to practice on. Listen to Gerka."

Fthon deas fthleman fthangafth," recited Gerka, punishing his bottom lip.

"Futhong deas—"

"Fthon," corrected Gerka. *"Fthon deas fthleman fthangafth."*

"It's better in a civilized tongue. Wet evenings are gnatless *futhong—"*

"Fthon!" insisted Gerka, playing catapults with his mouth.

The commission sat in an ornate hall containing semicircular rows of seats rising in ten tiers. There were four hundred present. The way in which attendants and minor officials fawned around them showed that this was an assembly of great importance.

It was, too. The four hundred represented the political and military power of a world that had created a space-empire extending through a score of solar systems and controlling twice as many planets. Up to a short time ago they had been, to the best of their knowledge and belief, the lords of creation. Now there was some doubt about it. They had a serious problem to settle, one that a later Terran historian irreverently described as 'a moot point.'

They ceased talking among themselves when a pair of guards arrived in charge of Hillder, led him to a seat facing the tiers. Four hundred pairs of eyes examined the stranger, some curiously, some doubtfully, some challengingly, many with unconcealed antagonism.

Sitting down, Hillder looked them over much as one looks into one of the more odorous cages at the zoo. That is to say, with faint distaste. Gently, he rubbed the side of his nose with a forefinger and sniffed. Deflatory gesture number twenty-two, suitable for use in the presence of massed authority. It brought its carefully calculated reward. Half a dozen of the most bellicose characters glared at him.

A frowning, furry-faced oldster stood up, spoke to Hillder as if reciting a well-rehearsed speech. "None but a highly intelligent and completely logical species can conquer space. It being self-evident that you are of such a kind, you will appreciate our position. Your very presence compels us to consider the ultimate alternatives of cooperation or competition, peace or war."

"There are no two alternatives to anything," Hillder asserted. "There is black and white and a thousand intermediate shades. There is yes and no and a thousand ifs, buts or maybes. For example: you could move farther out of reach."

Being tidy-minded, they didn't enjoy watching the thread of their logic being tangled. Neither did they like the resultant knot in the shape of the final suggestion. The oldster's frown grew deeper, his voice sharper.

'You should also appreciate your own position. You are one among countless millions. Regardless of whatever may be the strength of your kind, you, personally, are helpless. Therefore, it is for us to question and for you to answer. If our respective positions were reversed, the contrary would be true. That is logical. Are you ready to answer our questions?"

"I am ready."

Some showed surprise at that. Others looked resigned, taking it for granted that he would give all the information he saw fit and suppress the rest.

Resuming his seat, the oldster signaled to the Vard on his left, who stood up and asked, "Where is your base-world?"

"At the moment I don't know."

"You don't know?" His expression showed that he had expected awkwardness from the start. "How can you return to it if you don't know where it is?"

"When within its radio-sweep I pick up its beacon. I follow that."

"Aren't your space-charts sufficient to enable you to find it?"

"No."

"Why not?"

"Because," said Hillder," it isn't tied to a primary. It wanders around."

Registering incredulity, the other said, "Do you mean that it is a planet broken loose from a solar system?"

"Not at all. It's a scout-base. Surely you know what that is?"

"I do not," snapped the interrogator. "What is it?"

"A tiny, compact world equipped with all the necessary contraptions. An artificial sphere that functions as a frontier outpost."

There was a deal of fidgeting and murmuring among the audience as individuals tried to weigh the implications of this news.

Hiding his thoughts, the questioner continued, "You define it as a frontier outpost. That does not tell us where your home-world is located."

"You did not ask about my home-world. You asked about my base-world. I heard you with my own two ears."

"Then where is your home-world?"

"I cannot show you without a chart. Do you have charts of unknown regions?"

"Yes." The other smiled like a satisfied cat. With a dramatic flourish he produced them, unrolled them. "We obtained them from your ship."

"That was thoughtful of you," said Hillder, disappointingly pleased. Leaving his seat he placed a fingertip on the topmost chart and said, "There! Good old Earth!" Then he returned and sat down.

The Vard stared at the designated point, glanced around at his fellows as if about to make some remark, changed his mind and said nothing. Producing a pen he marked the chart, rolled it up with the others.

"This world you call Earth is the origin and center of your empire?"

"Yes."

"The mother-planet of your species?"

"Yes."

"Now," he went on, firmly, "how many of your kind are there?"

"Nobody knows."

"Don't you check your own numbers?"

"We did once upon a time. These days we're too scattered around." Hillder pondered a moment, added helpfully, "I can tell you that there are four billions of us spread over three planets in our own solar system. Outside of those the number is a guess. We can be divided into the rooted and the rootless and the latter can't be counted. They won't let themselves be counted because somebody might want to tax them. Take the grand total as four billions plus."

"That tells us nothing," the other objected. "We don't know the size of the plus."

"Neither do we," said Hillder, visibly awed at the thought of it. "Sometimes it frightens us." He surveyed the audience. "If nobody's ever been scared by a plus, now's the time."

Scowling, the questioner tried to get at it another way. "You say you are scattered. Over how many worlds?"

"Seven hundred fourteen at last report. That's already out of date. Every report is eight to ten planets behind the times."

"And you have mastery of that huge number?"

"Whoever mastered a planet? Why, we haven't yet dug into the heart of our own, and I doubt that we ever shall." He shrugged, finished, "No, we just amble around and maul them a bit. Same as you do."

"You mean you exploit them?"

"Put it that way if it makes you happy."

"Have you encountered no opposition at any time?"

"Feeble, friend, feeble," said Hillder.

"What did you do about it?"

"That depended upon circumstances. Some folk we ignored, some we smacked, some we led toward the light."

"What light?" asked the other, baffled.

"That of seeing things our way."

It was too much for a paunchy specimen in the third row. Coming to his feet he spoke in acidulated tones. "Do you expect *us* to see things your way?"

"Not immediately," Hillder said.

"Perhaps you consider us incapable of—"

The oldster who had first spoken now arose and interjected, "We must proceed with this inquisition logically or not at all. That means one line of questioning at a time and one questioner at a time." He gestured authoritatively toward the Vard with the charts. "Carry on, Thormin,"

Thormin carried on for two solid hours. Apparently he was an astronomical expert, because all his questions bore more or less on that subject. He wanted details of distances, velocities, solar classifications, planetary conditions, and a host of similar items. Willingly, Hillder answered all that he could, pleaded ignorance with regard to the rest.

Eventually Thormin sat down and concentrated on his notes in the manner of one absorbed in fundamental truth. He was succeeded by a hard-eyed individual named Grasud, who for the last half-hour had been fidgeting with impatience.

"Is your vessel the most recent example of its type?"

"No."

"There are better models?"

"Yes," agreed Hillder.

"Very much better?"

"I wouldn't know, not having been assigned one yet."

"Strange, is it not," said Grasud pointedly, "that an old-type ship should discover us while superior ones have failed to do so?"

"Not at all. It was sheer luck. I happened to head this way. Other scouts, in old or new ships, boosted other ways. How many directions are there in deep space? How many radii can be extended from a sphere?"

"Not being a mathematician I—"

"If you *were* a mathematician," Hillder interrupted, "you would know that the number works out at 2n." He glanced over the audience, added in tutorial manner, "The factor of two being determined by the demonstrable fact that a radius is half a diameter and 2n being defined as the smallest number that makes one boggle."

Grasud boggled as he tried to conceive it, gave it up, said, "Therefore, the total number of your exploring vessels is of equal magnitude?"

"No. We don't have to probe in every direction. It is necessary only to make for visible stars."

"Well, aren't there stars in every direction?"

"If distance is disregarded, yes. But one does not disregard distance. One makes for the nearest yet-unexplored solar systems and thus cuts down repeated jaunts to a reasonable number."

"You are evading the issue," said Grasud. "How many ships of your type are in actual operation?"

"Twenty."

"Twenty?" He made it sound anticlimactic. "Is that all?"

"It's enough, isn't it. How long do you expect us to keep antiquated models in service?"

"I am not asking about out-of-date vessels. How many scout-ships of all types are functioning?"

"I don't really know. I doubt whether anyone knows. In addition to Earth's fleets, some of the most advanced colonies are running expeditions of their own. What's more, a couple of allied lifeforms have learned things from us, caught the fever and started poking around. We can no more take a complete census of ships than we can of people."

Accepting that without argument, Grasud went on, "Your vessel is not large by our standards. Doubtless you have others of greater mass." He leaned forward, gazed fixedly. "What is the comparative size of your biggest ship?"

"The largest I've seen was the battleship *Lance.* Forty times the mass of my boat."

"How many people does it carry?"

"It has a crew numbering more than six hundred but in a pinch it can transport three times that."

"So you know of at least one ship with an emergency capacity of about two thousands?"

"Yes."

More murmurings and fidgetings among the audience. Disregarding them, Grasud carried on with the air of one determined to learn the worst.

"You have other battleships of equal size?"

"Yes."

"How many?"

"I don't know. If I did, I'd tell you. Sorry."

"You may have some even bigger?"

"That is quite possible," Hillder conceded. "If so, I haven't seen one yet. But that means nothing. One can go through a lifetime and not see everything. If you calculate the number of seeable things in existence, deduct the number already viewed, the remainder represents the number yet to be seen. And if you study them at the rate of one per second it would require—"

"I am not interested," snapped Grasud, refusing to be bollixed by alien argument.

"You should be," said Hillder. "Because infinity minus umpteen millions leaves infinity. Which means that you can take the part from the whole and leave the whole still intact. You can eat your cake and have it. Can't you?"

Grasud flopped into his seat, spoke moodily to the oldster. "I seek information, not a blatant denial of logic. His talk confuses me. Let Shahding have him."

Coming up warily, Shahding started on the subject of weapons, their design, mode of operation, range and effectiveness. He stuck with determination to this single line of inquiry and avoided all temptations to be side-tracked. His questions were astute and penetrating. Hillder answered all he could, freely, without hesitation.

"So," commented Shahding, toward the finish, "it seems that you put your trust in force-fields, certain rays that paralyze the nervous system, bacteriological techniques, demonstrations of number and strength, and a good deal of persuasiveness. Your science of ballistics cannot be advanced after so much neglect."

"It could never advance," said Hillder. "That's why we abandoned it. We dropped fiddling around with bows and arrows for the same reason. No initial thrust can outpace a continuous and prolonged one. Thus far and no farther shalt thou go." Then he added by way of speculative afterthought, "Anyway, it can be shown that no bullet can overtake a running man."

"Nonsense!" exclaimed Shahding, having once ducked a couple of slugs himself.

"By the time the bullet has reached the man's point of departure, the man has retreated," said Hillder. "The bullet then has to cover that extra distance but finds the man has retreated farther. It covers that, too, only to find that again the man is not there. And so on and so on."

"The lead is reduced each successive time until it ceases to exist," Shahding scoffed.

"Each successive advance occupies a finite length of time, no matter how small," Hillder pointed out. "You cannot divide and subdivide a fraction to produce zero. The series is infinite. An infinite series of finite time-periods totals an infinite time. Work it out for yourself. The bullet does not hit the man because it cannot get to him."

The reaction showed that the audience had never encountered this argument before or concocted anything like it of their own accord. None were stupid enough to accept it as serious assertion of fact. All were sufficiently intelligent to recognize it as logical or pseudo-logical denial of something self-evident and demonstrably true.

Forthwith they started hunting for the flaw in this alien reasoning, discussing it between themselves so noisily that Shahding stood in silence waiting for a break. He posed like a dummy for ten minutes while the clamor rose to a crescendo. A group in the front semicircle left their seats, knelt and commenced drawing diagrams on the floor while arguing vociferously and with some heat. A couple of Vards in the back tier showed signs of coming to blows.

Finally the oldster, Shahding and two others bellowed a united, "Quiet!"

The investigatory commission settled down with reluctance, still muttering, gesturing, showing each other sketches on pieces of paper. Shahding fixed ireful attention on Hillder, opened his mouth in readiness to resume.

Beating him to it, Hillder said casually, "It sounds silly, doesn't it? But anything is possible, anything at all. A man can marry his widow's sister."

"Impossible," declared Shahding, able to dispose of that without abstruse calculations. "He must be dead for her to have the status of a widow."

"A man married a woman who died. He then married her sister. He died. Wasn't his first wife his widow's sister?"

Shahding shouted, "I am not here to be tricked by the tortuous squirmings of an alien mind." He sat down hard, fumed a bit, said to his neighbor, "All right, Kadina, you can have him and welcome."

Confident and self-assured, Kadina stood up, gazed authoritatively around. He was tall for a Vard, and wore a well-cut uniform with crimson epaulettes and crimson-banded sleeves. For the first time in a while there was silence. Satisfied with the effect he had produced, he faced Hillder, spoke in tones deeper, less squeaky than any heard so far.

"Apart from the petty problems with which it has amused you to baffle my compatriots," he began in an oily manner, you have given candid, unhesitating answers to our questions. You have provided much information that is useful from the military viewpoint."

"I am glad you appreciate it," said Hillder.

"We do. Very much so," Kadina bestowed a craggy smile that looked sinister. "However, there is one matter that needs clarifying."

"What is that?"

"If the present situation were reversed, if a lone Vard-scout was subject to intensive cross-examination by an assembly of your lifeform, and if he surrendered information as willingly as you have done . . . " He let it die out while his eyes hardened, then growled, "We would consider him a traitor to his kind! The penalty would be death."

"How fortunate I am not to be a Vard," said Hillder.

"Do not congratulate yourself too early," Kadina retorted. "A death sentence is meaningless only to those already under such a sentence."

"What are you getting at?"

"I am wondering whether you are a major criminal seeking sanctuary among us. There may be some other reason. Whatever it is, you do not hesitate to betray your own kind." He put on the same smile again. "It would be nice to know why you have been so cooperative."

"That's an easy one," Hillder said, smiling back in a way that Kadina did not like. "I am a consistent liar."

With that, he left his seat and walked boldly to the exit. The guards led him to his cell.

He was there three days, eating regular meals and enjoying them with irritating gusto, amusing himself writing figures in a little notebook, as happy as a legendary space-scout named Larry. At the end of that time a ruminative Vard paid a visit.

"I am Bulak. Perhaps you remember me. I was seated at the end of the second row when you were before the commission."

"Four hundred were there," Hillder reminded. "I cannot recall all of them. Only the ones who suffered." He pushed forward a chair. "But never mind. Sit down and put your feet up—if you do have feet inside those funny-looking boots. What can I do for you?"

"I don't know."

"You must have come for some reason, surely?"

Bulak looked mournful. "I'm a refugee from the fog."

"What fog?"

"The one you've spread all over the place." He rubbed a fur-coated ear, examined his fingers, stared at the wall. "The commission's main purpose was to determine relative standards of intelligence, to settle the prime question of whether your kind's cleverness is less than, greater than, or equal to our own. Upon that and that alone depends our reaction to contact with another space-conqueror."

"I did my best to help, didn't I?"

"Help?" echoed Bulak as if it were a new and strange word. "Help? Do you call it that? The true test should be that of whether your logic has been extended farther than has ours, whether your premises have been developed to more advanced conclusions."

"Well?"

"You ended up by trampling all over the laws of logic. A bullet cannot kill anybody. After three days fifty of them are still arguing about it, and this morning one of them proved that a person cannot climb a ladder. Friends have fallen out, relatives are starting to hate the sight of each other. The remaining three hundred fifty are in little better state."

"What's troubling them?" inquired Hillder with interest.

"They are debating veracity with everything but brickbats," Bulak informed, somewhat as if compelled to mention an obscene subject. "You are a consistent liar. Therefore the statement itself must be a lie. Therefore you are not a consistent liar. The conclusion is that you can be a consistent liar only by not being a consistent liar. Yet you cannot be a consistent liar without being consistent."

"That's bad," Hillder sympathized.

"It's worse," Bulak gave back. "Because if you really are a consistent liar—which logically is a self-contradiction—none of your evidence is worth a sack of rotten muna-seeds. If you have told us the truth all the way through, then your final claim to be a liar must also be true. But if you are a consistent liar then none of it is true."

"Take a deep breath," advised Hillder.

"But," continued Bulak, taking a deep breath, "since that final statement must be untrue, all the rest may be true." A wild look came into his eyes and he started waving his arms around. "But the claim to consistency makes it impossible for any statement to be assessed as either true or untrue because, on analysis, there is an unresolvable contradiction that—"

"Now, now," said Hillder, patting his shoulder. "It is only natural that the lower should be confused by the higher. The trouble is that you've not yet advanced for enough. Your thinking remains a little primitive." He hesitated, added with the air of making a daring guess, "In fact it wouldn't surprise me if you still think *logically.*"

"In the name of the Big Sun," exclaimed Bulak, "how *else* can we think?"

"Like us," said Hillder. "But only when you're mentally developed." He strolled twice around the cell, said by way of musing afterthought, "Right now you couldn't cope with the problem of why a mouse when it spins."

"Why a mouse when it spins?" parroted Bulak, letting his jaw hang down.

"Or let's try an easier one, a problem any Earth-child could tackle."

"Such as what?"

"By definition an island is a body of land entirely surrounded by water?"

"Yes, that is correct."

"Then let us suppose that the whole of this planet's northern hemisphere is land and all the southern hemisphere is water. Is the northern half an island? Or is the southern half a lake?"

Bulak gave it five minutes' thought. Then he drew a circle on a sheet of paper, divided it, shaded the top half and contemplated the result. In the end he pocketed the paper and got to his feet.

"Some of them would gladly cut your throat but for the possibility that your kind may have a shrewd idea where you are and be capable of retribution. Others would send you home with honors but for the risk of bowing to inferiors."

"They'll have to make up their minds someday," Hillder commented, refusing to show concern about which way it went.

"Meanwhile," Bulak continued morbidly, "we've had a look over your ship, which may be old or new according to whether or not you have lied about it. We can see everything but the engines and remote controls, everything but the things that matter. To determine whether they're superior to ours we'd have to pull the vessel apart, ruining it and making you a prisoner."

"Well, what's stopping you?"

"The fact that you may be bait. If your kind has great power and is looking for trouble, they'll need a pretext. Our victimization of you would provide it. The spark that fires the powder-barrel." He made a gesture of futility. "What can one do when working utterly in the dark?"

"One could try settling the question of whether a green leaf remains a green leaf in complete absence of light."

"I have had enough," declared Bulak, making for the door. "I have had more than enough. An island or a lake? Who cares? I am going to see Mordafa."

With that he departed, working his fingers around while the fur quivered on his face. A couple of guards peered through the bars in the uneasy manner of those assigned to keep watch upon a dangerous maniac.

Mordafa turned up next day in the mid-afternoon. He was a thin, elderly, and somewhat wizened specimen with incongruously youthful eyes: Accepting a seat, he studied Hillder, spoke with smooth deliberation.

"From what I have heard, from all that I have been told, I deduce a basic rule applying to lifeforms deemed intelligent."

"You deduce it?"

"I have to. There is no choice about the matter. All the lifeforms we have discovered so far have not been truly intelligent. Some have been superficially so, but not genuinely so. It is obvious that you have had experiences that may come to us sooner or later but have not arrived yet. In that respect we may have been fortunate seeing that the results of such contact are highly speculative. There's just no way of telling."

"And what is this rule?"

"That the governing body of any lifeform such as ours will be composed of power-lovers rather than of specialists."

"Well, isn't it?"

"Unfortunately, it is. Government falls into the hands of those who desire authority and escapes those with other interests." He paused, went on, "That is not to say that those who govern us are stupid. They are quite clever in their own particular field of mass-organization. But by the same token they are pathetically ignorant of other fields. Knowing this, your tactic is to take advantage of their ignorance. The weakness of authority is that it cannot be diminished and retain strength. To play upon ignorance is to dull the voice of command."

"Hm!" Hillder surveyed him with mounting respect. "You're the first one I've encountered who can see beyond the end of his nose."

"Thank you," said Mordafa. "Now the very fact that you have taken the risk of landing here alone, and followed it up by confusing our leaders, proves that your kind has developed a technique for a given set of conditions and, in all probability, a series of techniques for various conditions."

"Go on," urged Hillder.

"Such techniques must be created empirically rather than theoretically," Mordafa continued. "In other words, they result from many experiences, the correcting of many errors, the search for workability, the effort to gain maximum results from minimum output." He glanced at the other. "Am I correct so far?"

"You're doing fine."

"To date we have established foothold on forty-two planets without ever having to combat other than primitive life. We may find foes worthy of our strength on the forty-third world, whenever that is discovered. Who knows? Let us assume for the sake of argument that intelligent life exists on one in every forty-three inhabitable planets."

"Where does that get us?" Hillder prompted.

"I would imagine," said Mordafa thoughtfully, "that the experience of making contact with at least six intelligent lifeforms would be necessary to enable you to evolve techniques for dealing with their like elsewhere. Therefore your kind must have discovered and explored not less than two hundred fifty worlds. That is an estimate in minimum terms. The correct figure may well be that stated by you."

"And I am not a consistent liar?" asked Hillder, grinning.

"That is beside the point, if only our leaders would hold on to their sanity long enough to see it. You may have distorted or exaggerated for purposes of your own. If so, there is nothing we can do about it. The prime fact holds fast, namely, that your space-venturings must be far more extensive than ours. Hence you must be older, more advanced, and numerically stronger."

"That's logical enough," conceded Hillder, broadening his grin.

"Now don't start on me," pleaded Mordafa. "If you fool me with an intriguing fallacy I won't rest until I get it straight. And that will do neither of us any good."

"Ah, so your intention is to do me good?"

"Somebody has to make a decision, seeing that the top brass is no longer capable of it. I am going to suggest that they set you free with our best wishes and assurances of friendship."

"Think they'll take any notice?"

"You know quite well they will. You've been counting on it all along." Mordafa eyed him shrewdly. "They'll grab at the advice to restore their self-esteem. If it works, they'll take the credit. If it doesn't, I'll get the blame." He brooded a few seconds, asked with open curiosity, "Do you find it the same elsewhere, among other peoples?"

"Exactly the same," Hillder assured him. "And there is always a Mordafa to settle the issue in the same way. Power and scapegoats go together like husband and wife."

"I'd like to meet my alien counterparts someday." Getting up, he moved to the door. "If I had not come along, how long would you have waited for your psychological mixture to congeal?"

"Until another of your type chipped in. If one doesn't arrive of his own accord, the powers-that-be lose patience and drag one in. The catalyst mined from its own kind. Authority lives by eating its vitals."

"That is putting it paradoxically," Mordafa observed, making it sound like a mild reproof. He went away.

Hillder stood behind the door and gazed through the bars in its top half. The pair of guards leaned against the opposite wall and stared back.

With amiable pleasantness, he said to them, "No cat has eight tails. Every cat has one tail more than no cat. Therefore every cat has nine tails."

They screwed up their eyes and scowled.

Quite an impressive deputation took him back to the ship. All the four hundred were there, about a quarter of them resplendent in uniforms, the rest in their Sunday best. An armed guard juggled guns at barked command. Kadina made an unctuous speech full of brotherly love and the glorious shape of things to come. Somebody presented a bouquet of evil-smelling weeds and Hillder made mental note of the difference in olfactory senses.

Climbing eighty yards to the lock, Hillder looked down. Kadina waved an officious farewell. The crowd chanted, "Hurrah!" in conducted rhythm. He blew his nose on a handkerchief, that being deflatory gesture number nine, closed the lock, sat at the control board.

The tubes fired into a low roar. A cloud of vapor climbed around and sprinkled ground-dirt over the mob. That touch was involuntary and not recorded in the book. A pity, he thought. Everything ought to be listed. We should be systematic about such things. The showering of dirt should be duly noted under the heading of the spaceman's farewell.

The ship snorted into the sky, left the Vard-world far behind. Hillder remained at the controls until free of the entire system's gravitational field. Then he headed for the beacon-area and locked the auto-pilot on that course.

For a while he sat gazing meditatively into star-spangled darkness. After a while he sighed, made notes in his logbook.

Cube K49, Sector 10, solar-grade D7, third planet. Name: Vard. Lifeform named Vards, cosmic intelligence rating BB, space-going, forty-two colonies. Comment: softened up.

He glanced over his tiny library fastened to a steel bulkhead. Two tomes were missing. They had swiped the two that were replete with diagrams and illustrations. They had left the rest, having no Rosetta Stone with which to translate cold print. They hadn't touched the nearest volume titled: *Diabologic, the Science of Driving People Nuts.*

Sighing again, he took paper from a drawer, commenced his hundredth, two hundredth or maybe three-hundredth try at concocting an Aleph number higher than aleph-one but lower than C. He mauled his hair until it stuck out in spikes, and although he didn't know it, he did not look especially well-balanced himself.

Fast Falls the Eventide

Astounding, May 1952

It was an old world, incredibly old, with a pitted moon and a dying sun and a sky too thin to hold a summer cloud. There were trees upon it but not the trees of yore, for these were the result of aeons of gradual accommodation. They inhaled and exhaled far less than did their distant forebears and they sucked more persistently at the aged soil.

So did the herbs.

And the flowers.

But the petal-lacking, rootless children of this sphere, the ones able to move around of their own volition, these could not compensate by sitting in one place and drawing from the ground. So slowly, ever so slowly they had dispensed with what once had been a basic need. They could manage quite well on the bare minimum of oxygen. Or at a pinch without any at all, experiencing no more than mild discomfort, a certain lassitude. All could do this without exception.

The children of this world were bugs.

And birds.

And bipeds.

Moth, magpie and man, all were related. All had the same mother: an ancient sphere rolling around a weakly glowing orange ball that some day would flicker and go out. Their preparation for this end had been long and arduous, partly involuntary, partly deliberate. This was their time: the age of fulfillment, shared between all, belonging to all.

Thus it was in no way odd that Melisande should talk to a small beetle. It sat attentively on the back of her pale, long-fingered hand, a tiny creature, black with crimson spots, clean and shiny as if subjected to hours of patient polishing. A ladybird. An amusingly toylike entity that seemed to lack a miniature handle in its side with which to wind it up.

Of course the ladybird could not understand a word of what was being said. It was not *that* intelligent. Time had run so far and the atmosphere become so thin that the insect's wings had adapted accordingly and now were twice the size of those owned by ladybirds of long ago. And with the physical alteration there had been mental alteration; its pin-sized brain was different too. By the standard of its own humble kind it had climbed several rungs up the ladder of life. Though it could not determine meanings, it knew when it was being addressed, sought human company, derived comfort from the sound of human voice.

And so with the others.

The birds.

The latter-day bees.

All the timid things that once had run for a hiding place or sought shelter in the dark.

Those who had survived—and many species had not—were shy no more. Regardless of whether or not they could understand the mouth-noises made, they liked to be spoken to, their existence acknowledged. They could and did listen for hours, extracting strange pleasure from the intimacy of sound. Or was the pleasure strange?

Perhaps not, for there were times when the sonic relationship was reversed and men stood fascinated while, in lilting language peculiarly its own, a blackbird or nightingale poured forth its very soul.

It was the same indefinable ecstasy.

You see?

So Melisande talked as she walked and Little Redspots listened with his own insectual pleasure until finally she gently flipped her hand and laughed, "Ladybird, ladybird, fly away home."

It raised colorful wing-cases, spread gauzy wings and fluttered from sight. Melisande paused to look at the stars. In these times they could be seen with brilliance and clarity by day as well as by night, a phenomenon that would have made her air-loving ancestors become filled with fear lest the breath of life soon depart.

No such sensation was within her as she studied the stars. There was only curiosity and speculation coming from a purely personal source. To her, the five-mileshigh atmosphere, the dim sun, the sparkling stars were all normal. Often she looked at the stars, sorting them out, identifying them, asking herself the same question again and again.

"Which one?"

And the heavens answered only, "Ah, which?"

Ceasing her speculation she tripped lightly onward along the narrow woodland path that led into the valley. Far to her left, on the verge of the horizon, something long, slender and metallic arrowed down from the sky and vanished beyond the curve of the earth. A little later a much muted thundering came to her ears.

Neither the sight nor the sound captured her attention. They were too ordinary. The ships of space came often to this ancient world, sometimes once in a month, sometimes twice in a day. Rarely were any two alike. Rarely did the people of one vessel resemble the crew of another.

They had no common language, these visitors from the glittering dark. They spoke a multitude of tongues. Some could talk only mentally, in powerfully projected thought-forms. Some were nonvocal and nontelepathic, could not speak at all, and communicated by means of dexterous finger-motions, ultra-rapid vibration of cilia or other gesticulatory devices.

Once, not so long ago, she had been briefly entertained by the slate-colored, armor-skinned personnel of a ship from Khva, a world unthinkable distances beyond Andromeda. They had been completely blind and totally dumb, making superfast limb-signals at each other and registering them through sensitive esp-organs. They had talked to her without voice and admired her without eyes.

All this was what made learning so hard. At seven hundred years of age she had just finished her final examinations and gained the status of an adult. Long, long ago one might have absorbed the wisdom of an era in a mere century. In the dimmer days still farther back one might have done it in ten years. But not today. Not today.

Now in these solemn times of the final centuries the knowledge to be imbibed was in quantity far too great for swift assimilation. It was an immense pile of data created by the impact of a mighty cosmos composed of worlds without end. Each new ship added a few modest grains to the mass, and the mountain already so built was as nothing to the titanic quantities yet to come—if this world lived long enough to receive them.

If!

There was the rub. Creation was conquered and made the slave of the shapes it had brought forth. The atom and the power within the atom were tools in the hands or pseudohands of matter forms able to think and move. Macrocosm and microcosm were equally the playthings of those whose ships roamed endlessly through the tremendous void.

But there were none who knew how to revive an expiring sun.

It could not be done in theory, much less in fact.

It was impossible.

So here and there, at great intervals, a senile sun would flare up a while, collapse into itself, flare again like a feeble thing making its last frantic snatch at life and then become extinguished for all time. A tiny spark in the dark suddenly blown out, unnoticed and unmissed from the limitless host that still blazed on.

Almost each vanishing marked tragedy, perhaps immediate in one case and delayed in another. Some life forms could resist cold longer than others but eventually succumbed just the same. By their superior techniques some could warm themselves and their worlds until the raw material sources of their heat were exhausted. Then they, too, became as if they had never been.

Any system whose primary reverted to an enormous cinder thereby became the property of a great, white, greedy idiot bearing the name of Supernal Frost. He would share his drear estates with none but the dead.

Melisande thought of all these things as she reached the valley. But the thoughts were not morbid; they held nothing of sadness or resentment. She was of her own kind and it was a life form old in experience and remarkably astute. It had faced the inevitable a thousand times before and had learned the futility of battering against it head-on. It knew what to do with an immovable object: one climbs over it or burrows under it or sneaks around it. One uses one's brains because they are there to be used.

Inevitability was not to be feared.

That which cannot be stayed must be avoided with skill and ingenuity.

A great marble palace sprawled across the end of the valley. Its farther side faced a long series of shrub-dotted and flower-carpeted terraces with narrow lawns and feathery fountains. Its nearer side was the back looking upon nothing but the valley. Melisande always approached it from the rear because the path through the woods was the short cut to home.

Mounting the steps she experienced a thrill of excitement as she entered the huge edifice. Wide, mosaic-floored corridors with walls bearing colorful murals led her to the east wing whence came a steady murmur of voices and occasionally the penetrating sound of a caller-trumpet.

Bright-eyed with anticipation, she went into a large hall whose seats rose in semicircular tiers to considerable height. It was a place originally designed to hold four thousand. The number of people now seated therein came to no more than two hundred—almost a score of empty seats for every one occupied. The place looked bare. The voices of the few floated hollowly around the emptiness, were echoed by the curved walls and reflected by the overhead cupola.

All the world was like this: facilities for thousands available to mere dozens. Cities with small-town populations; towns numbering no more citizens than a one-time village; and villages holding only three or four families. Whole streets of houses of which half a dozen were homes while the others, empty, silent and glassy-eyed, stared at the lowering sky.

There were just over one million people on this world. Once upon a time they had numbered four thousand millions. The vanished numbers had long since taken to the star-trails, not like rats leaving a sinking ship but boldly, confidently as those whose destiny has become magnified until too great for the confines of one planet.

The small remainder were to follow as soon as they were ready. And that was why the two hundred were here, waiting in the hall, fidgety, chattering, a little on edge as they listened for the fateful blare of the caller-trumpet.

"Eight-two-eight Hubert," it suddenly gave forth. "Room Six."

A blond giant came up from his seat, stalked down the aisle watched by almost two hundred pairs of eyes. Voices were temporarily silent. He went past Melisande who smiled and murmured low.

"Good luck!"

"Thanks!"

Then he was gone through the distant door. The chatterers resumed. Melisande sat herself at the end of a row next to a thin, swarthy youth of some seven and a half centuries, little older than herself.

"I'm a minute late," she whispered. "Have they been calling long?"

"No," he assured. "That last name was the fourth." He stretched out his legs, pulled them in, stretched them out again, surveyed his fingernails, shifted in his seat, registered vague discomfort. "I wish they'd hurry up with this. The strain is rather—"

"Nine-nine-one Jose-Pietro," boomed the trumpet. "Room Twenty."

He heard it with his mouth open, his eyes startled. The way he came to his feet was slow, uncertain. He licked thin lips suddenly gone dry, cast an appealing glance at Melisande.

"That's me!"

"They must have heard you," she laughed. "Well, don't you want to go?"

"Yes, of course." He edged past her, his gaze on the door through which the blond Hubert had gone. "But when it comes to the point I sort of go weak in the knees."

She made a negligent gesture. "Nobody's going to amputate your legs. They're simply waiting to give you a document—and maybe it'll be one with a gold seal."

Throwing her a look of silent gratitude, he speeded up, exited with a mite more self-assurance.

"Seven-seven Jocelyn—Room Twelve."

And immediately after, "Two-four-oh Betsibelle—Room Nineteen."

Two girls went out, one dark and plump and smiling, one tall, slender, red-haired and serious.

Came a series of names in quick succession: Lurton, Irene, George, Teresa-Maria, Robert and Elena. Then, after a short interval, the summons for which she was waiting.

"Four-four Melisande—Room Two!"

The man in Room Two had light gray eyes, snowy hair and smooth, unlined features. He might have been middle-aged—or old, extremely old. There was no way of telling at a time when a person can retain a seamless face and snowy locks for more than a thousand years.

Waiting for her to be seated, he said: "Well, Melisande, I am happy to say you have passed."

"Thank you, my tutor."

"I felt sure you would pass. I viewed it as almost a foregone conclusion." He smiled across at her, went on, "And now you want to know where you are weak, where you are strong. Those are the essential details, aren't they?"

"Yes, my tutor." She uttered it in low tones, her hands folded demurely in her lap.

"In general knowledge you are excellent," he informed. "That is something of which to be proud—that one should hold the immense storehouse of wisdom described by the inadequate name of general knowledge. You are also most satisfactory in sociology, mass-psychology, ancient and modern philosophies and transcosmic ethics." He leaned forward, looking at her. "But you are rather poor in general communications."

"I am sorry, my tutor." She bit her lower lip, vexed with herself.

"You are nontelepathic and seem quite unable to develop even rudimentary receptivity. When it comes to visual signaling you are somewhat better but still not good enough. Your communication-rate is sluggish, your mistakes numerous, and you appear to be handicapped by a form of tactile uncertainty."

She was now looking at the floor, her face wearing a blush of shame. "I regret it, my tutor."

"There is nothing to regret," he contradicted sharply. "One cannot excel in everything, much as one might like to do so." He waited for her eyes to come up, then proceeded, "As for purely vocal forms of communication, you are no more than fair in the guttural languages." A pause, then: "But you are superb in the liquid ones."

"Ah!" Her features brightened.

"Your oral and written tests for liquid languages were taken in the speech-patterns of the Valreans of Sirius. Your errors were exactly none. Your vocal rate was three hundred twenty words per minute. The average for the Valreans is three hundred fourteen. That means you can speak their language a little better than they can themselves." He smiled to himself, deriving much satisfaction from the thought that his pupil could outshine the very originators of a linguistic mode. "So now, Melisande, the time has come to make serious decisions."

"I am ready, my tutor." Her gaze forward was steady, level and unswerving.

"First I must give you this." He handed her a thin scroll from which dangled a crimson cord terminating in a gold seal. "I congratulate you."

"Thank you!" Her fingers took it, held it, fondled it like something infinitely precious.

"Melisande," he asked, gently, "do you desire children?"

Her answer came evenly, undisturbed, quite without trace of embarrassment. "Not yet, my tutor."

"Then you consider yourself free to go out?" He gestured toward the window beyond which a multimillion lights gleamed and beckoned.

"Yes."

His face became solemn. "But you will not abandon all thoughts of children of your own? You will not plunge so deeply and become so absorbed as to be forgetful of your own shape and kind?"

"I think not," she promised.

"I am glad of that, Melisande. We are scattered afar, in little groups and numbers over an immensity of places. There is no need to increase our count within the cosmos, no need at all. But we should not reduce that count. We should maintain it. That way lies immortality as a species."

"Yes, I know. I have thought of it often." She studied her scroll without really seeing it. "I shall play my little part when the right moment comes."

"You have plenty of time, anyway. You are very young." He sighed as if he wished he could say the same of himself. Crossing the room to where a machine stood by the wall, he opened a cabinet at its side, took out a thick wad of cards. "We'll sort the applications and narrow them down to those most suitable."

He fed the cards one by one into the machine. They were no more than rectangles of thin, white plastic each bearing a reference number at the head, the rest being perforated with many circular or square-shaped holes. When the lot had been inserted he opened a cover revealing a small keyboard. On this he typed, "Nonvocals," and pulled a lever at one side.

The machine clicked, whirred, expelled cards in rapid succession. When it had finished, he glanced at its retention-counter.

"Eighty-four left."

Again resorting to the keyboard, he picked out the word, "Gutturals." The machine responded by throwing out another spray of cards. "Supersonics." More cards. "Staccatos." Out shot a little bunch. "Whistlers." No result.

"Twenty-one." He glanced at his pupil. "They are all liquid speakers now but I think it would be as well if we eliminated the slow ones, don't you?" Getting her nod, he reset the keyboard, "300-max." Several cards emerged. Extracting the remainder, he shuffled them in sensitive fingers, eyed the stars through the window. "There are eleven, Melisande. You have eleven worlds from which to choose."

Filing the first card into a different part of the machine, he set a pair of dials and pressed a stud. The apparatus emitted a faint hum while it warmed up, then a voice came from its hidden speaker.

It said: "Application Number 109,747. Valrea, a union of four planets located in—"

Abruptly it cut off as he jabbed another stud in response to a wave of Melisande's hand.

"You are not interested?"

"No, my tutor. Perhaps I ought to be because I already know their language and that would save a lot of bother. But they have some of us already, haven't they?"

"Yes. They applied for four hundred. We sent them thirty-six and, much later on, another twenty." He regarded her with almost paternal solicitude. "You would have company there, Melisande. You would have others of your own kind, few as they are."

"That may be," she admitted. "But is it fair that people like the Valreans, who have gained some of what they want, should be given still more while others who have none should continue to be denied?"

"No, it is not." He fed in a second card.

"Application 118,451," said the machine. "Brank, a single planet located in the Horse's Head Nebula, Section A71, Subsection D19. Mass 1.2. Civilization type-F. The dominant life form is a bipedal vertebrate as shown."

A screen above the apparatus glowed in full colors, depicted several gaunt, greenish-skinned creatures with long, spindly arms and legs, seven-fingered hands, hairless skulls and enormous yellow eyes.

For another two minutes the voice poured forth a flood of data concerning Brank and its emaciated inhabitants. Then it ceased and the machine went quiescent.

"Thirty years ago they asked for a hundred of us," he told Melisande. "We sent ten. They have now been allocated another six of which you may be one if you so desire."

Seeing that she was noncommittal, he slid another card into the apparatus.

"Application 120,776. Nildeen, a planet with one large satellite, heavily populated, located in the Maelstrom, Section L7, Subsection CC3."

It went on and on. The appropriate life form displayed itself on the screen, a tentacular, eyeless type of being with esp-organs protruding from its head like an insect's antenna. The Nildeens already had had forty of Melisande's kind, still wanted more. She turned them down.

The eleventh and last card aroused her greatest interest, caused her to lean forward with ears alert and eyes alight.

"Application 141,048. Zelam, a single planet located on the fringe of the known, reference numbers and coordinates not yet filed. Recent contact. Mass I. Civilization type-J. Dominant life form is reptilian as shown."

They had a faint resemblance to erect alligators, though Melisande did not know it. All of her own planet's lizardlike species had vanished a million years ago. There were now no local forms to which she could liken these horny-skinned, long-jawed and toothy Zelamites. By the standards of the dim past they were appallingly ugly; but by the standards of her especial planet and her especial era they were not ugly. They were merely an individualistic aspect of the same universal thing which is named Intelligence.

True, the varying forms might also vary in the accuracy with which they reflected this elusive but cosmos-wide thing, yet, taking the long view, it was nothing but a variation in time. Some had more centuries to catch up than did others. Some had come early on the scene and that was their good fortune. Others had come late and that was their hard luck. They were like differently handicapped runners in the same field, spread out, panting, some in front, some behind, but all heading the same way, all destined to pass the finishing line. The Zelamites were held-back runners.

"I will go to those," she said, making it an irrevocable decision.

Spreading the eleven cards across his desk, he surveyed them with a bothered frown. "They asked for sixty. Everyone asks for far too many, especially the newcomers. We've none to spare just yet. But we don't like to refuse anyone."

"So?"

"It has been suggested that we send them one, just one, as a beginning. It would show willingness if nothing else."

"I am one," she pointed out.

"Yes, yes, I know." He had the resigned air of a person about to be cornered without hope of escape. "We would rather that one were masculine."

"Why?"

"Dear me!" It defeated him completely. "There is no reason at all except that we would prefer it."

"Surely, my tutor, it would be a retrograde step and quite unworthy of us to insist upon something without any reason?"

"Not if it does no harm," he countered. "There is the true test—whether it does harm or good."

"Does it do the Zelamites good to refuse them a suitable volunteer?"

"We are not refusing them, Melisande. There are others besides yourself. Someone else may also have chosen Zelam. A dozen may wish to go there. At this stage, with so many applications, we just can't send all of them. Only one can go now. Others may follow later."

"Find out for me, please," she begged.

A mite unwillingly he flicked the switch on his desk and spoke into the silver instrument beside it.

"How many have selected Zelam, Reference 141,048?"

There was quite a long wait before the answer came, "None."

Switching off, he leaned back, eyed her thoughtfully. "You will be lonely."

"All first arrivals are lonely."

"There may arise perils beyond imagining."

"Which will remain the same whether borne by one or shared by a hundred," she gave back, undismayed.

Searching around for one last item of discouragement, he told her, "The Zelamites are nocturnal. They will expect you to work at night and sleep by day."

"Those of us on Brank have been doing the same for years, and many more elsewhere. My tutor, should it be harder for me than for them?"

"No, it should not." He came across to her. "I see that you are determined in your choice. If it be your destiny, it is not for me to thwart it." Taking her hand, he raised it gently, impressed a light kiss upon her fingers in the conventional farewell. "Good luck, Melisande. I am glad to have had you as a pupil of mine."

"Thank you, my tutor." Holding her scroll tightly to her breast, she paused in the doorway as she went out, gave him a final bright-eyed smile. "And I am proud to have had you!"

Long after she had gone he sat and gazed absently at the door. They came and they went, one after another. Each arrived as an utter stranger, departed like a child of his very own taking some of his essential essence with them.

And each one that went forever among the vast concourse of stars made his dying world a fraction smaller, barer, less possessed of life. It is not easy to remain with a long-loved sphere which is nearing its end, to watch the flame die down, watch the shadows creep and grow.

Even at the terrific velocities of this age the journey to Zelam was long and tedious, stretching through days and weeks into many months. It involved several changes, first from a huge hyperspatial mainliner to a smaller branchliner, then to a light blue sphere crewed by dumb Xanthians, then to a battered old rocketship manned by a weirdly mixed mob among whom were two bipeds of Melisande's own kind. Finally to a strange, wedge-shaped and mysteriously powered contraption which sinuous and scintillant Haldisians employed for trading around a small group of systems in one of which was the planet called Zelam.

Beyond this point was a great sprawl of darkness in which reposed a coil of brilliant mist that eventually would be reached by bigger and better ships. Another island universe. Another mighty host of living shapes and forms the highest of which would share one thing in common—and therefore prove willing to share it yet again.

But the length of the trip had been useful. With the aid of a phonetic dictionary and a rudimentary phonograph provided by Zelam, plus her own natural aptitude, she had become an accomplished speaker of the language by the time the planet rolled into view.

Lacking ladder, ramps or anything of that nature, the Haldisians got rid of her by the simple expedient of throwing her through the outer door of the air lock. A power exerted by them personally or perhaps by some unseen apparatus within the vessel—she did not know which—took hold of her, lowered her gently the forty feet to earth. Her luggage followed the same way. So did two of the crew. Another two came out but floated upward, gained the ship's flat topside, commenced opening cargo hatches.

There was a small Zelamite deputation to meet her, the news of her coming having been received a few days before. They were bigger than she had expected for the screen on which she had first seen them had given no indication of relative size. The shortest of them towered head and shoulders above her, had sharp-toothed jaws the length of her arm and looked as if he could cut her in half at one savage snap.

The largest and oldest of the group, a heavily built and warty-faced individual, came forward to meet her as the others hastened to pick up her bags.

"You are the one named Melisande?"

"That's me," she admitted, smiling at him.

He responded with what looked remarkably like a threatening snarl. It did not mislead her in the least. Her kind had learned a thousand centuries ago that those with different facial contours and bony structure perforce must have different ranges of expressions. She knew that the alarming grimace was nothing but an answering smile.

The tone of his voice proved it as he went on, "We are pleased to have you." His orange-colored eyes with their slot-shaped pupils studied her a moment before he added in mild complaint, "We asked for a hundred and hoped to get ten, perhaps twenty."

"More will come in due course."

"It is to be hoped so." He threw a significant glance toward the ship from which items of cargo were floating down. "The Haldisians have twenty. We are tired of hearing them boast about it. We think we are entitled to at least as many."

"They started with two of us," she pointed out. "The others came later—as yours will do. We have no choice but to deal with applications in strict rotation."

"Oh, well—" He spread the long fingers of one hand in the Zelamite equivalent of a shrug, conducted her to a six-wheeled vehicle standing nearby, superintended the loading of her luggage, then got in beside her. "I must compliment you on your fluency. It is remarkable."

"Thank you."

She concentrated on the blue-moss coated and yellow-flowered landscape as he drove to town at a fast pace. His body exuded a faintly pungent odor which her nostrils noted but her brain ignored. That was another very ancient lesson: that different metabolisms produce different manifestations. How boring would the universe be if all its creatures were identically the same!

They drew up before a long, low stone-built edifice with high-tilted roofs and plastic windows. The place was imposing mostly because of its lengthy facade. It stretched at least half a mile, had a blue-moss carpet along its front and a railed yard at each end.

"This is your college." He pointed to the nearer end. "And there is your home." Observing her expression he added by way of explanation, "of course, we cannot expect more than one person can do. We built apartments for ten, with space for extensions if we were lucky enough to get more of you."

"I see." Getting out, she watched her bags being taken inside. Despite centuries of training, free choice of destination and months of anticipatory journeying, some adjustment still was necessary. "And there is your home," he had said. It would take her at least a week and perhaps a month to get used to thinking of it as home. Probably even more because domestic routine would be topsy-turvy so long as she slept daytimes and worked nights.

"Before you go in," he suggested, "what about something to eat?"

"Good heavens, no" She gave a tinkling laugh. "The Haldisians insisted on providing a farewell dinner. They didn't know when to stop. I don't feel like looking at any more food for days."

"Armph!" The twist on his reptilian face suggested that he'd have liked it better if the Haldisians had left well alone. "In that case, all I can offer you is the rest and relaxation you must need. Do you think you might be ready to start work tomorrow evening?"

"Most certainly."

"You can have longer if you wish."

"Tomorrow evening will do," she assured.

"Good—I will tell Nathame. He is our chief cultural supervisor and high in governmental affairs. He will call to see you shortly before you begin."

Giving her another wide-jawed and toothy smile, he drove away. She watched him go, then went and inspected her front door which the luggage-bearers had left invitingly open. It was a simple vertical shutter affair wound up and down by a side handle and could be fastened from the inside only by means of a small bolt.

Beyond it lay the passage, solid, motionless, solely to be walked upon and not for automatic transport. And lights that had to be switched because they knew nothing of perpetual illumination. But it was home-to-be.

She stepped inside.

Nathame came with the twilight on the next day. A sharp-eyed, alert specimen of Zelamite life, he wore glittering insignia on his shoulder-straps, bore himself with authoritative self-assurance. For a while he chatted inconsequentially, his keen gaze never shifting from her face, then added a grumble to the effect that if one person were another world's idea of a hundred it might be better to ask for ten thousand and thus obtain the number really required.

He fell silent for a bit, occupied by his own thoughts, then said: "Before we made contact with other people we had no history but our own. Now we've had to learn the lore of a whole galaxy. It is a record voluminous enough to absorb a lifetime. Nevertheless, I have specialized in it and have learned one thing: that your own particular kind of life is supremely clever."

"Do you think so?" She watched him curiously.

"I do not *think* it. I *know* it." He warmed to his subject. "History records that between sixty and seventy life forms have disappeared from the universal scene. Some warred together and exploded each other's worlds. Some were the victims of cosmic collisions that could be neither foreseen nor avoided. They vanished—*pouf!*—like that! The large majority died when their suns died and warmth went away from them and supernal cold took over." His orange-colored orbs still stared at her unblinking. "It proves one thing: that an entire species can be exterminated and become as though it had never been."

"Not necessarily," she contradicted, "because—"

"Ah!" He held up a hand to halt her. "Of a verity it is for *your* kind to deny the possibility. What or who can wipe out a life form scattered over a hundred million worlds? Nothing! Nobody!"

"I don't think anyone would wish to try."

"Not unless they were completely crazy," he agreed. "You have made yourselves invincible. You have preserved yourselves for eternity. I call that cleverness of the highest order." He pulled a face. "And how have you done it?"

"How do you imagine?" she invited.

"By using your great experience and immense wealth of wisdom to exploit the snobbery of lesser races."

"I don't see it that way."

Ignoring her, he went determinedly on, "Your people anticipated disaster. They foresaw that when your sun collapsed no other planet and no other system could or would accept a sudden influx of refugees numbering thousands of millions. But nobody minds a few dozen or hundreds, especially if they add to their hosts' prestige. Comes the master stroke: you persuade them to scramble for self-esteem like children clamoring for gifts. You made them *want* you."

"But surely—"

He silenced her again, clasped his hands together in a peculiarly artificial manner, minced across the room and spoke in high-pitched, long-drawn vowels, manifestly imitating a type of character with which she was not yet familiar.

"Really, Thasalmie, we wouldn't *dream* of sending *our* children to a *state* school. We've shipped them to the central college at Hei. *Terribly* expensive, of course. They have *Terran* tutors there and it makes *such* a difference in later life when one can say that one has been educated by *Terrans."*

Relaxing into a normal pose, he said, "You see? Since the first Haldisian ships discovered us we've had visits from about twenty life forms. Every one of them took up a patronizing attitude. What, you have no Terrans? By the stars, you must be backward! Why, we have twenty on our world—or forty, or fifty as the case may be." His nostrils twitched as he emitted a loud snort. "They boast and they brag and act so superior that everyone on this world develops a severe inferiority complex and starts screaming for an army of Terrans without delay."

"Braggarts and boasters are not Terran educated," she informed. "We don't produce that kind."

"Maybe you don't, but that's the effect of your presence among those you've not yet taught. They shine in reflected glory. So I say again that you are supremely clever, and on three counts. You are making use of the fact that the more intelligent a people the less they enjoy being thought stupid. Secondly, you have thus insured your own survival for all time. Thirdly, by being content merely to maintain your numbers and not increase them you are also maintaining the confidence of your various hosts. Nobody views with alarm an alien colony that never grows."

She smiled at him and remarked, "All along you've been inviting me to say, 'Look who's talking!' Haven't you?"

"Yes, but you were too diplomatic." Moving nearer and speaking with greater seriousness, he continued, "We asked for a hundred of your kind. Had we got them we would have asked for more. And more again. Not for prestige, but for other and better reasons."

"Such as?"

"We look far ahead. The Haldisians, who know more about it than we, say that ours is a short-term sun. That means an end similar to the end of your world. We must seek the same way out because we can conceive no other. The path your kind has made our kind can tread also. The demand for Terrans is greater than the supply—and there aren't many more of you, are there?"

"Not many," she admitted. "About a million. The old world hasn't long to go."

"Some day we shall be compelled to say that, too. It would be nice if by that time the Zelamites had become an acceptable substitute for Terrans." He made an imperative gesture. "So there is your job as far as one can take it. It's a hard job. Starting with our brightest children you must make us clever enough to share your salvation."

"We'll do our best," she promised, deliberately using the plural.

It did not escape him. Even his face could register gratification. Saluting her, he took his departure. Re-angling her mind and directing it exclusively to the task in hand, she hurried along the main corridor, reached the room from which was coming a shrill uproar.

Silence dropped like a heavy curtain as she entered. Taking her place by the desk, she surveyed the hundred small, thin-snouted, slot-eyed faces that in turn were examining her with youthful candidness.

"We shall commence tonight with the basic subject of transcosmic ethics," she informed. Turning around, she faced the dark rectangle that had no counterpart on Terra, picked up the white stick at its base and wrote upon the blackboard in a firm hand.

"Lesson One. Intelligence is like candy. It comes in an endless variety of shapes, sizes and colors, no one which is less delectable than others."

She glanced over her shoulder to insure that they were giving attention, found them copying it down, orange eyes intent. One had his tongue out, its purple tip laboriously following the movements of his writing instrument.

Involuntarily her gaze shifted to the transparent roof through which the galactic host looked down. Somewhere within that gleaming swam was a little red light, weak and dimming. Somewhere near to it was another, silvery blue, shining to the last.

The ancient fountain.

The guiding star.

Old Mother Earth.

Hobbyist

Astounding, September 1947

The ship arced out of a golden sky and landed with a whoop and a wallop that cut down a mile of lush vegetation. Another half mile of growths turned black and drooped to ashes under the final flicker of the tail rocket blasts. That arrival was spectacular, full of verve, and worthy of four columns in any man's paper. But the nearest sheet was distant by a goodly slice of a lifetime, and there was none to record what this far corner of the cosmos regarded as the pettiest of events. So the ship squatted tired and still at the foremost end of the ashy blast-track and the sky glowed down and the green world brooded solemnly all around.

Within the transpex control dome, Steve Ander sat and thought things over. It was his habit to think things over carefully. Astronauts were not the impulsive daredevils so dear to the stereopticon-loving public. They couldn't afford to be. The hazards of the profession required an infinite capacity for cautious, contemplative thought. Five minutes' consideration had prevented many a collapsed lung, many a leaky heart, many a fractured frame. Steve valued his skeleton. He wasn't conceited about it and he'd no reason to believe it in any way superior to anyone else's skeleton. But he'd had it a long time, found it quite satisfactory, and had an intense desire to keep it—intact.

Therefore, while the tail tubes cooled off with their usual creaking contractions, he sat in the control seat, stared through the dome with eyes made unseeing by deep preoccupation, and performed a few thinks.

Firstly, he'd made a rough estimate of this world during his hectic approach. As nearly as he could judge, it was ten times the size of Terra. But his weight didn't seem abnormal. Of course, one's notions of weight tended to be somewhat wild when for some weeks one's own weight has shot far up or far down in between periods of weightlessness. The most reasonable estimate had to be based on muscular reaction. If you felt as sluggish as a Saturnian sloth, your weight was way up. If you felt as powerful as Angus McKittrick's bull, your weight was down.

Normal weight meant Terrestrial mass despite this planet's tenfold volume. That meant light plasma. And that meant lack of heavy elements. No thorium. No nickel. No nickel-thorium alloy. Ergo, no getting back. The Kingston-Kane atomic motors demanded fuel in the form of ten gauge nickel-thorium alloy wire fed directly into the vaporizers. Denatured plutonium would do, but it didn't occur in natural form, and it had to be made. He had three yards nine and a quarter inches of nickel-thorium left on the feed-spool. Not enough. He was here for keeps.

A wonderful thing, logic. You could start from the simple premise that when you were seated your behind was no flatter than usual, and work your way to the inevitable conclusion that you were a wanderer no more. You'd become a native. Destiny had you tagged as suitable for the status of oldest inhabitant.

Steve pulled an ugly face and said, "Darn!"

The face didn't have to be pulled far. Nature had given said pan a good start. That is to say, it wasn't handsome. It was a long, lean, nut-brown face with pronounced jaw muscles, prominent cheekbones, and a thin, hooked nose. This, with his dark eyes and black hair, gave him a hawklike appearance. Friends talked to him about teepees and tomahawks whenever they wanted him to feel at home.

Well, he wasn't going to feel at home any more; not unless this brooding jungle held intelligent life dopey enough to swap ten gauge nickel-thorium wire for a pair of old boots. Or unless some dopey search party was intelligent enough to pick this cosmic dust mote out of a cloud of motes, and took him back. He estimated this as no less than a million-to-one chance. Like spitting at the Empire State hoping to hit a cent-sized mark on one of its walls.

Reaching for his everflo stylus and the ship's log, he opened the log, looked absently at some of the entries.

"Eighteenth day: The spatial convulsion has now flung me past rotal-range of Rigel. Am being tossed into uncharted regions.

"Twenty-fourth day: Arm of convulsion now tails back seven parsecs. Robot recorder now out of gear. Angle of throw changed seven times today.

"Twenty-ninth day: Now beyond arm of the convulsive sweep and regaining control. Speed far beyond range of the astrometer. Applying braking rockets cautiously. Fuel reserve: fourteen hundred yards.

"Thirty-seventh day: Making for planetary system now within reach."

He scowled, his jaw muscles lumped, and he wrote slowly and legibly, "Thirty-ninth day: Landed on planet unknown, primary unknown, galactic area standard reference and sector numbers unknown. No cosmic formations were recognizable when observed shortly before landing. Angles of offshoot and speed of transit not recorded, and impossible to estimate. Condition of ship: workable. Fuel reserve: three and one quarter yards."

Closing the log, he scowled again, rammed the stylus into its desk-grip, and muttered, "Now to check on the outside air and then see how the best girl's doing."

The Radson register had three simple dials. The first recorded outside pressure at thirteen point seven pounds, a reading he observed with much satisfaction. The second said that oxygen content was high. The third had a bi-colored dial, half white, half red, and its needle stood in the middle of the white.

"Breathable," he grunted, clipping down the register's lid. Crossing the tiny control room, he slid aside a metal panel, looked into the padded compartment behind. "Coming out, Beauteous?" he asked.

"Steve loves Laura?" inquired a plaintive voice.

"You bet he does!" he responded with becoming passion. He shoved an arm into the compartment, brought out a large, gaudily colored macaw. "Does Laura love Steve?"

"Hey-hey!" cackled Laura harshly. Climbing up his arm, the bird perched on his shoulder. He could feel the grip of its powerful claws. It regarded him with a beady and brilliant eye, then rubbed its crimson head against his left ear. "Hey-hey! Time flies!"

"Don't mention it," he reproved. "There's plenty to remind me of the fact without you chipping in."

Reaching up, he scratched her poll while she stretched and bowed with absurd delight. He was fond of Laura. She was more than a pet. She was a bona fide member of the crew, issued with her own rations and drawing her own pay. Every probe ship had a crew of two: one man, one macaw. When he'd first heard of it, the practice had seemed crazy—but when he got the reasons, it made sense.

"Lonely men, probing beyond the edge of the charts, get queer psychological troubles. They need an anchor to Earth. A macaw provides the necessary companionship—and more! It's the space-hardiest bird we've got, its weight is negligible, it can talk and amuse, and it can fend for itself when necessary. On land, it will often sense dangers before you do. Any strange fruit or food it may eat is safe for you to eat. Many a man's life has been saved by his macaw. Look after yours, my boy, and it'll look after you!"

Yes, they looked after each other, Terrestrials both. It was almost a symbiosis of the spaceways. Before the era of astronavigation nobody had thought of such an arrangement, though it had been done before. Miners and their canaries.

Moving over to the miniature air lock, he didn't bother to operate the pump. It wasn't necessary with so small a difference between internal and external pressures. Opening both doors, he let a little of his higher-pressured air sigh out, stood on the rim of the lock, jumped down. Laura fluttered from his shoulder as he leaped, followed him with a flurry of wings, got her talons into his jacket as he staggered upright.

The pair went around the ship, silently surveying its condition. Front braking nozzles O.K., rear steering flares O.K., tail propulsion tubes O.K. All were badly scored but still usable. The skin of the vessel likewise was scored but intact. Three months supply of food and maybe a thousand yards of wire could get her home, theoretically. But only theoretically, Steve had no delusions about the matter. The odds were still against him even if given the means to move. How do you navigate from you-don't-know-where to you-don't-know-where? Answer: you stroke a rabbit's foot and probably arrive you-don't-know-where-else.

"Well," he said, rounding the tail, "it's something in which to live. It'll save us building a shanty. Way back on Terra they want fifty thousand smackers for an all-metal, streamlined bungalow, so I guess we're mighty lucky. I'll make a garden here, and a rockery there, and build a swimming pool out back. You can wear a pretty frock and do all the cooking."

"Yawk!" said Laura derisively.

Turning, he had a look at the nearest vegetation. It was of all heights, shapes and sizes, of all shades of green with a few tending toward blueness. There was something peculiar about the stuff but he was unable to decide where the strangeness lay. It wasn't that the growths were alien and unfamiliar—one expected that on every new world—but an underlying something which they shared in common. They had a vague, shadowy air of being not quite right in some basic respect impossible to define.

A plant grew right at his feet. It was green in color, a foot high, and monocotyledonous. Looked at as a thing in itself, there was nothing wrong with it. Near to it flourished a bush of darker hue, a yard high, with green, firlike needles in lieu of leaves, and pale, waxy berries scattered over it. That, too, was innocent enough when studied apart from its neighbors. Beside it grew a similar plant, differing only in that its needles were longer and its berries a bright pink. Beyond these towered a cactus-like object dragged out of somebody's drunken dreams, and beside it stood an umbrella-frame which had taken root and produced little purple pods. Individually, they were acceptable. Collectively, they made the discerning mind search anxiously for it knew not what.

That eerie feature had Steve stumped. Whatever it was, he couldn't nail it down. There was something stranger than the mere strangeness of new forms of plant life, and that was all. He dismissed the problem with a shrug. Time enough to trouble about such matters after he'd dealt with others more urgent such as, for example, the location and purity of the nearest water supply.

A mile away lay a lake of some liquid that might be water. He'd seen it glittering in the sunlight as he'd made his descent, and he'd tried to land fairly near to it. If it wasn't water, well, it'd be just his tough luck and he'd have to look someplace else. At worst, the tiny fuel reserve would be enough to permit one circumnavigation of the planet before the ship became pinned down forever. Water he must have if he wasn't going to end up imitating the mummy of Rameses the Second.

Reaching high, he grasped the rim of the port, dexterously muscled himself upward and through it. For a minute he moved around inside the ship, then reappeared with a four-gallon freezocan which he tossed to the ground. Then he dug out his popgun, a belt of explosive shells, and let down the folding ladder from lock to surface. He'd need that ladder. He could muscle himself up through a hole seven feet high, but not with fifty pounds of can and water.

Finally, he locked both the inner and outer air lock doors, skipped down the ladder, picked up the can. From the way he'd made his landing the lake should be directly bow-on relative to the vessel, and somewhere the other side of those distant trees. Laura took a fresh grip on his shoulder as he started off. The can swung from his left hand. His right hand rested warily on the gun. He was perpendicular on this world instead of horizontal on another because, on two occasions, his hand had been ready on the gun, and because it was the most nervous hand he possessed.

The going was rough. It wasn't so much that the terrain was craggy as the fact that impeding growths got in his way. At one moment he was stepping over an ankle-high shrub, the next he was facing a burly plant struggling to become a tree.

Behind the plant would be a creeper, then a natural zareba of thorns, a fuzz of fine moss, followed by a giant fem. Progress consisted of stepping over one item, ducking beneath a second, going around a third, and crawling under a fourth.

It occurred to him, belatedly, that if he'd planted the ship tail-first to the lake instead of bow-on, or if he'd let the braking rockets blow after he'd touched down, he'd have saved himself much twisting and dodging. All this obstructing stuff would have been reduced to ashes for at least half the distance to the lake—together with any venomous life it might conceal.

That last thought rang like an alarm bell within his mind just as he doubled up to pass a low-swung creeper. On Venus were creepers that coiled and constricted, swiftly, viciously. Macaws played merry hell if taken within fifty yards of them. It was a comfort to know that, this time, Laura was riding his shoulder unperturbed—but he kept the hand on the gun.

The elusive peculiarity of the planet's vegetation bothered him all the more as he progressed through it. His inability to discover and name this unnamable queerness nagged at him as he went on. A frown of self-disgust was on his lean face when he dragged himself free of a clinging bush and sat on a rock in a tiny clearing.

Dumping the can at his feet, he glowered at it and promptly caught a glimpse of something bright and shining a few feet beyond the can. He raised his gaze. It was then he saw the beetle.

The creature was the biggest of its kind ever seen by human eyes. There were other things bigger, of course, but not of this type. Crabs, for instance. But this was no crab. The beetle ambling purposefully across the clearing was large enough to give any crab a severe inferiority complex, but it was a genuine, twenty-four-karat beetle. And a beautiful one. Like a scarab.

Except that he clung to the notion that little bugs were vicious and big ones companionable, Steve had no phobia about insects. The amiability of large ones was a theory inherited from schoolkid days when he'd been the doting owner of a three-inch stag-beetle afflicted with the name of Edgar.

So he knelt beside the creeping giant, placed his hand palm upward in its path. It investigated the hand with waving feelers, climbed onto his palm, paused there ruminatively. It shone with a sheen of brilliant metallic blue and it weighed about three pounds. He jogged it on his hand to get its weight, then put it down, let it wander on. Laura watched it go with a sharp but incurious eye.

"Scarabaeus Anderii," Steve said with glum satisfaction. "I pin my name on him—but nobody'll ever know it!"

"Dinna fash y'rsel'!" shouted Laura in a hoarse voice imported straight from Aberdeen. "Dinna fash! Stop chunnerin', wumman! Y' gie me a pain ahint ma sporran! Dinna—"

"Shut up!" Steve jerked his shoulder, momentarily unbalancing the bird. "Why d'you pick up that barbaric dialect quicker than anything else, eh?"

"McGillicuddy," shrieked Laura with earsplitting relish. "McGilli-Gilli-Gillicuddy! The great black—!" It ended with a word that pushed Steve's eyebrows into his hair and surprised even the bird itself. Filming its eyes with amazement, it tightened its claw-hold on his shoulder, opened the eyes, emitted a couple of raucous clucks, and joyfully repeated, "The great black—"

It didn't get the chance to complete the new and lovely word. A violent jerk of the shoulder unseated it in the nick of time and it fluttered to the ground, squawking protestingly. *Scarabaeus Anderii* lumbered out from behind a bush, his blue armor glistening as if freshly polished, and stared reprovingly at Laura.

Then something fifty yards away released a snort like the trumpet of doom and took one step that shook the earth. *Scarabaeus Anderii* took refuge under a projecting root. Laura made an agitated swoop for Steve's shoulder and clung there desperately. Steve's gun was out and pointing northward before the bird had found its perch. Another step. The ground quivered.

Silence for a while. Steve continued to stand like a statue. Then came a monstrous whistle more forceful than that of a locomotive blowing off steam. Something squat and wide and of tremendous length charged headlong through the half-concealing vegetation while the earth trembled beneath its weight.

Its mad onrush carried it blindly twenty yards to Steve's right, the gun swinging to cover its course, but not firing. Steve caught an extended glimpse of a slate-gray bulk with a serrated ridge on its back which, despite the thing's pace, took long to pass. It seemed several times the length of a fire ladder.

Bushes were flung roots topmost and small trees whipped aside as the creature pounded grimly onward in a straight line which carried it far past the ship and into the dim distance. It left behind a tattered swathe wide enough for a first-class road. Then the reverberations of its mighty tonnage died out, and it was gone.

Steve used his left hand to pull out a handkerchief and wipe the back of his neck. He kept the gun in his right hand. The explosive shells in that gun were somewhat wicked; any one of them could deprive a rhinoceros of a hunk of meat weighing two hundred pounds. If a man caught one, he just strewed himself over the landscape. By the looks of that slate-colored galloper, it would need half a dozen shells to feel incommoded. A seventy-five millimeter bazooka would be more effective for kicking it in the back teeth, but probe ship boys don't tote around such artillery. Steve finished the mopping, put the handkerchief back, picked up the can.

Laura said pensively, "I want my mother."

He scowled, made no reply, set out toward the lake. Her feathers still ruffled, Laura rode his shoulder and lapsed into surly silence.

The stuff in the lake was water, cold, faintly green and a little bitter to the taste. Coffee would camouflage the flavor. If anything, it might improve the coffee since he liked his java bitter, but the stuff would have to be tested before absorbing it in any quantity. Some poisons were accumulative. It wouldn't do to guzzle gayly while building up a death-dealing reserve of lead, for instance. Filling the freezocan, he lugged it to the ship in hundred yard stages. The swathe helped; it made an easier path to within a short distance of the ship's tail. He was perspiring freely by the time he reached the base of the ladder.

Once inside the vessel, he relocked both doors, opened the air vents, started the auxiliary lighting-set and plugged in the percolator, using water out of his depleted reserve supply. The golden sky had dulled to orange, with violet streamers creeping upward from the horizon. Looking at it through the transpex dome, he found that the perpetual haze still effectively concealed the sinking sun. A brighter area to one side was all that indicated its position. He'd need his lights soon.

Pulling out the collapsible table, he jammed its supporting leg into place, plugged into its rim the short rod which was Laura's official seat. She claimed the perch immediately, watched him beadily as he set out her meal of water, melon seeds, sunflower seeds, pecans and unshelled oleo nuts. Her manners were anything but ladylike and she started eagerly, without waiting for him.

A deep frown lay across his brown, muscular features as he sat at the table, poured out his coffee and commenced to eat. It persisted through the meal, was still there when he lit a cigarette and stared speculatively up at the dome.

Presently, he murmured, "I've seen the biggest bug that ever was. I've seen a few other bugs. There were a couple of little ones under a creeper. One was long and brown and many-legged, like an earwig. The other was round and black, with little red dots on its wing cases. I've seen a tiny purple spider and a tinier green one of different shape, also a bug that looked like an aphid. But not an ant."

"Ant, ant," hooted Laura. She dropped a piece of oleo nut, climbed down after it. "Yawk!" she added from the floor.

"Nor a bee."

"Bee," echoed Laura, companionably. "Bee-ant. Laura loves Steve."

Still keeping his attention on the dome, he went on, "And what's cockeyed about the plants is equally cockeyed about the bugs. I wish I could place it. Why can't I? Maybe I'm going nuts already."

"Laura loves nuts."

"I know it, you technicolored belly!" said Steve rudely.

And at that point night fell with a silent bang. The gold and orange and violet abruptly were swamped with deep, impenetrable blackness devoid of stars or any random gleam. Except for greenish glowings on the instrument panel, the control room was stygian, with Laura swearing steadily on the floor.

Putting out a hand, Steve switched on the indirect lighting. Laura got to her perch with the rescued tidbit, concentrated on the job of dealing with it and let him sink back into his thoughts.

"*Scarabaeus Anderii* and a pair of smaller bugs and a couple of spiders, all different. At the other end of the scale, that gigantosaurus. But no ant, or bee. Or rather, no ants, no bees." The switch from singular to plural stirred his back hairs queerly. In some vague way, he felt that he'd touched the heart of the mystery. "No ant—no ants," he thought. "No bee—no bees." Almost he had it—but still it evaded him.

Giving it up for the time being, he cleared the table, did a few minor chores. After that, he drew a standard sample from the freezocan, put it through its paces. The bitter flavor he identified as being due to the presence of magnesium sulfate in quantity far too small to prove embarrassing. Drinkable—that was something! Food, drink and shelter were the three essentials of survival. He'd enough of the first for six or seven weeks. The lake and the ship were his remaining guarantees of life.

Finding the log, he entered the day's report, bluntly, factually, without any embroidery. Partway through, he found himself stuck for a name for the planet. *Ander*, he decided, would cost him dear if the million-to-one chance put him back among the merciless playmates of the Probe Service. O.K. for a bug, but not for a world. *Laura* wasn't so hot, either—especially when you knew Laura. It wouldn't be seemly to name a big, gold planet after an oversized parrot. Thinking over the golden aspect of this world's sky, he hit upon the name of *Oro*, promptly made the christening authoritative by entering it in his log.

By the time he'd finished, Laura had her head buried deep under one wing. Occasionally she teetered and swung erect again. It always fascinated him to watch how her balance was maintained even in her slumbers. Studying her fondly, he remembered that unexpected addition to her vocabulary. This shifted his thoughts to a fiery-headed and fierier-tongued individual named Menzies, the sworn foe of another volcano named McGillicuddy. If ever the opportunity presented itself, he decided, the educative work of said Menzies was going to be rewarded with a bust on the snoot.

Sighing, he put away the log, wound up the forty-day chronometer, opened his folding bunk and lay down upon it. His hand switched off the lights. Ten years back, a first landing would have kept him awake all night in dithers of excitement. He'd got beyond that now. He'd done it often enough to have grown phlegmatic about it. His eyes closed in preparation for a good night's sleep, and he did sleep—for two hours.

What brought him awake within that short time he didn't know, but suddenly he found himself sitting bolt upright on the edge of the bunk, his ears and nerves stretched to their utmost, his legs quivering in a way they'd never done before. His whole body fizzed with that queer mixture of palpitation and shock which follows narrow escape from disaster.

This was something not within previous experience. Sure and certain in the intense darkness, his hand sought and found his gun. He cuddled the butt in his palm while his mind strove to recall a possible nightmare, though he knew he was not given to nightmares.

Laura moved restlessly on her perch, not truly awake, yet not asleep, and this was unusual in her.

Rejecting the dream theory, he stood up on the bunk, looked out through the dome. Blackness, the deepest, darkest, most impenetrable, blackness it was possible to conceive. And silence! The outside world slumbered in the blackness and the silence as in a sable shroud.

Yet never before had he felt so wide awake in this, his normal sleeping time. Puzzled, he turned slowly round to take in the full circle of unseeable view, and at one point he halted. The surrounding darkness was not complete. In the distance beyond the ship's tail moved a tall, stately glow. How far off it might be was not possible to estimate, but the sight of it stirred his soul and caused his heart to leap.

Uncontrollable emotions were not permitted to master his disciplined mind. Narrowing his eyes, he tried to discern the nature of the glow while his mind sought the reason why the mere sight of it should make him twang like a harp. Bending down, he felt at the head of the bunk, found a leather case, extracted a pair of powerful night glasses. The glow was still moving, slowly, deliberately, from right to left. He got the glasses on it, screwed the lenses into focus, and the phenomenon leaped into closer view.

The thing was a great column of golden haze much like that of the noonday sky except that small, intense gleams of silver sparkled within it. It was a shaft of lustrous mist bearing a sprinkling of tiny stars. It was like nothing known to or recorded by any form of life lower than the gods. But was it life?

It moved, though its mode of locomotion could not be determined. Self-motivation is the prime symptom of life. It could be life, conceivably though not credibly, from the Terrestrial viewpoint. Consciously, he preferred to think it a strange and purely local feature comparable with Saharan sand-devils. Subconsciously, he knew it was life, tall and terrifying.

He kept the glasses on it while slowly it receded into the darkness, foreshortening with increasing distance and gradually fading from view. To the very last the observable field shifted and shuddered as he failed to control the quiver in his hands. And when the sparkling haze had gone, leaving only a pall over his lenses, he sat down on the bunk and shivered with eerie cold.

Laura was dodging to and fro along her perch, now thoroughly awake and agitated, but he wasn't inclined to switch on the lights and make the dome a beacon in the night. His hand went out, feeling for her in the darkness, and she clambered eagerly onto his wrist, thence to his lap. She was fussy and demonstrative, pathetically yearning for comfort and companionship. He scratched her poll and fondled her while she pressed close against his chest with funny little crooning noises. For some time he soothed her and, while doing it, fell asleep. Gradually he slumped backward on the bunk. Laura perched on his forearm, clucked tiredly, put her head under a wing.

There was no further awakening until the outer blackness disappeared and the sky again sent its golden glow pouring through the dome. Steve got up, stood on the bunk, had a good look over the surrounding terrain. It remained precisely the same as it had been the day before. Things stewed within his mind while he got his breakfast; especially the jumpiness he'd experienced in the nighttime. Laura also was subdued and quiet. Only once before had she been like that—which was when he'd traipsed through the Venusian section of the Panplanetary Zoo and had shown her a crested eagle. The eagle had stared at her with contemptuous dignity.

Though he'd all the time in his life, he now felt a peculiar urge to hasten. Getting the gun and the freezocan, he made a full dozen trips to the lake, wasting no minutes, nor stopping to study the still enigmatic plants and bugs. It was late in the afternoon by the time he'd filled the ship's fifty-gallon reservoir, and had the satisfaction of knowing that he'd got a drinkable quota to match his food supply.

There had been no sign of gigantosaurus or any other animal. Once he'd seen something flying in the far distance, birdlike or batlike. Laura had cocked a sharp eye at it but betrayed no undue interest. Right now she was more concerned with a new fruit. Steve sat in the rim of the outer lock door, his legs dangling, and watched her clambering over a small tree thirty yards away. The gun lay in his lap; he was ready to take a crack at anything which might be ready to take a crack at Laura.

The bird sampled the tree's fruit, a crop resembling blue-shelled lychee nuts. She ate one with relish, grabbed another. Steve lay back in the lock, stretched to reach a bag, then dropped to the ground and went across to the tree. He tried a nut. Its flesh was soft, juicy, sweet and citrus. He filled the bag with the fruit, slung it into the ship.

Nearby stood another tree, not quite the same, but very similar. It bore nuts like the first except that they were larger. Picking one, he offered it to Laura who tried it, spat it out in disgust. Picking a second, he slit it, licked the flesh gingerly. As far as he could tell, it was the same. Evidently he couldn't tell far enough: Laura's diagnosis said it was not the same. The difference, too subtle for him to detect, might be sufficient to roll him up like a hoop and keep him that shape to the unpleasant end. He flung the thing away, went back to his seat in the lock, and ruminated.

That elusive, nagging feature of Oro's plants and bugs could be narrowed down to these two nuts. He felt sure of that. If he could discover why—parrotwise—one nut was a nut while the other nut was not, he'd have his finger right on the secret. The more he thought about those similar fruits the more he felt that, in sober fact, his finger was on the secret already—but he lacked the power to lift it and see what lay beneath.

Tantalizingly, his mulling-over the subject landed him the same place as before; namely, nowhere. It got his dander up, and he went back to the trees, subjected both to close examination. His sense of sight told him that they were different individuals of the same species. Laura's sense of whatchamacallit insisted that they were different species. Ergo, you can't believe the evidence of your eyes. He was aware of that fact, of course, since it was a platitude of the spaceways, but when you couldn't trust your optics it was legitimate to try to discover just why you couldn't trust 'em. And he couldn't discover even that!

It soured him so much that he returned to the ship, locked its doors, called Laura back to his shoulder and set off on a tailward exploration. The rules of first landings were simple and sensible. Go in slowly, come out quickly, and remember that all we want from you is evidence of suitability for human life. Thoroughly explore a small area rather than scout a big one—the mapping parties will do the rest. Use your ship as a base and centralize it where you can live—don't move it unnecessarily. Restrict your trips to a radius representing daylight-reach and lock yourself in after dark.

Was Oro suitable for human life? The unwritten law was that you don't jump to conclusions and say, "Of course! I'm still living, aren't I?" Cameron, who'd plonked his ship on Mithra, for instance, thought he'd found paradise until, on the seventeenth day, he'd discovered the fungoid plague. He'd left like a bat out of hell and had spent three sweaty, swearing days in the Lunar Purification Plant before becoming fit for society. The authorities had vaporized his ship. Mithra had been taboo ever since. Every world a potential trap baited with scenic delight. The job of the Probe Service was to enter the traps and jounce on the springs. Another dollop of real estate for Terra—if nothing broke your neck.

Maybe Oro was loaded for bear. The thing that walked in the night, Steve mused, bore awful suggestion of nonhuman power. So did a waterspout, and whoever heard of anyone successfully wrestling with a waterspout? If this Oro-spout were sentient, so much the worse for human prospects. He'd have to get the measure of it, he decided, even if he had to chase it through the blank avenues of night. Plodding steadily away from the tail, gun in hand, he pondered so deeply that he entirely overlooked the fact that he wasn't on a pukka probe job anyway, and that nothing else remotely human might reach Oro in a thousand years. Even spaceboys can be creatures of habit. Their job: to look for death; they were liable to go on looking long after the need had passed, in bland disregard of the certainty that if you look for a thing long enough, ultimately you find it!

The ship's chronometer had given him five hours to darkness. Two and a half hours each way; say ten miles out and ten back. The water had consumed his time. On the morrow, and henceforth, he'd increase the radius to twelve and take it easier.

Then all thoughts fled from his mind as he came to the edge of the vegetation. The stuff didn't dribble out of existence with hardy spurs and offshoots fighting for a hold in rocky ground. It stopped abruptly, in light loam, as if cut off with a machete, and from where it stopped spread a different crop. The new growths were tiny and crystalline.

He accepted the crystalline crop without surprise, knowing that novelty was the inevitable feature of any new locale. Things were ordinary only by Terrestrial standards. Outside of Terra, nothing was supernormal or abnormal except insofar as they failed to jibe with their own peculiar conditions. Besides, there were crystalline growths on Mars. The one unacceptable feature of the situation was the way in which vegetable growths ended and crystalline ones began. He stepped back to the verge and made another startled survey of the borderline. It was so straight that the sight screwed his brain around. Like a field. A cultivated field. Dead straightness of that sort couldn't be other than artificial. Little beads of moisture popped out on his back.

Squatting on the heel of his right boot, he gazed at the nearest crystals and said to Laura, "Chicken, I think these things got planted. Question is, who planted 'em?"

"McGillicuddy," suggested Laura brightly.

Putting out a finger, he flicked the crystal sprouting near the toe of his boot, a green, branchy object an inch high.

The crystal vibrated and said, *"Zing!"* in a sweet, high voice.

He flicked its neighbor, and that said, *"Zang!"* in lower tone.

He flicked a third. It emitted no note, but broke into a thousand shards.

Standing up, he scratched his head, making Laura fight for a claw-hold within the circle of his arm. One zinged and one zanged and one returned to dust. Two nuts. Zings and zangs and nuts. It was right in his grasp if only he could open his hand and look at what he'd got.

Then he lifted his puzzled and slightly ireful gaze, saw something fluttering erratically across the crystal field. It was making for the vegetation. Laura took off with a raucous cackle, her blue and crimson wings beating powerfully. She swooped over the object, frightening it so low that it dodged and sideslipped only a few feet above Steve's head. He saw that it was a large butterfly, full-winged, almost as gaudy as Laura. The bird swooped again, scaring the insect but not menacing it. He called her back, set out to cross the area ahead. Crystals crunched to powder under his heavy boots as he tramped on.

Half an hour later he was toiling up a steep, crystal-coated slope when his thoughts suddenly jelled and he stopped with such abruptness that Laura spilled from his shoulder and perforce took to wing. She beat round in a circle, came back to her perch, made bitter remarks in an unknown language.

"One of this and one of that," he said. "No twos or threes or dozen. Nothing I've seen has repeated itself. There's only one gigantosaurus, only one *Scarabaeus Anderii*, only one of every other danged thing. Ever item is unique, original, and an individual creation in its own right. What does that suggest?"

"McGillicuddy," offered Laura.

"For Pete's sake, forget McGillicuddy."

"For Pete's sake, for Pete's sake," yelled Laura, much taken by the phrase. "The great black—"

Again he upset her in the nick of time, making her take to flight while he continued talking to himself. "It suggests constant and all-pervading mutation. Everything breeds something quite different from itself and there aren't any dominant strains." He frowned at the obvious snag in this theory. "But how the blazes does anything breed? What fertilizes which?"

"McGilli—," began Laura, then changed her mind and shut up.

"Anyway, if nothing breeds true, it'll be tough on the food problem," he went on. "What's edible on one plant may be a killer on its offspring. Today's fodder is tomorrow's poison. How's a farmer to know what he's going to get? Hey-hey, if I'm guessing right, this planet won't support a couple of hogs."

"No, sir. No hogs. Laura loves hogs."

"Be quiet," he snapped. "Now, what shouldn't support a couple of hogs demonstrably does support gigantosaurus—and any other fancy animals which may be mooching around. It seems crazy to me. On Venus or any other place full of consistent fodder, gigantosaurus would thrive, but here, according to my calculations, the big lunk has no right to be alive. He ought to be dead."

So saying, he topped the rise and found the monster in question sprawling right across the opposite slope. It was dead.

The way in which he determined its deadness was appropriately swift, simple and effective. Its enormous bulk lay draped across the full length of the slope and its dragon-head, the size of a lifeboat, pointed toward him. The head had two dull, lackluster eyes like dinner plates. He planted a shell smack in the right eye and a sizable hunk of noggin promptly splashed in all directions. The body did not stir.

There was a shell ready for the other eye should the creature leap to frantic, vengeful life, but the mighty hulk remained supine.

His boots continued to desiccate crystals as he went down the slope, curved a hundred yards off his route to get around the corpse, and trudged up the farther rise. Momentarily, he wasn't much interested in the dead beast. Time was short and he could come again tomorrow, bringing a full-color stereoscopic camera with him. Gigantosaurus would go on record in style, but would have to wait.

This second rise was a good deal higher, and more trying a climb. Its crest represented the approximate limit of this day's trip, and he felt anxious to surmount it before turning back. Humanity's characteristic urge to see what lay over the hill remained as strong as on the day determined ancestors topped the Rockies. He had to have a look, firstly because elevation gave range to the vision, and secondly because of that prowler in the night—and, nearly as he could estimate, the prowler had gone down behind this rise. A column of mist, sucked down from the sky, might move around aimlessly, going nowhere, but instinct maintained that this had been no mere column of mist, and that it was going somewhere.

Where?

Out of breath, he pounded over the crest, looked down into an immense valley, and found the answer.

The crystal growths gave out on the crest, again in a perfectly straight line. Beyond them the light loam, devoid of rock, ran gently down to the valley and up the farther side. Both slopes were sparsely dotted with queer, jellylike lumps of matter which lay and quivered beneath the sky's golden glow.

From the closed end of the valley jutted a great, glistening fabrication, flat-roofed, flat-fronted, with a huge, square hole gaping in its midsection at front. It looked like a tremendous oblong slab of polished, milk-white plastic half-buried endwise in a sandy hill. No decoration disturbed its smooth, gleaming surface. No road led to the hole in front. Somehow, it had the new-old air of a house that struggles to look empty because it is full—of fiends.

Steve's back hairs prickled as he studied it. One thing was obvious—Oro bore intelligent life. One thing was possible—the golden column represented that life. One thing was probable—fleshly Terrestrials and hazy Orons would have difficulty in finding a basis for friendship and cooperation.

Whereas enmity needs no basis.

Curiosity and caution pulled him opposite ways. One urged him down into the valley while the other drove him back, back, while yet there was time. He consulted his watch. Less than three hours to go, within which he had to return to the ship, enter the log, prepare supper. That milky creation was at least two miles away, a good hour's journey there and back. Let it wait. Give it another day and he'd have more time for it, with the benefit of needful thought betweentimes.

Caution triumphed. He investigated the nearest jellyblob. It was flat, a yard in diameter, green, with bluish streaks and many tiny bubbles hiding in its semitransparency. The thing pulsated slowly. He poked it with the toe of his boot, and it contracted, humping itself in the middle, then sluggishly relaxed. No amoeba, he decided. A low form of life, but complicated withal. Laura didn't like the object. She skittered off as he bent over it, vented her anger by bashing a few crystals.

This jello dollop wasn't like its nearest neighbor, or like any other. One of each, only one. The same rule: one butterfly of a kind, one bug, one plant, one of these quivering things.

A final stare at the distant mystery down in the valley, then he retraced his steps. When the ship came into sight he speeded up like a gladsome voyager nearing home. There were new prints near the vessel, big, three-toed, deeply-impressed spoor which revealed that something large, heavy and two-legged had wandered past in his absence. Evidently an animal, for nothing intelligent would have meandered on so casually without circling and inspecting the nearby invader from space. He dismissed it from his mind. There was only one thingumbob, he felt certain of that.

Once inside the ship, he relocked the doors, gave Laura her feed, ate his supper. Then he dragged out the log, made his day's entry, had a look around from the dome. Violet streamers once more were creeping upward from the horizon. He frowned at the encompassing vegetation. What sort of stuff had bred all this in the past? What sort of stuff would this breed in the future? How did it progenerate, anyway?

Wholesale radical mutation presupposed modification of genes by hard radiation in persistent and considerable blasts. You shouldn't get hard radiation on lightweight planets—unless it poured in from the sky. Here, it didn't pour from the sky, or from any place else. In fact, there wasn't any.

He was pretty certain of that fact because he'd a special interest in it and had checked up on it. Hard radiation betokened the presence of radioactive elements which, at a pinch, might be usable as fuel. The ship was equipped to detect such stuff. Among the junk was a cosmiray counter, a radium hen, and a gold-leaf electroscope. The hen and the counter hadn't given so much as one heartening cluck, in fact the only clucks had been Laura's. The electroscope he'd charged on landing and its leaves still formed an inverted V. The air was dry, ionization negligible, and the leaves didn't look likely to collapse for a week.

"Something's wrong with my theorizing," he complained to Laura. "My thinkstuff's not doing its job."

"Not doing its job," echoed Laura faithfully. She cracked a pecan with a grating noise that set his teeth on edge. "I tell you it's a hoodoo ship. I won't sail. No, not even if you pray for me. I won't, I won't, I won't. Nope. Nix. Who's drunk? That hairy Lowlander Mc—"

"Laura!" he said sharply.

"Gillicuddy," she finished with bland defiance. Again she rasped his teeth. "Rings bigger'n Saturn's. I saw them myself. Who's a liar? Yawk! She's down in Grayway Bay, on Tethis. Boy, what a torso!"

He looked at her hard and said, "You're nuts!"

"Sure! Sure, pal! Laura loves nuts. Have one on me."

"O.K.," he accepted, holding out his hand.

Cocking her colorful pate, she pecked at his hand, gravely selected a pecan and gave it to him. He cracked it, chewed on the kernel while starting up the lighting-set. It was almost as if night were waiting for him. Blackness fell even as he switched on the lights.

With the darkness came a keen sense of unease. The dome was the trouble. It blazed like a beacon and there was no way of blacking it out except by turning off the lights. Beacons attracted things, and he'd no desire to become a center of attraction in present circumstances. That is to say, not at night.

Long experience had bred fine contempt for alien animals, no matter how whacky, but outlandish intelligences were a different proposition. So filled was he with the strange inward conviction that last night's phenomenon was something that knew its onions that it didn't occur to him to wonder whether a glowing column possessed eyes or anything equivalent to a sense of sight. If it had occurred to him, he'd have derived no comfort from it. His desire to be weighed in the balance in some eerie, extrasensory way was even less than his desire to be gaped at visually in his slumbers.

An unholy mess of thoughts and ideas was still cooking in his mind when he extinguished the lights, bunked down and went to sleep. Nothing disturbed him this time, but when he awoke with the golden dawn his chest was damp with perspiration and Laura again had sought refuge on his arm.

Digging out breakfast, his thoughts began to marshal themselves as he kept his hands busy. Pouring out a shot of hot coffee, he spoke to Laura.

"I'm durned if I'm going to go scatty trying to maintain a three-watch system single-handed, which is what I'm supposed to do if faced by powers unknown when I'm not able to beat it. Those armchair warriors at headquarters ought to get a taste of situations not precisely specified in the book of rules."

"Burp!" said Laura contemptuously.

"He who fights and runs away lives to fight another day," Steve quoted. "That's the Probe Law. It's a nice, smooth, lovely law—when you can run away. We can't!"

"Burrup!" said Laura with unnecessary emphasis.

"For a woman, your manners are downright disgusting," he told her. "Now I'm not going to spend the brief remainder of my life looking fearfully over my shoulder. The only way to get rid of powers unknown is to convert 'em into powers known and understood. As Uncle Joe told Willie when dragging him to the dentist, the longer we put it off the worse it'll feel."

"Dinna fash y'rsel'," declaimed Laura. "Burp-gollop-bop!"

Giving her a look of extreme distaste, he continued, "So we'll try tossing the bull. Such techniques disconcert bulls sometimes." Standing up, he grabbed Laura, shoved her into her traveling compartment, slid the pane shut. "We're going to blow off forthwith."

Climbing up to the control seat, he stamped on the energizer stud. The tail rockets popped a few times, broke into a subdued roar. Juggling the controls to get the preparatory feel of them, he stepped up the boost until the entire vessel trembled and the rear venturis began to glow cherry-red. Slowly the ship commenced to edge its bulk forward and, as it did so, he fed it the takeoff shot. A half-mile blast kicked backward and the probe ship plummeted into the sky.

Pulling it round in a wide and shallow sweep, he thundered over the borderline of vegetation, the fields of crystals and the hills beyond. In a flash he was plunging through the valley, braking rockets blazing from the nose. This was tricky. He had to co-ordinate forward shoot, backward thrust and downward surge, but like most of his kind he took pride in the stunts performable with these neat little vessels. An awe-inspired audience was all he lacked to make the exhibition perfect. The vessel landed fairly and squarely on the milk-white roof of the alien edifice, slid halfway to the cliff, then stopped.

"Boy," he breathed, "am I good!" He remained in his seat stared around through the dome, and felt that he ought to add, "And too young to die." Occasionally eyeing the chronometer, he waited awhile The boat must have handed that roof a thump sufficient to wake the dead. If anyone were in, they'd soon hotfoot out to see who was heaving hundred-ton bottles at their shingles. Nobody emerged. He gave them half an hour, his hawklike face strained, alert. Then he gave it up, said, "Ah, well," and got out of the seat.

He freed Laura. She came out with ruffled dignity, like a dowager who's paraded into the wrong room. Females were always curious critters, in his logic, and he ignored her attitude, got his gun, unlocked the doors, jumped down onto the roof. Laura followed reluctantly, came to his shoulder as if thereby conferring a great favor.

Walking past the tail to the edge of the roof, he looked down. The sheerness of the five-hundred-foot drop took him aback. Immediately below his feet, the entrance soared four hundred feet up from the ground and he was standing on the hundred-foot lintel surmounting it. The only way down was to walk to the side of the roof and reach the earthy slope in which the building was embedded, seeking a path down that.

He covered a quarter of a mile of roof to get to the slope, his eyes examining the roof's surface as he went, and failing to find one crack or joint in the uniformly smooth surface. Huge as it was, the erection appeared to have been molded all in one piece—a fact which did nothing to lessen inward misgivings. Whoever did this mighty job weren't Zulus!

From ground level the entrance loomed bigger than ever. If there had been a similar gap at the other side of the building, and a clear way through, he could have taken the ship in at one end and out at the other as easily as threading a needle.

Absence of doors didn't seem peculiar; it was difficult to imagine any sort of door huge enough to fill this opening yet sufficiently balanced to enable anyone—or anything—to pull open or shut. With a final, cautious look around which revealed nothing moving in the valley, he stepped boldly through the entrance, blinked his eyes, found interior darkness slowly fading as visual retention lapsed and gave up remembrance of the golden glow outside.

There was a glow inside, a different one, paler, ghastlier, greenish. It exuded from the floor, the walls, the ceiling and the total area of radiation was enough to light the place clearly, with no shadows. He sniffed as his vision adjusted itself. There was a strong smell of ozone mixed with other, unidentifiable odors.

To his right and left, rising hundreds of feet, stood great tiers of transparent cases. He went to the ones on his right and examined them. They were cubes, about a yard each way, made of something like transpex. Each contained three inches of loam from which sprouted a crystal. No two crystals were alike; some small and branchy, others large and indescribably complicated.

Dumb with thought, he went around to the back of the monster tier, found another ten yards behind it. And another behind that. And another and another. All with crystals. The number and variety of them made his head whirl. He could study only the two bottom rows of each rack, but row on row stepped themselves far above his head to within short distance of the roof. Their total number was beyond estimation.

It was the same on the left. Crystals by the thousands. Looking more closely at one especially fine example, he noticed that the front plate of its case bore a small, inobtrusive pattern of dots etched upon the outer surface. Investigation revealed that all cases were similarly marked, differing only in the number and arrangement of the dots. Undoubtedly, some sort of cosmic code used for classification purposes.

"The Oron Museum of Natural History," he guessed, in a whisper.

"You're a liar," squawked Laura violently. "I tell you it's a hoodoo—" She stopped, dumfounded, as her own voice roared through the building in deep, organlike tones, "A hoodoo— A hoodoo—"

"Holy smoke, will you keep quiet!" hissed Steve. He tried to keep watch on the exit and the interior simultaneously. But the voice rumbled away in the distance without bringing anyone to dispute their invasion.

Turning, he paced hurriedly past the first blocks of tiers to the next batteries of exhibits. Jelly blobs in this lot. Small ones, no bigger than his wrist watch, numberable in thousands. None appeared to be alive, he noted.

Sections three, four and five took him a mile into the building as nearly as he could estimate. He passed mosses, lichens and shrubs, all dead but wondrously preserved. By this time he was ready to guess at section six—plants. He was wrong. The sixth layout displayed bugs, including moths, butterflies, and strange, unfamiliar objects resembling chitinous hummingbirds. There was no sample of *Scarabaeus Anderii*, unless it were several hundred feet up. Or unless there was an empty box ready for it—when its day was done.

Who made the boxes? Had it prepared one for him? One for Laura? He visualized himself, petrified forever, squatting in the seventieth case of the twenty-fifth row of the tenth tier in section something-or-other, his front panel duly tagged with its appropriate dots. It was a lousy picture. It made his forehead wrinkle to think of it.

Looking for he knew not what, he plunged steadily on, advancing deeper and deeper into the heart of the building. Not a soul, not a sound, not a footprint. Only that all-pervading smell and the unvarying glow. He had a feeling that the place was visited frequently but never occupied for any worthwhile period of time.

Without bothering to stop and look, he passed an enormous case containing a creature faintly resembling a bison-headed rhinoceros, then other, still larger cases holding equally larger exhibits—all carefully dot-marked.

Finally, he rounded a box so tremendous that it sprawled across the full width of the hall. It contained the grand-pappy of all trees and the great-grand-pappy of all serpents. Behind, for a change, reared five hundred feet high racks of metal cupboards, each cupboard with a stud set in its polished door, each ornamented with more groups of mysteriously arranged dots.

Greatly daring, he pressed the stud on the nearest cupboard and its door swung open with a juicy click. The result proved disappointing. The cupboard was filled with stacks of small, glassy sheets each smothered with dots.

"Super filing-system," he grunted, closing the door. "Old Prof Heggarty would give his right arm to be here."

"Heggarty," said Laura, in a faltering voice. "For Pete's sake!"

He looked at her sharply. She was ruffled and fidgety, showing signs of increasing agitation.

"What's the matter, Chicken?"

She peeked at him, returned her anxious gaze the way they had come, sidestepped to and fro on his shoulder. Her neck feathers started to rise. A nervous cluck came from her beak and she cowered close to his jacket.

"Darn!" he muttered. Spinning on one heel, he raced past successive filing blocks, got into the ten yards' space between the end block and the wall. His gun was out and he kept watch on the front of the blocks while his free hand tried to soothe Laura. She snuggled up close, rubbing her head into his neck and trying to hide under the angle of his jaw.

"Quiet, Honey," he whispered. "Just you keep quiet and stay with Steve, and we'll be all right."

She kept quiet, though she'd begun to tremble. His heart speeded up in sympathy though he could see nothing, hear nothing to warrant it.

Then, while he watched and waited, and still in absolute silence, the interior brightness waxed, became less green, more golden. And suddenly he knew what it was that was coming. He *knew* what it was!

He sank on one knee to make himself as small and inconspicuous as possible. Now his heart was palpitating wildly and no coldness in his mind could freeze it down to slower, more normal beat. The silence, the awful silence of its approach was the unbearable feature. The crushing thud of a weighty foot or hoof would have been better. Colossi have no right to steal along like ghosts.

And the golden glow built up, drowning out the green radiance from floor to roof, setting the multitude of case-surfaces afire with its brilliance. It grew as strong as the golden sky, and stronger. It became all-pervading unendurable, leaving no darkness in which to hide, no sanctuary for little things.

It flamed like the rising sun or like something drawn from the heart of a sun, and the glory of its radiance sent the cowering watcher's mind awhirl. He struggled fiercely to control his brain, to discipline it, to bind it to his fading will—and failed.

With drawn face beaded by sweat, Steve caught the merest fragmentary glimpse of the column's edge appearing from between the stacks of the center aisle. He saw a blinding strip of burnished gold in which glittered a pure white star, then a violent effervescence seemed to occur within his brain and he fell forward into a cloud of tiny bubbles.

Down, down he sank through myriad bubbles and swirls and sprays of iridescent froth and foam which shone and changed and shone anew with every conceivable color. And all the time his mind strove frantically to battle upward and drag his soul to the surface.

Deep into the nethermost reaches he went while still the bubbles whirled around in their thousands and their colors were of numberless hues. Then his progress slowed. Gradually the froth and the foam ceased to rotate upward, stopped its circling, began to swirl in the reverse direction and sink. He was rising! He rose for a lifetime, floating weightlessly, in a dreamlike trance.

The last of the bubbles drifted eerily away, leaving him in a brief hiatus of non-existence—then he found himself sprawled full length on the floor with a dazed Laura clinging to his arm. He blinked his eyes, slowly, several times. They were strained and sore. His heart was still palpitating and his legs felt weak. There was a strange sensation in his stomach as if memory had sickened him with a shock from long, long ago.

He didn't get up from the floor right away; his body was too shaken and his mind too muddled for that. While his wits came back and his composure returned, he lay and noted that all the invading goldness had gone and that again the interior illumination was a dull, shadowless green. Then his eyes found his watch and he sat up, startled. Two hours had flown.

That fact brought him shakily to his feet. Peering around the end of the bank of filing cabinets, he saw that nothing had changed. Instinct told him that the golden visitor had gone and that once more he had this place to himself. Had it become aware of his presence? Had it made him lose consciousness or, if not, why had he lost it? Had it done anything about the ship on the roof?

Picking up his futile gun, he spun it by its stud guard and looked at it with contempt. Then he holstered it, helped Laura onto his shoulder where she perched groggily, went around the back of the racks and still deeper into the building.

"I reckon we're O.K., Honey," he told her. "I think we're too small to be noticed. We're like mice. Who bothers to trap mice when he's got bigger and more important things in mind?" He pulled a face, not liking the mouse comparison. It wasn't flattering either to him or his kind. But it was the best he could think of at the moment. "So, like little mice, let's look for cheese. I'm not giving up just because a big hunk of something has sneaked past and put a scare into us. We don't scare off, do we, Sweetness?"

"No," said Laura unenthusiastically. Her voice was still subdued and her eyes perked apprehensively this way and that. "No scare. I won't sail, I tell you. Blow my sternpipes! Laura loves nuts!"

"Don't you call me a nut!"

"Nuts! Stick to farming—it gets you more eggs. McGillicuddy, the great—"

"Hey!" he warned.

She shut up abruptly. He put the pace on, refusing to admit that his system felt slightly jittery with nervous strain or that anything had got him bothered. But he knew that he'd no desire to be near that sparkling giant again. Once was enough, more than enough. It wasn't that he feared it, but something else, something he was quite unable to define.

Passing the last bank of cabinets, he found himself facing a machine. It was complicated and bizarre—and it was making a crystalline growth. Near it, another and different machine was manufacturing a small, horned lizard. There could be no doubt at all about the process of fabrication because both objects were half-made and both progressed slightly even as he watched. In a couple of hours' time, perhaps less, they'd be finished, and all they'd need would be . . . would be—

The hairs stiffened on the back of his neck and he commenced to run. Endless machines, all different, all making different things, plants, bugs, birds and fungoids. It was done by electroponics, atom fed to atom like brick after brick to build a house. It wasn't synthesis because that's only assembly, and this was assembly plus growth in response to unknown laws. In each of these machines, he knew, was some key or code or cipher, some weird master-control of unimaginable complexity, determining the patterns each was building—and the patterns were infinitely variable.

Here and there a piece of apparatus stood silent, inactive, their tasks complete. Here and there other monstrous layouts were in pieces, either under repair or readied for modification. He stopped by one which had finished its job. It had fashioned a delicately shaded moth which perched motionless like a jeweled statue within its fabrication jar. The creature was perfect as far as he could tell, and all it was waiting for was . . . was—

Beads of moisture popped out on his forehead. All that moth needed was the breath of life!

He forced a multitude of notions to get out of his mind. It was the only way to retain a hold on himself. Divert your attention—take it off this and place it on that! Firmly, he fastened his attention on one tremendous, partly disassembled machine lying nearby. Its guts were exposed, revealing great field coils of dull gray wire. Bits of similar wire lay scattered around on the floor.

Picking up a short piece, he found it surprisingly heavy. He took off his wrist watch, opened its back, brought the wire near to its works. The Venusian jargoon bearing fluoresced immediately. V-jargoons invariably glowed in the presence of near radiation. This unknown metal was a possible fuel. His heart gave a jump at the mere thought of it.

Should he drag out a huge coil and lug it up to the ship? It was very heavy, and he'd need a considerable length of the stuff—if it was usable as fuel. Supposing the disappearance of the coil caused mousetraps to be set before he returned to search anew?

It pays to stop and think whenever you've got time to stop and think; that was a fundamental of Probe Service philosophy. Pocketing a sample of the wire, he sought around other disassembled machines for more. The search took him still deeper into the building and he fought harder to keep his attention concentrated solely on the task. It wasn't easy. There was that dog, for instance, standing there, statuelike, waiting, waiting. If only it had been anything but indubitably and recognizably an Earth-type dog. It was impossible to avoid seeing it. It would be equally impossible to avoid seeing other, even more familiar forms—if they were there.

He'd gained seven samples of different radioactive wires when he gave up the search. A cockatoo ended his peregrinations. The bird stood steadfastly in its jar, its blue plumage smooth and bright, its crimson crest raised, its bright eye fixed in what was not death but not yet life. Laura shrieked at it hysterically and the immense hall shrieked back at her with long-drawn roars and rumbles that reverberated into dim distances. Laura's reaction was too much; he wanted no cause for similar reaction of his own.

He sped through the building at top pace, passing the filing cabinets and the mighty array of exhibition cases unheedingly. Up the loamy side slopes he climbed almost as rapidly as he'd gone down, and he was breathing heavily by the time he got into the ship.

His first action was to check the ship for evidence of interference. There wasn't any. Next, he checked the instruments. The electroscope's leaves were collapsed. Charging them, he watched them flip open and flop together again. The counter showed radiation aplenty. The hen clucked energetically. He'd blundered somewhat—he should have checked up when first he landed on the roof. However, no matter. What lay beneath the roof was now known; the instruments would have advised him earlier but not as informatively.

Laura had her feed while he accompanied her with a swift meal. After that, he dug out his samples of wire. No two were the same gauge and one obviously was far too thick to enter the feed holes of the Kingston-Kanes. It took him half an hour to file it down to a suitable diameter. The original piece of dull gray wire took the first test. Feeding it in, he set the controls to minimum warming-up intensity, stepped on the energizer. Nothing happened.

He scowled to himself. Someday they'd have jobs better than the sturdy but finicky Kingston-Kanes, jobs that'd eat anything eatable. Density and radioactivity weren't enough for these motors; the stuff fed to them had to be right.

Going back to the Kingston-Kanes, he pulled out the wire, found its end fused into shapelessness. Definitely a failure. Inserting the second sample, another gray wire not so dull as the first, he returned to the controls, rammed the energizer. The tail rockets promptly blasted with a low, moaning note and the thrust dial showed sixty per cent normal surge.

Some people would have got mad at that point. Steve didn't. His lean, hawklike features quirked, he felt in his pocket for the third sample, tried that. No soap. The fourth likewise was a flop. The fifth produced a peculiar and rhythmic series of blasts which shook the vessel from end to end and caused the thrust-dial needle to waggle between one hundred twenty per cent and zero. He visualized the Probe patrols popping through space like outboard motors while he extracted the stuff and fed the sixth sample. The sixth roared joyously at one hundred seventy per cent. The seventh sample was another flop.

He discarded all but what was left of the sixth wire. The stuff was about twelve gauge and near enough for his purpose. It resembled deep-colored copper but was not as soft as copper nor as heavy. Hard, springy and light, like telephone wire. If there were at least a thousand yards of it below, and if he could manage to drag it up to the ship, and if the golden thing didn't come along and ball up the works, he might be able to blow free. Then he'd get to some place civilized—if he could find it. The future was based on an appalling selection of "ifs."

The easiest and most obvious way to salvage the needed treasure was to blow a hole in the roof, lower a cable through it, and wind up the wire with the aid of the ship's tiny winch. Problem: how to blow a hole without suitable explosives. Answer: drill the roof, insert unshelled pistol ammunition, say a prayer and pop the stuff off electrically. He tried it, using a hand drill. The bit promptly curled up as if gnawing on a diamond. He drew his gun, bounced a shell off the roof; the missile exploded with a sharp, hard crack and fragments of shell casing whined shrilly into the sky. Where it had struck, the roof bore a blast smudge and a couple of fine scratches.

There was nothing for it but to go down and heave on his shoulders, as much loot as he could carry. And do it right away. Darkness would fall before long, and he didn't want to encounter that golden thing in the dark. It was fateful enough in broad light of day, or in the queer, green glow of the building's interior, but to have it stealing softly behind him as he struggled through the nighttime with his plunder was something of which he didn't care to think.

Locking the ship and leaving Laura inside, he returned to the building, made his way past the mile of cases and cabinets to the machine section at back. He stopped to study nothing on his way. He didn't wish to study anything. The wire was the thing, only the wire. Besides mundane thoughts of mundane wire didn't twist one's mind around until one found it hard to concentrate.

Nevertheless, his mind was afire as he searched. Half of it was prickly with alertness, apprehensive of the golden column's sudden return; the other half burned with excitement at the possibility of release. Outwardly, his manner showed nothing of this; it was calm, assured, methodical.

Within ten minutes he'd found a great coil of the coppery metal, a huge ovoid, intricately wound, lying beside a disassembled machine. He tried to move it, could not shift it an inch. The thing was far too big, too heavy for one to handle. To get it onto the roof he'd have to cut it up and make four trips of it—and some of its inner windings were fused together. So near, so far! Freedom depended upon his ability to move a lump of metal a thousand feet vertically. He muttered some of Laura's words to himself.

Although the wire cutters were ready in his hand, he paused to think, decided to look farther before tackling this job. It was a wise decision which brought its reward, for at a point a mere hundred yards away he came across another, differently shaped coil, wheel-shaped, in good condition, easy to unreel. This again was too heavy to carry, but with a tremendous effort which made his muscles crack he got it up on its rim and proceeded to roll it along like a monster tire.

Several times he had to stop and let the coil lean against the nearest case while he rested a moment. The last such case trembled under the impact of the weighty coil and its shining, spidery occupant stirred in momentary simulation of life. His dislike of the spider shot up with its motion, he made his rest brief, bowled the coil onward.

Violet streaks again were creeping from the horizon when he rolled his loot out of the mighty exit and reached the bottom of the bank. Here, he stopped, clipped the wire with his cutters, took the free end, climbed the bank with it. The wire uncoiled without hindrance until he reached the ship, where he attached it to the winch, wound the loot in, rewound it on the feed spool.

Night fell in one ominous swoop. His hands were trembling slightly but his hawklike face was firm, phlegmatic as he carefully threaded the wire's end through the automatic injector and into the feed hole of the Kingston-Kanes. That done, he slid open Laura's door, gave her some of the fruit they'd picked off the Oron tree. She accepted it morbidly, her manner still subdued, and not inclined for speech.

"Stay inside, Honey," he soothed. "We're getting out of this and going home."

Shutting her in, he climbed into the control seat, switched on the nose beam, saw it pierce the darkness and light up the facing cliff. Then he stamped on the energizer, warmed the tubes. Their bellow was violent and comforting. At seventy per cent better thrust he'd have to be a lot more careful in all his adjustments: it wouldn't do to melt his own tail off when success was within his grasp. All the same, he felt strangely impatient, as if every minute counted, aye, every second!

But he contained himself, got the venturis heated, gave a discreet puff on his starboard steering flare, watched the cliff glide sidewise past as the ship slewed around on its belly. Another puff, then another, and he had the vessel nose-on to the front edge of the roof. There seemed to be a faint aura in the gloom ahead and he switched off his nose beam to study it better.

It was a faint yellow haze shining over the rim of the opposite slope. His back hairs quivered as he saw it. The haze strengthened, rose higher. His eyes strained into the outer pall as he watched it fascinatedly, and his hands were frozen on the controls. There was dampness on his back. Behind him, in her traveling compartment, Laura was completely silent, not even shuffling uneasily as was her wont. He wondered if she were cowering.

With a mighty effort of will which strained him as never before, he shifted his control a couple of notches, lengthened the tail blast. Trembling in its entire fabric, the ship edged forward. Summoning all he'd got, Steve forced his reluctant hands to administer the take-off boost. With a tearing crash that thundered from the cliffs, the little vessel leaped skyward on an arc of fire. Peering through the transpex, Steve caught a fragmentary and foreshortened glimpse of the great golden column advancing majestically over the crest, the next instant it had dropped far behind his tail and his bow was arrowing for the stars.

An immense relief flooded through though his soul though he knew not what there had been to fear. But the relief was there and so great was it that that he worried not at all about where he was bound or for how long. Somehow, he felt certain that if he swept in a wide, shallow curve he'd pick up a Probe beat-note sooner or later. Once he got a beat-note, from any source at all, it would lead him out of the celestial maze.

Luck remained with him, and his optimistic hunch proved correct, for while still among completely strange constellations he caught the faint throb of Hydra III on his twenty-seventh day of sweep. That throb was his cosmic lighthouse beckoning him home.

He let go a wild shriek of "Yipee!" thinking that only Laura heard him—but he was heard elsewhere.

Down on Oron, deep in the monster workshop, the golden giant paused blindly as if listening. Then it slid stealthily along the immense aisles, reached the filing system. A compartment opened, two glassy plates came out.

For a moment the plates contacted the Oron's strange, sparkling substance, became etched with an array of tiny dots. They were returned to the compartment, and the door closed. The golden glory with its imprisoned stars then glided quietly back to the machine section.

Something nearer to the gods had scribbled its notes. Nothing lower in the scale of life could have translated them or deduced their full purport.

In simplest sense, one plate may have been inscribed, "Biped, erect, pink, homo intelligens type P.739, planted on Sol III, Condensation Arm BDB—moderately successful."

Similarly, the other plate may have recorded, "Flapwing, large, hook-beaked, vari-colored, periquito macao type K.8, planted on Sol III, Condensation Arm BDB—moderately successful."

But already the sparkling hobbyist had forgotten his passing notes. He was breathing his essence upon a jeweled moth.

HOMO SAPS

Astounding, December 1941

Majestically the long caravan emerged from the thick belt of blue-green Martian *doltha* weed and paraded into the Saloma Desert. Forty-four camels stalked along with the swaying gait and high-faluting expression of their kind. All were loaded. Beneath the burdens their deliberate, unhurried feet dug deeply into the long waves of fine, pinkish sand.

The forty-fifth animal, which was in the lead, was not a camel. It was daintier, more shapely, had a beige-colored coat and only one hump. A racing dromedary. But its expression was fully as supercilious as that worn by the others.

Sugden had the dromedary, Mitchell was on the following camel, and Ali Fa'oum formed the rearguard of one. The forty-two burdened beasts in between had modest loads and immodest odors. Ali, at the back, got the benefit of the last. It didn't matter. He was used to it. He'd miss it if it wasn't there.

Twisting in his seat, Sugden tilted his head toward the sinking sun, and said, "They'll put on the brakes pretty soon, I guess."

Mitchell nodded lugubriously. He'd sworn camels across Arabia, cursed them through the Northern Territory of Australia, and had oathed them three times around Mars. His patience was no better than on the day he'd started. Within his bosom burned a theory that if there had never been camels there would have been no such thing as Oriental fatalism.

Abruptly the dromedary stopped, went down fore legs first, back legs next and settled with a sickening heave. It didn't bother to look behind. There wasn't any need, anyway. The rest of the cavalcade followed suit, front legs first, hind legs next, the same heave. A box with loose fastenings parted from its indifferent bearer and flopped into the sand.

Ali, now compelled to dismount, did so. He found the fodder, distributed it along the resting line. Ignoring the white men, the animals ate slowly and with maddening deliberation, their disinterested eyes studying the far horizon. Ali started grooming them as they ate. He'd groomed them in Port Tewfik thirty years ago. He was still doing it. They still let him get on with it, their expressions lordly.

Lighting a cigarette, Sugden gave it a savage suck, and said, "And they talk about mules!"

Slowly the dromedary turned its head, gave him a contemptuous look. Then it resumed its contemplation of distance. It chewed monotonously and methodically, its bottom lip pursed in silent scorn.

"Same distance, same time," voiced Mitchell sourly. Thumping the heel of his jackboot he killed a Martian twelve-legged sand spider. "Never more, never less. They clock on and clock off and they work no overtime."

"They've got us where they want us." Sugden blew a twin funnel of smoke from itching nostrils, stared distastefully at what had been the spider. "They're the only things that can cover these deserts apart from the Martians themselves. If we had tractors, we'd use tractors if there was any gasoline on this planet."

"Some day, when I'm bloated with riches," Mitchell pursued, "I'm going to be eccentric. I'm going to get them to build me a superhyperultra rocketship. One that'll carry some real tonnage."

"Then what?" inquired Sugden.

"Then start from where I left off here—only with elephants."

"Ha-ha!" laughed Sugden, with artificial violence.

The dromedary turned its head again. It made a squelching sound with its slowly moving mouth. The noise was repeated all the way along the line until the mount of Ali emitted the final salivary smack. Ali proceeded with his grooming.

Mitchell snorted and said, complainingly, "You'd think the whole darned lot had loose dental plates." He started to open up the thermic meal pack. "And they stink."

"And I don't like their faces," added Sugden.

"Me neither. Give me a cigarette, will you?" Mitchell lit it, let it hang from his bottom lip. "To think the Martians kowtow to them and treat us like dirt. Funny the way they've acted like that since the first camel was imported."

"Yeah, I'd like to get to the root of it sometime."

"Try talking to a Martian. Might as well talk to a gatepost, and—*yeouw,* this thermic's red-hot!" Mitchell coddled his fingers. "Sixty years and never a word out of them. They ought to be able to talk, but won't." He heaved the meal pack onto its telescopic legs, slid out its trays. "Hi, Ali, come and give us a hand."

"No, sah. Finish these first. One hour."

"See? Removing his solar topee, Mitchell flung it on the sand. "The stinkers first, us last."

The igloo-shaped lumps of Jenkinsville showed on the horizon at sunset next day. Nobody knew the Martian name of the place, but its first discoverer had been one Hiram Jenkins, originally of Key West, Florida. So from then on it was Jenkinsville. The place was precisely fourteen miles away. Nevertheless, the dromedary squatted and the rest did likewise.

Sugden dismounted with the usual scowl, raked out the usual battered cigarette, heard Mitchell air the usual curse. It couldn't have been a curse of much potency since the curve on the grief chart remained constant, with never a dip.

The same box fell into the sand again, making the same dismal thump. Phlegmatically, Ali got on with the feeding and grooming rigmarole. In superior silence the forty-five animals rested and masticated and gazed at nearby Jenkinsville much as Sugden had gazed at the squashed spider.

"I've a persistent notion," said Sugden, his sand-chafed eyes on the energetic Mr. Fa'oum, "that he sneaks up at midnight and worships them. First time I catch him I'll prove he can't salaam without presenting his rumps for suitable retaliation."

"Humph!" Mitchell wrestled with the meal pack, burned his fingers as he'd done a thousand times before, let out his thousandth *yeouw!* "Hi, Ali!"

"One hour," said Ali, firmly.

"I'm clinging to life," announced Mitchell, speaking to the general outlines of Jenkinsville, "so's I can outlive the lot. One by one, as they die on me, I'm going to skin 'em. I'll make foot mats of their stinking pelts. I'll get married, wipe my feet coming in and going out and every time the cuckoo clock puts the bean on me."

The sixth camel from the front rumbled its insides. Slowly the rumble moved from stomach to gullet, ended in an emphatic burp. Taking its blank eyes off Jenkinsville, the dromedary looked backward with open approval. Mitchell enjoyed a furious kick at the thermic, denting its side.

"Now, now!" said Sugden.

Mitchell gave him a look of sudden death, twitched a tray from the thermic. He did it wholeheartedly. The tray shot clean out of the container, tilted against his ineffectual grasp, poured a mess of hot beans in tomato sauce over his jackboots. Ali paused and watched as he brought a bundle of night coats to the complacent camels. Sugden stared at Mitchell. So did Ali. Also the camels.

Looking first at Sugden, then at his boots, Mitchell said, "Notice that?"

"Yes, I've noticed it," admitted Sugden, gravely.

"Funny, isn't it?"

"Not at all. I think it unfortunate."

"Well," said Mitchell, stabbing a finger at the observing line, "*they* think it's funny."

"Oh, forget it. All animals are curious."

"Curious? Hah!" Lugging off his boots, Mitchell hefted them, swung them around, gauged their weight and handiness. All the time his eyes were on the dromedary. In the end, he changed his mind, cleaned his boots in the sand, then put them on. "They're seeing the world at our expense—and they all look at me when I do this to myself."

"Aw, let's eat," soothed Sugden. "We're hungry, and hunger makes one short-tempered. We'll feel better afterward. Besides, we'll be in Jenkinsville early in the morning."

"Sure, we will. We'll be in Jenkinsville first thing in the morning. We'll offer our junk for all the mallow seeds we can get, and if we don't dispose of the lot—as we probably won't—we'll start another one-hundred-mile hike to Dead Plains to shoot the balance." Mitchell glowered at the cosmos. "If, by some miracle unique in the records of Martian trading, we switch all we've got, we'll start back on our one hundred fifty miles of purgatory to Lemport, accompanied by forty-four camels, forty-four double-humped skunks."

"And one dromedary," Sugden reminded, delicately.

"And one one-humped skunk," agreed Mitchell. He glared across the sands to where the said skunk was enjoying its own processes with true Arabian aplomb.

"If you're not going to eat," announced Sugden, "I am!" He slid another tray from the thermic, stabbed himself a couple of steaming pinnawursts. He was very partial to minced livers of the plump and succulent pinna birds.

As the food went cold in the Martian evening, Mitchell joined in. The pair ate ruminatively, in unconscious imitation the camels.

Three hours beyond the flaming dawn the caravan slouched the market place in Jenkinsville and unloaded with many animal grunts and much Terrestrial profanity. Martians came crowding in, more or less ignored the white men, took a little more notice of Ali Fa'oum, but paid most attention to the camels. For a long time they looked at the camels and the camels looked at them, each side examining the other with the aloofish interest of ghosts discovering fairies.

Mitchell and Sugden let them get on with it. They knew that in due time, when they thought fit, the natives would turn to business. Meanwhile, the interim could be used for making all the necessary preparations, setting up the stalls, displaying the stocks, getting the books and scales ready. Each Martian had his hoard of mallow seeds, some small bags, some big bags, some with two or three.

The seeds were what the traders were after. From this product of the Martian desert mallow could be distilled—a genuine cure for Terrestrial cancer. This disease would have been wiped out long ago if only the temperamental mallow were cultivatable—which it wasn't. It grew wherever it took the fancy and nowhere else. It didn't fancy anywhere on Earth. Hence, its short, glossy-leafed bushes had to be searched for, and Martians did the searching.

In ones and twos, and in complete silence, the Martians drifted from the camels to the stalls. They were large-eyed beings, with big chests and flop ears, but otherwise human in shape. Though literally dumb, they were fairly intelligent. Terrestrial surgeons opined that the Martian voice box once had functioned, but now was petrified by centuries of disuse. Maybe they were right. Mitchell and Sugden didn't know or very much care. The traders high-pressured their clients in deft sign language, sometimes helped out by writing and sketches.

An old Martian got his bag weighed, was credited with one hundred eighty dollars in gold, solid, heavy, international spondulics. Mitchell showed him a roll of batik-patterned broadcloth and a half-plate glossy photograph of Superba de la Fontaine attired in a sarong of the same material. He didn't mention that the fair Superba was originally Prunella Teitelbaum of Terre Haute. All the same, the old chap liked neither. He pulled a face at Mitchell, indicated that both were trash.

"They're getting finicky," complained Mitchell, addressing the God of Commerce. Irefully, he swung a roll of Harris tweed along the roughwood counter, fingered it, smelled it, held it up for his customers to enjoy the heathery odor of the fabric. The customer approved, indicated that he'd take three arm spans of same. Mitchell sliced off the required length, rolled it dexterously, tossed it over.

Way down in the Communal Hall beyond the serried rows of red granite igloos a band of tribal beaters started playing on a choir of gongs. The instruments ranged all the way from a tiny, tinkling silver hand disk up to an enormous copper cylinder twenty feet in diameter. Every note was powerful and pure, but the tune was blatant torture.

Scowling, Mitchell said to the old fellow, "Now how about a watch? So long as you've got the time, you'll never have to ask a policeman. Here's the very one, a magnificent, fifty-jeweled, ten-day chronometer, rectified for Mars, checked by the Deimos Observatory, and guaranteed by Mitchell & Sugden."

He tried to put it all into signs, sweating as he did it. The Martian sniffed, rejected the timepiece, chose five cheap alarm clocks. Moreover, he went right through the stock of several dozen in order to pick himself five with differing notes. Then he selected a gold bangle set with turquoises, a midget radio, an aluminum coffee percolator and a small silver pepper pot into which he solemnly emptied the inevitable packet of Martian snuff.

"That leaves you two bucks seventy," said Mitchell. The old fellow took his balance in cigarettes and canned coffee, toddled back to pay his respects to the camels. There was still a gang busy soul-mingling with the animals. "Damn the stinkers!" Mitchell heaved a huge bag of seeds onto the scales. The needle swung around. "Seven hundred smackers," he breathed. He scrawled the amount in big figures with a blue pencil, held it out to the new customer.

This one was a young Martian, taller than the average. He nodded, produced a five-year-old catalogue, opened it, pointed to illustrations, conveyed by many signs that he wanted the cash put to his credit until he had enough to get an automobile.

"No use," said Mitchell. "No gasoline. No go. No soap!" He made snakes of his arms in his efforts to explain the miserable and absolute impotence of an automobile sans juice. The Martian watched gravely, started to argue with many further references to the catalogue. Mitchell called in Sugden to help.

After ten minutes, Sugden said: "I get it. He wants a heap with a producer-gas plant. He thinks he can run it on local deadwood."

"For Pete's sake!" groaned Mitchell. "Now they're going Broadway on us! How in the name of the seven devils can we get one here?"

"In pieces," Sugden suggested. "We'll try, anyway. Why not? It may start a cult. We might end up with a million jujubes apiece. We might both be Martian producer-gas automobile tycoons, and be ambushed by blondes like they say in magazines. It'll cost this guy an unholy sum, but it's his sum. Attend to the customer, Jimson, and see that he's satisfied."

With doubtful gloom, Mitchell made out a credit slip for seven hundred, handed it across. Then he took a deep breath, looked around, noticed camels and Martians regarding each other with the same philosophical interest. Some of the animals were munching choice tidbits offered them by the natives.

More bags, more weighings, more arguments all through the rest of the day. As usual, the clients didn't want a good proportion of the Mitchell-Sugden stock and again as usual, some of them wanted things not in stock and difficult to obtain.

On the previous trip one Martian had taken a hundred phonograph records and had ordered some minor electrical apparatus. Now he turned up, claiming his apparatus, didn't want another disk, put in an urgent order for a couple of radio transmitter tubes of special design. After half an hour's semaphoring, he had to draw the tubes before Mitchell understood what was wanted. There was no law against supplying such stuff, so he booked the order.

"Oh, Jiminy," he said, wearily, "why can't you guys talk like civilized people?"

The Martian was faintly surprised by this comment. He considered it solemnly, his big, grave eyes wandering from the liverish Mitchell to the camels and back again. The dromedary nodded, smirked, and let the juice of an overripe *wushkin* drool from its bottom lip. The Martian signed Mitchell an invitation to follow him.

It was on the verge of dusk and time for ceasing operations, anyway. Leaving his exhausted partner to close the post, Mitchell trailed the Martian. Fifteen years before he had trailed one to an illegal still and had crawled back gloriously blotto. It might happen again.

They passed the camels now being groomed by the officious Ali Fa'oum, wandered through the town to a large igloo halfway between the market place and the northern outskirts. A mile to the south the gongs of Communal Hall were sounding a raucous evensong. The big tremblor caused dithers in the digestive system.

Inside the igloo was a room filled with a jumble of apparatus, some incomplete, some discarded but not thrown out. The sight did not surprise Mitchell, since it was well known that the Martians had scientific abilities along their own peculiar lines. His only emotion was a feeling of disappointment. No still.

Connecting up a thing looking like a homemade radio receiver with a tiny loud-speaker, the Martian drew from its innards a length of thin cable terminating in a small, silvery object which he promptly swallowed. With the cable hanging out of his mouth, his big eyes staring solemnly at Mitchell, he fiddled with dials. Suddenly, an inhuman, metallic voice oozed from the loud-speaker.

"Spich! This artificial spich! Just made him. Very hard—cannot do much!"

"Ah!" said Mitchell, faintly impressed.

"So you get me tubes. Do better then—see?"

"Sure," agreed Mitchell. Then the overwhelming thought struck him that he was the first Terrestrial to hold vocal conversation with a Martian. Front-page news! He was no pressman, but he was trader enough to feel that there ought to be a thousand frogskins in this interview if he handled it right. What would a journalist do? Oh, yes, ask questions. "Why can't you guys speak properly?" he asked, with unjournalistic awkwardness.

"Properly?" squawked the loud-speaker. The Martian was astonished. "We do talk properly. Ten thousand years ago we ceased this noise-talk of low-life forms and talked here"—he touched his forehead—"so!"

"You mean you converse telepathically?"

"Of course—same as camels."

"What?" yelled Mitchell.

"Sure! They are high form of life."

"Like hell they are," bawled Mitchell, his face purpling.

"Hah!" The Martian was amused. "I prove it. They talk here." Again he touched his forehead. "And not here, like you." He touched his throat. "They toil in moderation, eat reasonably, rest adequately, wear no clothes, pay no taxes, suffer no ills, have no worries, enjoy much contemplation and are happy."

"But they darned well work," shouted Mitchell. He smacked his chest. "And for me."

"As all must, high and low alike. You also work for them. Who works the hardest ? You see—*glug-glug!*" The loud-speaker gulped into silence. Hurriedly, the Martian made adjustments to the set and presently the speaker came to fresh but weaker life. "Battery nearly gone. So sorry!"

"Camels, a high form of life!" jeered Mitchell. "Ha-ha! I'll believe it when I've got a lemon-colored beard nine feet long."

"Does the delectable pinna know the superiority of our bellies? How can *you* measure the mental stature of a camel where there is no common basis? You cannot talk inside the head; you have never known at any time what a camel is thinking." The loud-speaker's fading crackle coincided with the Martian's patronizing chuckle. Mitchell disliked both noises.

"So long as it knows what I'm thinking, that's all that matters."

"Which is entirely your own point of view." Again the Martian registered his amusement. "There are others, you know, but all the same—*crackle, crackle, pop!*" The apparatus finally gave up the ghost and none of its operator's adjustments could bring it back to life. He took out the artificial larynx through which he had been talking, signed that the interview was over.

Mitchell returned to the camp in decidedly unsweet humor. Sugden met him, and said, "We shifted sixty percent. That means another hike starting tomorrow morning. A long one, too."

"Aaargh!" said Mitchell. He began to load the thermics. Sugden gave him a look, holed down in his sleeping bag and left him to work it off.

Jenkinsville was buried in slumber and Sugden was snoring loudly by the time he finished, He kept muttering to himself, "Homo saps, huh? Don't make me laugh!" all the while he worked. Then he got the last thermic sealed up, killed a spider he found scuttling around in an empty can, had a last look over the camp.

The camels were a row of blanketed, gurgling shapes in the general darkness, with the nursemaidish Ali Fa'oum a lesser shape somewhere near them.

Looking at them, Mitchell declaimed, "If I thought for one moment that you misshapen gobs of stink-meat knew what I was saying, I'd tell you something that'd take the supercilious expression off your faces for all time!"

With that blood-pressure reliever, he started back to his own sleeping bag, got nearly there, suddenly turned and raced toward the camels. His kick brought Ali into immediate wakefulness, and his bellow could be heard all over the camp.

"Which one of them made that noise?"

"No can tell," protested Ali, sleepily. "Forty-four of them an' dromedary. How tell who makes noise? Only Allah know!"

Sugden's voice came through the night, saying, "Mitch, for Heaven's sake!"

"Oh, all right." Mitchell returned, found his torch. "Telepathic bunk!" he muttered. "We'll see!" By the light of his torch he cut a playing card into forty-five pieces, numbered them with a pencil, shuffled them in the dark, shut his eyes and picked one. *Number twelve.*

Waking again, Sugden stuck his head out and said, suspiciously. "What're you doing now?"

"Crocheting for my bottom drawer," said Mitchell. Ignoring the other, he examined his gun by the light of the torch, found it fully loaded with ten powerful dynoshells. Smiling happily, he murmured, "Number twelve!" and lay down to sleep.

Ali shook him into wakefulness with the first flush of dawn. Sugden was already up, fully dressed and looking serious.

"One of the camels has scrammed," he announced. "Number twelve."

"Eh!" Mitchell shot up like a jack-in-the-box.

Sugden said, "And I don't like that funny look you put on when I told you it was my camel, not one of yours. Have you pinned an abracadabra on it?"

"Me? What, me?" Mitchell tried to look innocent. "Oh, no!"

"Because if you have, you'd better unhex it mighty quick."

"Oh, we'll find it," comforted Mitchell. He got dressed, stowed away his gun, made the mental reservation that he'd do nothing about number twelve, nothing at all. He made the thought as powerful as he could.

The missing animal was waiting for them beside the trail one hour out from Jenkinsville. It took its position in the string as of old habit. Nobody said anything. It was a long time since Mitchell had been so quiet.

After a while, Sugden's dromedary turned its neck and made a horrible face at Mitchell riding right behind. He still said nothing. Deliberately, the caravan swayed on.

I Am Nothing

Astounding, July 1952

David Korman rasped, "Send them the ultimatum."

"Yes, sir, but—"

"But what?"

"It may mean war."

"What of it?"

"Nothing, sir." The other sought a way out. "I merely thought—"

"You are not paid to think," said Korman, acidly. "You are paid only to obey orders."

"Of course, sir. Most certainly." Gathering his papers he backed away hurriedly. "I shall have the ultimatum forwarded to Lani at once."

"You better had!" Korman stared across his ornate desk, watched the door close. Then he voiced an emphatic, "Bah!"

A lickspittle. He was surrounded by lickspittles, cravens, weaklings. On all sides were the spineless ready to jump to his command, eager to fawn upon him. They smiled at him with false smiles, hastened into pseudo-agreement with every word he uttered, gave him exaggerated respect that served to cover their inward fears.

There was a reason for all this. He, David Korman, was strong. He was strong in the myriad ways that meant full and complete strength. With his broad body, big jowls, bushy brows and hard gray eyes he looked precisely what he was: a creature of measureless power, mental and physical.

It was good that he should be like this. It was a law of Nature that the weak must give way to the strong. A thoroughly sensible law. Besides, this world of Morcine needed a strong man. Morcine was one world in a cosmos full of potential competitors, all of them born of some misty, long-forgotten planet near a lost sun called Sol. Morcine's duty to itself was to grow strong at the expense of the weak. Follow the natural law.

His heavy thumb found the button on his desk, pressed it, and he said into the little silver microphone, "Send in Fleet Commander Rogers at once."

There was a knock at the door and he snapped, "Come in." Then, when Rogers had reached the desk, he informed, "We have sent the ultimatum."

"Really, sir? Do you suppose they'll accept it?"

"Doesn't matter whether they do or don't," Korman declared. "In either event we'll get our own way." His gaze upon the other became challenging. "Is the fleet disposed in readiness exactly as ordered?"

"It is, sir."

"You are certain of that? You have checked it in person?"

"Yes, sir."

"Very well. These are my orders: the fleet will observe the arrival on Lani of the courier bearing our demands. It will allow twenty-four hours, for receipt of a satisfactory reply."

"And if one does not come?"

"It will attack one minute later in full strength. Its immediate task will be to capture and hold an adequate ground base. Having gained it, reinforcements will be poured in and the territorial conquest of the planet can proceed."

"I understand, sir." Rogers prepared to leave. "Is there anything more?"

"Yes," said Korman. "I have one other order. When you are about to seize this base my son's vessel must be the first to land upon it."

Rogers blinked and protested nervously, "But, sir, as a young lieutenant he commands a small scout bearing twenty men. Surely one of our major battleships should be—"

"My son lands first!" Standing up, Korman leaned forward over his desk. His eyes were cold. "The knowledge that Reed Korman, my only child, was in the forefront of the battle will have an excellent psychological effect upon the ordinary masses here. I give it as my order."

"What if something happens?" murmured Rogers, aghast. "What if he should become a casualty, perhaps be killed?"

"That," Korman pointed out, "will enhance the effect."

"All right, sir." Rogers swallowed and hurried out, his features strained.

Had the responsibility for Reed Korman's safety been placed upon his own shoulders? Or was that character behind the desk genuine in his opportunist and dreadful fatalism? He did not know. He knew only that Korman could not be judged by ordinary standards.

Blank-faced and precise, the police escort stood around while Korman got out of the huge official car. He gave them his usual austere look-over while the chauffeur waited, his hand holding the door open. Then Korman mounted the steps to his home, heard the car door close at the sixth step. Invariably it was the sixth step, never the fifth or seventh.

Inside, the maid waited on the same corner of the carpet, her hands ready for his hat, gloves and cloak. She was stiff and starched and never looked directly at him. Not once in fourteen years had she met him eye to eye.

With a disdainful grunt he brushed past her and went into the dining room, took his seat, studied his wife across a long expanse of white cloth filled with silver and crystal.

She was tall and blond and blue-eyed and once had seemed supremely beautiful. Her willowy slenderness had made him think with pleasure of her moving in his arms with the sinuosity of a snake. Now, her slight curves had gained angularity. Her submissive eyes wore crinkles that were not the marks of laughter.

"I've had enough of Lani," he announced. "We're precipitating a showdown. An ultimatum has been sent."

"Yes, David."

That was what he had expected her to say. He could have said it for her. It was her trademark, so to speak; always had been, always would be.

Years ago, a quarter of a century back, he had said with becoming politeness, "Mary, I wish to marry you."

"Yes, David."

She had not wanted it—not in the sense that he had wanted it. Her family had pushed her into the arrangement and she had gone where shoved. Life was like that: the pushers and the pushed. Mary was of the latter class. The fact had taken the spice out of romance. The conquest had been too easy. Korman insisted on conquest but he liked it big. Not small.

Later on, when the proper time had come, he had told her, "Mary, I want a son."

She had arranged it precisely as ordered. No slipups. No presenting him with a fat and impudent daughter by way of hapless obstetrical rebellion. A son, eight pounds, afterward named Reed. He had chosen the name.

A faint scowl lay over his broad face as he informed, "Almost certainly it means war."

"Does it, David?"

It came without vibrancy or emotion. Dull-toned, her pale oval features expressionless, her eyes submissive. Now and again he wondered whether she hated him with a fierce, turbulent hatred so explosive that it had to be held in check at all costs. He could never be sure of that. Of one thing he was certain: she feared him and had from the very first.

Everyone feared him. Everyone without exception. Those who did not at first meeting soon learned to do so. He saw to that in one way or another. It was good to be feared. It was an excellent substitute for other emotions one has never had or known.

When a child he had feared his father long and ardently; also his mother. Both of them so greatly that their passing had come as a vast relief. Now it was his turn. That, too, was a natural law, fair and logical. What is gained from one generation should be passed to the next. What is denied should likewise be denied.

Justice.

"Reed's scoutship has joined the fleet in readiness for action."

"I know, David."

His eyebrows lifted. "How do you know?"

"I received a letter from him a couple of hours ago." She passed it across.

He was slow to unfold the stiff sheet of paper. He knew what the first two words would be. Getting it open, he found it upside-down, reversed it and looked.

"Dear Mother."

That was her revenge.

"Mary. I want a son."

So she had given him one—and then taken him away.

Now there were letters, perhaps two in one week or one in two months according to the ship's location. Always they were written as though addressing both, always they contained formal love to both, formal hope that both were keeping well.

But always they began, "Dear Mother."

Never, "Dear Father."

Revenge!

Zero hour came and went. Morcine was in a fever of excitement and preparation. Nobody knew what was happening far out in space, not even Korman. There was a time-lag due to sheer distance. Beamed signals from the fleet took many hours to come in.

The first word went straight to Korman's desk where he posed ready to receive it. It said the Lanians had replied with a protest and what they called an appeal to reason. In accordance with instructions the fleet commander had rejected this as unsatisfactory. The attack was on.

"They plead for reasonableness," he growled. "That means they want us to go soft. Life isn't made for the soft." He threw a glance forward. "Is it?"

"No, sir," agreed the messenger with alacrity.

"Tell Bathurst to put the tape on the air at once."

"Yes, sir."

When the other had gone he switched his midget radio and waited. It came in ten minutes, the long, rolling, grandiloquent speech he'd recorded more than a month before. It played on two themes: righteousness and strength, especially strength.

The alleged causes of the war were elucidated in detail, grimly but without ire. That lack of indignation was a telling touch because it suggested the utter inevitability of the present situation and the fact that the powerful have too much justified self-confidence to emote.

As for the causes, he listened to them with boredom. Only the strong know there is but one cause of war. All the other multitudinous reasons recorded in the history books were not real reasons at all. They were nothing but plausible pretexts. There was but one root-cause that persisted right back to the dim days of the jungle. When two monkeys want the same banana, that is war.

Of course, the broadcasting tape wisely refrained from putting the issue so bluntly and revealingly. Weak stomachs require pap. Red meat is exclusively for the strong. So the great antennae of the world network comported themselves accordingly and catered for the general dietary need.

After the broadcast had finished on a heartening note about Morcine's overwhelming power, he leaned back in his chair and thought things over. There was no question of bombing Lani into submission from the upper reaches of its atmosphere. All its cities cowered beneath bombproof hemispherical force fields. Even if they had been wide open he would not have ordered their destruction. It is empty victory to win a few mounds of rubble.

He'd had enough of empty victories. Instinctively, his gray eyes strayed toward the bookcase on which stood the photograph he seldom noticed and then no more than absently. For years it had been there, a subconsciously-observed, taken-for-granted object like the inkpot or radiant heat panel, but less useful than either.

She wasn't like her picture now. Come to think of it, she hadn't been really like it *then*. She had given him obedience and fear before he had learned the need for these in lieu of other needs. At that time he had wanted something else that had not been forthcoming. So long as he could remember, to his very earliest years, it had never been forthcoming, not from anyone, never, never, never.

He jerked his mind back to the subject of Lani. The location of that place and the nature of its defenses determined the pattern of conquest. A ground base must be won, constantly replenished with troops, arms and all auxiliary services. From there the forces of Morcine must expand and, bit by bit, take over all unshielded territory until at last the protected cities stood alone in fateful isolation. The cities would then be permitted to sit under their shields until starved into surrender.

Acquisition of enemy territory was the essential aim. This meant that despite space-going vessels, force shields and all the other redoubtable gadgets of ultra-modernism, the ordinary foot soldier remained the final arbiter of victory. Machines could assault and destroy. Only men could take and hold.

Therefore this was going to be no mere five-minute war. It would run on for a few months, perhaps even a year, with spasms of old style land-fighting as strong points were attacked and defended. There would be bombing perforce limited to road blocks, strategic junctions, enemy assembly and regrouping areas, unshielded but stubborn villages.

There would be some destruction, some casualties. But it was better that way. Real conquest comes only over real obstacles, not imaginary ones. In her hour of triumph Morcine would be feared. Korman would be feared. The feared are respected and that is proper and decent.

If one can have nothing more.

Pictorial records in full color and sound came at the end of the month. Their first showing was in the privacy of his own home to a small audience composed of himself, his wife, a group of government officials and assorted brass hats.

Unhampered by Lanian air defenses, weak from the beginning and now almost wiped out, the long black ships of Morcine dived into the constantly widening base and unloaded great quantities of supplies. Troops moved forward against tough but spasmodic opposition, a growing weight of armored and motorized equipment going with them.

The recording camera trundled across an enormous bridge with thick girders fantastically distorted and with great gaps temporarily filled in. It took them through seven battered villages which the enemy had either defended or given cause to believe they intended to defend. There were shots of crater-pocked roads, skeletal houses, a blackened barn with a swollen horse lying in a field nearby.

And an action-take of an assault on a farmhouse. A patrol, suddenly fired on, dug in and radioed back. A monster on huge, noisy tracks answered their call, rumbled laboriously to within four hundred yards of the objective, spat violently and lavishly from its front turret. A great splash of liquid fell on the farmhouse roof, burst into roaring flame. Figures ran out, seeking cover of an adjacent thicket. The sound track emitted rattling noises. The figures fell over, rolled, jerked, lay still.

The reel ended and Korman said, "I approve it for public exhibition." Getting out of his seat, he frowned around, added, "I have one criticism. My son has taken command of a company of infantry. He is doing a job, like any other man. Why wasn't he featured?"

"We would not depict him except with your approval, sir," said one.

"I not only approve—I order it. Make sure that he is shown next time. Not predominantly. Just sufficiently to let the people see for themselves that he is there, sharing the hardships and the risks."

"Very well, sir."

They packed up and went away. He strolled restlessly on the thick carpet in front of the electric radiator.

"Do them good to know Reed is among those present," he insisted.

"Yes, David." She had taken up some knitting, her needles going *click-click*.

"He's my son."

"Yes, David."

Stopping his pacing, he chewed his bottom lip with irritation. "Can't you say anything but that?"

She raised her eyes. "Do you wish me to?"

"Do I wish!" he echoed. His fists were tight as he resumed his movements to and fro while she returned to her needles.

What did she know of wishes?

What does anyone know?

By the end of four months the territorial grip on Lani had grown to one thousand square miles while men and guns continued to pour in. Progress had been slower than expected. There had been minor blunders at high level, a few of the unforeseeable difficulties that invariably crop up when fighting at long range, and resistance had been desperate where least expected. Nevertheless, progress was being made. Though a little postdated, the inevitable remained inevitable.

Korman came home, heard the car door snap shut at the sixth step. All was as before except that now a part of the populace insisted on assembling to cheer him indoors. The maid waited, took his things. He stumped heavily to the inner room,

"Reed is being promoted to captain."

She did not answer.

Standing squarely before her, he demanded. "Well, aren't you interested?"

"Of course, David." Putting aside her book, she folded long, thin-fingered hands, looked toward the window.

"What's the matter with you?"

"The matter?" The blond eyebrows arched as her eyes came up. "Nothing is the matter with me. Why do you ask?"

"I can tell." His tones harshened a little. "And I can guess. You don't like Reed being out there. You disapprove of me sending him away from you. You think of him as your son and not mine. You—"

She faced him calmly. "You're rather tired, David. And worried."

"I am not tired," he denied with unnecessary loudness. "Neither am I worried. It is the weak who worry."

"The weak have reason."

"I haven't."

"Then you're just plain hungry." She took a seat at the table. "Have something to eat. It will make you feel better."

Dissatisfied and disgruntled, he got through his evening meal. Mary was holding something back, he knew that with the sureness of one who had lived with her for half his lifetime. But he did not have to force it out of her by autocratic methods. When and only when he had finished eating she surrendered her secret voluntarily. The way in which she did it concealed the blow to come.

"There has been another letter from Reed."

"Yes?" He fingered a glass of wine, felt soothed by food but reluctant to show it. "I know he's happy, healthy, and in one piece. If anything went wrong, I'd be the first to learn of it."

"Don't you want to see what says?" She took it from a little walnut bureau, offered it to him.

He eyed it without reaching for it. "Oh, I suppose it's all the usual chitchat about the war."

"I think you ought to read it," she persisted.

"Do you?" Taking it from her hand he held it unopened, surveyed her curiously. "Why should this particular missive call for my attention? Is it any different from the others? I know without looking that it is addressed to you. Not to me. To you! Never in his life has Reed written a letter specifically to me."

"He writes to both of us."

"Then why can't he start with, 'Dear Father and Mother' ?"

"Probably it just hasn't occurred to him that you would feel touchy about it. Besides, it's cumbersome."

"Nonsense!"

"Well, you might as well look at it as argue about it unread. You'll have to know sooner or later."

That last remark stimulated him into action. Unfolding it, he grunted as he noted the opening words, then went through ten paragraphs descriptive of war service on another planet. It was the sort of stuff every fighting man sent home. Nothing especial about it. Turning the page, he perused the brief remainder. His face went taut and heightened in color.

"Better tell you I've become the willing slave of a Lanian girl. Found her in what little was left of the village of Bluelake which had taken a pretty bad beating from our heavies. She was all alone and, as far as I could discover, seemed to be the sole survivor. Mom, she's got nobody. I'm sending her home on the hospital ship *Istar*. The captain jibbed but dared not refuse a Korman. Please meet her for me and look after her until I get back."

Flinging it onto the table, he swore lengthily and with vim, finishing, "The young imbecile."

Saying nothing, Mary sat watching him, her hands clasped together

"The eyes of a whole world are on him," he raged. "As a public figure, as the son of his father, he is expected to be an example. And what does he do?"

She remained silent.

"Becomes the easy victim of some designing little skirt who is quick to play upon his sympathies. An enemy female!"

"She must be pretty," said Mary.

"*No* Lanians are pretty," he contradicted in what came near to a shout. "Have you taken leave of your senses?"

"No, David, of course not."

"Then why make such pointless remarks? One idiot in the family is enough." He punched his right fist several times into the palm of his left hand. "At the very time when anti-Lanian sentiment is at its height I can well imagine the effect on public opinion if it became known that we were harboring a specially favored enemy alien, pampering some painted and powdered hussy who has dug her claws into Reed. I can see her mincing proudly around, one of the vanquished who became a victor by making use of a dope. Reed must be out of his mind."

"Reed is twenty-three," she observed.

"What of it? Are you asserting that there's a specific age at which a man has a right to make a fool of himself?"

"David, I did not say that."

"You implied it." More hand-punching. "Reed has shown an unsuspected strain of weakness. It doesn't come from me."

"No, David, it doesn't."

He stared at her, seeking what lay unspoken behind that remark. It eluded him. His mind was not her mind. He could not think in her terms. Only in his own.

"I'll bring this madness to a drastic stop. If Reed lacks strength of character, it is for me to provide it." He found the telephone, remarked as he picked it up. "There are thousands of girls on Morcine. If Reed feels that he must have romance, he can find it at home."

"He's not home," Mary mentioned. "He is far away."

"For a few months. A mere nothing." The phone whirred and he barked into it, "Has the *Istar* left Lani yet?" He held on a while, then racked the instrument and rumbled aggrievedly, "I'd have had her thrown off but it's too late. The *Istar* departed soon after the mailboat that brought his letter." He made a face and it was not pleasant. "The girl is due here tomorrow. She's got a nerve, a blatant impudence. It reveals her character in advance."

Facing the big, slow-ticking clock that stood by the wall, he gazed at it as if tomorrow were due any moment. His mind was working on the problem so suddenly dumped in his lap. After a while, he spoke again.

"That scheming baggage is not going to carve herself a comfortable niche in my home, no matter what Reed thinks of her. I will not have her, see?"

"I see, David."

"If he is weak, I am not. So when she arrives I'm going to give her the roughest hour of her life. By the time I've finished she'll be more than glad of passage back to Lani on the next ship. She'll get out in a hurry and for keeps."

Mary remained quiet.

"But I'm not going to indulge a sordid domestic fracas in public. I won't allow her even the satisfaction of that. I want you to meet her at the spaceport, phone me immediately she arrives, then bring her to my office. I'll cope with her there."

"Yes, David."

"And don't forget to call me beforehand. It will give me time to clear the place and insure some privacy."

"I will remember," she promised.

It was three-thirty in the following afternoon when the call came through. He shooed out a fleet admiral, two generals and an intelligence service director, hurried through the most urgent of his papers, cleared the desk and mentally prepared himself for the distasteful task to come.

In short time his intercom squeaked and his secretary's voice announced, "Two people to see you, sir—Mrs. Korman and Miss Tatiana Hurst."

"Show them in."

He leaned backward, face suitably severe. Tatiana, he thought. An outlandish name. It was easy to visualize the sort of hoyden who owned it: a flouncy thing, aged beyond her years and with a sharp eye to the main chance. The sort who could make easy meat of someone young, inexperienced and impressionable, like Reed. Doubtless she had supreme confidence that she could butter the old man with equal effectiveness and no trouble whatsoever. Hah, that was her mistake.

The door opened and they came in and stood before him without speaking. For half a minute he studied them while his mind did sideslips, repeatedly strove to co-ordinate itself, and a dozen expressions came and went in his face. Finally, he arose slowly to his feet, spoke to Mary, his tones frankly bewildered.

"Well, where is she?"

"This," informed Mary, with unconcealed and inexplicable satisfaction, "is her."

He flopped back into his chair, looked incredulously at Miss Tatiana Hurst. She had skinny legs exposed to knee height. Her clothing was much the worse for wear. Her face was a pale, hollow-cheeked oval from which a pair of enormous dark eyes gazed in a non-focusing, introspective manner as if she continually kept watch within her rather than upon things outside. One small white hand held Mary's, the other arm was around a large and brand new teddy-bear gained from a source at which he could guess. Her age was about eight. Certainly no more than eight.

It was the eyes that got him most, terribly solemn, terribly grave and unwilling to see. There was a coldness in his stomach as he observed them. She was not blind. She could look at him all right—but she looked without really perceiving.

The great dark orbs could turn toward him and register the mere essential of his being while all the time they saw only the secret places within herself. It was eerie in the extreme and more than discomforting.

Watching her fascinatedly, he tried to analyze and define the peculiar quality in those optics. He had expected daring, defiance, impudence, passion, anything of which a predatory female was capable. Here, in these radically altered circumstances, one could expect childish embarrassment, self-consciousness, shyness. But she was not shy, he decided. It was something else. In the end he recognized the elusive factor as absentness. She was here yet somehow not with them. She was somewhere else, deep inside a world of her own.

Mary chipped in with a sudden, "Well, David?"

He started at the sound of her voice. Some confusion still cluttered his mind because this culmination differed so greatly from his preconceptions. Mary had enjoyed half an hour in which to accommodate herself to the shock. He had not. It was still fresh and potent.

"Leave her with me for a few minutes," he suggested. "I'll call you when I've finished."

Mary went, her manner that of a woman enjoying something deep and personal. An unexpected satisfaction long overdue.

Korman said with unaccustomed mildness, "Come here, Tatiana."

She moved toward him slowly, each step deliberate and careful, touched the desk, stopped.

"Round this side, please, near to my chair."

With the same almost robotic gait she did as instructed, her dark eyes looking expressionlessly to the front. Arriving at his chair, she waited in silence.

He drew in a deep breath. It seemed to him that her manner was born of a tiny voice insisting, "I must be obedient. I must do as I am told. I can do only what I am told to do."

So she did it as one compelled to accept those things she had no means of resisting. It was surrender to all demands in order to keep one hidden and precious place intact. There was no other way.

Rather appalled, he said, "You're able to speak, aren't you?"

She nodded, slightly and only once.

"But that isn't speech," he pointed out.

There was no desire to contradict or provide proof of ability. She accepted his statement as obvious and left it at that. Silent and immensely grave, she clung to her bear and waited for Korman's world to cease troubling her own.

"Are you glad you're here, or sorry?"

No reaction. Only inward contemplation. Absentness.

"Well, are you glad then?"

A vague half-nod.

"You are not sorry to be here?"

An even vaguer shake.

"Would you rather stay than go back?"

She looked at him, not so much to see him as to insure that he could see her.

He rang his bell, said to Mary, "Take her home."

"Home, David?"

"That's what I said." He did not like the exaggerated sweetness of her tone. It meant something, but he couldn't discern what.

The door closed behind the pair of them. His fingers tapped restlessly on the desk as he pictured those eyes. Something small and bitterly cold was in his insides.

During the next couple of weeks his mind seemed to be filled with more problems than ever before. Like most men of his caliber he had the ability to ponder several subjects at once, but not the insight to detect when one was gaining predominance over the others.

On the first two or three of these days he ignored the pale intruder in his household. Yet he could not deny her presence. She was always there, quiet, obedient, self-effacing, hollow-cheeked and huge-eyed. Often she sat around for long periods without stirring, like a discarded doll.

When addressed by Mary or one of the maids she remained deaf to inconsequential remarks, responded to direct and imperative questions or orders. She would answer with minimum head movements or hand gestures when these sufficed, spoke monosyllabically in a thin little voice only when speech was unavoidable. During that time Korman did not speak to her at all—but he was compelled to notice her fatalistic acceptance of the fact that she was no part of his complicated life.

After lunch on the fourth day he caught her alone, bent down to her height and demanded, "Tatiana, what is the matter with you? Are you unhappy here?"

One brief shake of her head.

"Then why don't you laugh and play like other—?" He ceased abruptly as Mary entered the room.

"You two having a private gossip?" she inquired.

"As if we could," he snapped.

That same evening he saw the latest pictorial record from the fighting front. It gave him little satisfaction. Indeed, it almost irked him. The zip was missing. Much of the thrill of conquest had mysteriously evaporated from the pictures.

By the end of the fortnight he'd had more than enough of listening for a voice that seldom spoke and meeting eyes that did not see. It was like living with a ghost—and it could not go on. A man is entitled to a modicum of relaxation in his own home.

Certainly he could kick her back to Lani as he had threatened to do at the first. That, however, would be admission of defeat. Korman just could not accept defeat at anyone's hands, much less those of a brooding child. She was not going to edge him out of his own home nor persuade him to throw her out. She was a challenge he had to overcome in a way thoroughly satisfactory to himself.

Summoning his chief scientific adviser to his office, he declaimed with irritation, "Look, I'm saddled with a maladjusted child. My son took a fancy to her and shipped her from Lani. She's getting in my hair. What can be done about it?"

"Afraid I cannot help much, sir."

"Why not?"

"I'm a physicist."

"Well, can you suggest anyone else?"

The other thought a bit, said, "There's nobody in my department, sir. But science isn't solely concerned with production of gadgets. You need a specialist in things less tangible." A pause, then, "The hospital authorities might put you on to someone suitable."

He tried the nearest hospital, got the answer, "A child psychologist is your man."

"Who's the best on this planet?"

"Dr. Jager."

"Contact him for me. I want him at my house this evening, not later than seven o'clock."

Fat, middle-aged and jovial, Jager fell easily into the role of a casual friend who had just dropped in. He chatted a lot of foolishness, included Tatiana in the conversation by throwing odd remarks at her, even held a pretended conversation with her teddy-bear. Twice in an hour she came into his world just long enough to register a fleeting smile—then swiftly she was back in her own.

At the end of this he hinted that he and Tatiana should be left by themselves. Korman went out, convinced that no progress was being or would be made. In the lounge Mary glanced up from her seat.

"Who's our visitor, David? Or is it no business of mine?"

"Some kind of mental specialist. He's examining Tatiana."

"Really?" Again the sweetness that was bitter.

"Yes" he rasped. "Really."

"I didn't think you were interested in her."

"I am not," he asserted. "But Reed is. Now and again I like to remind myself that Reed is my son."

She let the subject drop. Korman got on with some official papers until Jager had finished. Then he went back to the room, leaving Mary immersed in her book. He looked around.

"Where is she?"

"The maid took her. Said it was her bedtime."

"Oh." He found a seat, waited to hear more.

Resting against the edge of a table, Jager explained, "I've a playful little gag for dealing with children who are reluctant to talk. Nine times out of ten it works."

"What is it?"

"I persuade them to *write*. Strangely enough, they'll often do that, especially if I make a game of it. I cajole them into writing a story or essay about anything that created a great impression upon them. The results can be very revealing."

"And did you—?"

"A moment, please, Mr. Korman. Before I go further I'd like to impress upon you that children have an inherent ability many authors must envy. They can express themselves with remarkable vividness in simple language, with great economy of words. They create telling effect with what they leave out as much as by what they put in." He eyed Korman speculatively. "You know the circumstances in which your son found this child?"

"Yes, he told us in a letter."

"Well, bearing those circumstances in mind I think you'll find this something exceptional in the way of horror stories." He held out a sheet of paper. "She wrote it unaided." He reached for his hat and coat.

"You're going?" questioned Korman in surprise. "What about your diagnosis? What treatment do you suggest?"

Dr. Jager paused, hand on door. "Mr. Korman, you are an intelligent person." He indicated the sheet the other was holding. "I think that is all you require."

Then he departed. Korman eyed the sheet. It was not filled with words as he'd expected. For a story it was mighty short. He read it.

I am nothing and nobody. My house went bang. My cat was stuck to a wall. I wanted to pull it off. They wouldn't let me. They threw it away.

The cold thing in the pit of his stomach swelled up. He read it again. And again. He went to the base of the stairs and looked up toward where she was sleeping.

The enemy whom he had made nothing.

Slumber came hard that night. Usually he could compose his mind and snatch a nap any time, anywhere, at a moment's notice. Now he was strangely restless, unsettled. His brain was stimulated by he knew not what and it insisted on following tortuous paths.

The frequent waking periods were full of fantastic imaginings wherein he fumbled through a vast and cloying grayness in which was no sound, no voice, no other being. The dreams were worse, full of writhing landscapes spewing smoky columns, with things howling through the sky, with huge, toadlike monsters crawling on metal tracks, with long lines of dusty men singing an aeons-old and forgotten song.

"You've left behind a broken doll."

He awakened early with weary eyes and a tired mind. All morning at the office a multitude of trifling things conspired against him. His ability to concentrate was not up to the mark and several times he had to catch himself on minor errors just made or about to be made. Once or twice he found himself gazing meditatively forward with eyes that did not see to the front but were looking where they had never looked before.

At three in the afternoon his secretary called on the intercom, "Astroleader Warren would like to see you, sir."

"Astroleader?" he echoed, wondering whether he had heard aright. "There's no such title."

"It is a Drakan space-rank."

"Oh, yes, of course. I can tend to him now."

He waited with dull anticipation. The Drakans formed a powerful combine of ten planets at great distance from Morcine. They were so far away that contact came seldom. A battleship of theirs had paid a courtesy call about twice in his lifetime. So this occasion was a rare one.

The visitor entered, a big-built youngster in light-green uniform. Shaking hands with genuine pleasure and great cordiality, he accepted the indicated chair.

"A surprise, eh, Mr. Korman?"

"Very."

"We came in a deuce of a hurry but the trip can't be done in a day. Distance takes time unfortunately."

"I know."

"The position is this," explained Warren. "Long while back we received a call from Lani relayed by intervening minor planets. They said they were involved in a serious dispute and feared war. They appealed to us to negotiate as disinterested neutrals."

"Ah, so that's why you've come?"

"Yes, Mr. Korman. We knew the chance was small of arriving in time. There was nothing for it but to come as fast as we could and hope for the best. The role of peacemaker appeals to those with any claim to be civilized."

"Does it?" questioned Korman, watching him.

"It does to us." Leaning forward, Warren met him eye to eye. "We've called at Lani on the way here. They still want peace. They're losing the battle. Therefore we want to know only one thing: Are we too late?"

That was the leading question: Are we too late? Yes or no? Korman stewed it without realizing that not so long ago his answer would have been prompt and automatic. Today, he thought it over.

Yes or no? Yes meant military victory, power and fear. No meant—what? Well, no meant a display of reasonableness in lieu of stubbornness. No meant a considerable change of mind. It struck him suddenly that one must possess redoubtable force of character to throw away a long-nursed viewpoint and adopt a new one. It required moral courage. The weak and the faltering could never achieve it.

"No," he replied slowly. "It is not too late."

Warren stood up, his face showing that this was not the answer he had expected. "You mean, Mr. Korman—?"

"Your journey has not been in vain. You may negotiate."

"On what terms?"

"The fairest to both sides that you can contrive." He switched his microphone, spoke into it. "Tell Rogers that I order our forces to cease hostilities forthwith. Troops will guard the perimeter of the Lani ground base pending peace negotiations. Citizens of the Drakan Confederation will be permitted unobstructed passage through our lines in either direction."

"Very well, Mr. Korman."

Putting the microphone aside, he continued with Warren, "Though far off in mere miles, Lani is near to us as cosmic distances go. It would please me if the Lanians agreed to a union between our planets, with common citizenship, common development of natural resources. But I don't insist upon it. I merely express a wish—knowing that some wishes never come true."

"The notion will be given serious consideration all the same," assured Warren. He shook hands with boyish enthusiasm. "You're a big man, Mr. Korman."

"Am I?" He gave a wry smile. "I'm trying to do a bit of growing in another direction. The original one kind of got used up."

When the other had gone, he tossed a wad of documents into a drawer. Most of them were useless now. Strange how he seemed to be breathing better than ever before, his lungs drawing more fully.

In the outer office he informed, "It's early yet, but I'm going home. Phone me there if anything urgent comes along."

The chauffeur closed the car door at the sixth step. A weakling, thought Korman as he went into his home. A lamebrain lacking the strength to haul himself out of a self-created rut. One can stay in a rut too long.

He asked the maid, "Where is my wife?"

"Slipped out ten minutes ago, sir. She said she'd be back in half an hour."

"Did she take—"

"No, sir." The maid glanced toward the lounge.

Cautiously he entered the lounge, found the child resting on the settee, head back, eyes closed. A radio played softly nearby. He doubted whether she had turned it on of her own accord or was listening to it. More likely someone else had left it running.

Tiptoeing across the carpet, he cut off the faint music. She opened her eyes, sat upright. Going to the settee, he took the bear from her side and placed it on an arm, positioned himself next to her.

"Tatiana," he asked with rough gentleness, "why are you nothing?"

No answer. No change.

"Is it because you have nobody?"

Silence.

"Nobody of your own?" he persisted, feeling a queer kind of desperation. "Not even a kitten?"

She looked down at her shoes, her big eyes partly shielded under pale lids. There was no other reaction.

Defeat. Ah, the bitterness of defeat. It set his fingers fumbling with each other, like those of one in great and unbearable trouble. Phrases tumbled through his mind.

"I am nothing."

"My cat . . . they threw it away."

His gaze wandered blindly over the room while his mind ran round and round her wall of silence seeking a door it could not find. Was there no way in, no way at all?

There was.

He discovered it quite unwittingly.

To himself rather than to her he murmured in a bearable undertone, "Since I was very small I have been surrounded by people. All my life there have been lots of people. But none were mine. Not one was really mine. Not one. I, too, am nothing."

She patted his hand.

The shock was immense. Startled beyond measure, he glanced down at the first touch, watched her give three or four comforting little dabs and hastily withdraw. There was heavy pulsing in his veins. Something within him rapidly became too big to contain.

Twisting sidewise, he snatched her onto his lap, put his arms around her, buried his nose in the soft part of her neck, nuzzled behind her ear, ran his big hand through her hair. And all the time he rocked to and fro with low crooning noises.

She was weeping. She hadn't been able to weep before. She was weeping not as a woman does, softly and subdued, but like a child, with great racking sobs that she fought hard to suppress.

Her arm was around his neck, tightening, clinging and tightening more while he rocked and stroked and called her "Honey" and uttered silly sounds and wildly extravagant reassurances.

This was victory.

Not empty.

Full.

Victory over self is completely full.

Into Your Tent I'll Creep

Astounding, September 1957

Morfad sat in the midship cabin and gloomed at the wall. He was worried and couldn't conceal the fact. The present situation had the frustrating qualities of a gigantic rattrap. One could escape it only with the combined help of all the other rats.

But the others weren't likely to lift a finger either on his or their own behalf. He felt sure of that. How can you persuade people to try to escape a jam when you can't convince them that they're in it, right up to the neck?

A rat runs around a trap only because he is grimly aware of its existence. So long as he remains blissfully ignorant of it, he does nothing. On this very world a horde of intelligent aliens had done nothing about it through the whole of their history. Fifty skeptical Altairans weren't likely to step in where three thousand million Terrans had failed.

He was still sitting there when Haraka came in and announced, "We leave at sunset."

Morfad said nothing.

"I'll be sorry to go," added Haraka. He was the ship's captain, a big, burly sample of Altairan life. Rubbing flexible fingers together, he went on, "We've been lucky to discover this planet, exceedingly lucky. We've become blood brothers of a lifeform fully up to our own standard of intelligence, space-traversing like ourselves, friendly and cooperative."

Morfad said nothing.

"Their reception of us has been most cordial," Haraka continued enthusiastically. "Our people will be greatly heartened when they hear our report. A great future lies before us, no doubt of that. A Terran-Altairan combine will be invincible. Between us we can explore and exploit the entite galaxy."

Morfad said nothing.

Cooling down, Haraka frowned at him. "What's the matter with you, Misery?"

"I am not overjoyed."

"I can see that much. Your face resembles a very sour *shamsid* on an aged and withered bush. And at a time of triumph, too! Are you ill?"

"No." Turning slowly, Morfad looked him straight in the eyes. "Do you believe in psionic faculties?"

Haraka reacted as if caught on one foot. "Well, I don't know, I am a captain, a trained engineer-navigator, and as such I cannot pretend to be an expert upon extraordinary abilities. You ask me something I am not qualified to answer. How about you? Do you believe in them?"

"I do—*now.*"

"Now? Why now?"

"The belief has been thrust upon me." Morfad hesitated, went on with a touch of desperation. "I have discovered that I am telepathic."

Surveying him with slight incredulity, Haraka said, "You've discovered it? You mean it has come upon you recently?"

"Yes."

"Since when?"

"Since we arrived on Terra."

"I don't understand this at all," confessed Haraka, baffled. "Do you assert that some peculiarity in Terra's conditions has suddenly enabled you to read my thoughts?"

"No, I cannot read your thoughts."

"But you've just said that you have become telepathic."

"So I have. I can hear thoughts as clearly as if the words were being shouted aloud. But not your thoughts nor those of any member of our crew."

"Haraka leaned forward, his features intent. "Ah, you have been hearing *Terran* thoughts, eh? And what you've heard has got you bothered? Morfad, I am your captain, your commander. It is your bounden duty to tell me of anything suspicious about these Terrans." He waited a bit, urged impatiently, "Come on, speak up!"

"I know no more about these humanoids than you do." said Morfad. "I have every reason to believe them genuinely friendly, but I don't know what they think."

"But by the stars, man, you—"

"We are talking at cross-purposes," Morfad interrupted. "Whether I do or do not overhear Terran thoughts depends upon what one means by Terran."

"Look," said Haraka, "whose thoughts *do* you hear?"

Steeling himself, Monad said flatly, "Those of Terran dogs."

"Dogs?" Haraka lay back and stared at him. *"Dogs?* Are you serious?"

"I have never been more so. I can hear dogs and no others. Don't ask me why because I don't know. It is a freak of circumstance."

"And you have listened to their minds ever since we jumped to Earth?"

"Yes."

"What sort of things have you heard?"

"I have had pearls of alien wisdom cast before me," declared Morfad, "and the longer I look at them the more they scare the hell out of me."

"Get busy frightening me with a few examples," invited Haraka, suppressing a smile.

"Quote: the supreme test of intelligence is the ability to live as one pleases without working," recited Morfad. "Quote: the art of retribution is that of concealing it beyond all suspicion. Quote: the sharpest, most subtle, most effective weapon in the cosmos is flattery."

"Huh?"

"Quote: if a thing can think, it likes to think that it is God; treat it as God and it becomes your willing slave."

"Oh, no!" denied Haraka.

"Oh, *yes,*" insisted Morfad. He waved a hand toward the nearest port. "Out there are three thousand million petty gods. They are eagerly panted after, fawned upon, gazed upon with worshiping eyes. Gods are very gracious toward those who love them." He made a spitting sound that lent emphasis to what followed. "The lovers know it—and love comes cheap."

Haraka said, uneasily, "I think you're crazy."

"Quote: to rule successfully the ruled must be unconscious of it." Again the spitting sound. "Is that crazy? I don't think so. It makes sense. It works. It's working out there right now."

"But—"

"Take a look at this." He tossed a small object into Haraka's lap. "Recognize it?"

"Yes, it's what they call a cracker."

"Correct. To make it some Terrans plowed fields in all kinds of weather, rain, wind and sunshine, sowed wheat, reaped it with the aid of machinery other Terrans had sweated to build. They transported the wheat, stored it, milled it, enriched the flour by various processes, baked it, packaged it, shipped it all over the world. When humanoid Terrans want crackers, they've got to put in man-hours to get them."

"So?"

"When a dog wants one he sits up, waves his forepaws and admires his god. That's all. Just that."

"But, darn it, man, dogs are relatively stupid."

"So it seems," said Morfad, dryly.

"They can't really do anything effective."

"They haven't got hands."

"And don't need them—having brains."

"Now see here," declaimed Haraka, openly irritated, "we Altairans invented and constructed ships capable of roaming the spaces between the stars. The Terrans have done the same. Terran dogs have not done it and won't do it in the next million years. When one dog has the brains and ability to get to another planet, I'll eat my cap."

"You can do that right now," Morfad suggested. "We have two dogs on board."

Haraka let go a grunt of disdain. "The Terrans have given us those as a memento."

"Sure they gave them to us—but at whose behest?"

"It was wholly a spontaneous gesture."

"Was it?"

"Are you suggesting that dogs put the idea into their heads?" Haraka demanded.

"I know they did," retorted Morfad, looking grim. "And we've not been given two males or two females. Oh no, sir, not on your life. One male and one female. The givers said we could breed them. Thus in due course our own worlds can become illuminated with the undying love of man's best friend."

"Nuts!" said Haraka.

Morfad gave back, "You're obsessed with the old, out-of-date idea that conquest must be preceded by aggression. Can't you understand that a wholly alien species just naturally uses wholly alien methods? Dogs employ their own tactics, not ours. It isn't within their nature or abilities to take us over with the aid of ships, guns and a great hullabaloo. It *is* within their nature and abilities to creep in upon us, their eyes shining with hero worship. If we don't watch out, we'll be mastered by a horde of loving creepers."

"I can invent a word for your mental condition," said Haraka. "You're suffering from caniphobia."

"With good reasons."

"Imaginary ones."

"Yesterday I looked into a dogs' beauty shop, Who was doing the bathing, scenting, powdering, primping? Other dogs? Hah! Humanoid females were busy dolling 'em up. Was *that* imaginary?"

"You can call it a Terran eccentricity. It means nothing whatever. Besides, we've quite a few funny habits of our own."

"You're dead right there," Morfad agreed. "And I know one of yours. So does the entire crew."

Haraka narrowed his eyes. "You might as well name it. I am not afraid to see myself as others see me."

"All right. You've asked for it. You think a lot of Kashim. He always has your ear; you will listen to nobody else. Everything he says makes sound sense—to you."

"So you're jealous of Kashim, eh?"

"Not in the least," assured Monad, making a disparaging gesture. "I merely despise him for the same reason that every one else holds him in contempt. He is a professional toady. He spends most of his time fawning upon you, flattering you, pandering to your ego. He is a natural-born creeper who gives you the Terradog treatment. You like it. You bask in it. It affects you like an irresistible drug. It works—and don't tell me that it doesn't because all of us know that it *does.*"

"I am not a fool. I have Kashim sized up. He does not influence me to the extent you believe."

"Three thousand million Terrans have four hundred million dogs sized up and are equally convinced that no dog has a say in anything worth a hoot."

"I don't believe it."

"Of course you don't. I had little hope that you would. Morfad is telling you these things and Morfad is either crazy or a liar. But if Kashim were to tell you while prostrate at the foot of your throne, you would swallow his story hook, line and sinker. Kashim has a Terradog mind and uses Terradog logic, see?"

"My disbelief has better basis than that."

"For instance?" Morfad invited.

"Some Terrans are telepathic. Therefore, if this myth of subtle mastery by dogs were a fact, they'd know of it. Not a dog would be left alive on this world." Haraka paused, finished pointedly, "They don't know of it."

"Terran telepaths hear the minds of their own kind but not those of dogs. I hear the minds of dogs but not those of any other kind. As I said before, I don't know why this should be. I know only. that it *is.*"

"It seems nonsensical to me."

"It would. I suppose you can't be blamed for taking that viewpoint. My position is difficult; I'm like the only one with ears in a world that is stone-deaf."

Haraka thought it over, said after a while, "Suppose I were to accept everything you've said at face value—what do you think I should do about it?"

"Refuse to take the dogs," responded Morfad promptly.

"That's more easily said than done. Good relations with the Terrans are vitally important. How can I reject a warmhearted gift without offending the givers?"

"All right, don't reject it. Modify it instead. Ask for two male or two female dogs. Make it plausible by quoting an Altairan law against the importation of alien animals that are capable of natural increase."

"I can't do that. It's far too late. We've already accepted the animals and expressed our gratitude for them. Besides, their ability to breed is an essential part of the gift, the basic intention of the givers. They've presented us with a new species, an entire race of dogs."

"You said it!" confirmed Morfad.

"For the same reason we can't very well prevent them from breeding when we get back home," Haraka pointed out. "From now on we and the Terrans are going to do a lot of visiting. As soon as they discovered that our dogs failed to multiply, they'd become generous and sentimental and dump another dozen on us. Or maybe a hundred. We'd then be worse off than we were before."

"All right, all right," Morfad shrugged with weary resignation. "If you're going to concoct a major objection to every possible solution, we may as well surrender without a fight. Let's abandon ourselves to becoming yet another dog-dominated species. Requote: to rule successfully the ruled must be unconscious of it." He gave Haraka the sour eye. "If I had my way, I'd wait until we were far out in free space and then give those two dogs the hearty heave-ho out the hatch."

Haraka grinned in the manner of one about to nail down a cockeyed tale once and for all. "And if you did that it would be proof positive beyond all argument that you're afflicted with a delusion."

Emitting a deep sigh, Morfad asked, "Why would it?"

"You'd be slinging out two prime members of the master race. Some domination, eh?" Haraka grinned again. "Listen, Morfad, according to your own story you know something never before known or suspected and you're the only one who does know it. That should make you a mighty menace to the entire species of dogs. They wouldn't let you live long enough to thwart them or even to go around advertising the truth. You'd soon be deader than a low-strata fossil." He walked to the door, held it open while he made his parting shot. "You look healthy enough to me."

Morfad shouted at the closing door, "It doesn't follow that because I can hear their thoughts they must necessarily hear mine. I doubt that they can because it's just a freakish—"

The door clicked shut. He scowled at it, walked twenty times up and down the cabin, finally resumed his chair and sat in silence while he beat his brains around in search of a satisfactory solution.

The sharpest, most subtle, most effective weapon in the cosmos is flattery.

Yes, he was seeking a means of coping with four-footed warriors incredibly skilled in the use of Creation's sharpest weapon. Professional fawners, creepers, worshipers, man-lovers ego-boosters, trained to near-perfection through countless generations in an art against which there seemed no decisive defense.

How to beat off the coming attack, contain it, counter it?

Yes, God!

Certainly, God!

Anything you say, God!

How to protect oneself against this insidious technique, how to quarantine it or—

By the stars! That was it—*quarantine* them! On Pladamine, the useless world, the planet nobody wanted. They could be breed there to their limits and meanwhile dominate the herbs and bugs. And a soothing reply would be ready for any nosy Terran tourist.

The dogs? Oh, sure, we've still got them, lots of them. They're doing fine. Got a nice world of their very own. Place called Pladamine. If you wish to go see them, it can be arranged.

A wonderful idea. It would solve the problem while creating no hard feelings among the Terrans. It would prove useful in the future and to the end of time. Once planted on Pladamine no dog could ever escape by its own efforts. Any tourists from Terra who brought dogs along could be persuaded to leave them in the canine heaven specially created by Altair. There the dogs would find themselves unable to boss anything higher than other dogs, and, if they didn't like it, they could lump it.

No use putting the scheme to Haraka, who was obviously prejudiced. He'd save it for the authorities back home. Even if they found it hard to credit his story, they'd still take the necessary action on the principle that it is better to be safe than sorry. Yes, they'd play it safe and give Pladamine to the dogs.

Standing on a cabin seat, he gazed out and down through the port. A great mob of Terrans, far below, waited to witness the coming take-off and cheer them on their way. He noticed beyond the back of the crowd a small, absurdly groomed dog dragging a Terran female at the end of a thin, light chain. Poor girl, he thought. The dog leads, she follows yet believes *she* is taking *it* some place.

Finding his color camera, he checked its controls, walked along the corridor and into the open air lock, It would be nice to have a picture of the big send-off audience. Reaching the rim of the lock he tripped headlong over something four-legged and stubby-tailed that suddenly intruded itself between his feet. He dived outward, the camera still in his grip, and went down fast through the whistling wind while shrill feminine screams came from among the watching crowd.

Haraka said, "The funeral has delayed us two days. We'll have to make up the time as best we can." He brooded a moment, added, "I'm very sorry about Morfad. He had a brilliant mind but it was breaking up toward the end, Oh well, it's a comfort that the expedition has suffered only one fatality."

"It could have been worse, sir," responded Kashim. "It could have been you. Praise the heavens that it was not."

"Yes, it could have been me." Haraka regarded him curiously. "And would it have grieved you, Kashim?"

"Very much indeed, sir. I don't think anyone aboard would feel the loss more deeply. My respect and admiration was such that—"

He ceased as something padded softly into the cabin, laid its head in Haraka's lap, gazed soulfully up at the captain. Kashim frowned with annoyance.

"Good boy!" approved Haraka, scratching the newcomers ears.

"My respect and admiration," repeated Kashim in louder tones, "are such that—"

"Good boy!" said Haraka again. He gently pulled one ear, then the other, observed with pleasure the vibrating tail.

"As I was saying, sir, my respect—"

"Good boy!" Deaf to all else, Haraka slid a hand down from the ears and massaged under the jaw.

Kashim favored Good Boy with a glare of inutterable hatred. The dog rolled a brown eye sidewise and looked at him without expression. From that moment, Kashim's fate was sealed.

Jay Score

Astounding, May 1941

There are very good reasons for everything they do. To the uninitiated some of their little tricks and some of their regulations seem mighty peculiar—but rocketing through the cosmos isn't quite like paddling a bathtub across a farm pond, no, sir!

For instance, this stunt of using mixed crews is pretty sensible when you look into it. On the outward runs toward Mars, the Asteroids or beyond, they have white Terrestrials to tend the engines because they're the ones who perfected modern propulsion units, know most about them and can nurse them like nobody else. All ships' surgeons are black Terrestrials because for some reason none can explain no Negro gets gravity-bends or space nausea. Every outside repair gang is composed of Martians who use very little air, are tiptop metal workers and fairly immune to cosmic-ray burn.

As for the inward trips to Venus, they mix them similarly except that the emergency pilot is always a big clunker like Jay Score. There's a motive behind that; he's the one who provided it. I'm never likely to forget him. He sort of sticks in my mind, for keeps. What a character!

Destiny placed me at the top of the gangway the first time he appeared. Our ship was the *Upskadaska City,* a brand new freighter with limited passenger accommodation, registered in the Venusian space-port from which she took her name. Needless to say she was known among hardened spacemen as the *Upsydaisy.*

We were lying in the Colorado Rocket Basin, north of Denver, with a fair load aboard, mostly watch-making machinery, agricultural equipment, aeronautical jigs and tools for Upskadaska, as well as a case of radium needles for the Venusian Cancer Research Institute. There were eight passengers, all emigrating agriculturalists planning on making hay thirty million miles nearer the Sun. We had ramped the vessel and were waiting for the blow-brothers-blow siren due in forty minutes, when Jay Score arrived.

He was six feet nine, weighed at least three hundred pounds yet toted this bulk with the easy grace of a ballet dancer. A big guy like that, moving like that, was something worth watching. He came up the duralumin gangway with all the nonchalance of a tripper boarding the bus for Jackson's Creek. From his hamlike right fist dangled a rawhide case not quite big enough to contain his bed and maybe a wardrobe or two.

Reaching the top, he paused while he took in the crossed swords on my cap, said, "Morning, Sarge. I'm the new emergency pilot. I have to report to Captain McNulty."

I knew we were due for another pilot now that Jeff Durkin had been promoted to the snooty Martian scent-bottle *Prometheus.* So this was his successor. He was a Terrestrial all right, but neither black nor white. His expressionless but capable face looked as if covered with old, well-seasoned leather. His eyes held fires resembling phosphorescence. There was an air about him that marked him an exceptional individual the like of which I'd never met before.

"Welcome, Tiny," I offered, getting a crick in the neck as I stared up at him. I did not offer my hand because I wanted it for use later on. "Open your satchel and leave it in the sterilizing chamber. You'll find the skipper in the bow."

"Thanks," he responded without the glimmer of a smile. He stepped into the airlock, hauling the rawhide hay-barn with him.

"We blast in forty minutes," I warned.

Didn't see anything more of Jay Score until we were two hundred thousand out, with Earth a greenish moon at the end of our vapor-trail. Then I heard him in the passage asking someone where be could find the sergeant-at-arms. He was directed through my door.

"Sarge," he said, handing over his official requisition, "I've come to collect the trimmings." Then he leaned on the barrier, the whole framework creaked and the top tube sagged in the middle.

"Hey!" I shouted.

"Sorry!" He unleaned. The barrier stood much better when he kept his mass to himself.

Stamping his requisition, I went into the armory, dug out his needle-ray projector and a box of capsules for same. The biggest Venusian mud-skis I could find were about eleven sizes too small and a yard too short for him, but they'd have to do. I gave him a can of thin, multipurpose oil, a jar of graphite, a Lepanto power-pack for his microwave radiophone and, finally, a bunch of nutweed pellicules marked: "Compliments of the Bridal Planet Aromatic Herb Corporation."

Shoving back the spicy lumps, he said, "You can have 'em—they give me the staggers." The rest of the stuff he forced into his side-pack without so much as twitching an eyebrow. Long time since I'd seen anyone so poker-faced.

All the same, the way he eyed the space-suits seemed strangely wistful. There were thirty bifurcated ones for the Terrestrials, all hanging on the wall like sloughed skins. Also there were six head-and-shoulder helmets for the Martians, since they needed no more than three pounds of air. There wasn't a suit for him. I couldn't have fitted him with one if my life had depended upon it. It'd have been like trying to can an elephant.

Well, he lumbered out lightly, if you get what I mean. The casual, loose-limbed way he transported his tonnage made me think I'd like to be some place else if ever he got on the rampage. Not that I thought him likely to run amok; he was amiable enough though sphinxlike. But I was fascinated by his air of calm assurance and by his motion which was fast, silent and eerie. Maybe the latter was due to his habit of wearing an inch of sponge-rubber under his big dogs.

I kept an interested eye on Jay Score while the *Upsydaisy* made good time on her crawl through the void. Yes, I was more than curious about him because his type was a new one on me despite that I've met plenty in my time.

He remained uncommunicative but kind of quietly cordial. His work was smoothly efficient and in every way satisfactory. McNulty took a great fancy to him, though he'd never been one to greet a newcomer with love and kisses.

Three days out, Jay made a major hit with the Martians. As everyone knows, those goggle-eyed, ten-tentacled, half-breathing kibitzers have stuck harder than glue to the Solar System Chess Championship for more than two centuries. Nobody outside of Mars will ever pry them loose. They are nuts about the game and many's the time I've seen a bunch of them go through all the colors of the spectrum in sheer excitement when at last somebody has moved a pawn after thirty minutes of profound cogitation.

One rest-time Jay spent his entire eight hours under three pounds pressure in the starboard airlock. Through the lock's phones came long silences punctuated by wild and shrill twitterings as if he and the Martians were turning the place into a madhouse. At the end of the time we found our tentacled outside-crew exhausted. It turned out that Jay had consented to play Kli Yang and had forced him to a stalemate. Kli had been sixth runner-up in the last solar melee, had been beaten only ten times—each time by a brother Martian, of course.

The red-planet gang had a finger on him after that, or I should say a tentacle-tip. Every rest-time they waylaid him and dragged him into the airlock. When we were eleven days out he played the six of them simultaneously, lost two games, stalemated three, won one. They thought he was a veritable whizzbang—for a mere Terrestrial. Knowing their peculiar abilities in this respect, I thought so, too. So did McNulty. He went so far as to enter the sporting data in the log.

You may remember the stunt that the audiopress of 2270 boosted as 'McNulty's Miracle Move'? It's practically a legend of the spaceways. Afterward, when we'd got safely home, McNulty disclaimed the credit and put it where it rightfully belonged. The audiopress had a good excuse, as usual. They said he was the captain, wasn't he? And his name made the headline alliterative, didn't it? Seems that there must be a sect of audiojournalists who have to be alliterative to gain salvation.

What precipitated that crazy stunt and whitened my hair was a chunk of cosmic flotsam. Said object took the form of a gob of meteoric nickel-iron ambling along at the characteristic speed of *pssst!* Its orbit lay on the planetary plane and it approached at right angles to our sunward course.

It gave us the business. I'd never have believed anything so small could have made such a slam, To the present day I can hear the dreadful whistle of air as it made a mad break for freedom through that jagged hole.

We lost quite a bit of political juice before the autodoors sealed the damaged section. Pressure already had dropped to nine pounds when the compensators held it and slowly began to build it up again. The fall didn't worry the Martians; to them nine pounds was like inhaling pigwash.

There was one engineer in that sealed section. Another escaped the closing doors by the skin of his left ear. But the first, we thought, had drawn his fateful number and eventually would be floated out like so many spacemen who've come to the end of their duty.

The guy who got clear was leaning against a bulwark, white-faced from the narrowness of his squeak. Jay Score came pounding along. His jaw was working, his eyes were like lamps, but his voice was cool and easy.

He said, "Get out. Seal this room. I'll try make a snatch. Open up and let me out fast when I knock."

With that he shoved us from the room which we sealed by closing its autodoor. We couldn't see what the big hunk was doing but the telltale showed he'd released and opened the door to the damaged section. Couple of seconds later the light went out, showing the door had been closed again. Then came a hard, urgent knock. We opened. Jay plunged through with the engineer's limp body cuddled in his huge arms. He bore it as if it were no bigger and heavier than a kitten and the way he took it down the passage threatened to carry him clear through the end of the ship.

Meanwhile we found we were in a first-class mess. The rockets weren't functioning any more. The venturi tubes were okay and the combustion chambers undamaged. The injectors worked without a hitch—provided that they were pumped by hand. We had lost none of our precious fuel and the shell was intact save for that one jagged hole. What made us useless was the wrecking of our coordinated feeding and firing controls. They had been located where the big bullet went through and now they were so much scrap.

This was more than serious. General opinion called it certain death though nobody said so openly. I'm pretty certain that McNulty shared the morbid notion even if his official report did under-describe it as "an embarrassing predicament." That is just like McNulty. It's a wonder he didn't define our feelings by recording that we were somewhat nonplussed.

Anyway, the Martian squad poured out, some honest work being required of them for the first time in six trips. Pressure had crawled back to fourteen pounds and they had to come into it to be fitted with their head-and-shoulder contraptions.

Kli Yang sniffed offensively, waved a disgusted tentacle and chirruped, "I could swim!" He eased up when we got his dingbat fixed and exhausted it to his customary three pounds. That is the Martian idea of sarcasm: whenever the atmosphere is thicker than they like they make sinuous backstrokes and declaim, "I could swim!"

To give them their due, they were good. A Martian can cling to polished ice and work continuously for twelve hours on a ration of oxygen that wouldn't satisfy a Terrestrial for more than ninety minutes. I watched them beat it through the airlock, eyes goggling through inverted fishbowls, their tentacles clutching power lines, sealing plates and quasi-arc welders. Blue lights made little auroras outside the ports as they began to cut, shape and close up that ragged hole.

All the time we continued to bullet sunward. But for this accursed misfortune we'd have swung a curve into the orbit of Venus in four hours' time. Then we'd have let her catch us up while we decelerated to a safe landing.

But when that peewee planetoid picked on us we were still heading for the biggest and brightest furnace hereabouts. This was the way we continued to go, our original velocity being steadily increased by the pull of our fiery destination.

I wanted to be cremated—but not yet!

Up in the bow navigation-room Jay Score remained in constant conference with Captain McNulty and the two astro-computator operators. Outside, the Martians continued to crawl around, fizzing and spitting with flashes of ghastly blue light. The engineers, of course, weren't waiting for them to finish their job. Four space-suits entered the wrecked section and started the task of creating order out of chaos.

I envied all those busy guys and so did many others. There's a lot of consolation in being able to do something even in an apparently hopeless situation. There's a lot of misery in being compelled to play with one's fingers while others are active.

Two Martians came back through the lock, grabbed some more sealing-plates and crawled out again. One of them thought it might be a bright idea to take his pocket chess set as well, but I didn't let him. There are times and places for that sort of thing and knight to king's fourth on the skin of a busted boat isn't one of them. Then I went along to see Sam Hignett, our Negro surgeon.

Sam had managed to drag the engineer back from the rim of the grave. He'd done it with oxygen, adrenaline and heart-massage. Only his long, dexterous fingers could have achieved it. It was a feat of surgery that has been brought off before, but not often.

Seemed that Sam didn't know what had happened and didn't much care, either. He was like that when he had a patient on his hands. Deftly he closed the chest incision with silver clips, painted the pinched flesh with iodized plastic, cooled the stuff to immediate hardness with a spray of ether.

"Sam," I told him. "You're a marvel,"

"Jay gave me a fair chance," he said. "He got him here in time."

"Why put the blame on him?" I joked, unfunnily.

"Sergeant," he answered, very serious, "I'm the ship's doctor. I do the best I can. I couldn't have saved this man if Jay hadn't brought him when he did."

"All right, all right," I agreed. "Have it your own way."

A good fellow, Sam. But he was like all doctors—you know, ethical. I left him with his feebly breathing patient.

McNulty came strutting along the catwalk as I went back. He checked the fuel tanks. He was doing it personally, and that meant something. He looked worried, and that meant a lot. It meant that I need not bother to write my last will and testament because it would never be read by anything living.

His portly form disappeared into the bow navigation-room and I heard him say, "Jay, I guess you—" before the closing door cut off his voice.

He appeared to have a lot of faith in Jay Score. Well, that individual certainly looked capable enough. The skipper and the new emergency pilot continued to act like cronies even while heading for the final frizzle.

One of the emigrating agriculturalists came out of his cabin and caught me before I regained the armory. Studying me wide-eyed, he said, "Sergeant, there's a half-moon showing though my port."

He continued to pop them at me while I popped mine at him. Venus showing her half pan meant that we were now crossing her orbit. He knew it too—I could tell by the way he bugged them.

"Well," he persisted, with ill-concealed nervousness, "how long is this mishap likely to delay us?"

"No knowing." I scratched my head, trying to look stupid and confident at one and the same time. "Captain McNulty will do his utmost. Put your trust in him—Poppa knows best."

"You don't think we are . . . er . . . in any danger?"

"Oh, not at all."

"You're a liar," he said.

"I resent having to admit it," said I.

That unhorsed him. He returned to his cabin, dissatisfied, apprehensive. In short time he'd see Venus in three-quarter phase and would tell the others. Then the fat would be in the fire.

Our fat in the solar fire.

The last vestiges of hope had drained away just about the time when a terrific roar and violent trembling told that the long-dead rockets were back in action. The noise didn't last more than a few seconds. They shut off quickly, the brief burst serving to show that repairs were effective and satisfactory.

The noise brought out the agriculturalist at full gallop. He knew the worst by now and so did the others. It had been impossible to conceal the truth for three days since he'd seen Venus as a half-moon. She was far behind us now. We were cutting the orbit of Mercury. But still the passengers clung to desperate hope that someone would perform an unheard-of miracle.

Charging into the armory, he yipped, "The rockets are working again. Does that mean—?"

"Nothing," I gave back, seeing no point in building false hopes.

"But can't we turn around and go back?" He mopped perspiration trickling down his jowls. Maybe a little of it was forced out by fear, but most of it was due to the unpleasant fact that interior conditions had become anything but arctic.

"Sir," I said, feeling my shirt sticking to my back, "we've got more pull than any bunch of spacemen ever enjoyed before. And we're moving so fast that there's nothing left to do but hold a lily."

"My ranch," he growled, bitterly. "I've been allotted five thousand acres of the best Venusian tobacco-growing territory, not to mention a range of uplands for beef."

"Sorry, but I think you'll be lucky ever to see it."

Crrrump! went the rockets again. The burst bent me backward and made him bow forward like he had a bad bellyache. Up in the bow, McNulty or Jay Score or someone was blowing them whenever he felt the whim. I couldn't see any sense in it.

"What's that for?" demanded the complainant, regaining the perpendicular.

"Boys will be boys," I said.

Snorting his disgust he went to his cabin. A typical Terrestrial emigrant, big, healthy and tough, he was slow to crack and temporarily too peeved to be really worried in any genuinely soul-shaking way.

Half an hour later the general call sounded on buzzers all over the boat. It was a ground signal, never used in space. It meant that the entire crew and all other occupants of the vessel were summoned to the central cabin. Imagine guys being called from their posts in full flight!

Something unique in the history of space navigation must have been behind that call, probably a compose-yourselves-for-the-inevitable-end speech by McNulty.

Expecting the skipper to preside over the last rites, I wasn't surprised to find him standing on the tiny dais as we assembled. A faint scowl lay over his plump features but it changed to a ghost of a smile when the Martians mooched in and one of them did some imitation shark-dodging.

Erect beside McNulty, expressionless as usual, Jay Score looked at that swimming Martian as if he were a pane of glass. Then his strangely lit orbs shifted their aim as if they'd seen nothing more boring. The swim-joke was getting stale, anyway.

"Men and vedras," began McNulty—the latter being the Martian word for 'adults' and, by implication, another piece of Martian sarcasm—"I have no need to enlarge upon the awkwardness of our position." That man certainly could pick his words—awkward! "Already we are nearer the Sun than any vessel has been in the whole history of cosmic navigation."

"Comic navigation," murmured Kli Yang, with tactless wit.

"We'll need your humor to entertain us later," observed Jay Score in a voice so flat that Kli Yang subsided.

"We are moving toward the luminary," went on McNulty, his scowl reappearing, "faster than any ship moved before. Bluntly, there is not more than one chance in ten thousand of us getting out of this alive." He favored Kli Yang with a challenging stare but that tentacled individual was now subdued. "However, there is that one chance—and we are going to take it."

We gaped at him, wondering what he meant. Every one of us knew our terrific velocity made it impossible to describe a U-turn and get back without touching the Sun. Neither could we fight our way in the reverse direction with all that mighty drag upon us. There was nothing to do but go onward, onward, until the final searing blast scattered our disrupted molecules.

"What we intend is to try a cometary," continued McNulty. "Jay and myself and the astro-computators think it's remotely possible that we might achieve it and pull through."

That was plain enough. The stunt was a purely theoretical one frequently debated by mathematicians and astro-navigators but never tried out in grim reality. The idea is to build up all the velocity that can be got and at the same time to angle into the path of an elongated, elliptical orbit resembling that of a comet. In theory, the vessel might then skim close to the Sun so supremely fast that it would swing pendulumlike far out to the opposite side of the orbit whence it came. A sweet trick—but could we make it?

"Calculations show our present condition fair enough to permit a small chance of success," said McNulty. "We have power enough and fuel enough to build up the necessary velocity with the aid of the Sun-pull, to strike the necessary angle and to maintain it for the necessary time. The only point about which we have serious doubts is that of whether we can survive at our nearest to the Sun." He wiped perspiration, unconsciously emphasising the shape of things to come. "I won't mince words, men. It's going to be rotten!"

"We'll see it through, skipper," said someone. A low murmur of support sounded through the cabin.

Kli Yang stood up, simultaneously waggled four jointless arms for attention, and twittered, "It is an idea. It is excellent, I, Kli Yang, endorse it on behalf of my fellow vedras. We shall cram ourselves into the refrigerator and suffer the Terrestrial smell while the Sun goes past."

Ignoring that crack about human odor, McNulty nodded and said, "Everybody will be packed into the cold room and endure it as best they can."

"Exactly," said Kli. "Quite," he added with bland disregard of superfluity. Wiggling a tentacle-tip at McNulty, he carried on, "But we cannot control the ship while squatting in the ice-box like three and a half dozen strawberry sundaes. There will have to be a pilot in the bow. One individual can hold her on course—until he gets fried. So somebody has to be the fryee."

He gave the tip another sinuous wiggle being under the delusion that it was fascinating his listeners into complete attention. "And since it cannot be denied that we Martians are far less susceptible to extremes of heat, I suggest that—"

McNulty snapped a harsh remark. His gruffness deceived nobody. The Martians were nuisances—but grand guys.

"All right." Kli's chirrup rose to a shrill, protesting yelp. "Who else is entitled to become a crisp?"

"Me," said Jay Score. It was odd the way he voiced it. Just as if he were a candidate so obvious that only the stone-blind couldn't see him.

He was right, at that! Jay was the very one for the job. If anyone could take what was going to come through the fore observation ports it was Jay Score. He was big and tough, built for just such a task as this. He had a lot of stuff that none of us had got and, after all, he was a fully qualified emergency pilot. And most definitely this was an emergency, the greatest ever.

But it was funny the way I felt about him. I could imagine him up in front, all alone, nobody there, our lives depending on how much he could take, while the tremendous Sun extended its searing fingers—

"You!" ejaculated Kli Yang, breaking my train of thought. His goggle eyes bulged irefully at the big, laconic figure on the dais. "You would! I am ready to mate in four moves, as you are miserably aware, and promptly you scheme to lock yourself away."

"Six moves," contradicted Jay, airily. "You cannot do it in less than six."

"Four!" Kli Yang fairly howled. "And right at this point you—"

It was too much for the listening McNulty. He looked as if on the verge of a stroke. His purple face turned to the semaphoring Kli.

"Forget your blasted chess!" he roared. "Return to your stations, all of you. Make ready for maximum boost. I will sound the general call immediately when it becomes necessary to take cover and then you will all go to the cold room." He started around, the purple gradually fading as his blood pressure went down. "That is, everyone except Jay."

More like old times with the rockets going full belt. They thundered smoothly and steadily. Inside the vessel the atmosphere became hotter and hotter until moisture trickled continually down our backs and a steaminess lay over the gloss of the walls. What it was like in the bow navigation-room I didn't know and didn't care to discover. The Martians were not inconvenienced yet; for once their wacky composition was much to be envied.

I did not keep check on the time but I'd had two spells of duty with one intervening sleep period before the buzzers gave the general call. By then things had become bad. I was no longer sweating: I was slowly melting into my boots.

Sam, of course, endured it most easily of all the Terrestrials and had persisted long enough to drag his patient completely out of original danger. That engineer was lucky, if it's lucky to be saved for a bonfire. We put him in the cold room right away, with Sam in attendance.

The rest of us followed when the buzzer went. Our sanctuary was more than a mere refrigerator; it was the strongest and coolest section of the vessel, a heavily armored, triple shielded compartment holding the instrument lockers, two sick bays and a large lounge for the benefit of space-nauseated passengers. It held all of us comfortably.

All but the Martians. It held them, but not comfortably. They are never comfortable at fourteen pounds pressure which they regard as not only thick but also smelly—something like breathing molasses impregnated with aged goat.

Under our very eyes Kli Yang produced a bottle of *hooloo* scent, handed it to his half-parent Kli Morg. The latter took it, stared at us distastefully then sniffed the bottle in an ostentatious manner that was positively insulting. But nobody said anything.

All were present excepting McNulty and Jay Score. The skipper appeared two hours later. Things must have been raw up front, for he looked terrible. His haggard face was beaded and glossy, his once-plump cheeks sunken and blistered. His usually spruce, well-fitting uniform hung upon him sloppily. It needed only one glance to tell that he'd had a darned good roasting, as much as he could stand.

Walking unsteadily, he crossed the floor, went into the first-aid cubby, stripped himself with slow, painful movements. Sam rubbed him with tannic jelly. We could hear the tormented skipper grunting hoarsely as Sam put plenty of pep into the job.

The heat was now on us with a vengeance. It pervaded the walls, the floor, the air and created a multitude of fierce stinging sensations in every muscle of my body. Several of the engineers took off their boots and jerkins. In short time the passengers followed suit, discarding most of their outer clothing. My agriculturalist sat a miserable figure in tropical silks, moody over what might have been.

Emerging from the cubby, McNulty flopped into a bunk and said, "If we're all okay in four hours' time, we're through the worst part."

At that moment the rockets faltered. We knew at once what was wrong. A fuel tank had emptied and a relay had failed to cut in. An engineer should have been standing by to switch the conduits. In the heat and excitement, someone had blundered.

The fact barely had time to register before Kli Yang was out through the door. He'd been lolling nearest to it and was gone while we were trying to collect our overheated wits. Twenty seconds later the rockets renewed their steady thrum.

An intercom bell clanged right by my ear. Switching its mike, I croaked a throaty, "Well?" and heard Jay's voice coming back at me from the bow.

"Who did it?"

"Kli Yang," I told him. "He's still outside."

"Probably gone for their domes," guessed Jay. "Tell him I said thanks."

"What's it like around where you live?" I asked.

"Fierce. It isn't so good . . . for vision." Silence a moment, then, "Guess I can stick it . . . somehow. Strap down or hold on ready for next time I sound the . . . bell."

"Why?" I half yelled, half rasped.

"Going to rotate her. Try . . . distribute . . . the heat."

A faint squeak told that he'd switched off. I told the others to strap down. The Martians didn't have to bother about that because they owned enough saucer-sized suckers to weld them to a sunfishing meteor.

Kli came back, showed Jay's guess to be correct; he was dragging the squad's head-and-shoulder pieces. The load was as much as he could pull now that temperature had climbed to the point where even he began to wilt.

The Martian moochers gladly donned their gadgets, sealing the seams and evacuating them down to three pounds pressure. It made them considerably happier.

Remembering that we Terrestrials use spacesuits to keep air inside, it seemed peculiar to watch those guys using theirs to keep it outside.

They had just finished making themselves comfortable and had laid out a chessboard in readiness for a minor tourney when the bell sounded again. We braced ourselves. The Martians clamped down their suckers.

Slowly and steadily the *Upsydaisy* began to turn upon her longitudinal axis. The chessboard and pieces tried to stay put, failed, crawled along the floor, up the wall and across the ceiling. Solar pull was making them stick to the sunward side,

I saw Kli Morg's strained, heat-ridden features glooming at a black bishop while it skittered around, and I suppose that inside his goldfish bowl were resounding some potent samples of Martian invective.

"Three hours and a half," gasped McNulty.

That four hours estimate could only mean two hours of approach to the absolute deadline and two hours of retreat from it. So the moment when we had two hours to go would be the moment when we were at our nearest to the solar furnace, the moment of greatest peril.

I wasn't aware of that critical time, since I passed out twenty minutes before it arrived. No use enlarging upon the horror of that time. I think I went slightly nuts. I was a hog in an oven, being roasted alive. It's the only time I've ever thought the Sun ought to be extinguished for keeps. Soon afterward I became incapable of any thought at all.

I recovered consciousness and painfully moved in my straps ninety minutes alter passing the midway point. My dazed mind had difficulty in realizing that we had now only half an hour to go to reach theoretical safety.

What had happened in the interim was left to my imagination and I didn't care to try picture it just then. The Sun blazing with a ferocity multi-million times greater than that of a tiger's eye, and a hundred thousand times as hungry for our blood and bones. The flaming corona licking out toward this shipload of half-dead entities, imprisoned in a steel bottle.

And up in front of the vessel, behind its totally inadequate quartz observation-ports, Jay Score sitting alone, facing the mounting inferno, staring, staring, staring—

Getting to my feet I teetered uncertainly, went down like a bundle of rags. The ship wasn't rotating any longer and we appeared to be bulleting along in normal fashion. What dropped me was sheer weakness. I felt lousy.

The Martians already had recovered. I knew they'd be the first. One of them lugged me upright and held me steady while I regained a percentage of my former control. I noticed that another had sprawled right across the unconscious McNulty and three of the passengers. Yes, he'd shielded them from some of the heat and they were the next ones to come to life.

Struggling to the intercom, I switched it but got no response from the front. For three full minutes I hung by it dazedly before I tried again. Nothing doing. Jay wouldn't or couldn't answer.

I was stubborn about it, made several more attempts with no better result. The effort cost me a dizzy spell an down I flopped once more. The heat was still terrific. I felt more dehydrated than a mummy dug out of sand a million years old.

Kli Yang opened the door, crept out with dragging, pain-stricken motion. His air-helmet was secure on his shoulders. Five minutes later he came back, spoke through the helmet's diaphragm.

"Couldn't get near the bow navigation-room. At the midway catwalk the autodoors are closed, the atmosphere sealed off and it's like being inside a furnace." He stared around, met my gaze, answered the question in my eyes. "There's no air in the bow."

No air meant the observation-ports had gone *phut.* Nothing else could have emptied the navigation-room. Well, we carried spares for that job and could make good the damage once we got into the clear. Meanwhile here we were roaring along, maybe on correct course and maybe not, with an empty, airless navigation-room and with an intercom system that gave nothing but ghastly silence.

Sitting around we picked up strength. The last to come out of his coma was the sick engineer. Sam brought him through again. It was about then that McNulty wiped sweat, showed sudden excitement.

"Four hours, men," he said, with grim satisfaction. "We've done it!"

We raised a hollow cheer. By Jupiter, the superheated atmosphere seemed to grow ten degrees cooler with the news. Strange how relief from tension can breed strength; in one minute we had conquered former weakness and were ready to go. But it was yet another four hours before a quartet of spacesuited engineers penetrated the forward hell and bore their burden from the airless navigation-room,

They carried him into Sam's cubby-hole, a long, heavy, silent figure with face burned black.

Stupidly I hung around him saying, "Jay, Jay, how're you making out?"

He must have heard, for he moved the fingers of his right hand and emitted a chesty, grinding noise. Two of the engineers went to his cabin, brought back his huge rawhide case. They shut the door, staying in with Sam and leaving me and the Martians fidgeting outside. Kli Yang wandered up and down the passage as if he didn't know what to do with his tentacles.

Sam came out after more than an hour. We jumped him on the spot.

"How's Jay?"

"Blind as a statue." He shook his woolly head. "And his voice isn't there any more. He's taken an awful beating."

"So that's why he didn't answer the intercom." I looked him straight in the eyes. "Can you . . . can you do anything for him, Sam?"

"I only wish I could." His sepia face showed his feelings. "You know how much I'd like to put him right. But I can't." He made a gesture of futility. "He is completely beyond my modest skill, Nobody less than Johannsen can help him. Maybe when we get back to Earth—" His voice petered out and he went back inside.

Kli Yang said, miserably, "I am saddened."

A scene I'll never forget to my dying day was that evening we spent as guests of the Astro Club in New York. That club was then—as it is today—the most exclusive group of human beings ever gathered together. To qualify for membership one had to perform in dire emergency a feat of astro-navgation tantamount to a miracle. There were nine members in those days and there are only twelve now.

Mace Waldron, the famous pilot who saved that Martian liner in 2263, was the chairman. Classy in his soup and fish, he stood at the top of the table with Jay Score sitting at his side. At the opposite end of the table was McNulty, a broad smirk of satisfaction upon his plump pan. Beside the skipper was old, white-haired Knud Johannsen, the genius who designed the J-series and a scientific figure known to every spaceman.

Along the sides, manifestly self-conscious, sat the entire crew of the *Upsydaisy*, including the Martians, plus three of our passengers who'd postponed their trips for this occasion. There were also a couple of audiojournalists with scanners and mikes.

"Gentlemen and vedras," said Mace Waldron, "this is an event without precedent in the history of humanity, an event never thought-of, never imagined by this club. Because of that I feel it doubly an honor and a privilege to propose that Jay Score, Emergency Pilot, be accepted as a fully qualified and worthy member of the Astro Cub."

"Seconded!" shouted three members simultaneously.

"Thank you, gentlemen." He cocked an inquiring eyebrow. Eight hands went up in unison. "Carried," he said. "Unanimously." Glancing down at the taciturn and unmoved Jay Score, he launched into a eulogy. It went on and on and on, full of praise and superlatives, while Jay squatted beside him with a listless air.

Down at the other end I saw McNulty's gratified smirk grow stronger and stronger. Next to him, old Knud was gazing at Jay with a fatherly fondness that verged on the fatuous. The crew likewise gave full attention to the blank-faced subject of the talk, and the scanners were fixed upon him too.

I returned my attention to where all the others were looking, and the victim sat there, his restored eyes bright and glittering, but his face completely immobile despite the talk, the publicity, the beam of paternal pride from Johannsen.

But after ten minutes of this I saw J.20 begin to fidget with obvious embarrassment.

Don't let anyone tell you that a robot can't have feelings!

Last Blast

Astounding, November 1952

The blow was delivered in a manner full of logic and devoid of sentiment, that is to say, suddenly and without warning. It was a hundred or a thousand times more fearsome than the latest hell-bomb but took longer to demonstrate the fact. Nobody opposed it or tried to strike back for the plain reason that nobody knew they'd been hit.

And when realization came, it was too late—as had been intended.

A rather appalling simplicity was the outstanding characteristic of the unknown enemy's technique. One long, silvery cigar came out of the sky, dropped seven bombs in planned positions and went away. It wasn't noticed. At minimum altitude of twenty miles and lowest velocity of four thousand eight hundred per hour, the thing remained too high and fast to be discovered by the naked eye. Neither did radar screens register its passing. They were not alerted because in orthodox thought there was nothing for which to watch. The world was at peace, without fear, and had been for more than half a century.

The bombs landed and burst without spectacular brilliance or tremendous noise or detectable concussion. They looked as formidable as so many bottles of stale beer tossed overboard by an irresponsible spacehand for they were nothing but small, brittle spheres containing a thin, slightly cloudy liquid. The spheres hit Earth and shattered. The liquid splashed around.

This spread of droplets was the beginning of the end, creating the certitude that humankind would pass out not with a bang but with a whimper. The greatest scoop in history for any journalist able to see the shape of things to come. But no newspaper mentioned it the next day. No radio network voiced one excited word about it. They didn't know. They didn't suspect. They had been killed—but needed time to die.

Humanity remained untroubled for at least a little while when every second counted and every split-second added long steps to the march of death. Some folk worried but it was about health, babies, taxes, stocks and shares; other folk, hopes of heavenly salvation, anything but poison from the skies.

The first to gripe was Barton Maguire, a farmer in Iowa. The last to react were the seven human beings on the Moon. Maguire's surly complaints served as the original warning. One of the Lunar seven made the final move.

Men on the Moon were no novelty. Twenty successive landings had boiled away a world's capacity for amazement. A feat is remarkable only the first time. Do it again and it reduces to pretty good. Twenty times becomes ordinary.

Only a ship on Venus or Mars would bring a repeat of those wild international celebrations of sixteen years ago. Such another whoopee had yet to come and by the looks of things there would be a long wait. Thirty million miles come to more than a hop, skip and jump.

Meanwhile men had to be content with a satellite as their sole cosmic plaything. The group on the Moon were there because the playing had begun. Their task was not complicated, not immensely difficult, but it was valuable as a source of essential data. They were extracting a sample of the new toy.

To this purpose they had considerable tonnage of equipment ferried over in four loads. Within an air-tight sanctuary, shaped like an inverted ice-cream cone, they worked upon a minor crater that had no name, tended a nuclear engine and serviced a drill that brought up a constant succession of cores each of which told a story. An expert could cast a sharp eye over these cylinders of extraterrestrial plasma and declare that to the limit of the bore the Moon was made thus and so. Later, analysts would use them to list its riches in hydrocarbonates and metallic ores, if any.

Seven men consorting cheek by jowl under a dunce's cap and parted from the rest of humanity by a quarter million miles. There were moments when it irked; times when the engine moaned and the drill churned and the great rig trembled to its peak far beyond allotted hours—because men must battle the immediate task lest instead they battle each other.

Wilkin, government metallurgist, was the least sociable of the bunch. A gaunt, elderly individual with pale eyes fronted by steel-rimmed glasses, he had the dreary pessimism of the liverish and nursed the resentment of one handed a young man's job when near retirement. Somewhere back in the stuffy haunts of bureaucracy his tongue had stabbed a superior. The Moon was his sentence.

Liveliest of the lot was Yarbridge, thickset, tow-haired—the radio operator; a one-time ham who gloried in running a station where none had been run before. The small but powerful transmitter-receiver was his personal juju complete with call-name of Yarboo. He had an advantage over the rest—he had the comfort of his god and a thousand invisible friends behind the god. He had been conditioned to the company of voices in the dark. About the only thing he missed was the morning mail with its QSL cards.

The busiest and, therefore, the least touchy man was James Holland, tall, gangling, freckled. Though the youngest member of the party he was quiet, thoughtful, studious. He had to be. As the atomechanic he'd spent four years studying nuclear engines and reckoned he'd devote another forty to absorbing latest advances.

Some fast brainwork had been required to learn how to cope with the contraption he'd got here, for it was way ahead of anything he'd seen at the International Power Institute—one quarter the size, one eighth the mass, and it ran on thorium. It resembled a pair of Diesels coupled nose to nose with the hot-stuff cased between the fan-drives. Probably it would be out of date within a year. Holland tended to pore over books and blueprints in determination to keep up with the times.

The remaining quartet were curiously alike in many respects, big-chested, hard-eyed, untidy, ruthlessly expert at various card games and lavishly supplied with adjectives. All four had made a career from sticking pins in Earth's heart for the big oil companies. They knew how to do it and did it well, vituperatively but efficiently.

The day the bombs dropped there were forty-six cores, lying outside the Moon-dome. They reposed in a neat row, placed in order of extraction, each tagged at both ends with a plastic numeral by way of doubled check. The quantity of them indicated a bore-depth of nine hundred twenty feet. The nuclear engine moaned soft and low while the drill rotated and sank slowly, ever so slowly, toward the thousand mark.

An untouched case of whisky atop a small mountain of sealed food patiently bided this first celebration-point. At one thousand feet a bottle would be broached, some sort of petty celebration organized. There were twelve bottles in the case but that didn't mean a probing limit of twelve thousand feet. The drive would continue so long as the engine could rotate the lengthening mass of steel tube, so long as a ship could bring more shafts, more cutting-heads, more whisky.

Ambling to the dome's center point, Yarbridge eyed a white ring where the turning shaft had been touched with chalk at a measured point. He kept quiet while a driller timed the ring's descent to ground level. The chalk circle disappeared and the other put his watch away.

"How's she going?" asked Yarbridge, not really caring.

"Cool and steady." The driller bit a ragged end from a thumbnail. "What's the latest from over there?"

"Gale warning in the Atlantic. Vesuvius is spewing sky-high and the Italians are evacuating the area around it. A Czech stratoliner has crashed. Seventy dead, no survivors. They were burned alive."

"Humph! Nothing ever happens." He put spit on a finger, used it to make a wet ring on the shaft. "Luck!"

"What's that for? Hoping to hit a gold reef?"

"Hoping we don't have to change a cutter too soon."

Yarbridge nodded. He could see what it meant. Real sweat. They'd have to haul up most of a thousand feet of stuff, detach it section by section to get at the worn head. Then fix a new cutter and reverse the whole process, linking up section by section as the toothy bit went down. It would have to be done again and again and again but nobody was yearning for it.

In short time he tired of studying the shaft and started what they had come to call the Sing Sing hitch, namely, a bored, aimless walk to and fro or around the rim of the circular space in which they were confined. Day and night some fidgety soul was performing this trek. When two did it simultaneously and passed each other for the tenth time, each generated mild thoughts of mayhem.

He wouldn't have been mooching but for the home planet's Asiatic face. The great hemispherical antenna atop the dome did not trap much worth having when confronted by Chinese, Malays and Dyaks. Caterwaulings from Shanghai, tin prices from Singapore and a little boogie from Tokyo. The thousand with the kit to beam him were concentrated around the corner and temporarily silent. These were the siesta hours of his electronic god.

Finally he sat on a packing case near the engine, watched Holland check over the linked generator that provided heat, power and light. It struck him as faintly ironic that they could and did use electric razors while millions on Earth lacked the juice to run them.

"James," he said, "why am I like the Moon?"

Holland turned a freckled face toward him. "Don't you know?"

"Perhaps," said Yarbridge, "it's because I'm bored." He brooded a moment, asked, "Aren't you?"

"No."

"Why not?"

The other thought a while, said slowly, "Like you, I have an interest. But mine doesn't wax and wane with exterior conditions. It remains constant."

"I guess you're right. Maybe I've become too dependent upon a box of tricks. I should have learned to play poker."

"Fat lot of money you'd have coming at the end of this," opined Holland. "Those four would have stripped you."

"Or I might get their wads."

"I doubt it."

"Yes, and so do they judging by the number of times they've wanted me to join them." He glanced around. "Where's old Sourpuss? Hiding in a crate?"

Nodding toward the trap in the dome's wall, Holland informed, "Put on a headpiece and went out for another look at the last core. He muttered something about that inch-wide striation of red dirt being ferrous oxide."

"What does that signify?"

"Nothing of importance. It isn't worth digging up. Too thin and too deep."

"The truth is that he doesn't give a darn for that core or any other," suggested Yarbridge. "He's escaping six faces that give him the gripes. A two hours' supply of oxygen means that temporarily he can get away from it all. Why doesn't he join the Foreign Legion?"

"He's an old dog compelled to learn new tricks," said Holland solemnly. "As a young one in the same fix, I sympathize with him."

"They ought to let him go home," Yarbridge commented. "They ought to send us a guitar player in his place. Or, better still, half a dozen slinky brunettes from the chorus line. Rumor has it there are twenty more points selected for further test bores. If so, we'll be stuck here quite a spell."

"Suits me. I'm out of mischief, perfecting my education and making money fast." He gave a sly grin. "Being neither married nor brunette-starved, I can afford to wait."

Yarbridge stood up, stretched himself, made a face. "Oh, well, shortly the sunny side."

The other knew what he meant. They were swinging away from Earth's dark hemisphere and round to her illuminated face. That meant an additional diversion in circumstances where each one was precious, to be savored to the utmost. Some intelligent official back home had seen fit to include in their equipment a small telescope, only x200, with four-inch object lens. It had proved considerably a morale-booster. Men could and did stare through it for hours, drinking the scene with avid thirst, and telling each other thumping lies about the wealth of detail to be discerned in their own back yards.

They cleaned, polished and fondled the spyglass, treating it with loving care, for it made the faraway seem near. It provided illusionary comfort. Soon it would reverse that role and create realistic pain. It sharpened any eye in search of peace and beauty but magnified turmoil and tragedy with equal impartiality.

A direct pointer to coming trouble was not immediately recognized as such either by the seven on the Moon or the teeming masses of Earth. Even specialized minds summoned to deal with it were motivated more by curiosity than alarm. It formed a minor item in a news bulletin picked up from KDTH at Dubuque, Iowa.

"Experts from the Department of Agriculture at Washington are flying to the farm of Barton Maguire, near Dubuque. In an interview Maguire said that a field has developed grassrot."

It was forgotten before the succeeding item had been voiced halfway through. KDTH began to fade. Yarbridge searched around, picked up a lively performance of *"La Cumparsita"* from Rio de Janeiro, hummed in off-key accompaniment. Wilkin lay nearby on his oxygen-inflated mattress and frowned through his spectacles. Two drillers off duty played cards with deadly earnestness.

Two days later WCBM at Baltimore, made intermittent by static, let go half a sentence. ". . . Eminent botanists and biologists rushed by the United Nations Food Commission to the farm of Barton Maguire, in Iowa."

James Holland, having a turn at the telescope, removed his attention, said to nobody in particular, "Who's this Maguire? I'm sure I've heard his name before."

"There are millions of them," grunted a driller. He planted a queen on his opponent's nine, confiscated both cards. "They swarm out of the ground every St. Patrick's Day."

Letting it pass, Holland had another look at Earth. In full sunlight it was a spectacle of which one could never tire, a vision infinitely more satisfying than the other planets or the host of stars. And it kept steady, without faltering behind a shivering atmosphere. The chief snag was that if one stared too intently and too long one began to imagine things. The brain gained ascendancy over the eyes, forcing them to detect a nonexistent dot in mid-Atlantic and call it a liner. Or convert a line to a road and conjure vehicles along it.

He was again at the 'scope the next day when Yarbridge brought in a voice that for some time had been dimly muttering, "Yarboo! Come in Yarboo!" It boosted to fair strength. For a couple of minutes Yarbridge and the other slapped backs, chewed technicalities, exchanged love to Margaret for love to Jeannie, swapped a couple of corny insults. Then again Holland's attention was drawn away as the distant ham spoke more seriously and in lower tones.

"Something fishy is going on. Lot of rumors flying around. They say that troops have been rushed north with flame throwers. A guy told me he'd been turned back by the National Guard outside Dubuque. He thinks a flying saucer has landed and the authorities are keeping it quiet. You can take that as bunk. How many saucers have you found up there?"

"None," said Yarbridge.

"It's bound to happen some day," ventured the other. "But I don't believe it's happened yet. This saucer stuff is a lot of scuttlebutt. All the same, there's a general feeling of suspicion that something is going on and we're not being told. See if you can raise a station farther north—maybe you'll be given a hair-raiser."

"You could do that yourself." Digging a small book out of a breast pocket, Yarbridge consulted it. "There are a dozen or more in and around Dubuque."

"Hah! You're telling me? Their cards are stuck on my wall. Try getting them!"

"You mean they're not operating?"

"Definitely not!" A pause, then, "That's why I say there's something peculiar afoot. If anything of national or international interest were taking place up there, they'd be bawling all over the bands. But they aren't. You know what *that* means!"

"Shut down and sealed by official order."

"That's how it looks—and I don't like it."

"Me neither." Yarbridge glanced at an Earth-chronometer, ticking to one side of his rig. "Will you be around at eighteen hours G.M.T.?"

"Yes, if I'm not in clink."

"All right. I'll let you know what I find."

He added a bit more, switched off, turned in his swivel seat and said to Holland, "I've known that boy for ten years. He's as excitable as a porcelain Buddha and doesn't tell tales for the fun of it. Furthermore, all the hams in Dubuque won't drop dead on the same day."

A hairy driller passing by caught the last remark, stopped and informed, "They might, if they were holding a weekly meeting and some nut let go a bomb. Years ago we lost a complete crew that way during a native revolt."

Ignoring it, Yarbridge went on, "Can you see anything extraordinary in Iowa?"

"What, with this glass?" Holland made a disparaging gesture. "We need one umpteen times the size."

"I suppose so." He switched on, resumed probing the ether. "If we can't use our eyes, we'll have to depend on our ears. I'll try bringing in Jerry, who lives at—"

He broke off as his slow-motion dial hit a peaky point and a Canadian voice came out the speaker: ". . . At Ottawa this morning. After a hurried meal, the

Russian delegation left by air for Iowa, having refused press interviews. Circles close to the United States Government say that an exchange of agricultural technologists has been arranged and that an American party flew to Omsk last night."

Holland got up from the 'scope, put hands on lean hips and said, "That's Iowa again."

"I know." Yarbridge sounded a little grim. "How about adding another heater or two? I feel cold."

"You'll be colder if major ructions take place across there," remarked Wilkin, morbidly gratified. "Fine fix we'll be in, cut off from the rest."

"Why should there be trouble?" asked Yarbridge with a touch of defiance. "We have outgrown world wars. There hasn't been so much as a diplomatic clash for half a century. Everyone is peaceful and happy these days."

"Are they?" Wilkin cocked a sardonic eyebrow.

"They darned well ought to be!"

"*Ought* and *is* are different words," Wilkin pointed out.

"You should know!" snapped Yarbridge.

"What do you mean by that?" His pale eyes narrowing behind his glasses, Wilkin sat up.

Hurriedly Holland chipped in. "If people had the patience to wait for the heaters, there'd be no need to warm up their tempers." He started off toward the switchboard, adding, "I can take a hint. I'll turn them on at once. No rest for the wicked."

It served to crack up the acrimonious by-play. It was a conversational gambit frequently adopted by a third party when two men showed signs of rubbing each other the wrong way. Strange conditions breed strange conventions, including that of drowning other people's differences in one's own sorrows.

Here, the problem of how to live together perforce had been solved, haphazardly but adequately. On Earth it was soon to prove unsolvable. The unknown enemy had complicated it beyond solution merely by shifting its crux from the brain to the belly.

Possession of power creates a peculiar hiatus in the reasoning part of the brain. There's one lesson that authority is mentally incapable of learning, namely, that truth will out. The more determinedly and persistently truth is thrust down the well, the bigger the bounce when finally she emerges.

By the end of a week authority still wore a pin on its lips but the Lunar seven had learned via Yarbridge and a hundred hams that Iowa was under martial law and its state lines held by troops against all but those holding official permits to cross. Also that the German and Brazilian armies had been partially mobilized with the consent of the United Nations. The Australian Government had voted itself powers unheard-of except in time of war. Planes and unspecified supplies were being rushed to south China for reasons not stated.

Two more days and the stubborn secrecy of the powers-that-be was bust wide open by the sheer necessity of world-wide publicity. This point marked the second step forward in the natural march of events foreseen by those who had provided the root cause.

Yarbridge could have picked up the official announcement from any professional radio station in any known language. By luck he got it from WBAX at Wilkes-Barre.

"A previously unknown phenomenon afflicting the holding of Farmer Barton Maguire, outside Dubuque, Iowa, has been found by experts to be caused by the presence of a filterable virus that is responsible for the ultra-rapid decomposition of chlorophyll. The same virus has also appeared in Brazil, Germany, mid-Russia, China, Pakistan and Rhodesia. Its origin is unknown."

"Well, that's a consolation," commented Yarbridge as the faraway announcer paused for breath. "I'd expected something worse."

"You couldn't!" contradicted Wilkin.

WBAX continued with: "This disease can be spread by contact and borne from one place to another by animals or birds. The government, therefore, prohibits all movements of livestock whether near an affected area or not. Dogs, cats and other domestic creatures must be kept under control. Any found wandering loose will be destroyed on sight without compensation to owners."

"They're becoming tough," observed a driller, thoughtfully. "It can't be for nothing—the public wouldn't stand for it." He pulled at an ear, finished, "I reckon it's serious."

"Shut up and listen," ordered Yarbridge.

"Under the Emergency Powers Act of 1988 the government takes authority to seize any property found to be contaminated and use thereon any measures that may be deemed necessary to destroy the virus. All citizens are required to report affected areas without delay to the nearest post office, police station or military camp. Failure to do so is punishable by a fine of one thousand U.N. dollars or one year's imprisonment."

"Hell's bells!" the driller ejaculated. "Sounds like they're scared."

"Sh-h-h!"

"The following description of symptoms has been issued for the benefit of the public," went on WBAX. "First occurs a bleaching of green leaves which turn gray and dry within forty-eight hours. They are then brittle and lifeless, will readily crumble between the fingers. The process spreads from point of origin in a rapidly increasing circle, destroying plant life over a progressively greater area. The inside of such an area is not dangerous since the virus remains active only at the rim where it can continue to feed on chlorophyll. The rim, therefore, is the danger point; pending arrival of expert assistance the rim should be thoroughly burned by any means at hand and then given similar treatment at any point where advance is found to continue. The Department of Agriculture assures listeners that there is no reason for undue apprehension and that every effort is being made to find a satisfactory method of combating this menace."

Wilkin wiped his glasses and said, "That last lullaby tells two things. One, that they regard it as a genuine menace. Two, that they haven't found what they call a satisfactory method of dealing with it."

"They will," assured Yarbridge.

"Will they?" asked Wilkin.

"You like to think they won't, eh?" inquired the driller, glowering at him.

"I see things as they are and not as I'd prefer to see them," answered Wilkin, stiffly. "My dream world has long been dead."

"The real one is alive. It will go on living."

"The former is factual; the latter hypothetical."

The other let his fists dangle. "When a guy turns to ten-dollar words, I give up."

He went away, sadly shaking his head in the manner of one unable to cope with an idiot. Wilkin finished shining his glasses, carefully fitted them on his nose, eyed Holland as if inviting further comment.

Holland obliged with, "One thing they didn't tell us."

"What's that?"

"Rate of spread."

"Yes," agreed Wilkin. He fiddled his fingers, watched himself doing it. "They didn't tell us."

"Maybe they forgot," offered Yarbridge. "Or didn't think it especially important."

"It could be five inches a month," ventured Holland. "It could be twenty miles per day."

"Now don't start giving me the willies," Yarbridge protested.

"If you want a real headache," suggested Wilkin, "go to bed and think it over. Take away chlorophyll and see what's left."

"It means nothing to me. I don't eat the lousy stuff."

"You're lucky," said Wilkin in the same even tone. "You should survive as the last man."

Yarbridge scowled, said to Holland, "What is he talking about?"

"Something that may never happen."

"I might have guessed it." He sniffed his contempt.

"Or may," said Wilkin.

"There are the oceans," Holland told him, "full of fish."

"How nice!" said Wilkin. He lay down, closed his eyes.

Confused with having half his attention on the radio and only half on this erratic conversation, Yarbridge demanded, "Look here, what has fish got to do with it? Why bring them up?"

Wilkin did not bother to reply.

Holland said, "Oh, forget it," and strolled toward his engine.

"This can't go on for another couple of years," informed Yarbridge, speaking to thin air. "Not when guys go off the beam after four months."

He reached for his microphone, called a person named Jerry without enthusiasm—and without result.

At the thousand-foot mark the barber shop quartet didn't sound so hot and the whisky lacked zip. The celebration had all the joyous verve of a wake held around a frowning corpse. For one thing, they'd been delayed by need to replace a cutter. For another, there were those shenanigans next door, a quarter million miles away.

So they finished the bottle, listened while four cold sober drillers bellowed a bawdy song, put on one or two artificial grins, told one or two unfunny anecdotes. Then somehow they broke it up before properly begun, returned in silence to duty or to bed.

Men were quiet after that, speaking when necessary, tending to hang around the radio receiver or play with the 'scope. Faces became set. The nuclear engine gave out its low whine; the drill went round and round, was drawn up, forced down, rotated again. More cores were stacked outside without anyone knowing or caring whether they held dirt or diamonds. The task had been reduced to a job and the job to a mere function.

As the days drifted by the radio told that the British, Dutch and Belgian governments had brought in a complicated system of food rationing. The United States authorities took control of all cereals and fixed the retail price of bread. Canada followed suit. In the Argentine a million men slaved to build along the northern frontier something described as the Fire Curtain. The Ukrainian Republic made heated protest to the United Nations about what it called infringement of rights of sovereignty, but nothing was said about what had raised Ukrainian bile.

Obviously a thin, bedraggled veil of censorship continued to obscure the international scene. The dunkers of truth were still on the job. But Moonlisteners found significance in the occasional use of new words apparently coined on the spur of the moment and thrust into news bulletins.

"A gun battle took place in Milan early this morning when strong forces of Italian police surrounded a warehouse and trapped a band of chowjackers. Eighteen were killed, more than forty captured. The police lost six.

"New York state troopers grabbed a bunch of beefleggers. The British sent to jail a smooth gentleman described as a burp-baron. Not to be outdone, the Germans raided a noisy plant in the Black Forest wherein large humans and large canines were cooperating in the production of dogburgers."

"Hear that?" exclaimed Yarbridge. "How do guys like those get away with it?"

"They didn't," someone pointed out.

"What I mean is where's the money in it?"

"At the right time, in the right place and in the right conditions there is money in dead rats," Wilkin opined.

"If I remember correctly," put in Holland, seriously, "they actually did eat rats during the siege of Paris."

"Go easy, will you? " Yarbridge thinned his lips. "My stomach can stand only so much."

"Be thankful that you're not in the part of Asia where they have two or three thousands to the square mile," advised Wilkin. "You would stand for something a good deal worse there. Or better, according to your gastronomic viewpoint."

"Such as what?"

"Stiffburgers."

"What?"

"Mock-pork—the dead feeding the living."

Yarbridge yellowed around the jawline. An off-duty driller—apparently asleep—opened a dark eye and stared at Wilkin. He maintained the gaze while he mulled things over, then rolled off his mattress, lumbered across and spoke in a deep rumble.

"I've had too much of you, you four-eyed runt!" He jerked a thumb skyward. "I've a wife and three kids over there. I've worry enough without you trying to be funny. Keep your noisy trap shut, see?"

"I wasn't trying to be funny," Wilkin denied. He wiped his glasses, peered at the big bulk without visible intimidation. "My only daughter is in Iowa."

"More shame to you then, acting the way you do. Hold your teeth together if you want to keep them."

Another driller came along, glanced from one to another, said, "Something wrong, Hank?"

"Nothing much, Joe. Only that I'm working myself up to break a certain gab's neck."

"What'll that buy you?"

"Satisfaction," informed Hank.

James Holland said soothingly, "Not all folk worry the same way. Some nurse it. Some let it go bang; some hope for the best; some expect the worst."

"All right," conceded Hank. "Then he can switch fast from type four to type one."

"Thus shaping myself in your image," said Wilkin. Displaying unexpected nerve, he came to his feet, faced the other. "Why should I?"

"Because, Grandpop, I've got this." His opponent showed a knobby fist half the size of a ham. "And I'm not particular about—"

Wilkin opened a hand, revealed a vest-pocket automatic three inches long. "I've got this—and I'm not finicky either" He waited a moment, his pale eyes level, then ended, "We've got free speech here. You're not taking it away. Beat it, you hairy bum!"

The other studied him calculatingly, up and down, then spat on the ground, turned and headed for the mid-section. Joe went with him. Wilkin reposed on his oxygen bag.

"You blundered there," Holland told him. "He's bothered about his family, as is natural. Some people are touchy when worried."

"So am I," said Wilkin.

"You look it," scoffed Yarbridge. "In my opinion—"

He shut up as Holland nudged him. The latter continued, "Anyway, this is no place to wave a gun around."

"It will be!" Wilkin promised.

The third inevitable step began when the Indian delegate to the United Nations Assembly made a long, impassioned speech that might have been cribbed from the late nineteen thirties. It was upon the same subject: the haves and have-nots. It ended the same way—with an implied threat. It produced the same reaction: open pacification and secret preparation.

Dr. Francisca, chairman of the assembly, dexterously employed a procedural quibble to avoid a vote on the plain issue of who should give what to whom. He had a wary eye on the have-nots, present in full strength and ready to vote as one man. The danger of a complete split was avoided for twenty-four hours. At the end of that time India withdrew from the United Nations. China followed. So did every other nation whose crops could not keep pace with its needs.

Joe saw the first flash on Earth's dark side. The little telescope wasn't popular when Earth resembled a great black ball against a blinding Sun, but occasionally it was used as the terminator approached. He was staring through it in the angled blaze of false twilight when he spotted a flash on Earth's sickle of darkness. Then another and another.

Quietly he left the 'scope, shook Yarbridge awake and whispered, "I've just seen lights over there."

"What of it? Why spoil my sleep?"

"Nobody's seen them before."

"Maybe they weren't looking. There isn't a constant watch as you know quite well."

"I've got a queer feeling about them. They were mighty big flashes."

Yarbridge emitted an imitation snore.

Nearby, Holland stirred, awoke, propped himself on an elbow, asked, "What's the matter now?"

"I don't know," said Joe. "I can't be sure. I want this tramp to check up on the radio."

"Well, what makes you think something may be wrong?"

"I've just seen three great glares on Earth's dark strip."

"Meteors," suggested Holland."

"Do you think so?"

"Could be." He eyed the other. "What else?"

"Atom bombs," said Joe.

"Nuts!"

"Why not?"

"They aren't *that* crazy."

"How can we tell?" Joe asked. "We know only what we hear. And that isn't enough."

"You're morbid."

"Maybe I am," said Joe, doggedly, "but I saw what I saw. Aren't you interested?"

"No."

The other frowned. "Why not?"

"Because I've swallowed a pill that you've yet to take. You'll have to gulp it down sooner or later and whether you like it or not."

"Meaning—?"

"There's nothing we can do. Positively nothing!"

Musing it with much reluctance, Joe finally admitted, "Yes, that's it. Until the ship comes we're trapped. We've got to sit here and watch. We've got to eat our fingers down to the knuckles and—"

Raising an irritated face from where he was lying, Wilkin harshed, "Then go gnaw them some place else. I need sleep even if you don't."

"Earth's dying," said Joe, taking no notice. "The drills are still and the derricks are down and the fields are aflame—and none of you care. Technicians! Bigbrains! And none of you care!"

"Get some shuteye, Joe," advised Holland. "A few sparks in a glass don't signify the crack of doom."

"All, right." Resignedly he turned to leave, added with strange positiveness, "But we'll have that sleepy-eyed lunk at his bawl-box before breakfast—and we'll see who's right and who's wrong."

Yarbridge responded with another snore, a real one this time.

Reclining full length, James Holland stated at the stars visible through the transparency of the dome's conical cap. A blue one kept winking at him alongside the circular rim of the overhead antenna. After a while he closed his eyes but found it impossible to sleep. His brain droned drearily, "There's nothing we can do, nothing we can do."

In the small hours he ceased to court slumber, rolled off his mattress, crept silently past the others' feet and had a long look through the telescope.

There was a babble of insistent voices right across the ether, singsong ones, guttural ones, determined ones, hysterical ones. Ignoring the play of languages none could understand, Yarbridge felt around with his dials, picked up a station that did not identify itself with any call-sign or locale but was rapidly transmitting a series of figures in plain English.

It went on, "The first group of numbers will report for service by six clock this evening, the second group tomorrow, the third the day after. Unless he is totally blind or is certified under the Mental Deficiency Act, the failure of any citizen to report will result in the issue of a warrant for his arrest. This is the Federal Broadcasting Service radiating simultaneously from all stations."

"By hokey!" said Yarbridge. "Sounds like they've taken over the whole shebang from coast to—"

He broke off as the faraway voice continued, "Indian and Chinese forces crossed their borders in great strength at noon yesterday and are attempting to seize the Burmese rice-bowl and such wheat-growing areas of central Russia as the virus has not yet reached. A report that Germany is about to invade the Black Earth region of the Ukraine has been energetically denied in Berlin. The Italians indignantly repudiate a French accusation that they are preparing to attack the uncontaminated agricultural area of southeast France. In view of the serious international situation the President has declared a state of emergency and assumed all the powers to which he is entitled thereunder. His midnight speech emphasized that the time has come to honor our—"

The announcer ceased in mid-sentence. They waited a minute for him to resume but he didn't. Even the sizzle of background noise had gone.

Yarbridge turned a strained face over one shoulder, remarked to the small audience, "That's war—without saying so."

"I could have told you several hours ago," said Joe.

"I'd have bet on it a couple of weeks ago," capped Wilkin.

"How long is it since that virus stuff was first mentioned?" a driller inquired.

Consulting his logbook, Yarbridge informed, "Forty-seven days."

"And how long before the ship is due?"

"Thirty-two."

"Think it'll come?"

It was a shocking question.

Yarbridge passed a hand through tousled hair and growled, "Why not?"

"The ship isn't one of those thinking machines they have in stories," the other pointed out. "Men order it to be sent and other men bring it."

"Well?"

"Suppose they become too busy?"

"That's hardly—"

"Or the ship gets busted wide open?"

"There are two ships," Yarbridge reminded.

"So what? There's a war on. They're parked side by side, like stiffs in a morgue. Whatever wallops one will wallop both."

"The walloping won't be easy," put in Holland. "They've got formidable defenses over there."

"What, after fifty years of peace? They never had enough even when they were having wars."

Joe chipped in with, "How about asking the spaceport, to confirm date of arrival?"

Glooming at his instruments, Yarbridge said nothing.

"What's come over you?" persisted Joe. Suspicion grew into his beefy features. "You're here to maintain contact, aren't you? How about raising the spaceport?"

"I can try," said Yarbridge.

"Try? What d'you mean, try?" Joe glanced around at the listeners, added, "How long since you last spoke to the spaceport?"

"Nine days."

"Haven't you called since then?"

"Dozens of times. No reply."

"No reply," echoed Joe. He swallowed hard, stared at his feet, manifestly could think of nothing more to say.

Wilkin studied him with pale, calculating eyes.

"And you didn't tell us," broke in another driller with unconcealed ire. "These fancy mechanics knew we're cut off but didn't tell us. We're too dim to understand. We're only oil boys, see?"

Holland said, "Now don't start dividing us into rival trade unions just because four of you happen to share the same skill. We're all in this together. The spaceport has something better to do than chat and hold our hands day after day. We've gone many a full week without speaking to it."

"Not when it's being called," retorted the other.

"Radio apparatus isn't infallible," said Yarbridge, not very convincingly. "They may have a technical hitch."

"I always thought you guys were too clever to have hitches."

"I wish to heaven we were!" said Holland, fervently. He rubbed a freckled chin, glanced toward the engine steadily droning on the farther side.

The others followed his gaze and went silent. They knew what he meant. The engine and its coupled generator provided light and they could dispense with that if necessary. Also power for the drill, the radio, the cooker, and other items they could do without in a pinch. Also warmth via the numerous heaters placed equidistantly around the perimeter. They couldn't live through the Lunar nights without warmth. And finally oxygen by electrolysis of Moon-water eighty feet down. They couldn't survive without oxygen.

Frankly alarmed, one asked, "How much jollop have you got for that contraption?"

"You mean thorium oxide?"

"Yes."

"Sufficient for a couple of years."

"Then all you have to do is keep her going?"

"That's all," agreed Holland, straight-faced.

The other looked him up and down as if seeking an invisible joke at his expense. Then he moved away to tend the drill.

Yarbridge used his mike. "Yarboo calling Booster One. Come in Booster One. Come in Booster One!"

He wasted his breath.

As the days rolled by they developed a tendency to ignore the radio most times or treat it with open skepticism when the temptation to listen became too much. The thousand friends behind Yarbridge's god had shrunk to little more than a dozen, the technical qualifications of the missing ones having drawn them into the detection and communications services of the armed forces.

The few survivors told little, though they could have said much. But they did not dare. Vertical beam antenna were now prohibited and their calls were monitored, They spoke briefly and pointlessly, with the extreme wariness of those peculiarly susceptible to the capital charge of disseminating information that might be useful to an enemy.

Yarbridge said wearily to Holland one day, "This is grim. Doesn't matter whether I get George in Memphis or Jules in Toulouse, he can't tell me so much as whether it's raining because somebody across the battle line might need that datum."

"If there *are* any battle lines," said Holland. He pawed his freckles, went on, "What beats me is that in all that gabble nobody mentions who's fighting whom."

"Everyone is fighting everyone," opined Wilkin, coming up behind him. "What else do you expect"

"And when they do see fit to tell anything you get less than half of it," Yarbridge continued. "Listen to this."

"He turned the volume control, brought up a British voice that had been murmuring almost indistinguishably: ". . . And several more robot planes were shot down over London last night. The rest of the country—"

Switching off, he said, "There's a sample. He doesn't say how many. He doesn't say who sent them. He doesn't say what happened to the bomb loads when the planes dropped or what damage was caused."

"Of course he doesn't say," put in Wilkin. "In fact it's a wonder he says anything at all. But it won't be for much longer."

"Why?"

"The lights are going down across the world. Would *you* squat there and count them out loud for the benefit of an unimportant gang upon the Moon?"

"Who says we're unimportant?" inquired Hank, joining them and displaying aggressiveness.

"I do," Wilkin informed. "Who cares for someone looking out the top window when there's a free-for-all in the street?"

"It can't last," decided the other, not caring to argue the point. "They haven't got the stuff. Half a century back they'd have been using supersonic missiles and all kinds of other gadgets. These days they haven't got 'em. Armaments have hit an all-time low."

"Who told you that?" inquired Wilkin.

"Everybody knows it."

"Do they?" He put on a lopsided smile. "Pity we can't ask them today."

Hank scowled, edged nearer the radio and rasped at Yarbridge, "Unimportant or not, we're entitled to know what's happened to our wives and kids. Why doesn't the spaceport—"

It was a gag, for as he got alongside Wilkin he swung a huge fist into the metallurgist's face and grunted with the force of the blow. Wilkin crashed one way while his glasses flew the other. The thing was done with such suddenness that Hank was astride the victim and frisking his pockets before the others had time to interfere. Breathing heavily, he came erect holding the little automatic.

"I never did like sneery guys with guns." His eyes challenged them as beside him Wilkin sat up and held hands to features. He moved over to Yarbridge. "All right, Porky, get busy and raise the spaceport."

"How?"

"He asks me how!" His big hand gave the other's shoulder a shove. "You know how. Let's see you do it—and fast!"

Yarbridge obliged, then said, "There you are. I can call until my tonsils drop out. Now let us see you do better."

"How can I tell that you're calling them in the right place?" He pointed to the dials. "Or, for that matter, that you're correctly tuned to get anybody on that set?"

"How do I know when a cutter is due to be swapped?" asked Yarbridge.

"Don't be funny with me!" A pulse was beating heavily in his forehead, "If the drill goes bust while I stand here a month, I'm going to—"

"You're going to do nothing we don't like," interjected Holland. "And you'd better give me that gun."

"You crazy?"

"Not yet?"

"Me, neither," assured Hank. "So you can go take a walk."

"Thanks," said Holland. "I will." Shoving hands deep in pockets he ambled away, his lips pursed in a silent whistle.

Thirty seconds later the engine stopped. The drill ceased its weary grinding. The lights went out and there was no illumination save through the transparent peak of the otherwise opaque dome. The U-tubes set in the wall no longer fizzed and bubbled. No oxygen trickled into the interior and no hydrogen poured outside.

Hank crossed the circular area with a bull-like rush, gestured with the automatic. "Start her up."

"Sorry."

"I said start her up!"

"Do it yourself."

He examined the engine from end to end, seeking visible evidence of how to do it. Once or twice he toyed momentarily with a lever, stud or switch but thought better of it. He had all the layman's near-superstitious fear of hot-stuff.

"It's your job, not mine." He flourished the weapon again. "Go to it."

"I'm on strike," Holland informed. "My union has called me out."

"If you don't do as you're told, Spotty-pan, I'll put a slug through your bean."

"Well," hazarded Holland, thoughtfully, "that might be one way to get her operating. But I doubt it."

The other drillers had clustered around by now and one demanded, "What's the big idea, cutting the engine?"

"He's trying to show us who's boss," Hank growled. "And I won't have it. No kid's going to push me around."

"There's nothing for it but to make him see sense," put in Joe. He rolled up his sleeves, revealed brawny arms.

"That'll take you a couple of minutes," Holland pointed out.

"So what?"

"You won't have that long."

Joe took a hurried step backward. "No? Why won't we?"

Glancing significantly at the engine which could be trusted to remain quiescent for a million years, Holland advised, "Wait and see."

"Give him the gun, Hank," said Joe, nervously.

"Go on, give it him," urged the rest as panic mounted.

"I think he's a liar," declared Hank, mulish. "I think he's taking us for a ride. He wouldn't lounge there easylike if something were about to happen."

"I'm hoping it won't." Holland ostentatiously consulted his wrist watch. "Because I'm betting that your nerves will crack before mine." Extracting a handkerchief, he mopped his forehead, had another look at the watch.

It was an effective gesture. The driller alongside Hank decided that more waiting would be unendurable. He made a snatch at the gun, got it, strove to twist it out of the other's grip. Stubborn to the last, Hank hung on. The remaining pair suddenly made up their minds and joined the fray, ignoring Hank's grunts and curses. The disputed weapon emitted a thin, hard crack and planted a slug in the dirt between stamping feet. It came loose. One of them tossed it toward the onlooker who was still doing his best to maintain a phony expression of strained anxiety.

"Start her up! For Pete's sake start her up!"

The struggle ceased by mutual consent and all four tried to urge him with their eyes. He did things including several that weren't necessary and some they couldn't see. The engine moaned. He let in the generator clutch. The lights came on. The U-tubes bubbled and gassed.

"You big, awkward hophead!" one of them rumbled at Hank. "Why can't you leave well alone? Think we haven't got troubles enough?"

They went back to the drill. Hank stared a while at his own hands, opening and closing the fingers, favored Holland with a look of dark suspicion, then lumbered after the others.

Holland made for his sleeping space, picked up his helmet, checked the pressure in its little oxygen cylinder. He fitted the headpiece while Wilkin sat grimly nursing a split lip and Yarbridge watched in silence. Exiting via the double trap, he trudged through fine gray Lunar dust, past the stack of cores and at a suitable spot fired the gun until it was empty. Then he hurled it into the distance.

Returning, he removed the helmet, carefully placed it on its rack, lay down and studied the overhead circle of transparency. Wilkin still offered no remark.

After a while, Yarbridge said, "You were lucky to get away with that. I don't know that I'd have had the nerve to try it."

"Comes easier when you've done it once or twice before," Holland informed. "A few years ago I was compelled to learn that one needn't always be completely without means of defense. In the last resort there's often one thing that can be used and effectively."

"Such as what?"

"The other fellow's ignorance."

"Suppose he isn't ignorant?"

"Then it's your hard luck." He smiled to himself, went on, "But everybody is ignorant by one standard if not by another. I'd be a prize sucker for a radio gag if you could think up a good one."

"I guess so," agreed Yarbridge who had never given a thought to this aspect of his own ability.

He made up for lost time by commencing forthwith to examine the possibilities. As weeks and months rolled on and the situation worsened a crafty scheme or two might prove useful. Indeed, technical knowledge plus sharp wits might decide between life and death.

The ship did not come, neither on the appointed day nor a fortnight later. They required the extra two weeks to incubate to point of vocal expression the opinion that it would never arrive.

Other data supported this dread thought. The telescope had enough power to reveal numerous and sinister markings on Earth's land surface though not with clarity sufficient to determine their true nature. The instrument had to be used with imagination that might be over- or under-exercised according to the individual.

And night after night, day after day brilliant flashes had been observed on the mother-globe, waxing and waning until finally they ceased.

Only seven stations could be heard across the full widths of the long medium, short and ultra-short bands They were unintelligible, radiating high-speed but very weak signals in code. A week later there were four. Ten days afterward there was one. Then that, too, went off the air. The ether was silent. Earth rolled along her appointed course, a black ball on the night side, a shining picture on the day side, and gave forth no single voice.

At that point they took stock of food supplies. Originally enough packaged meals and emergency rations had been dumped to last seven men for twenty months and nearly a third of that time had now passed. If they reduced consumption to the minimum and rigorously prevented all waste the seven might live another sixteen months.

That much being known, the arithmetic of the situation became obvious to each man, though he kept it strictly to himself, coddling it within the secret recesses of his own mind. If one died, so much the better for the rest; they'd make out another eighteen or nineteen months. If two went under the survivors would gain a further spell of life. Three deaths would permit the remaining four to eat until the engine stopped—and beyond that if they could.

The environment was beginning to force a distorted picture into each mind, making it see that the others were not men with mouths, but mouths with men around them.

But this hidden reaction betrayed its presence in indirect ways. The hairy-chested quartet stopped the drill to cut down power consumption and—as they theorized—help eke out the precious reserve of hot-stuff. Holland noted the deed, deduced its purpose and did not bother to tell them that disintegration was held at a uniform rate regardless of power used. It could not be speeded up without danger nor slowed without ceasing to provide exploitable energy. Their action was futile.

One day Joe caught him away from the rest, sidled up, said, "I've been thinking."

"It's a healthy occupation," Holland approved.

"What if this gadget packs in?"

"Then it's my responsibility to get it going again."

"Yes, I know" He glanced around to make sure none were within hearing. "We're stuck here quite a spell. If anything happens to you, we're sunk."

"That's what I like about it," said Holland.

"I don't," declared Joe with some emphasis. "If you fall sick at the wrong time, it'll mean the end."

"Very true. So on no account must I become ill." He eyed the other shrewdly. "It might help if we reserved some whisky for an emergency. The way it's evaporating out of sealed bottles there won't be any left pretty soon."

"It isn't me—it's the others," said Joe.

"It would be!" endorsed Holland.

Joe blinked and went on, "Anyway, what I want to say is this: that it's your duty to teach someone else to handle this groan-machine. One isn't enough. We need another who knows how."

"Such as yourself."

"I could learn."

"I don't doubt it," said Holland.

"Well, why shouldn't you show somebody?"

"I may come to regret it—if one can have regret's in one's sleep."

"What d'you mean by that?

"If your thinking has been taken far enough, you know darned well what I mean."

"Smart, aren't you?" spat Joe, momentarily vicious.

"The circumstances compel me to be," assured Holland blandly. Crossing fingers, he held them under Joe's nose. "This is me. Don't you forget it."

Yarbridge came across as Joe stamped away. "He looks sour. You been rubbing him the wrong way?"

"He's just applied for the post of assistant atomechanic. I turned him down."

"Did you tell him you've been instructing me?"

"No." He pondered briefly, explained, "Three of us have completely different qualifications whereas the other four are and always have been birds of a feather. Each of those four knows what the others are doing and why they're doing it, at any given moment. They understand each other in a way they can't understand us. Our methods and functions defeat them. No matter how irrational it may be, people often tend to dislike what they're unable to understand."

"All the same, if there's a split in this group it's of their own making," Yarbridge observed.

"Yes, but we mustn't blame them for it. The division is in some ways as natural as the sunrise. So, if I'd told him I'd picked you instead of a driller as standby mechanic, it might aggravate matters."

Yarbridge gestured toward the food stack. "I fear they'll be more than aggravated by the time we've eaten most of the way down that. Sooner or later somebody's going to make us put on a local version of what's happened on Earth."

"While there's life there's hope," said Holland.

"Of what? A miracle?"

"A ship."

"That *would* be a miracle," declared Yarbridge, flatly.

He was wrong. In due time a ship came, deliberately and without benefit of supernatural forces.

It was ten months since those in the dome had first heard mention of the virus and by now they'd almost forgotten its existence. Events that followed had overshadowed the cause, like a prolonged riot in which none can recall who or what started it.

The food stack now stood at less than half its original height. The drill remained sunk to the best part of two thousand feet, its drive-gears motionless, its shaft red-brown with a fine layer of rust. The engine droned and shuddered, the lights still burned, the numerous heaters gave protection against night's exterior low of -150° C. Moon-water still surrendered its oxygen and maintained the breath of life. The radio remained serviceable but had not been in operation for weeks.

Four oxygen-inflated beds were lined together on the perimeter, three more at the opposite side. This sleeping arrangement was symbolic of psychological antagonisms that no man wished to boost to a crisis yet no man was able to cure. Civilized conditioning persisted enough to hold the issue in precarious suspense at least for a little while longer, though each man knew deep in his soul that a time might come when one would starve to death while another sat and watched unmoved.

They were loafing around, four at one side and three at the other, each indulging the vacuous occupation of deciding what he could do with most if only it were there. Conscious of his age, physique, and the shape of things to come, Wilkin yearned for his lost gun. Hank ached for his wife and kids but refused to show it or mention it. Yarbridge's need was no more than a familiar voice seeking him out and calling him in. Holland's choice, vividly and tantalizingly depicted in his mind, was a two-gallon can of pineapple juice, cold or warm.

And the ship came.

It screamed overhead and howled into the distance and turned in a wide sweep and came back with a rising roar. The sounds cut off. The dome trembled slightly as great tonnage sat itself outside.

Hank stood up with little beads of moisture on his forehead. He had the expression of a sleepwalker. The others came to their feet seeking visible confirmation that all ears had heard the same.

"The ship!" said Yarbridge on a note of incredulity. "It can't be anything but the ship!"

"Didn't make that sort of noise last time," observed Wilkin, unwilling to jump to conclusions. He felt vaguely around his pockets as if looking for something without knowing what. "Maybe it's a different one."

"Sounded different to me," confirmed Joe. "Bigger and faster."

"I'll take a look." Holland picked up his helmet.

A loud knocking sounded on the double-trap before he had time to fit the headpiece. He dumped it, went to the trap with six pair of eyes watching, manipulated the locks.

The three who entered were not human.

Gray uniformed, gray-blue skinned and hairless, they came into the dome with the casual, unsurprised air of neighbors wanting to borrow the mower. They had two arms and two legs apparently formed of cords and cartilage rather than muscle and bone, for they bent in a curve from end to end instead of at a mid-joint. The six fingers of each hand were similarly bendable and jointless.

Apart from these noteworthy features of strange coloring and rubber skeletons they approximated to human appearance. Their mouths looked natural, their eyes were of human type, their ears normal enough though somewhat large. All three stood a couple of inches above Holland, the tallest of his group. All three were bald and hatless.

Wilkin was the first to break the silence. He peered over the tops of his glasses as if to insure that they were not causing an optical illusion, and said, "Who are *you?*"

"That doesn't matter," responded the foremost of the trio. "Does it?"

"Where did you learn to speak English?" put in Holland, having expected communication by means of signs and gestures. He felt behind to check that he wasn't flat on his mattress and deep in a ridiculous dream. His hand prodded Yarbridge's paunch.

"On your own world of course. Where else could we learn it?"

"Can you take us back there?" inquired Hank, single-mindedly dismissing everything in favor of one aim.

"We have come for that purpose." The alien glanced around, noting everything but not curious. "We intend to leave with the minimum of delay. Do whatever is necessary before you depart and do it quickly."

It wasn't a request. It wasn't an order. It was a plain statement of plain fact, devoid of either politeness or authority. Somehow it created a cold impression that the speaker was not in the habit of asking or telling, but rather of presenting a realistic case and awaiting the inevitable result. An inhuman, unemotional mind concerned only with facts.

They packed in a hurry, their minds filled with a thousand questions postponed by the glorious vision of escape. It did not occur to any of them to view the newcomers as enemies or treat them with hostility. They had no data to go upon. So far as they were concerned the Martians—or whoever they were—had turned up at long last and at the most opportune time.

Each bearing a pack of personal belongings, they donned helmets, followed the three from the dome. Holland, the last out, switched off the nuclear engine, fastened the double-trap. Filing aboard a vessel several times the size of those with which they were familiar, they were conducted to a large cabin and left to themselves. The ship boosted immediately afterward, plunged toward Earth.

Nobody talked much. Shock of alien contact plus inward speculation of what was awaiting at the other end kept them fairly silent until the landing. The trip had taken fourteen hours, less than half the time they'd required on the outward journey nearly a year ago.

An alien not identifiable as one of those already seen appeared at the cabin, said, "We are grounded and you may leave. Follow me." Conducting them to the long ramp leading from the air lock, he pointed outward. "You will find food and accommodation in that camp. We'll summon you when required."

Descending the ramp, they set feet on bare brown earth, paused to survey their surroundings. Straight ahead stood a large collection of hutments typical of an army training center. To the left were the outskirts of a medium-sized town. Mountains loomed in the far background and a small river flowed on the right.

"Where's this?" Yarbridge glanced around, noted that no alien had stayed with them. "Anyone recognize the place?"

"We can find out." Hoisting his pack, Holland started forward "We've got tongues in our heads."

Hank moved up alongside him, recent differences forgotten. "What did that guy mean about calling us when wanted? Does he think we're going to squat in this dump until somebody whistles to us like dogs?"

Holland shrugged, offered no comment.

"If so, he's got another thing coming," Hank went on. "I'm more than grateful for the hitch from up there but that doesn't mean I've got to wait for the official thank-you ceremony. I'm going home and fast! What's the use of making for this camp?"

"Before you know which way to go and how to get there, you've got to find out where you are."

"You may be a thousand miles from home," Yarbridge contributed. "With all the world to pick from you can't expect those aliens to dump you in your own back yard."

"I don't care if it's a million miles. I'll make it if I have to crawl it. I've a wife and kids."

"I had a daughter," said Wilkin, dull-toned. "And I doubt whether I'll ever see her again."

"Shut up, Misery!" growled Hank.

Passing through the main gates they went to the first hut. It contained forty Chinese men and women who eyed them with blank indifference. They tried the second. That held a weird mixture of races including a half-naked brown man with a bone through his nose.

"Anyone know English?" called Holland.

A trembling oldster came from the back. He had a long, untended beard and hot but rheumy eyes.

"I do, my son."

"What goes here?"

"What goes?" He had a moment of muddled mystification before his features cleared. "Ah, my son, you seek enlightenment?"

"That is the idea," agreed Holland. "More or less."

"You are inspired," informed the other, grasping him by the arm. "For you have come to the right place and the right person. I have been privileged to save the world. I saved it upon my knees, a sinner crying at the gates of heaven. I prayed while the city fell and children screamed and the unrepentant died." The grip tightened, the eyes grew hotter. "Until finally my voice was heard and help came from the skies. Listen, my son, if you, too, will have the grace—"

"Sorry, dad, some other time." Holland pulled gently away.

They transferred attention to the third hut, leaving the oldster querulously mumbling in his beard. Outside the door of this adjoining place a big brawny man stood watching their approach.

He rasped as they reached him, "Another bunch, eh? Where did they find you?"

"On the Moon," Holland told him.

"So?" He studied them from beneath bushy brows, then offered, "Some folks don't know when they're well off. Why didn't you stay there?"

"Would you?"

"Hah! You bet your shirt I would!" He spat on the ground. "Unless I could find a way to drop it on this alien mob that has darned near wiped out humanity."

Hank pushed forward, his beefy features working. "It doesn't look wiped out to me."

"It wouldn't," agreed the other, giving him a calculating up and down. "We're all here in this camp and in that town. All sixty thousand of us. There aren't any more except a scattered few being found and dragged in like you."

"There aren't any more?" Hank had difficulty in understanding it. "You mean—?"

"The world is empty save for this collection of racial remnants." He waved a hand to indicate the local area. "This is us—Homer Saps."

"You sure you know what you're talking about?" asked Yarbridge.

"I ought to, mister. I've been here most of a month." He gave them another shrewdly estimating look-over, went on, "My name's Deacon. I'm an Australian, not that that means anything these days. If you fellows are wanting some place to bunk, you'd better come in here. We've room for ten and we'd rather have you than a gang of half-wild, half-witted Dyaks or Hottentots."

They followed him inside. Spring beds were lined against both walls, each with a cupboard and arms-rack. A tattered and faded military notice in English flapped behind the door. Some thirty men, mostly white, observed their entrance apathetically. One of them had the broad, flat, features and monkish haircut of an Eskimo.

Slinging his pack onto a vacant bed, Holland inquired, "Just where are we?"

"Outside a place called Kaystown in Alberta. It jumped up in two or three years after someone struck oil. Nearest dump of any size was Lethbridge."

"Was?"

"Half of it's flat and the rest is empty."

He sat on the springs, stared at the wall, subconsciously noted that the windows needed washing. After a while, he asked, "How do you know these aliens caused it all?"

"They told me so."

"They openly boasted of it?"

"No, I can't say they bragged," admitted Deacon with a mite of reluctance. He looked as though he'd have enjoyed another forceful spit had he been outside. "They're neither conscience-stricken nor triumphant. They mentioned it as an accomplished fact, like saying that two and two make four."

"I wonder," mused Holland.

"You wonder what?"

"Whether they're opportunists. Whether they're kidding. Maybe they're cashing in on a ready-made situation. Maybe they're grabbing the discredit in order to establish psychological mastery."

"You think they mightn't have done it?" Deacon's features hardened.

"It's possible."

"Won't pay you to talk that way around here."

"Why not?"

"You've had it easy on the Moon, little as you may know it. You've not tasted what most folk down here have experienced. And they're touchy, see? They don't like these aliens and they won't be amiable toward anyone who does like them." He leaned forward, "There's hatred all around, long, fierce, all-consuming. If you sniff, you can smell it. If you look, you can see it."

"Then why don't they do something about it? Sixty thousand against one ship—heck, they could swamp it!"

"The idea has been stewed until it's boiled to rags," Deacon informed. "For one thing, they have weapons and we haven't. For another, what they've done before they can do again."

"What are you getting at?"

"They dropped a virus. It ate green stuff at faster than walking pace. It killed the grass and everything that lives on grass directly or indirectly But it left the seeds lying below ground. So now they're coming up; the grass is returning. All that those rubber-legged caricatures need do is sling out another dose of poison. That would wipe out the new crop and the only seeds still down would be the ones that refused to germinate. It would mean finish!"

One of the listeners put in, "Besides what's the use of jumping the ship unless we can catch them all together? We can't. They've a flock of little boats constantly roaming the world"

"And there are plenty more aliens wherever they've come from," contributed another.

"Do you know where they came from?" Holland asked Deacon.

"Nowhere around this neck of the cosmos. Some faraway star that hasn't a number, much less a name. That's what they say."

"Hm-m-m!" He pondered it for quite a time, then remarked, "So they're a long, long way from home. I'd like to know more about them."

"You'll know plenty before you're through," Deacon promised. "For myself, I'd like to see them at the seventh layer of the seventh hell!"

The summons came late next morning. One alien appeared armed with no more than blank indifference to the looks with which he was greeted. He went from hut to hut until he found the seven.

"Come with me."

Hank bristled forthwith. "Who does he think he—?"

He closed his trap as Holland jogged him with a sharp elbow. "Let's not become noisy just yet."

The alien stood watching them with blue, humanlike eyes. His strangely colored and impassive face gave no indication of whether he had heard the brief exchange.

Holland went out with Yarbridge close behind. The others hesitated, then followed. They walked to the ship without further remark, trailed their guide to a cabin in the nose occupied by four more of his kind.

Without preamble the biggest of the four picked on Joe and asked, "What is your profession?"

"Boring engineer," informed Joe. "A driller, like these." He indicated the other three.

"Driller of what?"

Joe explained it more fully.

"So four of you do the same thing." The other thought it over, turned to the guide, said, "They should interest Klaeth, he being a geologist. Take them to him."

Yarbridge's turn came next. Admitting that he was a radio operator he was rewarded by being sent to be interviewed by an alien named Ygath. Then Wilkin was questioned.

"Ah!" exclaimed the alien. "A metallurgist, no less. That is gratifying. Mordan has been hoping to find one such as you."

Wilkin was conducted elsewhere. He followed his guide gloomily, his pale eyes dull behind his glasses. That left Holland as the last for treatment.

"And you?"

"Atomechanic."

"That tells us nothing. just what do you *do*?"

"I tend and service atomic-powered engines."

"What do you mean by atomic-powered?"

Holland's back hairs gave a twitch but he permitted no surprise to show in his features. "It is power derived from the controlled decomposition of certain unstable elements or compounds."

"Metals?"

"Certain rare metals or their oxides."

"You had better stay here," declared the other. "I shall deal with you myself." He switched to a sibilant language as he addressed one of his companions who went away, returned in short time with a wad of papers.

"These are the documents you require, Drhan," he said, handing them over.

Scanning them rapidly, Drhan nodded approval, pointed to a tubular chair, told Holland, "You will sit there." When he was seated Drhan studied him a while, frankly trying to estimate his intelligence and capabilities. Finally he informed, "It was as well that we picked you and your friends off that dead satellite. You are all technicians and we are badly in need of technicians."

"Why?"

"Because we have acquired a world replete with things we do not understand."

"Indeed?" Holland cast a significant glance at the huge and complicated instrument board beneath the bow observation port. "Yet you're miles ahead of us there."

"You think so?"

"That's how it looks."

"It would," agreed Drhan. "But appearances can be deceptive. We are backward in many branches of science. A ship such as this is something we might not have developed of our own accord for centuries to come. Fortunately others did the job for us. We have gained a big advance by proxy." Without bothering to explain in detail he indulged another unconcealed summing up of his listener. "Now these others teach us to build ships and run them. In return we permit them to eat."

"You permit them?" Holland sat up, feeling cold.

"Yes." The gray-blue face remained blank. "Though backward in some respects we are advanced in others. Like everyone else, we have developed weapons characteristic of the subjects which we excel. Ours are effective, as you have seen for yourself. We do not destroy people. We are content to destroy food and leave people to obliterate themselves in the battle for the remaining crumbs. We persuade the opposition to slaughter itself."

"That must save you an awful lot of bother and heartache," remarked Holland.

If the other perceived the sarcasm he did not show it, for he added with the air of one stating an obvious and incontrovertible fact, "Take away food and you take away life. No more is necessary, no more need be done."

"Why deprive us of ours? What have we done to you?"

The question did not accord with Drhan's logic because he had to mull it quite a time before he said, "You have done nothing to us. Why should you? How could you? We want your world because we need it. We have taken it because it would not have been given had we asked for it. We struck effectively and without warning because that is the best guarantee of success. Surely you can see the sense of that?"

"I can," admitted Holland, grimly.

Drhan went on, "Far, far in the past we stood urgently in need of another world reasonably similar to our own but could do nothing about it until we acquired ships. Then for four hundred of your years we searched the cosmos around us before we found one and seized it. In due time we had to have another. It took us twice as long to discover. Now we must have a third. There aren't many that fit our specification; they're rather rare. It has required almost two thousand years to find this one of yours."

"Two thousand? Do you live *that* long?"

"Of course not. Those two thousand years cover many expeditions sent out generation after generation."

"Do your people know that you've found this world?"

"Not yet. Not until some of us return to tell them. We have no means of sending signals so far. The ship will have to go back with precise details of location." His eyes gazed shrewdly into Holland's and for the first time his face showed the faintest glimmer of a smile. "From the viewpoint of your kind that is something worth knowing, as doubtless you have decided. It means that if you can permanently disable this vessel you will escape our attentions for another two thousand years. Doesn't it?"

"The idea is not without attraction," Holland admitted.

"Therefore I suggest that you discourage any hotheads from trying," advised Drhan. "There are few of you left. It would be a pity if there were none."

"Why leave any at all in the first place? You could have killed off the scattered survivors."

"And thus destroy the knowledge we must acquire?" He motioned toward the wad of papers lying on his desk. "Already we have done much exploring. And what have we found? That this world is full of ingenious machines some of which we understand, some of which we think we understand, and others of which we know nothing. But they are ours by right of conquest. They are a valuable part of our inheritance. We must learn to use them, know how they operate right down to basic principles. How are we to learn these things without waste of time?"

"How do you expect?"

"That those who know will teach us."

"Or what?"

"There is no 'or' about it," assured Drhan with all the positiveness of experience. "The will to resist weakens as the body shrivels and the belly becomes bloated with hunger. We know. We have seen it happen again and again."

"Unmoved?"

Once more his mind had to plow through unaccustomed labyrinths to catch the question and try to pin it down, And then he could not devise a satisfactory answer.

With mild complaint, he said, "I don't comprehend. The issue is a simple one, namely, we or you. The result is perfectly proper and natural: the weak become subject to the strong."

"And the stupid to the clever?" suggested Holland.

"It is the same thing," declared Drhan. Picking up the papers, he sought through them, his fingers bending either way with equal facility. "Now, we have here several reports of certain great power machines devoid of visible fuel supplies. I presume that these are the atomic mechanisms of which you speak?"

"Probably."

"Then you will explain them to us."

Obediently Holland got on with the job of explaining.

Deacon made the springs squeak as he sat up and asked, "They try to pick your brains?"

"That was their purpose," conceded Yarbridge. "They know something of radio but haven't got as far as frequency modulation, let alone stereoscopic T. V. and suchlike stuff. They're just emerging from the spark-signal stage."

"How much did you tell them?"

"A fat lot. I can't hand out in one day what took me about three years to acquire."

"Don't tell 'em anything," Deacon ordered, making it sound authoritative. "Feed them a lot of useless guff instead. That's what I did. I was sitting with a ton of food in the loneliest part of Northern Territory when one of their little boats picked me up. I'd been prospecting in happy ignorance of what was happening elsewhere. I'd found a dollop of slaty flakes in a river bed and knew I'd struck osmiridium. Think I told them all that? Not on your life! I misled them up the garden path. You do the same if you want peace!"

"It's not so easy for us," put in Joe. "We can't kid them our drills bring up lots of little brass Buddhas."

"Say you go round poking for fresh water. Make it sound scientific and say you plant a drill wherever a hazel twig jerks around. That'll get them playing with bits of stick."

"You don't credit them with much intelligence, do you?" inquired Holland.

"Do you?" Deacon countered aggressively.

"Certainly."

"You would!" said Deacon beginning to dislike Holland and not hesitating to show it. He glanced around the hut, found moral support in many faces. "I bet you think them a good deal sharper than what is left of your own kind?"

"Not necessarily."

"Backing out, eh?"

"Not at all. I say I don't think them dopey."

"Meaning you think we are dopey?"

"When you consider the present state of affairs there is much to be said for that theory," said Holland. "But I don't agree with it. Not just yet."

"Not here, you don't," observed Deacon, pointedly. "On that ship it may be different. Perhaps you change your mind to suit the company you keep. How much have you been telling them of what you know?"

"As much as can be told in a few hours."

"A Kahsam!" pronounced Deacon gaining color.

Low murmurs sounded around the hut. Men fidgeted, rubbed their knuckles, eyed Holland with antagonism; all but the one who resembled an Eskimo and didn't know a word of English.

Holland began, "Not knowing what a Kahsam is supposed to be, I—"

"I'll tell you." Deacon stood up, walked heavily to the other's bedside. "First wise-boy they took on board was a bleary little goat named Kahsam, a professor of languages from some snoot college. He spent a fortnight teaching them English and was tickled to bits because they learned so fast. He was overjoyed to help those who'd filled his college with corpses."

"Did he know that at the time?"

"Shut up and listen, will you? He did his stuff for two weeks and thought himself mighty cute. When they'd finished with him they dumped him in one of the most comfortable apartments in town, gave him a food priority certificate."

"That was nice," said Holland, lying back and surveying the other's angry features.

"First chance that came along we pulled him to pieces," informed Deacon, displaying savage satisfaction. "His playmates haven't missed him yet." Licking thick lips, he added with sinister meaning, "Since then we've got a name for any guy who willingly and persistently collaborates with the enemy. He's a Kahsam. A traitor to his kind is a Kahsam. Sooner or later he goes the same way."

"I wouldn't care for that," admitted Holland, rubbing his freckles and grinning upward.

Irritated further by this airiness, Deacon went on, "I invited you and your bunch in here so as to keep other types out. That means I've a duty to warn you when you're sticking out your necks. You've an equal duty to take notice and not try us too far." He paused a moment, added, "Because what I've said isn't just talk!"

With that he returned to his bed-space, lay down and scowled at the roof. Other men studied him in silence, now and again frowned at the culprit. The Eskimo gazed steadily at nothing while Wilkin blinked at him through thick glasses and the four drillers proceeded to deal a worn and filthy pack of cards.

After a while Holland sighed introspectively, went out for a breath of night air and a look at the stars. A minute later Yarbridge joined him.

"That Deacon is a natural ringleader," whispered the radio operator.

"I know."

"He's a decent enough guy providing you don't offend his sense of what's right."

"True, brother, true."

"Then why try making an enemy of him?"

"I need enemies."

"Jumping jiminy!" said Yarbridge, low-voiced. "We're in enough of a mess without stirring up more."

"Worry not nor weep tears of dire despair," advised Holland, patting him on the back. "I am the Kahsam, not you."

"It's nothing to joke about," Yarbridge insisted, looking serious. "These survivors are jumpier than a flea in a hot oven and they can't be blamed for it. They've seen, heard and felt things that we avoided while on the Moon. They are pinned down here with too little to do and they can't escape because a man must eat while on the run."

"I am not lacking in imagination," Holland reminded.

"Then why don't you use some of it? If you insist on flaunting treachery in their faces, you're liable to beat it to the ship six yards ahead of a lynching party."

"You must have precognition," said Holland, patting him again. "Such a fate is my purpose, my desired aim."

Staring at him in the starlight, Yarbridge muttered, "I'll keep you out of trouble whether you like it or not."

"How?"

"First time you're not around I'll warn them that you're off your nut."

The warning was effective for a time. He went to the ship every morning, returned to the hut each evening and was met with uneasy suspicion rather than open hostility. Their ready acceptance of Yarbridge's diagnosis was natural in the strange circumstances for not a day passed without some man running amuck in the nearby town or some woman creating an hysterical scene as overtaxed nerves finally snapped. It was understood by everyone that at any time a man or woman might prove unable to take it, be calm today, completely crazy tomorrow.

Thus the mental conditioning born of the situation impelled them to treat him much as one would a prospective lunatic and it was ten days before they found cause to revert to their original attitude. He entered the hut at dusk, sat on the end of his bed, spoke to Yarbridge.

"I won't be here tomorrow."

"How's that?"

"They're flying me south."

"Only you? Not the rest of us?"

"Only me. I'm going down in one of their little lifeboats. They want samples of hot-stuff to take back to their own world."

Erupting from his bed-space, Deacon loudly demanded, "Are you helping them get it?"

"Of course. It's buried deep in an abandoned plant covering six square miles. They don't even know what to look for—so how can they dig it out without help?"

"So much the better," said Deacon. "Left to themselves they'd never find it or recognize it when it was right in their rubbery mitts. But you have to open your dirty big trap!"

Somewhat mordantly, Wilkin chipped in, "We've got to look at things as they are rather than as we'd like them to be. I don't see how we can get by without playing ball even if we play no more than we can help."

"You wouldn't see," growled Deacon. "You're old and already half dead behind those weak eyes." He put big fists on big hips. "Let me tell you something, mister: that virus can't live without food any more than we can. I got that straight from the rubber boys who invented the stuff. Twenty hours without chlorophyll kills it stone dead. Know what that means?"

Staring stonily forward, Wilkin did not reply.

"It means that this world has been virus-free for weeks, maybe some of it for months. If birds hadn't carted it around, it might have been free before then. The virus has eaten itself out of existence. Untouched seeds are coming up. North of the town are skeletal trees already forcing out new buds and leaves. There are acres of tiny shoots that will become badly thinned-out corn. When those lousy invaders beat it we shall be able to cope for keeps providing we can last out on canned stuff the first couple of months."

"They know we can cope," Wilkin, answered dully. "Mordan said so."

"What else did he say?"

"They'd leave us in cold storage, be gone two and a half years and come back in great strength with many ships. By that time we should have far more food growing around than sixty thousand can eat—and if we want to keep it we'd better have the bands out and the flags flying for them."

"I'd as soon kiss a flock of crocodiles."

"What alternatives do you suggest?" invited Holland.

"Not the one you've chosen," snapped Deacon, his complexion darkening. "I'll be a Kahsam for nobody."

"I'm with you there," declared Hank, standing up and scowling at Holland.

"Me, too," supported Joe. "Knuckling down can go too far. When a guy hands over atomic power for the asking, I reckon—"

Yarbridge shot to his feet and flapped pudgy hands. "Quit snapping and snarling. What do you bums know of atomics?"

"Not much," said Deacon. He jerked a heavy thumb in the general direction of the ship. "But it's more than those stinkers have any right to know. It's enough to tell me that atomic power is a gift too big for those we don't love."

"You said it!" endorsed a dozen voices emphatically.

"Furthermore," continued Deacon, encouraged without needing it, "you're a radio guy, not a nuclear specialist. So what do *you* know about it?"

"The stuff is dangerous to handle. It has to be moved with tongs half the length of a flagpole or, better still, by remote control. What will it do to that crowd if in their innocence they start playing with it like sand?"

Taken aback, Deacon eyed him uncertainly. "You think the radiations will burn them to crisps?"

"I don't know for sure." Yarbridge gestured toward Holland, who was reposing carelessly on his bed and listening with academic interest. "But he does! And on the Moon he made a remark I haven't forgotten. He said that when you're without any other means of resistance you can take advantage of your opponent's ignorance."

"So that's the idea!" Deacon stewed it a moment, said to Holland, "Why didn't you tell us instead of lolling around and watching us go on the boil?"

"Because it is not the idea," Holland informed. "They know that radiation is highly lethal and that the stuff must be handled with extreme care. I told them."

"You did?" Deacon seemed unable to believe his ears. Eventually he rasped, "There you are, men, a Kahsam!"

"He's kidding us," suggested Yarbridge, bewildered and reproachful.

"I told them," repeated Holland, irritatingly matter of fact. Putting feet on the floor he braced himself. "They took a steel safe out of one of the town's banks this morning and have lugged it on board as a suitable cupboard for samples."

"That's right," endorsed a gaunt, blue-jowled man at the other end of the hut. "I saw them carting it away and wondered—"

"They're not having it *all* their own way," asserted Deacon, veins swelling in his neck. "Without this dirty Kahsam they'll be stumped!"

So saying, he made a mad-bull rush for the traitor's bed-space. A dozen others jumped with him. Anticipating this, Holland had come to his feet, ready and prepared even while looking casual. Now he leaped the Eskimo, bed and all, shot through the door into outer darkness. He ran for the ship, moving in long, lithe strides that heavier men would find hard to overtake.

Behind him occurred the precise sort of delay for which he had hoped. Fury is impetuous, possessed of no time or inclination for thought; therefore the enraged dozen attempted the impossible by trying to get through the door in a solid bunch. They jammed together, cursing vividly, until Deacon, Hank and a couple of others tore themselves free by main force and raced after the fugitive. Forty or fifty from neighboring huts emerged and joined the chase on general principles.

It was most of a mile to the space vessel and Holland made it two hundred yards ahead of a skinny but whipcord-muscled pursuer who had shown a surprising turn of speed. A bright light bloomed above the ship's lowered ramp as an alien guard detected the oncoming rush of feet. Holland ran up the ramp and through the open luck unopposed by the guard. Two more guards appeared, motioned him farther inward before they joined the third at the lock.

The one who had switched the light bawled, "Hold it!" About to mount the ramp, the skinny runner paused, glanced behind in search of support, glowered up at the guard. The rest of the pack arrived, milled around and oathed while each waited for someone to bell the cat.

"Go away," ordered the guard.

Deacon planted a big boot on the ramp, told him, "We want that louse you've just taken aboard."

"What've you got against lice?" called a voice from the back. "He's a stinking Kahsam!"

"Go away," repeated the guard, not interested in reasons or causes.

For a moment it seemed as if Deacon were about to take the lead and thus precipitate the general rush, but he thought better of it when the guard produced a high-pressure hand-spray. His companions continued to fidget around murmuring oaths and threats.

His eyes gleaming as he scowled up toward the ship's light, Deacon said to the guard, "All right, you can keep the dirty scut and welcome! And we mean keep him—for good!"

"Go away," repeated the guard, impassively.

They went slowly and defiantly, balked of their prey and voicing their disappointment with lavish use of adjectives. Standing behind an observation port, Holland watched them depart, then spoke to Drhan and Ygath at his side

"They're in an ugly mood. It is hard for people to be coldly realistic after many highly emotional experiences."

"I suppose so," commented Drhan. He scratched a large ear with a flexible finger. "It is well that you have kept telling us of rising danger to yourself and that we held the lock open as you requested."

"We could have foreseen it without being told," remarked Ygath, "had we known the importance of this atomic power."

"Naturally they don't like us taking the biggest thing they've got," agreed Drhan. "I might feel the same way myself if the Shadids grabbed our best biological weapons." He glanced at Holland, went on, "Therefore we're so much the more indebted to one mentally capable of looking facts in the face. And that in turn creates a minor problem."

"Meaning me?" Holland asked.

"Yes. We cannot take you with us. We dare not leave you here, especially since we want your services when we return."

Ygath suggested, "We can establish him with adequate food supplies either on the other side of this world or upon the satellite. He would be beyond reach of petty vengeance and should be safe enough until we return. The he would have our protection."

"Don't let it bother you," said Holland. "You can dump me here."

"What, after that scene outside?"

"I know my own kind. You're departing in two days' time. By then they'll have simmered down."

"Are you certain?"

"I'm fairly sure. They aren't without logic. They will realize that what has been done can't be undone. A few may argue that perhaps it's all for the best. The others will be soothed by your going even though you're coming back. Probably they'll get busy trying to plot a hot reception for you."

"Which will be more than futile," Drhan assured.

"I know it," agreed Holland.

They eyed him, seeking a double meaning, found his features showing the confidence of one who knows himself to be on the winning side. It pleased them even though deep in their hearts each had a mite of sympathy for Deacon.

Nobody likes a traitor, not even those who use him.

Mid-morning two days later a repeated thrum of propulsors drew the attention of those in the camp and the nearest outskirts of the town. Assembling, they watched in sour silence while several lifeboats zoomed back to the mother-ship and were taken on board. The large vessel then belly-slid through sandy soil, flared and roared, made a bound, finished at an upward tilt on the side of a small hill four miles farther away. Its tubes ceased their bellowing.

"Must be making ready to beat it," remarked Hank.

"Can't be too soon for me," said Joe.

"Wonder what's happened to Holland," Yarbridge ventured. He shifted restlessly, expecting vituperative reproof for mentioning the name. "Somehow I don't think he'll go with them."

"They'll dump him some place else," suggested a burly, red-haired man. "The devil looks after his own."

"I'd like to find him where he's planted," topped another, lending it menace.

Several voices supported that. They continued to observe the vessel now made too small by distance for them to discern individual activity around it. Nobody had binoculars; in bygone weeks that now seemed aeons all such instruments had been confiscated for the use of armies now dead and gone.

After most of an hour somebody reported, "One of them is coming this way. Maybe he wants to shake hands all round. No hard feelings and all that. It was just in fun. Rubber Boy loves Homer Sap."

Shading his eyes with a hairy hand Deacon stared lengthily. "It isn't one of them. It's the Kahsam, no less!"

"He wouldn't dare," said the redhead incredulously.

"He would and he is," Deacon asserted. Again he studied the distant figure tramping steadily toward "And I can guess why."

"Why?" invited the other.

"Bet you he's bringing a message from his lords and masters telling us what they'll do to us if we touch one hair of his precious head."

"I'll take my chance on that," declared the redhead. He examined a clenched fist. It was big and raw-boned.

"Lay off him, Lindsay," Deacon ordered. He cast a warning frown at all within hearing. "That goes for the rest of you, too. If the rubber boys are taking it skyward, we can well afford to wait until they're out of sight." His authoritative gaze went over each surly face. "Then we'll have him all to our little selves and what the eye doesn't see the heart won't grieve over!"

"Yes, that makes sense," Lindsay admitted with reluctance. Shoving hands in pockets, he controlled his emotions.

Following this cue, the others forced themselves to cool down. Presently Holland arrived at rapid pace, stopped a few yards from the mob and immediately in front of Deacon.

"They're waiting for the last lifeboat," he informed. "When they've got it aboard they're going home."

Nobody made remark. They stood together, hard-eyed, content to bide their time.

Licking his lips, Holland went on, "All right, if that's the way you feel." He moved forward. "Me, I'm not going to stand when I can sit."

"You'll neither stand nor sit pretty soon," screamed a nerve-strained voice at the back.

"Shut up!" roared Deacon, glaring over the heads of the front ranks. He threw a meaningful glance toward the alien ship, pretended to consult the watch he didn't possess.

They got it. Opening a path to permit Holland to pass, they closed in behind him, escorted him to the hut. Fifty crowded him. Three or four hundred massed outside the door. One man held a needle-sharp fishing spear made from a prong of a garden fork. Another carried a length of nylon cord scorched at both ends.

Squatting on the end of his bed, Holland wearily rubbed his freckles, favored Yarbridge with a tired grin and said, "I suppose all these gloomy looking gumps resent me shoveling hot-stuff aboard by the ton?"

"Well, haven't you?" inquired Yarbridge, hopefully.

"I gave them enough."

"One ounce is too much!" harshed Deacon, chipping in.

"What can you do with a mere ounce?" Holland asked.

"Close your gab!" advised Lindsay, scowling at him.

"Or use it to say prayers," suggested another.

A man outside called through the door, "The lifeboat's come back. It won't be long now!"

Everyone stared the same way: at Holland.

He said to nobody in particular, "Naturally they wanted the whole works, blueprints, formulae, extraction techniques, samples of thorium, radium, uranium, plutonium, neptunium, the entire shebang. They wanted sufficient to enable them to set up in business way back home. I couldn't give it all—the stuff wasn't there."

"But, you gave all you could?" invited Deacon.

"Yes, Beefy, I did. I gave them precisely enough. They will stash it in the safe and—"

A light of near-blinding brilliance flashed through the west-side windows. Beyond the door a man howled like a hungry wolf. Then the ground shuddered. The hut gave four violent jerks, a sidewall cracked and let more light pour in. There was no sound other than that of witnesses outside.

The bunch at the door ran west with one accord. Several in the hut chased after them. Deacon stood up, his heavy features mystified.

"In the name of glory, what was *that*?"

"I told you," said Holland. "I gave them enough."

Making up his mind, Deacon rushed out, looked westward. The others pressed behind, gazed at an immense gout of vapor rising more than four miles away. It was monstrous, frightening despite its familiarity. Nothing could be seen of the alien ship.

Swiveling on one heel, Deacon said in stilled tones, "That was your sweet trick."

"I needed hate here to establish trust and confidence there," explained Holland. "I got it—and it worked."

Turning his back upon him, Deacon bent down with elbows resting on knees. "You know what to do."

Holland surveyed the proffered rear end. "Great as the temptation may be, I resist it. Not because I forgive you. I think we can arrange a wallop more effective."

Coming up quickly, Deacon eyed him suspiciously. "Such as what?"

"According to statistics they had on that ship," Holland continued, ignoring the question, "humanity clung to a basic convention even in its death throes, namely, women and children first. Result: we survivors number more females than males."

"That's right," a voice endorsed. "About five to three."

"If we double our number every thirty years we'll be a formidable swarm before one thousand, let alone two thousand. And we aren't starting from trees and caves. We're starting with salvable parts of civilization and we still have the know-how." He jerked an indicative thumb to the town. "Ten to one that somewhere in there are a couple of nuclear physicists and umpteen other experts who've been making like bricklayers while nosy aliens were around." He paused thoughtfully, finished, "And between the lot of us we must have learned some useful things about that ship. The next one just won't get this far. It will regret the attempt."

"So did that one!" bawled a voice.

It was like the snapping of a tense cord and brought a roar of triumphant cheers.

When the noise had died down, Holland said, "Large families will help. So when we get around to lawmaking"—he studied Deacon, walked round him a couple of times looking him up and down as if inspecting a prime hunk of beef—"we'll have to make bachelordom illegal."

Deacon flushed and let out an agonized yelp of, "Hey, you can't do that to me!"

"We can," assured Holland amid surrounding laughter. "And what's more, we shall!"

He was wrong there. Ten days before such a law was passed a buxom widow put the bee on Deacon.

Late Night Final

Astounding, December 1948

Commander Cruin went down the extending metal ladder, paused a rung from the bottom, placed one important foot on the new territory, and then the other. That made him the first of his kind on an unknown world.

He posed there in the sunlight, a big bull of a man meticulously attired for the occasion. Not a spot marred his faultlessly cut uniform of gray-green on which jeweled orders of merit sparkled and flashed. His jack boots glistened as they had never done since the day of launching from the home planet. The golden bells of his rank tinkled on his heel-hooks as he shifted his feet slightly. In the deep shadow beneath the visor of his ornate helmet his hard eyes held a glow of self-satisfaction.

A microphone came swinging down to him from the air lock he'd just left. Taking it in a huge left hand, he looked straight ahead with the blank intentness of one who sees long visions of the past and longer visions of the future. Indeed, this was as visionary a moment as any there had been in his world's history.

"In the name of Huld and the people of Huld," he enunciated officiously, "I take this planet." Then he saluted swiftly, slickly, like an automaton.

Facing him, twenty-two long, black spaceships simultaneously thrust from their forward ports their glorypoles ringed with the red-black-gold colors of Huld. Inside the vessels twenty-two crews of seventy men apiece stood rigidly erect, saluted, broke into well-drilled song, "Oh, heavenly fatherland of Huld."

When they had finished, Commander Cruin saluted again. The crews repeated their salute. The glorypoles were drawn in. Cruin mounted the ladder, entered his flagship. All locks were closed. Along the valley the twenty-two invaders lay in military formation, spaced equidistantly, noses and tails dead in line.

On a low hill a mile to the east a fire sent up a column of thick smoke. It spat and blazed amid the remnants of what had been the twenty-third vessel—and the eighth successive loss since the fleet had set forth three years ago. Thirty then. Twenty-two now.

The price of empire.

Reaching his cabin, Commander Cruin lowered his bulk into the seat behind his desk, took off his heavy helmet, adjusted an order of merit which was hiding modestly behind its neighbor.

"Step four," he commented with satisfaction.

Second Commander Jusik nodded respectfully. He handed the other a book. Opening it, Cruin meditated aloud.

"Step one: Check planet's certain suitability for our form of life." He rubbed his big jowls. "We know it's suitable."

"Yes, sir. This is a great triumph for you."

"Thank you, Jusik." A craggy smile played momentarily on one side of Cruin's broad face. "Step two: Remain in planetary shadow at distance of not less than one diameter while scout boats survey world for evidence of superior life forms. Three: Select landing place far from largest sources of possible resistance but adjacent to a source small enough to be mastered. Four: Declare Huld's claim ceremoniously, as prescribed in manual on procedure and discipline." He worked his jowls again. "We've done all that."

The smile returned, and he glanced with satisfaction out of the small port near his chair. The port framed the smoke column on the hill. His expression changed to a scowl, and his jaw muscles lumped.

"Fully trained and completely qualified," he growled sardonically. "Yet he had to smash up. Another ship and crew lost in the very moment we reach our goal. The eighth such loss. There will be a purge in the astronautical training center when I return."

"Yes, sir," approved Jusik, dutifully. "There is no excuse for it."

"There are no excuses for anything," Cruin retorted.

"No, sir."

Snorting his contempt, Cruin looked at his book. "Step five: Make all protective preparations as detailed in defense manual." He glanced up into Jusik's lean, clear-cut features. "Every captain has been issued with a defense manual. Are they carrying out its orders?"

"Yes, sir. They have started already."

"They better had! I shall arrange a demotion of the slowest." Wetting a large thumb, he flipped a page over. "Step six: If planet does hold life forms of suspected intelligence, obtain specimens."

Lying back in his seat he mused a moment, then barked: "Well, for what are you waiting?"

"I beg your pardon, sir?"

"Get some examples," roared Cruin.

"Very well, sir." Without blinking, Jusik saluted, marched out.

The self-closer swung the door behind him. Cruin surveyed it with a jaundiced eye.

"Curse the training center," he rumbled. "It has deteriorated since I was there."

Putting his feet on the desk, he waggled his heels to make the bells tinkle while he waited for the examples.

Three specimens turned up of their own accord. They were seen standing wide-eyed in a row near the prow of number twenty-two, the endmost ship of the line. Captain Somir brought them along personally.

"Step six calls for specimens, sir," he explained to Commander Cruin. "I know that you require ones better than these, but I found these under our nose."

"Under your nose? You land and within short time other life forms are sightseeing around your vessel? What about your protective precautions?"

"They are not completed yet, sir. They take some time."

"What were your lookouts doing—sleeping?"

"No, sir," assured Somir desperately. "They did not think it necessary to sound a general alarm for such as these."

Reluctantly, Cruin granted the point. His gaze ran contemptuously over the trio. Three kids. One was a boy, knee-high, snub-nosed, chewing at a chubby fist. The next, a skinny-legged, pigtailed girl obviously older than the boy. The third was another girl almost as tall as Somir, somewhat skinny, but with a hint of coming shapeliness hiding in her thin attire. All three were freckled, all had violently red hair.

The tall girl said to Cruin: "I'm Marva—Marva Meredith." She indicated her companions. "This is Sue and this is Sam. We live over there, in Williamsville." She smiled at him and suddenly he noticed that her eyes were a rich and startling green. "We were looking for blueberries when we saw you come down."

Cruin grunted, rested his hands on his paunch. The fact that this planet's life manifestly was of his own shape and form impressed him not at all. It had never occurred to him that it could have proved otherwise. In Huldian thought, all superior life must be humanoid and no exploration had yet provided evidence to the contrary.

"I don't understand her alien gabble and she doesn't understand Huldian," he complained to Somir. "She must he dull-witted to waste her breath thus."

"Yes, sir," agreed Somir. "Do you wish me to hand them over to the tutors?"

"No. They're not worth it." He eyed the small boy's freckles with distaste, never having seen such a phenomenon before. "They are badly spotted and may be diseased. *Pfaugh!*" He grimaced with disgust. "Did they pass through the ray-sterilizing chamber as they came in?"

"Certainly, sir. I was most careful about that."

"Be equally careful about any more you may encounter." Slowly, his authoritative stare went from the boy to the pigtailed girl and finally to the tall one. He didn't want to look at her, yet knew that he was going to. Her cool green eyes held something that made him vaguely uncomfortable. Unwillingly he met those eyes. She smiled again, with little dimples. "Kick 'em out!" he rapped at Somir.

"As you order, sir."

Nudging them, Somir gestured toward the door. The three took hold of each other's hands, filed out.

"Bye!" chirped the boy, solemnly.

"Bye!" said pigtails, shyly.

The tall girl turned in the doorway. "Good-by!"

Gazing at her uncomprehendingly, Cruin fidgeted in his chair. She dimpled at him, then the door swung to.

"Good-by." He mouthed the strange word to himself. Considering the circumstances in which it had been tittered, evidently it meant farewell. Already be had picked up one word of their language.

"Step seven: Gain communication by tutoring specimens until they are proficient in Huldian."

Teach them. Do not let them teach you—teach *them.* The slaves must learn from the masters, not the masters from the slaves.

"Good-by." He repeated it with savage self-accusation. A minor matter, but still an infringement of the book of rules. There are no excuses for anything.

Teach them.

The slaves—

Rockets rumbled and blasted deafeningly as ships maneuvered themselves into the positions laid down in the manual of defense. Several hours of careful belly-edging were required for this. In the end, the line had reshaped itself into two groups of eleven-pointed stars, noses at the centers, tails outward. Ash of blast-destroyed grasses, shrubs and trees covered a wide area beyond the two menacing rings of main propulsion tubes which could incinerate anything within one mile.

This done, perspiring, dirt-coated crews lugged out their forward armaments, remounted them pointing outward in the spaces between the vessels' splayed tails. Rear armaments still aboard already were directed upward and outward. Armaments plus tubes now provided a formidable field of fire completely surrounding the double encampment. It was the Huldian master plan conceived by Huldian master planners. In other more alien estimation, it was the old covered-wagon technique, so incredibly ancient that it had been forgotten by all but most earnest students of the past. But none of the invaders knew that.

Around the perimeter they stacked the small, fast, well-armed scouts of which there were two per ship. Noses outward, tails inward, in readiness for quick take-off, they were paired just beyond the parent vessels, below the propulsion tubes, and out of line of the remounted batteries. There was a lot of moving around to get the scouts positioned at precisely the same distances apart and making precisely the same angles. The whole arrangement had that geometrical exactness beloved of the military mind.

Pacing the narrow catwalk running along the top surface of his flagship, Commander Cruin observed his toiling crews with satisfaction. Organization, discipline, energy, unquestioning obedience—those were the prime essentials of efficiency. On such had Huld grown great. On such would Huld grow greater.

Reaching the tail-end, he leaned on the stop-rail, gazed down upon the concentric rings of wide, stubby venturis. His own crew were checking the angles of their two scouts already positioned. Four guards, heavily armed, came marching through the ash with Jusik in the lead. They had six prisoners.

Seeing him, Jusik bawled: "Halt!" Guard and guarded stopped with a thud of boots and a rise of dust. Looking up, Jusik saluted.

"Six specimens, sir."

Cruin eyed them indifferently. Half a dozen middle-aged men in drab, sloppily fitting clothes. He would not have given a snap of the fingers for six thousand of them.

The biggest of the captives, the one second from the left, had red hair and was sucking something that gave off smoke. His shoulders were wider than Cruin's own though he didn't look half the weight. Idly, the commander wondered whether the fellow had green eyes; he couldn't tell that from where he was standing.

Calmly surveying Cruin, this prisoner took the smoke-thing from his mouth and said, tonelessly: "By hokey, a brasshat!" Then he shoved the thing back between his lips and dribbled blue vapor.

The others looked doubtful, as if either they did not comprehend or found it past belief.

"Jeepers, *no!*" said the one on the right, a gaunt individual with thin, saturnine features.

"I'm telling you." assured Redhead in the same flat voice.

"Shall I take them to the tutors, sir?" asked Jusik.

"Yes." Unleaning from the rail, Cruin carefully adjusted his white gloves. "Don't bother me with them again until they are certified as competent to talk." Answering the other's salute, he paraded back along the catwalk.

"See?" said Redhead, picking up his feet in time with the guard. He seemed to take an obscure pleasure in keeping in step with the guard. Winking at the nearest prisoner, he let a curl of aromatic smoke trickle from the side of his mouth.

Tutors Fane and Parth sought an interview the following evening. Jusik ushered them in, and Cruin looked up irritably from the report he was writing.

"Well?"

Fane said: "Sir, these prisoners suggest that we share their homes for a while and teach them to converse there."

"How did they suggest that?"

"Mostly by signs," explained Fane.

"And what made you think that so nonsensical a plan had sufficient merit to make it worthy of my attention?"

"There are aspects about which you should be consulted," Fane continued stubbornly. "The manual of procedure and discipline declares that such matters must be placed before the commanding officer whose decision is final."

"Quite right, quite right." He regarded Fane with a little more favor. "What are these matters?"

"Time is important to us, and the quicker these prisoners learn our language the better it will be. Here, their minds are occupied by their predicament. They think too much of their friends and families. In their own homes it would be different, and they could learn at great speed."

"A weak pretext," scoffed Cruin.

"That is not all. By nature they are naive and friendly. I feel that we have little to fear from them. Had they been hostile they would have attacked by now."

"Not necessarily. It is wise to be cautious. The manual of defense emphasizes that fact repeatedly. These creatures may wish first to gain the measure of us before they try to deal with us."

Fane was prompt to snatch the opportunity. "Your point, sir, is also my final one. Here, they are six pairs of eyes and six pairs of ears in the middle of us, and their absence is likely to give cause for alarm in their home town. Were they there, complacency would replace that alarm—and *we* would be the eyes and ears!"

"Well put," commented Jusik, momentarily forgetting himself.

"Be silent!" Cruin glared at him. "I do not recall any ruling in the manual pertaining to such a suggestion as this. Let me check up." Grabbing his books, he sought through them. He took a long time about it, gave up, and said: "The only pertinent rule appears to be that in circumstances not specified in the manual the decision is wholly mine, to be made in light of said circumstances providing that they do not conflict with the rulings of any other manual which may be applicable to the situation, and providing that my decision does not effectively countermand that or those of any senior ranking officer whose authority extends to the same area." He took a deep breath.

"Yes, sir," said Fane.

"Quite, sir," said Parth.

Cruin frowned heavily. "How far away are these prisoners' homes?"

"One hour's walk." Fane made a persuasive gesture. "If anything did happen to us—which I consider extremely unlikely—one scout could wipe out their little town before they'd time to realize what had happened. One scout, one bomb, one minute!" Dexterously, he added, "At your order, sir."

Cruin preened himself visibly. "I see no reason why we should not take advantage of their stupidity." His eyes asked Jusik what he thought, but that person failed to notice. "Since you two tutors have brought this plan to me, I hereby approve it, and I appoint you to carry it through." He consulted a list which he extracted from a drawer. "Take two psychologists with you—Kalma and Hefni."

"Very well, sir." Impassively, Fane saluted and went out, Parth following.

Staring absently at his half-written report, Cruin fiddled with his pen for a while, glanced at Jusik, and spat: "At what are you smiling?"

Jusik wiped it from his face, looked solemn.

"Come on. Out with it!"

"I was thinking, sir," replied Jusik, slowly, "that three years in a ship is a very long time."

Slamming his pen on the desk, Cruin stood up. "Has it been any longer for others than for me?"

"For you," said Jusik, daringly but respectfully, "I think it has been longest of all."

"Get out!" shouted Cruin.

He watched the other go, watched the self-closer push the door, waited for its last click. He shifted his gaze to the port, stared hard-eyed into the gathering dusk. His heel-bells were silent as he stood unmoving and saw the invisible sun sucking its last rays from the sky.

In short time, ten figures strolled through the twilight toward the distant, tree-topped hill. Four were uniformed; six in drab, shapeless clothes. They went by conversing with many gestures, and one of them laughed. He gnawed his bottom lip as his gaze followed them until they were gone.

The price of rank.

"Step eight: Repel initial attacks in accordance with techniques detailed in manual of defense." Cruin snorted, put up one hand, tidied his orders of merit.

"There have been no attacks," said Jusik.

"I am not unaware of the fact." The commander glowered at him. "I'd have preferred an onslaught. We are ready for them. The sooner they match their strength against ours the sooner they'll learn who's boss now!" He hooked big thumbs in his silver-braided belt. "And besides, it would give the men something to do. I cannot have them everlastingly repeating their drills of procedure. We've been here nine days and nothing has happened." His attention returned to the book. "Step nine: Follow defeat of initial attacks by taking aggressive action as detailed in manual of defense." He gave another snort. "How can one follow something that has not occurred?"

"It is impossible," Jusik ventured.

"Nothing is impossible," Cruin contradicted, harshly. "Step ten: In the unlikely event that intelligent life displays indifference or amity, remain in protective formation while specimens are being tutored, meanwhile employing scout vessels to survey surrounding area to the limit of their flight-duration, using no more than one-fifth of the numbers available at any time."

"That allows us eight or nine scouts on survey," observed Jusik, thoughtfully. "What is our authorized step if they fail to return?"

"Why d'you ask that?"

"Those eight scouts I sent out on your orders forty periods ago are overdue."

Viciously, Commander Cruin thrust away his book. His broad, heavy face was dark red.

"Second Commander Jusik, it was your duty to report this fact to me the moment those vessels became overdue."

"Which I have," said Jusik, imperturbably. "They have a flight-duration of forty periods, as you know. That, sir, made them due a short time ago. They are now late."

Cruin tramped twice across the room, medals clinking, heel-bells jangling. "The answer to nonappearance is immediately to obliterate the areas in which they are held. No half-measures. A salutary lesson."

"Which areas, sir?"

Stopping in mid-stride, Cruin bawled: "*You* ought to know that. Those scouts had properly formulated route orders, didn't they? It's a simple matter to—"

He ceased as a shrill whine passed overhead, lowered to a dull moan in the distance, curved hack on a rising note again.

"Number one." Jusik looked at the little timemeter on the wall. "Late, but here. Maybe the others will turn up now."

"Somebody's going to get a sharp lesson if they don't!"

"I'll see what he has to report." Saluting, Jusik hurried through the doorway.

Gazing out of his port, Cruin observed the delinquent scout belly-sliding up to the nearest formation. He chewed steadily at his bottom lip, a slow, persistent chew which showed his thoughts to be wandering around in labyrinths of their own.

Beyond the fringe of dank, dead ash were golden buttercups in the grasses, and a hum of bees, and the gentle rustle of leaves on trees. Four engine-room wranglers of ship number seventeen had found this sanctuary and sprawled flat on their backs in the shade of a big-leafed and blossom-ornamented growth. With eyes closed, their hands plucked idly at surrounding grasses while they maintained a lazy, desultory conversation through which they failed to hear the ring of Cruin's approaching bells.

Standing before them, his complexion florid, he roared: "Get up!"

Shooting to their feet, they stood stiffly shoulder to shoulder, faces expressionless, eyes level, hands at their sides.

"Your names?" He wrote them in his notebook while obediently they repeated them in precise, unemotional voices. "I'll deal with you later," he promised. "March!"

Together, they saluted, marched off with a rhythmic pounding of boots, one-two-three-hup! His angry stare followed them until they reached the shadow of their ship. Not until then did he turn and proceed. Mounting the hill, one cautious hand continually on the cold butt of his gun, he reached the crest, gazed down into the valley he'd just left. In neat, exact positioning, the two star-formations of the ships of Huld were silent and ominous.

His hard, authoritative eyes turned to the other side of the hill. There, the landscape was pastoral. A wooded slope ran down to a little river which meandered into the hazy distance, and on its farther side was a broad patchwork of cultivated fields in which three houses were visible.

Seating himself on a large rock, Cruin loosened his gun in its holster, took a wary look around extracted a small wad of reports from his pocket and glanced over them for the twentieth time A faint smell of herbs and resin came to his nostrils as he read.

"I circled this landing place at low altitude and recorded it photographically, taking care to include all the machines standing thereon. Two other machines which were in the air went on their way without attempting to interfere. It then occurred to me that the signals they were making from the ground might be an invitation to land, and I decided to utilize opportunism as recommended in the manual of procedure. Therefore I landed. They conducted my scout vessel to a dispersal point off the runway and made me welcome."

Something fluted liquidly in a nearby tree. Cruin looked up, his hand automatically seeking his holster. It was only a bird. Skipping parts of the report, he frowned over the concluding words.

" . . . lack of common speech made it difficult for me to refuse and after the sixth drink during my tour of the town I was suddenly afflicted with a strange paralysis in the legs and collapsed into the arms of my companions. Believing that they had poisoned me by guile, I prepared for death . . . tickled my throat while making jocular remarks . . . I was a little sick." Cruin rubbed his chin in puzzlement. "Not until they were satisfied about my recovery did they take me back to my vessel. They waved their hands at me as I took off. I apologize to my captain for overdue return and plead that it was because of factors beyond my control."

The fluter came down to Cruin's feet, piped at him plaintively. It cocked its head sidewise as it examined him with bright, beady eyes.

Shifting the sheet he'd been reading, he scanned the next one. It was neatly typewritten, and signed jointly by Parth, Fane, Kalma and Hefni.

"Do not appear fully to appreciate what has occurred . . . seem to view the arrival of a Huldian fleet as just another incident. They have a remarkable self-assurance which is incomprehensible inasmuch as we can find nothing to justify such an attitude. Mastery of them should be so easy that if our homing vessel does not leave too soon it should be possible for it to bear tidings of conquest as well as of mere discovery."

"Conquest," he murmured. It had a mighty imposing sound. A word like that would send a tremendous thrill of excitement throughout the entire world of Huld.

Five before him had sent back ships telling of discovery, but none had gone so far as he, none had traveled so long and wearily, none had been rewarded with a planet so big, lush, desirable—and none had reported the subjection of their finds. One cannot conquer a rocky waste. But this—

In peculiarly accented Huldian, a voice behind him said, brightly: "Good morning!"

He came up fast, his hand sliding to his side, his face hard with authority.

She was laughing at him with her clear green eyes. "Remember me—Marva Meredith?" Her flaming hair was windblown. "You see," she went on, in slow, awkward tones, "I know a little Huldian already. Just a few words."

"Who taught you?" he asked, bluntly.

"Fane and Parth."

"It is your house to which they have gone?"

"Oh, yes. Kalma and Hefni are guesting with Bill Gleeson; Fane and Parth with us. Father brought them to us. They share the welcome room."

"Welcome room?"

"Of course." Perching herself on his rock, she drew up her slender legs, rested her chin on her knees. He noticed that the legs, like her face, were freckled. "Of course. Everyone has a welcome room, haven't they?"

Cruin said nothing.

"Haven't you a welcome room in your home?"

"Home?" His eyes strayed away from hers, sought the fluting bird. It wasn't there. Somehow, his hand had left his holster without realizing it. He was holding his hands together, each nursing the other, clinging, finding company, soothing each other.

Her gaze was on his hands as she said, softly and hesitantly, "You have got a home . . . somewhere . . . haven't you?"

"No."

Lowering her legs, she stood up. "I'm so sorry."

"You are sorry for *me?"* His gaze switched back to her. It held incredulity, amazement, a mite of anger. His voice was harsh. "You must be singularly stupid."

"Am I?" she asked, humbly.

"No member of my expedition has a home," he went on. "Every man was carefully selected. Every man passed through a screen, suffered the most exacting tests. Intelligence and technical competence were not enough; each had also to be young, healthy, without ties of any sort. They were chosen for ability to concentrate on the task in hand without indulging morale-lowering sentimentalities about people left behind."

"I don't understand some of your long words," she complained. "And you are speaking far too fast."

He repeated it more slowly and with added emphasis, finishing, "Spaceships undertaking long absence from base cannot be handicapped by homesick crews. We picked men without homes because they can leave Huld and not care a hoot. They are pioneers!"

" 'Young, healthy, without ties,' " she quoted. "That makes them strong?"

"Definitely," he asserted.

"Men especially selected for space. Strong men." Her lashes hid her eyes as she looked down at her narrow feet. "But now they are not in space. They are here, on firm ground."

"What of it," he demanded.

"Nothing." Stretching her arms wide she took a deep breath, then dimpled at him. "Nothing at all."

"You're only a child," he responded scornfully. "When you grow older—"

"You'll have more sense," she finished for him, chanting it in a high, sweet voice. "You'll have more sense, you'll have more sense. When you grow older you'll have more sense, tra-la-la-lala!"

Gnawing irritatedly at his lip, he walked past her, started down the hill toward the ships.

"Where are you going?"

"Back!" he snapped.

"Do you like it down there?" Her eyebrows arched in surprise.

Stopping ten paces away, he scowled at her. "Is it any of your business?"

"I didn't mean to be inquisitive," she apologized. "I asked because . . . because—"

"Because what?"

"I was wondering whether you would care to visit my house."

"Nonsense! Impossible!" He turned to continue downhill.

"Father suggested it. He thought you might like to share a meal. A fresh one. A change of diet. Something to break the monotony of your supplies." The wind lifted her crimson hair and played with it as she regarded him speculatively. "He consulted Vane and Parth. They said it was an excellent idea."

"They did, did they?" His features seemed molded in iron. "Tell Vane and Parth they are to report to me at sunset." He paused, added, "Without fail!"

Resuming her seat on the rock, she watched him stride heavily down the slope toward the double star-formation. Her hands were together in her lap, much as he had held his. But hers sought nothing of each other. In complete repose, they merely rested with the ineffable patience of hands as old as time.

Seeing at a glance that he was liverish, Jusik promptly postponed certain suggestions that he had in mind.

"Summon captains Drek and Belthan," Cruin ordered. When the other had gone, he flung his helmet onto the desk, surveyed himself in a mirror. He was still smoothing the tired lines on his face when approaching footsteps sent him officiously behind his desk.

Entering, the two captains saluted, remained rigidly at attention. Cruin studied them irefully while they preserved wooden expressions.

Eventually, he said: "I found four men lounging like undisciplined hoboes outside the safety zone." He stared at Drek. "They were from your vessel." The stare shifted to Belthan. "You are today's commander of the guard. Have either of you anything to say?"

"They were off-duty and free to leave the ship," explained Drek. "They had been warned not to go beyond the perimeter of ash."

"I don't know how they slipped through," said Belthan, in official monotone. "Obviously the guards were lax. The fault is mine."

"It will count against you in your promotion records," Cruin promised. " Punish these four, and the responsible guards, as laid down in the manual of procedure and discipline." He leaned across the desk to survey them more closely. "A repetition will bring ceremonial demotion!"

"Yes, sir," they chorused.

Dismissing them, he glanced at Jusik. "When tutors Fane and Parth report here, send them in to me without delay."

"As you order, sir."

Cruin dropped the glance momentarily, brought it back. "What's the matter with you?"

"Me?" Jusik became self-conscious. "Nothing, sir."

"You lie! One has to live with a person to know him. I've lived on your neck for three years. I know you too well to be deceived. You have something on your mind."

"It's the men," admitted Jusik, resignedly.

"What of them?"

"They are restless."

"Are they? Well, I can devise a cure for that. What's making them restless?"

"Several things, sir."

Cruin waited while Jusik stayed dumb, then roared: "Do I have to prompt you?"

"No, sir." Jusik protested, unwillingly. "It's many things. Inactivity. The substitution of tedious routine. The constant waiting, waiting, waiting right on top of three years' close incarceration. They wait—and nothing happens."

"What else?"

"The sight and knowledge of familiar life just beyond the ash. The realization that Fane and Parth and the others are enjoying it with your consent. The stories told by the scouts about their experiences on landing." His gaze was steady as he went on. "We've now sent out five squadrons of scouts, a total of forty vessels. Only six came back on time. All the rest were late on one plausible pretext or another. The pilots have talked, and shown the men various souvenir photographs and a few gifts. One of them is undergoing punishment for bringing back some bottles of paralysis-mixture. But the damage has been done. Their stories have unsettled the men."

"Anything more?"

"Begging your pardon, sir, there was also the sight of you taking a stroll to the top of the hill. They envied you even that!" He looked squarely at Cruin. "I envied you myself."

"I am the commander," said Cruin.

"Yes, sir." Jusik kept his gaze on him but added nothing more.

If the second commander expected a delayed outburst, he was disappointed. A complicated series of emotions chased each other across his superior's broad, beefy features. Lying back in his chair, Cruin's eyes looked absently through the port while his mind juggled with Jusik's words.

Suddenly, he rasped: "I have observed more, anticipated more and given matters more thought than perhaps you realize. I can see something which you may have failed to perceive. It has caused me some anxiety. Briefly, if we don't keep pace with the march of time we're going to find ourselves in a fix."

"Indeed, sir?"

"I don't wish you to mention this to anyone else: I suspect that we are trapped in a situation bearing no resemblance to any dealt with in the manuals."

"Really, sir?" Jusik licked his lips, felt that his own outspokenness was leading into unexpected paths.

"Consider our present circumstances," Cruin went on. "We are established here and in possession of power sufficient to enslave this planet. Any one of our supply of bombs could blast a portion of this earth stretching from horizon to horizon. But they're of no use unless we apply them effectively. We can't drop them anywhere, haphazardly. If parting with them in so improvident a manner proved unconvincing to our opponents, and failed to smash the hard core of their resistance, we would find ourselves unarmed in a hostile world. No more bombs. None nearer than six long years away, three there and three back. Therefore we must apply our power where it will do the most good." He began to massage his heavy chin. "We don't know where to apply it."

"No, sir," agreed Jusik, pointlessly.

"We've got to determine which cities are the key points of their civilization, which persons are this planet's acknowledged leaders, and where they're located. When we strike, it must be at the nerve-centers. That means we're impotent until we get the necessary in formation. In turn, that means we've got to establish communication with the aid of the tutors." He started plucking at his jaw muscles. "And that takes time!"

"Quite, sir, but—"

"But while time crawls past the men's morale evaporates. This is our twelfth day and already the crews are restless. Tomorrow they'll be more so."

"I have a solution to that, sir, if you will forgive me for offering it," said Jusik, eagerly. "On Huld everyone gets one day's rest in five. They are free to do as they like, go where they like. Now if you promulgated an order permitting the men say one day's liberty in ten, it would mean that no more than ten percent of our strength would be lost on any one day. We could stand that reduction considering our power, especially if more of the others are on protective duty."

"So at last I get what was occupying your mind. It comes out in a swift flow of words." He smiled grimly as the other flushed. "I have thought of it. I am not quite so unimaginative as you may consider me."

"I don't look upon you that way, sir," Jusik protested.

"Never mind. We'll let that pass. To return to this subject of liberty—there lies the trap! There is the very quandary with which no manual deals, the situation for which I can find no officially prescribed formula." Putting a hand on his desk he tapped the polished surface impatiently. "If I refuse these men a little freedom, they will become increasingly restless—naturally. If I permit them the liberty they desire, they will experience contact with life more normal even though alien, and again become more restless—naturally!"

"Permit me to doubt the latter, sir. Our crews are loyal to Huld. Blackest space forbid that it should be otherwise!"

"They were loyal. Probably they are still loyal." Cruin's face quirked as his memory brought forward the words that followed. "They are young, healthy, without ties. In space, that means one thing. Here, another." He came slowly to his feet, big, bulky and imposing. "I *know!*"

Looking at him, Jusik felt that indeed he did know. "Yes, sir," he parroted, obediently.

"Therefore the onus of what to do for the best falls squarely upon me. I must use my initiative. As second commander it is for you to see that my orders are carried out to the letter."

"I know my duty, sir." Jusik's thinly-drawn features registered growing uneasiness.

"And it is my final decision that the men must be restrained from contact with our opponents, with no exceptions other than the four technicians operating under my orders. The crews are to be permitted no liberty, no freedom to go beyond the ash. Any form of resentment on their part must be countered immediately and ruthlessly. You will instruct the captains to watch for murmurers in their respective crews and take appropriate action to silence them as soon as found." His jowls lumped, and his eyes were cold as he regarded the other. "All scout-flights are canceled as from now, and all scout-vessels remain grounded. None moves without my personal instructions."

"That is going to deprive us of a lot of information," Jusik observed. "The last flight to the south reported discovery of ten cities completely deserted, and that's got some significance which we ought to—"

"I said the flights are canceled!" Cruin shouted. "If I say the scout-vessels are to be painted pale pink, they will be painted pale pink, thoroughly, completely, from end to end. I am the commander!"

"As you order, sir."

"Finally, you may instruct the captains that their vessels are to be prepared for my inspection at midday tomorrow. That will give the crews something to do."

"Very well, sir."

With a worried salute, Jusik opened the door, glanced out and said: "Here are Fane, Kalma, Parth and Hefni, sir."

"Show them in."

After Cruin had given forcible expression to his views, Fane said: "We appreciate the urgency, sir, and we are doing our best, but it is doubtful whether they will be fluent before another four weeks have passed. They are slow to learn."

"I don't want fluency," Cruin growled. "All they need are enough words to tell us the things we want to know, the things we *must* know before we can get anywhere."

"I said sufficient fluency," Fane reminded. "They communicate mostly by signs even now."

"That flame-headed girl didn't."

"She has been quick," admitted Fane. "Possibly she has an above-normal aptitude for languages. Unfortunately she knows the least in any military sense and therefore is of little use to us."

Cruin's gaze ran over him balefully. His voice became low and menacing. "You have lived with these people many days. I look upon your features and find them different. Why is that?"

"Different?" The four exchanged wondering looks.

"Your faces have lost their lines, their space-gauntness. Your cheeks have become plump, well-colored. Your eyes are no longer tired. They are bright. They hold the self-satisfied expression of a fat *skodar* wallowing in its trough. It is obvious that you have done well for yourselves." He bent forward, his mouth ugly. "Can it be that you are in no great hurry to complete your task?"

They were suitably shocked.

"We have eaten well and slept regularly," Fane said. "We feel better for it. Our physical improvement has enabled us to work so much the harder. In our view, the foe is supporting us unwittingly with his own hospitality, and since the manual of—"

"Hospitality?" Cruin cut in, sharply.

Fane went mentally off-balance as vainly he sought for a less complimentary synonym.

"I give you another week," the commander harshed. "No more. Not one day more. At this time, one week from today, you will report here with the six prisoners adequately tutored to understand my questions and answer them."

"It will be difficult, sir."

"Nothing is difficult. Nothing is impossible. There are no excuses for anything." He studied Vane from beneath forbidding brows. "You have my orders—obey them!"

"Yes, sir."

His hard stare shifted to Kalma and Hefni. "So much for the tutors; now *you*. What have you to tell me? How much have you discovered?"

Blinking nervously, Hefni said: "It is not a lot. The language trouble is—"

"May the Giant Sun burn up and perish the language trouble! How much have you learned while enjoyably larding your bellies?"

Glancing down at his uniform-belt as if suddenly and painfully conscious of its tightness, Hefni recited: "They are exceedingly strange in so far as they appear to be highly civilized in a purely domestic sense but quite primitive in all others. This Meredith family lives in a substantial, well-equipped house. They have every comfort, including a color-television receiver."

"You're dreaming! We are still seeking the secrets of plain television even on Huld. Color is unthinkable."

Kalma chipped in with: "Nevertheless, sir, they have it. We have seen it for ourselves."

"That is so," confirmed Fane.

"Shut up!" Cruin burned him with a glare. "I have finished with you. I am now dealing with these two." His attention returned to the quaking Hefni: "Carry on."

"There is something decidedly queer about them which we've not yet been able to understand. They have no medium of exchange. They barter goods for goods without any regard for the relative values of either. They work when they feel like it. If they don't feel like it, they don't work. Yet, in spite of this, they work most of the time."

"Why?" demanded Cruin, incredulously.

"We asked them. They said that one works to avoid boredom. We cannot comprehend that viewpoint." Hefni made a defeated gesture. "In many places they have small factories which, with their strange, perverted logic, they use as amusement centers. These plants operate only when people turn up to work."

"Eh?" Cruin looked baffled.

"For example, in Williamsville, a small town an hour's walk beyond the Meredith home, there is a shoe factory. It operates every day. Some days there may be only ten workers there, other days fifty or a hundred, but nobody can remember a time when the place stood idle for lack of one voluntary worker. Meredith's elder daughter, Marva, has worked there three days during our stay with them. We asked her the reason."

"What did she say?"

"For fun."

"Fun . . . fun . . . fun?" Cruin struggled with the concept. "What does that mean?"

"We don't know," Hefni confessed. "The barrier of speech—"

"Red flames lick up the barrier of speech!" Cruin bawled. "Was her attendance compulsory?"

"No, sir."

"You are certain of that?"

"We are positive. One works in a factory for no other reason than because one feels like it."

"For what reward?" topped Cruin, shrewdly.

"Anything or nothing." Hefni uttered it like one in a dream. "One day she brought back a pair of shoes for her mother. We asked if they were her reward for the work she had done. She said they were not, and that someone named George had made them and given them to her. Apparently the rest of the factory's output for that week was shipped to another town where shoes were required. This other town is going to send back a supply of leather, nobody knows how much—and nobody seems to care."

"Senseless," defined Cruin. "It is downright imbecility." He examined Hefni as if suspecting him of inventing confusing data. "It is impossible for even the most primitive of organizations to operate so haphazardly. Obviously you have seen only part of the picture; the rest has been concealed from you, or you have been too dull-witted to perceive it."

"I assure you, sir," began Hefni.

"Let it pass," Cruin cut in. "Why should I care how they function economically? In the end, they'll work the way *we* want them to!" He rested his heavy jaw in one hand. "There are other matters which interest me more. For instance, our scouts have brought in reports of many cities. Some are organized but grossly underpopulated; others are completely deserted. The former have well-constructed landing places with air-machines making use of them. How is it that people so primitive have air-machines?"

"Some make shoes, some make air-machines, some play with television. They work according to their aptitudes as well as their inclinations."

"Has this Meredith got an air-machine?"

"No." The look of defeat was etched more deeply on Helni's face. "If he wanted one he would have his desire inserted in the television supply-and-demand program."

"Then what?"

"Sooner or later, he'd get one, new or secondhand, either in exchange for something or as a gift."

"Just by asking for it?"

"Yes."

Getting up, Cruin strode to and fro across his office. The steel heel-plates on his boots clanked on the metal floor in rhythm with the bells. He was ireful, impatient, dissatisfied.

"In all this madness is nothing which tells us anything of their true character or their organization." Stopping his stride, he faced Hefni. "You boasted that *you* were to be the eyes and ears." He released a loud snort. "Blind eyes and deaf ears! Not one word about their numerical strength, not one—"

"Pardon me, sir," said Hefni, quickly, "there are twenty-seven millions of them."

"Ah!" Cruin registered sharp interest. "Only twenty-seven millions? Why, there's a hundred times that number on Huld which has no greater area of land surface." He mused a moment. "Greatly underpopulated. Many cities devoid of a living soul. They have air-machines and other items suggestive of a civilization greater than the one they now enjoy. They operate the remnants of an economic system. You realize what all this means?"

Hefni blinked, made no reply. Kalma looked thoughtful. Fane and Parth remained blank-faced and tight-lipped.

"It means two things," Cruin pursued. "War or disease. One or the other, or perhaps both—and on a large scale. I want information on that. I've got to learn what sort of weapons they employed in their war, how many of them remain available, and where. Or, alternatively, what disease ravished their numbers, its source, and its cure." He tapped Hefni's chest to emphasize his words. "I want to know what they've got hidden away, what they're trying to keep from your knowledge against the time when they can bring it out and use it against us. Above all, I want to know which people will issue orders for their general offensive and where they are located."

"I understand, sir," said Hefni, doubtfully.

"That's the sort of information I need from your six specimens. I want information, not invitations to meals!" His grin was ugly as he noted Hefni's wince. "If you can get it out of them before they're due here, I shall enter the fact on the credit side of your records. But if I, your commander, have to do you job by extracting it from them myself—" Ominously, he left the sentence unfinished.

Hefni opened his mouth, closed it, glanced nervously at Kalma who stood stiff and dumb at his side.

"You may go," Cruin snapped at the four of them. "You have one week. If you fail me, I shall deem it a front-line offense and deal with it in accordance with the active-service section of the manual of procedure and discipline."

They were pale as they saluted. He watched them file out, his lips curling contemptuously. Going to the port, he gazed into the gathering darkness, saw a pale star winking in the east. Low and far it was—but not so far as Huld.

In the mid-period of the sixteenth day, Commander Cruin strode forth polished and bemedaled, directed his bell-jangling feet toward the hill. A sour-faced guard saluted him at the edge of the ash and made a slovenly job of it.

"Is that the best you can do?" He glared into the other's surly eyes. "Repeat it!"

The guard saluted a fraction more swiftly.

"You're out of practice," Cruin informed. "Probably all the crews are out of practice. We'll find a remedy for that. We'll have a period of saluting drill every day." His glare went slowly up and down the guard's face. "Are you dumb?"

"No, sir."

"Shut up!" roared Cruin. He expanded his chest. "Continue with your patrol."

The guard's optics burned with resentment as he saluted for the third time, turned with the regulation heel-click and marched along the perimeter.

Mounting the hill, Cruin sat on the stone at the top. Alternately he viewed the ships lying in the valley and the opposite scene with its trees, fields and distant houses. The metal helmet with its ornamental wings was heavy upon his head but he did not remove it. In the shadow beneath the projecting visor, his cold eyes brooded over the landscape to one side amid the other.

She came eventually. He had been sitting there for one and a half periods when she came as he had known she would—without knowing what weird instinct had made him certain of this. Certainly, he had no desire to see her—no desire at all.

Through the trees she tripped light-footed, with Sue and Sam and three other girls of her own age. The newcomers had large, dark, humorous eyes, their hair was dark, and they were leggy.

"Oh, hello!" She paused as she saw him.

"Hello!" echoed Sue, swinging her pigtails.

"'Lo!" piped Sam, determined not to be left out.

Cruin frowned at them. There was a high gloss on his jack boots, and his helmet glittered in the sun.

"These are my friends," said Marva, in her alien-accented Huldian. "Becky, Rita and Joyce."

The three smiled at him.

"I brought them to see the ships."

Cruin said nothing.

"You don't mind them looking at the ships, do you?"

"No," he growled with reluctance.

Lankily but gracefully she seated herself on the grass. The others followed suit with the exception of Sam who stood with fat legs braced apart sucking his thumb, and solemnly studying Cruin's decorated jacket.

"Father was disappointed because you could not visit us."

Cruin made no reply.

"Mother was sorry, too. She's a wonderful cook. She loves a guest."

No reply.

"Would you care to come this evening?"

"No."

"Some other evening?"

"Young lady," he harshed, severely, "I do not pay visits. Nobody pays visits."

She translated this to the others. They laughed so heartily that Cruin reddened and stood up.

"What's funny about that?" he demanded.

"Nothing, nothing." Marva was embarrassed. "If I told you, I fear that you would not understand."

"I would not understand." His grim eyes became alert, calculating as they went over her three friends. "I do not think, somehow, that they were laughing at me. Therefore they were laughing at what I do not know. They were laughing at something I ought to know but which you do not wish to tell me." He bent over her, huge and muscular, while she looked up at him with her great green eyes. "And what remark of mine revealed my amusing ignorance?"

Her steady gaze remained on him while she made no answer. A faint but sweet scent exuded from her hair.

"I said that nobody pays visits," he repeated. "That was the amusing remark—nobody pays visits. And I am not a fool!" Straightening, he turned away. "So I am going to call the rolls!"

He could feel their eyes upon him as he started down the valley. They were silent except for Sam's high-pitched, childish, "Bye!" which he ignored.

Without once looking back, he gained his flagship, mounted its metal ladder, made his way to the office and summoned Jusik.

"Order the captains to call their rolls at once."

"Is something wrong, sir?" inquired Jusik, anxiously.

"Call the rolls!" Cruin bellowed, whipping off his helmet. "Then we'll know whether anything is wrong." Savagely, he flung the helmet onto a wall hook, sat down, mopped his forehead.

Jusik was gone for most of a period. In the end he returned, set-faced, grave.

"I regret to report that eighteen men are absent, sir."

"They laughed," said Cruin, bitterly. "They laughed—because they *knew!*" His knuckles were white as his hands gripped the arms of his chair.

"I beg your pardon, sir?" Jusik's eyebrows lifted.

"How long have they been absent?"

"Eleven of them were on duty this morning."

"That means the other seven have been missing since yesterday?"

"I'm afraid so, sir."

"But no one saw fit to inform me of this fact?"

Jusik fidgeted. "No, sir."

"Have you discovered anything else of which I have not been informed?"

The other fidgeted again, looked pained.

"Out with it, man!"

"It is not the absentees' first offense," Jusik said with difficulty. "Nor their second. Perhaps not their sixth."

"How long has this been going on?" Cruin waited a while, then bawled: "Come on! You are capable of speech!"

"About ten days, sir."

"How many captains were aware of this and failed to report it?"

"Nine, sir. Four of them await your bidding outside."

"And what of the other five?"

"They . . . they—" Jusik licked his lips.

Cruin arose, his expression dangerous. "You cannot conceal the truth by delaying it."

"They are among the absentees, sir."

"I see!" Cruin stamped to the door, stood by it. "We can take it for granted that others have absented themselves without permission, but were fortunate enough to be here when the rolls were called. That is their good luck. The real total of the disobedient cannot be discovered. They have sneaked away like nocturnal animals, and in the same manner they sneak back. All are guilty of desertion in the face of the enemy. There is one penalty for that."

"Surely, sir, considering the circ—"

"Considering nothing!" Cruin's voice shot up to an enraged shout. "Death! The penalty is death!" Striding to the table, he hammered the books lying upon it. "Summary execution as laid down in the manual of procedure and discipline. Desertion, mutinous conduct, defiance of a superior officer, conspiracy to thwart regulations and defy my orders—all punishable by death!" His voice lowered as swiftly as it had gone up. "Besides, my dear Jusik, if we fail through disintegration attributable to our own deliberate disregard of the manuals, what will be the penalty payable by *us?* What will it be, eh?"

"Death." admitted Jusik. He looked at Cruin. "On Huld, anyway."

"We are on Huld! *This* is Huld! I have claimed this planet in the name of Huld and therefore it is part of it."

"A mere claim, sir, if I may say—"

"Jusik, are *you* with these conspirators in opposing my authority?" Cruin's eyes glinted. His hand lay over his gun.

"Oh, no, sir!" The second commander's features mirrored the emotions conflicting within him. "But permit me to point out, sir, that we are a brotherly band who've been cooped together a long, long time and already have suffered losses getting here as we shall do getting back. One can hardly expect the men to—"

"I expect obedience!" Cruin's hand remained on the gun. "I expect iron discipline and immediate, willing, unquestionable obedience. With those, we conquer. Without them, we fail." He gestured to the door. "Are those captains properly prepared for examination as directed in the manuals?"

"Yes, sir. They are disarmed and under guard."

"Parade them in." Leaning on the edge of his desk, Cruin prepared to pass judgment on his fellows. The minute he waited for them was long, long as any minute he had ever known.

There had been scent in her hair.
And her eyes were cool and green.
Iron discipline must be maintained.
The price of power.

The manual provided an escape. Facing the four captains, he found himself taking advantage of the legal loophole to substitute demotion for the more drastic and final penalty.

Tramping the room before them while they stood in a row, pale-faced and rigid, their tunics unbuttoned, their ceremonial belts missing, the guards impassive on either side of them, he rampaged and swore and sprinkled them with verbal vitriol while his right fist hammered steadily into the palm of his left hand.

"But since you were present at the roll call, and therefore are not technically guilty of desertion, and since you surrendered yourselves to my judgment immediately you were called upon to do so, I hereby sentence you to be demoted to the basic rank, the circumstances attending this sentence to be entered in your records." He dismissed them with a curt flourish of his white-gloved hand. "That is all."

They filed out silently.

He looked at Jusik. "Inform the respective lieutenant captains that they are promoted to full captains and now must enter recommendations for their vacated positions. These must be received by me before nightfall."

"As you order, sir."

"Also warn them to prepare to attend a commanding officer's court which will deal with the lower-ranking absentees as and when they reappear. Inform Captain Somir that he is appointed commander of the firing squad which will carry out the decisions of the court immediately they are pronounced."

"Yes, sir." Gaunt and hollow-eyed, Jusik turned with a click of heels and departed.

When the closer had shut the door, Cruin sat at his desk, placed his elbows on its surface, held his face in his hands. If the deserters did not return, they could not be so punished. No power, no authority could vent its wrath upon an absent body. The law was impotent if its subject lacked the essential feature of being present. All the laws of Huld could not put memories of lost men before a firing squad.

It was imperative that he make an example of the offenders. Their shy, furtive trips into the enemy's camp, he suspected, had been repeated often enough to have become a habit. Doubtless by now they were settled wherever they were visiting, sharing homes—welcome rooms—sharing food, company, laughter. Doubtless they had started to regain weight, to lose the space hues on their cheeks and foreheads, and the light in their eyes had begun to burn anew; and they had talked with signs and pictures, played games, tried to suck smoke things, and strolled with girls through the fields and the glades.

A pulse was beating steadily in the thickness of his neck as he stared through the port and waited for some sign that the tripled ring of guards had caught the first on his way in. Down, down, deep down inside him at a depth too great for him to admit that it was there, lay the disloyal hope that none would return.

One deserter would mean the slow, shuffling tread of the squad, the hoarse calls of, "Aim!" and "Fire," and the stepping forward of Somir, gun in hand, to administer the mercy shot.

Damn the manuals.

At the end of the first period after nightfall Jusik burst into the office, saluted, breathed heavily. The glare of the ceiling illumination deepened the lines on his thin features, magnified the bristles on his unshaven chin.

"Sir, I have to report that the men are getting out of control."

"What d'you mean?" Cruin's heavy brows came down as he stared fiercely at the other.

"They know of the recent demotions, of course. They know also that a court will assemble to deal with the absentees." He took another long-drawn breath. "And they also know the penalty these absentees must face."

"So?"

"So more of them have deserted—they've gone to warn the others not to return."

"Ah!" Cruin smiled lopsidedly. "The guards let them walk out, eh? Just like that?"

"Ten of the guards went with them," said Jusik.

"Ten?" Coming up fast, Cruin moved near to the other, studied him searchingly. "How many went altogether?"

"Ninety-seven."

Grabbing his helmet, Cruin slammed it on, pulled the metal chin strap over his jaw muscles. "More than one complete crew." He examined his gun, shoved it back, strapped on a second one. "At that rate they'll all be gone by morning." He eyed Jusik. "Don't you think so?"

"That's what I'm afraid of, sir."

Cruin patted his shoulder. "The answer, Jusik, is an easy one—we take off immediately."

"Take off?"

"Most certainly. The whole fleet. We'll strike a balanced orbit where it will be impossible for any man to leave. I will then give the situation more thought. Probably we'll make a new landing in some locality where none will be tempted to sneak away because there'll be nowhere to go. A scout can pick up Fane and his party in due course."

"I doubt whether they'll obey orders for departure, sir."

"We'll see, we'll see." He smiled again, hard and craggy. "As you would know if you'd studied the manuals properly, it is not difficult to smash incipient mutiny. All one has to do is remove the ringleaders. No mob is composed of men, as such. It is made up of a few ringleaders and a horde of stupid followers." He patted his guns. "You can always tell a ringleader—invariably he is the first to open his mouth!"

"Yes, sir," mouthed Jusik, with misgivings.

"Sound the call for general assembly."

The flagship's siren wailed dismally in the night. Lights flashed from ship to ship, and startled birds woke up and squawked in the trees beyond the ash.

Slowly, deliberately, impressively, Cruin came down the ladder, faced the audience whose features were a mass of white blobs in the glare of the ships' beams. The captains and lieutenant captains ranged themselves behind him and to either side. Each carried an extra gun.

"After three years of devoted service to Huld," he enunciated pompously, "some men have failed me. It seems that we have weaklings among us, weaklings unable to stand the strain of a few extra days before our triumph. Careless of their duty they disobey orders, fraternize with the enemy, consort with our opponents' females, and try to snatch a few creature comforts at the expense of the many." His hard, accusing eyes went over them. "In due time they will be punished with the utmost severity."

They stared back at him expressionlessly. He could shoot the ears off a running man at twenty-five yards, and he was waiting for his target to name itself. So were those at his side.

None spoke.

"Among you may be others equally guilty but not discovered. They need not congratulate themselves, for they are about to be deprived of further opportunities to exercise their disloyalty." His stare kept flickering over them while his hand remained ready at his side. "We are going to trim the ships and take off, seeking a balanced orbit. That means lost sleep and plenty of hard work for which you have your treacherous comrades to thank." He paused a moment, finished with: "Has anyone anything to say?"

One man holding a thousand.

Silence.

"Prepare for departure," he snapped, and turned his back upon them.

Captain Somir, now facing him, yelped: "Look out, commander!" and whipped up his gun to fire over Cruin's shoulder.

Cruin made to turn, conscious of a roar behind him, his guns coming out as he twisted around. He heard no crack from Somir's weapon, saw no more of his men as their roar cut off abruptly. There seemed to be an intolerable weight upon his skull, the grass came up to meet him, he let go his guns and put out his hands to save himself. Then the hazily dancing lights faded from his eyesight and all was black.

Deep in his sleep he heard vaguely and uneasily a prolonged stamping of feet, many dull, elusive sounds as of people shouting far, far away. This went on for a considerable time, and ended with a series of violent reports that shook the ground beneath his body.

Someone splashed water over his face.

Sitting up, he held his throbbing head, saw pale fingers of dawn feeling through the sky to one side. Blinking his aching eyes to clear then, he perceived Jusik, Somir and eighteen others. All were smothered in dirt, their faces bruised, their uniforms torn and bedraggled.

"They rushed us the moment you turned away from them," explained Jusik, morbidly. "A hundred of them in the front. They rushed us in one united frenzy, and the rest followed. There were too many for us." He regarded his superior with red-rimmed optics. "You have been flat all night."

Unsteadily, Cruin got to his feet, teetered to and fro. "How many were killed?"

"None. We fired over their heads. After that—it was too late."

"Over their heads?" Squaring his massive shoulders, Cruin felt a sharp pain in the middle of his back, ignored it. "What are guns for if not to kill?"

"It isn't easy," said Jusik, with the faintest touch of defiance. "Not when they're one's own comrades."

"Do you agree?" The commander's glare challenged the others.

They nodded miserably, and Somir said: "There was little time, sir, and if one hesitates, as we did, it becomes—"

"There are no excuses for anything. You had your orders; it was for you to obey them." His hot gaze burned one, then the other. "You are incompetent for your rank. You are both demoted!" His jaw came forward, ugly, aggressive, as he roared: "Get out of my sight!"

They mooched away. Savagely, he climbed the ladder, entered his ship, explored it from end to end. There was not a soul on board. His lips were tight as he reached the tail, found the cause of the earth-rocking detonations. The fuel tanks had been exploded, wrecking the engines and reducing the whole vessel to a useless mass of metal.

Leaving, he inspected the rest of his fleet. Every ship was the same, empty and wrecked beyond possibility of repair. At least the mutineers had been thorough and logical in their sabotage. Until a report vessel arrived, the home world of Huld had no mean of knowing where the expedition had landed. Despite even a systematic and wide-scale search it might well be a thousand years before Huldians found this particular planet again. Effectively the rebels had marooned themselves for the rest of their natural lives and placed themselves beyond reach of Huldian retribution.

Tasting to the full the bitterness of defeat, he squatted on the bottom rung of the twenty-second vessel's ladder, surveyed the double star-formations that represented his ruined armada. Futilely, their guns pointed over surrounding terrain. Twelve of the scouts, he noted, had gone. The others had been rendered as useless as their parent vessels.

Raising his gaze to the hill, he perceived silhouettes against the dawn where Jusik, Somir and the others were walking over the crest, walking away from him, making for the farther valley he had viewed so often. Four children joined them at the top, romped beside them as they proceeded. Slowly the whole group sank from sight under the rising sun.

Returning to the flagship, Cruin packed a patrol sack with personal possessions, strapped it on his shoulders. Without a final glance at the remains of his once-mighty command he set forth away from the sun, in the direction opposite to that taken by the last of his men.

His jack boots were dull, dirty. His orders of merit hung lopsidedly and had a gap where one had been torn off in the fracas. The bell was missing from his right boot; he endured the pad-*ding*, pad-*ding* of its fellow for twenty steps before he unscrewed it and slung it away.

The sack on his back was heavy, but not so heavy as the immense burden upon his mind. Grimly, stubbornly he plodded on, away from the ships, far, far into the morning mists—facing the new world alone.

Three and a half years had bitten deep into the ships of Huld. Still they lay in the valley, arranged with mathematical precision, noses in, tails out, as only authority could place them. But the rust had eaten a quarter of the way through the thickness of their tough shells, and their metal ladders were rotten and treacherous. The field mice and the voles had found refuge beneath them; the birds and spiders had sought sanctuary within them. A lush growth had sprung from encompassing ash, hiding the perimeter for all time.

The man who came by them in the midafternoon rested his pack and studied them silently, from a distance. He was big, burly, with a skin the color of old leather. His deep gray eyes were calm, thoughtful as they observed the thick ivy climbing over the flagship's tail.

Having looked at them for a musing half hour he hoisted his pack and went on, up the hill, over the crest and into the farther valley. Moving easily in his plain, loose-fitting clothes, his pace was deliberate, methodical.

Presently he struck a road, followed it to a stone-built cottage in the garden of which a lithe, dark-haired woman was cutting flowers. Leaning on the gate, he spoke to her. His speech was fluent but strangely accented. His tones were gruff but pleasant.

"Good afternoon."

She stood up, her arms full of gaudy blooms, looked at him with rich, black eyes. "Good afternoon." Her full lips parted with pleasure. "Are you touring? Would you care to guest with us? I am sure that Jusik—my husband—would be delighted to have you. Our welcome room has not been occupied for—"

"I am sorry," he chipped in. "I am seeking the Merediths. Could you direct me?"

"The next house up the lane." Deftly, she caught a falling bloom, held it to her breast. "If their welcome room has a guest, please remember us."

"I will remember," he promised. Eyeing her approvingly, his broad, muscular face lit up with a smile. "Thank you so much."

Shouldering his pack he marched on, conscious of her eyes following him. He reached the gate of the next place, a long, rambling, picturesque house fronted by a flowering garden. A boy was playing by the gate.

Glancing up as the other stopped near him, the boy said: "Are you touring, sir?"

"Sir?" echoed the man. *"Sir?"* His face quirked. "Yes, sonny, I am touring. I'm looking for the Merediths."

"Why, I'm Sam Meredith!" The boy's face flushed with sudden excitement. "You wish to guest with us?"

"If I may."

"Yow-ee!" He fled frantically along the garden path, shrieking at the top of his voice, "Mom, Pop, Marva, Sue—we've got a guest!"

A tall, red-headed man came to the door; pipe in mouth. Coolly, calmly, he surveyed the visitor.

After a little while, the man removed the pipe and said: "I'm Jake Meredith. Please come in." Standing aside, he let the other enter, then called, "Mary, Mary, can you get a meal for a guest?"

"Right away," assured a cheerful voice from the back.

"Come with me." Meredith led the other to the veranda, found him an easy-chair. "Might as well rest while you're waiting. Mary takes time. She isn't satisfied until the legs of the table are near to collapse—and woe betide you if you leave anything."

"It is good of you." Seating himself, the visitor drew a long breath, gazed over the pastoral scene before him.

Taking another chair, Meredith applied a light to his pipe. "Have you seen the mail ship?"

"Yes, it arrived early yesterday. I was lucky enough to view it as it passed overhead."

"You certainly were lucky considering that it comes only once in four years. I've seen it only twice, myself. It came right over this house. An imposing sight."

"Very!" indorsed the visitor, with unusual emphasis. "It looked to me about five miles long, a tremendous creation. Its mass must be many times greater than that of all those alien ships in the valley."

"Many times," agreed Meredith. The other leaned forward, watching his host. "I often wonder whether those aliens attributed smallness of numbers to war or disease, not thinking of large-scale emigration, nor realizing what it means."

"I doubt whether they cared very much seeing that they burned their boats and settled among us." He pointed with the stem of his pipe. "One of then lives in that cottage down there. Jusik's his name. Nice fellow. He married a local girl eventually. They are very happy."

"I'm sure they are."

They were quiet a long time, then Meredith spoke absently, as if thinking aloud. "They brought with them weapons of considerable might, not knowing that we have a weapon truly invincible." Waving one hand, he indicated the world at large. "It took us thousands of years to learn about the sheer invincibility of an idea. That's what we've got—a way of life, an idea. Nothing can blast that to shreds. Nothing can defeat an idea—except a better one." He put the pipe back in his mouth. "So far, we have failed to find a better one."

"They came at the wrong time," Meredith went on. "Ten thousand years too late." He glanced sidewise at his listener. "Our history covers a long, long day. It was so lurid that it came out in a new edition every minute. But this one's the late night final."

"You philosophize, eh?"

Meredith smiled. "I often sit here to enjoy my silences. I sit here and think. Invariably I end up with the same conclusion."

"What may that be?"

"That if I, personally, were in complete possession of all the visible stars and their multitude of planets I would still be subject to one fundamental limitation"—bending, he tapped his pipe on his heel—"in this respect—that no man can eat more than his belly can hold." He stood up, tall, wide-chested. "Here comes my daughter, Marva. Would you like her to show you your room?"

Standing inside the welcome room, the visitor surveyed it appreciatively. The comfortable bed, the bright furnishings.

"Like it?" Marva asked.

"Yes, indeed." Facing her, his gray eyes examined her. She was tall, red-haired, green-eyed, and her figure was ripe with the beauty of young womanhood. Pulling slowly at his jaw muscles, he asked: "Do you think that I resemble Cruin?"

"Cruin?" Her finely curved brows crinkled in puzzlement.

"The commander of that alien expedition."

"Oh, him!" Her eyes laughed, and the dimples came into her cheeks. "How absurd! You don't look the least bit like him. He was old and severe. You are *young*—and far more handsome."

"It is kind of you to say so," he murmured. His hands moved aimlessly around in obvious embarrassment. He fidgeted a little under her frank, self-possessed gaze. Finally, he went to his pack, opened it. "It is conventional for the guest to bring his hosts a present." A tinge of pride crept into his voice. "So I have brought one. I made it myself. It took me a long time to learn . . . a long time . . . with these clumsy hands. About three years."

Marva looked at it, raced through the doorway, leaned over the balustrade and called excitedly down the stairs. "Pop, Mom, our guest has a wonderful present for us. A clock. A clock with a little metal bird that calls the time."

Beneath her, feet bustled along the passage and Mary's voice came up saying: "May I see it? Please let me see it." Eagerly, she mounted the stairs.

As he waited for them within the welcome room, his shoulders squared, body erect as if on parade, the clock whirred in Cruin's hands and its little bird solemnly fluted twice.

The hour of triumph.

A Little Oil

Galaxy, October 1952

The ship hummed and thrummed and drummed. It was a low-cycle note, sonorous and penetrating like that produced by the big-pipe octave of a mighty organ. It moaned through hull-plates, groaned out of girders, throbbed along nerves and bones, beat upon tired ears and could not be ignored. Not after a week, a month or a year. Certainly not after most of four years.

There was no effective cure for the noise. It was the inevitable, unavoidable result of bottling an atomic propulsor within a cylinder of highly conductive metal. The first ship had screeched one hundred cycles higher, minute after minute, hour after hour, and had never returned. Somewhere amid the waste spaces of the infinite, it might still be howling, unheard, unheeded, after thirty years.

Ship number two had started out with a slag-wool padded engine room and silicone-lined venturis. The low note. The drone of a burdened bee amplified twenty thousand times. And the bee had not come back to the hive. Eighteen years into the star field and blindly heading onward for another hundred, thousand or ten thousand years.

The vessel now thundering along was number three, not going outward, but on its way back, heading for home. Nosing toward a not-yet-visible red dot lost in the mist of stars, a strayed soul fumbling for salvation, it was determined not to be damned as others had been damned. Ship number three—that meant something.

Sea sailors cherish sea superstitions. Space sailors coddle space superstitions. In the captain's cabin where Kinrade sat writing the log, a superstition was pinned to the wall and functioned as a morale booster.

THIRD TIME DOES IT!

They had believed it at the start when the crew had numbered nine. They would believe it at the finish, though reduced to six. But in between times there had been and might again be bad moments of shaken faith when men wanted out at any cost, even the cost of death and to hell with the ultimate purpose of the flight.

Moments when men fought other men in effort to break loose from audiophobia, claustrophobia, half a dozen other phobias.

Kinrade wrote with the pen in his right hand, a blue-steeled automatic within easy reach of his left. His eyes concentrated on the log, his ears on the ship and its everlasting drumming. The noise might hesitate, falter or cease, and the blessing of its cessation would be equally a curse. Or other sounds might rise above this persistent background, an oath, a shout, a shot. It had happened once before, when Weygarth cracked. It could happen again.

Kinrade was somewhat edgy himself, for he jerked in his seat and slid his left hand sidewise when Bertelli came in unexpectedly. Recovering, he swung his chair round on its socket, gazed into the other's sad gray eyes.

"Well, have they marked it yet?"

The question startled Bertelli. His long, lugubrious, hollow-cheeked face grew longer. His great gash of a mouth drooped at the corners. The sad eyes took on an expression of hopeless bafflement. He was clumsily embarrassed.

Recognizing those familiar symptoms, Kinrade became more explicit. "Is Sol visible on the screen?"

"Sol?" Bertelli's hands tangled together, the fingers like carrots.

"Our own sun, you imbecile!"

"Oh, *that*!" The eyes widened in delightful comprehension. "I haven't asked."

"I thought maybe you'd come to tell me they've got it spotted at last."

"No, Captain. It's just that I wondered whether you need any help." His expression switched from its accustomed glumness to the eager smile of a fool more than willing to serve. The mouth lifted, widened so much that it made the ears stick out and reminded the onlooker of a slice of melon.

"Thanks," said Kinrade, more kindly. "Not right now."

Bertelli's embarrassment came back in painful strength. His face was humbly apologetic for having asked. After shifting around on his big, ugly feet, he went out. As always, he skidded violently on the steel-floored catwalk, regained balance with a clatter of heavy boots. Nobody else slipped at that spot, but he invariably did.

Kinrade suddenly realized that he was smiling and changed it to a troubled frown. For the hundredth time he consulted the ship's register, found it no more informative than on the ninety-nine other occasions. There was the little roster with three names of the nine crossed out. And the same entry halfway down: *Enrico Bertelli, thirty-two, psychologist.*

It was the bunk. If Bertelli were a psychologist or any thing remotely connected with scientific expertness, then, he, Robert Kinrade, was a bright blue giraffe. For almost four years they'd been locked together in this groaning cylinder, six men carefully chosen from the great mass of humanity, six men supposed to be the salt of the Earth, the cream of their kind. But the six were five men and a fool.

There was a puzzle here. It intrigued him in spare moments when he had time to think with a mind untrammeled by serious matters. It dangled before him tantalizingly, making him repeatedly picture its subject all the way down from sad eyes to flat feet. During rare moments of meditation, he found himself vainly trying to analyze Bertelli and deduce the real reason for his being, concentrating upon him to the temporary exclusion of the others.

As opportunity occurred, Kinrade watched him, too, marveling that any so-called expert could be so thoroughly and unfailingly nitwitted. He studied Bertelli with such intentness that he failed to notice whether the others might be doing the same for similar reasons born of similar thoughts.

Yet this concentration was his answer—and he did not know it.

Marsden was duty navigator and Vail stood guard in the engine room when Kinrade went to lunch. The other three already were at the table in the tiny galley. He nodded briefly and took his place.

Big blond Nilsen, atomic engineer by choice, plus botanist by official coercion, eyed Kinrade skeptically and said, "No sun."

"I know."

"There ought to be."

Kinrade shrugged.

"But there isn't," Nilsen persisted.

"I know."

"Do you care?"

"Don't be a sap." Breaking open a packaged meal, Kinrade tossed it into his compartmented plastic plate.

Thrum-thrum went the ship from floor, walls and ceiling.

"So you think I'm a sap, do you?" Nilsen leaned forward, stared with aggressive expectancy.

"Let's eat," suggested Aram, the thin, dark and nervous cosmogeologist at his side. "One bellyache's enough without hunting another."

"That's not the point," declared Nilsen. "I want to know—"

He shut up as Bertelli mumbled "Pardon me," and reached across him for salt in a container fastened to the other end of the table.

Unscrewing it, Bertelli brought it to his end, sat down, found himself on the extreme edge of his seat. His eyes popped very slightly in mild surprise. He stood, slid the seat forward on its runners, sat again, knocked the salt off the table. Radiating shame and self-consciousness he picked it up, used it in the manner of one emptying a large bucket, practically lay full length on the table to screw it in its original position. That task performed, he squirmed backward with his behind in the air, gained the seat again.

It was the edge and so near that he began to slide off it. The eyes bulged a fraction more widely than before and once again he went through the seat-sliding performance. Finally he sat down, smoothed out an invisible napkin, favored every one with a look of abject apology.

Taking in a deep breath, Nilsen said to him, "Sure you wouldn't care for a little more salt?"

Bertelli's eyes dulled under the impact of the problem, sought his plate, examined it with idiotic care. "No, I don't think so, thank you."

Surveying his own plate a moment, Nilsen looked up, met Kinrade's eyes, asked, "What's this guy got that others haven't got?"

Grinning at him, Kinrade replied, "That problem is a corker. I've been trying to figure it out and I can't."

A half-smile came into Nilsen's features as he confessed, "Neither can I."

Bertelli said nothing. He went on with his meal, eating in characteristic manner with elbows held high and his hand uncertainly seeking a mouth it could not miss.

Putting a pencil-tip to the screen, Marsden said, "That one looks pink to me. But it may be my imagination."

Kinrade bent close and had a look. "Too small to be sure. A mere pinpoint."

"Then I'd been kidding myself."

"Not necessarily. Your eyes may be more color-sensitive than mine."

"Ask Goofy here," suggested Marsden.

Bertelli examined the brilliant dot from ten different distances and as many angles. Finally he squinted at it.

"That can't be it," he announced, triumphant with discovery, "because our sun is orange-red."

"The fluorescent coating of the screen would make it look pink," informed Marsden with a touch of impatience. "Does that dot look pink?"

"I don't know," Bertelli admitted miserably.

"You're a great help."

"It's too far away for more than mere guesswork," said Kinrade. "Resolution isn't good enough to cope with such a distance. We'll have to wait until we get a good deal closer."

"I'm fed up waiting," said Marsden, scowling at the screen.

"But we're going home," Bertelli reminded him.

"I know. That's what's killing me."

"Don't you *want* to go home?" Bertelli puzzledly asked.

"I want to too much." Irritatedly, Marsden rammed the pencil back into his pocket. "I thought I'd stand the inward trip better than the outward one just because it would be homeward. I was wrong. I want green grass, blue skies and plenty of room to move around. I can't wait."

"I can," said Bertelli, virtuously. "Because I've got to. If I were unable to wait, I'd go nuts."

"Would you?" Marsden looked him over, the grouch slowly fading from his face. The change went as far as a chuckle. "How much of a trip would that be?"

Leaving the navigation room, he headed toward the galley, still chuckling as he went. Rounding the farther corner, he let out a low guffaw.

"What's funny?" asked Bertelli, vacantly mystified.

Straightening up from the screen, Kinrade eyed him with care. "How is it that whenever somebody starts blowing his—" Changing his mind, he let the sentence die out.

"Yes, Captain?"

"Oh, forget it."

The ship plunged onward, moaning at every plate.

Vail appeared presently, coming off duty and on his way to eat. He was a short man of great width, with long arms and powerful hands.

"Any luck?"

"We're not sure." Kinrade indicated the dot burning amid a confusing host of others. "Marsden thinks that's it. He may be wrong."

"Don't you *know?*" asked Vail, looking at him and ignoring the screen Kinrade was pointing to.

"We will in due time. It's a bit early yet."

"Changing your tune, aren't you?"

"What do you mean?" Kinrade's tone was sharp.

"Three days ago you told us that Sol should become visible in the screen almost anytime. That gave us a lift. We needed it. I'm no sniveling babe myself, but I must admit I wanted that boost." He surveyed the other with a touch of resentment. "The higher hopes go, the lower they fall when they drop."

"I'm not dropping mine," Kinrade said. "Three days plus or minus is a tiny margin of error in a return trip taking two years."

"That would be true if we're on correct course. Maybe we aren't."

"Are you suggesting that I'm not competent to work out the proper coordinates?"

"I'm suggesting that even the best of us can blunder," Vail gave back stubbornly. "In proof of which, two ships have gone to pot."

"Not because of navigational errors," put in Bertelli, looking unconvincingly profound.

Pursing his lips, Vail stared at him and inquired, "What the hell do you know about space navigation?"

"Nothing," Bertelli confessed with the air of one surrendering a back tooth. He nodded toward Kinrade. "But he knows enough."

"I wonder!"

"The route for return was worked out in full detail by Captain Sanderson before he died," said Kinrade, his color a little heightened. "I've checked and rechecked at least a dozen times. So has Marsden. If you're not satisfied, you can have the calculations and go through them yourself."

"I'm not a trained navigator."

"Then shut your trap and leave other—"

Bertelli broke in with a note of protest. "But I didn't have it open!"

Shifting attention to him, Kinrade asked, "You didn't have what open?"

"My mouth," said Bertelli. He registered personal injury. "Don't know why you have to pick on me. Everyone picks on me."

"You're wrong," Vail told him. "He—"

"There you are. I'm wrong. I'm always wrong. I'm never right." Emitting a deep sigh, Bertelli wandered out, dragging big feet. His face was a picture of misery.

Vail watched him in faint amazement, then said, "That looks to me like a persecution complex. And he's supposed to be a psychologist. What a laugh!"

"Yes," agreed Kinrade, without humor. "What a laugh!"

Going to the screen, Vail examined it. "Which one does Marsden think is Sol?"

"That one." Kinrade pointed it out for him.

Staring at it hungrily for quite a time, Vail finished, "Oh, well, let's hope he's right." Then he departed.

Left alone, Kinrade sat in the navigator's chair and looked at the screen without seeing it. His mind was on a problem that might be real or might be imaginary.

When does science become an art? Or should it be: when does art become a science?

Aram cracked next day. He got a dose of "Charlie," the same psychotic behavior pattern that had put an end to Weygarth. There was a technical name for it, but few knew it and fewer could pronounce it. The slang term came from an ancient, almost forgotten war in which the rear-gunner of a big aircraft—Tail End Charlie—would think too long of the heavy bomb-load and the thousands of gallons of high octane spirit right behind his perspex parrot-cage, and all of a sudden he'd batter upon the walls of his prison, screaming.

The way Aram broke was characteristic of this space affliction. He sat next to Nilsen, quietly downing his meal, but picking at the compartmented plastic tray as though completely indifferent to food or drink. Then, without a word or the slightest change of expression, he pushed away the tray, got up and ran like hell. Nilsen tried to trip him and failed. Aram shot through the door like a bolting rabbit, raced headlong down the passage toward the airlock.

Slamming his own chair back to the limit of its holding rails, Nilsen went after him with Kinrade one jump behind. Bertelli stayed in his seat, a forkful of food halfway to his mouth, his gaze fixed blankly on the facing wall while his big ears remained perked for outer sounds.

They caught Aram frantically struggling with the airlock wheel and trying to force it the wrong way around. Even if he had rotated it the right way, he wouldn't have had time to open it. His thin features were pale and he was snuffling with exertion.

Reaching him, Nilsen jerked him around by one shoulder, smacked him in the jaw. There was plenty of force behind that blow. Aram, a small, lightly built man, caromed along the passage and ended up as an unconscious bundle by the forward door. Rubbing his knuckles, Nilsen grunted to himself, checked the airlock wheel to make sure it was holding good and tight.

Then he grasped the victim's feet while Kinrade lifted the shoulders and between them they bore the sagging Aram to his tiny cabin, laid him in his bunk. Nilsen remained on watch while Kinrade went for the hypodermic needle and a shot of dope. They put Aram out of the running for the next twelve hours. This was the only known countermeasure: an enforced sleep during which an overactive brain could rest and strained nerves recuperate.

Returning to the galley, Nilsen resumed his interrupted meal, said to Kinrade, "Good thing he didn't think to swipe a gun."

Kinrade nodded without answering. He knew what the other meant. Weygarth had tried to hold them off with a gun while he prepared his dash to false freedom on a blast of air. They could not rush him without risking serious loss. They'd had to shoot him down quickly, ruthlessly, before it was too late. Weygarth had been their first bitter casualty only twenty months out.

And now they dared not suffer another loss. Five men could run the ship, control it, steer it, land it. Five represented the absolute minimum. Four would be damned forever to a great metal coffin thundering blindly amid the host of stars.

It brought up yet another of the problems that Kinrade had not been able to resolve, at least to his own satisfaction. Should an airlock be fastened with a real lock to which only the captain held the key? Or might that cost them dear in a sudden and grave emergency? Which was the greater risk, lunatic escape for one or balked escape for all?

Oh, well, they were homeward bound, and when they got back he'd hand over the log and the detailed reports and leave the big brains to work it out for themselves. That was their job; his to make landfall safely.

Kinrade glanced at Nilsen, noted the introspective frown on his face and knew what he was thinking of Weygarth. Scientists and top-grade technicians are people with highly trained minds, but that does not make them less or more than other men. Their status does not keep them in splendid isolation from humanity. Outside of their especial interests, they are plain, ordinary folks subject to the strains and tensions of every man. Their minds are not and cannot be solely and everlastingly occupied with one subject. Sometimes they think of other men and sometimes of themselves. Nilsen's was a trained mind, intelligent and sensitive, therefore so much the more liable to crack. Kinrade knew instinctively that if and when Nilsen made a break for the lock, he would not forget the gun.

It took less intelligent, less imaginative types—the cow-mind—to endure long incarceration in a huge steel boiler on which a dozen devils hammered hour after hour, day after day, without cease or let-up. There was another problem for Earth's bigbrains to mull a while: dull-witted people were tops for endurance, but useless functionally. Bright minds were essential to run the ship, yet somewhat more likely to go *phut,* even though only temporarily.

What did this add up to? Answer: the ideal space crew should be composed of hopeless dopes with high I.Q. A contradiction in terms.

Now that he came to consider it, the thought struck him that here might be the solution to the mystery of Bertelli. Those who had designed and built the ship and hand-picked the crew were people of formidable craftiness. It was incredible that they'd dig up a formless character like Bertelli in a spirit of not giving a damn. The selection had been deliberate and carefully calculated, of that Kinrade was certain. Perhaps the loss of two ships had convinced them that they'd have to be more modest in their choice of crews. Maybe Bertelli had been planted to test how a dope made out.

If so, they had something—but it wasn't enough. Without a doubt, Bertelli would be the last to crack, the last to race for the airlock. Beyond that, nothing could be said in his favor purely from the technical viewpoint. He knew little worth knowing and that he had learned from the others. Any responsibility with which he was entrusted invariably got fouled up in masterly style. Indeed, with his big, clumsy mitts on any of the controls, he would be a major menace.

He was liked, all right. In fact, he was popular in a way. Bertelli had other accomplishments about as genuinely useful on a spaceship as a skunk's smell-gun at a convention. He could play several musical instruments, sing in a cracked voice, mime in really funny manner, tap-dance with a peculiar sort of loose-jointed clumsiness. After they'd got over their initial irritation with him, they had found him amusing and pathetic—a bumbler they were sorry to feel superior to, because they couldn't think of anyone who wouldn't be superior to him.

The schemers back home would learn that a spaceship is better without non-technical thickheads, Kinrade decided rather uncertainly. They had made their test and it hadn't come off. It hadn't come off. It hadn't come off. The more he repeated it to himself, the less sure he felt about it.

Vail came in, paused at the sight of them. "I thought you'd finished ten minutes ago."

"It's all right." Nilsen stood up, brushed away crumbs, gestured toward his chair. "I'll go watch the engines."

Getting his tray and meal, Vail seated himself, eyed the others. "What's up?"

"Aram's in bed with Charlie," Kinrade told him.

Not the flicker of emotion crossed Vail's face. He made a vicious stab at his food, said, "The Sun would bring him out of that condition. That's what we all want, a sight of the Sun."

"There are millions of suns," informed Bertelli, eagerly offering the lot.

Leaning his elbows on the table, Vail said in a harsh voice and with great significance, "That is precisely the point!"

Bertelli's eyes dulled into complete confusion. He fidgeted with his tray, knocked his fork around without noticing it. Still looking at Vail, he felt for the fork, picked it up by the prongs, absently poked at the tray with the handle. Then he lifted the handle toward his mouth.

"I'd try the other end," advised Vail, watching with interest. "It's sharper."

The eyes lowered, studied the fork while gradually they took on an expression of vacant surprise. He made a childish motion indicative of helplessness. Finally he bestowed on both his usual apologetic grin and at the same time gave a casual twitch of finger and thumb that landed the handle smack in his palm.

Kinrade noticed that flip. Vail didn't, but he did—and for once he got a strange, uncanny feeling that Bertelli had made a very small mistake, a tiny error that might have passed unseen.

When Kinrade was in his cabin, the intercom called on the desk and Marsden's voice said, "Aram's just come out of it. He's got a sore jaw, but he seems cooled down. I don't think he needs another shot—yet."

"We'll let him run loose, but keep an eye on him for a while," Kinrade decided. "Tell Bertelli to stick close. He has nothing better to do."

"All right." Marsden paused, added in lower tones, "Vail is pretty surly lately. Have you noticed?"

"He's okay. Just gets jumpy now and again. Don't we all?"

"I suppose so." Marsden sounded as if he'd like to say more, but he didn't. He cut off and the intercom went silent.

Finishing the day's entry on the log, Kinrade examined himself at the mirror, decided he'd put off a shave a little longer. This was his idea of petty luxury; he disliked the chore, but lacked the courage to grow a beard. Other men, other notions.

He lay back in his chair and enjoyed a quiet think, first about the planet called home, then the men who had sent this ship into space, then the men who were flying it with him. They'd been trained for the job, these six who, for the first time, had reached another star, and their training had incorporated a certain amount of useful flexibility. The three spacemen among them had been given superswift education in some branch of science. The scientists had undergone courses in space navigation or atomic engineering. Two aptitudes per men. Then he thought again and eliminated Bertelli.

Pre-flight education had gone further than that. A bald-headed old coot who bossed a lunatic asylum had lectured them on space etiquette with every air of knowing what he was talking about. Each man, he had explained, would know only three things about his fellows, to wit: name, age and qualification. No man must ask for more nor seek to pry into another's private life. Unknown lives provide no basis for irrational prejudices, antagonisms or insults, he had said. Empty personalities don't clash so readily. So it was established that none might urge another to reveal what made him tick.

Thus Kinrade could not probe the reasons why Vail was irritable above the average or what made Marsden more impatient than others. He could not determine from past data why Nilsen potentially was the most dangerous or Aram the least stable. Neither could he insist that Bertelli explain his presence in understandable terms. Pending successful completion of the flight, each man's history remained hidden behind a curtain through which, from time to time, only insignificant items had been glimpsed.

After most of four years existing cheek by jowl with these people, he had come to know them as never before—but not as he would know them some day in the green fields of Earth when the flight was a bygone event, the tabu was broken and they had memories for free discussion.

He liked to muse on these matters because he had developed a theory that he intended to dump right in the laps of the experts. It concerned lifers in penitentiaries. Not all criminals are stupid, he believed. Many might be intelligent, sensitive men somehow pushed or kicked off the path called straight and narrow. Walled up, some of them would get a dose of Charlie, try to bust out, beat up a warder, anything, *anything* to escape—and be rewarded for their efforts with solitary confinement. It was like treating a poisoned man with an even more powerful dose of what made him ill. It was wrong, wrong. He was convinced of that. There was a reformist streak in Kinrade.

Upon his desk he had a neatly written scheme for the treatment of lifers likely to go psycho. It involved constant individual observation and the timely use of occupational therapy. Whether or not it was practical, he didn't know, but at least it was constructive. The plan was his pet. He wanted leading penologists to play with it, give it a serious tryout. If it worked—and he felt that it should—the world would have derived one benefit from this flight in a way not originally contemplated. Even that alone made it profitable.

At that point, his thoughts were brought to an abrupt end by the arrival of Nilsen, Vail and Marsden. Behind them, waiting in the doorway, but not entering, was Aram with Bertelli in attendance. Kinrade braced himself in his seat and spoke gruffly.

"This is great. Nobody at the controls."

"I switched on the autopilot," Marsden said. "It will hold her on course four or five hours. You said so yourself."

"True." His eyes examined them. "Well, why the scowling deputation?"

"This is the end of the fourth day," Nilsen pointed out. "Soon we'll be into the fifth. And we're still looking for Sol."

"So?"

"I'm not satisfied that you know where we're going."

"I am."

"Is that a fact or more face-saving?"

Kinrade stood up, said, "For the sake of argument, suppose I admitted that we're running blind—what could you do about it?"

"That's an easy one." Nilsen's air was that of one whose suspicions have almost been confirmed. "We picked you for captain after Sanderson died. We'd withdraw the vote and choose somebody else."

"And then?"

"Make for the nearest star, hunt around for a planet we can live on."

"Sol *is* the nearest star."

"It is if we're heading right," Nilsen retorted.

Sliding open a drawer in his desk, Kinrade took out a large roll of paper, spread it across the top. Its multitude of tiny squares bore a large number of dots and crosses amid which a thick, black line ran in a steady curve.

"This is the return course." His fingers indicated several crosses and dots. "We can tell by direct observation of these bodies whether or not we are on course. There's only one thing we can't check with absolute accuracy."

"What's that?" inquired Vail, frowning at the chart.

"Our velocity. It can be estimated only with a five per cent margin of error, plus or minus. I know we're on course, but not precisely how far along it. Hence the four-day lag. I warn you that it can extend to as much as ten."

Nilsen said, heavily, "They took photos of the star formation on the way out. We've just been putting the transparencies over the screen. They don't match."

"Of course they don't." Kinrade displayed impatience. "We're not at the same point. The star field will have circumferential displacement."

"We aren't without brains despite not being trained navigators," Nilsen gave back. "There is displacement. It progresses radially from a focal point that is not the pink spot you claim is Sol. The point is about halfway between that and the left edge of the screen." He gave a loud sniff, invited. "Can you talk yourself out of that one?"

Kinrade sighed, put a finger on the chart. "This line is a curve, as you can see. The outward course was a similar curve bending the reverse way. The tail camera focused along the line of the ship's axis. A few thousand miles out, it was pointing sunward, but the farther the ship got, the more its axis pointed to one side. By the time we crossed the orbit of Pluto, it was aiming to hell and away."

Peering at the chart, Nilsen thought a while, asked shrewdly, "If you are sincere, what's the absolute margin of error?"

"I told you—ten days."

"Nearly half of those have gone. We'll give you the other half."

"Thanks!" said Kinrade, faintly sarcastic.

"After which we'll either see Sol and identify it beyond doubt or we'll have a new captain and be heading for the nearest light."

"We'll draw lots for captain," suggested Bertelli from the back. "I'd like the chance to boss a ship."

"Heaven help us!" exclaimed Marsden.

"We'll pick the man best qualified," said Nilsen.

"That's why you chose Kinrade in the first place," Bertelli reminded him.

"Maybe. But we'll find someone else."

"Then I insist on being considered. One dope is as good as another for making a mess of things."

"When it comes to that, we're not in the same class," replied Nilsen, feeling that his efforts were being subtly sabotaged. "You can out-boob me with your big hands pinned to your big ears. He looked over the others. "Isn't that so?"

They grinned assent.

It wasn't Nilsen's triumph. It was somebody else's.

Merely because they did grin.

Bertelli organized another party that night. For once his birthday was not the pretext. Somehow he'd managed to celebrate seven birthdays in four years without anyone seeing fit to count them all. But an excuse can be overdone, so he announced his candidacy for the post of captain, explaining that he wished to curry favor with voters. It was as good as any.

They cleared the galley as they'd done a score of times before. They broke a bottle of gin, shared it between them, sipped with introspective glumness. Aram did his party-piece by bird-calling between two fingers, received the usual polite applause. Marsden recited something about the brown eye of the little yellow dog. By that time Nilsen had warmed up sufficiently to sing two songs in a deep, rich bass. He gained louder applause for having varied his repertoire.

Weygarth, of course, wasn't there to do his sleight-of-hand tricks. Sanderson and Dawkins were also missing from the bill. Temporarily, their absence was forgotten as the tiny audience awaited the star turn.

Bertilli, of course. This was the sort of thing at which he excelled and the chief reason why a major nuisance had become tolerated, liked, perhaps loved.

When they'd held the alien landfall spree, he'd played an oboe for most of an hour, doing more things with the instrument than they had believed possible. He had ended with a sonic impression of an automobile collision, the agitated toot of horns, the crash, the heated argument between oboe-voiced drivers that finished with decidedly rude noises. Nilsen had almost rolled out of his seat.

On the way home, there had been a couple more whoopees arranged for no particular reason. Bertelli had mimed for these, his dental plates removed, his features rubbery, his arms like snakes. First the eager sailor leaping ashore and seeking feminine company. The search, the discovery, pursuit, encounter, rebuff, the persuasion, the going to a show, the strolling home, the pause on the doorstep rewarded with a black eye.

Another time he'd reversed the roll, became a plump blonde followed by an eager sailor. Wordlessly, but with motions, gestures, posturings and facial expressions equal to if not better than speech, he had taken them on the night's prowl ending with the fight on the doorstep.

This time he pretended to be a bashful sculptor shaping a statue of Venus de Milo with invisible clay. Piling up a column of what wasn't there, he hesitantly stroked it, nervously patted it, embarrassedly smoothed it into near-visible form. He rolled two cannon-balls, plonked them on her chest while covering his eyes, rolled two pills and shyly put them on top, delicately molded them into shape.

It took him twenty hilarious minutes to make her almost, but not quite, complete, at which point he took idiotic alarm. He scanned horizon, looked out the door, peered under the table to insure that they two were alone. Satisfied, yet full of embarrassment he made a faltering approach, withdrew, plucked up fresh courage, lost it again, had a spasm of daring that failed at the critical moment.

Vail offered pungent advice while Nilsen sprawled in the next seat and held an aching diaphragm. Summoning up every thing he had in an effort to finish the job, Bertelli made a mad rush at it, fell over his own feet, slid on his face along the steel floor-plates. Nilsen made choking sounds. Stupidly enraged with himself, Bertelli shot to his feet, drew his bottom lip over the tip of his nose, waggled his bat-ears, closed his eyes, made one violent stab with a forefinger—and provided Venus with a navel.

For days afterward, they chuckled over that performance, making curvaceous motions with their hands or prodding each other in the paunch at odd moments. The ghostly Venus stayed good for a laugh until . . . the Sun came up.

Making another of his frequent checks late in the eighth day, Marsden found that one of the transparencies now coincided dot for dot with a focal point two inches leftward of an enlarged pink glow. He let go a howl that brought the rest of the crew racing to the bow.

Sol was identified. They looked at it, licked lips over it, looked again. Four years in a bottle is like forty years in the star fields—and they had been bottled too long. One by one they visited Kinrade's cabin and exulted over the superstition on the wall.

THIRD TIME DOES IT!

Morale boosted way up. The ship's drumming and thrumming somehow lost its hellishness and took on a heartening note of urgency. Jangled nerves accepted the new and different strain of anticipation right to the glorious moment when a voice from Earth came feebly through the radio receiver. The voice strengthened day by day, week by week, until finally it bawled from the speaker while the fore observation-port was filled with half a planet.

"From where I'm standing, I can see an ocean of faces turned toward the sky," said the announcer. "There must be half a million people present, sharing the most eventful hour in history. At any moment now, folks, you will hear the distant drone of the first spaceship to return from another star. I just can't tell you how much—"

What followed the landing was the worst part. The blaring bands, the thunder of cheers. The handshakes, speeches, the posing for press photographers, newsreels, television scanners, the cameras of countless frantic amateurs.

It ended at last. Kinrade said farewell to his crew, felt the beartrap grip of Nilsen's hand, the soft, frank clasp of Aram, the shy, self-conscious touch of Bertelli.

Looking into the latter's mournful eyes, he said, "The authorities will now start howling for all the data we've got. I suppose you've finished your book."

"What book?"

"Now, now, don't kid me." He offered a knowing wink. "You're the official psychologist, aren't you?"

He didn't wait for an answer. While the others busied themselves collecting personal belongings, he got the log and the file of reports, took them to the Administration Building.

Looking no different for the passage of time, Bancroft sat paunchily behind his desk, said with satirical satisfaction, "You are now looking at a fat man wallowing in the joys of promotion and higher salary."

"Congratulations." Kinrade dumped the books and sat down.

"I would swap both for youth and adventure." Casting an anticipatory glance at what the other had brought, Bancroft went on, "There are questions I'm bursting to ask. But the answers are hidden somewhere in that pile and I guess you're in a hurry to go home."

"A 'copter will pick me up when it can get through the overcrowded air. I have twenty minutes to spare."

"In that case I'll use them." Bancroft leaned forward, eyes intent. "What about the first two ships?"

"We searched seven planets. Not a sign."

"They hadn't landed or crashed?"

"No."

"So they must have gone on?"

"Evidently."

"Any idea why?"

Kinrade hesitated, said, "It's a hunch and nothing more. I think their numbers were reduced by accident, sickness or whatever. They became too few to retain control of the ship." He paused, added, "We lost three men ourselves."

"Tough luck." Bancroft looked unhappy. "Who were they?"

"Weygarth, Dawkins and Sanderson. The first died on the way out. He never saw the new sun, much less his own. The story is there." He gestured toward the reports. "The other two were killed on the fourth planet, which I've established as unsafe for human habitation."

"What's wrong with it?"

"A big and hungry life-form exists under the surface, sitting with traps held open beneath a six-inch crust of soil. Sanderson walked around, fell into a red, sloppy mouth four feet wide by ten long. He was gulped from sight. Dawkins rushed to his rescue, but dropped into another." His fingers fumbled with each other as he finished, "There was nothing we could do, not a damned thing."

"A pity, a great pity." Bancroft shook his head slowly from side to side. "How about the other planets?"

"Four are useless. Two are made to measure for us."

"Hah, that's something!" He glanced at the small clock on his desk, continued hurriedly. "And now the ship. Doubtless your reports are full of criticisms. Nothing is perfect, not even the best we've produced. What do you consider its most outstanding fault?"

"The noise. It could drive you out of your mind. It needs cutting out."

"Not completely," Bancroft contradicted. "There is psychic terror in absolute silence."

"All right. Then it needs cutting down to a more endurable level. Try it yourself for a week and see how you like it."

"I wouldn't. The problem is being beaten, although slowly. We have a new and quieter type of engine already on the test-bench. Four years' progress, you know."

"We need it," said Kinrade.

Bancroft went on, "And what do you think of the crew?"

"Best ever."

"They ought to be. We skimmed the world for the cream—nothing less was good enough. Each man was tops in his own particular line."

"Including Bertelli?"

"I knew you'd ask about him." Bancroft smiled as if at a secret thought. "You want me to explain him, eh?"

"I've no right to insist, but I'd certainly like to know why you included such a dead weight."

"We lost two ships," said Bancroft, looking serious. "One could be an accident. Two were not. It's hard to believe that an exceptional kind of breakdown or a collision with a lump of rock or some other million-to-one chance would occur twice running."

"I don't believe it myself."

"We spent years studying the problem," Bancroft continued. "Every time we got the same answer: it wasn't due to any defect in the vessels. The cause lay somewhere in the human element. Short of a four-year test on living men, we could do no more than speculate. Then one day the likely solution popped up by sheer chance."

"How?"

"We were in this very room, beating our brains for the hundredth or two-hundredth time, when that clock stopped." He indicated the timepiece facing him.

"A fellow named Whittaker from the Space Medicine Research Station wound it up, shook it, got it going. Immediately afterward a brainwave hit him, kerplonk!"

Picking up the clock, Bancroft opened its back, turned it toward his listener. "What do you see?"

"Cogs and wheels."

"Nothing else?"

"Couple of coiled springs."

Are you sure that is all?"

"All that matters," declared Kinrade, having no doubt .

"Wrong, dead wrong," said Bancroft, positively, "You have made precisely the mistake we made with ships number one and two. We built giant metal clocks, fitted them with human cogs and wheels accurately designed for their purpose. Cogs and wheels of flesh and blood, chosen with the same care as one would choose parts for a fine watch. But the clocks stopped. We had overlooked something that Whittaker suddenly thought of."

"Well, what was it?"

Bancroft smiled and said. "A little oil."

"Oil?" exclaimed Kinrade, sitting up.

"Our error was natural. In a technological age, we technicians tend to think we're the whole cheese. We aren't. Maybe we're a very considerable slice, but we are not the lot. Civilization is composed of others also, the housewife, the taxi driver, the dime store salesgirl, the postman, the hospital nurse, the corner cop. It would be a hell of a civilization built solely on boys pushing studs of computor-machines and without the butcher, the baker, the candlestick-maker. That's a lesson some of us needed to learn."

"You've got something," Kinrade agreed, "but I don't see what."

"We had another problem in our laps," said Bancroft. "What sort of oil must you use for human cogs and wheels? Answer: human oil. What kind of individual specializes in being oil?"

"And you dug up Bertelli?"

"We did. His family has been oil for twenty generations. He is the present holder of a great tradition—and internationally famous."

"Never heard of him. I suppose he traveled with us under a false name?"

"He went under his own."

"I didn't recognize him," Kinrade persisted. "Neither did anyone else. So how can he be famous? Or did he have his face altered by plastic surgery?"

"He changed it completely in one minute flat." Getting up, Bancroft lumbered to a filing cabinet, opened it, sought through several folders. Extracting a full-plate glossy photograph, he slid it across the desk. "All he did to his face was wash it."

Picking up the picture, Kinrade stared at the chalk-white features, the cone-shaped hat set rakishly on a high, false skull, the huge eyebrows arched in perpetual surprise, the red diamonds painted around the mournful eyes, the grotesque, bulbous nose, the crimson ear-to-ear mouth, the thick ruff of lace around the neck.

"Coco!"

"The twentieth Coco with which this world has been blessed." Bancroft confirmed.

Kinrade had another long look. "May I keep this?"

"Certainly. I can get a thousand more copies any time I want."

Kinrade emerged from the Administration Building just in time to see the subject of his thoughts in hot pursuit of a ground-taxi.

With a shapeless and hurriedly packed bag swinging wildly from one hand, Bertelli went along in exaggerated, loose-jointed bounds with big boots rising waist-high, while his long neck protruded forward and his face bore a ludicrous expression of woe.

Many a time the onlooker had been puzzled by the fleeting familiarity of one of Bertelli's poses or gestures. Now, knowing what he did know, he recognized instantly the circus jester's classic anxiety-gallop across a sawdust ring. To make it complete, Bertelli should have been casting frightened glances over one shoulder at a floating skeleton attached to him by a long cord.

Bertelli caught up with the taxi, bestowed an inane smile, slung his bag inside and clambered after it. The taxi whirled away with twin spurts of vapor from its underbody jets.

For a long minute, Kinrade stood looking absently at the poised spaceships and the sky. His mind was viewing the world as a gigantic stage on which every man, woman and child played a wonderful and necessary part.

And holding the whole show together with laughter, exaggerating temper and hostility and conflict into absurdity, was the clown.

If he'd had to assemble the crew, he couldn't have picked a better psychologist than Bertelli.

Meeting On Kangsham

If, March 1965

Warhurst leaned on a tubular rail and watched the passengers boarding the ship. This was one of his favorite occupations, there being nothing more sinful available. Nice to see a change of faces once in a while. Nicer still to see an occasional female one as reminder of the fact that the human race is not an all-male society. And, anyway, he liked to speculate about who these people were and what particular talents they possessed and why they were going wherever they were going.

Up the duralumin gangway they came, the fat and the thin, the short and the tall. The majority were men in their twenties or thirties. Adventurous types willing to live in loneliness and beat an existence out of alien soil. Fodder for the faraway. Among them might be a criminal or two as well as a few misanthropes. One man, a little balding and slightly older than the rest, wore a calm, phlegmatic air. Warhurst weighed him up as some kind of scientist or maybe a doctor. The three girls following immediately behind had a brisk, professional manner and might be nurses. There was a serious shortage of doctors and nurses out there.

Van Someren joined him at the rail, draped himself over it and gazed down. He was the ship's agent and, as the local representative of the owner, was entitled to enough respect to avoid a charge of mutiny. Chewing a splinter of wood, he watched the ascending passengers as if seeking the one escaping with the green eye of the little yellow god. After a while he removed the splinter, straightened himself and spoke.

"Take a look at Methuselah."

Obediently Warhurst took a look. A gangling and skinny oldster was coming aboard dragging a large and badly battered case. A ship's loader tried to lend a hand with the case. The ancient repelled him fiercely with emphatic but unhearable words. Defiantly he lugged the case upward. His face became more visible as it neared: it was complete with two eyes, a nose and a pure white Fancy Dan mustache. The eyes were rheumy but shrewd, the nose was suffering from battle fatigue but still breathing.

"Eighty if a day," said Warhurst. "They must be scraping the bottom of the barrel."

"He's all yours," said Van Someren.

"What d'you mean, all mine?"

"You're the deck officer. He's a privileged passenger. Count it up on your fingers."

"Jeepers! Is he a big stockholder or something?"

"As far as I know he isn't worth a cent. All I can say is that I have my orders and those are to tell you that old geezer's name is William Harlow and that he's a privileged passenger. I am further instructed to state with suitable emphasis that you will be held personally responsible for his safe arrival and that if you fail in this duty your offal will be required for feeding to the vultures."

"Nuts to that," said Warhurst. "If he's a chronic invalid he belongs to the ship's medic."

"Since when have invalids been toted into the wilds?"

"There has to be a first time," Warhurst protested.

"Well, this ain't it. He's not a sick man as far as I know. They wouldn't ship him if he were."

"I should think so, too. We've no geriatric ward on this vessel."

"There's no psychiatric one either but they let you zoom around." Van Someren smirked triumphantly, had a brief chew on his hunk of wood, then diagnosed, "I know what's the matter with you. You've figured on squiring those three dames around—on company time and with full pay."

"No harm in that, is there?"

"I wouldn't know, never having experienced your in-flight technique. But orders are orders and you obey them or walk the plank into shark-infested seas. The owners say you're to nursemaid this Harlow relic. Think of him as your poor old father and treat him with filial care."

"Get out of my sight, you darned woodpecker," said Warhurst.

"All right, all right, have it your own way." Van Someren smirked again and wandered off.

Leaving the rail, Warhurst went below, pushed through a group of passengers cluttering a narrow corridor, found his man standing firmly astride his big case. He went up to him.

"Mr. Harlow?"

"Correct. Who told you?"

"It's my business to know these things. I'm Steve Warhurst."

"That's a heck of a coincidence."

"What is?"

"That being your name. Could easily have been anything else, Joe Snape, Theophilus Bagley or whatever. But it had to be . . . what did you say?"

"Steve Warhurst. I'm the deck officer."

"That so? What do you do for a crust?"

"I look after the welfare of the passengers," explained Warhurst, patiently.

"Man, you've got it made," said Harlow.

"I do plenty of other things," Warhurst persisted, not liking the insinuation. "Taking care of the human load is only one of my jobs."

"I should think so, too. You're wearing enough gold to be worth mining." Harlow let his watery, yellow-tinged eyes examine the passengers within visual range. "Real bunch of sissies. In my young days they needed no fancy-pants deck officers. A man climbed aboard and strapped himself down good and tight. If a strap busted he got an eye knocked out."

"Things have changed," Warhurst reminded.

"So I've heard."

"Nobody has to be mummy-wrapped or encapsulated. We've got null-G. You'll float like a feather as we rise. When the siren yowls we'll both go up without the aid of nets."

"Human race is getting soft," opined Mr. Harlow.

"I'd like to see your transit voucher," Warhurst prompted.

"What for?"

"It records your cabin number. I'll take you to it."

"Listen," ordered Harlow, baring a set of beaten-up teeth, "I know my cabin number and I'm capable of reaching it under my own steam."

"I wasn't suggesting wheeling you there. I merely want to show you where it is."

"Show me?" Harlow registered incredulity. "Let me tell you I've found my way through places that'd give you the holy horrors. I don't need any snub-nosed kid to tell me which way to go."

"No offense," soothed Warhurst. "How about me helping you with your case?"

"Scoot!" bawled Harlow.

First Officer Winterton, who happened to be passing, stopped and asked, "Is something wrong?"

"This gilded cutie," informed Harlow, nodding at Warhurst, "thinks I'm a cripple."

"I offered to help with his case," explained Warhurst.

"There you are—what did I tell you?" said Harlow.

"It was quite proper of him," Winterton assured Harlow. "Mr. Warhurst is the ship's host so far as the passengers are concerned."

"Then why doesn't he pick on the others? Some of 'em are making ready to faint."

"Why didn't you?" Winterton asked Warhurst, secretly beginning to regret his intervention.

"The agent said he was a P.P."

Harlow let go his grip on his case, grabbed Warhurst's tie, pulled its knot to quarter size and growled, "if you want to call me names call 'em proper, as man to man."

"A P.P. is a privileged passenger," said Warhurst, fighting for breath.

"Privileged?" He let go the tie, irritated and baffled. "Never asked for a privilege in my life and I'm not starting now."

"You don't have to ask. The status is thrust upon you."

"Why?"

"How the devil should I know why?" retorted Warhurst, feeling far from jovial himself. He freed his neck and pumped oxygen. "I get orders and I don't question the reasons for them."

"There aren't any reasons," Harlow informed. "Some jerk of a clerk must have got things mixed up. Is there a big shot named Barlow on board?"

"No."

"Can't be him then, can it? Not if he isn't here. Anyway, nobody's going to coddle me, see? Prize fool I'd look being baby-sitted by some young squirt dolled up like a Christmas tree."

"The young squirt," Winterton pointed out, "happens to be forty-two years old and has twenty years of space service behind him."

"Just as I thought," said Harlow. "Still wet behind the ears and got plenty to learn. I could eat six like him before breakfast and still be all set for a real feed." He gripped his case and heaved it off the floor, his fingers thin and veined, with knuckles like knobs. "You decorated dummies go and prop up the staggerers. I can fend for myself," he grunted.

Case in hand, he went along the corridor and peered at the number on each cabin door. His pace was slow, laborious. Turning the end corner, he passed from sight.

"Awkward customer, huh?" said Warhurst

"A savage old-timer," decided Winterton. "Aren't many of them left these days. Wonder why he's been rated a P.P. The last one I came across was a retired employee. Been fifty years with the company. They gave him free passage to Earth along with the full treatment."

"We're not heading for home," said Warhurst.

"Yeah, I know. We're making for six underpopulated underdeveloped planets reserved exclusively for the young and healthy. The powers-that-be seem to have made an exception for this Harlow character. I can't imagine why."

"Maybe he's not fit to live with so they're isolating him in the never-never."

"Oh, he's not that bad."

"I know," said Warhurst. "I was only kidding."

They were four days out before Warhurst renewed the encounter. He'd been kept busy awhile on various matters that always crowded up immediately after departure or shortly before arrival. The interim period was the time when he could pay more attention to social duties.

In dress uniform, with face closely shaved and pants pressed, he went to the lounge all set to play the part of guide, companion and father confessor to any lonely hearts who might be moping around. It was a job that had endless possibilities none of which ever came to anything. As he expressed it in his more complaining moments, whenever the basket of fruit was being handed around he invariably got the lemon.

And again it was so. The feminine portion of the ship's load obviously was neither solitary nor bored. There was a clinking of glasses and a steady babble of conversation and no sweet face was visibly yearning for his company. Only old Harlow sat by himself, hunched in a corner behind a small and empty table.

With a shrug of resignation Warhurst crossed the lounge, said, "Mind if I sit here?"

"I can suffer it. Had plenty of worse things happen to me."

"You seem to have survived," said Warhurst, offering a wary smile.

"What comes of pulling my head in every time the chopper fell." Harlow inspected him with faint disapproval. "Done yourself up for Sunday, huh? How come your picking on me? Those girls refuse to be fascinated?"

"The ladies are being entertained, as you can see."

"Good thing, too. Keep 'em out of mischief." He glowered across the room and muttered something under his breath. Then he informed, "Soon as I came in one of 'em put on a sloppy smile and said, 'Hello, Pop!' Must think I'm a penny balloon or something. Pop! Put her in her place, I did. Told her my name is Bill and not to forget it."

"Mind if *I* call you Bill?"

"Call me any durned thing you like so long as it ain't Pop."

"Same with me. I don't care what I'm called so long as it isn't a gilded cutie or a snub-nosed kid."

"Oh, well, fair's fair, I guess."

"You can call me Steve."

"Knew a fellow of that name once. Went into Reedstar and never came out. Tough luck—but that's the way it is."

"The way what is?"

"Life," said Harlow. "They come and they go and some never come back."

Warhurst changed the subject. "Care to have a drink with me?"

"Depends. Wouldn't give belly room to all this cocktail muck. Strictly for women that stuff is. Hammerhead juice is the only thing fit to drink and they don't know what it is these days. Human race is going down the drain."

"Leave it to me." Warhurst got up and went to the bar. "Joe, the old fellow I'm with likes a blowtorch pointed down his gullet. Says there's nothing like hammerhead juice. What have you got that he might consider a few cuts above goat's milk?"

With narrowed eyes Joe gazed across the lounge and studied Harlow. He seemed to be struggling with a problem. Finally he bent under the counter and came up with a bottle and poured a measure of green, oily liquid.

"This should be diluted with gin. He's getting it raw. Comes as near as it can get to being unfit for human consumption. Same for you?"

"No, sir. Got to think of the fire hazard. I'll have a shot of crew-rum, official issue."

Joe served that too, leaned over the bar and whispered, "Know who that old dodderer is?"

"No. Do you?"

"No."

"Then we're back where we started."

"Listen," urged Joe, "and I'll tell you something. I've been at this job as long as you've been at yours. I've never seen hammerhead juice and nobody's ever asked for it and I haven't got any."

"It's just his figure of speech," suggested Warhurst. "He means some kind of rotgut."

"Listen," ordered Joe for the second time. "I've never seen the stuff but I have heard of it. My father used to mention it when he conned me into growing up and following him into the space service. According to him only one bunch ever asked for it and had the intestinal fortitude to beat it into submission." He paused to give a well-calculated touch of drama, finished, "The Legion of Planetary Scouts."

"It adds up," said Warhurst impassively. Picking up the drinks, he took them across, carefully placed them on the table. He sat down and looked at Harlow. "In the long ago those drinks would have been two tantalizing globules floating around in mid-air. We'd have had to swim after them, gulping like goldfish. But now we can lay gravity on the floor like a carpet or roll it up and hide it in the attic when we don't want it. Things have changed. I told you that before, didn't I?"

"You did."

"Well, I apologize for doing so. I took it for granted that you hadn't been on a ship in years—and you said nothing to disillusion me. I was wrong."

"How have you figured it out?" asked Harlow, eyeing him carefully.

Warhurst jerked a thumb toward the bar, "Joe there says nobody but planetary scouts ever asked for hammerhead juice."

"Fat lot he knows about it. He's not old enough to remember."

"His father told him,"

"That so? Maybe he was right. I dunno."

"You do know," Warhurst insisted. "I think you've been a planetary scout and that you may be one of the last of the original legion."

"There'll never be a last, not so long as photographic reconnaissance isn't enough and somebody has to trudge on foot to see what's under the mist and the trees." Harlow gulped his drink, clamped his eyes shut and gripped the rim of the table. Then he opened the eyes, let out a brief gasp and said, "Not bad for cough medicine. Gives a feller a slight jolt."

"Joe thinks it verges on cyanide."

"He would. They're weak at the knees these days."

"See here, Bill, tell me something. When were you last on a ship?"

"Couple of years ago."

"A passenger liner?"

"No—it was a government survey ship."

"With null-G?"

"You bet," said Harlow emphatically. "Couldn't have gone the distance otherwise. Even at that it took plenty long enough to return to base."

"How long?"

"What's it to you?"

"Nothing at all," admitted Warhurst. "I'm just plain nosey. How long did it take?"

"Fourteen years," informed Harlow with some reluctance.

Warhurst rocked back. "Fourteen? Ye gods! Any G-less ship using up that much time must have been out to the very edge of exploration."

"That's right. Fourteen out and fourteen back. And I was stuck there for eight years as well, given up for lost. That makes thirty-six in all. A slice out of a man's life." He took a good suck at his drink, repeated the eye-closing and table-gripping business, said, "Hah!" and then finished, "After which I had a fight on my hands."

"Over what?"

"Feller called me a liar."

"Didn't he believe you'd been gone that long?"

"He believed it all right. Couldn't deny the facts. Made a long, oily speech about the time I'd put in and the immense value of the reports I'd made. Real greasy type he was, with medals and badges and gold rings on his sleeves and a fancied-up cap like yours. Buttered me all over—and then called me a liar."

"Why?"

"Said that around the time I had left—which was before he was born—I'd not told the truth about my age and that he had the documentary evidence to prove it. Said I should never have been sent out in the first place and that it was a damned disgrace."

"Had you told the truth?" Warhurst pressed.

"Didn't tell a lie," Harlow evaded. "Told 'em I was plenty young enough to go ten times round the galaxy."

"And were you?"

"Yes, sir! I still am." Harlow scowled at the floor. "This pudding-headed pipsqueak wasn't buying that. Said I was far too old for further service and that I'd be given free passage back to Terra. Durn it, I'm only eighty-eight and that's me, bang, slap, finish. A dead dog. I got riled. Terra, I yelled, Terra? Haven't seen the place in nearly seventy years and don't know a soul there. What's on Terra for me? Nothing! If you're exporting the garbage you can ship me to Kangshan. At least I've got an old partner there."

"What did he say to that?"

"Wouldn't look me straight in the eyes. Muttered something about how Kangshan was strictly for characters a lot younger than me. Said be didn't think they'd have me there even if he got down on his knees and begged."

"You had an answer to that one, I guess?"

"Sure did. Told him he wasn't old enough to speak for others. Told him to signal Kangshan and ask if they'd take me."

"Which I presume he did."

"Must have done, though he took long enough about it. Eventually another official nincompoop handed me my sailing orders and made another oily speech. I tell you, Warble—"

"Warhurst. Steve Warhurst."

"I tell you if brass-hat gab could be boosted through tubes we'd all be way out beyond. Seems more talk than action these days. Human race is losing its capacity to suffer."

"I wouldn't say that, Bill. Things done the hard way aren't necessarily done better. Nor are they done badly because done the easy way. The essence of progress consists of finding ways of avoiding old-time difficulties."

"That may be, but—" Harlow paused, mused a short while, ventured, "Well, maybe I'm not as young as I used to be. But that doesn't make me a dead dog, does it?"

"Not at all,"

"Kangshan doesn't think so."

"You say you've got a partner there?"

"Yes, Jim Lacey. He's all I've got in creation. No scout operates alone except by accident. They go places in small bunches or often in pairs. You fellows who zoom around in shiploads don't know what partnership really means, A man's sidekick is his only contact with the human race when the rest of it is multi-million miles away. He's another brain to help solve problems, another pair of hands to work and fight. With each other a couple of trouble-seekers can get by in circumstances where if alone they'd go nuts. So I'm telling you that in faraway places partnership is something very special."

"I can well imagine," said Warhurst.

"Lacey was my first and longest space-partner. We were born in the same town, lived on the same street, went to the same schools and eventually joined the service together. We were dropped into some hot spots and shared the grief when things became rough and tough. Now I'm going to Kangshan. I promised I'd meet him there."

"After best part of forty years he wouldn't figure on seeing you again, would he?"

With a stubborn set to his jaw, Harlow repeated, "I said I'd meet him and that's all that matters." He stood up, a little creakily, "My turn. Same again?" Warhurst nodded.

Taking the empty glasses, Harlow carried them to the bar. "A crew-rum and another shot of that green hair oil."

"Like it, Pop?" asked Joe, willing to be sociable.

Harlow hammered on the bar and bawled, "Don't call me Pop, you bottle-juggling ape! I could out-march you with a ninety-pound pack and then do a tap dance." Grabbing the drinks, he brought them back, seated himself and snarled, "Booze-slingers in space. They'll be organizing beauty contests next. Human race is on the skids."

"Here's to the old days," said Warhurst. He drank, wobbled his Adam's apple, closed his eyes and held on tight.

"For a beginner you show promise, Wharton."

"Warhurst, if you don't mind."

There was the inevitable spell of rushed work before the landing but Warhurst got through it in good time and stationed himself at the head of the gangway. The formality was always the same; as each passenger began the descent Warhurst put on his most cordial smile and speeded the parting guest with a word of good cheer.

"Hope you've enjoyed your trip, Mr. Soandso. Good-by! Best of luck!"

Harlow came last, having listened to the swan song a dozen times while waiting beside his big case. Heaving the case forward, he stopped at the top of the steps.

"Why don't they tape it and save you the bother? Thought you said there's nothing wrong with doing things the easy way."

"Passengers like the personal touch."

"They would. Mothers' pets. Think they're mighty tough but I could beat 'em away with my hat." His watery eyes gazed across the primitive spaceport and into the far distance. "Last landing for me. Just as well, I reckon. Got to come sometime and it might as well be now."

Warhurst held out a hand. "Goodby, Bill. Glad to have known you."

Giving the hand a couple of prim shakes, Harlow responded with, "We got along, Warburton." Then he lugged his case down the steps and across the tarmac. A big, beefy man met him, chatted briefly, tried to take the case and was fiercely repelled. The big man then led him to a private floater and climbed aboard. Harlow got his case in and followed. A few seconds later the floater emitted a high-pitched whine, shuddered a couple of times, then soared. Heading swiftly northward, it diminished to a dot and vanished.

Winterton appeared at the exit, said with satisfaction, "All off. That's got rid of another menagerie."

"I often wonder just what happens to them," Warhurst ventured.

"I don't," said Winterton. "Couldn't care less. Got more than enough to worry about."

Soon afterward the ship took off and headed back to base with little load aboard. Outward cargo was always plentiful, inward usually small. All they took out of Kangshan was ten tons of osmiridium and two passengers.

The ship made six relatively short hauls from base and one long run to Terra. Then it arrived at Kangshan again. Three years had passed since its last visit but the scene had changed only slightly. The spaceport was now a fraction larger and had a new control tower. The adjacent capital town of Wingbury had added a couple of hundred houses and that was all.

Winterton came along and asked, "Want to go out?"

"Who wouldn't?" responded Warhurst. "Aren't we beating it yet?"

"The refinery says it can boost the return load if we'll wait four days. The agent says we're to stand by and take it. Anyone who wants to run around on solid earth can do so." He waved an arm in the general direction of Wingbury. "Go help yourself."

"Thanks," said Warhurst. "Nine thousand population and one soda-bar."

"You don't have to go."

"I'll go. Give my legs some exercise if nothing else."

Donning his dress uniform, he went into town. He'd been there a couple of times before and knew what to expect. One main street with forty quiet, understocked shops. It was a settlement right on the space frontier, growing and developing with chronic slowness. One could not expect the sophisticated joys of civilization on a planet with two small towns, thirty villages and a total population of less than fifty thousands.

He strolled ten times up and down the main street and stared into the half-empty windows of shops. Becoming bored, he visited the soda-bar, took a stool near to the only other customer, a leathery-faced character in his early thirties.

The customer nodded. "Hi, sailor! What ship?"

"Salamander."

"Should have known she was due. I lose touch these days, being well out of town. When are they going to start sending the really big boats?"

"Darned if I know."

The other nodded again, mused a bit, went on, "Hard luck on you fellows. Nothing for you here. Progress takes time. But things will be different if you can live long enough to see 'em."

"I know," said Warhurst.

"Got no relatives here, no friends, nobody you can visit?"

"Not a soul."

"Too bad."

"I palled on with a fellow who landed on the last trip, three years ago. Wouldn't mind seeing how he's making out."

"Well, what's to stop you?"

"Lost track of him," Warhurst explained. "Saw him off the ship and don't know where he went."

The other twisted around on his stool and pointed across the road. "Try the governmental building over there, department of immigration. They register every arrival and should be able to tell you where he is."

"Thanks!" Finishing his drink, Warhurst crossed the road, entered the building and found the department on the second floor. He spoke to the young clerk behind the counter. "I'm trying to trace a recent immigrant."

"Date of arrival and full name?"

Warhurst gave the information.

Digging out a ledger, the clerk thumbed through it, asked "Ex the *Salamander*?"

"Yes, that's my ship."

"William Harlow," said the clerk. "Exempted from age restriction. Taken into the charge of Joseph Buhl. I don't know what—"

Another clerk standing nearby interrupted with, "Buhl? I saw Joe Buhl a couple of minutes ago. He went up the road as I was looking through the window."

"He's your man," informed the first clerk. "You should have no trouble finding him." He extracted a register and consulted it. "His floater is numbered D117. You'll find it in the park alongside the spaceport."

"What does he look like?"

"As tall as you but a lot heavier. Has a slight paunch, big red face and bushy eyebrows."

"I'll track him down," Warhurst said. "It'll give me something to do."

Trudging back to the spaceport, he reached the floaterpark and found machine D117. He sat on the fat tire of a landing wheel and waited. There were twelve other floaters in the park. Far across the tarmac stood only one spaceship, his own, waiting for its promised payload. After forty minutes a hefty, florid-faced man approached. Warhurst came to his feet.

"Mr. Buhl?"

"That's right?"

"Thought I'd like to see Bill Harlow. I've been told that you should know where he is."

Buhl studied him levelly. "Got bad news for you."

"Is he—?"

"Died a year ago, aged ninety."

"I'm sorry to hear that."

"You an old friend of his?" Buhl inquired.

"Couldn't be, having only half his years. I kept him company on the last trip. Took a liking to the cantankerous old cuss and he seemed to find me bearable."

"I understand. Why did you figure on looking him up—got some time on your hands?"

"A bit."

"Well, maybe I can fill it in for you, mister—?"

"Steve Warhurst."

"I'll give you a ride and show you something mighty interesting."

Buhl unlocked the floater's door and motioned the other to enter. Warhurst got in and settled himself. Buhl plumped heavily into the pilot's seat, slammed the door, took the machine up and turned its nose to the north.

"Know much about this planet?"

"Not a lot," Warhurst confessed. "There are so many newly settled worlds these days that we space wanderers get to learn little about any of them. On each planet the spaceport and adjacent town is about all we're familiar with."

"Then I'll educate you somewhat," Buhl said. "This planet was discovered by a survey ship called the *Kangshan* and its captain named it after his ship. He made the usual aerial survey but—as is always the case—it wasn't enough. He came down low to test the atmosphere and found it satisfactory. So he dumped a couple of scouts and took off, leaving them to face a forty days' survival test."

"Bait," Warhurst contributed.

"Correct. Scouts are bait. That's what they're for—among other things." Buhl gazed meditatively forward while the floater hissed steadily on. "The two were Jim Lacey and Bill Harlow."

"Ah! I never knew that."

"You know now. They tramped around looking for exploitable prospects—and trouble. Eventually they arrived at a big quartzite monolith known today as The Needle. Mineral-rich mountains lay to the west, a big river and falls to the east. Time was pressing. Guess what?"

"They split," Warhurst hazarded.

"Correct. They broke the rules and split up. It was no crime but it was a risk. Harlow headed west and Lacey went east. They agreed to meet at The Needle four days later. Harlow returned on time lugging a load of stuff for assay. He camped at The Needle for a couple of days and then went looking for Lacey. He found him near the river, dead."

"Huh?" Warhurst looked baffled. "The old fellow talked as if Lacey were still alive."

"He would," said Buhl. "That's the way these old-timers were made." He dropped the floater's nose and began to lose altitude. "Lacey had had his feet bitten off by a mud-wallower. He'd blasted it as he fell and thus didn't get eaten. But then he went under from loss of blood. Harlow buried him, marked the grave, examined the wallower and made careful notes about it. In due time the *Kangshan* homed on his tiny beacon and picked him up. The planet was settled on the strength of his report and wallowers have since been hunted down and exterminated."

"Harlow didn't say a word about all this," complained Warhurst.

"Typical of him. If he bragged it was always about how he could keep going long after us softer types had dropped." Buhl pointed downward. A wide river now wound beneath with a monster cascade straight ahead. "Lacey Falls." Turning away from the river he brought the floater down to twenty feet above a rough dirt road. He followed the road for a few miles until a small town rolled into sight. "Look to your right."

Obediently, Warhurst looked and was in time to see a large roadside sign that said: HARLOW. Pop. 820.

"Named after him, eh?"

"That's right. I'm the mayor. We gave him a home, comfort and companionship in his last days. It was all we could do for him."

"I'm glad of that."

"Wasn't much use, though. He'd been kept alive beyond his years by change, activity and danger. He was killed by leisure and safety. There was no solution to the problem and he knew it. Often he'd leave town, walk out to The Needle and brood."

"Why?"

"Because he'd told Lacey he'd meet him there. He never forgot it. It became an obsession towards the end. His last words were, 'I told Jim I'd meet him.' "

They crossed the town, landed at the base of an enormous quartzite rock. They got out and stared up at it. It soared for two hundred feet, the facets of its crystals glittering in the sun.

"The Needle," informed Buhl. "It's not unique. There are other formations like it. We dug up Lacey's bones and buried them here. We buried Harlow with them."

He led the way around to the front of The Needle. A plain, unadorned grave lay at its foot. On the face of the rock a skilled mason had polished a square yard of crystal and cut a neat inscription thereon.

All it said was:

James Lacey
and
William Harlow
THEY MET.

METAMORPHOSITE

Astounding, December 1946

They let him pause halfway along the gangway so that his eyes could absorb the imposing scene. He stood in the middle of the high metal track, his left hand firmly grasping a side rail, and gazed into the four-hundred-foot chasm beneath. Then he studied the immense space vessels lying in adjacent berths, his stare tracing their gangways to their respective elevator towers behind which stood a great cluster of buildings whence the spaceport control column soared to the clouds. The height at which he stood, and the enormous dimensions of his surroundings, made him a little, doll-like figure, a man dwarfed by the mightiest works of man.

Watching him closely, his guards noted that be did not seem especially impressed. His eyes appeared to discard sheer dimensions while they sought the true meaning behind it all. His face was quite impassive as he looked around, but all his glances were swift, intelligent and assured. He comprehended things with that quick confidence which denotes an agile mind. One feature was prominent in the mystery enveloping him; it was evident that he was no dope.

Lieutenant Roka pushed past the two rearmost guards, leaned on the rail beside the silent watcher, and explained, "This is Madistine Spaceport. There are twenty others like it upon this planet. There are from two to twenty more on every one of four thousand other planets, and a few of them considerably bigger. The Empire is the greatest thing ever known or ever likely to be known. Now you see what you're up against."

" 'Numbers and size,' "quoth the other. He smiled faintly and shrugged. "What of them?"

"You'll learn what!" Roka promised. He, too, smiled, his teeth showing white and clean. "An organization can grow so tremendous that it's far, far bigger than the men who maintain it. From then on, its continued growth and development are well-nigh inevitable. It's an irresistible force with no immovable object big enough to stop it. It's a juggernaut. It's destiny, or whatever you care to call it."

"Bigness," murmured the other. "How you love bigness." He leaned over the railing, peered into the chasm. "In all probability down there is an enemy you've not conquered yet."

"Such as what?" demanded Roka.

"A cancer bug." The other's eyes swung up, gazed amusedly into the lieutenant's. "Eh?" He shrugged again. "Alas, for brief mortality!"

"Move on," snapped Roka to the leading guard.

The procession shuffled on, two guards, then the prisoner, then Roka, then two more guards. Reaching the tower at the end of the track, the sextet took an elevator to ground level, found a jet car waiting for them, a long, black sedan with the Silver Comet of the Empire embossed on its sides. Two men uniformed in myrtle green occupied its front seats while a third stood by the open door at the rear.

"Lieutenant Roka with the specimen and appropriate documents," said Roka. He indicated the prisoner with a brief gesture, then handed the third man a leather dispatch case. After that, he felt in one pocket, extracted a printed pad, added, "Sign here, please."

The official signed, returned the pad, tossed the dispatch case into the back of the car.

"All right," he said to the prisoner. "Get in."

Still impassive, the other got into the car, relaxed on the rear seat. Roka bent through the doorway, offered a hand.

"Well, sorry to see the last of you. We were just getting to know each other, weren't we? Don't get any funny ideas, will you? You're here under duress, but remember that you're also somewhat of an ambassador—that'll give you the right angle on things. Best of luck!"

"Thanks." The prisoner shook the proffered hand, shifted over as the green-uniformed official clambered in beside him. The door slammed, the jets roared, the car shot smoothly off. The prisoner smiled faintly as he caught Roka's final wave.

"Nice guy, Roka," offered the official.

"Quite."

"Specimen," the official chuckled. "Always they call 'em specimens. Whether of human shape or not, any seemingly high or presumably intelligent form of life imported from any newly discovered planet is, in bureaucratic jargon, a specimen. So that's what you are, whether you like it or whether you don't. Mustn't let it worry you, though. Nearly every worthwhile specimen has grabbed himself a high official post when his planet has become part of the Empire."

"Nothing worries me," assured the specimen easily.

"No?"

"No."

The official became self-conscious. He picked the dispatch case off the floor, jiggled it aimlessly around, judged its weight, then flopped it on his lap. The two in front maintained grim silence and scowled steadily through the windshield as the car swung along a broad avenue.

At good speed they swooped over a humpback crossing, overtook a couple of highly colored, streamlined cars, swung left at the end of the avenue. This brought them up against a huge pair of metal gates set in a great stone wall. The place would have looked like a jail to the newcomer if he'd known what jails look like—which he didn't.

The gates heaved themselves open, revealing a broad drive which ran between well-tended lawns to the main entrance of a long, low building with a clock tower at its center. The entrance, another metal job heavy enough to withstand a howitzer, lay directly beneath the tower. The black sedan curved sideways before it, stopped with a faint hiss of air brakes.

"This is it." The official at the back of the car opened a door, heaved himself out, dragging the case after him. His prisoner followed, shut the door, and the sedan swooped away.

"You see," said the man in green uniform. He gestured toward the lawns and the distant wall. "There's the wall, the gate, and a space from here to there in which you'd be immediately seen by the patrols. Beyond that wall are a thousand other hazards of which you know nothing. I'm telling you this because here's where you'll have your home until matters get settled. I would advise you not to let your impatience overcome your judgment, as others have done. It's no use running away when you've nowhere to run."

"Thanks," acknowledged the other. "I won't run until I've good reason and think I know where I'm going."

The official gave him a sharp look. A rather ordinary fellow, he decided, a little under Empire average in height, slender, dark, thirtyish and moderately good-looking. But possessed of the cockiness of youth. Under examination he'd probably prove boastful and misleading. He sighed his misgiving. A pity that they hadn't snatched somebody a good deal older.

"Harumph!" he said apropos of nothing.

He approached the door, the other following. The door opened of its own accord, the pair entered a big hall, were met by another official in myrtle green.

"A specimen from a new world," said the escort, "for immediate examination."

The second official stared curiously at the newcomer, sniffed in disdain, said, "O.K.—you know where to take him."

Their destination proved to be a large examination room at one end of a marble corridor. Here, the official handed over the dispatch case to a man in white, departed without further comment. There were seven men and one woman in the room, all garbed in white.

They studied the specimen calculatingly, then the woman asked, "You have learned our language?"

"Yes."

"Very well, then, you may undress. Remove all your clothes."

"Not likely!" said the victim in a level voice.

The woman didn't change expression. She bent over an official form lying on her desk, wrote in a neat hand in the proper section: "Sex convention normal." Then she went out.

When the door had shut behind her, the clothes came off. The seven got to work on the prisoner, completing the form as they went along. They did the job quietly, methodically, as an obvious matter of old-established routine. Height:

four point two lineal units. Weight: seventy-seven migrads. Hair: type-S, with front peaked. No wisdom teeth. All fingers double-jointed. Every piece of data was accepted as if it were perfectly normal, and jotted down on the official form. Evidently they were accustomed to dealing with entities differing from whatever was regarded as the Empire norm.

They X-rayed his cranium, throat, chest and abdomen from front, back and both sides and dutifully recorded that something that wasn't an appendix was located where his appendix ought to be. Down went the details, every one of them. Membraned epiglottis. Optical astigmatism: left eye point seven, right eye point four. Lapped glands in throat in lieu of tonsils. Crenated ear lobes. Cerebral serrations complex and deep.

"Satisfied?" he asked when apparently they'd finished with him.

"You can put on your clothes."

The head man of the seven studied the almost-completed form thoughtfully. He watched the subject dressing himself, noted the careful, deliberate manner in which the garments were resumed one by one. He called three of his assistants, conferred with them in low tones.

Finally he wrote at the bottom of the form: "Not necessarily a more advanced type, but definitely a variation. Possibly dangerous. Should be watched." Unlocking the dispatch case, he shoved the form in on top of the other papers it contained, locked the case, gave it to an assistant. "Take him along to the next stage."

Stage two was another room almost as large as its predecessor and made to look larger by virtue of comparative emptiness. Its sole furnishings consisted of an enormous carpet with pile so heavy it had to be waded through, also a large desk of glossy plastic and two pneumatic chairs. The walls were of translucite and the ceiling emitted a frosty glow.

In the chair behind the desk reposed a swarthy, saturnine individual with lean features and a hooked nose. His dress was dapper and a jeweled ring ornamented his left index finger. His black eyes gazed speculatively as the prisoner was marched the full length of the carpet and seated in the second chair. He accepted the leather case, unlocked it, spent a long time submitting its contents to careful examination.

In the end, he said, "So it took them eight months to get you here even at supra-spatial speed. *Tut tut,* how we grow! Life won't be long enough if this goes on. They've brought you a devil of a distance, eh? And they taught you our language on the way. Did you have much difficulty in learning it?"

"None," said the prisoner.

"You have a natural aptitude for languages, I suppose?"

"I wouldn't know."

The dark man leaned forward, a sudden gleam in his eyes. A faint smell of morocco leather exuded from him. His speech was smooth.

"Your answer implies that there is only one language employed on your home world."

"Does it?" The prisoner stared blankly at his questioner.

The other sat back again, thought for a moment, then went on, "It is easy to discern that you are not in the humor to be cooperative. I don't know why. You've been treated with every courtesy and consideration, or should have been. Have you any complaint to make on that score?"

"No," said the prisoner bluntly.

"Why not?" The dark man made no attempt to conceal his surprise. "This is the point where almost invariably I am treated to an impassioned tirade about kidnapping. But you don't complain?"

"What good would it do me?"

"No good whatever," assured the other.

"See?" The prisoner settled himself more comfortably in his chair. His smile was grim.

For a while, the dark man contemplated the jewel in his ring, twisting it this way and that to catch the lights from its facets. Eventually he wrote upon the form the one word: "Fatalistic," after which he murmured, "Well, we'll see how far we can get, anyway." He picked up a paper. "Your name is Harold Harold-Myra?"

"That's correct."

"Mine's Helman, by the way. Remember it, because you may need me sometime. Now this Harold-Myra—is that your family name?"

"It is the compound of my father's and mother's names."

"Hm-m-m! I suppose that that's the usual practice on your world?"

"Yes."

"What if you marry a girl named Betty?"

"My name would still be Harold-Myra," the prisoner informed. "Hers would still be the compound of her own parents' names. But our children would be called Harold-Betty."

"I see. Now according to this report, you were removed from a satellite after two of our ships had landed on its parent planet and failed to take off again."

"I was certainly removed from a satellite. I know nothing about your ships."

"Do you know why they failed to take off?"

"How could I? I wasn't there!"

Helman frowned, chewed his lower lip, then rasped, "It is I who am supposed to be putting the questions."

"Go ahead then," said Harold Harold-Myra.

"Your unspoken thought being, 'And a lot of good it may do you,' " put in Helman shrewdly. He frowned again, added the word: "Stubborn" to the form before him. "It seems to me," he went on, "that both of us are behaving rather childishly. Mutual antagonism profits no one. Why can't we adopt the right attitude toward each other? Let's be frank, eh?" He smiled, revealing bright dentures. "I'll put my cards on the table and you put yours."

"Let's see yours."

Helman's smile vanished as quickly as it had appeared. He looked momentarily pained. "Distrustful" went down on the form. He spoke, choosing his words carefully.

"I take it that you learned a lot about the Empire during your trip here. You know that it is a mighty organization of various forms of intelligent life, most of them, as it happens, strongly resembling yours and mine, and all of them owing allegiance to the particular solar system in which you're now located. You have been told, or should have been told, that the Empire sprang from here, that throughout many, many centuries it has spread over four thousand worlds, and that it's still spreading."

"I've heard all of that," admitted the other.

"Good! Then you'll be able to understand that you're no more than a temporary victim of our further growth, but, in many ways, a lucky man."

"I fail to perceive the luck."

"You will, you will," soothed Helman. "All in good time." Mechanically, his smile had returned, and he was making an attempt at joviality. "Now I can assure you that an organization so old and so widespread as ours is not without a modicum of wisdom. Our science has given us incredible powers, including the power to blow whole worlds apart and desiccate them utterly, but that doesn't make us disregard caution. After a wealth of experience covering a multitude of planets we've learned that we're still not too great to be brought low. Indeed, for all our mighty power, we can err in manner disastrous to us all. So we step carefully."

"Sounds as if someone once put a scare into you," commented Harold Harold-Myra.

Helman hesitated, then said, "As a matter of fact, someone did. I'll tell you about it. Many decades ago we made a first landing on a new planet. The ship failed to take off. Our exploratory vessels always travel in threes, so a second vessel went down to the aid of its fellow. That didn't take off either. But the third ship, waiting in space, got a despairing message warning that the world held highly intelligent life of an elusive and parasitic type."

"And they confiscated the bodies you'd so kindly provided," suggested Harold.

"You know all about this life form?" Helman asked. His fingers slid toward an invisible spot on the surface of his desk.

"It's the first I've heard of them," replied the other. "Confiscation was logical."

"I suppose so," Helman admitted with some reluctance. He went on, his keen eyes on his listener. "They didn't get the chance to take over everyone. A few men realized their peril in the nick of time, locked themselves in one vessel away from the parasites and away from their stricken fellows. There weren't enough of them to take off, so they beamed a warning. The third ship saw the menace at once; if action wasn't taken swiftly it meant that we'd handed the keys of the cosmos to unknown powers. They destroyed both ships with one atomic bomb. Later, a task ship arrived, took the stern action we deemed necessary, and dropped a planet wrecker. The world dissolved into flashing gases. It was an exceedingly narrow squeak. The Empire, for all its wealth, ingenuity and might, could not stand if no citizen knew the real nature of his neighbor."

"A sticky situation," admitted Harold Harold-Myra. "I see now where I come in—I am a sample."

"Precisely." Helman was jovial again. "All we wish to discover is whether your world is a safe one."

"Safe for what?"

"For straightforward contact."

"Contact for what?" Harold persisted.

"Dear me! I'd have thought a person of your intelligence would see the mutual advantages to be gained from a meeting of different cultures."

"I can see the advantages all right. I can also see the consequences."

"To what do you refer?" Helman's amiability began to evaporate.

"Embodiment in your Empire."

"Tut," said Helman impatiently. "Your world would join us only of its own free will. In the second place, what's wrong with being part of the Empire? In the third, how d'you know that your opinions coincide with those of your fellows? They may think differently. They may prove eager to come in."

"It looks like it seeing that you've got two ships stuck there."

"Ah, then you admit that they're forcibly detained?"

"I admit nothing. For all I know, your crews may be sitting there congratulating themselves on getting away from the Empire—while my people are taking steps to throw them out."

Helman's lean face went a shade darker. His long, slender hands clenched and unclenched while his disciplined mind exerted itself to suppress the retort which his emotion strove to voice.

Then he said, "Citizens of the Empire don't run away from it. Those who do run don't get very far."

"A denial and an affirmative," commented Harold amusedly. "All in one breath. You can't have it both ways. Either they run or they don't."

"You know perfectly well what I meant." Helman, speaking slowly and evenly, wasn't going to let this specimen bait him. "The desire to flee is as remote as the uselessness of it is complete."

"The former being due to the latter?"

"Not at all!" said Helman sharply.

"You damn your ramshackle Empire with every remark you make," Harold informed. "I reckon I know it better than you do."

"And how do you presume to know our Empire?" inquired Helman. His brows arched in sarcastic interrogation. "On what basis do you consider yourself competent to judge it?"

"On the basis of history," Harold told him. "Your people are sufficiently like us to be like us—and if you can't understand that remark, well, I can't help it. On my world we're old, incredibly old, and we've learned a lot from a past which is long and lurid. We've had empires by the dozens, though none as great as yours. They all went the same way—down the sinkhole. They all vanished for the same fundamental and inevitable reasons. Empires come and empires go, but little men go on forever."

"Thanks," said Helman quickly. He wrote on the form: "Anarchistic," then, after further thought, added: "Somewhat of a crackpot."

Harold Harold-Myra smiled slowly and a little sadly. The writing was not within line of his vision, but he knew what had been written as surely as if he'd written it himself. To the people of his ancient planet it was not necessary to look at things in order to see them.

Pushing the form to one side, Helman said, "The position is that every time we make a landing we take the tremendous risk of presenting our secrets of space conquest to people of unknown abilities and doubtful ambitions. It's a chance that has to be taken. You understand that?" He noted the other's curt nod, then went on, "As matters stand at present, your world holds two of our best vessels. Your people, for all we can tell, may be able to gain a perfect understanding of them, copy them in large numbers, even improve on them. Your people may take to the cosmos, spreading ideas that don't coincide with ours. Therefore, in theory, the choice is war or peace. Actually, the choice for your people will be a simple one: cooperation or desiccation. I hate to tell you this, but your hostile manner forces me to do so."

"Uncommunicative might be a better word than hostile," suggested Harold Harold-Myra.

"Those who're not with us are against us," retorted Helman. "We're not being dictatorial; merely realistic. Upon what sort of information we can get out of you depends the action we take regarding your world. You are, you must understand, the representative of your kind. We are quite willing to accept that your people resemble you to within reasonable degree, and from our analysis of you we'll decide whether—"

"We get canonized or vaporized," put in Harold.

"If you like." Helman refused to be disturbed. He'd now acquired the sang-froid of one conscious of mastery. "It is for you to decide the fate of your planet. It's an enormous responsibility to place on one man's shoulders, but there it is, and you've got to bear it. And remember, we've other methods of extracting from you the information we require. Now, for the last time, are you willing to subject yourself to my cross-examination, or are you not?"

"The answer is," said Harold carefully, "not!"

"Very well then." Helman accepted it phlegmatically. He pressed the spot on his desk. "You compel me to turn from friendly interrogation to forcible analysis. I regret it, but it is your own choice." Two attendants entered, and he said to them, "Take him to stage three."

The escorting pair left him in this third and smaller room and he had plenty of time to look around before the three men engaged therein condescended to notice him. They were all in white, this trio, but more alert and less automatic than the white-garbed personnel of the medical examination room. Two of them were young, tall, muscular, and hard of countenance. The third was short, thickset, middle-aged and had a neatly clipped beard.

Briskly they were switching on a huge array of apparatus covering one wall of the room. The setup was a mass of plastic panels, dials, meters, buttons, switches, sockets with corded plugs, and multi-connection pieces. From inside or close behind this affair came a low, steady hum. Before it, centrally positioned, was a chair.

Satisfied that all was in readiness, the bearded man said to Harold, "O.K., be seated." He signed to his two assistants, who stepped forward as if eager to cope with a refusal.

Harold smiled, waved a negligent hand, sat himself in the chair. Working swiftly, the three attached cushioned metal bands to his ankles, calves, thighs, chest, neck and head. Flexible metal tubes ran from the bands to the middle of the apparatus while, in addition, the one about his head was connected to a thin, multicore cable.

They adjusted the controls to give certain readings on particular meters, after which the bearded one fixed glasses on his nose, picked up a paper, stared at it myopically. He spoke to the subject in the chair.

"I am about to ask you a series of questions. They will be so phrased that the answers may be given as simple negatives or affirmatives. You can please yourself whether or not you reply vocally—it is a matter of total indifference to me."

He glanced at Harold and his eyes, distorted into hugeness behind thick-lensed glasses, were cold and blank. His finger pressed a button; across the room a camera whirred into action, began to record the readings on the various meters.

Disregarding everything else, and keeping his attention wholly on the man in the chair, the bearded one said, "You were discovered on a satellite—yes or no?"

Harold grinned reminiscently, did not reply.

"Therefore your people know how to traverse space?"

No reply.

"In fact they can go further than to a mere satellite. They can reach neighboring planets—yes or no?"

No reply.

"Already they have explored neighboring planets?"

No reply.

"The truth is that they can do even better than that—they have reached other solar systems?"

He smiled once more, enigmatically.

"Your world is a world by itself?"

Silence.

"It is one of an association of worlds?"

Silence.

"It is the outpost world of another Empire?"

Silence.

"But that Empire is smaller than ours?"

No response.

"Greater than ours?"

"Heavens, I've been led to believe that yours is the greatest ever," said Harold sardonically.

"Be quiet!" One of the young ones standing at his side gave him an irate thrust on the shoulder.

"Or what?"

"Or we'll slap your ears off!"

The bearded man, who had paused expressionlessly through this brief interlude, carried on nonchalantly.

"Your kind are the highest form of life on your planet? There is no other intelligent life thereon? You knew of no other intelligent life anywhere previous to encountering emissaries of the Empire?"

The questioner was in no way disturbed by his victim's complete lack of response, and his bearing made that fact clear. Occasionally peering at the papers in his hand, but mostly favoring his listener with a cold, owlish stare, he plowed steadily on. The questions reached one hundred, two hundred, then Harold lost count of them. Some were substitutes or alternatives for others, some made cross reference with others asked before or to be asked later, some were obvious traps. All were cogent and pointed. All met stubborn silence.

They finished at length, and the bearded one put away his papers with the grumbling comment, "It's going to take us all night to rationalize this lot!" He gave Harold a reproving stare. "You might just as well have talked in the first place. It would have saved us a lot of bother and gained you a lot of credit."

"Would it?" Harold was incredulous.

"Take him away," snapped the bearded man.

One of the young men looked questioningly at the oldster, who understood the unspoken query and responded, "No, not there. Not yet, anyway. It mightn't be necessary. Let's see what we've got first." He took off his glasses, scratched his beard. "Put him in his apartment. Give him something to eat." He cackled gratingly. "Let the condemned man eat a hearty meal."

The apartment proved to be compact, well-appointed, comfortable. Three rooms: bathroom, bedroom, sitting room, the last with a filled bookcase, a large electric radiator, sunken heating panels for extra warmth, and a magniscreen television set.

Harold sprawled at ease in a soft, enveloping chair, watched a short-haired, burly man wheel in a generous meal. Hungry as he was, his attention didn't turn to the food. He kept it fixed on the burly man, who, unconscious of the persistent scrutiny, methodically put out the meat, bread, fruit, cakes and coffee.

As the other finished his task, Harold said casually, "What are those lizardlike things that wear black uniforms with silver braid?"

"Dranes." Short-hair turned around, gazed dully at the prisoner. His face was heavy, muscular, his eyes small, his forehead low. "We calls 'em Dranes."

"Yes, but what are they?"

"Oh, just another life form, I guess. From some other planet—maybe from one called Drane. I dunno. I used to know, but I've forgotten."

"You don't like them, eh?" suggested Harold.

"Who does?" He frowned with the unusual strain of thought, his small eyes shrinking still smaller. "I like to have ideas of my own, see? I don't care for any lizards reading my mind and telling the world what I'd sooner keep to myself, see? A man wants privacy—especially sometimes."

"So they're telepaths!" It was Harold's turn to frown. "Hm-m-m!" He mused anxiously. The other began to shove his empty meal trolley toward the door, and Harold went on hurriedly, "Any of them hereabouts?"

"No, it's too late in the evening. And there ain't a lot of them on this planet, thank Pete! Only a few here. They do some sort of official work, I dunno what. A couple of them got important jobs right in this dump, but they'll be home now. Good riddance, I says!" He scowled to show his intense dislike of the mysterious Dranes. "A guy can think what he likes while they're away." He pushed his trolley outside, followed it and closed the door. The lock clicked quietly, ominously.

Harold got on with his meal while he waited for angry men to come for him. Beardface and his two assistants had indicated that nothing more would be done with him before morning, but this last episode would speed things up considerably. He hastened his eating, vaguely surprised that he was getting it finished without interruption. They were less quick on the uptake than he'd anticipated. He employed the time usefully in working out a plan of campaign.

The apartment made his problem tough. He'd already given it a thorough scrutiny, noted that its decorated walls and doors were all of heavy metal. The windows were of armorglass molded in one piece over metal frames with sturdy, closely set bars. It was more than an apartment; it was a vault.

There was a very tiny lens cunningly concealed in the wall high up in one corner. It would have escaped discovery by anyone with lesser powers of observation. He'd found another mounted on the stem of the hour hand of the clock. It looked like a jewel. He knew it to be a scanner of some kind, and suspected that there were others yet to be found. Where there were scanners there would also be microphones, midget jobs hard to dig out when you don't want to make a search too obvious. Oh, yes, they'd know all about his little conversation with Short-hair—and they'd be along.

They were. The lock clicked open just as he ended his meal. Helman came in, followed by a huge fellow in uniform. The latter closed the door, leaned his broad back against it, pursed his lips in a silent whistle while he studied the room with obvious boredom. Helman went to a chair, sat in it, crossed his legs, looked intently at the prisoner. A vein pulsed in his forehead and the effect of it was menacing.

He said, "I've been on the televox to Roka. He swears that he's never mentioned the Dranes in your presence. He's positive that they've never been mentioned or described in your hearing by anyone on the ship. Nothing was said about them by the guards who brought you here. You've seen none in this building. So how d'you know about them?"

"Mystifying, isn't it?" commented Harold pleasantly.

"There is only one way in which you could have found out about the Dranes," Helman went on. "When the examiners finished with you in stage three an assistant pondered the notion of passing you along to stage four, but the idea was dropped for the time being. Stage four is operated by the Dranes."

"Really?" said Harold. He affected polite surprise.

"The Dranes were never mentioned," persisted Helman, his hard eyes fixed on his listener, "but they were thought of. You read those thoughts. You are a telepath!"

"And you're surprised by the obvious?"

"It wasn't obvious because it wasn't expected," Helman retorted. "On four thousand worlds there are only eleven truly telepathic life forms and not one of them human in shape. You're the first humanoid possessing that power we've discovered to date."

"Nevertheless," persisted Harold, "it should have been obvious. My refusal to cooperate—or my stubbornness, as you insist on calling it—had good reason. I perceived all the thoughts behind your questions. I didn't like them. I still don't like them."

"Then you'll like even less the ones I'm thinking now," snapped Helman.

"I don't," Harold agreed. "You've sent out a call for the Dranes, ordered them to come fast, and you think they'll be here pretty soon. You expect them to suck me dry. You've great confidence in their powers even though you can't conceive the full extent of mine." He stood up, smiled as Helman uncrossed his legs with a look of sudden alarm. He stared into Helman's black eyes, and his own were sparkling queerly. "I think," he said, "that this is a good time for us to go trundle our hoops—don't you?"

"Yes," Helman murmured. Clumsily he got to his feet, stood there with an air of troubled preoccupation. "Yes, sure!"

The guard at the door straightened up, his big hands held close to his sides. He looked inquiringly at the vacant Helman. When Helman failed to respond, he shifted his gaze to the prisoner, kept the gaze fixed while slowly the alertness faded from his own optics.

Then, although he'd not been spoken to, he said hoarsely, "O.K., we'll get along. We'll get a move on." He opened the door.

The three filed out, the guard leading, Helman in the rear. They moved rapidly along the corridors, passing other uniformed individuals without challenge or comment until they reached the main hall. Here, the man in myrtle green, whose little office held the lever controlling the automatic doors, sat at his desk and felt disposed to be officious.

"You can't take him out until you've signed him out, stating where he's being taken, and on whose authority," he enunciated flatly.

"On my authority," said Helman. He voiced the words in stilted tones as if he were a ventriloquist's dummy, but the officious one failed to notice it.

"Oh, all right," he growled. He shoved a large, heavy tome to one end of his desk. "Sign there. Name in column one, destination in column two, time of return in column three." He looked at the huge guard who was watching dumbly, emitted a resigned sigh, inquired, "I suppose you need a car?"

"Yes," said Helman mechanically.

The official pressed a button; a sonorous gong clanged somewhere outside the building. Then he pulled his tiny lever; the great doors swung open. The trio strolled out with deceptive casualness, waited a moment while the doors closed behind them. It was fairly dark now, but not completely so, for a powdering of stars lay across the sky, and a steady glow of light emanated from the surrounding city.

Presently a jet car swept around one end of the building, stopped before them. The three got in. Harold sat at the back between Helman and the big guard, both of whom were strangely silent, ruminative. The driver turned around, showed them a face with raised eyebrows.

"Downtown," uttered Helman curtly.

The driver nodded, faced front. The car rolled toward the gates in the distant wall, reached them, but they remained closed. Two men in green emerged from the shadow of the wall, focused light beams on the vehicle's occupants.

One said, "Inquisitor Helman, one specimen—I guess it's O.K." He waved his light beam toward the gates, which parted slowly and ponderously. Emitting a roar from its jets, the car swept through.

They dropped Harold Harold-Myra in the mid-southern section of the city, where buildings grew tallest and crowds swarmed thickest. Helman and the guard got out of the car, talked with him while the driver waited out of earshot.

"You will both go home," Harold ordered, "remembering nothing of this and behaving normally. Your forgetfulness will persist until sunrise. Until you see the sun you will be quite unable to recall anything which has occurred since you entered my room. Do you understand?"

"We understand."

Obediently they got back into the car. They were a pair of automatons. He stood on the sidewalk, watched their machine merge into the swirl of traffic and disappear. The sky was quite dark now, but the street was colorful with lights that shifted and flickered and sent eccentric shadows skittering across the pavement.

For a few minutes he stood quietly regarding the shadows and musing. He was alone—alone against a world. It didn't bother him particularly. His situation was no different from that of his own people, who formed a solitary world on the edge of a great Empire. He'd one advantage which so far stood him in good stead: he knew his own powers. His opponents were ignorant in that respect. On the other hand, he suffered the disadvantage of being equally ignorant, for although he'd learned much about the people of the Empire, he still did not know the full extent of their powers. And theirs were likely to be worthy of respect. Alliance of varied life forms with varied talents could make a formidable combination. The battle was to be one of Homo superior versus Homo sapiens plus the Dranes plus other things of unknown abilities—with the odds much in favor of the combine.

Now that he was footloose and fancy-free he could appreciate that guard's argument that there's no point in being free unless one knows where to nurse one's freedom. The guard, though, had implied something and overlooked something else. He'd implied that there were places in which freedom could be preserved, and he'd forgotten that escapees have a flair for discovering unadvertised sanctuaries. If his own kind were half as wise and a quarter as crafty as they ought to be, thought Harold, the tracing of such a sanctuary should not be difficult.

He shrugged, turned to go, found himself confronted by a tall, thin fellow in black uniform with silver buttons and silver braid. The newcomer's features were gaunt and tough, and they changed color from gold to blood-red as the light from a nearby electric sign flickered over it.

Harold could hear the other's mind murmuring, *"Queer outlandish clothes this fellow's wearing. Evidently a recent importee—maybe a specimen on the lam,"* even as the thinker's mouth opened and he said audibly, "Let me see your identity card!"

"Why?" asked Harold, stalling for time. Curse the clothes—he'd not had time to do anything about them yet.

"It's the regulation," the other returned irritably. "You should know that every citizen must produce his card when called upon to do so by the police." His eyes narrowed, his mind spoke silently but discernibly. *"Ah, he hesitates. It must be that he doesn't possess a card. This looks bad."* He took a step forward.

Harold's eyes flamed with an odd glow. "You don't really want to see my card?" he said gently. "Do you?"

The policeman had a momentary struggle with himself before he answered, "No . . . no . . . of course not!"

"It was just your mistake?"

"Just my mistake!" admitted the other slowly. His mind was now completely muddled. A random thought, *"He's dangerous!"* fled wildly through the cerebral maze, pursued, outshouted and finally silenced by other, violently imposed thoughts saying, *"Silly mistake. Of course he's got a card. I interfere too much."*

With shocking suddenness, another thought broke in, registering clearly and succinctly despite the telepathic hubbub of a hundred surrounding minds. *"By the Blue Sun, did you catch that, Gaeta? A fragment of hypnotic projection! Something about a card. Turn the car around!"*

A cold sweat beaded on Harold's spine; he closed his mind like a trap, sent his sharp gaze along the road. There was too great a flood of cars and too many swiftly changing lights to enable him to pick out any one vehicle turning in the distance. But he'd know that car if it came charging down upon him. Its driver might be of human shape, but its passengers would be lizard-like.

Machines whirled past him four, five and sometimes six abreast. The eerie voice, which had faded, suddenly came back, waxed strong, faded away again.

It said, *"I might be wrong, of course. But I'm sure the amplitude was sufficient for hypnosis. No, it's gone now—I can't pick it up at all. All these people make too much of a jumble on the neural band."*

Another thought, a new one, answered impatiently, *"Oh, let it pass, you're not on duty now. If we don't—"* It waned to indiscernibility.

Then the policeman's mind came back, saying, *"Well, why am I standing here like a dummy? Why was I picking on this guy? It must've been for something! I didn't stop him for the fun of it—unless I'm scatty!"*

Harold said quickly and sharply, "You didn't stop me. I stopped you. Intelligence Service—remember?"

"Eh?" The cop opened his mouth, closed it, looked confused.

"Wait a moment," added Harold, a strong note of authority in his voice. He strained his perception anxiously. A river of surrounding thoughts flowed through his mind, but none with the power and clarity of the invisible Gaeta and his alert companion. Could they, too, close their minds? There wasn't any way of telling!

He gave it up, returned his attention to the cop, and said, "Intelligence Service. I showed you my official warrant. Good heavens, man, have you forgotten it already?"

"No." The man in black was disconcerted by this unexpected aggressiveness. The reference to a nonexistent Intelligence Service warrant made his confusion worse confounded. "No," he protested, "I haven't forgotten." Then, in weak effort to make some sort of a comeback: "But you started to say something, and I'm waiting to hear the rest."

Harold smiled, took him by the arm. "Look, I'm authorized to call upon you for assistance whenever needed. You know that, don't you?"

"Yes, sure, but—"

"What I want you to do is very simple. It's necessary that I change attire with a certain suspected individual and that he be kept out of circulation overnight. I'll point him out to you when he comes along. You're to tell him that you're taking him in for interrogation. You'll then conduct us somewhere where we can change clothes, preferably your own apartment if you've got one. I'll give you further instructions when we get there."

"All right," agreed the cop. He blinked as he tried to rationalize his mind. Thoughts gyrated bafflingly in his cranium. *"Not for you to reason why. Do your duty and ask no questions. Let higher-ups take the responsibility. This guy's got all the authority in the world—and he knows what he's doing."* There was something not quite right about those thoughts. They seemed to condense inward instead of expanding outward, as thoughts ought to do. But they were powerful enough, sensible enough, and he wasn't able to give birth to any contrary ideas. "All right," he repeated.

Studying the passers-by, Harold picked a man of his own height and build. Of all the apparel streaming past, this fellow's looked made to fit him to a nicety. He nudged the cop.

"That's the man."

The officer strode majestically forward, stopped the victim, said, "Police! I'm taking you in for interrogation."

"Me?" The man was dumbfounded. "I've done nothing!"

"Then what've you got to worry about?"

"Nothing," hastily assured the other. He scowled with annoyance. "I guess I'll have to go. But it's a waste of time and a nuisance."

"So you think the Empire's business is a nuisance?" inquired Harold, joining the cop.

The victim favored him with a look of intense dislike, and complained, "Go on, try making a case against me. Having it stick will be something else!"

"We'll see!"

Cutting down a side street, the trio hit a broad avenue at its farther end. No cars here; it was solely for pedestrians. The road was divided into six moving strips, three traveling in each direction, slowest on the outsides, fastest in the middle. Small groups of people, some chatting volubly, some plunged in boredom, glided swiftly along the road and shrank in the distance. A steady rumbling sound came from beneath the rubbery surface of the road.

The three skipped onto an outer slow strip, thence to the medium fast strip, finally to the central rapid strip. The road bore them ten blocks before they left it. Harold could see it rolling on for at least ten blocks more.

The cop's apartment proved to be a modernistic, three-roomed bachelor flat on the second floor of a tall, graystone building. Here, the captive started to renew his protests, looked at Harold, found his opinions changing even as he formed them. He waxed cooperative, though in a manner more stupefied than willing. Emptying the contents of his pockets on a table, he exchanged clothes.

Now dressed in formal, less outlandish manner, Harold said to the police officer, "Take off your jacket and make yourself at home. No need to be formal on this job. We may be here some time yet. Get us a drink while I tell this fellow what's afoot." He waited until the cop had vanished into an adjoining room, then his eyes flamed at the vaguely disgruntled victim. "Sleep!" he commanded, "sleep!"

The man stirred in futile opposition, closed his eyes, let his head hang forward. His whole body slumped wearily in its chair. Raking rapidly through the personal possessions on the table, Harold found the fellow's identity card. Although he'd never seen such a document before, he wasted no time examining it, neither did he keep it. With quick dexterity, he dug the cop's wallet out of his discarded jacket, extracted the police identity card, substituted the other, replaced the wallet. The police card he put in his own pocket. Way back on the home planet it was an ancient adage that double moves are more confusing than single ones.

He was barely in time. The cop returned with a bottle of pink, oily liquid, sat down, looked dully at the sleeper, said, "Huh?" and transferred his lackluster stare to Harold. Then he blinked several times, each time more slowly than before, as if striving to keep his eyes open against an irresistible urge to keep them shut. He failed. Imitating his captive, he hung his head—and began to snore.

"Sleep," murmured Harold, "sleep on toward the dawn. Then you may awake. But not before!"

Leaning forward, he lifted a small, highly polished instrument from its leather case beneath the policeman's armpit. A weapon of some sort. Pointing it toward the window, he pressed the stud set in its butt. There was a sharp, hard crack, but no recoil. A perfect disk of glassite vanished from the center of the window. Cold air came in through the gap, bringing with it a smell like that of roasted resin. Giving the weapon a grim look, he shoved it back into its holster, dusted his fingers distastefully.

"So," he murmured, "discipline may be enforced by death. Verily, I'm back in the dark ages!"

Ignoring the sleepers, he made swift search of the room. The more he knew about the Empire's ordinary, everyday citizens the better it'd be for him. Knowledge—the right knowledge—was a powerful arm in its own right. His people understood the value of intangibles.

Finished, he was about to leave when a tiny bell whirred somewhere within the wall. He traced the sound as emanating from behind a panel, debated the matter before investigating further. Potential danger lurked here; but nothing ventured, nothing gained. He slid the panel aside, found himself facing a tiny loudspeaker, a microphone, a lens, and a small circular screen.

The screen was alive and vivid with color, and a stern, heavily jowled face posed in sharp focus within its frame. The caller raked the room with one quick, comprehending glance, switched his attention to Harold.

"So the missing Guarda *is* indisposed," he growled. "He slumbers before a bottle. He awaits three charges: absent from duty, improperly dressed, and drunk! We'll deal with this at once." He thinned his lips. "What is your name and the number of your identity card, citizen?"

"Find out," suggested Harold. He slammed the panel before the tiny scanner could make a permanent record of his features—if it had not done so already.

That was an unfortunate episode: it cut down his self-donated hours of grace to a few minutes. They'd be on their way already, and he'd have to move out fast.

He was out of the apartment and the building in a trice. A passing car stopped of its own accord and took him downtown. Its driver was blissfully unaware of the helplessness of his own helpfulness.

Here, the city seemed brighter than ever mostly because the deeper darkness of the sky enhanced the multitude of lights. A few stars still shone, and a string of colored balls drifted high against the backdrop, where some unidentifiable vessel drove into space.

He merged with the crowds still thronging the sidewalks. There was safety in numbers. It's hard to pick one guy out of the mob, especially when he's dressed like the mob, behaves like the mob. For some time he moved around with the human swarm though his movements were not as aimless. He was listening to thoughts, seeking either of two thought-forms, one no more than slightly helpful, the other important. He found the former, not the latter.

A fat man wandered past him and broadcast the pleasurable notion of food shared in large company. He turned and followed the fat man, tracking him along three streets and another moving avenue. The fat man entered a huge restaurant with Harold at his heels. They took an unoccupied table together.

Plenty of active thoughts here. In fact the trouble was that there were far too many. They made a constant roar right across the telepathic band; it was difficult to separate one from another, still more difficult to determine who was emanating which. Nevertheless, he persisted in his effort to sort out individual broadcasts, taking his food slowly to justify remaining there as long as possible. Long after the fat man had left he was still seated there, listening, listening. There were many thoughts he found interesting, some revealing, some making near approach to the notions he sought, but none quite on the mark, not one.

In the end, he gave it up, took his check from the waiter. It was readily apparent what the waiter had on his mind, namely, this crazy stuff called money. Roka had told him a lot about money, even showing him samples of the junk. He remembered that Roka had been dumbfounded by his ignorance concerning a common medium of exchange. With amusing superiority, the worthy lieutenant had assumed that Harold's people had yet to discover what they'd long since forgotten.

There had been some of this money—he didn't know just how much—in the pockets of this suit, but he'd left it all with the suit's hapless donor. There wasn't any point in snatching someone else's tokens. Besides, having managed without it all his life, he wasn't going to become a slave to it now.

He paid the waiter with nothing, putting it into the fellow's hand with the lordly air of one dispensing a sizable sum. The waiter gratefully accepted nothing, put nothing into his pocket, initialed the check, bowed obsequiously. Then he rubbed his forehead, looked vague and confused, but said nothing. Harold went out.

It was on the sidewalk that Harold made the contact he was seeking, though not in the manner he'd expected. He was looking for a mutinous thinker who might lead him to the underworld of mutinous thinkers. Instead, he found a friend.

The fellow was twenty yards away and walking toward him with a peculiarly loose-jointed gait. He was humanoid in all respects but one—his skin was reptilian. It was a smooth but scaly skin of silvery gray in which shone an underlying sheen of metallic blue. The pupils of his eyes were a very light gray, alert, intelligent.

Those eyes looked straight into Harold's as they came abreast, a flood of amity poured invisibly from them as he smiled and said in an undertone, "Come with me." He walked straight on, without a pause. He didn't look back to see whether Harold followed.

Harold didn't wait to consider the matter. This was a time for quick decision. Swiveling on one heel, he trailed along behind the speaker. And as he trod warily after the other, his mind was active with thoughts, and his thinking was done within a mental shell through which nothing could probe.

Evidently the scaly man was an outsider, a product of some other world. His queer skin was proof of that. There were other factors, too. He hadn't read Harold's mind—Harold was positive of that—yet in some strange, inexplicable way he'd recognized a kinship between them and had acknowledged it without hesitation. Moreover, he was strolling along with his mind wide open, but Harold was totally unable to analyze his thoughts. Those thoughts, in all probability, were straightforward and logical enough, but they oscillated in and out of the extreme edge of the neural band. Picking them up was like trying to get frequency modulation on a receiver designed for amplitude modulation. Those thought-forms might be normal, but their wave-forms were weird.

Still not looking back, the subject of his speculations turned into an apartment building, took a levitator to the tenth floor. Here he unlocked a door, gazed around for the first time, smiled again at his follower, motioned him inside.

Harold went in. The other closed the door after him. There were two similar entities in the apartment. One sat on the edge of a table idly swinging his legs; the other lounged on a settee and was absorbed in a magazine.

"Oh, Melor, there's a—" began the one on the settee. He glanced up, saw the visitor, grinned in friendly fashion. Then his expression changed to one of surprise, and he said, "By the everlasting light, it's *you*! Where did you find him, Melor?"

This one's mind was fully as baffling and Harold found himself unable to get anything out of it. The same applied to the being perched upon the table: his thoughts wavered in and out of the borderline of detection.

"I found him on the street," replied the one called Melor, "and I invited him along. He has a most attractive smell." He sat down, invited Harold to do likewise. Looking at the one on the settee, he went on, "What did you mean by, 'Oh, it's *you*'? D'you know him?"

"No." The other switched on a teleset at his side. "They broadcast a call for him a few minutes ago. He's wanted—badly." He moved a second switch. "Here's the recording. Watch!"

The set's big screen lit up. A sour-faced man in flamboyant uniform appeared on the screen, spoke with official ponderousness.

"All citizens are warned to keep watch for and, if possible, apprehend an escaped specimen recently brought from the Frontier. Name: Harold Harold-Myra. Description—" He went on at great length, giving everything in minute detail, then finished, "His attire is noticeably unconventional and he has not yet been provided with an identity card. Citizens should bear in mind that he may possess attributes not familiar to Empire races and that he is wanted alive. In case of necessity, call Police Emergency on Stud Four. Here is his likeness."

The screen went blank, lit up again, showed Harold's features in full color. He recognized part of his former prison in the background. Those midget scanners had done their job!

"Tush!" scoffed the being on the settee. He switched off, turned to Harold. "Well, you're in good hands. That's something. We wouldn't give anyone in authority a magni-belt to hold up his pants. My name's Tor. The one industriously doing nothing on the table is Vern. The one who brought you here is Melor. Our other names don't matter much. As maybe you've guessed, we aren't of this lousy, over-organized world. We're from Linga, a planet which is a devil of a long way off, too far away for my liking. The more I think of it, the farther it seems."

"It's no farther than my own world," said Harold. He leaned forward. "Look, can you read my mind?"

"Not a possibility of it," Tor answered. "You're like the local breed in that respect—you think pulsatingly and much too far down for us. Can you read ours?"

"I can't. You wobble in and out of my limit." He frowned. "What beats me is what made Melor pick me out if he can't read my thoughts."

"I smelled you," Melor put in.

"Huh?"

"That's not strictly correct, but it's the best way I can explain it. Most of the Empire's peoples have some peculiar faculty they call a sense of smell. We don't possess it. They talk about bad odors and sweet ones, which is gibberish to us. But we can sense affinities and oppositions, we can sort of 'smell' friends and enemies, instantly, infallibly. Don't ask me how we do it, for how can I tell you?"

"I see the difficulty," agreed Harold.

"On our world," Melor continued, "most life forms have this sense which seems peculiar to Linga. We've no tame animals and no wild ones—they're tame if you like them, wild if you don't. None would be driven by curiosity to make close approach to a hunter, none would flee timidly from someone anxious to pet them. Instinctively they know which is friend and which is enemy. They know it as certainly as you know black from white or night from day."

Tor put in, "Which is an additional reason why we're not very popular. Skin trouble's the basic one, d'you understand? So among an appalling mixture of hostile smells we welcome an occasional friendly one—as yours is."

"Do the Dranes smell friendly?"

Tor pulled a face. "They stink!" he said with much emphasis. Gazing ruminatively at the blank television screen, he went on, "Well, the powers-that-be are after your earthly body, and I'm afraid we can't offer you much encouragement though we're willing to give you all the help we can. Something like twenty specimens have escaped in the last ten or twelve years. All of them broke loose by suddenly displaying long-concealed and quite unexpected powers which caught their captors by surprise. But none stayed free. One by one they were roped in, some sooner than others. You can't use your strength without revealing what you've got, and once the authorities know what you've got they take steps to cope with it. Sooner or later the fugitive makes a try for his home planet—and finds the trappers waiting."

"They're going to have a long, long wait," Harold told him, "for I'm not contemplating a return to my home world. Leastways, not yet. What's the use of coming all the way here just to go all the way back again?"

"We took it that you hadn't much choice about the coming," said Tor.

"Nor had I. Circumstances made it necessary for me to come. Circumstances make it necessary for me to stay awhile."

The three were mildly surprised by this phlegmatic attitude.

"I'm more of a nuisance here," Harold pointed out. "This is the Empire's key planet. Whoever bosses this world bosses the Empire. It may be one man, it may be a small clique, but on this planet is the mind or minds which make the Empire tick. I'd like to retime that tick."

"You've *some* hopes!" opined Tor gloomily. "The Big Noise is Burkinshaw Three, the Lord of Terror. You've got to have forty-two permits, signed and countersigned, plus an armed escort, to get within sight of him. He's exclusive!"

"That's tough, but the situation is tougher," He relaxed in his chair and thought awhile. "There's a Lord of Terror on every planet, isn't there. It's a cockeyed title for the bosses of imperial freedom!"

"Terror means greatness, superior wisdom, intellect of godlike quality," explained Tor.

"Oh, does it? My mistake! We use the same-sounding word on my planet, and there it means fear." Suddenly a strange expression came into his face. He ejaculated, "Burkinshaw! Burkinshaw! Ye gods!"

"What's the matter?" Melor inquired.

"Nothing much. It's only that evidence is piling up on top of a theory. It should help. Yes, it ought to help a lot." Getting up, he paced the room restlessly. "Is there an underground independence movement on Linga?" he asked.

Tor grinned with relish, and said, "I'd not be far from the truth if I guessed that there's such a movement on every planet excepting this one. Imperially speaking, we're all in the same adolescent condition: not quite ripe for self-government. We'll all get independence tomorrow, but not today." He heaved a resigned sigh. "Linga's been getting it tomorrow for the last seven hundred years."

"As I thought," Harold commented. "The same old setup. The same old stresses, strains and inherent weaknesses. The same blindness and procrastination. We've known it all before—it's an old, old tale to us."

"What is?" persisted the curious Melor.

"History," Harold told him.

Melor looked puzzled.

"There's an ancient saying," Harold continued, "to the effect that the bigger they come the harder they fall. The more ponderous and top-heavy a structure the riper it is for toppling." He rubbed his chin, studied his listeners with a peculiarly elfish gaze. "So the problem is whether we can shove hard enough to make it teeter."

"Never!" exclaimed Tor. "Nor a thousand either. It's been tried times without number. The triers got buried—whenever there was enough to bury."

"Which means that they tried in the wrong way, and/or at the wrong time. It's up to us to push in the right way at the right time."

"How can you tell the right time?"

"I can't. I can choose only the time which, when everything's taken into account, seems the most favorable—and then hope that it's the right time. It'll be just my hard luck if I'm wrong." He reflected a moment, then went on, "The best time ought to be nine days hence. If you can help me to keep under cover that long, I'll promise not to involve you in anything risky in the meanwhile. Can you keep me nine days?"

"Sure we can." Tor regarded him levelly. "But what do we get out of it other than the prospect of premature burial?"

"Nothing except the satisfaction of having had a finger in the pie."

"Is that all?" Tor asked.

"That's all," declared Harold positively. "You Lingans must fight your way as we're fighting ours. If ever my people help you, it will be for the sake of mutual benefit or our own satisfaction. It won't be by way of reward."

"That suits me." Tor said flatly. "I like good, plain talk, with no frills. We're tired of worthless promises. Count us with you to the base of the scaffold, but not up the steps—we'd like to indulge second thoughts before we mount those!"

"Thanks a lot," acknowledged Harold gratefully. "Now here are some ideas I've got which—"

He stopped as the television set emitted a loud chime. Tor reached over, switched on the apparatus. Its screen came to life, depicting the same uniformed sourpuss as before.

The official rumbled, "Urgent call! Citizens are warned that the escaped specimen Harold Harold-Myra, for whom a call was broadcast half an hour ago, is now known to be a telepath, a mesman, a seer and a recorder. It is possible that he may also possess telekinetic powers of unknown extent. Facts recently brought to light suggest that he's a decoy and therefore doubly dangerous. Study his likeness; he must be brought in as soon as possible."

The screen blanked, lit up again, showed Harold's face for a full minute. Then the telecast cut off.

"What does he mean, a seer and a recorder?" inquired Harold, mystified.

"A seer is one who makes moves in anticipation of two, three, four or more of his opponent's moves. A chessmaster is a seer."

"Heavens, do they play chess here, too?"

"Chess is popular all over the Empire. What of it?"

"Never mind," said Harold. "We'll stick the fact on top of the pile. Go on."

"A recorder," explained Tor, "is someone with a photographic memory. He doesn't write anything down. He remembers it all, accurately, in full detail."

"Humph! I don't think there's anything extraordinary about that."

"We Lingans can't do it. In fact, we know of only four life forms that can." Respect crept into Tor's snake-skinned face. "And do you really have telekinetic power as well?"

"No. It's a false conclusion to which they've jumped. They appear to think I'm a poltergeist or something—goodness only knows why." He mused a moment. "Maybe it's because of that analysis in stage three. I can control my heartbeats, my blood pressure, my thoughts, and I made their analytical apparatus go haywire. They can get out of it nothing but contradictory nonsense. Evidently they suspect that I sabotaged its innards by some form of remote control."

"Oh!" Tor was openly disappointed.

Before any of them could venture further remark, the television set called for attention and Sourpuss appeared for the third time.

"All nonnative citizens will observe a curfew tonight from midnight until one hour after dawn," he droned. "During this period the police may call at certain apartments. Any nonnative citizens found absent from their apartments and unable to give satisfactory reason therefor, or any nonnative citizens who obstruct the police in the execution of their duty, will be dealt with in accordance with pan-planetary law." He paused, stared out of the screen. He looked bellicose. "The fugitive, Harold Harold-Myra, is in possession of identity card number AMB 307-40781, entered in the name of Robertus Bron. That is all."

"Bron," echoed Harold. "Bron . . . Burkinshaw . . . chessmasters. Dear me!"

The three Lingans were apprehensive, and Melor ventured, "You can see their moves. One: they're satisfied that by now you've found a hiding place. Two: they know you're hiding with outsiders and not with natives. Since there aren't more than sixty thousand outsiders on this planet, sharing one third that number of apartments, it's not impossible to pounce on the lot at one go." His forehead wrinkled with thought. "It's no use you fleeing elsewhere because this curfew is planet-wide. It covers everywhere. I reckon your easiest way out would be to hypnotize a native and stay in his apartment overnight. If, as they say, you're a mesman, it should be easy."

"Except for one thing."

"What is that?"

"It's what they expect me to do. In fact, it's what they're trying to make me do."

"Even so," persisted Melor, "what's to stop you?"

"The routine. A master race always has a routine. It's drilled into them; it's part of their education. Having been warned that a badly wanted specimen is on the loose and about to bolt, they will take the officially prescribed precautions." He grinned at them reassuringly, but they didn't derive much comfort from it. "I can only guess what that routine will be, but I reckon it'll include some method of advertising my presence in a native's apartment even though its occupant is helpless. Scanners coupled to the Police Emergency system and switched in by the opening of a door, or something like that. When I take risks, I pick my own. It's asking for trouble to let the opposition pick 'em for you."

"Maybe you're right," agreed Melor. "We do know that local people have certain facilities denied to outsiders."

"Now if a couple of cops come along to give this place a look over, and I take control of their minds and send them away convinced that I'm just another Lingan, the powers-that-be will have been fooled, won't they?"

"I hadn't thought of that," put in Tor. He was disgusted with his own lack of imagination. "It was so obvious that I didn't see it."

"So obvious," Harold pointed out, "that the authorities know that's just what would occur should they find me here."

"Then why the curfew and the search?"

"Bluff!" defined Harold. "They hope to make me move or, failing that, put scare into those harboring me. They're banging on the walls hoping the rat will run. I won't run! With your kind permission, I'll sit tight."

"You're welcome to stay," Tor assured. "We can find you a spare bed, and if you—"

"Thanks!" Harold interrupted, "but I don't need one. I don't sleep."

"You don't!" They were dumbfounded.

"Never slept a wink in my life. It's a habit we've abandoned." He walked around the room, studying its fittings. "Impatience is the curse of plotters. Nothing bores me more than waiting for time to ripen. I've simply got to wait nine days. Are you really willing to put up with me that long or, if not, can you find me some place else?"

"Stay here," said Tor. "You repay us with your company. We can talk to each other of homes beyond reach. We can talk about the freedom of subject peoples and of things it is not wise to discuss outside. It is sweet to dream dreams. It is good to play with notions of what one might do if only one could find a way to do it."

"You're a little pessimistic," gibed Harold.

On the fourth day his idleness became too much to bear. He went out, strolled along the streets of the city. Two more irate broadcasts had advertised his extended liberty, but the last of them had been three days before. Since then, silence.

His trust reposed in the inability of the public to remember that morning's broadcast, let alone the details of the twentieth one before it, and his confidence was not misplaced. People wandered past him with vacant expressions and preoccupied minds. In most cases, their eyes looked at him without seeing him. In a few cases, his features registered, but no significance registered with them. The farther he walked, the safer he felt.

Downtown he found a smart, modernistic store well stocked with scientific instruments. This simplified matters. He'd been trying to solve the problem of how to get Melor to shop for him without using this silly stuff called money. The Lingan's respect for it equaled his own contempt for it, therefore he couldn't ask his hosts to spend their own on his behalf. Instinct rather than deliberate reasoning had made him recognize this simple ethic of a moneyed world.

Boldly entering the store, he examined its stock. Here were some things he wanted, others capable of ready adaptation to what he desired. Different cultures evolved differing modes of manufacture. Conventional jobs would need alteration to become conventional according to his other-worldly notions, but the simplest tools would enable him to deal with these. Making a list of his requirements, he prowled around until it was complete, handed it to a salesman.

The latter, a shrewd individual, looked the list over, said sharply, "This stuff is for microwave radiation."

"I know it," said Harold blandly.

"It is not for sale to the public except on production of an official permit," he went on. Then, stiffly, "Have you such a permit? May I see your identity card?"

Harold showed him the card.

"Ah!" mouthed the salesman, his manner changing, "the police!" His laugh was apologetic and forced. "Well, you didn't catch me disregarding regulations!"

"I'm not trying to catch you. I've come to get some necessary equipment. Pack it up and let me have it. I'm on urgent business and in a hurry."

"Certainly, certainly." Bustling to and fro, anxious to placate, the salesman collected the equipment, packaged it. Then he made careful note of the name and number on Harold's identity card. "We charge this to the Police Department, as usual?"

"No," Harold contradicted. "Charge it to the Analysis Division of the Immigration Department, Stage Three."

He had a satisfied smile as he went out. When the Bearded One got the bill he could stick it in his analyzer and watch the meters whirl. Which reminded him now that he came to think of it—there didn't seem to be an overmuch sense of humor on this world.

Safely back in the Lingans' apartment, he unloaded his loot, got started on it. His hosts were out. He kept the door locked, concentrated on his task and progressed with speed and dexterity which would have astounded his former captors. When he'd been at work an hour the set in the corner chimed urgently, but he ignored it and was still engrossed in his task when the Lingans came in some time later.

Carefully closing and fastening the door, Melor said, "Well, they've got worried about you again."

"Have they?"

"Didn't you catch the recent broadcast?"

"I was too busy," explained Harold.

"They've discovered that you've got a police card and not the card they first announced. They broadcast a correction and a further warning. The announcer was somewhat annoyed."

"So'd I be," said Harold, "if I were Sourpuss."

Melor's eyes, which had been staring absently at the litter of stuff on which Harold was working, suddenly realized what they saw.

"Hey, where did you get all that?" he asked, with alarm. "Have you been outdoors?"

"Sure! I had to get this junk somehow or other and I couldn't think of how to get it any other way. I couldn't wish it into existence. We've not progressed quite *that* far—yet!" He glanced at the uneasy Lingan. "Take it easy. There's nothing to worry about. I was out for less than a couple of hours, and I might have been born and bred in this city for all the notice anyone took of me."

"Maybe so." Melor flopped into a chair, massaged his scaly chin. Ripples of underlying blueness ran through it as his skin moved. "But if you do it too often you'll meet a cop, or a spaceman, or a Drane. Cops are too inquisitive. Spacemen recognize outsiders and rarely forget a face. Dranes know too much and can divine too much. It's risky." He looked again at the litter of apparatus. "What're you making, anyway?"

"A simple contactor."

"What's that for?"

"Making contact with someone else." Harold wangled an electric iron into the heart of the mess, deftly inserted a condenser smaller than a button, linked it into the circuit with two dabs of solder. "If two people, uncertain of each other's whereabouts, are seeking each other within the limits of the same horizon, they can trace each other with contactors."

"I see," said Melor, not seeing at all. "Why not make mental contact?"

"Because the telepathic range is far too short. Thoughts fade swiftly with distance, especially when blanketed by obstacles."

The three were still watching him curiously when he finished the job shortly before midnight. Now he had a small transmitter-receiver fitted with three antennae, one being a short, vertical rod, the second a tiny silver loop rotatable through its horizontal plane, the third a short silver tube, slightly curved, also rotatable horizontally.

"Now to tune it up," he told them.

Connecting the setup to the power supply, he let it warm through before he started tuning it with a glassite screwdriver. It was a tricky job. The oscillatory circuit had to be steered a delicate margin past peak so that it would swing dead on to resonance when hand-capacity was removed. And, strangely enough, hand-capacity was greater on this planet. The correct margin had to be discovered by trial and error, by delicate adjustment and readjustment.

He manipulated the tuning with fingers as firm and sensitive as any surgeon's. His jawbone ached. Tuning the set onward, he took his hand away. The circuit swung short. He tried again and again. Eventually he stood away from the apparatus, rubbed his aching jaw, in which dull pain was throbbing, switched off the power.

"That'll do," he remarked.

"Aren't you going to use it now?" Melor inquired.

"I can't. Nobody's looking for me yet."

"Oh!" The trio were more puzzled than ever. They gave it up and went to bed.

Putting away his apparatus, Harold dug a book on ancient history out of the Lingans' small but excellent library, setting himself down to the fourth successive night of self-education. There was dynamite in these books for those who had eyes to see. No Lord of Terror had seen them in the light in which he saw them!

The ninth day dawned in manner no different from any other. The sun came up and the Empire's boss city stirred to officially conducted life.

When Melor appeared, Harold said to him, "I believe this is your free day. Have you any plans for it?"

"Nothing important. Why?"

"The fun starts today, or ought to start if my calculations are correct. I could do with your help."

"In what way?"

"You're going to be mighty useful if I come up against someone who can control his thoughts or shield them entirely. Hatred or animosity aren't thoughts—they're emotions of which antagonistic thoughts are born. You Lingans respond to such emotions. You can go on reading the heart long after the mind is closed to me."

"I get the point but not the purpose," confessed Melor.

"Look," said Harold patiently, "when I say the fun starts I don't mean that there's going to be wholesale violence. We've found better ways. It's possible, for instance, to talk oneself into anything or out of anything provided one says the right things to the right person at the right time. The waving blade hasn't half the potency of the wagging tongue. And the tongue isn't messy." He smiled grimly. "My people have had more than their fill of messy methods. We don't bother with them these days. We're grown up."

"So?" prompted Melor.

"So I need you to tell me how I'm doing if, mayhap, I'm working on someone with a closed mind."

"That's easy. I could tell you when hatred, fear or friendliness intensifies or lessens by one degree."

"Just what I need," enthused Harold. "My form of life has its shortcomings as well as its talents, and we don't let ourselves forget it. Last time some of us forgot it, the forgetters thought themselves a collective form of God. The delusion bred death!"

His tongue gently explored a back tooth as his gaze went to the transmitter-receiver waiting at one side of the room.

Nothing happened until midday. The two kept company through the morning, the fugitive expectant and alert, his host uneasy and silently speculative. At noon the television set chimed and Melor switched it on.

Helman came on the screen. He stared straight at the watching pair in manner suggesting that he saw them as clearly as they saw him. His dark features were surly.

"This is a personal broadcast for the benefit of the specimen known as Harold Harold-Myra," Helman enunciated, "or to any citizen illegally maintaining contact with him. Be it known, Harold Harold-Myra, that a summary of all the available data on your world type has been laid before the Council of Action, which Council, after due consideration thereof, has decided that it is to the essential interest of the Empire that your life form be exterminated with the minimum of delay. By midday tomorrow an order will be sent to appropriate war vessels requiring them to vaporize your native planet—unless, in the meantime, you have surrendered yourself and provided new evidence which may persuade the Council of Action to reconsider its decision."

Helman stopped, licked his lips. His air was that of one still nursing a severe reprimand.

He went on, "This notification will be rebroadcast in one hour's time. Watchers in touch with the fugitive are advised to bring it to his attention as this will be the last warning." His surliness increased as he finished, "In the event of his prompt surrender, the Council of Action will extend gracious pardon to those who have been harboring this specimen."

The screen blanked.

"Mate in one move," said Melor glumly. "We told you that it was a waste of time to sit and plot. They get 'em all, one way or another."

"It's check—and your move."

"All right then—what's your move?"

"I don't know yet. We've still got to wait. If you sit by the chimney long enough, Santa Claus comes down."

"In the name of the Blue Sun, who is Santa Claus?" asked Melor peevishly.

"The man with a million lollies."

"Lollies?"

"Things you lick."

"Oh, cosmos!" said Melor. "What madman wants to own a million things to lick? Is this anything to do with your sermon about wagging tongues? If so, *we're* licked!"

"Forget it," Harold advised. "I talk in riddles to pass the time."

A pain suddenly pulsed in his jawbone. It brought an exclamation from him which stirred the nervous Melor. Putting two fingers into his mouth, Harold unscrewed the crown of a back molar, took it out, put it on the table. A tiny splinter of crystal glittered within the base of the crown. The crystal was fluorescent. Melor gaped at it fascinatedly.

Swiftly powering the transmitter-receiver, Harold let it warm up. A faint, high-pitched whistle crept into its little phone. He swung the loop slowly while the whistle strengthened, then weakened, finally faded out. Slightly offsetting the loop to bring back the signal, he pressed a stud. The note grew stronger.

"That side," he murmured, indicating the face of the loop nearest to the watching Melor.

Returning the loop to fade-out position, he switched in the transmitter, swung its curved tube antenna until it paralleled the direction faced by the receiver's loop. Again he offset the loop, and the signal returned. He waited expectantly. In a little while, the signal broke into three short pips, then resumed its steady note. He flipped his transmitter switch three times.

For half an hour the two sat and waited while the whistle maintained itself and gave triple pips at regular intervals. Then, suddenly, it soared up in power and gave one pip.

Carefully, Harold repeated all the rigmarole with the antenna, this time obtaining a different direction. Three pips came as his reward, and again he switched his transmitter in acknowledgment. Another long wait. Then, slowly, weakly and distantly, a voice crept into his mind.

"A blue car. A blue car."

Going to the window, he looked down into the street. From his height of ten floors he had a clear view extending several blocks in both directions. He found a score of automobiles on the street, half a dozen of them blue.

"Stop, step out, get in again," he thought. He repeated the mental impulse, driving it outward with maximum intensity.

A car stopped, a human shape got out, looked around, stepped back into the vehicle. It was a blue car.

Harold crossed the room, disconnected the contactor, and returned to the window. Looking downward, he thought powerfully.

"I believe I've got you. Drive on slowly . . . slowly . . . here you are . . . stop there! The building immediately on your right. Ten floors up."

He continued to keep watch as the car pulled in by the opposite sidewalk. Two men emerged from it, crossed the road with casual nonchalance, disappeared beneath him. No other cars halted, nobody followed the men into the building.

A voice reached him strongly, *"Are we dragging anything?"*

"Not that I can see."

"Good!"

Melor said plaintively, "I know that you're communicating with someone. Santa Claus, I presume? How you can read each other's toothache is a mystery to me."

"Our throbs are no worse than your wobbles."

"You bounce around," said Melor, "and, according to you, we dither. Some day we'll come across some other life form which spins around in circles, like a mental dervish. Or even an entity capable of logical reasoning without thought at all; a sort of Bohr-thinker who skips straight from premise to conclusion without covering the intervening distance." His eyes found the crystal still on the table, noted that it had ceased to glow. "Better plant your key-frequency back in your face before somebody sets it in a ring."

Harold smiled, took up the crystal, screwed it back into place. Opening the door, he looked out just as the pair from the car arrived on the landing. He beckoned them in, locked the door behind them, introduced them to the Lingan.

"This is Melor, a friend from Linga. Melor, meet George Richard-Eve and Burt Ken-Claudette."

Melor looked askance at the newcomers' neat space uniforms and the silver comet insignia glittering on their epaulettes. He commented, "Well, they smell as good as they look bad. You'll produce a pally Drane next!"

"Not likely!" Harold assured.

Burt sat down, said to Harold, "You know the locals by now. Are they crafty enough to have drawn a bead on that transmission and if so, how long d'you think they'll give us? If time's short, we can beat it in the car and delay matters a little."

"They know how I got the stuff, where I got it, and its purpose, and they're not too dopey to listen out," Harold replied. "As I guess, I give them half an hour."

"That'll do."

Melor put in, "Talk mentally if it suits you better. I don't mind."

"You're in this," Harold told him, "so we'll talk vocally. You're entitled to listen." He turned to Burt. "What's cooking?"

"There's fun and games on four out of the five. The fifth proved useless for our purpose: it held nothing but a few time-serving bureaucrats on high pay. But four should do, I reckon."

"Go on."

"All the appointed ones have gone beyond and the first of them ought to have reached their destinations by now. It's six days to the nearest system, so they've a good margin." He smoothed his dark hair, looked reminiscent. "*Nemo* is due to pop off any moment now. That was a tough job! We took forty people off it, but had to scour the place from end to end to find the last pair of them. We got 'em, though. They've been dumped in safety."

"Good!"

"This has been an education," Burt went on. "Better than going to the zoo. There's an underground message system on number three, for instance, which has to be seen to be believed. By 'underground' they mean ten thousand feet up! How d'you think they do it?"

"I've no idea," said Harold.

"With birds! Among the minority life forms there is one which is beaked and feathered. They talk with birds. They chirrup and squawk at them, and every bird understands what's said."

"Orniths," informed Melor. "They came originally from Gronat, the Empire's eight hundredth conquest. They're scattered around and there are a few of them here, maybe a dozen or so. When you've had time to tour the Empire you'll find it contains even stranger forms. And the humanoids don't even dislike them all."

"It would seem that the humanoids don't even like each other much," Burt commented. "To most of them, a brother from a neighboring planet is a foreigner."

"Still in the schoolkid stage," said Harold. "Rah-rah and all that."

Burt nodded and continued, "As you know, we've had to move too fast in too little time to put over anything really drastic, but what's been done ought to be enough to show what could be done—which is all that matters." A faraway look came into his eyes. "When we triumphantly cast our bread upon the waters we little thought it'd come back—all wet."

"So you've found confirmation of that?"

"Plenty," Burt replied. "Have you?"

"Any amount of it." Harold went to the bookshelf, selected a heavy tome titled *The Imperial Elect*. He skimmed through its pages, found an illustration, showed it to Burt. "Look!"

"Phew!" said Burt.

"The Budding Cross," breathed George, looking over Burt's shoulder. "And the Circle of Infinity!"

"That shelf is crammed with stuff," Harold told them as he replaced the book. "I've been going through it like a man in a strange dream." He came back, sat down. "Anything more to report?"

"Not much. Jon has stayed on number three. He had a stroke of luck and got at the Lord, a fat personage named Amilcare. Temporarily, His Eminence doesn't know which shoe is on which foot."

Harold opened his mouth to comment, closed it without saying anything. His mental perception perked up, listened intently. Burt and George listened likewise. Melor began to fidget. For the first time, Harold noticed that a fringe of fine hairs lay along the rims of the Lingan's ears, and that these hairs were now fully extended and quivering.

"There's a stink of hostility," complained Melor uneasily. In his lithe, loose-jointed gait, he went to the window.

A hubbub lay across the ether, a confused mixture of thoughts from which it was impossible to extract more than odd, disjointed phrases.

"Line 'em across that end . . . rumble, rumble . . . yes, take the ground floor . . . rumble, buzz, buzz . . . work upward . . . rumble . . . ten of you . . . look out for . . . rumble . . . they may be . . ."

"I expect visitors," remarked George, easily. He joined Melor at the window.

The others followed, and the four looked down at the street. It was a hive of activity. A dozen cars were drawn across one end, blocking it completely. Another dozen jockeyed for position to block the opposite end. Cars plugged the three side streets in between. Something invisible droned steadily overhead; it sounded like a squadron of helicopters. More than two hundred black-uniformed men were scattered along the sidewalk in little groups.

"Their bearings must have been rough." Burt pulled a face at the cohort below. "It got them this section of the street but not the building. I'd be ashamed of such a sloppy job."

"It's good enough," Harold answered. He filtered the telepathic surge once again. It was entirely human, involuntary and nonreceptive. "We could go down and save them some bother, but I'm a bit curious about those butterfly minds down there. Surely they'd have brought something potent along with them."

"Test it," suggested Burt.

Dropping their mental shields, the three let their thoughts flow forth bearing a perfect picture of their location. Instantly the hubbub was overwhelmed by an alien mind which imposed itself upon the ether. It was clear, sharp, penetrating, and of remarkable strength.

"They're in that building there! Ten floors high! Three of them and a Lingan. They contemplate no resistance!"

"A Drane!" said Harold.

It was impossible to locate the creature amid the mass of men and automobiles beneath, nor could he sense its general direction, for, having said all it considered essential, it had closed its mind and its powerful impulse was gone.

"Judging by the throb, there was a Drane down there," offered Melor belatedly. "Did you hear it? I couldn't understand what it said."

"It got us fixed. It identified your erratic thought-flow and said that a Lingan was with us."

"And what are we going to do about it? Do we stand like sheep and wait to be taken away?"

"Yes," Harold informed.

Melor's face registered approaching martyrdom, but he offered no further remark.

There wasn't an immediate response to the Drane's revelation. For reasons unknown to the watchers, a short time-lag intervened. It ended when a car roared along the street with a silver-spangled official bawling orders from its side window. As one man, the uniformed clusters made a determined rush for the front entrance of the building.

It was Melor who opened the door and admitted a police captain and six men. All seven wore the strained expressions of people called upon to deal with things unimaginable, and all seven were armed. Little blasters, similar to the one Harold had found so objectionable, were ready in their hands.

The captain, a big, burly man, but pale of face, entered the room with his blaster held forward, and gabbled hastily through his prepared speech.

"Listen to me, you four, before you try any tricks. We've reversed the controls on these guns. They stay safe while they're gripped but go off immediately our hands loosen—and hypnosis causes involuntary relaxation of the muscles which you can't prevent!" He swallowed hard. "Any clever stunts will do no more than turn this place into a shambles. In addition, there are more men outside, more on every floor, more in the street. You can't cope with the lot!"

Smiling amiably, Harold said, "You tempt us to persuade you to toss those toys out of the window, and your pants after them. But we want to talk to the Council of Action and have no time for amusement. Let's go."

The captain didn't know whether to scowl or look relieved. Cautiously he stood to one side, his gun held level, as the four filed out through the door. The escorts were equally leery. They surrounded the quartet, but not too closely, bearing themselves with the air of men compelled to nurse vipers to their bosoms.

As they marched along the landing toward the levitators Burt nudged the nearest guard and demanded, "What's your name?"

The fellow, a lanky, beetle-browed individual, was startled and apprehensive as he answered, "Walt Bron."

"Tut!" said Burt.

The guard didn't like that *"tut."* His brows came down, his small eyes held a stupefied expression as his mind said to itself, *"Why should he want my name? Why pick on me? I ain't done him any harm. What's he up to now?"*

Burt smiled broadly and his own mind reached out to George's and Harold's, saying, *"Something has got them worried, though the higher-ups aren't likely to have told them much."*

"Yes—it looks as if there's irritation in influential circles and the cops got bawled out in consequence. Evidently news is coming through." Pause. *"Did you feel any probe?"*

"No."

"Neither did we. That Drane must have gone." Pause. *"Pity we can't talk with Melor this way. He's walking behind like a fatalist pacing to certain death."* Pause. *"Got plenty of guts, the way he's taken us on trust."*

"Yes—but we'll look after him!"

They reached the levitators. The entire landing was now solid with armed police and a number of them were pressing eagerly into the deserted apartment, intent on a thorough search.

Herded into a levitator, the captured quartet and their escort of seven crammed it to capacity. The glassite doors slid shut. The burly captain pressed a button and the levitator soared smoothly upward while its occupants watched the rising indicator with offhand interest. They stopped at the twenty-seventh floor.

The captain didn't permit the doors to open. He stood with his attention fixed upon the indicator while slowly his beefy face changed color. Suddenly, he rammed his big thumb on the ground-level button and the levitator shot downward.

Harold: *"Who did that?"*

Burt: *"Me. I couldn't resist it."* Then, vocally, and loudly, "I didn't notice any guns go off. Did you?"

The other captives grinned. The captain glared at the up-flying shaft but said nothing. The escort's uneasiness registered more openly on their faces.

A veritable guard of honor had lined up between the front entrance and the waiting car. About sixty guns were held in readiness on either side—in flat disregard of the fact that one had only to start something and let the fire of one rank bring down half the opposite rank, thus providing plentiful company in death.

The four got into the car, and its driver, a thin-featured, pessimistic individual, looked even less happy for their arrival. He had a cop for company in front. The car blew its jets and started off with half a dozen cars leading and a full dozen following. It was a cavalcade worthy of the year's best burial, and its pace was suitably funereal as it wended its way through a succession of side streets to the outskirts of the city. A thousand feet above them a helicopter and two gyros drifted along, carefully following every bend and turn on their route.

The destination proved to be an immense, needlelike skyscraper, tall, slender, graceful. It soared majestically from spacious, well-tended grounds around which stood a high wall surmounted by the spidery wiring of a photoelectric telltale system. As they swept through the great gateway, the prisoners caught a glimpse of the telltale marker-board in the granite lodge and a group of heavily armed guards lounging behind the gates.

"The palace of the Council," Melor informed. "This is where they make worlds and break them—or so they claim."

"Be quiet!" snapped the cop in front. Then, in a high, squeaky voice, he added, "There are fairies at the bottom of my garden!"

"Indeed?" said Burt, affecting polite surprise.

The cop's sour face whitened. His grip tightened on his blaster, forgetting in his emotion that a stronger hold was supposed to be ineffective.

"Let him alone, Burt!" thought Harold.

"I don't like him," Burt came back. *"His ears stick out."*

"How he smells of fury!" criticized Melor, openly.

Conversation ended as the procession halted in front of the skyscraper's ornate entrance. The quartet climbed out, paraded through another wary guard of honor, entered the building. Here, more black-uniformed men conducted them two levels below ground, ushered them into an apartment which, ominously, had a beryllium-steel grille in lieu of a door. The last man out turned a monster key in the grille and departed.

Before the inmates had time thoroughly to examine their new prison, an attendant appeared, thrust packaged foods through the bars of the grille, and told them, "I haven't got the key and don't know who has. Neither can I find out. If you want anything, call for me, but don't think you can make me open up. I couldn't do it even if I wanted—which I don't!"

"Dear me," said Burt, "that's unkind of you." Going to the grille, he swung it open, looked out at the astounded attendant and continued, "Tell the Council that we are very comfortable and appreciate their forethought. We shall be pleased to call upon them shortly."

The attendant's scattered wits came together. He took to his heels as if the breath of death was on his neck.

"How did you do that?" demanded Melor, his eyes wide. He ambled loose-jointedly to the grille, looked at its lock, swung it to and fro on its hinges.

"The gentleman with the key locked it, then unlocked it, and wandered away satisfied that duty had been done," Burt released a sigh. "Life is full of delusions." Opening a packet, he examined its contents. "Calorbix!" he said disgustedly, and tossed the package on a table.

"Here they come," George announced.

A horde arrived. They locked the grille, put two heavy chains around its end post, padlocked those. The four watched in amused silence. A pompous little man, with much silver braid strewn over his chest, then tried the grille, shaking it furiously. Satisfied, he scowled at the four, went away, the horde following.

Burt mooched restlessly around the room. "There are scanners watching us, microphones listening to us and, for all I know, some cockeyed gadget tasting us. I'm fed up with this. Let's go see the Council."

"Yes, it's about time we did," George agreed.

"The sooner the better," added Harold.

Melor offered no comment. The conversation of his friends, he decided, oft was confusing and seemingly illogical. They had a habit of going off at the queerest slants. So he contented himself with staring at the grille, through which nothing but some liquid form of life could pass, while he wondered whether Tor and Vern had yet been dragged into the net. He hoped not. It was better to execute one Lingan than three.

A minute later the man with the keys came back accompanied by two guards and a tall, gray-haired official clad in myrtle green. The badge of the Silver Comet glittered on the latter's shoulder straps. His keen gaze rested on the warden as that worthy surlily unlocked the padlocks, withdrew the chains, freed the grille.

Then he said to the four, "Most remarkable!" He waited for a response, but none came, so he carried on. "This warder hasn't the least notion of what he's doing. As the Council expected, you influenced him to return and unlock the gate. We kept him under observation. It has been an interesting demonstration of what hypnosis can achieve." His smile was amiable. "But you didn't expect him to return accompanied, eh?"

"What does it matter?" Harold answered. "Your brain advertises that the Council is ready to deal with us."

"I waste my breath talking." The official made a gesture of futility. "All right. Come with me."

The Council looked small. Its strength a mere eight, all but two of them human. They sat at a long table, the six humans in the middle, a nonhuman at each end. The thing on the extreme right had a head like a purple globe, smooth, shining, hairless, possessing no features except a pair of retractable eyes. Below was a cloaked shapelessness suggesting no shoulders and no arms. It was as repulsive as the sample on the left was beautiful. The one on the left had a flat, circular, golden face surrounded by golden petals, large and glossy. The head was supported by a short, fibrous green neck from the knot of which depended long, delicate arms terminating in five tentacles. Two black-knobbed stamens jutted from the face, and a wide, mobile mouth was visible beneath them. It was lovely, like a flower.

Between this table and the staring captives hung a barrier of wire. Harold, Burt and George could *see* that it was loaded, and their perceptions examined it gingerly. They diagnosed its purpose simultaneously; it bore an alternating current imposed upon a pulsing potential. Two hundred cycles per second, with a minimum pressure of four thousand volts rising to peak points of seven thousand every tenth cycle.

"Hypnocast jammer!" reported Burt. He was puzzled. "But that doesn't blank neural sprays. They're different bands. Can you hear what they're thinking?"

"Not a thing," answered Harold. "Neither could I get your thoughts while you were speaking."

"I've lost contact, too," put in George. "Something which isn't that screen is droning out a bass beat note that makes a mess of the telepathic band."

Sniffing with distaste, Melor said, "This is where I come in. I know what's the matter. There's a Drane in the room. He's doing it."

"Are you sure of that?"

"I can sense him." He pointed at the flowerlike being on the left. "Furthermore, Dranes can't speak. They've no vocal cords. The Florans function as their interpreters—that's why this one's here."

One of the humans on the Council, a bull-headed, heavily jowled man, leaned forward, fixed glittering eyes on the four. His voice was harsh.

"The Lingan is right. Since we are not assembled to be entertained by your alien antics, nor to listen to your lies, but solely for the purpose of weighing fresh truths with justice and with wisdom, we find it necessary to employ a Drane."

So saying, he made a dramatic gesture. The Floran reached a tentacled hand down behind the table, lifted the hidden Drane, placed it on the polished surface.

Mental visualization, Harold realized had proved correct with regard to shape and appearance but had misled him in the matter of size. He'd taken it for granted that a Drane possessed bulk comparable with his own. But this creature was no larger than his fist. Its very smallness shocked him.

It was lizardlike, but not so completely as first appeared, and now that he could see it closely, its tiny but perfect uniform looked absurd. While they regarded it, the thing sat there and stared at them with eyes like pinpoints of flaming crimson, and as it stared the strange beat note disappeared, a psychic flood poured through the screen and lapped around their minds.

But already the three shields were up, while the fourth—the Lingan—felt the force only as an acute throb. The pressure went up and up; it was amazing that such a midget brain could emit so mighty a mental flow of power. It felt and probed and thrust and stabbed, its violence increasing without abate.

Perspiration beaded the features of the trio as they gazed fixedly at the same spot on the Drane's jacket while maintaining their shields against its invisible assault. Melor sat down, cradled his head in his arms, began to rock slowly from side to side. The Council watched impassively. The Drane's optics were jewels of fire.

"Keep it up," whispered Harold. "It's almost on the boil."

Like the lizards it resembled, the Drane's pose was fixed, unmoving. It had remained as motionless as a carved ornament since it had reached the table, and its baleful eyes had never blinked. Still its psychic output went up.

Then, suddenly, it pawed at its jacket, snatched the paw away. A thin wisp of smoke crawled out of the cloth. The next instant, the creature had fled from the table, the mental pressure collapsing as its source disappeared. Its sharp, peaky voice came into their minds as the thing snaked through a tiny door, fled along the outer passage. The voice faded with distance.

"Burning . . . burning . . . burning!"

The Council member who had spoken originally now sat staring through the screen at the prisoners. His hand was on the table, and his fingers rapped its surface nervously. The other members maintained blank expressions. He turned his head, looked at the Floran.

"What happened?"

"The Drane said he was burning," enunciated the mouth in the flowerlike head. Its tones were weak, but precise. "His mind was very agitated. The peril destroyed his ability to concentrate, and he had to flee lest worse befall."

"Pyrotics!" said the Council member incredulously. "There are legends of such." His attention returned to the captives. "So you're pyrotics—fire-raisers!"

"Some of your people can do it—but don't know it themselves," Harold told him. "They've caused most of any seemingly inexplicable fires you've experienced." He made a gesture of impatience. "Now that we've got rid of that Drane how about giving way to what's on your mind? We can read what is written there, and we know the next move: you're to call Burkinshaw, Helman and Roka, after which the parley will start."

Frowning, but making no retort, the Council member pressed a red button on his desk. His attitude was one of expectancy.

In short time, Helman and Roka entered the room, took seats at the table. The former's bearing was surly and disgruntled. The latter grinned sheepishly at the quartet, even nodded amiably to Harold.

One minute after them, Burkinshaw Three, the Supreme Lord, came in and took the center seat. His awesome name and imposing title fitted him like somebody else's glove, for he was a small, thin man, round-shouldered, narrow-chested, with a pale, lined face. His balding head had wisps of gray hair at the sides, and his eyes peered myopically through rimless pince-nez. His whole appearance was that of a mild and perpetually preoccupied professor—but his mind was cold, cold.

That mind was now wide open to the three. It was a punctilious mind, clear and sharp in form, operating deliberately and calculatingly through the mixed output of the other humans at the Council table.

Arranging some papers before him, and keeping his gaze fixed upon the top sheets, Burkinshaw spoke in measured, unhurried tones, saying, "I don't doubt that you can read my mind and are reading it now, but in justice to the Lingan, who cannot do so, and for the benefit of my fellows, who are not telepathic either, I must use ordinary speech." He adjusted the pince-nez, turned over a sheet of paper and continued.

"We, of the Imperial Council of Action, have decided that the safety of the Empire demands that we obliterate the planet known to us as KX-724 together with any adjacent planets, satellites or asteroids harboring its dominant life form. We are now met to consider this life form's final plea for preservation, and it is the duty of each of us to listen carefully to what new evidence may be offered, weighing it not with favor or with prejudice, but with justice."

Having thus spoken, the Supreme Lord removed his pince-nez, polished each lens, clipped them carefully on his nose, stared owlishly over their tops at the prisoners. His eyes were a very pale blue, looked weak, but were not weak.

"Have you chosen your spokesman?"

Their minds conferred swiftly, then Harold said, "I shall speak."

"Very well then." Burkinshaw relaxed in his seat. "Before you commence it is necessary to warn you that our grave decision concerning the fate of your people is neither frivolous nor heartless. In fact, it was reached with the greatest reluctance. We were driven to it by the weight of evidence and, I regret to say, additional data which we've recently gained is of a nature calculated to support our judgment. Bluntly, your kind of life is a menace to our kind. The responsibility now rests with you to prove otherwise—to our satisfaction."

"And if I can't?" queried Harold.

"We shall destroy you utterly."

"If you can," said Harold.

The assembled minds reacted promptly. He could hear them, aggressive and fuming. The purple thing exuded no thoughts but did give out a queer suggestion of imbecilic amusement. The Floran's attitude was one of mild surprise mixed with interest.

Burkinshaw wasn't fazed. "If we can," he agreed blandly, while his brain held little doubt that they could. "Proceed in your own way," he invited. "You have about fourteen hours in which to convince us that our decision was wrong, or impracticable."

"You've tempted us into giving minor demonstrations of our powers," Harold began. "The Drane was planted here for a similar purpose; you used him as a yardstick with which to measure our mental abilities. From your viewpoint, I guess, the results have strengthened your case and weakened ours. Only the yardstick wasn't long enough."

Burkinshaw refused to rise to the bait. Placing his fingertips together as if about to pray, he stared absently at the ceiling, said nothing. His mind was well disciplined, for it registered no more than the comment, "*A negative point.*"

"Let it pass," Harold went on, "while I talk about coincidences. On my world, a coincidence is a purely fortuitous lining-up of circumstances and either is isolated or recurs haphazardly. But when a seeming coincidence repeats itself often enough, it ceases to be a coincidence. You know that, too—or ought to know it. For example, let's take the once-alleged coincidence of meteoric phenomena appearing simultaneously with earthquakes. It occurred so frequently that eventually one of your scientists became curious, investigated the matter, discovered solar-dynamic space-strain, the very force which since has been utilized to boost your astrovessels to supra-spatial speeds. The lesson, of course, is that one just can't dismiss coincidences as such when there are too many of them."

"A thrust—toward where?" mused the Floran.

"No point yet apparent," thought Burkinshaw.

"I don't like the way he gabbles," said Helman's mind uneasily. *"He's talking to gain time. Maybe the three of them are trying to push something through that screen. They burned the Drane through it, didn't they?"* He fidgeted in his seat. *"I don't share B's faith in that screen. Curses on Roka and all the rest of the pioneering crowd—they'll be the end of us yet!"*

Smiling to himself, Harold continued, "We've found out that the game of chess is generally known all over the Empire."

"Pshaw!" burst out the harsh-voiced man seated on Burkinshaw's left. "That's no coincidence. It spread from a central source, as anyone with a modicum of intelligence should have deduced."

"Be quiet, Dykstra," reproved Burkinshaw.

"Which source?" Harold asked him.

Dykstra looked peeved as he replied, "Us! We spread it around. What of it?"

"We had it long before you contacted us," Harold told him.

Dykstra opened his mouth, glanced at Burkinshaw, closed his mouth and swallowed hard. Burkinshaw continued to survey the ceiling.

Harold pursued, "We've had it so long that we don't know how long. The same board, same pieces, same moves, same rules. If you work it out, you'll find that that involves a very large number of coincidences."

They didn't comment vocally, but he got their reactions.

Four of the Council were confused.

"Surprising, but possible," mused the Floran.

"What of it, anyway?" inquired Dykstra's mind.

"No point yet apparent," thought Burkinshaw coolly.

The purple thing's brain emitted a giggle.

"Bron," said Harold. "Walt Bron, Robertus Bron and umpteen other Brons. Your directory of citizens is full of them. My world, likewise, is full of them, always coupled with the other parent's name, of course, and occasionally spelled Brown, but pronounced the same. We've also got Roberts and Walters." He looked at Helman. "I know four men named Hillman." He shifted his gaze to the Supreme Lord. "And among our minor musicians is one named Theodore Burkinshaw-May."

Burkinshaw removed his stare from the ceiling and concentrated on the wall. *"I see where he's going. Reserve judgment until he arrives."*

"The vessel which brought us here was named the *Fenix*, in characters resembling those of our own alphabet," Harold continued. "And in days long gone by when we had warships, there was one named the *Phoenix*. We found your language amazingly easy to learn. Why? Because one-fifth of your vocabulary is identical with ours. Another fifth is composed of perversions of our words. The remainder consists of words which have changed beyond all recognition or words you've acquired from the peoples you've conquered. But, basically, your language is ours. Have you had enough coincidences?"

"Nonsense!" exclaimed Dykstra loudly. "Impossible!"

Burkinshaw turned and looked at Dykstra with eye that were reproving behind their lenses. "Nothing is impossible," he contradicted mildly. "Continue," he ordered Harold, while his thoughts ran on, *"The pleader is making the inevitable point—too late."*

"So you can see where I'm going," Harold remarked to him. "Just for one final coincidence, let me say I was stupid enough to misunderstand the imperial title. I thought they called themselves Lords of Terror. A silly mistake." His voice slowed down. "Their title is a mystic one rooted deep in your past. They call themselves Lords of Terra!"

"Dear me," said Dykstra, "isn't that nice!"

Ignoring him, Harold spoke to Roka. "You're awake by now. Last night something clicked in your mind and you found yourself remembering things you didn't know you'd forgotten. Do you remember what my people call their parent planet?"

"Terra," Roka responded promptly. "I reported it to the Supreme Lord this morning. You call yourselves Terrestrials."

Dykstra's heavy face went dark red, and accusations of blasphemy were welling within his mind when Burkinshaw beat him to it.

"This morning's revised report of Lieutenant Roka and certain survivors of his crew now lies before the Council." He indicated the papers on the table. "It has already been analyzed by the police commissioner, Inquisitor Hellman and myself. We now believe that the pleaders assertions are founded in truth and that in discovering KX-724 we have discovered our long-lost point of origin. We have found our mother planet. The *Fenix,* unknown to any of us, was homeward bound!"

Half the Council were dumbfounded. The purple creature was not; it registered that human rediscoveries were of little consequence to purple things. The Floran thought similarly. Dykstra's mind was a turmoil of confusion.

"A difference of three light-years has separated us for two thousand centuries," Harold told them quietly. "In that tremendous past we'd grown great and venturesome. We sent several convoys of colonists to the nearest system four and a half light-years away. We never knew what happened to them, for then followed the final atomic war which reduced us to wandering tribes sunk lower than savages. We've been climbing back ever since. The path of our climb has been very different from yours, for roving particles had done strange things to us. Some of those things died out, some were rooted out, others persisted and made us what we are today."

"What are you?" inquired the member next to Roka.

"Humanity metamorphosed," Burkinshaw answered for him.

"In the awful struggle for life on new and hostile worlds, you, too, sank," Harold continued. "But you climbed again, and once more reached for the stars. Naturally, you sought the nearest system, one and a half light-years away, for you had forgotten the location of your home, which was spoken of only in ancient legends. We were three light-years farther away than your nearest neighboring system. Logically, you picked that—and went away from us. You sank again, climbed again, went on again, and you never came back until you'd built a mighty Empire on the rim of which we waited, and changed, and changed."

Now they were all staring at him fascinatedly. Even Dykstra was silent, his mind full of the mighty argosy across the ages. Half of it was schoolbook stuff to him, but not when presented in this new light.

"Those of you who are of the Brotherhood of the Budding Cross know that this is true—that you have completed the circle and reached the Seat of Sol." He made a swift and peculiar sign. Two of his audience responded automatically.

"It's of little use," Burt's thought came over strongly. *"They're too factual."*

"Wait!"

"The Council was silent a long time, and eventually the Floran said, "All this is very touching—but how touching will it be when they take over our Empire?" To which its mind added, *"And we Florans swap one master for another. I am against it. Better the devil you know than the devil you don't."*

Resting his thin arms on the table, Burkinshaw Three blinked apologetically at the Terrans and spoke smoothly. "If they knew what we know, the Empire's sentimentalists might be against your destruction. However, the fabric of our cosmic edifice cannot be sustained by anything so soft as sentiment. Moreover, the prodigal sons have no intention of presenting this fatted calf to their long-lost fathers. Your removal from the scheme of things appears to me as necessary as ever—perhaps even more necessary—and that it will be patricide makes no difference to the fact." His thin, ascetic face held an ingratiating wish to please. "I feel sure that you understand our position. Have you anything more to say?"

"No luck," whispered Melor. "The hatred has gone—to be replaced by fear."

Harold grimaced, said to the Supreme Lord, "Yes, I'd like to say that you can blast Terra out of existence and its system along with it, but it'll do you no good."

"We are not under the delusion that it will do us any good," declared Burkinshaw. "Nor would we sanction so drastic an act for such a purpose." He removed his pince-nez, screwed up his eyes as he looked at his listeners. "The motive is more reasonable and more urgent—it is to prevent harm."

"It won't do that, either."

"Why not?"

"Because you're too late."

"I feared you'd say that." Burkinshaw leaned back in his seat, tapped his glasses on a thumbnail. *"If he can't satisfy me that his claim is well based, I shall advance the hour!"* Then he said, "You'll have to prove that."

"There's trouble on four out of the five other planets in this system. You've just had news of it. Nothing serious, merely some absenteeism, sabotage, demonstrations, but no violence. It's trouble all the same—and it could be worse."

"There's always trouble on one planet or another," put Helman sourly. "When you're nursing four thousand of them, you get used to unrest."

"You overlook the significance of coincidences, I fear. Normal troubles pop up here and there, haphazardly. These have come together. They've kept an appointment in time!"

"We'll deal with them," Helman snapped.

"I don't doubt it," said Harold evenly. "You'll also deal with an uproar in the next system when you get news of it soon. You'll deal with four planets simultaneously, or forty planets—simultaneously. But four hundred planets—simultaneously—and then four thousand! Somewhere is the number that'll prove too much for even the best of organizations."

"It's not possible," Helman asserted stubbornly. "Only two dozen of you Terrans got here, Roka told us that. You took over his ship, substituted two dozen Terrestrials for part of his crew, impressed false memories on his and the other's minds, causing them to suspect nothing until their true memories suddenly returned." He scowled. The pulse in his forehead was beating visibly. "Very clever of you. Very, very clever. But twenty-four aren't enough."

"We know it. Irrespective of relative powers, some numbers are needed to deal with numbers." Harold's sharp-eyed gaze went from Helman to Burkinshaw. "If you people are no more and no less human than you were two hundred thousand years ago—and I think that your expansive path *has* kept you much the same—I'd say that your bureaucrats still live in watertight compartments. So long as supposedly missing ships fail to observe the officially prescribed rigmarole for reporting, it's taken that they're still missing. And, ten to one, your Department of Commerce doesn't even know that the Navy has mislaid anything."

It was a tribute to the Supreme Lord's quick-wittedness that his mind was way ahead of his confreres', for he acted while they were still stewing it over. He switched on the televisor set in the wall on one side.

Looking at its scanner, he said sharply, "Get me the Department of Commerce, Movements Section."

The screen colored, a fat man in civilian attire appeared. An expression of intense respect covered his ample features as he identified his caller.

"Yes, your excellency?"

"The Navy has reported two vessels immobilized beyond the Frontier. They're the *Callan* and the *Mathra*. Have they been recorded recently in any movements bulletins?"

"A moment, your excellency." The fat man disappeared. After some time, he came back, a puzzled frown on his face. "Your excellency, we have those two ships recorded as obsolete war vessels functioning as freighters. Their conversion was assumed by us, since they are transporting passengers and tonnage. The *Callan* has cleared four ports in the Frontier Zone, Sector B, in the last eight days. The *Mathra* departed from the system of Hyperion after landing passengers and freight on each of its nine planets. Its destination was given as external to the Frontier Zone, Sector J."

"Inform the Navy Department," Burkinshaw ordered, and switched off. He was the least disturbed individual at the table. His manner was calm, unruffled as he spoke to Harold. "So they're busily bringing in Terrans or Terrestrials or whatever you call yourselves. The logical play is to have those two vessels blown out of existence. Can it be done?"

"I'm afraid not. It depends largely upon whether the ships getting such an order have or have not already come under our control. The trouble with warships and atom bombs and planet-wreckers is that they're useful only when they work when and where you want them to work. Otherwise, they're liabilities." He gestured to indicate Burt and George. "According to my friends, the bomb allocated to Terra is on the ship *Warcat* clearing from your third neighbor. Ask Amilcare about it."

It required some minutes to get the third planet's Lord on the screen, and then his image was cloudy with static.

"Where's the *Warcat*?" rasped Burkinshaw.

The image moved, clouded still more, then cleared slightly. "Gone," said Amilcare jovially. "I don't know where."

"On whose authority?"

"Mine," Amilcare answered. His chuckle was oily and a little crazy. "Jon wanted it so I told him to take it. I couldn't think of anything you'd find more gratifying. Don't you worry about Jon—I'm looking after him for you."

Burkinshaw cut him off. "This Jon is a Terran, I suppose?"

"A Terrestrial," Harold corrected.

"Put a call out for him," urged Dykstra irefully. "The police won't all be bereft of their senses even if Amilcare is."

"Let me handle this," Burkinshaw said. Then, to Harold, "What has he done with the *Warcat*?"

"He'll have put somebody on it to control the crew and they'll be giving you a demonstration of what a nuisance planet-wreckers can be when they drop where they shouldn't."

"So your defense is attack? The bloodshed has started? In that case, the war is on, and we're all wasting our—"

"There will be no bloodshed," Harold interrupted. "We're not so infantile as that. None's been shed so far, and none will be shed if it can be avoided. That's what we're here for—to avoid it. The fact that we'd inevitably win any knock-down and drag-out affair you care to start hasn't blinded us to the fact that losers can lose very bloodily." He waved a hand toward the televisor. "Check up with your watertight bureaucrats. Ask your astronomers whether that refueling asteroid of yours is still circling."

Burkinshaw resorted to the televisor for the third time. All eyes were on its screen as he said, "Where is *Nemo* now?"

"*Nemo*? Well, your excellency, at the present moment it is approaching alignment with the last planet *Drufa* and about twenty hours farther out."

"I'm not asking where it ought to be! I want to know whether it's actually there!"

"Pardon me, your excellency." The figure slid off the screen and was gone a long time. When it returned, its voice crept out of the speaker hushed and frightened. "Your excellency, it would seem that some strange disaster has overtaken the body. I cannot explain why we've failed to observe—"

"Is it there?" rapped Burkinshaw impatiently.

"'Yes, your excellency. But it is in gaseous condition. One would almost believe that a planet-wrecker had—"

"Enough!" Without waiting to hear the rest, he switched off.

Lying back in his chair, he brooded in complete disregard of the fact that his mind was wide open to some even though not to all. He didn't care who picked up his impressions.

"We may be too late. Possibly we were already too late the day Roka came back. At long last we've fallen into the trap we've always feared, the trap we avoided when we vaporized that world of parasites. Nevertheless, we can still destroy Terra—they can't possibly have taken over every world and every ship and we can still wipe her out. But to what avail? Revenge is sweet only when it's profitable. Will it profit us? It all depends on how many of these people have sneaked into our ranks, and how many more can get in before we destroy their base."

Helman thought, *"This is it! Any fool could tell it had to come sooner or later. Every new world is a risk. We've been lucky to get through four thousand of them without getting in bad. Well, the end could have been worse. At least, these are our own kind and should favor us above all other shapes."*

Melor murmured, "Their hate has weakened, and their fear turns to personal worry. Excepting the Purple One and the Floran. The Purple One, who was amused, is now angry. The Floran, who was interested and amiable, now fears."

"That's because we're not of their shape. Racial antagonisms and color antagonisms are as nothing to the mutual distrust between different shapes. There lies the Empire's weak spot. Every shape desires mastery of its own territory. So far as we're concerned, they can have it," Harold commented.

Putting his glasses back on his nose, Burkinshaw sighed and said, "Since you intend to take over the Empire, our only remaining move is to issue a general order for the immediate destruction of Terra. No matter how many confiscated ships try to thwart my purpose, obedience by one loyal vessel will suffice." His hand reached out toward the televisor switch.

"We aren't taking over your Empire," Harold told him swiftly. "Neither do we wish to do so. We're concerned only that you don't take over our world. All we want is a pact of noninterference in each other's affairs, and the appointment of a few Lingans to act as ambassadors through whom we can maintain such contact as suits us. We want to go our own way along our own path, we've the ability to defend our right to do so, and the present situation is our way of demonstrating the fact. No more than that. If, peevishly, you destroy our world, then, vengefully, we shall disrupt your ramshackle collection of worlds, not with our own strength, but by judiciously utilizing yours! Leave us in peace and we shall leave you in peace."

"Where's our guarantee of that?" asked Burkinshaw cynically. "How do we know that a century of insidious penetration will not follow such a pact?" He stared at the four, his blue eyes shrewd and calculating to a degree not apparent before. "In dealing with us you've been able to use an advantage you possess which Florans, Lingans, Rethrans and others have not got, namely, you know us as surely as you know your own kith and kin." He bent forward. "Likewise, *we* know *you*! If you're of sound and sane mind, you'll absorb gradually what you can't gulp down in one lump. That's the way we acquired the Empire, and that's the way you'll get it."

"We've proved to you that we can take it over," Harold agreed evenly, "and that is our protection. Your distrust is the measure of ours. You'll never know how many of us are within your Empire and you'll never find out—but obliteration of our parent world will no longer obliterate our life form. We have made our own guarantee. Get it into your head, there is no winner in this game. It's stalemate!" He watched interestedly as Burkinshaw's forefinger rested light on the switch. "You're too late, much too late. We don't want your Empire because we're in the same fix—we're too late."

Burkinshaw's eyes narrowed and he said, "I don't see why it's too late for you to do what you've been so anxious to prove you can do."

"The desire doesn't exist. We've greater desires. It's because we have wended our way through a hell of our own creation that we have changed, and our ambitions have changed with us. Why should we care about territorial conquests when we face prospects infinitely greater? Why should we gallivant in spaceships around the petty limits of a galaxy when some day we shall range unhampered through infinity? How d'you think we knew you were coming, and prepared for you, even though we were uncertain of your shape and unsure your intentions?"

"I'm listening," observed Burkinshaw, his fingers still toying with the switch, "but all I hear is words. Despite your many differences from us, which I acknowledge, the ancient law holds good: that shape runs true to shape."

Harold glanced at Burt and George. There was swift communion between them.

Then he said, "Time has been long, and the little angle between the paths of our fathers has opened to a mighty span. Our changes have been violent and many. A world of hard radiation has molded us anew, has made us what you cannot conceive, and you see us in a guise temporarily suitable for our purpose." Without warning, his eyes glowed at the Purple One. "Even that creature, which lives on life force and has been sucking steadily at us all this time, would now be dead had he succeeded in drawing one thin beam of what he craves!"

Burkinshaw didn't bother to look at the purple thing but commented boredly, "The Rethran was an experiment that failed. If he was of any use, he'd have got you long before now." He rubbed his gray side-hairs, kept his hand on the switch. "I grow tired of meaningless noises. You are now hinting that you are no longer our shape. I prefer to believe the evidence of my eyes." His optics sought the miniature time-recorder set in a ring on his finger. "If I switch on, it may mean the end of us all, but you cannot hypnotize a scanner, and the scene registered in this room will be equivalent to my unspoken order—death to Terra! I suspect you of playing for time. We can ill afford further time. I give you one minute to prove that you are now as different from us as is this Floran or this Rethran or that Lingan. If you do so, we'll deal with this matter sensibly and make a pact such as you desire. If not"—he waggled the switch suggestively—"the slaughter starts. We may lose—or we may not. It's a chance we've got to take."

The three Terrestrials made no reply. Their minds were in complete accord and their response was simultaneous.

Dykstra sobbed, "Look! Oh, eternity, look!" then sank to his knees and began to gabble. The purple creature withdrew its eyes right into its head so that it could not see. Burkinshaw's hand came away from the switch; his glasses fell to the floor and lay there, shattered, unheeded. Roka and Helman and the other humans on the Council covered their faces with their hands, which slowly took on a tropical tan.

Only the Floran came upright. It arose to full height, its golden petals completely extended, its greenish arms trembling with ecstasy.

All flowers love the sun.

Minor Ingredient

Astounding, Mach 1956

He dragged his bags and cases out of the car dumped them on the concrete, paid off the driver. Then he turned and looked at the doors that were going to swallow him for four long years.

Big doors, huge ones of solid oak. They could have been the doors of a penitentiary save for what was hand-carved in the center of a great panel. Just a circle containing a four-pointed star. And underneath in small neat letters the words: "God bless you."

Such a motto in such a place looked incongruous, in fact somewhat silly. A star was all right for a badge, yes. Or an engraved, stylized rocketship, yes. But underneath should have been "Onward, Ever Onward" or "Excelsior" or something like that.

He rang the doorbell. A porter appeared, took the bags and cases into a huge ornate hall, asked him to wait a moment. Dwarfed by the immensity of the place he fidgeted around uneasily, refrained from reading the long roll of names embossed upon one wall. Four men in uniform came out of a corridor, marched across the hall in dead-straight line with even step, glanced at him wordlessly and expressionlessly went out the front. He wondered whether they despised his civilian clothes.

The porter reappeared, conducted him to a small room in which a wizened, bald-headed man sat behind a desk. Baldhead gazed at him myopically through old-fashioned and slightly lopsided spectacles.

"May I have your entry papers, please." He took them, sought through them, muttering to himself in an undertone. "Umph, umph! Warner McShane for pilot-navigator course and leader commission." He stood up, offered a thin, soft band. "Glad to meet you, Mr. McShane. Welcome to Space Training College."

"Thank you," said McShane, blank-faced.

"God bless you," said Baldhead. He turned to the waiting porter. "Mr. McShane has been assigned Room Twenty, Mercer's House."

They traipsed across a five-acre square of neatly trimmed grass around which stood a dozen blocks of apartments. Behind them, low and far, could be seen an array of laboratories, engineering shops, test-pits, lecture halls, classrooms and places of yet unknown purpose. Farther still, a mile or more behind those, a model spaceport holding four Earthbound ships cemented down for keeps.

Entering a building whose big lintel was inscribed "Mercer's," they took an elevator to the first floor, reached Room 20. It was compact, modestly furnished but comfortable. A small bedroom led off it to one side, a bathroom on the other.

Stacking the luggage against a wall the porter informed, "Commodore Mercer commands this house, sir, and Mr. Billings is your man. Mr. Billings will be along shortly."

"Thank you," said McShane.

When the porter had gone he sat on the arm of a chair and pondered his arrival. This wasn't quite as expected. The place had a reputation equaled by no other in a hundred solar systems. Its fame rang among the stars, all the way from here to the steadily expanding frontiers. The man fully trained by S. T. C. was somebody, really somebody. The man accepted for training was lucky, the one who got through it was much to be envied.

Grand Admiral Kennedy, supreme commander of all space forces, was a graduate of S. T. C. So were a hundred more now of formidable rank and importance. Things must have changed a lot since their day. The system must have been plenty tough long, long ago but had softened up considerably since. Perhaps the entire staff had been here too long and were suffering from senile decay.

A discreet knock sounded on the door and he snapped, "Come in."

The one who entered looked like visible confirmation of his theory. A bent-backed oldster with a thousand wrinkles at the corners of his eyes and white muttonchop whiskers sticking grotesquely from his cheeks.

"I am Billings, sir. I shall be attending to your needs while you are here." His aged eyes turned to the luggage. "Do you mind if I unpack now, sir?"

"I can manage quite well for myself, thank you." McShane stifled a grim smile. By the looks of it the other stood in more need of helpful service.

"If you will permit me to assist—"

"The day I can't do my own unpacking will be the day I'm paralyzed or dead," said McShane. "Don't trouble yourself for me."

"As you wish, sir, but—"

"Beat it, Billings."

"Permit me to point out, sir, that—"

"No, Billings, you may not point out," declared McShane, very firmly.

"Very well." Billings withdrew quietly and with dignity.

Old fusspot, thought McShane. Heaving a case toward the window he unlocked it, commenced rummaging among its contents. Another knock sounded.

"Come in." The newcomer was tall, stern-featured, wore the full uniform of a commodore. McShane instinctively came erect feet together, hands stiffly at sides.

"Ah, Mr. McShane. Very glad to know you. I am Mercer, your housemaster." His sharp eyes went over the other from head to feet. "I am sure that we shall get along together very well."

"I hope so, sir," said McShane respectfully.

"All that is required of you is to pay full attention to your tutors, work hard, study hard, be obedient to the house rules and loyal to the college."

"Yes, sir."

"Billings is your man, is he not?"

"Yes, sir."

"He should be unpacking for you."

"I told him not to bother, sir."

"Ah, so he has been here already." The eyes studied McShane again, hardening slightly. "And you told him not to bother. Did he accept that?"

"Well, sir, he tried to argue but I chased him out."

"I see." Commodore Mercer firmed his lips, crossed the room, jerked open a top drawer. "You have brought your full kit, I presume. It includes three uniforms as well as working dress. The ceremonial uniforms first and second will be suspended on the right and left-hand sides of the wardrobe, jackets over pants, buttons outward."

He glanced at McShane who said nothing.

"The drill uniform will be placed in this drawer and no other, pants at bottom folded twice only, jacket on top with sleeves doubled across breast, buttons uppermost, collar to the left." He slammed the drawer shut. "Did you know all that? And where everything else goes?"

"No, sir," admitted McShane flushing.

"Then why did you dismiss your man?"

"I thought—"

"Mr. McShane, I would advise to postpone thinking until you have accumulated sufficient facts to form a useful basis. That is the intelligent thing to do, is it not?"

"Yes, sir."

Commodore Mercer went out, closing the door gently. McShane aimed a hearty kick at the wall, muttered something under his breath. Another knock sounded on the door.

"Come in."

"May I help you now, sir?"

"Yes, Billings, I'd appreciate it if you'd unpack for me."

"With pleasure, sir."

He started on the job, putting things away with trained precision. His motions were slow but careful and exact. Two pairs of boots, one of slippers, one of gym shoes aligned on the small shoe rack in the officially approved order. One crimson-lined uniform cloak placed on a hanger, buttons to the front, in the center of the wardrobe.

"Billings," said McShane, after a while, "just what would happen to me if I dumped my boots on the window ledge and chucked my cloak across the bed?"

"Nothing, sir."

"Nothing?" He raised his eyebrows.

"No, sir. But I would receive a severe reprimand."

"I see."

He flopped into a chair, watched Billings and stewed the matter in his mind. They were a cunning bunch in this place. They had things nicely worked out. A tough customer feeling his oats could run wild and take his punishment like a man. But only a louse would do it at the expense of an aged servant.

They don't make officers of lice if they can help it. So they'd got things nicely organized in such a manner that bad material would reveal itself as bad, the good would show up as good. That meant he'd have to walk warily and watch his step. For four years. Four years at the time of life when blood runs hot and surplus energies need an aggressive outlet.

"Billings, when does one eat here?"

"Lunch is at twelve-thirty, sir. You will be able to hear the gong sound from the dining ball. If I may say so, sir, you would do well to attend with the minimum of delay."

"Why? Will the rats get at the food if it has to wait a while?"

"It is considered courteous to be prompt, sir. An officer and a gentleman is always courteous."

"Thank you, Billings." He lifted a quizzical eyebrow. "And just how long have *you* been an officer?"

"It has never been my good fortune, sir."

McShane studied him carefully, said, "If that isn't a rebuke it ought to be."

"Indeed, sir, I would not dream of—"

"When I am rude," interrupted McShane, still watching him, "it is because I am raw. Newcomers usually are more than somewhat raw. At such moments, Billings, I would like you to ignore me."

"I cannot do that, sir. It is my job to look after you. Besides I am accustomed to jocularity from young gentlemen." He dipped into a case, took out a twelve by eight pin-up of Sylvia Lafontaine attired in one small ostrich feather. Holding it at arm length, he surveyed it expressionlessly, without twitching a facial muscle.

"Like it?" asked McShane.

"Most charming, sir. However, It would be unwise to display this picture upon the wall."

"Why not? This is my room, isn't it?"

"Definitely, sir. I fear me the commodore would not approve."

"What has it got to do with him? My taste in females is my own business."

"Without a doubt, sir. But this is an officer's room. An officer must be a gentleman. A gentleman consorts only with ladies."

"Are you asserting that Sylvia is no lady?"

"A lady," declared Billings, very, very firmly, "would never expose her bosom to public exhibition."

"Oh, hell!" said McShane, holding his head.

"If I replace it in your case, sir, I would advise you to keep it locked. Or would you prefer me to dispose of it in the furnace room?"

"Take it home and gloat over it yourself."

"That would be most indecent, sir. I am more than old enough to be this person's father."

"Sorry, Billings." He mooched self-consciously around the room, stopped by the window, gazed down upon the campus. "I've a heck of a lot to learn."

"You'll get through all right, sir. All the best ones get through. I know. I have been here many years. I have seen them come and watched them go and once in a while I've seen them come back."

"Come back?"

"Yes, sir. Occasionally one of them is kind enough to visit us. We had such a one about two months ago. He used to be in this very house, Room 32 on the floor above. A real young scamp but we kept his nose to the grindstone and got him through very successfully." The muttonchop whiskers bristled as his face became suffused with pride. "Today, sir, he is Grand Admiral Kennedy."

The first lectures commenced the following morning and were not listed in the printed curriculum. They were given in the guise of introductory talks. Commodore Mercer made the start in person. Impeccably attired, he stood on a small platform with his authoritative gaze stabbing the forty members of the new intake with such expertness that each felt himself the subject of individual attention.

"You've come here for a purpose—see that it is achieved . . . The trier who fails is a far better man than the failure who has not tried . . . We hate to send a man down but will not hesitate if he lets the college down . . . Get it fixed firmly in your minds that space-navy leadership is not a pleasant game; it is a tough, responsible job and you're here to learn it."

In that strain he carried on a speech evidently made many times before to many previous intakes. It included plenty of gunk about keeping right on to the end of the road, what shall we do with a drunken sailor, the honor of the Space Service, the prestige of the College, the lights in the sky are stars, glory, glory, hallelujah, and so forth.

After an hour of this he finished with, "Technical knowledge is essential. Don't make the mistake of thinking it enough to get top marks in technical examinations. Officers are required to handle men as well as instruments and machines. We have our own ways of checking on your fitness in that respect." He paused, said, "That is all from me, gentlemen. You will now proceed in orderly, manner to the main lecture room where Captain Saunders will deal with you."

Captain Saunders proved to be a powerfully built individual with a leathery face, a flattened nose, and an artificial left hand permanently hidden in a glove. He studied the forty newcomers as though weighing them against their predecessors, emitted a non-committal grunt.

He devoted half an hour to saying most of the things Mercer had said, but in blunter manner. Then, "I'll take you on a tour to familiarize you with the layout. You'll be given a book of rules, regulations and conventions; if you don't read them and observe them, you've only yourselves to blame. Tuition proper will commence at nine-thirty tomorrow morning. Parade in working dress immediately outside your house. Any questions?"

Nobody ventured to put any questions. Saunders led them forth on the tour which occupied the rest of the day. Conscious of their newness and junior status, they absorbed various items of information in complete silence, grinned apologetically at some six hundred second-, third- and fourth-year men hard at work in laboratories and lecture rooms.

Receiving their books of rules and regulations, they attended the evening meal, returned to Mercer's House. By this time McShane had formed a tentative friendship with two fellow sufferers named Simcox and Fane.

"It says here," announced Simcox, mooching along the corridor with his book open in his hands, "that we are confined to college for the first month, after which we are permitted to go to town three evenings per week."

"That means we start off with one month's imprisonment," growled Fane. "Just at the very time when we need a splurge to break the ice."

McShane lowered his voice to a whisper. "You two come to my room, At least we can have a good gab and a few gripes. I've a full bottle of whiskey in the cupboard."

"It's a deal," enthused Fane, his face brightening.

They slipped into Room 20, unobserved by other students. Simcox rubbed his hands together and Fane licked anticipatory lips while McShane went to the cupboard.

"What're we going to use for glasses?" asked Fane, staring around.

"What're we going to use for whiskey?" retorted McShane straightening up and backing away from the cupboard. He looked at them, his face thunderous. "It's not here."

"Maybe you moved it and forgot," suggested Simcox. "Or perhaps your man has stashed it some place where Mercer can't see it."

"Why should he?" demanded Fane, waving his book of rules. "It says nothing about bottles being forbidden."

"I'd better search the place before I blow my top," said McShane, still grim. He did just that and did it thoroughly. "It's gone. Some dirty scut swiped it."

"That means we've a thief in the house," commented Simcox unhappily. "The staff ought to be told."

Fane consulted his book again. "According to this, complaints and requests must be taken to the House Proctor, a fourth-year man residing in Room 1."

"All right, watch me dump this in his lap." McShane bolted out, down the stairs, hammered on the door of Room 1.

"Come in."

He entered. The proctor, a tall, dark-haired fellow in the mid-twenties, was reclining in a chair, legs crossed, a heavy book before him. His dark eyes coldly viewed the visitor.

"Your name?"

"Warner McShane."

"Mr. McShane, you will go outside, close the door, knock in a way that credits me with normal hearing, and re-enter in proper manner."

McShane went red. "I regret to say I am not aware of what you consider the proper manner."

"You will march in at regulation pace, halt smartly, and stand at attention while addressing me."

Going out, McShane did exactly as instructed, blank-faced but inwardly seething. He halted, hands stiffly at sides, shoulders squared.

"That's better," said the proctor. His gaze was shrewd as he surveyed the other. "Possibly you think I got malicious satisfaction out of that?"

No reply.

"If so, you're wrong. You're learning exactly as I learned—the hard way. An officer must command obedience by example as well as by authority. He must be willing to give to have the right to receive." Another pause inviting comment that did not come. "Well, what's your trouble?"

"A bottle of whiskey has been stolen from my room."

"How do you know that it stolen?"

"It was there this morning. It isn't there now. Whoever took it did so without my knowledge and permission. That is theft."

"Not necessarily. Your man may have removed it."

"It's still theft."

"Very well. It will be treated as such if you insist." His bearing lent peculiar significance to his final question. "Do you insist?"

McShane's mind whirled around at superfast pace. The darned place was a trap. The entire college was carpeted with traps. This very question was a trap. Evade it! Get out of it while the going is good!

"If you don't mind, I'll first ask my man whether he took it and why."

The change in the proctor was remarkable. He beamed at the other as he said, "I am very glad to hear you say that."

McShane departed with the weird but gratifying feeling that in some inexplicable way he had gained a small victory, a positive mark on his record-sheet that might cancel out an unwittingly-earned negative mark. Going upstairs, he reached his door, bawled down the corridor, "Billings! Billings!" then went into his room.

"Two minutes passed before Billings appeared. "You called me, sir?"

"Yes, I did. I had a bottle of whiskey in the cupboard. It has disappeared. Do you know anything about it?"

"Yes, sir. I removed it myself."

"Removed it?" McShane threw Simcox and Fane a look of half-suppressed exasperation. "What on earth for?"

"I have obtained your first issue of technical books and placed them on the rack in readiness, sir. It would be advisable to commence your studies at once, if I may say so."

"Why the rush?"

"The examination at the end of the first month is designed to check on the qualifications that new entrants are alleged to possess. Occasionally they prove not to the complete satisfaction of the college. In such a case, the person concerned is sent home as unsuitable." The old eye acquired a touch of desperation. "You will have to pass, sir. It is extremely important. You will pardon me for saying that an officer can manage without drink when it is expedient to do so."

Taking a deep breath, McShane asked, "Exactly what have you done with the bottle?"

"I have concealed it, sir, in a place reserved by the staff for that purpose."

"And don't I ever get it back?"

Billings was shocked. "Please understand, sir, that the whiskey has been removed and not confiscated. I will be most happy to return it in time for you to celebrate your success in the examination."

"Get out of my sight," said McShane.

"Very well, sir."

When he had gone, McShane told the others, "See what I've got? It's worse than living with a maiden aunt."

"Mine's no better," said Fane gloomily.

"Mine neither," endorsed Simcox

"Well, what are we going to do about it, if anything?" McShane invited.

They thought it over and after a while Simcox said, "I'm taking the line of least resistance." He raised his tone to passable imitation of childish treble. "I am going to go home and do my sums because my Nanny will think I'm naughty if I don't."

"Me, too," Fane decided. "A officer and a gentleman, sir, never blows his nose with a ferocious blast. Sometimes the specimen I've got scares hell out of me. One spit on the floor and you're expelled with ignominy."

They ambled out, moody-faced. McShane flung himself into a chair, spent twenty minutes scowling at the wall. Then, becoming bored with that, he reached for the top book in the stack. It was thrillingly titled *"Astromathematical Foundations of Space Navigation."* It looked ten times drier than a bone. For lack of anything else to do, he stayed with it. He became engrossed despite himself. He was still with it at midnight, mentally bulleting through the starwhorls and faraway mists of light.

Billings tapped on the door-panels, looked in, murmured apologetically, "I realized that you are not yet in bed, sir, and wondered whether you had failed to notice the time. It is twelve o'clock. If I may make so bold—"

He ducked out fast as McShane hurled the book at him.

Question Eleven: The motto of the Space Training College is *"God Bless You."* As briefly as possible explain its origin and purpose.

McShane scribbled rapidly. "The motto is based upon three incontrovertible points. Firstly, a theory need not be correct or even visibly sensible; it is sufficient for it to be workable. Secondly, any life form definable as intelligent must have imagination and curiosity. Thirdly, any life form possessed of imagination and curiosity cannot help but speculate about prime causes."

He sharpened his thoughts a bit, went on, "Four hundred years ago a certain Captain Anderson, taking a brief vacation on Earth, stopped to listen to a religious orator who was being heckled by several members of the audience. He noticed that the orator answered every witticism and insult with the words, 'God bless you, brother!' and that the critics lacked an effective reply. He also noted that in a short time the interrupters gave up their efforts one by one, eventually leaving the orator to continue unhampered."

What next? He chewed his pen, then, "Captain Anderson, an eccentric but shrewd character, was sufficiently impressed to try the same tactic on alien races encountered in the cosmos. He found that it worked nine times out of ten. Since then it has been generally adopted as a condensed, easily employed and easily understood form of space-diplomacy."

He looked it over. Seemed all right but not quite enough. The question insisted upon brevity but it had to be answered in full, if at all.

"The tactic has not resolved all differences or averted all space wars but, it is workable in that it has reduced both to about ten per cent of the potential number. The words 'God bless you' are neither voiced nor interpreted in conventional Earth terms. From the cosmic viewpoint they may be said to mean, 'May the prime cause of everything be beneficial to you!' "

Yes, that looked all right. He read it right through, felt satisfied, was about to pass on to the next question when a tiny bubble of suspicion lurking deep in his subconscious suddenly rose to the surface and burst with a mentally hearable pop.

The preceding ten questions and the following ones all inquired about subjects on which he was supposed to be informed. Question Eleven did not. Nobody at any time had seen fit to explain the college motto. The examiners had no right to assume that any examinee could answer it.

So why had they asked? It now became obvious—they were still trapping.

Impelled by curiosity, he, McShane, had looked up the answer in the college library, this Holy Joe aspect of space travel being too much to let pass unsolved. But for that he'd have been stuck.

The implication was that anyone unable to deal with Question Eleven would be recognized as lacking in curiosity and disinterested. Or, if interested, too lazy and devoid of initiative to do anything about it.

He glanced surreptitiously around the room in which forty bothered figures were seated at forty widely separated desks. About a dozen examinees were writing or pretending to do so. One was busily training his left ear to droop to shoulder level. Four were masticating their digits. Most of the others were feeling around their own skulls as if seeking confirmation of the presence or absence of brains.

The discovery of one trap slowed him up considerably. He reconsidered all the questions already answered treating each one as a potential pitfall. The unanswered questions got the same treatment.

Number Thirty-four looked mighty suspicious. It was planted amid a series of technical queries from which it stuck out like a Sirian's prehensile nose. It was much too artless for comfort. All it said was: In not more than six words define courage.

Well, for better or for worse here goes. "Courage is fear faced with resolution."

He wiped off the fiftieth question with vast relief, left the room, wandered thoughtfully around the campus.

Simcox joined him in short time asked, "How did it go with you?"

"Could have been worse."

"Yes, that's how I felt about it. If you don't hit the minimum of seventy-five per cent, you're out on your neck. I think I've made it all right."

They waited until Fane arrived. He came half an hour later and wore the sad expression of a frustrated spaniel.

"I got jammed on four stinkers. Every time there's an exam I go loaded with knowledge that evaporates the moment I sit down."

Two days afterward the results went up on the board. McShane muscled through the crowd and took a look.

McShane, Warner. 91%. Pass with credit.

He sprinted headlong for Mercer's House, reached his room with Simcox and Fane panting at his heels.

"Billings! Hey, Billings!"

"You want me, sir?"

"We got through. All three of us," He performed a brief fandango. "Now's the time. The bottle, man. Come on, give with that bottle."

"I am most pleased to learn of your success, sir," said Billings, openly tickled pink.

"Thank you, Billings. And now's the time to celebrate. Get us the bottle and some glasses."

"At eight-thirty, sir."

McShane glanced at his watch. "Hey, that's in one hour's time. What's the idea?"

"I have readied paper and envelopes on your desk, sir. Naturally you will wish to inform your parents of the result. Your mother especially will be happy to learn of your progress."

"My mother especially?" McShane stared at him. "Why not my father?"

"Your father will be most pleased also," assured Billings. "But generally speaking, sir, mothers tend to be less confident and more anxious."

"That comes straight from one who knows," commented McShane for the benefit of the others. He returned attention to Billings. "How long have you been a mother?"

"For forty years, sir."

The three went silent. McShane's features softened and his voice became unusually gentle.

"I know what you mean, Billings. We'll have our little party just when you say."

"At eight-thirty to the minute, sir," said Billings. "I will bring glasses and soda."

He departed, Simcox and Fane following. McShane brooded out the window for a while, then went to his desk, reached for pen and paper.

"Dear Mother—"

The long, vast, incredibly complicated whirl of four years sufficiently jam-packed to simulate a lifetime. Lectures, advice, the din of machine shops, the deafening roar of testpits, banks of instruments with winking lights and flickering needles, starfields on the cinema screen, equations six pages long, ball games, ceremonial parades with bands playing and banners flying, medical check-ups, bloodcounts, blackouts in the centrifuge, snap questions, examinations.

More examinations, more stinkers, more traps. More lectures each deeper than its predecessor. More advice from all quarters high and low.

"You've got to be saturated with a powerful and potent education to handle space and all its problems. We're giving you a long, strong dose of it here. It's a very complex medicine of which every number of the staff is a part. Even your personal servant is a minor ingredient."

"The moment you take up active service as an officer every virtue and every fault is enlarged ten diameters by those under you. A little conceit then gets magnified into insufferable arrogance."

"The latter half of the fourth year is always extremely wearing, sir. May I venture to suggest that a little less relaxation in the noisiest quarter of town and a little more in bed—"

"You fellows must get it into your heads that it doesn't matter a hoot whether you've practiced it fifty or five hundred times. You aren't good enough until you've reduced it to an instinctive reaction. A ship and a couple of hundred men can go to hell while you're seeking time for thought."

"Even your personal servant is a minor ingredient."

"If I may be permitted the remark, sir, an officer is only as strong as the men who support him."

For the last six months McShane functioned as House Proctor of Mercer's, a dignified and learned figure to be viewed with becoming reverence by young and brash first-year men, Simcox and Fane were still with him but the original forty were down to twenty-six.

The final examination was an iron-cased, red-hot heller. It took eight days.

McShane, Warner. 82%. Pass with credit.

After that, a week of wild confusion dominated by a sense of an impending break, of something about to snap loose. Documents, speeches, the last parade with thudding feet and *oompah-oompah,* relatives crowding around, mothers, brothers, sisters in their Sunday best, bags, cases and boxes packed, cheers, handshakes, a blur of faces saying things not heard. And then an aching silence broken only by the purr of the departing car.

He spent a nervy, restless fortnight at home, kissed farewells with a hidden mixture of sadness and relief, reported on the assigned date to the survey-frigate *Manasca.* Lieutenant McShane, fourth officer, with three men above him, thirty below.

The *Manasca* soared skyward, became an unseeable dot amid the mighty concourse of stars. Compared with the great battleships and heavy cruisers roaming the far reaches she was a tiny vessel—but well capable of putting Earth beyond communicative distance and almost beyond memory.

It was a long, imposing, official-looking car with two men sitting erect in the front, its sole passenger in the back. With a low hum it came up the drive and stopped. One of the men in front got out, opened the rear door, posed stiffly at attention.

Dismounting, the passenger walked toward the great doors which bore a circled star on one panel. He was a big man, wise-eyed, gray-haired. The silver joint under his right kneecap made him move with a slight limp.

Finding the doors ajar, he pushed one open, entered a big hall. Momentarily it was empty. For some minutes he studied the long roster of names embossed upon one wall.

Six uniformed men entered from a corridor, marching with even step in two ranks of three. They registered a touch of awe and their arms snapped up in a sixfold salute to which he responded automatically.

Limping through the hall, he found his way out back, across the campus to what once had been Mercer's House. A different name, Lysaght's, was engraved upon its lintel now. Going inside, he reached the first floor, stopped undecided in the corridor.

A middle-aged civilian came into the corridor from the other end, observed him with surprise, hastened up.

"I am Jackson, sir. May I help you?"

The other hesitated, said, "I have a sentimental desire to look out the window of Room Twenty."

Jackson's features showed immediate understanding as he felt in his pocket and produced a master key. "Room Twenty is Mr. Cain's, sir. I know he would be only too glad to have you look around. I take it that it was once your own room, sir?"

"Yes, Jackson, about thirty year ago."

The door clicked open and he walked in. For five minutes he absorbed the old, familiar scene.

"Thirty years ago," standing in the doorway. "That would be in Commodore Mercer's time."

"That's right. Did you know him?"

"Oh yes, sir." He smiled deprecatingly. "I was just a boy message-runner then. It's unlikely that you ever encountered me."

"Probably you remember Billings, too?"

Yes, indeed." Jackson's face lit up. "A most estimable person, sir. He has been dead these many years." He saw the other's expression, added, "I am very sorry, sir."

"So am I." A pause. "I never said good-by to him."

"Really, sir, you need have no regrets about that, When a young gentleman passes his final and leaves us we expect great excitement and a little forgetfulness. It is quite natural and we are accustomed to it." He smiled reassurance. "Besides, sir, soon after one goes another one comes. We have plenty to keep us busy."

"I'm sure you have."

"If you've sufficient time to spare, sir," continued Jackson, "would you care to visit the staff quarters?"

"Aren't they out of bounds?"

"Not to you, sir. We have a modest collection of photographs going back many years. Some of them are certain to interest you."

"I would much like to see them."

They walked downstairs, across to staff quarters, entered a lounge. Carefully Jackson positioned a chair, placed a large album on a table.

"While you are looking through this, sir, may I prepare you some coffee?"

"Thank you, Jackson. It is very kind of you."

He opened the album as the other went to the kitchens. First page: a big photo of six hundred men marching in column of platoons. The saluting-base in the mid-background, the band playing on the left.

The next twenty pages depicted nobody he had known. Then came one of a group of house-masters among whom was Commodore Mercer. Then several clusters of staff members, service and tutorial, among which were a few familiar faces.

Then came a campus shot. One of the figures strolling across the grass was Fane. The last he'd seen of Fane had been twelve years back, out beyond Aldebaran. Fane had been lying in hospital, his skin pale green, his body bloated, but cheerful and on the road to recovery. He'd seen nothing of Fane since that day. He'd seen nothing of Simcox for thirty years and had heard of him only twice.

The middle of the book held an old face with a thousand wrinkles at the corners of its steady, understanding eyes, with muttonchop whiskers on its cheeks. He looked at that one a long time while it seemed to come at him out of the mists of the past.

"If I may say so, sir, an officer and a gentleman is never willfully unkind."

He was still meditating over the face when the sounds of distant footsteps and a rattling coffee tray brought him back to the present.

Squaring his gold-braided shoulders, Fleet Commander McShane said in soft, low tones, "God bless you!"

And turned the page.

Now Inhale

Astounding, April 1959

His leg irons clanked and his wrist chains jingled as they led him into the room. The bonds on his ankles compelled him to move at an awkward shuffle and the guards delighted in urging him onward faster than he could go. Somebody pointed to a chair facing the long table. Somebody else shoved him into it with such force that he lost balance and sat down hard.

The black brush of his hair jerked as his scalp twitched and that was his only visible reaction. Then he gazed across the desk with light gray eyes so pale that the pupils seemed set in ice. The look in them was neither friendly nor hostile, submissive nor angry; it was just impassively and impartially cold, cold.

On the other side of the desk seven Gombarians surveyed him with various expressions: triumph, disdain, satisfaction, boredom, curiosity, glee and arrogance. They were a humanoid bunch in the same sense that gorillas are humanoid. At that point the resemblance ended.

"Now," began the one in the middle, making every third syllable a grunt, "your name is Wayne Taylor?"

No answer.

"You have come from a planet called Terra?"

No response.

"Let us not waste any more time, Palamin," suggested the one on the left. "If he will not talk by invitation, let him talk by compulsion."

"You are right, Eckster." Putting a hand under the desk Palamin came up with a hammer. It had a pear-shaped head with flattened base. "How would you like every bone in your hands cracked finger by finger, joint by joint?"

"I wouldn't," admitted Wayne Taylor.

"A very sensible reply," approved Palamin. He placed the hammer in the middle of the desk, positioning it significantly. "Already many days have been spent teaching you our language. By this time a child could have learned it sufficiently well to understand and answer questions." He favored the prisoner with a hard stare. "You have pretended to be abnormally slow to learn. But you can deceive us no longer. You will now provide all the information for which we ask."

"Willingly or unwillingly," put in Eckster, licking thin lips, "but you'll provide it anyway."

"Correct," agreed Palamin. "Let us start all over again and see if we can avoid painful scenes. Your name is Wayne Taylor and you come from a planet called Terra?"

"I admitted that much when I was captured."

"I know. But you were not fluent at that time and we want no misunderstandings. Why did you land on Gombar?"

"I've told my tutor at least twenty times that I did it involuntarily. It was an emergency landing. My ship was disabled."

"Then why did you blow it up? Why did you not make open contact with us and invite us to repair it for you?"

"No Terran vessel must be allowed to fall intact into hostile hands," said Taylor flatly.

"Hostile?" Palamin tried to assume a look of pained surprise but his face wasn't made for it. "Since you Terrans know nothing whatever about us what right have you to consider us hostile?"

"I wasn't kissed on arrival," Taylor retorted. "I was shot at coming down. I was shot at getting away. I was hunted across twenty miles of land, grabbed and beaten up."

"Our soldiers do their duty," observed Palamin virtuously.

"I'd be dead by now if they were not the lousiest marksmen this side of Cygni."

"And what is Cygni?"

"A star."

"Who are you to criticize our soldiers?" interjected Eckster, glowering.

"A Terran," informed Taylor as if that were more than enough.

"That means nothing to me," Eckster gave back with open contempt.

"It will."

Palamin took over again. "If friendly contact were wanted the Terran authorities would send a large ship with an official deputation on board, wouldn't they?"

"I don't think so."

"Why not?"

"We don't risk big boats and important people without knowing what sort of a reception they're likely to get."

"And who digs up that information?"

'Space scouts."

"Ah!" Palamin gazed around with the pride of a pygmy who has trapped an elephant. "So at last you admit that you are a spy?"

"I am a spy only in the estimation of the hostile."

"On the contrary," broke in a heavily jowled specimen seated on the right, "you are whatever we say you are—because we say it."

"Have it your own way," conceded Taylor.

"We intend to."

"You can be sure of that, my dear Borkor," soothed Palamin. He returned attention to the prisoner. "How many Terrans are there in existence?"

"About twelve thousand millions."

"He is lying," exclaimed Borkor, hungrily eyeing the hammer.

"One planet could not support such a number," Eckster contributed.

"They are scattered over a hundred planets," said Taylor.

"He is still lying," Borkor maintained.

Waving them down, Palamin asked, "And how many ships have they got ?"

"I regret that mere space scouts are not entrusted with fleet statistics," replied Taylor coolly. "I can tell you only that I haven't the slightest idea."

"You must have *some* idea."

"If you want guesses, you can have them for what they are worth."

"Then make a guess."

"One million."

"Nonsense!" declared Palamin. "Utterly absurd!"

"All right. One thousand. Or any other number you consider reasonable."

"This is getting us nowhere," Borkor complained.

Palamin said to the others, "What do you expect? If we were to send a spy to Terra would we fill him up with top-secret information to give the enemy when caught? Or would we tell him just enough and only enough to enable him to carry out his task? The ideal spy is a shrewd ignoramus, able to take all, unable to give anything."

"The ideal spy wouldn't be trapped in the first place," commented Eckster maliciously.

"Thank you for those kind words," Taylor chipped in. "If I had come here as a spy, you'd have seen nothing of my ship much less me."

"Well, exactly where were you heading for when forced to land on Gombar?" invited Palamin.

"For the next system beyond."

"Ignoring this one?"

"Yes."

"Why?"

"I go where I'm told."

"Your story is weak and implausible." Palamin lay back and eyed him judicially. "It is not credible that a space explorer should bypass one system in favor of another that is farther away."

"I was aiming for a binary said to have at least forty planets," said Taylor. "This system has only three. Doubtless it was considered relatively unimportant."

"What, with us inhabiting all three worlds?"

"How were we to know that? Nobody has been this way before."

"They know it now," put in Eckster, managing to make it sound sinister.

"This one knows it," Palamin corrected. "The others do not. And the longer they don't, the better for us. When another life form starts poking its snout into our system we need time to muster our strength."

This brought a murmur of general agreement.

"It's your state of mind," offered Taylor.

"What d'you mean?"

"You're taking it for granted that a meeting must lead to a clash and in turn to a war."

"We'd be prize fools to assume anything else and let ourselves be caught unprepared," Palamin pointed out.

Taylor sighed. "To date we have established ourselves on a hundred planets without a single fight. The reason: we don't go where we're not wanted."

"I can imagine that," Palamin gave back sarcastically. "Someone tells you to beat it and you obligingly beat it. It's contrary to instinct."

"Your instinct," said Taylor. "We see no sense in wasting time and money fighting when we can spend both exploring and exploiting."

"Meaning that your space fleets include no warships?"

"Of course we have warships."

"Many?"

"Enough to cope."

"Pacifists armed to the teeth," said Palamin to the others. He registered a knowing smile.

"Liars are always inconsistent," pronounced Eckster with an air of authority. He fixed a stony gaze upon the prisoner. "If you are so careful to avoid trouble, why do you *need* warships?"

"Because we have no guarantee that the entire cosmos shares our policy of live and let live."

"Be more explicit."

"We chivvy nobody. But someday somebody may take it into their heads to chivvy us."

"Then you will start a fight ?"

"No. The other party will have started it. We shall finish it."

"Sheer evasion," scoffed Eckster to Palamin and the rest. "The technique is obvious to anyone but an idiot. They settle themselves upon a hundred planets—if we can believe that number, which I don't! On most there is no opposition because nobody is there to oppose. On the others the natives are weak and backward, know that a struggle is doomed to failure and therefore offer none. But on any planet sufficiently strong and determined to resist—such as Gombar for instance—the Terrans will promptly treat that resistance as unwarranted interference with themselves. They will say they are being chivvied. It will be their moral justification for a war.

Palamin looked at Taylor. "What do you say to that?"

Giving a deep shrug, Taylor said, "That kind of political cynicism has been long out of date where I come from. I can't help it if mentally you're about ten millennia behind us."

"Are we going to sit here and allow ourselves to be insulted by a prisoner in chains?" Eckster angrily demanded of Palamin. "Let us recommend that he be executed. Then we can all go home. I for one have had enough of this futile rigmarole."

Another said, "Me, too." He looked an habitual me-tooer.

"Patience," advised Palamin. He spoke to Taylor. "You claim that you were under orders to examine the twin system of Halor and Ridi?"

"If by that you mean the adjacent binary, the answer is yes. That was my prescribed destination."

"Let us suppose that instead you had been told to take a look over our Gombarian system. Would you have done so?"

"I obey orders."

"You would have come upon us quietly and surreptitiously for a good snoop around?"

"Not necessarily. If my first impression had been one of friendliness, I'd have presented myself openly."

"He is dodging the question," insisted Eckster, still full of ire.

"What would you have done if you had been uncertain of our reaction?" continued Palamin.

"What anyone else would do," Taylor retorted. "I'd hang around until I'd got the measure of it one way or the other."

"Meanwhile taking care to evade capture?"

"Of course."

"And if you had not been satisfied with our attitude you'd have reported us as hostile?"

"Potentially so."

"That is all we require," decided Palamin. "Your admissions are tantamount to a confession that you are a spy. It does not matter in the least whether you were under orders to poke your inquisitive nose into this system or some other system, you are still a spy." He turned to the others. "Are we all agreed?"

They chorused, "Yes."

"There is only one proper fate for such as you," Palamin finished. "You will be returned to your cell pending official execution." He made a gesture of dismissal. "Take him away."

The guards took him by simple process of jerking the chair from under him and kicking him erect. They tried to rush him out faster than he could go, he stumbled in his leg irons and almost fell. But he found time to throw one swift glance back from the doorway and his strangely pale eyes looked frozen.

When the elderly warder brought in his evening meal, Taylor asked, "How do they execute people here?"

"How do they do it where you come from?"

"We don't."

"You don't?" The warder blinked in amazement. Putting the tray on the floor, he took a seat on the bench beside Taylor and left the heavily-barred grille wide open. The butt of his gun protruded from its holster within easy reach of the prisoner's grasp. "Then how do you handle dangerous criminals?"

"We cure the curable by whatever means are effective no matter how drastic, including brain surgery. The incurable we export to a lonely planet reserved exclusively for them. There they can fight it out between themselves."

"What a waste of a world," opined the warder. In casual manner he drew his gun, pointed it at the wall and pressed the button. Nothing happened. "Empty," he said.

Taylor made no remark.

"No use you snatching it. No use you running for it. The armored doors, multiple locks and loaded guns are all outside."

"I'd have to get rid of these manacles before I could start something with any hope of success," Taylor pointed out. "Are you open to bribery?"

"With what? You have nothing save the clothes you're wearing. And even those will be burned after you're dead."

"All right, forget it." Taylor rattled his irons loudly and looked disgusted. "You haven't yet told me how I'm to die."

"Oh, you'll be strangled in public," informed the warder. He smacked his lips for no apparent reason. "All executions take place in the presence of the populace. It is not enough that justice be done, it must also be seen to be done. So everybody sees it. And it has an excellent disciplinary effect." Again the lip smacking. "It is quite a spectacle."

"I'm sure it must be."

"You will be made to kneel with your back to a post, your arms and ankles tied behind it," explained the warder in tutorial manner. "There is a hole drilled through the post at the level of your neck. A loop of cord goes round your neck, through the hole and around a stick on the other side. The executioner twists the stick, thereby tightening the loop quickly or slowly according to his mood."

"I suppose that when he feels really artistic he prolongs the agony quite a piece by slackening and retightening the loop a few times?" Taylor ventured.

"No, no, he is not permitted to do that," assured the warden, blind to the sarcasm. "Not in a final execution. That method is used only to extract confessions from the stubborn. We are a fair-minded and tender-hearted people, see?"

"You're a great comfort to me," said Taylor.

"So you will be handled swiftly and efficiently. I have witnessed many executions and have yet to see a sloppy, badly performed one. The body heaves and strains against its bonds, the eyes stick out, the tongue protrudes and turns black and complete collapse follows. The effect is invariably the same and is a tribute to the executioner's skill. Really you have nothing to worry about, nothing at all."

"Looks like I haven't, the way you put it," observed Taylor dryly. "I'm right on top of the world without anything to lose except my breath." He brooded a bit, then asked, "*When* am I due for the noose?"

"Immediately after you've finished your game," the warder informed.

Taylor eyed him blankly. "Game? What game? What do you mean?"

"It is conventional to allow a condemned man a last game against a skilled player chosen by us. When the game ends he is taken away and strangled."

"Win or lose?"

"The result makes no difference. He is executed regardless of whether he is the winner or the loser."

"Sounds crazy to me," said Taylor frowning.

"It would, being an alien," replied the warder. "But surely you'll agree that a person facing death is entitled to a little bit of consideration if only the privilege of putting up a last minute fight for his life."

"A pretty useless fight."

"That may be. But every minute of delay is precious to the one concerned." The warder rubbed hands together appreciatively. "I can tell you that nothing is more exciting, more thrilling than a person's death-match against a clever player."

"Is that so?"

"Yes. You see, he cannot possibly play in normal manner. For one thing, his mind is obsessed by his impending fate while his opponent is bothered by no such burden. For another, he dare not let the other win—and he dare not let him lose, either. He has to concentrate all his faculties on preventing a decisive result and prolonging the game as much as possible. And, of course, all the time he is mentally and morally handicapped by the knowledge that the end is bound to come."

"Bet it gives you a heck of a kick," said Taylor.

The warder sucked his lips before smacking them. "Many a felon have I watched playing in a cold sweat with the ingenuity of desperation. Then at last the final move. He has fainted and rolled off his chair. We've carried him out as limp as an empty sack. He has come to his senses on his knees facing a crowd waiting for the first twist."

"It isn't worth the bother," decided Taylor. "No player can last long."

"Usually they don't but I've known exceptions, tough and expert gamesters who've managed to postpone death for four or five days. There was one fellow, a professional *alizik* player, who naturally chose his own game and contrived to avoid a decision for sixteen days. He was so good it was a pity he had to die. A lot of video-watchers were sorry when the end came."

"Oh, so you put these death-matches on the video?"

"It's the most popular show. Pins them in their chairs, I can tell you."

"Hm-m-m!" Taylor thought a bit, asked, "Suppose this video-star had been able to keep the game on the boil for a year or more, would he have been allowed to do so?"

"Of course. Nobody can be put to death until he has completed his last game. You could call it a superstition, I suppose. What's more, the rule is that he gets well fed while playing. If he wishes he can eat like a king. All the same, they rarely eat much."

"Don't they?"

"No—they're so nervous that their stomachs refuse to hold a square meal. Occasionally one of them is actually sick in the middle of a game. When I see one do that I know he won't last another day."

"You've had plenty of fun in your time," Taylor offered.

"Quite often," the warder admitted. "But not always. Bad players bore me beyond description. They give the video-watchers the gripes. They start a game, fumble it right away, go to the strangling-post and that's the end of them. The greatest pleasure for all is when some character makes a battle of it."

"Fat chance I've got. I know no Gombarian games and you people know no Terran ones."

"Any game can be learned in short time and the choice is yours. Naturally you won't be permitted to pick one that involves letting you loose in a field without your irons. It has to be something that can be played in this cell. Want some good advice?"

"Give."

"This evening an official will arrive to arrange the contest after which he will find you a suitable partner. Don't ask to be taught one of our games. No matter how clever you may try to be your opponent will be better because he'll be handling the familiar while you're coping with the strange. Select one of your own planet's games and thus give yourself an advantage."

"Thanks for the suggestion. It might do me some good if defeat meant death—but victory meant life."

"I've told you already that the result makes no difference."

"There you are then. Some choice, huh?"

"You can choose between death in the morning and death the morning after or even the one after that." Getting up from the bench, the warder walked out, closed the grille, said through the bars, "Anyway, I'll bring you a book giving full details of our indoor games. You'll have plenty of time to read it before the official arrives."

"Nice of you," said Taylor. "But I think you're wasting your time."

Left alone, Wayne Taylor let his thoughts mill around. They weren't pleasant ones. Space scouts belonged to a high-risk profession and none knew it better than themselves. Each and every one cheerfully accepted the dangers on the ages-old principle that it always happens to the other fellow, never to oneself. But now it had happened and to him. He ran a forefinger around the inside of his collar which felt a little tight.

When he'd dived through the clouds with two air-machines blasting fire to port and starboard he had pressed alarm button D. This caused his transmitter to start flashing a brief but complicated number giving his coordinates and defining the planet as enemy territory.

Earlier and many thousands of miles out in space he had reported his intention of making an emergency landing and identified the chosen world with the same coordinates. Button D, therefore, would confirm his first message and add serious doubts about his fate. He estimated that between the time he'd pressed the button and the time he had landed the alarm-signal should have been transmitted at least forty times.

Immediately after the landing he'd switched the delayed-action charge and taken to his heels. The planes were still buzzing around. One of them swooped low over the grounded ship just as it blew up. It disintegrated in the blast. The other one gained altitude and circled overhead, directing the search. To judge by the speed with which troops arrived he must have had the misfortune to have dumped himself in a military area full of uniformed goons eager for blood. All the same, he'd kept them on the run for six hours and covered twenty miles before they got him. They'd expressed their disapproval with fists and feet.

Right now there was no way of telling whether Terran listening-posts had picked up his repeated D-alarm. Odds were vastly in favor of it since it was a top priority channel on which was kept a round-the-clock watch. He didn't doubt for a moment that, having received the message, they'd do something about it.

The trouble was that whatever they did would come too late. In this very sector patrolled the *Macklin,* Terra's latest, biggest, most powerful battleship. If the *Macklin* happened to be on the prowl, and at her nearest routine point, it would take her ten months to reach Gombar at maximum velocity. If she had returned to port, temporarily replaced by an older and slower vessel, the delay might last two years.

Two years was two years too long. Ten months was too long. He could not wait ten weeks. In fact it was highly probable that he hadn't got ten days. Oh, time, time, how impossible it is to stretch it for a man or compress it for a ship.

The warder reappeared, shoved a book between the bars. "Here you are. You have learned enough to understand it."

"Thanks."

Lying full length on the bench he read right through it swiftly but comprehensively. Some pages he skipped after brief perusal because they described games too short, simple and childish to be worth considering. He was not surprised to find several games that were alien variations of ones well-known upon Terra. The Gombarians had playing cards, for instance, eighty to a pack with ten suits.

Alizik proved to be a bigger and more complicated version of chess with four hundred squares and forty pieces per side. This was the one that somebody had dragged out for sixteen days and it was the only one in the book that seemed capable of such extension. For a while he pondered *Alizik,* wondering whether the authorities—and the video audience—would tolerate play at the rate of one move in ten hours. He doubted it. Anyway, he could not prevent his skilled opponent from making each answering move in five seconds.

Yes, that was what he really wanted: a game that slowed down the other fellow despite his efforts to speed up. A game that was obviously a game and not a gag because any fool could see with half an eye that it was possible to finish it once and for all. Yet a game that the other fellow could not finish, win or lose, no matter how hard he tried.

There wasn't any such game on the three worlds of Gombar or the hundred worlds of Terra or the multimillion worlds yet unfound. There couldn't be because, if there were, nobody would play it. People like results. Nobody is sufficiently cracked to waste time, thought and patience riding a hobbyhorse that got nowhere, indulging a rigmarole that cannot be terminated to the satisfaction of all concerned including kibitzers.

But nobody!

No?

"When the last move is made God's Plan will be fulfilled; on that day and at that hour and at that moment the universe will vanish in a mighty thunderclap."

He got off the bench, his cold eyes expressionless, and began to pace his cell like a restless tiger.

* * * * * * * * *

The official had an enormous potbelly, small, piggy eyes and an unctuous smile that remained permanently fixed. His manner was that of a circus ringmaster about to introduce his best act.

"Ah," he said, noting the book, "so you have been studying our games, eh?"

"Yes."

"I hope you've found none of them suitable."

"Do you?" Taylor surveyed him quizzically. "Why?"

"It would be a welcome change to witness a contest based on something right out of this world. A genuinely new game would give a lot of satisfaction to everybody. Providing, of course," he added hurriedly, "that it was easy to understand and that you didn't win it too quickly."

"Well," said Taylor, "I must admit I'd rather handle something I know than something I don't."

"Good, good!" enthused the other. "You prefer to play a Terran game?"

"That's right."

"There are limitations on your choice."

"What are they?" asked Taylor.

"Once we had a condemned murderer who wanted to oppose his games-partner in seeing who could be the first to catch a sunbeam and put it in a bottle. It was nonsensical. You must choose something that obviously and beyond argument can be accomplished."

"I see."

"Secondly, you may not select something involving the use of intricate and expensive apparatus that will take us a long time to manufacture. If apparatus is needed, it must be cheap and easy to construct."

"Is that all?"

"Yes—except that the complete rules of the game must be inscribed by you unambiguously and in clear writing. Once play begins those rules will be strictly followed and no variation of them will be permitted."

"And who approves my choice after I've described it?"

"I do."

"All right. Here's what I'd like to play." Taylor explained it in detail, borrowed pen and paper and made a rough sketch. When he had finished the other folded the drawing and put it in a pocket.

"A strange game," admitted the official, "but it seems to me disappointingly uncomplicated. Do you really think you can make the contest last a full day?"

"I hope so."

"Even two days perhaps?"

"With luck."

"You'll need it!" He was silent with thought a while, then shook his head doubtfully. "It's a pity you didn't think up something like a better and trickier version of *alizik.* The audience would have enjoyed it and you might have gained yourself a longer lease of life. Everyone would get a great kick out of it if you beat the record for delay before your execution."

"Would they really?"

"They sort of expect something extra-special from an alien life form."

"They're getting it, aren't they?"

"Yes, I suppose so." He still seemed vaguely dissatisfied. "Oh, well, it's your life and your struggle to keep it a bit longer."

"I'll have only myself to blame when the end comes."

"True. Play will commence promptly at midday tomorrow. After that it's up to you."

He lumbered away, his heavy footsteps dying along the corridor. A few minutes later the warder appeared.

"What did you pick?"

"Arky-malarkey."

"Huh? What's that?"

"A Terran game."

"That's fine, real fine." He rubbed appreciative hands together. "He approved it, I suppose?"

"Yes he did."

"So you're all set to justify your continued existence. You'll have to take care to avoid the trap."

"What trap?" Taylor asked.

"Your partner will play to win as quickly and conclusively as possible. That is expected of him. But once he gets it into his head that he can't win he'll start playing to lose. You've no way of telling exactly when he'll change his tactics. Many a one has been caught out by the sudden switch and found the game finished before he had time to realize it."

"But he must keep to the rules, mustn't he?"

"Certainly. Neither you nor he will be allowed to ignore them. Otherwise the game would become a farce."

"That suits me."

Somewhere outside sounded a high screech like that of a bobcat backing into a cactus. It was followed by a scuffle of feet, a dull thud and dragging noises. A distant door creaked open and banged shut.

"What goes? said Taylor.

"Lagartine's game must have ended."

"Who's Lagartine?"

"A political assassin." The warder glanced at his watch. "He chose *ramsid,* a card game. It has lasted a mere four hours. Serves him right. Good riddance to bad rubbish."

"And now they're giving him the big squeeze?"

"Of course." Eyeing him, the warder said, "Nervous?"

"Ha-ha," said Taylor without mirth.

The performance did not commence in his cell as he had expected. A contest involving an alien life form playing an alien game was too big an event for that. They took him through the prison corridors to a large room in which stood a table with three chairs. Six more chairs formed a line against the wall, each occupied by a uniformed plug-ugly complete with hand gun. This was the knock-down-and-drag-out squad ready for action the moment the game terminated.

At one end stood a big, black cabinet with two rectangular portholes through which gleamed a pair of lenses. From it came faint ticking sounds and muffled voices. This presumably contained the video camera.

Taking a chair at the table, Taylor sat down and gave the armed audience a frozen stare. A thin-faced individual with the beady eyes of a rat took the chair opposite. The potbellied official dumped himself in the remaining seat. Taylor and Rat-eyes weighed each other up, the former with cold assurance, the latter with sadistic speculation.

Upon the table stood a board from which arose three long wooden pegs. The left-hand peg held a column of sixty-four disks evenly graduated in diameter, the largest at the bottom, smallest at the top. The effect was that of a tapering tower built from a nursery do-it-yourself kit.

Wasting no time, Potbelly said, "This is the Terran game of Arky-malarkey. The column of disks must be transferred from the peg on which it sits to either of the other two pegs. They must remain graduated in the same order, smallest at the top, biggest at the bottom. The player whose move completes the stack is the winner. Do you both understand?"

"Yes," said Taylor.

Rat-eyes assented with a grunt.

"There are three rules," continued Potbelly, "which will be strictly observed. You will make your moves alternately, turn and turn about. You may move only one disk at a time. You may not place a disk upon any other smaller than itself. Do you both understand?"

"Yes," said Taylor.

Rat-eyes gave another grunt.

From his pocket Potbelly took a tiny white ball and carelessly tossed it onto the table. It bounced a couple of times, rolled across and fell off on Rat-eyes' side.

"You start," he said.

Without hesitation Rat-eyes took the smallest disk from the top of the first peg and placed it on the third.

"Bad move," thought Taylor, blank of face. He shifted the second smallest disk from the first peg to the second.

Smirking for no obvious reason, Rat-eyes now removed the smallest disk from the third peg, placed it on top of Taylor's disk on the second. Taylor promptly switched another disk from the pile on the first peg to the empty third peg.

After an hour of this it had become plain to Rat-eyes that the first peg was not there merely to hold the stock. It had to be used. The smirk faded from his face, was replaced by mounting annoyance as hours crawled by and the situation became progressively more complicated.

By bedtime they were still at it, swapping disks around like crazy, and neither had got very far. Rat-eyes now hated the sight of the first peg, especially when he was forced to put a disk back on it instead of taking one off it. Potbelly, still wearing his fixed, meaningless smile, announced that play would cease until sunrise tomorrow.

The next day provided a long, arduous session lasting from dawn to dark and broken only by two meals. Both players worked fast and hard, setting the pace for each other and seeming to vie with one another in effort to reach a swift conclusion. No onlooker could find cause to complain about the slowness of the game. Four times Rat-eyed mistakenly tried to place a disk on top of a smaller one and was promptly called to order by the referee in the obese shape of Potbelly.

A third, fourth, fifth and sixth day went by. Rat-eyes now played with a mixture of dark suspicion and desperation while the column on the first peg appeared to go up as often as it went down. Though afflicted by his emotions he was no fool. He knew quite well that they were making progress in the task of transferring the column. But it was progress at an appalling rate. What's more, it became worse as time went on. Finally, he could see no way of losing the game, much less winning it.

By the fourteenth day Rat-eyes had reduced himself to an automaton wearily moving disks to and fro in the soulless, disinterested manner of one compelled to perform a horrid chore. Taylor remained as impassive as a bronze Buddha and that fact didn't please Rat-eyes either.

Danger neared on the sixteenth day though Taylor did not know it. The moment he entered the room he sensed an atmosphere of heightened interest and excitement. Rat-eyes looked extra glum. Potbelly had taken on added importance. Even the stolid dull-witted guards displayed faint signs of mental animation. Four off-duty warders joined the audience. There was more activity than usual within the video cabinet.

Ignoring all this, Taylor took his seat and play continued. This endless moving of disks from peg to peg was a lousy way to waste one's life but the strangling-post was lousier. He had every inducement to carry on. Naturally he did so, shifting a disk when his turn came and watching his opponent with his pale gray eyes.

In the midafternoon Rat-eyes suddenly left the table, went to the wall, kicked it good and hard and shouted a remark about the amazing similarity between Terrans and farmyard manure. Then he returned and made his next move. There was some stirring within the video cabinet. Potbelly mildly reproved him for taking time to advertise his patriotism. Rat-eyes went on playing with the surly air of a delinquent whose mother has forgotten to kiss him.

Late in the evening, Potbelly stopped the game, faced the video lenses and said in portentous manner, "Play will resume tomorrow—the seventeenth day!"

He voiced it as though it meant something or other.

When the warder shoved his breakfast through the grille in the morning, Taylor said, "Late, aren't you? I should be at play by now."

"They say you won't be wanted before this afternoon."

"That so? What's all the fuss about?"

"You broke the record yesterday," informed the other with reluctant admiration. "Nobody has ever lasted to the seventeenth day."

"So they're giving me a morning off to celebrate, eh? Charitable of them."

"I've no idea why there's a delay," said the warder. "I've never known them to interrupt a game before."

"You think they'll stop it altogether?" Taylor asked, feeling a constriction around his neck. "You think they'll officially declare it finished?"

"Oh, no, they couldn't do that." He looked horrified at the thought of it. "We mustn't bring the curse of the dead upon us. It's absolutely essential that condemned people should be made to choose their own time of execution."

"Why is it?"

"Because it always has been since the start of time."

He wandered off to deliver other breakfasts, leaving Taylor to stew the explanation. "Because it always has been." It wasn't a bad reason. Indeed, some would consider it a good one. He could think of several pointless, illogical things done on Terra solely because they always had been done. In this matter of unchallenged habit the Gombarians were no better or worse than his own kind.

Though a little soothed by the warder's remarks he couldn't help feeling more and more uneasy as the morning wore on without anything happening. After sixteen days of moving disks from peg to peg it had got so that he was doing it in his sleep. Didn't seem right that he should be enjoying a spell of aimless loafing around his cell. There was something ominous about it.

Again and again he found himself nursing the strong suspicion that officialdom was seeking an effective way of ending the play without appearing to flout convention. When they found it—if they found it—they'd pull a fast one on him, declare the game finished, take him away and fix him up with a very tight necktie.

He was still wallowing in pessimism when the call came in the afternoon. They hustled him along to the same room as before. Play was resumed as if it had never been interrupted. It lasted a mere thirty minutes. Somebody tapped twice on the inside of the video cabinet and Potbelly responded by calling a halt. Taylor went back to his cell and sat there baffled.

Late in the evening he was summoned again. He went with bad grace because these short and sudden performances were more wearing on the nerves than continual day-long ones. Previously he had known for certain that he was being taken to play Arky-malarkey with Rat-eyes. Now he could never be sure that he was not about to become the lead character in a literally breathless scene.

On entering the room he realized at once that things were going to be different this time. The board with its pegs and disks still stood in the center of the table. But Rat-eyes was absent and so was the armed squad. Three people awaited him: Potbelly, Palamin, and a squat, heavily built character who had the peculiar air of being of this world but not with it.

Potbelly was wearing the offended frown of someone burdened with a load of stock in a nonexistent oil well. Palamin looked singularly unpleased and expressed it by snorting like an impatient horse. The third appeared to be contemplating a phenomenon on the other side of the galaxy.

"Sit," ordered Palamin, spitting it out.

Taylor sat.

"Now, Marnikot, you tell him."

The squat one showed belated awareness of being on Gombar, said pedantically to Taylor, "I rarely look at the video. It is suitable only for the masses with nothing better to do."

"Get to the point," urged Palamin.

"But having heard that you were about to break an ages-old record," continued Marnikot, undisturbed, "I watched the video last night." He made a brief gesture to show that he could identify a foul smell at first sniff. "It was immediately obvious to me that to finish your game would require a minimum number of moves of the order of two to the sixty-fourth power minus one." He took flight into momentary dreamland, came back and added mildly, "That is a large number."

"Large!" said Palamin. He let go a snort that rocked the pegs.

"Let us suppose," Marnikot went on, "that you were to transfer these disks one at a time as fast as you could go, morning, noon and night without pause for meals or sleep, do you know how long it would take to complete the game?"

"Nearly six billion Terran centuries," said Taylor as if talking about next Thursday week.

"I have no knowledge of Terran time-terms. But I can tell you that neither you nor a thousand generations of your successors could live long enough to see the end of it. Correct?"

"Correct," Taylor admitted.

"Yet you say that this is a Terran game?"

"I do."

Marnikot spread hands helplessly to show that as far as he was concerned there was nothing more to be said.

Wearing a forbidding scowl, Palamin now took over. "A game cannot be defined as a genuine one unless it is actually played. Do you claim that this so-called game really is played on Terra?"

"Yes."

"By whom?"

"By priests in the Temple of Benares."

"And how long have they been playing it?" he asked.

"About two thousand years."

"Generation after generation?"

"That's right."

"Each player contributing to the end of his days without hope of seeing the result?"

"Yes."

Palamin fumed a bit. "Then *why* do they play it?"

"It's part of their religious faith. They believe that the moment the last disk is placed the entire universe will go bang."

"Are they crazy?"

"No more so than people who have played *alizik* for equally as long and to just as little purpose."

"We have played *alizik* as a series of separate games and not as one never-ending game. A rigmarole without possible end cannot be called a game by any stretch of the imagination."

"Arky-malarkey is not endless. It has a conclusive finish." Taylor appealed to Marnikot as the indisputed authority. "Hasn't it?"

"It is definitely finite," pronounced Marnikot, unable to deny the fact.

"So!" exclaimed Palamin, going a note higher. "You think you are very clever, don't you?"

"I get by," said Taylor, seriously doubting it.

"But we are cleverer," insisted Palamin, using his nastiest manner. "You have tricked us and now we shall trick you. The game is finite. It can be concluded. Therefore it will continue until it reaches its natural end. You will go on playing it days, weeks, months, years until eventually you expire of old age and chronic frustration. There will be times when the very sight of these disks will drive you crazy and you will beg for merciful death. But we shall not grant that favor—and you will continue to play." He waved a hand in triumphant dismissal. "Take him away."

Taylor returned to his cell.

When supper came the warder offered, "I am told that play will go on regularly as from tomorrow morning. I don't understand why they messed it up today."

"They've decided that I'm to suffer a fate worse than death," Taylor informed.

The warder stared at him.

"I have been very naughty," said Taylor.

Rat-eyes evidently had been advised of the new setup because he donned the armor of philosophical acceptance and played steadily but without interest. All the same, long sessions of repetitive motions ate corrosively into the armor and gradually found its way through.

In the early afternoon of the fifty-second day Rat-eyes found himself faced with the prospect of returning most of the disks to the first peg, one by one. He took off the clompers he used for boots. Then he ran barefooted four times around the room, bleating like a sheep. Potbelly got a crick in the neck watching him. Two guards led Rat-eyes away still bleating. They forgot to take his clompers with them.

By the table Taylor sat gazing at the disks while he strove to suppress his inward alarm. What would happen now? If Rat-eyes had given up for keeps it could be argued that he had lost, the game had concluded and the time had come to play okey-chokey with a piece of cord. It could be said with equal truth that an unfinished game remains an unfinished game even though one of the players is in a mental home giving his hair a molasses shampoo.

If the authorities took the former view his only defense was to assert the latter one. He'd have to maintain with all the energy at his command that since he had not won or lost his time could not possibly have come. It wouldn't be easy if he had to make his protest while being dragged by the heels to his doom. His chief hope lay in Gombarian unwillingness to outrage an ancient convention. Millions of video viewers would take a poor look at officialdom mauling a pet superstition. Yes, man, there were times when the Idiot's Lantern had its uses.

He need not have worried. Having decided that to keep the game going would be a highly refined form of hell, the Gombarians had already prepared a roster of relief players drawn from the ranks of minor offenders whose ambitions never rose high enough to earn a strangling. So after a short time another opponent appeared.

The newcomer was a shifty character with a long face and hanging dewlaps. He resembled an especially dopey bloodhound and looked barely capable of articulating three words, to wit, "Ain't talking, copper." It must have taken at least a month to teach him that he must move only one disk at a time and never, never, never place it upon a smaller one. But somehow he had learned. The game went on.

Dopey lasted a week. He played slowly and doggedly as if in fear of punishment for making a mistake. Often he was irritated by the video cabinet which emitted ticking noises at brief but regular intervals. These sounds indicated the short times they were on the air.

For reasons best known to himself Dopey detested having his face broadcasted all over the planet and near the end of the seventh day he'd had enough. Without warning he left his seat, faced the cabinet and made a number of swift and peculiar gestures at the lenses. The signs meant nothing to the onlooking Taylor. But Potbelly almost fell off his chair. The guards sprang forward, grabbed Dopey and frog-marched him through the door.

He was replaced by a huge-jowled, truculent character who dumped himself into the chair, glared at Taylor and wiggled his hairy ears. Taylor, who regarded this feat as one of his own accomplishments, promptly wiggled his own ears back. The other then looked fit to burst a blood vessel.

"This Terran sneak," he roared at Potbelly, "is throwing dirt at me. Do I *have* to put up with that?"

"You will cease to throw dirt," ordered Potbelly.

"I only wiggled my ears," said Taylor.

"That is the same thing as throwing dirt," Potbelly said mysteriously. "You will refrain from doing it and you will concentrate upon the game."

And so it went on with disks being moved from peg to peg hour after hour, day after day, while a steady parade of opponents arrived and departed. Around the two hundredth day Potbelly himself started to pull his chair apart with the apparent intention of building a camp fire in the middle of the floor. The guards led him out. A new referee appeared. He had an even bigger paunch and Taylor promptly named him Potbelly Two.

How Taylor himself stood the soul-deadening pace he never knew. But he kept going while the others cracked. He was playing for a big stake while they were not. All the same, there were times when he awoke from horrid dreams in which he was sinking through the black depths of an alien sea with a monster disk like a millstone around his neck. He lost count of the days and once in a while his hands developed the shakes. The strain was not made any easier by several nighttime uproars that took place during this time. He asked the warder about one of them.

"Yasko refused to go. They had to beat him into submission."

"His game had ended?"

"Yes. The stupid fool matched a five of anchors with a five of stars. Immediately he realized what he'd done. He tried to kill his opponent." He wagged his head in sorrowful reproof. "Such behavior never does them any good. They go to the post cut and bruised. And if the guards are angry with them they ask the executioner to twist slowly."

"Ugh!" Taylor didn't like to think of it. "Surprises me that none have chosen my game. Everybody must know of it by now."

"They are not permitted to," said the warder. "There is now a law that only a recognized Gombarian game may be selected."

He ambled away. Taylor lay full length on his bench and hoped for a silent, undisturbed night. What was the Earth-date? How long had he been here? How much longer would he remain? How soon would he lose control of himself and go nuts? What would they do with him if and when he became too crazy to play?

Often in the thought-period preceding sleep he concocted wild plans of escape. None of them were of any use whatever. Conceivably he could break out of this prison despite its grilles, armored doors, locks, bolts, bars and armed guards. It was a matter of waiting for a rare opportunity and seizing it with both hands. But suppose he got out, what then? Any place on the planet he would be as conspicuous as a kangaroo on the sidewalks of New York. If it were possible to look remotely like a Gombarian, he'd have a slight chance. It was not possible. He could do nothing save play for time.

This he continued to do. On and on and on without cease except for meals and sleep. By the three-hundredth day he had to admit to himself that he was feeling somewhat moth-eaten. By the four-hundredth he was under the delusion that he had been playing for at least five years and was doomed to play forever, come what may. The four-twentieth day was no different from the rest except in one respect of which he was completely unaware—it was the last.

At dawn of day four twenty-one no call came for him to play. Perforce he waited a couple of hours and still no summons. Maybe they'd decided to break him with a cat-and-mouse technique, calling him when he didn't expect it and not calling him when he did. A sort of psychological water torture. When the warder passed along the corridor Taylor went to the bars and questioned him. The fellow knew nothing and was as puzzled as himself.

The midday meal arrived. Taylor had just finished it when the squad of guards arrived accompanied by an officer. They entered the cell and removed his irons. Ye gods, this was something! He stretched his limbs luxuriously, fired questions at the officer and his plug-uglies. They took no notice, behaved as if he had stolen the green eye of the little yellow god. Then they marched him out of the cell, along the corridors and past the games room.

Finally they passed through a large doorway and into an open yard. In the middle of this area stood six short steel posts each with a hole near its top and a coarse kneeling-mat at its base. Stolidly the squad tramped straight toward the posts. Taylor's stomach turned over. The squad pounded on past the posts and toward a pair of gates. Taylor's stomach turned thankfully back and settled itself.

Outside the gates they climbed aboard a troop-carrier which at once drove off. It took him around the outskirts of the city to a spaceport. They all piled out, marched past the control tower and onto the concrete. There they halted.

Across the spaceport, about half a mile away, Taylor could see a Terran vessel sitting on its fins. It was far too small for a warship, too short and fat for a scoutship. After staring at it with incredulous delight he decided that it was a battleship's lifeboat. He wanted to do a wild dance and yell silly things. He wanted to run like mad towards it but the guards stood close around and would not let him move.

They waited there for four long, tedious hours at the end of which another lifeboat screamed down from the sky and landed alongside its fellow. A bunch of figures came out of it, mostly Gombarians. The guards urged him forward.

He was dimly conscious of some sort of exchange ceremony at the half-way mark. A line of surly Gombarians passed him, going the opposite way. Many of them were ornamented with plenty of brass and had the angry faces of colonels come fresh from a general demotion. He recognized one civilian, Borkor, and wiggled his ears at him as he went by.

Then willing hands helped him through an air lock and he found himself sitting in the cabin of a ship going up. A young and eager lieutenant was talking to him but he heard only half of it.

" . . . Landed, snatched twenty and beat it into space. We cross-examined them by signs . . . bit surprised to learn you were still alive . . . released one with an offer to exchange prisoners. Nineteen Gombarian bums for one Terran is a fair swap, isn't it?"

"Yes," said Taylor, looking around and absorbing every mark upon the walls.

"We'll have you aboard the *Thunderer* pretty soon . . . *Macklin* couldn't make it with that trouble near Cygni . . . got here as soon as we could." The lieutenant eyed him sympathetically. "You'll be heading for home within a few hours. Hungry?"

"No, not at all. The one thing they didn't do was starve me."

"Like a drink?"

"Thanks, I don't drink."

Fidgeting around embarrassedly, the lieutenant asked, "Well, how about a nice, quiet game of draughts?"

Taylor ran a finger around the inside of his collar and said, "Sorry, I don't know how to play and don't want to learn. I am allergic to games."

"You'll change."

"I'll be hanged if I do," said Taylor.

Nuisance Value

Astounding, January 1957

The ship was small, streamlined and little better than junk. It lay uselessly in deep grass, its term of service finished and over. The name *Elsie II* was engraved either side of its bow. There was no romantic connection, the cognomen being derived from L.C.2, or Long-range Craft Number Two. At its midpoint it bore the silver star of the Space Union and that meant nothing either—for it was now in enemy possession.

Also in the hands of the foe was the complete crew of seven, all Terrans. They posed in a lugubrious line, tired, fed up, deprived of weapons, and waited for someone to push them around.

Twenty Kastans stood guard over them while three others sought through the ship for anyone who might have remained in hiding. They were very humanlike, these Kastans, except in matter of size. The shortest of them topped the tallest Terran by head and shoulders. They ranged from seven and a half to eight feet in height.

The Terrans waited in glum silence while big, heavy feet tramped through their stricken vessel from bow to stern. Finally an officer squeezed out the air lock, followed by two lesser ranks.

Strolling importantly to the group, the officer spoke to a Kastan whose left sleeve was adorned with three crimson circles. His language seemed to be composed of snorts and grunts. Next, he faced the prisoners and switched to fluent Extralingua.

"Who was in command of this ship?"

"I was," responded Frank Wardle.

"Sir."

Wardle gazed at him cold-eyed.

"Say, 'Sir,' when you speak to me," ordered the officer, impatiently.

"What is your rank?" inquired Wardle, unimpressed.

The other put a spade-sized hand on a holster holding a huge machine-pistol. "That is no concern of yours. You are a prisoner. You will do as you are told—as from now."

"I will say, 'sir,' to an officer of superior rank," informed Wardle in the tones of one who knows his rights. "I will also accept his ruling as to whether or not that form of address is reserved only for military superiors."

Chronic uncertainty afflicted the hearer. Knowing his own superiors he could give a shrewd guess as to whose side they'd take in any dispute concerning their rights and privileges. The curse of being an officer is that one is outranked by other officers. Maybe he'd better let the matter drop, it being a dangerous subject to dwell upon. He glanced at the onlooking troops to see whether they were aware that he had been defied. Their faces were blank, uncomprehending.

Reasserting himself by making his tones harsh and authoritative, he said to Wardle, "I am not disposed to argue with a mere prisoner. You have plenty left to learn. And very soon you will learn it."

"Yes, teacher," agreed Wardle.

Ignoring that, the officer went on, "You will follow this sergeant. You will walk behind him in single file. You will be guarded on both sides and in the rear. If any one of you attempts to escape the escort will shoot—to kill. Do you understand?"

"I do."

"Then so inform your companions."

"There is no need. They understand Extralingua. On Terra one gets educated."

"Also on Kasta," the officer riposted, "as you are about to discover." He turned to the sergeant. "Take them away."

The crew of the *Elsie* marched off, obediently following the sergeant. Three guards on either side kept pace with them at ten feet distance, just too far for a sudden jump and a successful snatch at a gun. Four more trudged weightily behind.

They struck a wide path between enormous trees and moved in contemplative silence. A thing like a small frilled lizard scuttled along a branch fifty feet up, stared down at them beady-eyed and uttered a few sympathetic squeaks. Nobody took any notice.

The sergeant's yard-wide shoulders swung in front of them while his size twenty boots went *thud-thud-thud.* There was no difficulty in keeping up with him because his slow pace compensated for his great strides. The escort's boots also thudded on the right, the left and in the rear. The Terrans felt like pygmies trapped by elephants in human form.

Eventually they reached a small encampment consisting of half a dozen huts set in a clearing. Here, the seven were herded into a truck, a troop-carrier with seats along both sides. They sat in line on one side, their feet dangling a few inches above the floor. The guards squatted on the other, machine-pistols in laps.

The truck roared to life, pulled out, rocked and swayed along a dirt road, reached a wide, paved artery, sped at top pace for three hours. During this time the Terrans said not a word but their eyes absorbed the passing scenery as though memorizing it for all time.

With a sudden turn to the right that shot the prisoners onto the floor the truck lumbered into a military center and stopped before a long stone building. The guards guffawed deep in their chests, nudged the struggling captives with their boots. A bunch of uniformed Kastans gathered around and gaped curiously as the Terrans dismounted and were conducted inside.

The sergeant lined them up against a wall, snorted and grunted a few warning words to the guard, hastened through a doorway. After a while an officer stuck his head out the same doorway, surveyed the silent seven and withdrew. A bit later the sergeant reappeared, urged them along a high-ceilinged corridor and into a room in which two officers were seated behind a long desk.

For twenty minutes the officers fiddled around with papers and pointedly ignored the arrivals. That keep-'em-waiting technique was deliberate and of malice aforethought, being calculated to impress upon the prisoners that they were trash to be swept up at leisure.

Finally one of the officers looked up, made a grimace of displeasure, pushed his papers to one side. He nudged his companion who also condescended to become aware of alien company.

"Who speaks Kastan?" asked the first officer, in that language.

No reply.

"Well, do any of you speak Extralingua?" he persisted.

"They all do, sir," chipped in the sergeant without waiting for anyone else to reply.

"So! Then let's get on with the interrogation."

He pointed a pen at random. "You there—what's your name?"

"Robert Cheminais."

"Number?"

"105697."

"Rank?"

"Captain."

The second officer scribbled all this on a sheet while the pen shifted and aimed at the next one.

"And you?"

"William Holden."

"Number?"

"112481."

"Rank?"

"Captain."

Another move as the pen selected the third one.

"Frank Wardle. 103882. Captain."

Then the rest in rapid succession.

"James Foley. 109018. Captain."

"Alpin McAlpin. 122474. Captain."

"Henry Casasola. 114086. Captain."

"Ludovic Pye. 101323. Captain."

"Seven captains on one ship," commented the officer. He let go a loud sniff. "That's the way the Terrans run their navy. Everyone a captain—if he isn't an admiral. And doubtless every one of them has forty medals." His sour eye examined the captives, then picked on Wardle. "How many medals have you got?"

"None—yet."

"Yet? You've a fat lot of hopes of getting one *now.* Not unless we give you one, having become crazy." He waited for an answer that did not come, went on, "But you are a captain?"

"That's right."

"And all the others are captains?"

"Correct."

"Then who commanded the ship?"

"I did," said Wardle.

"In that case," rasped the officer, "you can tell me something. You can tell me exactly why you're here."

"We're here because we've been made prisoners."

"I know that much, fool! I want to know why a Terran vessel has appeared in this locality where none has ventured before."

"We were on a long-range reconnaissance patrol. Our engines went haywire, propulsion became dangerously erratic, we were forced down. Your troops grabbed us before we could make repairs." Wardle gave a shrug of complete resignation. "Our luck ran out. That's war."

"Your luck ran out? Seems to me that you were let down by inferior equipment. Our space-navy would not tolerate that sort of thing. Our standard of efficiency is pretty high." He gazed steadily at his listener, continued, "Experts are on the way to examine these Terran engines. I don't suppose they'll discover anything worth learning."

Wardle offered no remark.

"So you were on a spying trip, eh? It hasn't done you much good, has it?"

No answer.

"We've a very useful labor force of four hundred thousand Union prisoners. The addition of seven Terrans won't make much difference one way or the other. You are undersized and puny creatures." He studied each of the seven in turn, his lips pursed in contempt. "However, we shall add you to the crowd. In time of war every little helps—even a bunch of weak-muscled captains." He turned to the stolidly listening sergeant. "Have them shipped to Gathin forthwith. I will forward their papers immediately we've dealt with them here."

He made a gesture of dismissal. The sergeant led the seven back to the truck, chivvied them aboard, took a seat facing them with the guard beside him, guns in laps. The truck lurched ahead, got onto the main road, hit up top speed. Its axles emitted a high-pitched whine.

Holden, hawk-nosed and lean-faced, bent forward, said to the sergeant in Extralingua, "Where's Gathin?"

"Up there." The other jerked a hammerlike thumb toward the sky. "Twelve days' flight. Anthracite mines, lead mines, machine-shops. Plenty of work for the dead." He showed big teeth. "Those taken in war are as dead. Therefore one should not be taken."

"Do you understand Terran?" asked Holden, switching to that language.

The sergeant looked blank.

Radiating a cordial smile, Holden said, "You dirty big stinking bum! Hail the Union!"

"Please?" said the sergeant, answering the smile with a cracked one.

"You flatfooted, hamhanded numbskull," responded Holden, oozing amiability. "May all your children have violent squints and may you be smothered to death in a heap of manure. Hail the Union!"

"Please?" repeated the sergeant, baffled but gratified.

"Take it easy, Bill," warned Wardle.

"Shaddap!" Switching back to Extralingua, Holden said to the sergeant, "I will teach you a little Terran if you wish."

The sergeant approved, thinking that every item of education was a step nearer to officership. Lessons commenced while the truck rocked along. Prisoners and guards listened with interest as Holden carefully enunciated words and phrases and the sergeant got them perfectly.

Such fluency had been gained that at the spaceport farewells were exchanged in the specified manner.

Holden, giving a vaudeville salute, "Drop dead, you fat rat!"

The sergeant, proud of his linguistic ability, "Thank you, my lord! Hail the Union!"

They trudged down the ship's gangway, stared at their new surroundings, and Wardle said in an undertone, "Item one: we've arrived without getting our throats slit. Item two: we now know exactly where Gathin is."

"Yair," agreed Holden. "We now where it is. But it's going to be easier to get in than get out."

"Oh, I don't know," opined Wardle, airily. "We've got a considerable advantage in that they won't expect us to try. Remember, chum, it's a cosmos-wide convention that a prisoner of war is a member of the living dead, properly resigned to his fate. Everyone recognizes that fact excepting Terrans—who are wholly crazy."

"Not all Terrans had that viewpoint once," offered Holden. "Around the time they learned to walk on their hind legs the Japanese considered capture more disgraceful than death. Some went so far as to commit suicide first chance they got."

"That was a heck of a long time ago and—"

"Silence!" bawled a paunchy Kastan who was standing near the bottom of the gangway with the inevitable guard in attendance. He glowered at the seven as they lined up in front of him. "So you are Terrans, eh? We have heard your kind mentioned by the Stames and Aluesines who"—he put on a grin of self-satisfaction—"are now our slaves by right of conquest. But they did not say you were so small. Or have we been sent a group of selected dwarfs?"

"Seven dwarfs, sonny," said Holden. "Snow White's coming on the next boat."

"Snow White?" The paunchy one frowned, consulted a wad of papers in his hand, searching through them one by one. "I have here documents for seven Terrans. There is nothing about an eighth due on this ship or the next."

"She must have missed it," said Holden, helpfully.

"*She?* You mean a female was captured with you?"

"Evidently she wasn't. She took to the woods." Holden put on a look of grudging admiration. "1 wouldn't have thought she'd have got away with it."

Paunchy took a deep breath. "Did you inform our Interrogation Center about this Snow White?"

"No, sonny. They didn't ask."

"Imbeciles!" he spat out. "Now we shall have to send a signal to Kasta and set up a widespread hunt for her. It will put our forces to much time and trouble."

"Hallelujah!" said Holden, fervently.

"What does that mean?"

"It is much to be deplored."

"You are right," agreed Paunchy, with some menace. "And in due course she will do much deploring." His eyes shifted along the rank, settled on Ludovic Pye. "Well, what are you laughing about? Is your brain afflicted?"

"He suffers from hysterics," put in Holden. "It is the shock of capture."

"Humph!" said Paunchy, openly contemptuous. "Weak in mind as well as in body. The Aluesines and Stames have more moral fiber, low-grade lifeforms though they be. They collapse from physical weakness but none have gone mad." He spat on the ground, vigorously. "Terrans!" Then he motioned toward a nearby truck. "Get in!"

They got in. It was the same procedure as before. They sat along one side with a line of surly guards facing them. The truck set off through a countryside different from that of Kasta. Here, trees were smaller though still big by Earth-standards. They grew more thickly and soon resembled a jungle through which the road cut in a wide, perfectly straight line.

Halfway to their destination they passed a gang of Aluesines toiling at the roadside. They were human-shaped characters nearly as tall as the Kastans but of skinnier physique. They had slot-shaped pupils, like cats, and by nature were nocturnal. Only they could know the torture of slaving in full sunlight.

The Aluesines observed the Terrans without interest or surprise. Every one of them had the appalling apathy of a creature resigned by custom to his fate and who takes for granted a similar attitude on the part of all others.

Holden, who was seated near the tailboard, leaned over it as the truck roared past and let go a yell of, *"Floreat Aluesia!"*

It caused no visible excitement. A guard leaned forward and belted Holden on the knee with his gun-butt.

"Fosham gubitsch!" he growled in incomprehensible Kastan.

"Hush yo mouf!" said Holden in equally incomprehensible Terran.

"Shut your own!" ordered Wardle. "We'll have trouble enough before we are through."

"You will not talk in dwarf-language," chipped in Paunchy, cutting a scowl into seven parts and handing a piece to each. "All speech will be in Extralingua. That is, until you have learned Kastan."

"Hah!" said Holden, determined to have the last word.

The officer was big even for one of his race. He wore a skin-tight uniform of dark green ornamented with silver braid. A couple of small white arrows decorated the flap of his top pocket. His face was broad, heavy and slightly gross, his expression severe.

"I am the commander of this prison. Over you I hold the power of pain and suffering, of life and death. Therefore you will strive to please me at all times. Henceforth that is your only aim, your sole purpose of existence—to please me."

The seven stood in silence as he did a bit of important strutting up and down the carpet.

"We have not had any Terrans before and now that we have I don't think much of them. All the same, we shall make full use of such work as you are capable of doing. That is our proper reward for victory and your proper penalty for defeat."

Holden opened his mouth, closed it as Wardle's heel rammed down on his toes.

"You will be conducted to your quarters," concluded the officer. "In the morning you will be cross-examined concerning your training and aptitudes. You will then be assigned appropriate tasks." He sat down, leaned back in his chair, put on an expression of boredom. "Take them away, sergeant."

They were marched out in single file, made to wait an hour in the middle of a great concrete yard. Barrack-blocks of solid stone reared ten floors high on each side of the yard. Beyond the blocks rose the wall to a height of sixty feet. The whole place seemed empty, there being no other prisoners in sight.

Eventually a guard-major appeared, took over from the sergeant, led them into the right-hand block and up stone steps to the sixth floor. Then along a corridor and into a large room with bare stone walls.

"Do you understand Kastan?"

They stared at him without response.

"Extralingua?"

"Yes," said Wardle, speaking for the bunch.

The guard-major drew himself up to full height, expanded his chest and gave forth "I am Guard-Major Slovits. I command this block. Over you I hold the power of life and death. Therefore you will strive to please me at all times."

"Henceforth that is your only aim," prompted Holden.

"Eh?"

"I was remarking that we understand," explained Holden, blank-faced. "Our only aim shall be to please you, Guard-Major Slobovitch."

"Slovits," corrected Slovits. He carried on, "You will remain here until the great gong sounds outside. You will then parade in the yard along with the others for your evening meal. Is that understood?"

"Yes," said Wardle, beating the gabby Holden to any further remarks.

"There will be no jostling of other prisoners, no unruly fighting for food. Disorder will be cured with the whip. Is that understood?"

"Yes, Guard-Major Slobovitch," assured Holden, beating Wardle out of his role as spokesman.

"Slovits!" said Slovits, glowering at him. He stumped out, slamming the door behind him.

Wardle prophesied to Holden, "One of these days you'll be trapped by your own trap."

"That's happened already. I volunteered for this nutty mission, didn't I?"

"You did. Let it be a warning to you."

There were twelve beds in the room, each consisting of plain wooden planks fastened to a wooden framework. The beds were nine feet in length and covered with one nine-foot blanket slightly threadbare and none too clean. At the end of the room was a faucet and one washbasin.

"Every modern inconvenience," growled Foley, to whom the chief curse of military service was lack of comfort.

"Twelve beds," observed Alpin McAlpin. "I wonder if that means we're getting some Stames or Aluesines with us. If so, it'll make contact easy right at the start."

"We'll have to wait and see," said Wardle. He strolled to the door, tried it. The door held firm. "Self-locking and solid metal. Hm-m-m! Wouldn't have surprised me if they'd left it open."

He crossed to one of the four windows. There were no bars to impede exit. The windows were hinged and opened without trouble. A baby elephant could have clambered through and escaped—given that it had been born with wings.

The others joined him for a look-see. Immediately beneath them the side of the block dropped six floors to the ground. Above, it rose four to the top. There were no ridges, no ledges, no breaks other than those provided by window-gaps.

At bottom lay a concrete space of bone-breaking hardness, forty feet wide, terminated by the outer wall. Evidently they'd been accommodated on the side of the block farthest from the yard, though whether or not this would prove an advantage remained to be seen.

The great exterior wall of the prison soared a full sixty feet from ground, its top being a couple of feet below the floor-level of their room. Thus they could look down upon the top, also see much of the country beyond.

As nearly as they could judge from their vantage-point the wall's top was about five feet wide. On each side one foot of this width was fringed with a triple row of metal spikes about six inches long and spaced three inches apart. The middle three feet formed a sentry-walk along which armed guards mooched from time to time with their attention directed mostly outward rather than inward.

Foley said to Holden, "Now there's a choice set-up for knocking them off the easy way."

"How d'you mean?"

"You call the attention of a sentry from here. He looks this way, sees your horrible face. He faints at the sight of it, collapses on the spikes and gets impaled."

"Wittiest speech I've heard in years," said Holden, sourly. "Look at me rolling all over the floor."

"Shut up, you bums," ordered Wardle. He left the window, sat on the edge of a bed, counted off his fingers as he continued talking and made his points one by one. "Let's review the situation."

They assented, sat around and listened.

"The know-alls on Earth said the Union is handicapped by an alien psychology which applies to enemies and allies alike. In this respect we Terrans appear to be unique—though someday we may encounter a yet unknown lifeform that uses what we regard as hoss-sense. Correct?"

They nodded.

"All right. This alien viewpoint asserts that to be taken prisoner is to be eternally disgraced. Even a released prisoner refuses to go back home; his family prefers to consider him dead for keeps rather than admit the shame of him. So there's no point in any prisoner attempting to escape except for the purpose of committing a nice, quiet, uninterrupted suicide. That gives us an advantage in dealing with enemies—but it's a hell of a handicap to our allies. Eh?"

Again they nodded.

"The Stames' and Aluesines' casualties consist only of killed and wounded. Officially there are none missing. So they've a powerful army here which, they say, does not exist." He paused, added, "And they say Terrans are crazy!"

"If we aren't," put in Holden, "why are we here?"

Taking no notice, Wardle went on, "The know-alls promised that we'd find ourselves in circumstances shaped by the enemy's unavoidable supposition that we would never dream of escaping for any purpose other than that of self-destruction. They said, for instance, that we'd be searched for weapons and documents but not for escape material. So far, they've proved right, haven't they?"

"Yair," said Holden, feeling around for a pocket-watch that wasn't a pocket-watch.

"They said that all the enemy would demand of us would be absolute obedience because the only problem he has in dealing with captives is that of reluctance to work. Naturally a gump who considers himself dead isn't going to sweat any harder than he has to. So the Kastans have never experienced any trouble with prisoners other than of two kinds, namely, slow working and occasional suicides. They've never come up against ridicule, sabotage, organized escapes or suchlike. Not sharing our state of mind, they don't and can't anticipate any difficulty in handling a few Terrans." He stopped, rubbed his chin thoughtfully and asked, "Do you fellows think the way we've been handled so far shows that the know-alls were again right?"

"Yair," said Holden, the others agreeing with him.

"Good! Then what we've got to do next is check up on whether they're correct about everything else because, if not, we're in a real jam—and we could remain in it until death us do part."

He counted another finger as he made the next point. "The bigbrains claim that Kastan prisons should be fully as well-built as any of ours but with one significant difference: defenses will be against attack from outside rather than mass escape from inside. The Kastans expect the former but not the latter, taking it for granted that the Union's motive would not be to release their own men but rather to rob the Kastan economy of a valuable labor force."

"It's all a lot of long-range supposition," put in Alpin McAlpin. "I wouldn't take any Kastan's mentality for granted on the strength of some Terran expert's guesses. We've a lot of checking-up to do before we know where we're going."

"That's what I'm getting at," said Wardle, staring hard at Holden. "Let's be humble and obedient for a while. Let's become willing and patient beasts of burden while keeping our eyes skinned for confirmatory evidence. From now on we'll confer every night and correlate whatever data we've gathered."

"Why give *me* the hard eye?" demanded Holden, bristling at him.

"You're a bit too full of bounce, chum. You're supposed to play a part and you're a bad actor."

"Nuts to that! I consider myself a cut above these Kastans, having been conceived in holy wedlock."

"So do we all. But we must conceal the fact for as long as seems expedient. Good manners is the art of pretending that one is not superior."

Foley let go with a violent laugh at that, and said, "You're like a troop of Tibetans."

"Why?" asked Wardle.

"You're always good for a few yaks."

A huge gong clamored somewhere across the yard.

"Food," added Foley, starting the line-up by the door. "Prison food. Let's see you laugh this lot off."

The door clicked open, they went through into an empty corridor, clattered down the stairs and into the yard. Here a guard met them, handed each man one circular wooden bowl and one wooden spoon.

"You will keep those and take care of them. Loss or damage will earn punishment." He pointed across the concrete, his forefinger the size of a banana. "At all mealtimes you will attend with those Stames. You will not join any of the other groups unless ordered to do so."

They traipsed across the yard, tagged on at the end of the indicated line of Stames. Ahead of them the line wound snakelike a couple of hundred yards, went through a gap between barrack-blocks and round to the cookhouse at back. Nearby were four other lines slowly shuffling forward, one wholly of Stames, two of Aluesines, and one of mixed species.

The Stames also were humanlike, towering head and shoulders above the Terrans. This unanimity of shape surprised nobody. Every intelligent lifeform yet encountered had been found only on planets approximating more or less to Terra's conditions, and every one had been of the same shape with no more than minor variations. A library of books had been written on the subject, with such titles as *Cosmic Domination of the Simian Structure.*

The similarities served to emphasize the differences. The Stames were first-class fighters in their own area but not aggressively warlike as were the Kastans. They were not nocturnal like the Aluesines. They lacked any appreciation of the ludicrous such as is enjoyed by Terrans. They were a serious-minded, humorless lifeform, producers of broody literature and moody music.

Holden nudged the one immediately in front of him. The Stame turned round, looked down upon him from his greater height. He had a mournful face, a lugubrious expression, and resembled a founder-member of the Society of the Disenchanted.

"How's the chow here, Happy?" asked Holden.

"Little and bad."

"It would be."

"So now they are taking Terrans," commented the Stame. "They have progressed that far, *houne?* The war is almost lost, *houne?*"

"What do you care? You've been thrown to the crocodiles, anyway."

"Crackodales? What are those, please?"

"Kastans wearing a grin," informed Holden. "But don't quote me."

The line edged onward. More Stames appeared, joined in behind the Terrans. They did not speak unless spoken to. Every one of them was thin, under-nourished, dull-eyed and apathetic. Stames and Aluesines in parallel lines were in no better condition. Their clothes were worn and shabby. A third of them lacked boots or shoes and trod the concrete bare-footed.

At the cookhouse forty impassive Aluesines stood in pairs beside twenty big, steaming boilers and ladled out the contents under the sharp eyes of as many guards. One scoop just about filled one bowl.

Holden, first in the Terran file, got his, examined it closely, smelled it, rasped, "What is this foul potion?"

A guard eyed him. "You say?"

"I say it's a crying shame, you lumbering clunker."

"You will speak only in Extralingua," reproved the guard. "To use your own language is forbidden."

Carrying their bowls clear of the several line-ups, they followed the example of those already served, sat on the hard surface of the yard and ate. Plying their spoons they dipped and sucked in unison. The concoction tasted like mixed vegetable soup. Unidentifiable portions of stuff floated around in it and to Terran nostrils it had the fragrance of the cathouse at the zoo.

Without enthusiasm they finished the stew, washed spoons and bowls under a faucet, hung around to see what next. Nothing much happened for a while. Prisoners who had been fed lolled listlessly around the yard while those yet to be fed shuffled forward with bowls in hands. As the last few of the latter reached the cookhouse a strange stirring, a kind of subtle animation went through the crowd. Tenseness could almost be felt.

Then behind the block a guard bawled something unhearable. Immediately a mob of prisoners made a mad rush to the cookhouse. There came noises of scuffling feet, shouted orders, Kastan curses and cracking whips. Soon the mob mooched back.

One of them, a weary-eyed Aluesine, sat near the Terrans, tilted his bowl to his mouth and drank greedily. Then he sighed, lay back propped on his elbows, looked idly around. His clothes were black with anthracite dust and a fresh weal showed across his face.

Wardle edged across to him, asked, "What caused the fracas?"

"Extra," said the other.

"Extra?" Wardle was puzzled. "Extra what?"

"Soup," said the Aluesine. "Sometimes after all have been served there is a little left over. So the guards give a shout. First comers get it, just a mouthful apiece."

"And for that you ran like an animal?"

"We are prisoners," reminded the Aluesine, with dreadful philosophy. "A prisoner is no more than an animal. What else can he be?"

"A warrior," snapped Wardle.

"What, without a gun and without honor? You speak stupidly."

He got up and walked away.

"Hear that?" Wardle glanced at the others. "It shows what we're up against."

"Hell of a note," said Holden, disgustedly.

"We mustn't condemn them," Wardle warned. "They think the way they've been brought up to think and the result isn't their fault. Besides, the Aluesines are having a hard time. They work when they ought to be sleeping and they try to sleep when normally they'd be active. Their nature is being turned upside-down. I'll bet that character feels like he's on his last lap."

"The Stames aren't having it good either," put in Ludovic Pye. "I've just had a word with that one." He pointed to a distant mourner following an invisible coffin. "Says he's been here four years, worked like a dog, and hasn't tasted meat since he bit his tongue."

"Well, we've another small advantage," Wardle commented. "The Kastans are doling out their lousy food on the basis of the minimum quantity needed to maintain useful life in people half as big again as ourselves. They're giving us the same as the rest. So in proportion to our requirements we're getting more than the others. We'll be only a quarter starved instead of half-starved."

"With all the numerous advantages we've got or are alleged to have," remarked Pye, sarcastically, "it's a wonder the Kastans don't give up."

"They will, chum, they will," Holden told him.

Heaving himself erect, Wardle said, "Let's make some sort of a start while the going is good. Split up and work individually around the yard. Question anyone who's got a spark of animation and see if we can find out who is the senior officer among this crowd."

They went their several ways. Holden was the first to pop the question. He picked upon a Stame one degree less miserable than the rest.

"Who is the senior officer in this dump?"

"The Kastan commander of course. You were taken before him when you arrived, weren't you?"

"I don't mean Festerhead. I mean who is the senior officer among the prisoners?"

"There are no officers."

"That so? Were they all sent elsewhere?"

"There are no officers," asserted the Stame, as if speaking to an idiot, "because a prisoner has no rank. We are all prisoners. Therefore there are no officers."

"Yair," said Holden. "That's right."

He scowled, gave up the search, but ambled aimlessly on. Presently he met Casasola, the silent one who was heard when and only when speech was unavoidable.

"No ranks, therefore no officers," Holden said.

Casasola pulled a face and walked onward without remark. Next came Foley.

"No rank, therefore no officers."

"You're telling me?" said Foley disgustedly, and continued his futile questioning.

In short time Holden became bored. Selecting an unpopulated corner of the yard, he sat down cross-legged, placed the bowl between his knees, hammered it with his spoon to attract attention and let go with a peculiar whine.

"No momma, no poppa. Have pity, Sahib. Baksheesh in the name of Allah."

"You will not talk in dwarf-language," ordered a voice situated high above size twenty boots.

Holden looked upward. "Oh, good evening, Guard-Major Slobovitch."

"The name is *Slovits,"* shouted Slovits, showing horse's teeth.

Nobody shared their room when the door clicked shut for the night. The five spare beds remained unoccupied. Wardle eyed the beds speculatively.

"Either this pokey isn't yet full yet to capacity or else they're keeping us apart from the rest night-times. I hope it's the former."

"Does it matter?" asked Pye.

"It might. If they're segregating us within the block it could be because they know more about Terrans than we think. By the same token they could know too much about our military tactics. I like an enemy to be big, clumsy and ignorant."

"They can't know much," scoffed Pye. "They're numerically the strongest lifeform yet known, and they control some sixty scattered planets, but their intelligence service has never probed as far as the Terran sphere of operations. The Kastans have been spending all their time fighting Stames and Aluesines and lesser types; up to when we left home they'd heard of us only by repute." He gave a sniff of disdain. "Bet they've crawled all over *Elsie* and think she's the best we've got."

"What, you dare to speak lightly of a woman's name?" interjected Holden, pretendedly shocked.

"Anyway," continued Wardle, we now know that the experts have proved correct about imprisoned allies and have weighed them up fairly accurately. It's obvious that not one of these prisoners would lift a finger to get back home. He knows that if he did return he'd be scorned by the populace, denied a living, repudiated by his family and become a social outcast. He's no inducement to make a break."

"Not yet," said Holden.

"No, not yet. Our experts think they've found a way to crack the hard crust of alien convention, to the great advantage of the Union and the confoundment of the Kastans. We've got to make it work. We've now had a close look at the set-up—what do you fellows think of our chances?"

"Too early to judge," Holden opined. "We can make some better guesses after another week."

"I thought they were exaggerating back on Terra," ventured Pye. "But they weren't. Not one little bit. We're expected to perform miracles with a mob of exhausted zombies. It's a tough task, in my opinion."

"That's because you're letting yourself be bemused by their alien viewpoint," said Wardle. "The more baffling you permit it to seem, the harder the job looks. Try simplifying it in your own mind."

"How d'you mean?"

"This way: basically the Stames and Aluesines are topnotch fighters, full of guts and ready for anything—so long as they've got guns in their hands and retain what they choose to regard as personal honor. Take away their guns and kick them in the britches and you destroy that honor. So they are bollixed by what is, in effect, a tribal custom that's been established for many centuries."

"But it doesn't make sense."

"Neither do some of our habits. Maybe it did make sense in the long, long ago. Maybe it was a natural and necessary way of eliminating the weak at a time when explosives and paralyzing gases weren't thought of. Anyway, the only real difference between these prisoners and ourselves is that we can be stripped naked and still retain an item of which they are deprived."

"Such as?"

"An invisible something called morale."

"Humph!" said Pye, unimpressed.

"Either a prisoner has it or hasn't," Wardle went on. "This mob has not got it and it isn't their fault. They've been kidded by long-standing custom into believing there's no such thing. Or rather I should say they've been made blind to it. What we've got to do is help them see clear and straight."

"I know all that," Pye grumbled, "But once I spent five years on Hermione. As maybe you know, the Hermies have good, sharp sight but see only black, white and shades of gray. They're not to blame for that; it's the way they're made. You can argue with them from now to the crack of doom and never succeed in describing colors or telling them what they're missing."

"So what? We aren't here to try to give the Stames and Aluesines something mysterious that they've never had. Our concern is to restore something they've lost, something they had aplenty when their guns were loaded and in their hands. It may be difficult. It isn't impossible."

"What does that mean?" inquired Holden.

"What does *what* mean?"

"Impossible?"

"Forget it," advised Wardle, grinning. "There is no such word."

Holden leaned across toward Pye and said in tutorial manner, "You heard what the nice gentlemen said—there is no such word."

"Humph!" repeated Pye, determined to coddle his mood of temporary skepticism.

Wardle ambled to a window and looked out. Darkness had fallen, the purplish sky was sprinkled with stars. A pale primrose glow rippled across the landscape as one of Gathin's three minor moons arced overhead.

The top of the prison wall was illuminated by narrow-beamed flares horizontally along it. Apparently the sole purpose of the lighting was to make clear the path of patrolling sentinels lest otherwise they should step on the spikes and take a sixty-foot dive.

"We must time the movements of these guards," said Wardle. "We'd better take turns at keeping watch on them. As soon as possible we must acquire precise details of their nightly routine."

"We must also dig up a small crate from somewhere," Holden put in, "or, better still, a three-foot folding ladder."

"What for?" demanded Wardle.

"Sooner or later we may have to slug one of them. The slugger will need a ladder to lay out a chump eight feet tall. Takes brains to think of everything." Selecting a bed, he sprawled on it, glanced sidewise, met the gaze of the ever-silent Casasola. "So you're still with us, eh? Just a rose in a garden of weeds."

Casasola did not deign to reply.

Came the dawn. It was sweetened by the majesty of Guard-Major Slovits. He flung wide the door, marched in, prodded each blanket-covered shape with his whip-handle.

"You will dress at once. You will go for your morning food. Immediately you have eaten you will parade outside the commander's office." He distributed a few more impartial jabs. "Is that understood?"

"It is," said Wardle.

Slovits marched out. Foley rolled over, groaned, sat up, rubbed red-rimmed eyes. "What did he say?"

"In effect, get moving," Wardle informed.

"After breakfast we're invited to drinks with Festerhead," Holden added.

"Like hell we are," said Foley. "What's Festerhead want us for, anyway?"

"I'll tell you for a small fee," offered Alpin McAlpin.

In due time they reached the head of the line-up and received one quart apiece of cat-house soup. They sat on the ground and ate.

"Good, *houne*?" remarked a nearby Stame, as though guzzling the stuff was the only remaining joy in life.

"Think so?" Foley scowled at him. "I say it stinks."

"An insult to the belly," offered Cheminais in support.

"Not fit for hogs," declared Ludovic Pye.

"Down, down, you mutinous dogs!" bellowed Holden at the top of his voice.

Ten thousand pairs of eyes turned simultaneously their way, ten thousand wooden spoons poised motionless over as many bowls. A dozen guards raced toward the center of general attention.

The first of them arrived and demanded breathlessly, "Now, what is this?"

"What is what?" said Holden, childlike and bland.

"You have screamed. Why have you screamed?"

"I *always* scream two hours after sunrise on Thursdays."

"Thursdays? What are those?"

"Holy days."

"And why do you scream then?"

"It is my religion," assured Holden, oozing piety.

"A prisoner has no religion," stated the guard, with considerable emphasis. "There will be no more screaming."

He stamped away impatiently. The other guards went with him. Ten thousand pairs of eyes lost interest, ten thousand spoons resumed scooping at as many bowls.

"That mug," said Holden, "is so dumb he thinks fuller's earth is a planet."

The nearby Stame glanced warily around, whispered in confidential manner, "I will tell you something. All Terrans are crazy."

"Not all of us," Wardle denied. "Just one of us. Only one."

"Which one?" asked the Stame.

"Not telling," said Holden. "It's a military secret."

"Prisoners have no secrets," said the Stame with much positiveness.

"*We* have!" Holden sucked soup loudly. "Good, *houne*?"

The Stame got up and walked away. For reasons best known to himself he was slightly dazed.

"Is this your idea of behaving quietly and humbly for a piece?" asked Wardle. "If so, what's going to happen when we decide to get uppish? Were you ever a juvenile delinquent?"

Holden finished his soup, then, "Obedience has its limits so far as I'm concerned. Besides, we're fighting a state of mind. It's a mental condition that sticks in my craw. The sooner we cure them of it, the better."

"That may be. But we've got to be careful we don't overreach ourselves by starting off too fast. We've got to show these Stames and Aluesines that victory and self-respect can both be gained. It won't help us any if they explain all our words and deeds in terms of lunacy."

"Neither will it help us to mope around kowtowing to all and sundry."

"Have it your own way," said Wardle, giving up.

The Stames and Aluesines started forming in close-packed columns and marching out through the main gate. They still carried their bowls and spoons. None bore tools, these presumably being stored at wherever they labored. Guards chivvied them continually as they trudged along, urging them to move faster. Several who stumbled and fell out of the ranks were promptly booted back into place.

Meanwhile the Terrans paraded as ordered outside the commander's office. A great Kastan banner flapped and fluttered from its pole above the building. Holden watched the flag, seemingly fascinated by its movements.

They were still waiting when the last of the working parties left the yard and the big gates clanged shut. Now the space was empty, the barrack-blocks deserted. There were no sounds other than the thump of boots along the wall-top, the receding shouts of guards accompanying the columns and vague noises in the distance where other slaves already had resumed their daily tasks.

After they had fidgeted aimlessly around for more than an hour, Slovits appeared. "You will come inside and answer all questions."

They traipsed in, found themselves facing five officers of whom the middle one was the prison commandeer. All five had the bored attitude of farmers about to compile the milk records of a herd of cows.

"You," said Festerhead, pointing. "Which one are you?"

"Alpin McAlpin."

"In what have you been trained?"

"Radio communications."

"So you are a technician?"

"Yes."

"Good!" approved Festerhead. "We can use skilled personnel. Far too many of these Union captives are common soldiers fit for nothing save drudgery." He conferred with the officer seated on his left, finished, "Yes, let Raduma have him." He returned attention to the seven and pointed again. "You?"

"Ludovic Pye."

"Training?"

"Electronics engineer."

"Raduma," said Festerhead to the one on his left. "Next?"

"Henry Casasola. Engineer-armorer."

"Main workshops," decided Festerhead. "Next?"

"Robert Cheminais. Propulsion engineer."

"Main workshops. Next?"

"James Foley. Fleet doctor."

"Prison hospital," said Festerhead, promptly. "Next?"

"Frank Wardle. Pilot-commander."

"A pilot? We have no use whatever for alien pilots. How long is it since you were inducted into the Terran forces?"

"Eight years ago."

"And what were you before then?"

"A forestry expert," informed Wardle, forcing his face to keep straight.

Festerhead slapped a hand on the desk and exclaimed with a gratified air, "Superb! Put him in the jungle gang. We'll then have one of them who can turn round twice and still know north from south." He stared inquiringly at the last Terran.

"William Holden. Navigator."

"What can we do with a navigator? Nothing! Have you no other technical qualification?"

"No."

"What were you originally?"

"A quarry manager."

Almost beaming, Festerhead said, "This one's for the stone gang."

Holden smirked back. He couldn't help it. Running through his mind was a brief speech made back on Terra by a gray-haired oldster.

"Without exception all intelligent lifeforms are builders. All large-scale builders employ natural resources, especially stone. One obtains stone from quarries. One quarries it by blasting. Therefore a quarry worker has access to explosives which, nine times out of ten, are not under military protection." A pause while he waited for it to sink in, followed by, "You will now undergo a course on quarrying techniques with particular reference to explosives."

Not noticing Holden's expression Festerhead returned attention to Wardle. "You were in charge of this Terran vessel that made a forced landing?"

"I was."

"Yet all of your crew were of the same rank, all captains. Why is that?"

"Each of us had risen to a captaincy in his own specialized profession."

"It seems strange to me," commented Festerhead. "The Terrans must have peculiar ways of doing things. However, it is of no consequence. I am concerned with something more important. He fixed a cold gaze on his listener. "This morning we received a signal from Kasta. They are taking all necessary measures to capture Snow White."

Wardle fought within himself to remain silent and impassive. It was an awful strain.

"Why was this female aboard?"

"We were transporting her to sector headquarters," lied Wardle, not daring to look at his six companions.

"Why?"

"I don't know. We had our orders and did not question them."

"Why is her name not recorded in the documents we have seized from your ship?"

"I don't know. The papers are prepared by Terran authorities. I cannot accept responsibility for what is or what is not written upon them."

"How did this female succeed in escaping while you seven were captured?" Festerhead persisted.

"She fled into the woods the moment we landed. We stayed by the ship, trying to repair it."

"Did she take anything with her? A weapon, or an instrument"—he bent forward, gave it emphasis—"such as a long-range transmitter?"

"I don't know. We were too busy to notice."

"Answer me truthfully or it will go hard with you! Is this Snow White an intelligence agent?"

"Not that I know of." Wardle made a deprecating gesture. "If she were, we wouldn't necessarily be told."

"Is she young or old?"

"Fairly young."

"And attractive?"

"Yes, I would call her that." Wardle felt a couple of beads of sweat sneaking down his spine.

Festerhead put on the knowing look of one who's been nicked by every nightclub and head waiter in town. "Have you any reason to suppose that she may have been the favorite of a high military commander?"

"Could be," conceded Wardle, radiating the admiration due from a yokel.

"And so, to us, a valuable hostage?" continued Festerhead, soaking up the worship of a hick.

"Could be," repeated Wardle, upping the output.

Preening himself, Festerhead said, "Describe her in full detail."

Wardle did it, right down to her stud earrings. It was a masterly picture worthy of Ananias at his best. Festerhead listened carefully while one of his officers wrote it down word for word.

"Have these details radiated to Kasta at once," ordered Festerhead when finally Wardle dried up. He switched attention to Slovits. "These Terrans will commence work today. See that they are taken where assigned."

Slovits led them away.

The seven were split up and conducted their various ways. They did not meet again until the Stame-line formed for the evening meal.

"No talking," greeted Wardle. "Leave it until later when we'll be alone."

Holden turned to Casasola, who was immediately behind him, empty bowl in hand. "You heard what the nice gentleman said. No talking. So keep your trap shut."

As usual, Casasola said nothing.

When they were in their room with the door fastened for the night, Wardle said, "Like me to start with the yap?"

"Might as well," agreed Pye, for the rest.

"All right. I've been with a gang of Stames cutting and hauling lumber. Six guards were with us, every one of them lazy and careless. They sat in a hut playing a kind of card game, knowing that nobody would take it on the lam because there's nowhere to go—not even home. Discipline gets pretty slack out there in the jungle."

"You want more of it?" asked Holden.

Ignoring the interruption, Wardle continued, "I talked plenty with those Stames and no guard ordered me to shut up. Seems that the Kastans have kept to their native timekeeping despite that the day here is more than twenty-eight hours long. Their routine is based on the Kastan hour which measures just over forty-two of our minutes. All walls are patrolled four times per hour. Roughly, once every ten minutes."

"That's what we made it when we watched them last night," Pye reminded.

"So anyone who wants to get over that sixty-foot wall has got to do it in under ten minutes. If he's spotted he'll be shot on sight—not for trying to escape but for disobedience. Ten minutes isn't much of a margin." He shrugged, went on, "The wall-patrols haven't been established to prevent escapes because they don't expect any. They're merely performing a wartime routine of keeping watch against outside attack. But that doesn't help us any. They've got eyes in their heads no matter which way they're looking."

"How about the gate?" asked Foley.

"There's an all-night guard on it; twelve men and another twelve within call. There's a total of four hundred guards in this jail. There are forty similar prisons in Gathin. A dozen are within easy reach of here, some so near that their lumbering gangs are cutting timber alongside our mob."

"How near?"

"One of them is only a mile away. You could see it from the window but for the rise of land and the trees." Wardle paused, finished, "I've saved the best bit to the last. You've noticed that extension back of Festerhead's building? It's the garrison armory. It holds at least four hundred guns and plenty of ammo."

"Did any Stame get roused from his lethargy by your questions?" inquired Holden.

"Not that I noticed." Wardle pulled a face. "They attributed them to idle curiosity. How did you get on?"

Holden laughed with a rasping, knocking sound like that of a burial casket falling downstairs. Taking from his pocket a lump of soft, grayish substance, he tossed it into the air, caught it, juggled it dexterously. Then he molded it with his fingers.

"What's that?" asked Foley.

"Alamite."

"And what might alamite be?"

"Plastic explosive," said Holden.

"For heaven's sake!" Foley fell over a bed in his haste to make distance.

"Put it away," begged Pye. "You make me nervous."

"Bah!" said Holden. "You could bite it and chew it and nothing would happen. It needs a detonator."

"You wouldn't happen to have one with you?"

"No, I didn't bother to bring one. I can get fifty any time I want. And a ton of alamite to go with it. The stuff is touchy. The guards don't go near it. They leave the slaves to handle it and blow themselves apart." He gave the same laugh again. "I am a slave."

"How's that, fellows?" said Wardle, with great satisfaction. "One blast at the armory doors and we've got four hundred guns."

"I've something else, too." Putting the alamite back in a pocket, Holden removed his jacket and shirt, unwound from his middle a long coil of thin but strong cord. "It was lying around begging to be taken. Good, *houne?*"

"Hide it some place," urged Wardle. "We're going to need that rope before we're through." He turned to McAlpin. "What's your report?"

"They let Pye and me work together. In a big repair shop. All sorts of electronic stuff. The work is mostly radio and video servicing, the ordinary checking, adjusting or repairing of spaceship equipment. They kept close watch on the two of us until they became satisfied that we really know our job. After that they left us alone to get on with it."

"Any chance of sabotaging their junk?"

"Not just yet," said McAlpin, regretfully. "Maybe later on. Raduma, who's in charge of the place, is a fussy character and to give him his due he's an expert. He likes everything perfect and regards a substandard job as a slur on his professional competence. Whenever we finish a piece of work he puts the equipment on the test-bench and checks its functioning personally. That doesn't leave us much scope, does it?"

"No, I guess not. But he's persnickety rather than suspicious?"

"That's right. And like all of his type he wastes no time or thought on apparatus which is beyond repair or not worth repairing. It gets tossed in the yard at back and is left there to rot."

"So—?"

"So we can help ourselves *ad lib* providing we do it surreptitiously and providing work goes on satisfactorily. There is a mountain of stuff from which we can take our pick—if nobody sees us picking. Some dexterous cannibalizing will get us everything we want. Our chief trouble is going to be that of smuggling it far from sight."

"Can you get it into the edge of the jungle?" asked Wardle.

"Sure thing. But no farther. We can't risk being missed more than five or six minutes at a time."

"Leave the rest to me. You get it into the jungle's fringe and let me know when and where. I'll have it dragged away somehow. I'm not in a timber gang for nothing. How long do you reckon it will take to swipe all the parts you need?"

McAlpin thought a bit. "We can make the booster in the workshop right under their noses. The bowl antenna will have to be sneaked piece by piece and assembled elsewhere. To make or steal the lot and get it away will take at least a fortnight—and that's assuming we're not caught."

"It won't be enough merely to make some equipment disappear," chipped in Pye. "We've also got to find a small clearing some place where we can set up the beacon without interference. It'll have to be off the forest tracks where no Kastan or gabby prisoner is likely to see it. It will also have to be within reach of power lines that we can tap."

"How near to power lines?"

"Say not more than eight hundred yards away," offered Pye. "I think we can grab enough cable to cover that distance."

"O. K. You tend to teleportating the stuff as far as the trees. I'll find a site and have it taken there."

"How?"

"Don't know yet. But it's my grief. I'll do it if it kills me." Wardle now turned attention to Foley. "Anything to say?"

"Not much. The prison hospital is a blot on so-called civilization. Its chief concern is to get half-dead slaves back to work with the minimum of cost, trouble and delay. Even sick guards have a rough time of it there. The equipment is poor, the treatment inhuman, and Doctor-Major Machimbar, who bosses the place, is a disgrace to the medical profession."

"A warning, fellows," said Wardle, looking at the others. "Nobody falls sick if he can help it."

"Give you one guess at Machimbar's greeting when I reported to him," said Foley.

"Henceforth your sole purpose in life will be to please me," Holden suggested.

"Correct." Foley brooded a while, added, "There's two items of interest. For one, the hospital is outside the prison and within a short sprint of the jungle. Theoretically it's an easy escape route. In grim fact you've got to be *in extremis* to be taken there."

"And the other item?" Wardle prompted.

"I found a Stame colonel."

"You did?"

"I asked an emaciated Stame what he'd been before capture. He said a colonel of infantry. He and his troop had been paralyzed with gas and were in manacles when they recovered. They never had a chance but that doesn't stop him thinking himself a shame to his race."

"We can use him," said Wardle.

"We can do better," Foley replied. "According to him there are four more ex-colonels somewhere in this clink. There is also a former Aluesine major-general."

"Name?"

"General Partha-ak-Waym."

"We've got to find that character. We've got to get him into a corner and talk."

"And make him see reason," contributed Pye, openly doubting the ability of any foreigner to do so.

Holden said, "The night is young. There is one among us, name of Cheminais, specially trained to bust any lock yet devised by the thinking mind. Being able to count, I have estimated that there are four barrack-blocks in this emporium. Therefore there's one chance in four that our block holds this Pat Ak-Whatzit."

"Partha-ak-Waym," Foley corrected.

"That is what I said," declared Holden. "Well, what are we waiting for? You fellows crippled or something?"

"Can you open the door?" Wardle asked Cheminais.

That worthy, a burly and blue-jowled specimen, felt around his clothes, produced a festoon of lockpicks. "I have not spent a day in the main workshops for nothing." He started operating on the door.

"You were with him in the workshops," said Wardle to Casasola. "Did you get anything worth having?"

Without comment Casasola felt at the back of his neck, found a loop of string, pulled it and hauled up what had been hanging down his back. It was the middle leaf of a Kastan truck-spring, a piece of steel thirty inches long, one inch wide, slightly curved. Two countersunk holes had been drilled either side of its center, also one hole at each end. He gave it to Wardle.

"Did you drill it yourself, without being spotted?" Wardle asked.

Casasola nodded.

"Good for you! Get any wire?"

Impassively Casasola handed over a coil of wire. Also a dozen six-inch nails with their heads cut off, their sheared ends slotted, their points ground needle sharp.

"Been quite a busy little bee, haven't you?" said Wardle, greatly pleased.

Casasola gave a faint smile and nodded again.

"The stupid, cockeyed thing!" swore Cheminais from the door. "Just because they're Kastans doesn't mean they've got to fix it upside-down." He did something to the lock. It squeaked in protest, surrendered with a click. The door swung open. "That's it. Dead easy once you've got the hang of it."

"Anyone coming with me?" Wardle glanced inquiringly around.

"Count me out," yawned Holden. "I'm too tired."

"I'll have to go," Cheminais pointed out. "There's a lock on every room."

"Maybe I should go, too," suggested Foley. "I've practically got an introduction from that Stame colonel. It may help to establish confidence at the start."

"Yes, you've made a point there." Wardle slipped cautiously into the corridor. It was empty. "Three of us are plenty. No sense in the lot of us trooping around.

If a guard catches us, act dopey. The door didn't shut and we don't know we're doing wrong, see?" He thought a moment. "We'll start at the top floor and work down. That way we're less likely to walk into a beating-up."

Swiftly but quietly he moved along the corridor, reached the stairs. Despite lack of a lighting system within the building it was not difficult to see where one was going. Darkness was never absolute on Gathin, what with the shine of three moons and a multitude of stars. Moreover the flarepath along the wall-top contributed its share to interior illumination.

At the foot of the stairs Wardle paused, motioned the others to stay still while he listened. Not a sound came down from above, no stamp of patrolling boots, no creak of leather, not even a restless stirring of prisoners.

The thought raced through his mind that if those incarcerated in this block had all been Terrans the entire building would have resounded with the noises of energetic and mostly mutinous activity. The trouble with Terrans was that they were persistent practitioners of naughtiness. All the same, there were circumstances in which they had very considerable nuisance value.

He mounted the stairs, turned the end of another unguarded corridor, listened again, went up the next flight. Cheminais padded silently behind him. Foley followed in the rear, no more than a dark shadow.

At the top Wardle stopped. The others halted promptly, thinking he'd heard something. They listened but detected no cause for alarm.

"What's the matter?" whispered Foley.

"Just thought of something. Holden—he wouldn't come. It's not like him to refuse activity."

"He said he was tired."

"Yes, I know," Wardle murmured. "And he's a liar. I've just realized he had a conspiratorial expression when he said it. He wanted me out of the way. If he starts an uproar while we're up here—"

"Forget it," urged Foley. "We've got to take a chance. We can't go back now."

"Darn Holden!" swore Wardle in an undertone. "And his Snow White. He's the most undisciplined—"

"Aren't we all?" Foley gave him a gentle shove. "Move on. I want some sleep tonight even if you don't."

Wardle glided forward, scowling in the gloom. He found a door, put his ear to it, heard grunts and faint snores.

"Try this one."

Cheminais felt around the lock, fumbled with it until it clicked. The door emitted loud creaks as he shoved it open. Wardle went in. A Stame sat up hurriedly in bed, stared at him with incredulous eyes as big as an owl's.

"Any Aluesines in here?" asked Wardle, in low tones.

The Stame opened his mouth, shut it, opened it again. His eyes were straining to grow larger. He seemed stuck for words.

"Quick!—any Aluesines?"

"Two doors along." It came out in a gasp.

"Thanks." Wardle departed, carefully closing the door.

Behind him, the Stame crawled out of bed, shook awake the one in the next. "A Terran just came in. D'you hear me, Vermer? A Terran is wandering around contrary to orders."

"Then why should he come here?" said the other, with much disdain. "You have been dreaming." He rolled over and went back to sleep.

The second door swung inward without a sound. The three passed through, quiet as ghosts. Nevertheless they were heard and seen the moment they entered. These nocturnal Aluesines could never reconcile themselves to sleeping in their normally wakeful hours, they had sharp ears and superb nightsight.

All twenty were sitting up, their cat-eyes watching the door as the trio of Terrans came in.

In low tones Wardle said without preamble, "We are looking for Partha-ak-Waym. Do any of you know where he is?"

One of them had enough self-possession to speak up promptly. "He is in this block, on the second floor, the middle room facing the yard."

Wardle eyed him with approval. "What is your rank?"

"A prisoner has no rank. Surely you know that?"

Foley chipped in with his own tactic. "What was your rank before capture?"

"I was a flight leader."

"Ah, a space-navy officer?"

"Yes—but there are no officers now."

"Your name?" asked Foley.

"Dareuth."

"Thanks! We shall remember it."

They made to depart but Dareuth was not prepared to leave it at that. "Earthmen, permit me to advise you—the latrines are best."

"Best?" Wardle paused in the doorway, looked back baffled. "Best for what?"

"For killing oneself. In any other place your comrades will be punished for allowing you to do it."

"Thank you, Dareuth," said Wardle, very courteously. He went into the corridor, closed the door. "God, what a state of mind! Anyone who breaks loose contrary to regulations is either looney or seeking a gibbet."

"Save your breath," Foley advised. "Do we try the second floor right now or do we leave it until another night?"

"We'll try now, while the going is good."

They got down to the second floor without mishap, found the right door. Cheminais unlocked it and they walked in. This room was a duplicate of their own, held twelve beds. A dozen Aluesines immediately sat up, wide awake and glowing-eyed.

Wardle whispered to the one on the nearest bed. The Aluesine pointed to the sixth and said, "There."

The three knew exactly what to do. They marched to the foot of the indicated bed, stood in line, shoulders squared, heads erect. Three arms flicked up in a precise salute.

"Captain Wardle and two officers reporting to General Partha-ak-Waym!"

General Partha retained full self-control and much dignity. Clambering out, he folded his one dirty blanket, pulled on his tattered and threadbare clothes. Then he gazed down upon the diminutive Terrans. He was older than the average prisoner, with many seams and wrinkles around the corners of his eyes.

"It does not help to be mocked," he said, quietly. "Former officers should know better than to behave in such a way."

"There is nothing 'former' about us, sir," replied Wardle, showing firmness. "We are still officers. I am still a captain. You are still a general."

"Really?" His features quirked. "A general in what army?"

By hokey, this was it! He'd asked for it and he was going to get it. Right where it would do the most good.

"I have the honor to inform you, sir, that you are a general of the Free Gath Republic."

"Indeed? Who says so?"

'The Space Union, sir. The Gaths need every officer they can muster."

"What nonsense is this?" said Partha, impatiently. "I have never heard of Gaths, never in my life. I do not believe that there is such a race. If there is, where are they located?"

"On Gathin, sir."

Hah, that hit him.

Partha rocked back. "But *this* is Gathin."

"That's correct, sir."

"I am not a native of Gathin."

"Neither are the Kastans."

"I am a . . . I am a—"

Wardle eyed him steadily. "You are a *what*, sir?"

There was no answer.

"Either you are a Gath or you are nothing," said Wardle. "And you cannot be nothing."

General Partha made no reply. He stood perfectly still as if on parade, his attention toward a window, his eyes upon the stars. Eleven other Aluesines got off their beds and stood with him, motivated by they knew not what.

"On this world of *ours*," continued Wardle, "there is a horde of a quarter million Kastan invaders. There is also an army of four hundred thousand fighting Gaths who lack one thing and one only—guns."

"The Stames—"

"What Stames? There are no Stames here, sir. There are only Gaths."

It took Partha quite a time to cope with his churning thoughts. He had to win a mental battle against the fixed idea that a prisoner is of the damned, forever without hope of salvation, without escape other than in the grave. A topsy-turvy viewpoint is extremely hard to assimilate and, metaphorically speaking, these three Terrans had come at him walking on the ceiling.

But he was a general—and as such was helped to moral victory by swift realization of the military advantages of doing what comes unnaturally.

Studying Wardle with sudden shrewdness, he said, "A few questions. Firstly, what is the response you have obtained from the Gaths who resemble Stames?"

"None—for the reason that we haven't approached them yet. We had to start somewhere. We started with you, sir."

"You intend to put the matter to them?"

"Most certainly, sir."

"Secondly," continued Partha, "you have stated that we need guns. Can they be obtained and, if so, when?"

"Guns will become available when the Gath army has the guts to use them, sir."

He did not flinch. On the contrary, he became more dignified than ever. "I accept that without resentment. To regain honor we must earn it." He paused, went on, "Thirdly, my past training enables me to see the tactical benefits of the rise of a Gath army. I would like to know whether such a rise is a plan in itself or essential part of a greater scheme."

"It is part of a greater Union plan," said Wardle.

"Meaning that an established Gath Republic would find itself with allies?"

"Yes, sir. It would be officially recognized and supported by the Space Union."

"*All* the Union, including—?"

"Including the Aluesine Empire," Wardle assured. "Is there any reason why conquering Aluesines should not recognize triumphant Gaths?"

At that moment the stream of burning thoughts and the surge of violent emotions became too much for Partha. He sat on time edge of his bed, held his face in his hands. Terrans and Aluesines watched in awkward silence.

Finally he recovered and said, "Give me time to discuss these things with my comrades. Do you think you might be able to visit me again tomorrow night?"

"I cannot agree to do so, sir, unless you state it properly."

"Properly?"

"Yes, sir. You must stand to attention and say, 'Captain Wardle, I wish to consult my staff. Report to me at the same time tomorrow.' "

General Partha-ak-Waym came erect. Instinctively the Aluesines lined up on either side of him. There was a visible glow in his eyes, a firmness in his voice.

"Captain Wardle, I wish to consult my staff. Report to me at the same time tomorrow."

"Very well, sir." Wardle saluted. So did Cheminais and Foley. The three marched out.

Halfway up the stairs to the third floor, Foley said, "Hooked, by gosh!"

Halfway up the stairs to the fifth floor a shot split the silence of the night somewhere outside. The three bolted to their room like scared rats.

Wardle reacted with the speed of one who has hidden reasons to expect the worst. Leaving Cheminais to relock the door, he took one swift look around the room, booted a blanket covered behind on the nearest bed.

"Where is he?"

Pye rolled over, struggled to raise himself on his elbows, bleared at the questioner. "Huh? 'Smatter?"

"Where's Holden?" Wardle bawled.

"Gone out," yawned Pye, cozily indifferent. He let the elbows slide from under him, sank back.

"Gone *where*?" cried Wardle, vastly irritated.

"That way." Pye pointed more or less toward an open window. Apparently this effort was too much for him because he let his arm drop, closed his eyes, gobbled and gulped a couple of times, settled down to a steady and rhythmic snore.

Wardle voiced five disconnected words none of which were in Extralingua. Crossing to the window he looked out and down. Sixty feet below the ground was vague, obscure, and he could detect nobody lurking there. A cord hung out the window, swaying slackly in the thin breeze of night. Within the room the cord was tied around the leg of a bed with about forty feet of surplus length coiled neatly alongside.

Even as he looked out a guard ran along the facing wall-top, disappeared from sight far over to the left. In that direction several voices could be heard arguing in the dark. What they were saying was indistinct, but they sounded querulous.

Returning to his own bed, Wardle flopped on it and stared fixedly at the window-gap. Foley and Cheminais washed at the one basin, lay down in the manner of men conspicuously unworried. Presently their snores were added to those of the others. Wardle continued to watch the window.

After half an hour the dangling cord went taut and emitted faint squeaks as it pressed hard on the woodwork of the window-frame. A head appeared in the gap, a body followed. Holden clambered through, pulled up the cord, carefully coiled it, closed the window. Then he spat on his hands and rubbed them against his pants.

"You cockeyed coot," said Wardle. "You'd try the patience of a sanctimony of bishops."

Holden started, recovered, said pleasantly, "You're looking well this evening—just had your tongue back from the cleaners?"

"This isn't funny. We heard a gun go off sometime back. It's going to endanger the whole set-up if we invite the Kastans to start shooting at us before we're ready."

"Nobody's been shooting at *me*, see?" said Holden.

"I suppose the gun exploded by sheer accident?"

"Dead right, chum. It was accidental but not quite sheer." Sitting on the edge of his bed, Holden started taking off his boots. "This joker had propped himself against the corner of the armory, being in need of more support than he gets from his sergeant. His gun was propped likewise. He'd worked it out very neatly that a weight on the ground isn't felt on the shoulder, see?"

"Yes, yes—get on with the story," urged Wardle.

"Well, I broke a piece of wire off the armory fence, bent each end to form a hook. It took me ten minutes to crawl to the corner. I hooked one end of the wire around his trigger, the other end to the fence. Then I crawled back and left the rest to nature."

"You lunatic. If he'd seen you, he'd have put a stream of slugs through your belly then and there."

"He didn't see me. He wasn't seeing anything except Jeanie with the light brown hair." Kicking his boots under the bed, Holden stood up. Undoing his pants, he felt around inside the seat, got a hold, commenced pulling out a long length of cloth. There seemed to be several yards of it.

Unable to suppress his curiosity, Wardle crossed to the other's bed, examined the stuff in the dim light. Then he grabbed it up, took it to the window for a better look.

"Holy cow! This is their flag!"

"Yair," agreed Holden.

"Where'd you get it?"

"I found it in the bulrushes." He let go a snicker. "What's good enough for Pharoah's daughter is good enough for me."

"The truth, man! You sneaked it right off the pole, didn't you?"

"Might as well admit it," said Holden, with mock resignation. "And a devil of a time I had getting it. Up on Festerhead's roof the wind is like a gale. I nearly fell off twice. If I'd held my jacket wide open I'd have become airborne."

"But . . . but—" Wardle waved the stolen banner and found himself temporarily lost for words.

"Four times a sentry passed below while I was struggling to get the thing down and stuff it in my pants. Never once did the stupid gump look upward."

"But—"

"We can use that rag. Cut off the crimson stripe at its end, convert the two white arrows into a six-pointed star, and what have you got? One white star on a blue background. For whom has the Union designed that kind of flag?"

"The Gath Republic."

"Correct. You can be quite bright at times." Rolling onto his bed, Holden arranged his blanket to give maximum warmth.

"Where are we going to hide it until it's needed?" asked Wardle.

"That's your worry. I got it— you stash it. Anyway, they never do any systematic searching."

"There's always got to be a first time," Wardle pointed out. "I don't like this situation. Pandemonium will break loose when they discover their flag has been thieved overnight."

"They won't stir a hair. After I'd cut the cord I frayed the ends to look like a break. Ten to one they'll jump to the conclusion that the wind whisked it into the jungle. If they do, I'm going to volunteer to lead some of the forest gang in search of it. That'll give us a sweet excuse to go looking for a beacon site."

"You've got a hell of a nerve," said Wardle, with grudging admiration.

Holden made a gesture of modest rebuttal. "I'd rather not see myself as others see me—I'm conceited enough already."

With that, he went to sleep. But Wardle remained awake some time, nursing the flag and thinking. His final conclusion was that Holden could not be blamed.

After all, a Terran must do *something*.

Over the next four days the flag-hunters led by Holden failed to find so much as a loose thread. At the end of that time Festerhead's patience ran out. He put them back onto timber work, produced another banner from somewhere and had it nailed to the pole.

But efforts had not been wasted. In those four days they had discovered a suitable place amid the thickest tangle of growths, cleared a small area, dug a pit six feet square by four deep. This they filled with rocks then left in readiness for concreting-in the beacon legs at first opportunity.

It was on the twenty-first day of Terran captivity that a threat to carefully laid plans came from a completely unexpected quarter. It proved yet again that not everything can be foreseen even by the shrewdest, most painstaking minds.

Over every conglomeration of intelligent beings hangs an invisible something called atmosphere. It cannot be seen, tasted or smelled. It can be sensed. It can almost be felt.

After the evening meal on that day, Wardle stood in the yard and suddenly was struck by a powerful impression of change. A thrill of alarm ran through his mind as he sought to pin down and analyze the reasons. The atmosphere of the prison yard was different from what it had been three weeks ago; the cause or causes should be identifiable.

Now that his brain had become aware of the phenomenon it didn't take his eyes long to relate cause and effect. The usual mob of Stames and Aluesines were milling aimlessly around the yard. In the mass, they were still whipped dogs—individually they were not. A change had taken place in personal behavior.

They no longer slouched. They walked and some actually marched. They did not creep past guards with their heads lowered and their attention focused on the ground. On the contrary, they kept heads erect and stared straight at the guards, man to man, eye to eye. Even the persistently humorless, unsmiling Stames had switched expressions from glumness to grimness.

Over all lay that vague, indefinable but strong impression of a calm before a storm, a power held in check with no guarantee that it could bide its time.

The guards, too, sensed it without knowing what they sensed. Alien convention prevented them from recognizing the undercurrents and subtle stir-rumblings familiar to Terran wardens. So they were uneasy without knowing why. They fidgeted, kept guns in hands, grouped together in the yard, walked at faster pace along the wall-tops.

With back hairs rising, Wardle set off on a hurried tour of the yard. In such a crowd it was difficult to find at once the individual he was seeking. Near one corner he encountered Pye.

"Help find Partha for me. Also grab any Stame brasshats you happen to see."

"Something wrong?" asked Pye.

"Take a look around. This lot's making ready to go bang any time. It's the old story of the pendulum swinging to the other extreme." He jerked a thumb toward a small cluster of guards standing together in the shadow of the wall. "Even the Kastans are jumpy. When that type goes round the bend they're liable to start shooting at whoever happens to be handy. And that means *us*."

Partha and two Stame colonels were found a few minutes later and shepherded into an unoccupied corner of the yard. There, Wardle made them a brief speech pointing out the giveaway symptoms, contrasting the controllability of an army with the indiscipline of a mob.

"Previously your men waited with complete despair," he said. "Now they wait with renewed hope that comes harder. It is trying to the patience."

"You created the disease," commented Partha. "It is for you to suggest a cure."

"All right. Pass the word around as fast as your words can go that we're holding a conference tonight and that we'll be wanting volunteers tomorrow."

"Volunteers for what?"

"I don't know, I just don't know," admitted Wardle, momentarily at his wit's end. "We'll have to concoct a scheme of some sort, any sort so long as it pipes off the mounting steam. It's the philosophy of the trapped rat—when nothing can be done, do *anything*."

"Very well," agreed Partha. He made to go.

"And tell everyone it's essential not to let the Kastans take alarm," Wardle added, with much emphasis. "That means all prisoners must look like slaves, behave like slaves."

Partha and the Stames went off, mixed in with the crowd, talked briefly to various groups and moved on. Within twenty minutes results became visible but Wardle did not feel happy about them.

Like all amateurs, the captives tended to overact. Many of those who'd been walking erect and secretly incubating a lovely spirit of defiance now put on grossly exaggerated expressions of humility and made a point of exhibiting them to baffled guards. Twenty Stames ceremoniously sat down in front of three Kastans and favored them with a unanimous look of oh-death-where-is-thy-sting.

Holden ambled up and Wardle greeted him bitterly with, "Look at that mob of raw beginners. They were feeling their oats and have been told to relax. Now you'd think the entire bunch was sickening for something."

"That's an idea," said Holden.

"Eh?"

"The Kastan war economy is partly dependent on slave labor. An epidemic would make a nice, effective form of sabotage, not to mention the hob it would play with their organization here."

"An epidemic of what?"

"Soap," said Holden.

"How about talking sense, just for a pleasant change?" Wardle suggested.

Ignoring that, Holden exclaimed, "Here's Foley." He waited until the other arrived, went on, "Just the man we want. What's the capacity of the hospital?"

"Thirty," said Foley. "Why?"

"What do you think this butcher Machimbar would do if three hundred prisoners flopped together?"

"Nothing. Not a thing. He'd let 'em die. He'd say the hospital is full and that Kastan guards have first call on his services. Machimbar is the sort who does only the minimum necessary to justify his rank and position and, if possible, prevent himself from being drafted to a combat area."

"A shirker of responsibility, is he?"

"More than that—he's a thoroughly selfish swine."

"He'll get his," promised Holden, "before we're through."

"What's on your mind—other than water?" asked Wardle.

A whistle shrilled across the yard before the other could reply. Prisoners assembled in long lines and started filing into their barrack-blocks. Guards prowled along the lines, bawling and blustering, urging them to hurry.

There was one small but significant incident. A lame Stame stumbled and fell out of the shuffling ranks. Swearing at him, a guard raised his whip. The Stame straightened, gazed coldly into the eyes of his enemy until the other gave way and the whip drooped unused.

"We haven't a lot of time," commented Wardle. "Let's hope we've got enough or can make enough."

Cheminais put in some fast manipulating that night. He tended to three doors in his own block, two in the adjoining one. A dozen prisoners made the twenty-yard dash between blocks in semidarkness, got across unheard, unseen. A council of war was held in the Terrans' room.

"We've several problems," began Wardle. "They've got to be settled in any way solvable within existing circumstances. First, there's the beacon."

"Has it been discovered?" asked Partha-ak-Waym.

"Not so far. We've built it, linked it to a power line and that's all. If the Kastans happen to find it, there's a good chance they'll assume it to be the work of one of their own signal corps. Even if they do get incurably curious it may take them a couple of months to make sure that no Kastan outfit knows anything about it."

"Not sharing our outlook," put in Holden, "they won't take it for granted that it's a product of naughty prisoners."

"Well, what's the problem?" Partha persisted.

"The forest gang did hard but unskilled work. They sneaked away all the stuff that McAlpin and Pye hid among the trees, erected it according to their instructions. Now it needs technicians to make final adjustments and start it radiating. Daytimes McAlpin and Pye can't slip away for more than five minutes at a go. They say they've got to have three or four uninterrupted hours to get the beacon functioning." He paused, added pointedly, "Union forces don't know the location of Gathin—until the beacon tells 'em."

"I can find some technicians among my men," suggested Partha. "If you can get them into the forest gang—"

"This is our own problem and we're going to cope with it in our own way," declared Wardle. "We'll give McAlpin and Pye a night out. They'll go over the wall."

"You mean—*escape?"* Partha voiced the word as though even now it had a slight touch of blasphemy.

"Not for keeps. They'll come back and report for work in the morning as usual. As I said before, we've got to keep the Kastans soothed. However, it might give all prisoners a boost if you let the news go round that we've been outside. Better warn them, though, not to mess things up by behaving as if they're as good as out themselves. They aren't out—yet."

"But to get over that wall is impossible."

"We'll admit it after we've found it can't be done," said Wardle. "And not before." Dismissing the point, he carried on to the second problem. "About ten thousand are in this jail but four hundred thousand on Gathin. We're a mere tithe of the whole. We've got to contact other prisons, persuade them to join in with us and take action at the same time. There are seven within easy reach. If they're the same size as this one, that means another seventy thousand men available."

Partha pursed his lips and frowned. "There is no communication between prisons."

"Then communication must be established. It's got to be done and will be done—and here's how." Wardle registered a faint smile as he continued, "You may not realize it, but to Terran eyes most Aluesines look remarkably alike. So also do Stames."

"Terrans look much alike to us," said Partha.

"It's highly probable that Kastans have similar trouble in distinguishing one from another," Wardle pointed out. "Adjacent prisons have forestry parties working almost alongside ours. If some prisoners swapped places, their respective guards wouldn't notice the difference."

"If they did notice, they wouldn't care," suggested Holden. "One bunch of slaves is as good as another."

"Maybe," Wardle conceded. "But a scheme can always be wrecked by one individual's officiousness." He returned attention to Partha. "You must find a number of volunteers, all officers capable of restoring and exercising their own authority, all able propagandists for the new viewpoint. They will join a forestry gang and switch into one from another prison."

"That can be done," agreed Partha. "There is one difficulty. An exchange is a two-way arrangement. It needs the co-operation of others who mentally are still slaves conditioned never to disobey."

"The Kastans haven't issued any orders about captives returning to their own jail. You can't disobey a command that has never been given. Besides, to change prisons is not to escape."

"Yes, that is true. Leave this task to me."

"We'll have to. We've no choice. A Terran can't swap. Among a bunch of eight-footers he'd be as conspicuous as a circus midget." Leaving it at that, Wardle said, "Now to our third problem. Prisoners must hold themselves in restraint until arrives the right moment to strike together and effectively. Premature action by individuals or groups could be fatal to our plans. We've got to insure that they don't jump the gun. Any suggestions?"

"They need a diversion," opined Holden. "One good hullabaloo would keep them happy for a month."

"Can you offer a suitable gag?"

"Yair," said Holden. He chewed vigorously, let go with a soul-shaking, "A-a-argh!" and fell flat. Then he curled up violently until his knees rammed into his chest, his eyes rolled under the lids to show only the whites, a long spurt of foam came from his writhing lips. It was a sight sufficiently revolting to turn the onlookers' stomachs.

"A-a-argh!" groaned Holden, most horribly. More foam appeared. Watching Stames and Aluesines bugged their eyes at him. Even Wardle felt a spasm of alarm.

Making a remarkable recovery, Holden got up, went to the basin, washed his mouth out, gargled a couple of times. "All it needs is a little practice."

"What good will it do?" inquired Partha, studying him as one would a maniac.

"A sick slave cannot work. A hundred sick slaves cannot work. A thousand sick—"

"Show me how," ordered Partha, making up his mind.

Shaving off a sliver of soap, Holden put it in the other's mouth, doing it like mailing a letter. "Now chew. All right, fall down. Curl up and moan. Louder than that, much louder. Your eyes, man, your eyes—roll them up until you can look at your brains!"

General Partha-ak-Waym lay curled up and rolled 'em. It was extremely effective since Aluesine eyeballs were pale orange in color. He looked awful.

Within short time ten Aluesines and eight Stames were groaning and foaming on the floor. It was, thought Wardle privately, the most beautiful chore ever thought up for a bunch of military brasshats.

"Good," he said when the horrid performance ended. "Find a battalion of volunteers for that and get them busy rehearsing. The show goes on at breakfast-time tomorrow. It should provide a satisfactory emotional outlet and bollix the Kastans more than somewhat."

The council of war ended. The members departed accompanied by Cheminais who was to lock them back in.

When they'd all gone, Wardle turned to Holden. "You said it needed practice. You've had plenty. Where'd you get it?"

"At about age four. Whenever I rolled and foamed my loving mother would give me the moon."

"What a repulsive little brat you must have been. If I were your father, I'd have given you a taste of hickory."

"He did," admitted Holden, grimacing. "Whenever he caught me at it." He switched attention to the silently listening Casasola. "For Pete's sake shut up and let me get a word in edgewise."

"We're wasting time," commented Wardle, impatiently. "The longest night doesn't last forever. We've got to get two fellows over the wall—we've not erected a secret beacon for nothing."

Lying on his back he edged beneath his bed, fiddled around with the underside of it, edged out again. He was now gripping a grooved wooden stock with the truck-spring fastened across one end. A wire ran taut across the spring's curve. Farther back in the stock was a winder and a simple trigger mechanism which Casasola had made in the workshops.

"This," he remarked "is where we put to use our training in the exploitation of rudimentary supplies. Learn to make the best of what is available, they said. And do not despise primitive things, for man conquered the animal world with no better." He held a hand out to Casasola. "The bolts."

Casasola gave him the machined nails which by now had small aluminum vanes fitted into their slots.

"The string."

Impassively Casasola handed over a ball of fine twine. Measuring it along the room, Wardle cut off a length of approximately a hundred and twenty feet, doubled it, fastened its middle to the tail of a bolt. Six inches behind the bolt he knotted-in a sliver of wood to act as a spreader, holding the strings some three or four inches apart.

"Open a window, someone, and watch for a guard." He stood waiting while Pye tied one of the string's two ends to the coil of stronger cord that Holden had stolen from the quarry. "Remember," he said to Pye, "when everything is ready, you'll have less than ten minutes."

"I know."

"Too much delay will get you a dozen slugs in the guts."

"So what?"

"If you or Mac want to back out, say so—we'll understand."

"Go jump," suggested Pye.

"What d'you think I am?" put in McAlpin, indignantly.

"Guard coming," hissed Holden from the window. "Here he is, the big, flat-footed lug. Right opposite." A pause, followed by, "Now he's passed."

He stepped aside. Wardle knelt by the window and steadied the crossbow on its ledge. Taking careful aim at the distant wall-top, he squeezed the trigger. The arbelest gave a slight jerk as its driving-wire slapped dully against two small silencers neatly carved from Holden's rubber heels.

The bolt shot into the night, fled three-quarters of the way to the wall, pulled up sharp as its trailing string snagged on a window-frame splinter and failed to pay out. In the darkness the bolt swooped back, hit the barrack-block two floors lower down. There sounded a loud clunk, a clatter of broken glass, a startled Stame exclamation.

Wardle cussed in a low voice, peered out and down for signs of Stame activity beneath. There wasn't any. Whoever had been shaken out of his beauty sleep had wisely decided to do nothing about it, probably because nothing effective could be done.

"A minute and a half gone," announced Pye.

They pulled back the tethered bolt, shaved the splinter from the ledge, rearranged the string to run more freely. Again Wardle took aim a few inches above the flarepath. The bolt sped out, went straight over the wall, stopped as it reached the following string's limit.

Slowly and with care they drew on the string. Infuriatingly, the bolt wriggled between the spikes and fell clear. Now they reeled in with frantic haste but again it clunked the barrack-block with a sound hugely magnified by the stillness of night. However, no glass was busted this time.

"Four minutes gone," said Pye.

The third shot proved just as futile, produced yet another crack of metal against stone. When the bolt came in they found the string-separator had broken. Hurriedly they replaced it.

"Six and a half minutes," informed Pye, morbidly.

"He's on his way back by now," said Wardle. "We'd better wait for him to pass again."

Clustering in the gloom, they listened and waited, hearing little save each other's breathing. Presently the guard went by along the wall-top, his big figure magnified to the monstrous by the flare of light. He did not look unusually alert, showed no sign of having been alarmed by strange noises.

When he'd gone from view, Wardle fired again. The bolt shot out with a very faint hiss. Its aluminum vanes shone briefly as it crossed the wall-top. Holden gently drew on the string and a few feet came into the room before it went taut.

"Hallelujah!" he said.

He now pulled only one end, giving a couple of fierce jerks to dislodge the distant separator. It stuck stubbornly a short time, came free. The string then reeled in easily. As it did so its other end went out the window taking with it the strong cord.

Before long Holden found himself pulling in cord instead of string. There was now a double line of cord extending from the room, across a forty-foot gap with a sixty-foot drop below, and terminating at one or more wall-top spikes over which it was looped.

"How long have we now?" asked Wardle.

"Four minutes."

"Not enough. We'll have to wait again. Got your own cord ready?"

"Sure thing," said Pye.

They waited. The guard's footsteps could be heard coming back. He seemed to take an inordinate time to get near. Everything depended on where his attention lay, how observant he was. The flarepath was a brilliant but narrow beam directed dead along the wall-top but there was enough side-glow to reveal the horizontally stretched string for a distance of several feet.

The guard neared the critical point. They held their breaths as they watched him. Strolling boredly along, he halted beside the looped spike, looked outward instead of inward, gave a wide yawn and moved onward.

"Thank heaven we blacked that rope," exclaimed Holden.

"Now!" urged Wardle.

Pye scrambled out the window, let himself hang from the cords by holding one in each grip. With body dangling over the drop he worked himself along hand over hand. His legs swung wildly as he strove to make speed. The cord creaked but held.

In this manner he reached the wall-top and still had come no raucous shout, no crack of a gun. Desperately he swung himself up sidewise, got handholds on two spikes, a toehold between two more. Levering himself over the triple row he rolled right into the flarepath.

Still prone, fearful of the light and whoever might look along its beam, he grabbed his own coil of rope, looped it around one of the opposite spikes. How he got over this other triple row was not clear to the watchers. His body humped itself, there was some momentary fumbling, and he vanished from sight as he slid down outside the wall.

"It took him four and a half minutes," said Holden.

"Seemed like ten years to me," contributed Wardle.

The guard mooched back. There were now two looped spikes for him to discover, one on each side of his path. Would he see them? He did not. In the same manner as before he ambled by and his footsteps faded.

McAlpin was swinging in midair almost before the guard had disappeared. He crossed the gap a good deal faster than Pye had done but had more difficulty in getting over the spikes. All the same, he made it. His shape vanished over the other side of the wall.

Unfastening one end of the cord, Holden pulled on the other end, got it all back into the room. To leave it out for several hours would be to tempt Providence. Perforce the outer rope would have to remain dangling, but only the couple of inches around the spike could be visible to the guard, the rest hanging in darkness down the wall.

"Just thought of something," said Holden. "A fellow parading along a flarepath can see pretty well to the right or left but is somewhat blinded if he looks straight ahead. I doubt whether that clunker could find Pye's rope even if you told him it was there."

"We're not counting on that," Wardle told him. "We are betting on a state of mind. Excepting on a peculiar dump called Terra nobody ever breaks out of jail—but nobody!"

After that they organized a constant watch at the window, taking turns one at a time while the others slept. It was an hour before dawn when the escapees returned.

Cheminais, keeping red-rimmed eyes directed on the wall, knew that their rope was still in position because every guard had been observed and none had so far interfered.

A guard went past, gun clasped in a spade-sized hand. A minute later McAlpin heaved himself over the outer spikes, pulled up half of the doubled cord and slung it down the inside wall. Then he rolled across the flarepath, got over the next lot of spikes with the same difficulty as before, slid down into darkness.

Apparently his thirty pounds of extra weight helped heave his companion up the outer wall as he went down the inner one. He'd no sooner gone than Pye popped up like a cork from a bottle, looped the cord and followed the other down inside. The cord shook violently, fell to ground.

Awakening the others, Cheminais informed, "They're back."

They let the guard pass again before tossing their own cord out the window. A weight came upon it, they hauled together. McAlpin rose into the window-gap, struggled through, trod on someone's toes and received a couple of choice oaths by way of welcome. The cord went down again, fished up Pye.

"How did it go?" Wardle asked them, anxiously.

"Topnotch," assured McAlpin. "The beacon is now bawling its head off."

"What d'you think will happen if it's picked up by a Kastan ship ahead of one of ours?"

"They'll trace it to Gathin. They know Gathin is a Kastan stronghold. Therefore the beacon must be an official one even if they haven't been notified of it. That's logical, isn't it? The alternative is an illegal beacon and that's plain silly."

"Let's hope you're right. You've done a good job."

"Like to know the toughest part of it?" McAlpin showed him a pair of red-seared palms. "Climbing sixty feet of thin cord."

"Dead easy," scoffed Holden.

"It would be for you," McAlpin retorted, "being several generations nearer to the monkeys."

Holden let that pass with the contempt it deserved.

"Well," prompted Casasola, shocking him with sudden speech, "why don't you *say* something?"

The multiple line-ups for breakfast were divisible into two parts: those aware and those unaware of what was brewing. Partha had considered it desirable to keep a goodly number in ignorance and thus support the play with an audience that could be depended upon to behave plausibly.

Stewed sludge was served. Ten thousand sat around scooping at their wooden bowls. The last and slowest had hardly finished when Guard-Major Slovits blew the whistle.

Eighty prisoners judiciously scattered around the yard promptly collapsed, doubled up, foamed, yelled bloody murder. The mob about to make for the gates stopped and stared. Near the gates four hefty guards gazed aghast at an afflicted Stame who was making like a circus acrobat with a thousand devils in his belly.

Among the guards there followed the inevitable moment of chronic indecision during which another fifty prisoners artistically added themselves to the sufferers on the floor. They vied with each other in producing the most foam, the loudest screams, the worst agonies.

Prisoners not in the plot milled around like scared sheep, watched themselves for similar symptoms. A number of guards became pinned within the mob, strove to force their way out. Stames and Aluesines dropped and had six fits in front of them, alongside of them, impeding them to the utmost. The mob pushed and shoved as those nearest tried to back away from each successive victim.

One Stame standing in what looked like shocked silence suddenly let go with an ear-splitting shriek, flung long, skinny arms around an adjacent guard, slid down foaming and slobbering all over the Kastan's pants and jack-boots. He got away with it, receiving not so much as a flick of the whip. The guard looked down in horror, made for some place else good and fast.

Slovits pounded heavily into the office building, reappeared a moment later with the prison commander. A solid rank of sixteen Aluesines immediately strove to please both of them by falling flat, foaming, groaning, dribbling and rolling orange-colored eyeballs.

Noting that Festerhead himself was now among those present another couple of hundred piled into the act all over the yard, added their howls to the general uproar. Guards shouted unhearable orders, Festerhead bellowed and waved his arms, Slovits blew the whistle ten times.

More individuals collapsed here and there in response to surreptitious signals from officers. Some of them were decided whole-hoggers who worked themselves into such a frenzy they swallowed their soap and began to puke in dead earnest.

At this point the captives who were uninformed got into a panic. The rumor went around like wildfire that something called "the black death" was highly contagious. There followed a concerted rush for the open gates.

Four guards who still had their wits about them moved swiftly, slammed shut the gates in the faces of the leading rank. The mob churned around a piece, made up its collective mind, headed for the sanctuary of the barrack-blocks. It split into a hundred racing lines threading their ways through a carpet of rolling bodies. Among the runners were many more plotters ordered to hold off until the last. These now made confusion worse confounded by collapsing in the most obstructive places including the barrack-blocks' doorways.

By now over a thousand were on their backs in the yard, screaming, hooting, hugging their bellies, voicing death rattles and other versions of last gasps. A form of rivalry had arisen between Aluesines and Stames, each striving to outdo the other in putting over a melodramatic picture of hell's torments. The resulting scene was like something out of the galaxy's maddest madhouse. The din was deafening.

Festerhead and his forces were swamped by the sheer magnitude and enthusiasm of this mass-display. Grouping together outside the office building, they scowled at the littered yard but did nothing. This wasn't mutiny, it wasn't disobedience. It was a phenomenon unheard-of, unthought-of. No mention of it existed in the Kastan book of rules and there was no official formula for coping with it.

A Stame who secretly admired his own talent as an actor crawled laboriously on all fours up to Guard-Major Slovits, hung out a purple tongue and croaked, "Water! For mercy's sake, water."

The guard next to Slovits swung a huge boot and kicked him straight in the teeth. The Stame flopped sidewise, spat blood and emitted moans that were real. Among the prone army of mock-sufferers several hundreds of eyes made vengeful note of the kicker's identity. Unaware of this, the guard drew back his foot for a second belt at the victim.

"What are you doing, fool?" rasped Festerhead. "Is that the way to make them ready for work?"

Putting down the foot, the guard furtively shifted behind a couple of his fellows. From that vantage point he stared sullenly at the injured Stame.

"Where is Doctor-Major Machimbar?" Festerhead demanded of Slovits.

"He is absent today, may it please you, commander," informed Slovits.

"He would be. And it does not please me." Festerhead thought hard and fast. "Something must be done. Within the hour headquarters will be pestering us with awkward questions as to why our working parties have not appeared."

"Yes, commander. What do you suggest?"

"Send twelve men into each barrack-block. They will march out all the fit prisoners and make them carry the sick ones inside. After that has been done, parade the fit ones in the yard, select from them any with medical experience, rush the rest to work—at the double."

"As you order, commander."

Slovits saluted, faced his men, favored them with the necessary bellowing. Parties of twelve split off and headed for each block.

The fit came out, picked up the sick, commenced bearing them to their respective dormitories. It took quite a time because every now and then a body-bearer would collapse and have to be carried in his turn. Thus it happened that the entire complement of one room, consisting of twenty opportunist Aluesines, contrived to have themselves borne to bed by a bunch of sour-faced Stames who did not see the obvious way of dodging the chore until it was too late.

Finally the fit were paraded in the yard, the fit being defined as those able to stand. Two dozen of them dropped in their tracks just as Slovits opened his mouth to bawl. Slovits closed the mouth while the end files wearily picked up the bodies and lugged them away. Five of the luggers swiftly decided that it requires less effort to be carried than to carry, whereupon they flopped and put on the foaming act. More end files broke off to take those away.

At that point Slovits came to the end of his patience. Stabbing a large finger at those still perpendicular, be roared, "All former doctors, surgeons, hospital orderlies and similar personnel will take six paces to the front."

Foley marched forward bawling with equal loudness, "One, two, three, four, five, *six*." He halted.

Eight Aluesines and eleven Stames did likewise, yelling in unison and finishing with a simultaneous, *"Six."* As if that were a signal, two of them bit the dust.

Slovits glared a moment at the two, his face twitching, his fingers working around. Then he said to the survivors, "Follow me."

Obediently they traipsed behind him to the office building. Three who preferred bed to Festerhead shamelessly gained their ends by collapsing on the way. Four more did the same during the ten minutes' wait outside the open door through which Festerhead could be heard shouting indistinguishable remarks into a telephone.

At the prison gates the situation was no better. Long files of captives shuffled outward, bowls and spoons clutched in boney hands, worn boots flapping or bare feet padding on the concrete. Every fifty yards or so the files halted, doubled-up bodies were dragged out of the way and borne back to the blocks. Then another fifty yards advance, a halt, more bodies.

For once the escorting Kastans did not yell, swear or swing their whips. They marched with the column, urging it onward but viewing its gradual loss of numbers with cold-blooded indifference. So far as they were concerned an epidemic was a calamity strictly for the brasshats. Let them do the worrying. That's what they were paid for, wasn't it?

Festerhead slammed down the phone, came out the door, cast a savage eye over the waiting eleven and harshed, "You will remain in the blocks and tend to the sick. I hold you responsible for restoring them to work with the minimum of delay. If you fail, you will be punished." He let his glare linger a moment upon each in turn. "The punishment will be severe."

"If we do fail," answered Foley, calmly positive, "the consequences will be more severe—the entire prison will be down and out, Kastans included."

"It is for you to prevent it."

"With what?" demanded Foley, greatly daring. "We have no medical kit, no supplies of any sort."

"I authorize you to make use of whatever facilities are in the hospital," Festerhead snapped.

"What if Doctor-Major Machimbar refuses us those facilities?"

"He will do nothing of the kind," declared Festerhead. "I am the prison commander. My orders will be obeyed. You will employ whatever supplies are available within the hospital and get the prisoners back to work." He turned to go, added as a pointed afterthought, "Or you will suffer."

One of the listening Stames started suffering then and there, flat on his back, with his feet trying to tuck themselves behind his ears.

Holden paced up and down the room, glanced through the windows at the starlit night and mused aloud. "It was a spectacular show but very much overdone. A Terran guard wouldn't have been fooled. They'd have had the high-pressure hoses out in one minute flat."

"How come you're such an authority on Terran prison techniques?" asked Alpin McAlpin.

"I know what I know."

"Sure thing you do. Bet your past is buried in the mists of iniquity."

"Quit needling," ordered Wardle, with some impatience. "Here's Partha and his boys. Let's get down to business."

Cheminais entered first, the lock-picks jangling carelessly in one hand. Then Partha followed by twenty Stames and Aluesines. The Terrans made sitting-space for them on the beds. Outside, a guard mooched along the flarepath and was blissfully ignorant of conspiratorial activity almost within hearing distance.

Wardle started the discussion with, "As probably you know, twenty-one managed to exchange with adjacent forest-parties today. Some of them will have to swap over a second or third time to spread themselves evenly around the local jails." He fixed attention on Partha. "The number isn't enough. Twice as many are needed. Can you raise more volunteers?"

"After today's performance," said Partha, permitting himself the ghost of a smile, "I don't think volunteers will be hard to find."

"According to what we've learned," Wardle went on, "there are twelve prisons within one day's march of here. Seven of these are almost within sight. We are getting some of our own men into those seven. "We'd better send more, just in case they can find a way of wangling themselves into the other five."

"It's worth a try," Partha agreed. "An army of one hundred and twenty thousand is better than one of seventy thousand. I have heard that there are forty prisons on Gathin, also several new ones not yet completed but possibly holding recently captured men. How nice if we could extend our influence over the whole lot."

"I've thought of that. The others are far away, some halfway around the planet. We could get at them by desperate and tedious measures, that's for sure. But it would take too long and the trouble isn't worth it. If we can make a major break in this area, and snatch enough guns, we can seize all the other prisons, one at a time, by main force."

Partha thought it over, objected, "The sole object of capturing prisons is to free the prisoners and thereby pile up the strength of the Gath Army. That's correct, isn't it?"

"Yes," said Wardle.

"There will be a formidable difference between prisoners conditioned by freedom propaganda and those who've never heard of it, never imagined it. Here we're building a mass of potential warriors filled with new hope and eager to fight. Elsewhere, a prison will give up no more than a mob of bewildered slaves."

"How long d'you think it will take a bewildered slave to see his chance to bust a Kastan right on the nose?" inquired Wardle.

"I can judge only by myself," Partha confessed, "and in my case it took too long."

"That's because you're a general. You're trained to be militarily correct, to look at everything from the viewpoint of personal responsibility. The lower ranks have no such inhibitions. Put guns in their hands, tell them that they are Gaths, that honor may be regained by kicking Kastans in the guts and"—he made an emphatic gesture—"I give them two minutes to absorb the facts and start shooting."

"I hope you're right," said Partha, doubtfully.

"Wait and see. Who put over the most extravagant displays this morning? The boys in the ranks. It wasn't an officer who sicked all over a guard's shiny boots."

Partha looked pained.

"Anyway, let's leave it at that. The real test will come before long. Right now we've something important to be settled." Standing in front of Partha, and speaking with great seriousness, Wardle said, "When the proper time arrives there will be two ways of obtaining guns."

"Two?"

"Yes. And it's for you to decide which way is preferred."

'Why me?"

"Because at the moment you are the only serving general in the forces of the Gath Republic. Therefore you are in command of those forces *and* the spokesman for that republic."

"I see. What is my choice?"

"Terran task forces will drop guns and other war supplies into prisons ready to receive and use them. They will also drop paratroops and special combat teams to take nearby barracks, armories and strongpoints." He paused to let that sink in, added, "Alternatively, the Gath Republic will fight its own battles and win its own victory with arms seized from its enemies."

Getting to his feet, Partha held himself erect, hands at sides, and said quietly, "The fight will be harder, the losses more grievous—but we prefer to face the struggle on our own." Behind him the listening Stames and Aluesines gave a murmur of agreement.

"Back on Earth," commented Wardle, smiling, "the betting was forty to one that you'd make that decision. The entire Gath Republic idea was based on the supposition that every intelligent being has his pride, that he measures it by his own ability to restore it and maintain it. That goes even for a prisoner, even for a slave." He smiled again. "So Terra asks a favor of you."

"A favor?" Partha was startled.

"We ask that the Gath Republic times its first assault to suit our convenience."

"The greater plan?"

"Correct. The chief curse of space-war is that of detecting and intercepting an enemy fleet. The void is so vast and velocities so tremendous that a blip on a screen can come ten seconds too late and a hundred thousand miles wide of the mark."

"So—?"

"So a great revolt on Gathin will bring the major part of the Kastan fleet here as fast as it can come. They'll just naturally concentrate on a danger-point so near to their home-world of Kasta. Remember, we're only twelve days' flight from there." He gave the same smile once more. "Terra would consider it neighborly of the Gath Republic if you timed your shenanigans for when we've taken up positions to intercept the Kastan fleet."

"And when is that likely to be?"

"Not more than eight days after our beacon has given them Gathin's location."

"It may be a month before they pick up the beacon," complained Partha. "Or two months, perhaps three."

"Not with what we've got zooming around and listening out," answered Wardle. "They are expecting a beacon to function sooner or later, they're hoping for it and constantly seeking it. Finding it is a matter of systematic search and not of haphazard luck. They're likely to trace the beacon and react to it almost any time as from now."

"All right. We'll strike when Terran fleets are ready to take advantage of the situation. Anything more?"

"One item. The doctors have got to make some pretence of coping with the epidemic. But we don't want to play the Kastans' game by curing everyone without exception. So we'd better reduce the number falling sick tomorrow morning. Let's cut it down to two or three hundred and maintain it at that until everyone has had a turn. Foley can explain to Festerhead that he's keeping the trouble in check but it's got to run its course."

"Yes, we can arrange it that way," agreed Partha. "The prisoners are getting psychological satisfaction out of that form of rebellion and so we mustn't drop it altogether. I'll order the number to be kept down to a judicious size."

"I'd like you also to order the doctors to support Foley a hundred per cent next time he argues with Festerhead," Wardle went on. "He wants to blame everything on poor and insufficient food. That diagnosis has got to be unanimous. Maybe it'll get us something better, maybe it won't, but there's no harm in trying."

"The doctors will be told." Partha wet thin lips as he thought of a few crusts of bread in addition to the lousy stew. "Enfeebled Gaths versus overfed Kastans is tough enough. One extra mouthful per meal would serve as a big step toward victory."

"You took a thousand steps when you switched from slaves to potential conquerors. There's less than another hundred steps to go. You'll make it even if you have to crawl, even with empty bellies."

"We shall," affirmed Partha, thoroughly determined. He followed Cheminais outside, his military staff trailing after him.

The door closed. A guard wandered past along the wall-top, kept dozey attention upon the jungle and the sky.

"Things are building up nicely," opined Holden, "to a wholesale massacre by soup-maddened Gaths."

Wardle stretched himself tiredly on his bed. "Let me sleep. I wish to dream of T-bone steaks smothered with button mushrooms."

He closed his eyes, gradually slipped into the unconscious. Holden lay drooling a bit, got off his bed, went to Wardle and shook him awake.

"Aloysius, why are you so cruel to me?"

"Drop dead!" bawled Wardle, aggravated beyond measure.

The guard came to an abrupt halt in the flarepath, stared straight toward the open windows and yelled, *"Fosham gubitsch!"*

Holden went to the window and shouted back, "You heard what the nice gentleman said—drop dead."

"You will not speak dwarf-language," ordered the guard, tough and menacing. "You will go to sleep."

"Yair," said Holden. "That's an idea." Finding his bed, he reposed on it and in due course awoke everyone else with his snores.

Thirteen days crawled past. The sufferers from what Holden called "saponic mastication" had now been further reduced to eighty every morning, merely to keep Festerhead soothed. Doctor-Major Machimbar continued to display lordly indifference to any sick other than guards, but did allow Foley and the others the free run of the hospital.

The beacon functioned twenty-eight hours per day. Nobody knew for certain whether the Kastans were still unaware of it or whether they had found it and were seeking an official reason for its existence. The latter possibility was now filling Partha and his staff with mounting apprehension.

One hundred and forty Stames and Aluesines had changed places with forestry parties from elsewhere, smuggled themselves into all seven adjacent prisons and three of the five that were farther away. They had done good work. All ten jails were now mentally conditioned for revolt and had riddled themselves with soap-disease as a means of maintaining morale through the waiting period.

In the middle of that night Pye was taking his turn to remain awake. He sprawled across his bed, gazed wearily at a spangle of stars gleaming in the window gaps, counted the minutes toward the time when Casasola would take over. He yawned for the hundredth stretch, fidgeted with boredom.

Faint clicks came from Holden's bed.

Pye sat up wide-eyed and listened.

The bed went on clicking.

Scrambling hurriedly across, Pye snatched up the other's jacket, extracted his pocket-watch. Opening its case he slowly rotated it in the horizontal plane. The clicks faded, ceased, resumed, suddenly became loud enough to awake the whole room.

Pop-pop, pipper-pop.

"Eureka!" exclaimed Wardle. He rubbed hands together in delight and satisfaction. "They're halfway through. Never mind, they'll repeat until they know we've got it."

The seven sat around and listened carefully while the pseudo-watch continued to emit pipper-pops. The sounds went on for ten minutes, ceased for one, started all over again.

"How about me sneaking out to interrupt the beacon?" asked Alpin McAlpin, eagerly.

"Not worth the trouble of getting over the wall," Wardle decided. "I can tend to it myself while working out there tomorrow. Cut off and on twelve times at one minute intervals, that's what you said, didn't you?"

"Yes. We've got to give them an intermittent period to show that we've heard them."

"It'll be done. Doesn't need a radio technician just to work a switch up and down."

"One hour before dawn, five days hence," commented Pye, still listening to the pipper-pops. "That's quicker than we anticipated."

"No matter. They'll keep postponing it so long as they get no assenting signal from us," said Wardle. "We'll interrupt the beacon early tomorrow. Five days should be enough. Besides, I want to get back to Terra. I've had nearly as much as I can take of this dump."

"Me, too," indorsed Pye, fervently.

Holden chose that moment to let go with an unmusical howl of, "Home, home, swe-e-eet home. Be it ever so humble—"

Outside, a guard blundered heavy-footed along the flarepath, shouted a string of incomprehensible words toward the barrack-block. He sounded arrogant and liverish.

Going to a window, Holden looked out and said with mock humility, "You will not speak louse-language. You will go take a walk." Then he ducked out of sight and flopped on his bed.

The watch, now closed and back in his pocket, was still emitting faint clicks in the morning. The same theme over and over again: five days hence, one hour before dawn.

On time last day there reappeared the old menace of a betraying atmosphere. In the yard at eventide ten thousand sat or mooched around with studied listlessness that gave no visual hint of what was coming. Yet over all lay a strange, invisible tenseness that could be smelled and felt.

Again the guards responded to instinct, sixth-sense or whatever it was. They became fidgety, nervous and tended to group together with fingers on or near triggers. But such was their conditioning that each inwardly sought the cause of his hunch outside the walls or in the sky, anywhere but inside the prison.

Partha came up to Wardle and said, "The men are behaving very well. All the same, the Kastans are sniffing around for trouble. Do you suppose it might be better if everyone left the yard and went to their rooms?"

"It would be a radical break in routine," Wardle pointed out. "Prisoners value this period of petty freedom in which to mix and talk. They never go indoors until they have to. A sudden eagerness to get themselves locked up for the night would arouse the suspicions of a halfwit."

"You may be right. But there's another hour to go. I fear that among so many may be one or two who'll crack under the strain of waiting and do something stupid."

"I don't think that would spoil our plans," opined Wardle. "The Kastans are used to such foolishness. How many prisoners have committed suicide these last four years, and how many did it by inviting a bullet from a guard?"

Partha frowned, said nothing.

"An hour is an hour," finished Wardle. "We've got to sit it out."

He watched Partha walk apprehensively away. Then he leaned against the wall and let his gaze linger on the armory.

Behind those big steel doors lay a treasure that must be won. A direct assault on the armory, or on the platoon at the gate, would bring the attackers under murderous fire from twenty-two guards high up atop the wall. Therefore the wall-top guards would have to be dealt with first. It was going to be tricky and need excellent timing.

Agreed plans were still being viewed and reviewed in his mind when the hour ended and prisoners filed into the barrack-blocks. They shuffled indoors, striving hard to maintain the usual appearance of slowness and reluctance. The natural glumness of the Stames gave them a considerable advantage over the Aluesines at such moments as this.

Now there was only the long night in which to make final preparations. Door-locks clicked shut, guards left the blocks, crossed the yard to their own quarters.

The last of them had not gone from sight before Cheminais was out and busily unlocking. He'd had to make an early start, there being enough doors to occupy his attention for three hours.

"Your part of the game completed?" Wardle asked Holden.

"Sure thing. Dareuth will lead the quarry gang in a rush to the garbage-dump. On it are forty old tin cans filled with alamite and complete with detonators." He gave a wistful sigh. "Wish we could have smuggled more in. There's a big steel barrel down at the quarry. It would have made a beautiful bang if we could have trundled it through the gates."

Wardle gave a shrug of indifference, lay down, arranged his blanket over himself. "I for one am going to get some sleep."

"Can you, at a time like this?" asked Pye.

"Dunno. But I'm going to try." He shut his eyes. The room went silent. Sleep did not come to any of them.

Eventually Wardle found himself at a window watching the regular passing and repassing of a guard and impatiently counting off the hours, the minutes. Now and again he eyed the twinkling starfield. Out in the dark, high up and far away, a big array of black, snouty spaceships waited in ambush. He knew they were there and found the knowledge comforting.

At ten minutes before deadline they were all by the windows. They let a guard go past, dropped a rope to ground-level. Holden climbed over the window-ledge, got a grip, made ready to slide down.

He paused, grinned up into their faces and said with unnecessary loudness, "Hoot M'Goot rides again."

"S-s-sh!" hissed Wardle, "Get down, you imbecile!" He glanced anxiously along the wall-top, was relieved to see no angry figure pounding back.

Holden slid into lower darkness. When the rope ceased vibrating they hauled it up. Looking out and down, they saw his vague, shadowy figure flit across to the base of the wall.

"Two minutes to go," announced Wardle.

They took up cross-bows, wound springs to full tension, placed bolts in grooves and positioned themselves abreast by the windows. Elsewhere were similar scenes, one figure silently lurking by the bottom of the wall, half a dozen armed ones standing behind sixth-floor windows. The night was slightly darker than usual, the flarepath looked more brilliant by contrast.

The guard came back. His movements seemed abnormally slow and lethargic. To nerves drawn taut he appeared to be taking one step per minute.

Wardle whispered, "I'll break the neck of the fellow who shoots prematurely. We want that clunker's gun to fall inside the wall, not outside or on top."

"Don't worry," said Pye, icily calm.

Now the guard came level with the window. Far below, Holden rattled a tin can. The guard halted, stared around. Holden rattled again. The guard unhitched his automatic gun from his shoulder, gripped it in his right hand, bent over and peered down toward the source of the noise.

"Now!"

Six arbelests went *whup-whup*.

For a horrid moment they thought they'd missed. The guard stayed bent, unmoving, apparently still looking down. An instant later he plunged headlong, not having uttered a sound. Spikes caught and tore the legs of his pants, ripped a boot from his foot before he disappeared. His gun landed with a metallic crash that sounded preternaturally loud. The body hit a second later with a sickening crunch of bone on concrete.

Over to the left, just out of sight, somebody atop the wall was giving queer whistling gasps. Farther away, on the other side of the jail, a Kastan voice was screaming bloody murder. A light machine-gun, presumably dropped by the screamer, suddenly came into action with a sharp, hard *taketa-taketa* and the screaming ceased.

Bolting through the door the six Terrans tried to race downstairs and join Holden in the yard. It wasn't easy. In front a solid column of Stames lurched, jostled and half-fell down the steps, jammed together on every bend and stuck until rearward pressure forced them loose. Behind, a bunch of Aluesines yipped with impatience and used their weight to try to drive the mass outdoors. Thus the smaller Terrans became submerged in a raging stream of seven-to-eight-footers and remained there until practically flung into the yard.

Already a thousand were out and on the rampage, sprinting to their assigned objectives. Two hundred from the block adjoining the gates had been briefed to attack the twelve guards there, also the twelve relief-guards sleeping nearby. Most of these were now within fifty yards of the gates and going fast with no opposition.

Wardle and the others kept anxious eyes in that direction as the mob from their own block raced across the yard toward the guards' dormitories.

Those heading for the gates made another thirty yards before astonished guards accepted the evidence of their own eyes. By then it was too late. A big, gaunt Aluesine in the lead swung up a shaped and sharp-edged piece of steel resembling a butcher's cleaver. He flung it at the quickest-witted guard who'd brought gun to shoulder and was fumbling for the trigger. The cleaver missed its target as the guard ducked. A moment later all twelve went down beneath the vengeful mob, not a shot having been fired.

Over to the right another gang was heading for the garbage-dump. Beyond them, a large group of former engineers hustled for the power-plant and the vehicle-park. Prisoners continued to pour out the blocks in their hundreds, adding themselves to various groups as previously ordered.

The two Kastans patrolling the vehicle-park proved more alert and less dumfounded than their fellows had been. Warned by the rising uproar they took refuge behind a couple of huge trucks, rested guns across steel bonnets and opened fire. Nine oncoming prisoners collapsed and lay still. *Taketa-taketa* went the guns, hosing slugs into the yard.

Splitting up, the engineers dodged around trucks, climbed over them, crawled underneath them. The guards tried to aim and fire ten ways at once. It couldn't be done. Fighting figures came at them from all directions, they went down for keeps, their weapons were snatched from dead hands.

At that point the Terrans lost sight of what was going on elsewhere. Reaching the dormitory building, they were swept headlong through its doors. In front of them a dozen cat-eyed Aluesines raced along a dark corridor as though it were fully illuminated. A few Stames with them were handicapped by lack of light, tended to falter and stumble. Other Aluesines brushed the Stames impatiently aside and dashed after their fellows.

Glimpsing narrow stairs at one side, Wardle gladly seized the chance to escape the press of bigger, heavier bodies. He jerked sidewise out of the crowd, gained the steps, pounded upward as fast as he could go. Somebody was puffing and blowing close upon his heels. Glancing over one shoulder he found Foley following and—somewhat to his surprise—the missing Holden who had joined up somehow. Holden was gripping an automatic gun and was the only one of them armed with a weapon worth a hoot. Of the others there was no sign. Presumably they were engaged in the melee lower down.

On the first floor the slumbering guards had been brought rudely awake by the general hullabaloo and especially by sounds of strife immediately beneath them. Just as Wardle reached the top of the stairs a huge Kastan, attired only in his underpants, came running out of a room with machine-pistol in hand.

The Terran lacked weight and inches but had the advantage of surprise. What the Kastan had expected to see will never be known but his reaction showed that a recalcitrant prisoner came last on the list. He wasted a valuable moment by letting his mouth hang open and looking thunderstruck

Wardle used the same moment to belt him in the belly with the butt of his cross-bow. The Kastan let out an elephantine grunt and bowed low, bringing his head down to convenient reach. Wardle promptly walloped him on the nut with all the strength he could muster. The guard flopped with a crash that shook the floor.

Flinging away his cross-bow, Wardle stooped to grab up the precious machine-pistol. It was the luckiest movement of his life. A dozen slugs blasted out the open door, went a few inches above his back, knocked chips from the opposite wall. Plunging flat, Wardle rolled madly out of the field of fire.

"Stay put," warned Holden, still at the top of the stairs. He edged past Foley, crawled cautiously toward the door, poked the snout of his gun around the corner and let fly into the room. Another shower of slugs was his answer.

Obviously those in the room had no intention of surrendering. Their automatic guns were stacked in the armory but each of them retained his machine-pistol. They were going to fight as long as strength and ammunition held out. The grim alternative was lifelong slavery, without honor, without hope. And this was a mighty poor time to try converting them to a strange Terran viewpoint.

Momentarily there was an impasse as the Terrans lay in wait outside and dared not rush in, while the Kastans waited inside and dared not charge out. Then sheer pressure of attackers down below forced the surplus upstairs. The first was an excited Aluesine ceremoniously bearing a large and rusty can on which was the legend IMFAT NOGOLY 111, whatever that meant.

"Give it to me," snarled Holden. He tossed his gun into Foley's arms, snatched the can from the Aluesine. His fingers fiddled a moment at the top of the can, then his arm swung across the doorway and slung it into the room. "Down!"

They all lay flat. IMFAT NOGOLY 111 went off with one hell of a bang that draped a glassless window-frame around a Stame colonel two hundred yards away. Together they dashed into the room. Eleven Kastans were scattered around with some indecision as to which piece was whose.

The take was eleven more machine-pistols. Now supported by the flood coming up from below, they charged straight into the next room farther along the corridor. It held twelve beds, twelve neatly folded uniforms, but was empty. So also were the remaining rooms on that floor.

Meanwhile the flood swept higher, was greeted on the third floor with heavily concentrated fire. Bodies rolled down the stairs, blocked the way to others. Stames and Aluesines worked frantically to remove the dead. They made another rush, were again repelled.

Evidently the Kastans missing from the second floor had joined those above. Some officer of the guard must have had enough time to organize a stand. Since there were eight floors in the building the defenders had plenty of room in which to retreat higher and higher, making the building's capture costly in the extreme.

It was now plain that Kastans could and would fight with great tenacity. The conquest of the prison was proving harder than anticipated.

Wardle found an Aluesine officer, suggested, "Dead Gaths are no use to the Gath Army. Better withdraw your men from the attack."

"But we've got to take this building at whatever cost," protested the other. "Most of four hundred Kastans are in there."

"Maybe we can get rid of them more cheaply."

"How?"

"We can blow them out. With enough stuff stacked inside we can lift them high enough to meet their own fleet. How's the rest of the battle going?"

"I haven't the remotest notion," admitted the officer.

Then he rocked forward, clutched Wardle around the neck and almost brought him down with the weight. The walls groaned, the ceilings showered dust, the ground quivered. A long strip of distorted steel buzzed through one window and out the other, hitting nobody. Glass rained from windows above.

"The armory doors," exclaimed Wardle. "Now we should have plenty of teeth."

He scooted into the yard, headed for the armory. Halfway there something went *taketa-taketa* and invisible bees buzzed over his head. After that he ran in a sort of leaping zigzag but no more bullets came.

Near the armory the great steel doors sprawled upon the ground, twisted as if by a giant hand. Prisoners were taking out weapons as fast as they could be snatched.

Just as he arrived Cheminais and two Stames shoved out a heavy machine-gun mounted on two wheels.

"Four more of these gadgets in there," informed Cheminais. He narrowed his eyes at the yard, part of which was conspicuously unoccupied. "The gate guard went down like skittles but the relief-guard is holding out. They've locked themselves in the guardhouse and are well armed."

"Oh, so that's who fired at me just now?"

"Yes, they've light automatic guns covering half a dozen narrow arcs around the building."

"But now we smack back at them, *houne*?" put in a Stame, mournfully happy. "We teach them a lesson, *houne*?"

"Any explosive in there?" asked Wardle, jerking a thumb.

"Only a dozen kegs of that quarrying junk," said Cheminais.

"That'll do. I'd better find Holden fast. He knows how best to use it."

So saying, he hastened back, his mind occupied with the potency of a ton or more of alamite. The distant gun opened up immediately he entered its arc. He took a dive, lay still. The gun ceased. Carefully he edged forward. *Taketa-taketa.* Whoever was behind that gun had good sight and poor patience.

The bullets came very close. One plucked at his shoulder padding, ripped a slice out of the cloth. Another struck concrete a foot from his nose, ricocheted skyward with a noise like that of a buzz-saw.

Another pause, during which sweat trickled down his spine. Slowly he raised his head. *Taketa-taketa.* This was not more than a one-second burst because immediately it was answered by a faster, heavier hammering from the yard. *Gamma-gamma-gamma* sounded Cheminais and his Stames. The distant gunpost dissolved into chaos as a stream of small explosive shells sprayed all over it.

That was good marksmanship in the hazy half-light of coming sunrise. Wardle got up and ran. In two minutes he was back with Holden who examined the kegs and pronounced them very bangworthy. Thirty Stames at once dragged the lethal load to the dormitories, lugged it up to the second floor, stacked it in a middle room.

Not knowing what was taking place the Kastans on the third and higher floors made no attempt to interfere. They sat tight and awaited further attacks from enemies swarming beneath.

While well-armed Stames and Aluesines kept close watch on the rising stairs, Holden primed the pyramid of kegs, got everything ready.

At that point Wardle appeared with one of the captured gate-guards. The huge Kastan was completely submissive and already had assumed the status of a slave who exists only to obey.

"You will go up to the next floor," ordered Wardle, "protecting yourself by shouting your identity in your own language. You will tell all those above that they must surrender at once or be blown sky-high."

Unhesitatingly the Kastan agreed, as a prisoner must. No thought of refusal or trickery entered his mind despite the current bad example of which he'd become a victim. He mounted the stairs, bawling a warning.

"This is Rifada. Do not shoot—I am Rifada."

He reached the top, turned out of sight onto the third floor. There was a brief silence while those below strained their ears to listen.

Then, "Guard-Sergeant Kling, I am ordered to tell you that all must surrender or be blown up."

"So! And you a prisoner of prisoners, eh?" A pause, followed by, "He comes up here and invites us to share his disgrace. Death is better than that." Another pause, then a short, sharp, "Kill him!"

A dozen shots blasted. Something made a dull thud on the floor. Aluesines and Stames cast each other the knowing looks of those who'd expected nothing less from a piece of Terran super-optimism.

Wardle made a gesture of mixed despair and disgust. "That settles it. We can do no more in these circumstances. Let 'em have it."

Two Aluesines remained at the bottom of the stairs to oppose a possible last-minute rush from above. All the rest hastened out of the building, placed themselves at a safe distance. Holden went into the middle room, stayed there a few seconds, came out like he'd been seared with a red-hot poker.

Taking their cue from this, the pair of Aluesines abandoned their post, followed him down and out at breakneck pace. They joined the crowd, turned to watch results.

For a short time the big building stood stark and silent against the growing light of morning. Then its walls bulged. Came a tremendous roar and the whole edifice burst apart. A great vertical column of dirt, dust and vapor arose skyward with darker lumps soaring and falling within it.

By a freak of chance characteristic of explosions eighteen Kastans survived the blast, bruised and badly shocked but otherwise whole. The dirtiest and most bedraggled of these was Guard-Major Slovits. He crawled out of the mess, stood up, felt himself all over, gazed around with a completely befuddled expression.

Holden brought him to his senses by tapping him on the chest and announcing, "Henceforth your sole purpose in life will be to please me. Is that understood?"

"Yes," agreed Slovits, demonstrating that one man's poison is another man's meat.

"In no circumstances will you disobey."

"No," confirmed Slovits, horrified at the thought of outraging a well-established convention.

"Therefore," finished Holden, pointing across the yard, "you will march these former guards in a smart and military manner to General Partha-ak-Waym and apply to him for immediate enlistment in the army of the Gath Republic."

Slovits stood staring down at him from his greater height. His heavy body swayed slightly while a peculiar series of emotions chased each other across his broad, leathery face. His lips worked but no words came out. Then suddenly his eyes closed and he slumped without a sound.

"Holy smoke!" exclaimed Holden, surprised. "The big ape has fainted."

"What do you expect when a warrior plunges into his living grave and is immediately hauled out by his enemy?" asked Wardle.

The guardhouse fell within half an hour, gave up twelve Kastan dead who'd fought to the last gasp. The prison's conquest was now complete but activity did not lessen in the slightest.

A blue flag with white star was nailed to the pole above the administration building, formally saluted and informally cheered. Stretcher parties collected the wounded, rushed them to the hospital where the doctors took charge. Other parties sought among the dead for Festerhead and Machimbar, found neither, both having had the good fortune to be absent when the balloon went up.

A triumphant column one thousand strong roared out in captured trucks and thundered along slave-built jungle roads. Four hundred were armed with light automatic guns, four hundred with machine-pistols, two hundred with hastily-made alamite grenades.

They reached the next nearest jail in time to take part in the final assault. Again the Kastans had fought with bitter determination born of the belief that the only alternative was a lifetime of damnation. Three hundred and seventy died in their boots. Forty-eight dazed Kastans accepted salvation in the ranks of the growing Gath Army.

The column sped forth again, now doubled in size and fire-power. It passed Festerhead and Machimbar on its way to the next jail, meeting them sitting pop-eyed in an official car, leaving them dead-eyed in a smoking wreck. The third and other prisons toppled in turn. By the fall of the tenth the column had become an army of which only one in seven carried a modern weapon.

A surprise assault in full strength upon a garrison town remedied the arms-shortage, provided lavish quantities of ammunition, added seven hundred mentally confused Kastans to the ranks. Here, the Gaths also gained their first heavy artillery in the form of ten mobile batteries of dual-purpose guns.

A side-swipe in force at an inadequately defended airfield won them four small space-cruisers in fighting trim, also sixty-two jet planes. One-time painters daubed out the double-arrow insignia, replaced them with a white star. Former pilots, navigators, space-engineers and gunners piled joyfully into the ships, took them up, plastered enemy airfields elsewhere.

Electricians and telephone engineers cut power cables, tapped lines, listened to unwitting Kastans talking from afar, bollixed them with fake messages, passed constant information to the Gath Field Intelligence Service. Scout-planes fed the headquarters staff with news of enemy movements. Radio technicians monitored Kastan broadcasts with captured equipment, added their quota of valuable details. Swiftly the Gaths had reached the stage of waging war systematically, knowing what they were doing and why they were doing it.

A small, judiciously estimated quantity of nuisance value had been placed in a suitable environment where it had fermented like yeast in a brewery vat.

On the ninth day of the revolt a flaming battleship fell through the sky from somewhere where twinklings and vivid flashings had concentrated among the stars. On a hilltop it made a meteorlike crater surrounded by gobs of molten metal. Faintly discernible upon one distorted slab were the tips of two white arrows

The same night eleven more ships plunged down white-hot, illuminating the jungle for miles. One was unidentifiable. One carried the sign of a Terran comet. Nine bore paired arrows.

Upon the tenth day Wardle and the others bounced and jolted in a racing truck that was part of a gigantic column pushing forward nearly a thousand miles south of the prison. Their driver was Gath-Major Slovits, the only one aboard big enough to hold the huge steering-wheel and reach the big foot-pedals. Slovits, reveling in unexpected freedom and new-found honor, was by now the Gathiest of the Gaths.

A mobile radio unit operating by the wayside drew their attention as an Aluesine sergeant, standing near it, waved them down. The sergeant came close, his cat-eyes examining them curiously.

"You Terrans are wanted at Langasime."

"That's a day's run rearward," complained Wardle. "The fighting is ahead. What's the idea?"

"They're calling for you over the air. You're wanted at Langasime as soon as you can get there."

"Who wants us?"

"A Terran frigate has landed. They say the enemy fleet has suffered severe loss and that our conquest of Gathin is only a matter of time. Union forces are massing to attack Kasta itself."

"Hm-m-m! By the looks of it we're being ordered home."

Wardle showed disappointment, stood coping with a moment of chronic indecision. A truck lumbered past hauling a tank of paralyzing gas and its long-range projector. Three white-starred jetplanes swooped over the advancing column, rocked and swayed into the distance. The horizon spewed smoke and faint noises, the *taketa-taketa* of light automatics, the *gamma-gamma-gamma* of heavy machine-guns, the brief, deep *whoomps* of alamite bombs, large caliber mortars and dual-purpose guns.

Reluctantly he gave way. "Oh, well, maybe they've something else in mind for us." Then to Slovits, "Take us back good and fast."

At the dilapidated and bomb-cratered Langasime spaceport the frigate's captain came down his gangway to meet them. He was tall, young, dapper, and spoke with an air of weary resignation.

"At H.Q. they need their heads examined. I've been ordered to pick up the Special Task Force—in a frigate." His attention settled on Casasola. "I suppose you fellows are part of it?"

Casasola said nothing.

"We fellows," informed Holden, "are *all* of it."

The captain frowned disapproval while he sought around for the gag. Failing to find it, he remarked incredulously, "What, only seven of you?"

"Yair," said Holden, donating an irritating smirk. "Good, *houne*?" He turned, made a motion of farewell. "Best of luck, Slobovitch."

"Slovits," reminded Slovits, with extreme politeness.

Panic Button

Astounding, November 1959

"The law of chance," said Lagasta ponderously, "lays it down that one cannot remain dead out of luck for everlasting." He had the fat oiliness typical of many Antareans; his voice was equally fat and oily. "Sooner or later the time must come when one finds a jewel in one's hair instead of a bug."

"Speak for yourself," invited Kaznitz, not caring for the analogy.

"That time has arrived," Lagasta went on. "Let us rejoice."

"I am rejoicing," Kaznitz responded with no visible enthusiasm.

"You look it," said Lagasta. He plucked a stalk of grass and chewed it without caring what alien bacteria might be lurking thereon. "We have found a new and empty world suitable for settlement. Such worlds are plenty hard to discover in spite of somebody's estimate that there must be at least a hundred million of them. The vastness of space." He ate a bit more grass, finished, "But we have found one. It becomes the property of our species by right of first discovery. That makes us heroes worthy of rich reward. Yet I fail to see delirious happiness on what purports to be your face."

"I take nothing for granted," said Kaznitz.

"You mean you sit right here on an enormous lump of real estate and don't believe it?"

"We have yet to make sure that nobody has prior title."

"You know quite well that we subjected this planet to most careful examination as we approached. Intelligent life cannot help betraying its presence with unmistakable signs for which we sought thoroughly. What did we see? Nothing! Not a city, not a village, not a road, not a bridge, not one cultivated field. Absolutely nothing!"

"It was a long-range survey of the illuminated side only," Kaznitz pointed out. "We need to take a much closer look—and at both sides."

Havarre lumbered over and sat beside them. "I have ordered the crew to get out the scout boats after they have finished their meal."

"Good!" said Lagasta. "That should soothe Kaznitz. He refuses to believe that the planet is devoid of intelligent life."

"It is not a matter of belief or disbelief," Kaznitz gave back. "It is a matter of making sure."

"We are soon to do that," Havarre told him. "But I am not worried. The place looks completely uninhabited."

"You can't weigh up a world with one incoming stare no matter how long and hard you make it." Kaznitz asserted. "The absence of people spread widely and in large numbers doesn't necessarily mean no concentration of them in small number."

"You mean Terrans?" queried Havarre, twitching his horsy ears.

"Yes."

"He's been obsessed with Terrans ever since Plaksted found them encamped on B417," remarked Lagasta.

"And why shouldn't I be? Plaksted had gone a long, long way merely to suffer a disappointment. The Terrans had got there first. We've been told that they're running around doing the same as we're doing, grabbing planets as fast as they can find them. We've been warned that in no circumstances must we clash with them. We've strict orders to recognize the principle of first come first served."

"That makes sense," opined Havarre. "In spite of years of haphazard contact we and the Terrans don't really know what makes the other tick. Each side has carefully refrained from telling the other anything more than is necessary. They don't know what we've got—but we don't know what they've got. That situation is inevitable. It takes intelligence to conquer space and an intelligent species does not weaken itself by revealing its true strength. Neither does it start a fight with someone of unmeasured and immeasurable size, power and resources. What d'you think we ought to do with Terrans—knock off their heads?"

"Certainly not!" said Kaznitz. "But I shall feel far happier when I know for certain that a task force of one thousand Terrans is not snoring its collective head off somewhere on the dark side of this planet. Until then I don't assume that the world is ours."

"Always the pessimist," jibed Lagasta.

"He who hopes for nothing will never be disappointed," Kaznitz retorted.

"What a way to go through life," Lagasta said. "Reveling in gloom."

"I fail to see anything gloomy about recognizing the fact that someone must get here first."

"How right you are. And this time it's us. I am looking forward to seeing the glum faces of the Terrans when they arrive tomorrow or next month or next year and find us already here. What do you say, Havarre?"

"I don't think the subject worthy of argument," answered Havarre, refusing to take sides. "The scout boats will settle the issue before long." He got to his feet, ambled toward the ship. "I'll chase the crew into action."

Lagasta frowned after him. "The company I keep. One has no opinions. The other wallows in defeat."

"And you wag your tail while the door is still shut," Kaznitz riposted.

Ignoring that, Lagasta gnawed more grass. They sat in silence until the first scout boat came out, watched it take off with a loud boom and a rising whine. A bit later a second boat bulleted into the sky. Then more of them at regular intervals until all ten had gone.

"Waste of time, patience and fuel," declared Lagasta. "There's nobody here but us first-comers."

Kaznitz refused to take the bait. He gazed at the ragged horizon toward which a red sun sank slowly. "The dark side will become the light side pretty soon. Those boats won't get back much before dawn. Think I'll go and enjoy my bunk. A good sleep is long overdue."

"It's a wonder you can enjoy anything with all the worries you've got," observed Lagasta with sarcasm.

"I shall slumber with the peace of the fatalistic. I shall not sit up all night eating weeds while tormented with the desire to be proved right and the fear of being proved wrong."

So saying, he went to the ship conscious of the other scowling after him. Like all of the crew he was sufficiently weary to fall asleep quickly. Soon after dark he was awakened by the switching on of the radio beacon and the faint but hearable sound of the subsequent *bip-bip-yidder-bip*. Much later he was disturbed by Havarre going to bed and, later still, by Lagasta.

By dawn they were so deep in their dreams that none heard the return of the scout boats despite the outside uproar ten times repeated. They grunted and snuffled in unconscious unison while nine pilots emerged from their vessels looking exhausted and bored. The tenth came out kicking the grass and jerking his ears with temper.

One of the nine stared curiously at the tenth and asked, "What's nibbling your offal, Yaksid?"

"Terrans," spat Yaksid. "The snitgobbers!"

Which was a very vulgar word indeed.

"Now," said Lagasta, displaying his bile, "tell us exactly what you saw."

"He saw Terrans," put in Kaznitz. "Isn't that enough?"

"I want no interference from you," Lagasta shouted. "Go squat in a thorny tree." He switched attention back to Yaksid and repeated, "Tell us exactly what you saw."

"I spotted a building in a valley, swept down and circled it several times. It was a very small house, square in shape, neatly built of rock slabs and cement. A Terran came out of the door, presumably attracted by the noise of my boat. He stood watching me zoom round and round and as I shot past the front he waved to me."

"Whereupon you waved back," suggested Lagasta in his most unpleasant manner.

"I made muck-face at him," said Yaksid indignantly, "but I don't think he saw me. I was going too fast."

"There was only this one house in the valley?"

"Yes."

"A very small house?"

"Yes."

"How small?"

"It could be described as little better than a stone hut."

"And only one Terran came out?"

"That's right. If any more were inside, they didn't bother to show themselves."

"There couldn't have been many within if the dump was almost a hut," Lagasta suggested.

"Correct. Six at the most."

"Did you see a ship or a scout boat lying nearby?"

"No, not a sign of one. There was just this house and nothing more," said Yaksid.

"What did you do next?"

"I decided that this lonely building must be an outpost belonging to a Terran encampment somewhere in the vicinity. So I made a close search of the district. I circled wider and wider until I'd examined an area covering twenty horizons. I found nothing."

"You're quite certain of that?"

"I'm positive. I went plenty low enough to detect a camp half-buried or well camouflaged; I couldn't find even the smell of a Terran."

Lagasta stared at him in silence a while and then said, "There is something wrong about this. A Terran garrison could not cram itself into one hut."

"That's what I think," Yaksid agreed.

"And since it cannot be within the building it must be some place else."

"Correct. But there was no sign of it anywhere within the area I covered. Perhaps one of the other scout boats passed over it and failed to see it."

"If it did, the pilot must have been stone-blind or asleep at his controls."

Kaznitz interjected, "That wouldn't surprise me. We landed short of sleep and the pilots haven't been given a chance to catch up. You can't expect them to be in full possession of their wits when they're mentally whirly."

"It was necessary to make a check with the minimum of delay," said Lagasta defensively.

"That's news to me."

"What d'you mean?"

"You gave me clearly to understand that the check was a waste of time, patience and fuel."

"I said nothing of the sort."

Havarre chipped in with, "What was said or not said is entirely beside the point. The point is that we have to deal with the situation as it exists. We have landed in expectation of claiming a planet. Yaksid has since found Terrans. Therefore the Terrans were here first. What are we going to do about it?"

"There is no problem to be solved," said Kaznitz before Lagasta had time to answer. "We have been given orders simple enough for a fool to understand. If we arrive first, we claim the planet, sit tight and invite any later Terrans to take a high dive onto solid rock. If the Terrans arrive first, we admit their claim without argument, shoot back into space and waste no time beating them to the next planet."

"Where *is* the next one?" inquired Lagasta with mock pleasantness. "And how long is it going to take us to find it? Inhabitable worlds don't cluster like ripe fruit, do they?"

"Certainly not. But what alternative do you suggest?"

"I think we'd do well to discover this missing garrison and estimate its strength."

"That would make sense if we were at war or permitted to start a war," said Kaznitz. "We are not permitted. We are under strict instructions to avoid a clash."

"I should think so, too," contributed Havarre. "Before we enter a war we must know exactly what we're fighting."

"There is nothing to stop us gathering useful information," Lagasta insisted.

"It's impossible for us to collect military data worth the effort of writing it down," Kaznitz gave back. "For the obvious reason that it will be years out of date by the time we get back home."

"So you think we should surrender a hard-earned world for the sake of one crummy Terran in a vermin-infested hut?"

"You know quite well there must be more of them somewhere around."

"I don't know it. I know only what I've been told. And I've been told that Yaksid has found one Terran in a hut. Nobody has seen a trace of any others. We should make further and closer search for others and satisfy ourselves that they really are here."

"Why?"

"It's possible that these others don't exist."

"Possible but highly improbable," Kaznitz opined. "I can't see Terran explorers contenting themselves with placing one man on a world."

"Perhaps they didn't. Perhaps he placed himself. The lone survivor of a space disaster who managed to get here in a lifeboat. What would be the worth of a Terran claim in those circumstances? We could easily remove every trace of the man and the hut and deny all knowledge of either. It couldn't be called a clash. One Terran just wouldn't get the chance to clash with a crew six hundred strong."

"That may be, but—"

"If we make more systematic search and find other Terrans in garrison strength, that will settle the matter and we'll take off. But if it proves that there are no others—" He let his voice tail off to add significance, finished, "All that stands between us and a world is one hunk of alien meat."

Kaznitz thought it over. "I dislike giving up a new planet fully as much as you do. But I'd dislike it even more if we were saddled with the blame for starting something that can't be finished. I think we'd like death and love it rather than endure the prolonged pain."

"Blame cannot be laid without someone to do the blaming," said Lagasta, "and a dead Terran positively refuses to talk. You worry too much. If you had nothing else with which to occupy your mind you'd grieve over the shape of your feet." He turned to Havarre. "You've had little enough to say. Have you no opinion about this?"

Immediately leery, Havarre replied, "If we stay put while we look around, I think we should be careful."

"Have you any reason to suppose that I intend to be rash?"

"No, no, not at all."

"Then why the advice?"

"You asked my opinion and I gave it. I don't trust these Terrans."

"Who does?" said Lagasta. He made a gesture indicative of ending the subject. "All right. We'll allow the pilots a good, long sleep. After their brains have been thoroughly rested we'll send them out again. Our next step will depend upon whether more Terrans have been found and, if so, whether they have been discovered in strength."

"What do you mean by strength?" Kaznitz asked.

"Any number in possession of a ship or a long-range transmitter. Or any number too large for us to remove without leaving evidence of it."

"Have it your own way," said Kaznitz.

"I intend to," Lagasta assured.

The first boat returned with the same news as before, namely, no Terrans, no sign that a Terran had ever been within a million miles of the planet. Eight more boats came back at varying intervals and made identical reports vouching for a total lack of Terrans in their respective sectors. One pilot added that he became so convinced that Yaksid must have suffered a delusion that on his return he had gone out of his way to cut through that worthy's sector. Yes, he had seen the stone house with his own two eyes. No, he had not observed any sign of life around the place.

Yaksid appeared last.

"I went straight to the house and circled it as before. Again a Terran came out and watched me. He also waved to me."

"It was the same Terran?" demanded Lagasta.

"He may have been. I don't know. One cannot study a face on the ground when flying a scout boat. Besides, all Terrans look alike to me. I can't tell one from another."

"Well, what happened after that?"

"I made low-level inspection of a surrounding area ten times larger than last time. In fact I overlapped by quite a piece the search lines of boats seven and eight. There was not another house or even a tent, much less an encampment."

Lagasta brooded over this information, eventually said, "The occupants of that house are by themselves in a strange world. That's a form of loneliness sufficiently appalling to guarantee that they'd rush out headlong for a look at a ship. If six, ten or twelve Terrans were crammed in that hut, they'd get stuck in the doorway in their haste to see Yaksid's boat. But only one showed himself the first time. Only one showed himself the second time. I think there's not more than one in that hut."

"So do I," offered Yaksid.

Kaznitz said to Yaksid, "He waved to you on both occasions. Did he appear to be waving for help?"

"No."

"Does it matter?" Lagasta asked.

"If he were a marooned survivor, one would expect him to jump at a chance of rescue."

"Not at our hands. He could see at a glance that the scout boat was not a Terran one. He'd take no chance with another species."

"Then why did he show himself? Why didn't he hide and leave us in sweet ignorance of his existence?"

"Because he couldn't conceal the hut," replied Lagasta, showing lack of patience.

"He wouldn't need to," Kaznitz persisted. "When you seek cover from a prospective enemy you don't take your house with you."

"Kaznitz, there are times when you irritate me beyond measure. Just what have you got on your mind?"

"Look, you believe that in that building is the only Terran upon this world. Right?"

"Right!"

"He can have got here in only one of two ways, namely, by accident or by design. Right?"

"Right!"

"If he doesn't want help, he's not here by accident. He's here by design. Right?"

Lagasta evaded the point. "I don't care if he's here by a miracle. It will take more than the presence of one lousy alien to make me give up a new world."

"I suspect there *is* more—more to it than meets the eye."

"That may be so. I am no fool, Kaznitz. Your suspicion of Terrans is no greater than mine. But I refuse to flee at first sight of one of them."

"Then what do you think we should do?"

"There are eight of us with enough knowledge of Terran gabble to limp through a conversation. We should have a talk with this character. If he's here for a purpose, we must discover what it is."

"And afterward?"

"It may prove expedient to make him disappear. A deplorable necessity. But, as you never cease to remind me, Kaznitz, life is full of deplorable things. And, like everyone else, this Terran must expect to have an unlucky day sooner or later. When he and his hut have vanished from the face of creation we can defy anyone to prove that we were not here first."

"Somehow I don't think it's going to be as easy as that," opined Kaznitz.

"You wouldn't. You were alarmed at birth and the feeling has never worn off."

Havarre put in uneasily, "As I said before, we should be very careful. But I see no harm in having a talk with this Terran. Neither his authorities nor ours can object to that. Nothing in our orders forbids us to speak."

"Thanks be to the suns for at least one bit of half-hearted support," said Lagasta piously. "We'll move the ship to where this stone hut is located. No need to load the scout boats on board. Let them fly with us. They'll help to make us look more imposing."

"Want me to order the crew to make ready right now?" inquired Havarre.

"Yes, you do that. We'll invite our prospective victim to dinner. Some of his kind are said to be fond of strong drink. We'll feed him plenty, sufficient to loosen his tongue. If he talks enough, he may save his neck. If he talks too much, he may get his throat cut. It all depends. We'll see."

"Bet you ten days' pay you're wasting your time," offered Kaznitz.

"Taken," agreed Lagasta with alacrity. "It will be a pleasant change to have you go moody over your losses and my gains."

As the ship came down Lagasta stood by a port and studied the rising house. "Neat and solid. He could possibly have built it himself. The door and windows could have come from a dismantled lifeboat. The rock slabs are local material and what looks like cement is probably hard mud."

"Still clinging to the theory of a lone survivor from some cosmic wreck?" asked Kaznitz.

"It's a likely explanation of why there is one Terran and only one." Lagasta glanced at the other. "Can you offer a better solution?"

"Yes. They've isolated a plague carrier."

"What?"

"Could be. What do we know of their diseases?"

"Kaznitz, why do you persist in producing the most unpleasant ideas?"

"Somebody has to consider the possibilities. When one knows almost nothing about another species what can one do but speculate? The only available substitutes for facts are guesses."

"They don't have to be repulsive guesses."

"They do—if your main purpose is to take no risks."

"If this character is bulging with alien bacteria to which we have no resistance, he could wipe out the lot of us without straining a muscle."

"That could happen," agreed Kaznitz cheerfully.

"Look here, Kaznitz, your morbid mind has put us in a fix. Therefore it is for you to get us out of it."

"How?"

"I am appointing you to go to that house and find out why that Terran is here. It's your job to make sure that he's safe and sanitary before we allow him aboard."

"He may refuse to come aboard. It could seem much like walking into a trap."

"If he won't come to us, we'll go to him. All you need do, Kaznitz, is first make sure that he is not loaded with death and corruption. I've no wish to expire as the result of breathing in bad company."

At that point the ship grounded with crunching sounds under the keel. The ten scout boats circled overhead, came down one by one and positioned themselves in a neat row. Lagasta had another look at the house now two hundred yards away. The alien occupant could be seen standing in the doorway gazing at the arrivals but his face was hidden in deep shadow.

"On your way, Kaznitz."

With a shrug of resignation, Kaznitz got going. While many pairs of eyes looked on he went down the gangway, trudged to the house, halted at the door. For a short while he and the Terran chatted. Then they went inside, remained for twenty minutes before they reappeared. They headed for the ship. Lagasta met them at the mid air lock.

"This," introduced Kaznitz, "is Leonard Nash. He says we should call him Len."

"Glad to know you," responded Lagasta with false cordiality. "It's all too seldom we meet your kind." He studied the Terran carefully. The fellow was short, broad and swarthy with restless eyes that seemed to be trying to look six ways at once. There was something peculiar about him that Lagasta could not place; a vague, indefinable air of being more different than was warranted even in an alien. Lagasta went on, "I don't think I've spoken to more than twenty Terrans in all my life. And then only very briefly."

"Is that so?" said Len.

"Yes," Lagasta assured.

"Too bad," said Len. His eyes flickered around. "Where do we eat?"

Slightly disconcerted, Lagasta took the lead. "This way to the officers' mess. We are honored to have you as our guest."

"That's nice," responded Len, following.

At the table Lagasta seated the newcomer on his right, said to Havarrre, "You speak some Terran so you sit on his other side." Then surreptitiously to Kaznitz, "You sit on my left—I want a word with you soon."

The ship's officers filed in, took their places. Lagasta made formal introduction while Len favored each in turn with a blank stare and a curt nod. Dinner was served. The Terran tasted the first dish with suspicion, pulled a face and pushed it away. The next course was much to his liking and he started scooping it up with single-minded concentration. He was an unashamed guzzle-guts and didn't care who knew it.

Lagasta grabbed the opportunity to lean sidewise and question Kaznitz in his own language. "You sure he's not full of disease?"

"Yes."

"How d'you know?"

"Because he's expecting to be picked up and taken home before long. In fact he has recorded the date of his return."

"Ah! So the Terrans *do* know he's here?" Lagasta suppressed a scowl.

"Yes. They dumped him here in the first place."

"Alone?"

"That's right."

"Why?"

"He doesn't know."

After digesting this information, Lagasta growled, "It doesn't make sense. I think he's lying."

"Could be," said Kaznitz.

Stewards brought bottles. Len's reaction to drink was the same as that to food: a wary and suspicious sip followed by lip-smacking approval and greedy swallowing. Whenever a new course was brought in his active eyes examined all the other plates as if to check that they didn't hold more than was on his own. Frequently he signed for his glass to be filled. His general manner was that of one cashing in on a free feed. Perhaps, thought Lagasta, it was excusable in one who'd had an entire world to himself and may have gone hungry most of the time. All the same, he, Lagasta, didn't like Terrans and liked this one even less.

With the long meal over and the officers gone, Lagasta, Kaznitz and Havarre settled down to more drinking and an informative conversation with their guest. By this time Len was feeling good, sprawling in his chair, a full glass in one hand, his face flushed with an inward glow. Obviously he was mellow and in the mood to talk.

Lagasta began politely with, "Company, even strange company, must be more than welcome to one leading such a lonely life as yours."

"Sure is," said Len. "There've been times when I've talked to myself for hours. Too much of that can send a fellow off his head." He took an appreciative swig from the glass. "Thank God I've a date marked on the wall."

"You mean you're here for a limited time?"

"I was dumped for four years maximum. Most of it's now behind me. I've only seven more months to go—then it's home, sweet home."

Seeing no satisfactory way of getting to the point obliquely, Lagasta decided to approach it on the straight. "How did you come to be put here in the first place?"

"Well, it was like this: I was a three-time loser and—"

"A what?"

"I'd done two stretches in prison when I qualified for a third. The judge gave me fifteen to twenty years, that being mandatory. So I was slung into the jug." He sipped his drink reminiscently. "Hadn't been there a week when I was called to the warden's office. Two fellows there waiting for me. Don't know who they were. Said to me, 'We've been taking a look at you. You're in good physical condition. You're also in a jam and plenty young enough to have regrets. How'd you like to do four years in solitary?' "

"Go on," urged Lagasta, managing to understand about three-quarters of it.

"Naturally, I asked who was crazy. I'd been plastered with fifteen to twenty and that was suffering enough. So they said they weren't trying to pin something more on me. They didn't mean four years in addition to—they meant four instead of. If I wanted it I could have it and, what's more, I'd come out with a clean sheet."

"You accepted?"

"After crawling all over them with a magnifying glass looking for the gag. There had to be one somewhere. The law doesn't suddenly ease up and go soft without good reason."

"What did they tell you?"

"Wanted me to take a ride in a spaceship. Said it might plant me on an empty world. They weren't sure about that but thought it likely. Said if I did get dumped all I had to do was sit tight for four years and behave myself. At the end of that time I'd be picked up and brought home and my prison records would be destroyed."

"So you're a criminal?"

"Was once. Not now. Officially I'm a solid citizen. Or soon will be."

Kaznitz put in with mild interest, "Do you intend to remain a solid citizen after your return?"

Giving a short laugh, Len said, "Depends."

Staring at him as if seeing him for the first time, Lagasta remarked, "If it were possible to make a person acquire respect for society by depriving him of the company of his fellows, it could be done in jail. There would be no need to go to the enormous trouble and expense of putting him on some faraway uninhabited planet. So there must be some motive other than the reformation of a criminal. There must be an obscure but worthwhile purpose in placing you here."

"Search me," said Len indifferently. "So long as I get the benefit, why should I care?"

"You say you've been here about three and a half Earth-years?"

"Correct."

"And nobody has visited you in all that time?"

"Not a soul," declared Len. "Yours are the first voices I've heard."

"Then," persisted Lagasta, "how have you managed to live?"

"No trouble at all. When the ship landed the crew prospected for water. After they'd found it they put down a bore and built the shack over it. They fixed a small atomic engine in the basement; it pumps water, heats it, warms and lights the place. They also swamped me with food, books, games, tape-recordings and whatever. I've got all the comforts of the Ritz, or most of them."

"Then they left you to do nothing for four years?"

"That's right. Just eat, sleep, amuse myself." Then by way of afterthought, "And keep watch."

"Ah!" Lagasta's long ears twitched as he pounced on that remark. "Keep watch for what?"

"Anyone coming here."

Leaning back in his seat, Lagasta eyed the other with ill-concealed contempt. Under clever questioning and the influence of drink the fellow's evasions had been driven from the sublime to the ridiculous. Persistent liars usually gave themselves away by not knowing when to stop.

"Quite a job," commented Lagasta, dangerously oily, "keeping watch over an entire planet."

"Didn't give me any gray hairs," assured Len. He exhibited an empty glass and Havarre promptly filled it for him.

"In fact," Lagasta went on, "seeing that you have to eat and sleep, it would be a major task merely to keep watch on the relatively tiny area within your own horizon."

"Sure would," Len agreed.

"Then how is it possible for one man to stand guard over a planet?"

"I asked them about that. I said, 'Hey, d'you chumps think I'm clairvoyant?' "

"And what was their reply?"

"They said, 'Don't worry your head, boy. If anyone lands north pole or south pole, your side or the other side, by day or by night, you don't have to go looking for them. *They'll come looking for you!*' " A smirk, lopsided and peculiarly irritating, came into Len's face. "Seems they were dead right, eh?"

Lagasta's temporary sensation of impending triumph faded away and was replaced by vague alarm. He slid a glance at Kaznitz and Havarre, found their expressions studiously blank.

"One can hardly describe it as keeping watch if one waits for people to knock on the door," he suggested.

"Oh, there was more to it than that," informed Len. "When they knock I press the button."

"What button?"

"The one in the wall. Got a blue lens above it. If anyone comes, I press the button and make sure the blue lens lights up. If the lens fails to shine, it shows I've not pressed hard enough. I ram the button deep enough to get the blue light. That's all there is to it."

"In view of our arrival I presume the button has been pressed?" asked Lagasta.

"Yeah, couple of days ago. Something came snoring around the roof. I looked out the window, saw your bubble boat, recognized the pilot as non-Terran. So I did my chore with the button. Then I went outside and waved to him. Fat lot of notice he took. Did he think I was thumbing a lift or something?"

Ignoring that question, Lagasta said, "What happens when the button is pressed?"

"Darned if I know. They didn't bother to tell me and I didn't bother to ask. What's it to me, anyway?"

"There is no antenna on your roof," Lagasta pointed out.

"Should there be?" Len held his drink up to the light and studied it with approval. "Say, this stuff varies quite a lot. We're on a bottle much better than the last one."

"For the button to transmit a signal there'd have to be an antenna."

"I'll take your word for it."

"Therefore," Lagasta baited, "it does not transmit a signal. It does something else."

"I told you what it does—it makes the blue lens light up."

"What good does that do?"

"Does me lots of good. Earns me a remission. I get out in four instead of fifteen to twenty." Strumming an invisible guitar, Len sang a discordant line about his little gray cell in the west. Then he struggled to his feet and teetered slightly. "Great stuff that varnish of yours. The longer you hold it the stronger it works. Either I go now under my own steam or I stay another hour and you carry me home."

The three stood up and Lagasta said, "Perhaps you'd like to take a bottle with you. After we've gone you can drink a toast to absent friends."

Len clutched it gratefully. "Friends is right. You've made my life. Don't know what I'd do without you. So far as I'm concerned you're welcome to stick around for keeps." Rather unsteadily he followed Kaznitz out, turned in the doorway and added, "Remember asking 'em, 'Where am I if some outlandish bunch want to play rough with me?' And they said, 'They won't—because there'll be no dividends in it.' " He put on the same smirk as before but it was more distorted by drink. "Real prophets, those guys. Hit the nail smack-bang on the head every time."

He went, nursing his bottle. Lagasta flopped into a chair and stared at the wall. So did Havarre. Neither stirred until Kaznitz came back.

Lagasta said viciously, "I'd lop off his fool head without the slightest compunction if it weren't for that button business."

"And that may be a lie," offered Havarre.

"It isn't," Kaznitz contradicted. "He told the truth. I saw the button and the lens for myself. I also heard the faint whine of a power plant somewhere in the foundations." He mused a moment, went on, "As for the lack of an antenna, all we know is that in similar circumstances we'd need one. But do they? We can't assume that in all respects their science is identical with our own."

"Logic's the same everywhere, though," Lagasta gave back. "So let's try and look at this logically. It's obvious that this Len character is no intellectual. I think it's safe to accept that he is what he purports to be, namely, a criminal, an antisocial type of less than average intelligence. That raises three questions. Firstly, why have the Terrans put only one man on this planet instead of a proper garrison? Secondly, why did they choose a person of poor mentality? Thirdly, why did they select a criminal?"

"For the first, I have no idea," responded Kaznitz. "But I can give a guess at the others."

"Well?"

"They used someone none too bright because it is impossible to coax, drug, hypnotize, torture or otherwise extract valuable information from an empty head. The Terrans don't know what we've got but one thing they do know: no power in creation can force out of a skull anything that isn't in it in the first place."

"I'll give you that," Lagasta conceded.

"As for picking on a criminal rather than any ordinary dope, seems to me that such a person could be given a very strong inducement to follow instructions to the letter. He'd be meticulous about pressing a button because he had everything to gain and nothing to lose."

"All right," said Lagasta, accepting this reasoning without argument. "Now let's consider the button itself. One thing is certain: it wasn't installed for nothing. Therefore it was fixed up for something. It has a purpose that makes sense even if it's alien sense. The mere pressing of it would be meaningless unless it produced a result of some kind. What's your guess on that?"

Havarre interjected, "The only possible conclusion is that it sounds an alarm somehow, somewhere."

"That's what I think," Kaznitz supported.

"Me, too," said Lagasta. "But it does more than just that. By sending the alarm it vouches for the fact that this watchman Len was still alive and in possession of his wits when we landed. And if we put him down a deep hole it will also vouch for the fact that he disappeared immediately after our arrival. Therefore it may provide proof of claim-jumping should such proof be necessary." He breathed deeply and angrily, finished, "It's highly likely that a fast Terran squadron is already bulleting this way. How soon it gets here depends upon how near its base happens to be."

"Doesn't matter if they catch us sitting on their world," Kaznitz pointed out. "We've done nothing wrong. We've shown hospitality to their sentinel and we've made no claim to the planet."

"I *want* to claim the planet," shouted Lagasta. "How'm I going to do it *now?*"

"You can't," said Kaznitz. "It's far too risky."

"It'd be asking for trouble in very large lumps," opined Havarre. "I know what I'd do if it were left to me."

"You'd do what?"

"I'd beat it at top speed. With luck we might get to the next new world an hour ahead of the Terrans. If we do we'll be more than glad that we didn't waste that hour on this world."

"I hate giving up a discovery," Lagasta declared.

"I hate giving up two of them in rapid succession," retorted Havarre with considerable point.

Lagasta growled, "You win. Order the crew to bring the scout boats aboard and prepare for take-off." He watched Havarre hasten out, turned to Kaznitz and rasped, "Curse them!"

"Who? The crew?"

"No, the Terrans." Then he stamped a couple of times around the cabin and added, "Snitgobbers!"

The vessel that swooped from the sky and made a descending curve toward the rock house was not a warship. It was pencil-thin, ultra-fast, had a small crew and was known as a courier boat. Landing lightly and easily, it put forth a gangway.

Two technicians emerged and hurried to the house, intent on checking the atomic engine and the power circuits. The relief watchman appeared, scuffed grass with his feet, stared curiously around. He was built like a bear, had an underslung jaw, small, sunken eyes. His arms were thick, hairy and lavishly tattooed.

Moving fast, the crew manhandled crates and cartons out of the ship and into the house. The bulkiest item consisted of forty thousand cigarettes in air-tight cans. The beneficiary of this forethought, a thug able to spell simple words, was a heavy smoker.

Leonard Nash went on board the ship, gave his successor a sardonic smirk in passing. The crew finished their task. The technicians returned. Leaning from the air-lock door, an officer bawled final injunctions at the lone spectator.

"Remember, you *must* press until the blue lens lights up. Keep away from the local gin-traps and girlie shows—they'll ruin your constitution. See you in four years."

The metal disk clanged shut and screwed itself inward. With a boom the ship went up while the man with a world to himself became a midget, a dot, nothing.

Navigator Reece sat in the fore cabin gazing meditatively at the starfield when Copilot McKechnie arrived to keep him company. Dumping himself in a pneumatic chair, McKechnie stretched out long legs.

"Been gabbing with that bum we picked up. He's not delirious with happiness. Got as much emotion as a lump of rock. And as many brains. It's a safe bet his clean sheet means nothing whatever; he won't be back a year before the cops are after him again."

"Did he have any trouble on that last world?"

"None at all. Says a bunch of weirdies landed six or seven months ago. They pushed a hunk of brotherly love at him and then scooted. He says they seemed to be in a hurry."

"Probably had a nice grab in prospect somewhere."

"Or perhaps we've got them on the run. Maybe they've discovered at long last that we're outgrabbing them in the ratio of seven to one. Those Antareans are still staking claims by the old method. Ship finds a planet, beams the news home, sits tight on the claim until a garrison arrives. That might take five, ten or twenty years, during which time the ship is out of commission. Meanwhile, a ship of ours discovers A, dumps one man, pushes on to B, dumps another man, and with any luck at all has nailed down C and D by the time we've transported a garrison to A. The time problem is a tough one and the only way to cope is to hustle."

"Dead right," agreed Reece. "It's bound to dawn on them sooner or later. It's a wonder they didn't knock that fellow on the head."

"They wouldn't do that, seeing he'd pressed the button," McKechnie observed.

"Button? What button?"

"There's a button in that house. Pressing it switches on a blue light."

"Is that so?" said Reece. "And what else?"

"Nothing else. Just that. A blue light."

Reece frowned heavily to himself while he thought it over. "I don't get it."

"Neither do unwanted visitors. That's why they scoot."

"I still don't get it."

"See here, to get into space a species must have a high standard of intelligence. Agreed?"

"Yes."

"Unlike lunatics, the intelligent are predictable in that they can be depended upon always to do the intelligent thing. They never, never, never do things that are pointless and mean nothing. Therefore a button and a blue light must have purpose, intelligent purpose."

"You mean we're kidding the Antareans with a phony setup, a rigmarole that is fundamentally stupid?"

"No, boy, not at all. We're fooling them by exploiting a way of thinking that you are demonstrating right now."

"Me?" Reece was indignant.

"Don't get mad about it. The outlook is natural enough. You're a spaceman in the space age. Therefore you have a great reverence for physics, astronautics and everything else that created the space age. You're so full of respect for the cogent sciences that you're apt to forget something."

"Forget what?"

McKechnie said, "That psychology is also a science."

Plus X

Astounding, June 1956

One thing was certain: he was out of the war. Perhaps for a long time to come or possibly for keeps—dead, maimed or a prisoner. The next few seconds would decide the manner of his exit from the fray.

The little ship made another crazy spin on its longitudinal axis. In the fore observation port the gray-green face of a planet swirled the opposite way. John Leeming's brains seemed to rotate in sympathy, causing momentary confusion. Behind the ship the distorted fire-trail shaped itself into an elongated spiral.

Ground came up fast, mere crinkles expanding into hills and valleys, surface fuzz swelling into massed trees. His straining eyes saw a cluster of rooftops turn upside down then swing right way round.

Choice needs time even if only the minimum required to make selection. When there's no time there's no choice. Leeming's sole concern was to land the ship any place, anywhere, even slap in the middle of the foe, so long as it hit belly-down with nothing to oppose its forward skidding.

He made it either by sheer good luck or, more likely, happy absence of bad luck. A gentle upward slope magnified toward the nose at precisely the right moment. He maneuvered somehow, heaven alone knew how, dropped the damaged tail, cut power, struck dirt, slid halfway up the slope amid a twin spray of dust, sparks and grinding noises.

For half a minute he sat still and sweated while feeling peculiarly cold. Then he glanced at the atmospheric analyzer. It said the local air had nothing wrong with it.

Clambering through the lock, Leeming bolted to the tail end. He looked at the array of drivers and found them a mess. Five tubes lacked linings and had warped under resulting heat. Four more were on the point of going cockeyed. He'd come in on the remaining seven and that was a feat verging on the miraculous.

Back home they'd warned him that the vessel might not stand up to the task imposed upon it. "We're giving you a special scout-boat with battleship tubes and improved linings. The ship is light and unarmed but fast and exceptionally long-ranged. Whether it will hold together over such a vast trip is something that can be determined only by actual test. Right now it's the best we can offer. In four or five years' time we may have one fifty times better. But we can't wait four or five years.

"I understand."

"So you'll be taking a risk, a big one. You may never return. All the same, we've got to learn what lies behind the enemy's spatial frontier, how deeply his authority extends, how far his hidden resources go. Somebody's got to stick out his neck to get that information. Somebody's got to wander loose behind the lines."

"I'm willing."

They'd patted his shoulder, given him a heavily escorted send-off that had taken him through the area of battle. Then, on his own, he'd slipped through a hostile frontier, a tiny, unstoppable speck in the immensity of space.

For weeks of which he'd lost count he had beamed data of all kinds, penetrating deeper and deeper into the starfield until the first tube blew a tormented and desiccated lining along the vapor-trail. Even as he turned belatedly for home the second one went. Then a third. After that, it was a matter of getting down in one piece on the nearest inhabitable hunk of plasma.

At the bottom of the slope, a thousand yards away, lay a large village stirred to active life by his overhead thunder and nearby landing. Already its small garrison was charging out, weapons in hand, heading for the ship.

Diving back through the lock, Leeming jerked a lever in the tiny control room, got out fast, raced up the slope, counting to himself as he ran. Down at the bottom the enemy troops paused in their advance, let go hoarse yells but failed to open fire.

"Sixty-nine, seventy!" gasped Leeming, and threw himself flat.

The ship flew apart with a mighty roar that shook the hills. Wind pressed powerfully in all directions. Shrapnel rained from the sky. A seven-pound lump of metal thumped to ground a yard from Leeming's head and he could not recognize it as any part of what once had arrowed past strange suns and unknown planets.

He stood up, saw that he now had the enemy on both sides. A thin line of armed figures had come over the crest of the slope. They had weapons pointed his way and were gazing awestruck at the great crater halfway down.

At the bottom the troops from the village picked themselves up, having either thrown themselves flat or been blown flat. None appeared to be injured, none looked delighted either.

Leeming raised his arms in universal token of surrender. He felt bitter as he did it. Good luck followed by bad luck. If only the ship had hit ten miles farther back or ten farther on, he could have taken to the woods and played hard to get for weeks, months or, if necessary, years.

Anyway, this was the end of the trail.

The enemy came up fast. They were two-legged, on the short side, tremendously broad and powerful. Their gait was the typical stumping of squat, heavy men. Close up, they were seen to have scaly skins, horn-covered eyes, no eyelids. The first one to arrive made Leeming think of a sidewinder that somehow had taken on monkeylike shape.

Though obviously made jumpy by his forced landing and the big bang, they did not treat him with open antagonism. Their manner was suspicious and reserved. After a little reflection he guessed the reason for this. They'd seen nobody quite like him before, had no means of determining whether he was friend or foe, and temporarily were reserving judgment.

This was excusable. On Leeming's side of the battle was a federation of eighteen life forms, four of them human and five more very human-like. Against these was an uneasy, precarious union of at least twenty life forms of which two were also very humanlike. Pending examination, this particular bunch of quasi-reptilians just couldn't tell enemy from ally. Neither did they know whether the ship's spectacular destruction was accidental or a piece of deliberate naughtiness.

Nevertheless they were taking no chances. Half a dozen kept him covered while an officer inspected the crater. The officer came back, favored Leeming with an unwinking stare, voiced an incomprehensible gabble. Leeming spread his hands and shrugged.

Accepting this lack of understanding as something that proved nothing one way or the other, the officer shouted commands at his troops. They formed up, marched to the village with the suspect in their midst.

Arriving, they shoved Leeming into the back room of a rock house with two guards for company, two more outside the door. He sat on a low, hard chair; sighed, stared blankly at the wall for two hours. The guards also sat, watched him as expressionlessly as a pair of snakes, and never said a word.

At the end of that time a trooper brought food and water. The meal tasted strange but proved satisfying. Leeming ate and drank in silence, studied the wall for another two hours.

He could imagine what was going on while they kept him waiting. The officer would grab the telephone—or whatever they used in lieu thereof—and call the nearest garrison town. The highest ranker there would promptly transfer responsibility to military headquarters. A ten-star panjandrum would pass the query to the main beam station. An operator would then ask the two humanlike allies whether they'd lost track of a scout in this region.

If a signal came back saying, "No," the local toughies would realize that they'd caught a rare bird deep within their spatial empire and menacingly far from the area of conflict. If a thing can be either of two things, and it isn't one of them, it's got to be the other. Therefore if he wasn't a friend he had to be a foe despite his appearance where no foe had ever penetrated before.

When they learned the truth they weren't going to like it. Holding-troops far behind the lines share all the glory and little of the grief. They're happy to let it stay that way. A sudden intrusion of the enemy where he's no right to be is an event disturbing to the even tenor of life and not to be greeted with cries of martial joy. Besides, where one can sneak in a host of armies can follow and it is disconcerting to be taken in force from the rear.

What would they do to him when they identified him as a creature of the Federation? He was far from sure, never having seen or heard of this especial life form before. One thing was probable: they'd refrain from shooting him out of hand. If sufficiently civilized, they'd imprison him for the duration of the war and that might mean for the rest of his natural life. If uncivilized, they'd bring in an ally able to talk Earth language and proceed to milk the prisoner of every item of information he possessed, by methods ruthless and bloody.

Back toward the dawn of history when conflicts had been Earth-wars there had existed a protective device known as the Geneva Convention. It had organized neutral inspection of prison camps, brought occasional letters from home, provided Red Cross parcels that had kept alive many a captive who otherwise would have died.

There was nothing like that today. A prisoner now had only two forms of protection, those being his own resources and the power of his side to retaliate against the prisoners they'd got. And the latter was a threat more potential than real. There cannot be retaliation without actual knowledge of maltreatment.

Leeming was still brooding over these matters when the guards were changed. Six hours had now dragged by. The one window showed that darkness was falling. He eyed the window furtively, decided that it would be suicidal to take a running jump at it under two guns. It was small and high.

A prisoner's first duty is to escape. That means biding one's time with appalling patience until occurs a chance that may be seized and exploited to the utmost. Or if no opportunity appears, one must be created—by brawn and brains, mostly the latter.

The prospect before him was tough indeed. And before long it was likely to look a deal tougher. The best moment in which to organize a successful getaway had come immediately after landing. If only he'd been able to talk the local language, he might have convinced them that black was white. With smooth, plausible words, unlimited self-assurance and just the right touch of arrogance he might have persuaded them to repair his boat and cheer him on his way, never suspecting that they had been argued into providing aid and comfort for the enemy.

Lack of ability to communicate had balled up that prospect at the start. You can't chivvy a sucker into donating his pants merely by making noises at him. Some other chance must now be watched for and grabbed, swiftly and with both hands—providing they were fools enough to permit a chance.

Which was most unlikely.

He remained in the house four days, eating and drinking at regular intervals, sleeping night-times, cogitating for hours, occasionally glowering at the impassive guards. Mentally he concocted, examined and rejected a thousand ways of regaining freedom, most of them spectacular, fantastic and impossible.

At one time he went so far as to try to stare the guards into an hypnotic trance, gazing intently at them until his own eyeballs felt locked for keeps. It did not faze them in the least. They had the lizardlike ability to remain motionless and outstare him until kingdom come.

Mid-morning of the fourth day the officer strutted in, yelled, *"Amash! Amash!"* and gestured toward the door. His tone and attitude were both unfriendly. Evidently they'd received a signal defining the prisoner as a Federation space-louse.

Leeming got up from his seat and walked out, two guards ahead, two behind, the officer following. A steel-sheathed car waited in the road. They shoved him into it, locked it. Two guards stood on the rear platform, one joined the driver at front. The journey took thirteen hours which the inmate spent jolting around in complete darkness.

By the time the car halted Leeming had invented one new and exceedingly repulsive word. He used it as the rear doors opened.

"Amash!" bawled a guard, unappreciative of alien contributions to the vocabulary of invective.

With poor grace Leeming amashed. He glimpsed great walls rearing against the night and a zone of bright light high up before he was pushed through a metal portal into a large room. Here a reception committee of six thuglike samples awaited him. One of the six signed a paper presented by the escort. The guards withdrew, the door closed, the six eyed the visitor with lack of amiability.

One of them said something in an authoritative voice, made motions illustrative of undressing.

Leeming used the word.

It did him no good. The six grabbed him, stripped him naked, searched every vestige of his clothing, paying special attention to seams and linings. None showed the slightest interest in his alien physique despite that it stood fully revealed in the raw.

Everything he possessed was put to one side, pen, compass, knife, lighter, lucky piece, the whole lot. Then they shied his clothes back at him. He dressed himself while they pawed through the loot and gabbled together. They seemed slightly baffled and he guessed that they were surprised by his lack of anything resembling a lethal weapon.

Amid the litter was a two-ounce matchbox-sized camera that any ignorant bunch would have regarded with suspicion. It took the searchers a couple of minutes to discover what it was and how it worked. Evidently they weren't too backward.

Satisfied that the captive now owned nothing more dangerous than the somewhat bedraggled clothes in which he stood, they led him through the farther door, up a flight of thick stone stairs, along a stone corridor and into a cell. The door slammed shut with a sound like the crack of doom.

In the dark of night four small stars winked and glittered through a heavily barred opening high up in one wall. Along the bottom of the gap shone a faint yellow glow from some outside illumination.

He fumbled around in the gloom, found a wooden bench against one wall. It moved when he lugged at it. Dragging it beneath the opening, he stood on it but found himself a couple of feet too low to gain a view. Though heavy, he struggled with it until he got it upended against the wall. Then he clambered up it, had a look between the bars.

Forty feet below lay a bare stone-floored space fifty yards wide and extending to the limited distance he could see in both directions. Beyond that, a smooth-surfaced stone wall rising to his own level. The top of the wall angled at about sixty degrees to form a sharp apex and ten inches above that ran a single line of taut wire, plain, without barbs.

From unseeable sources to the right and left poured powerful beams of light which flooded the entire area between cell and wall, also a similar area beyond the wall. Nothing moved. There was no sign of life. There was only the wall, the flares of light, the overhanging night and the distant stars.

"So I'm in the jug," he said. "That's torn it!"

He jumped to the invisible floor and the slight thrust of his feet made the bench fall with a resounding crash. Feet raced along the outer passage, light poured through a suddenly opened spyhole in the heavy metal door. An eye appeared in the hole.

"Sach invigia, faplap!" shouted the guard.

Leeming used the word again and added six more, older, time-worn but still potent. The spyhole slammed shut. He lay on the bench and tried to sleep.

An hour later he kicked hell out of the door and when the spyhole opened he said, "Faplap yourself!"

After that, he did sleep.

Breakfast consisted of one lukewarm bowl of stewed grain resembling millet, and a mug of water. Both were served with disdain. Soon afterward a thin-lipped specimen arrived accompanied by two guards. With a long series of complicated gestures the newcomer explained that the prisoner was to learn a civilized language and, what was more, would learn it fast, by order. Education would commence forthwith.

In businesslike manner the tutor produced a stack of juvenile picture books and started the imparting process while the guards lounged against the wall and looked bored. Leeming co-operated as one does with the enemy, namely, by misunderstanding everything, mispronouncing everything, overlooking nothing that would prove him a linguistic moron.

The lesson ended at noon and was celebrated by the arrival of another bowl of gruel containing a hunk of stringy, rubberish substance resembling the hind end of a rat. He ate the gruel, sucked the portion of animal, shoved the bowl aside.

Then he pondered the significance of their decision to teach him how to talk. Firstly, it meant that they'd got nothing resembling Earth's electronic brain-pryers and could extract information only by question-and-answer methods aided by unknown forms of persuasion. Secondly, they wanted to know things and intended to learn them if possible. Thirdly, the slower he was to gain fluency the longer it would be before they put him on the rack, if that was their intention.

His speculations ended when guards opened the door and called him out. Along the passage, down long stairs, into a great yard filled with figures mooching around under a sickly sun.

He halted in surprise. Rigellians! About two thousand of them. These were allies, members of the Federation. He looked them over with mounting excitement, seeking a few more familiar shapes amid the mob. Perhaps an Earthman or two. Or even a few humanlike Centaurians.

But there were none. Only rubber-limbed, pop-eyed Rigellians shuffling around in the aimless manner of those confronted with many wasted years and no perceivable future.

Even as he looked at them he sensed something peculiar. They could see him just as well as he could see them and, being the only Earthman, he was a legitimate object of attention. He was a friend from another star. They should have been crowding up to him, full of talk, seeking the latest news of the war, asking questions, offering information.

They took no notice of him. He walked slowly and deliberately right across the yard and they got out of his way. A few eyed him furtively, the majority pretended to be unaware of his existence. Nobody offered him a word. They were giving him the conspicuous brush-off.

He trapped a small bunch of them in a corner of the wall and said, "Any of you speak Terran?"

They looked at the sky, the wall, the ground, or at each other, and remained silent.

"Anyone know Centaurian?"

No answer.

"Well, how about Cosmoglotta?"

No answer.

He walked away feeling riled, tried another bunch. No luck. And another bunch. No luck. Within an hour he had questioned five hundred without getting a single response.

Giving up, he sat on a stone step and watched them irefully until a shrill whistle signaled that exercise time was over. The Rigellians formed up in long lines in readiness to march back to their quarters. Leeming's guards gave him a kick in the pants and chivvied him to his cell.

Temporarily he dismissed the problem of unsociable allies. After dark was the time for thinking: he wanted to use remaining hours of light to study the picture books and get well ahead with the local lingo while appearing to lag far behind. Fluency might prove an advantage some day. Too bad he'd never learned Rigellian, for instance.

So he applied himself fully to the task until print and pictures ceased to be visible. He ate his evening portion of mush. After that he lay on the bench, closed his eyes, set his brains to work.

In all his life he'd met no more than a couple of dozen Rigellians. Never once had he visited their systems. What little he knew of them was hearsay evidence. It was said their standard of intelligence was good, they were technologically efficient, they had been consistently friendly toward men of Earth since first contact. Fifty per cent of them spoke Cosmoglotta, maybe one per cent knew the Terran tongue.

Therefore, if the average held up, several hundreds of those met in the yard should have been able to converse with him in one language or another. Why had they remained silent? And why had they been so unanimous about it?

He invented, examined and discarded a dozen theories. It was two hours before he hit upon the obvious solution.

These Rigellians were prisoners, deprived of liberty perhaps for years to come. Some of them must have seen an Earthman at one time or another. But all of them knew that in the ranks of the foe were two races superficially humanlike. Therefore they suspected him of being a stooge, an ear of the enemy listening for plots.

That in turn meant something else. When a big mob of prisoners become excessively wary of a spy in their midst it's because they have something to hide. Yes, that was it! He slapped his knee in delight. The Rigellians had an escape plot in process of hatching and meanwhile were taking no chances.

How to get in on it?

Next day, at the end of exercise time, a guard administered the usual kick. Leeming upped and punched him clean on the snout. Four guards jumped in and gave the culprit a going over. They did it good and proper, in a way that no onlooking Rigellian could mistake for an act. It was an object lesson and intended as such. The limp body was carried upstairs with its face a mess of blood.

It was a week before Leeming was fit enough to reappear in the yard. His features were still an ugly sight. He strolled through the crowd, ignored as before, chose a spot in the sun and sat.

Soon afterward a prisoner sprawled tiredly on the ground a couple of yards away, watched distant guards and spoke in little more than a whisper.

"How'd you get here?"

Leeming told him.

"How's the war going on?"

"We're pushing them back slowly but surely. But it'll take time—a long time."

"How long do you suppose?"

"I don't know. It's anyone's guess." Leeming eyed him curiously. "What brought this crowd here?"

"We're colonists. We were advance parties, all male, planted on four new planets that were ours by right of discovery. Twelve thousand of us altogether." The Rigellian went silent a moment, looked carefully around. "They descended on us in force. That was two years ago. It was easy. We weren't prepared. We didn't even know a war was on."

"They grabbed the planets?"

"You bet they did. And laughed in our faces."

Leeming nodded understanding. Claim-jumping had been the original cause of the fracas now extending across a sizable slice of a galaxy. On one planet a colony had put up an heroic resistance and died to the last man. The sacrifice had fired a blaze of fury, the Federation had struck back and the war was on.

"Twelve thousand you said. Where are the others?"

"Scattered around in prisons like this one. You picked a choice dump in which to sit out the war. The enemy has made this his chief penal planet. It's far from the fighting front, unlikely ever to be discovered.

"The local life form isn't much good for space battles but plenty good enough to hold what others have captured. They're throwing up big jails all over the world. If the war goes on long enough, the planet will get solid with Federation prisoners."

"So your mob has been here most of two years?"

"Yes."

"And done nothing about it?"

"Nothing much," agreed the Rigellian. "Just enough to get forty of us shot for trying."

"Sorry," said Leeming, sincerely.

"Don't let it bother you. I know how you feel. The first few weeks are the worst." He pointed surreptitiously toward a heavily built guard across the yard. "Few days ago that lying swine boasted that there are already two hundred thousand Federation prisoners on this planet. He said that by this time next year there'll be two million. I hope he never lives to see it."

"I'm getting out of here," said Leeming.

"How?"

"I don't know yet. But I'm getting out. I'm not going to just squat and rot." He waited expectantly, hoping for some comment about others feeling the same way he did, maybe some evasive mention of a coming break, a hint that he might be invited to join in.

The Rigellian stood up. murmured, "Well, *I* wish you luck. You'll need it aplenty!"

He ambled off. A whistle blew and the guards shouted, *"Merse, faplaps! Amash!"* And that was that.

Over the next four weeks he had frequent conversations with the same Rigellian and about twenty others, picking up odd items of information but finding them peculiarly evasive whenever the subject of freedom came up.

He was having a concealed chat with one of them and asked, "Why does everyone insist on talking to me secretively and in whispers? The guards don't seem to care how much you yap to one another."

"You haven't been cross-examined yet. If in the meantime they notice we've had plenty to say to you, they will try to get out of you everything we've said—with particular reference to ideas on escape."

Leeming pounced on the lovely word. "Escape, that's all there is to live for right now. If anyone's thinking of making a bid, maybe I can help them and they can help me. I'm a competent space pilot and that fact is worth something."

The other cooled off at once. "Nothing doing."

"Why not?"

"We've been behind walls a long time. We've learned at bitter cost that escape attempts fail when too many know what is going on. Some planted spy betrays us. Or some selfish fool messes things up by pushing in at the wrong moment."

"I see."

"Imprisonment creates its own especial conventions," the Rigellian went on. "And one we've established here is that an escape-plot is the exclusive property of those who thought it up and only they can make the attempt. Nobody else is told. Nobody else knows until the resulting hullabaloo starts going.

"So I'm strictly on my own?"

"Afraid so. You're on your own in any case. We're in dormitories, fifty to a room. You're in a cell all by yourself. You're in no position to help anyone with anything."

"I can darned well help myself," he retorted angrily.

And it was his turn to walk away.

He'd been there just thirteen weeks when the tutor handed him a metaphorical firecracker. Finishing a lesson, the tutor compressed thin lips, looked at him with severity.

"You are pleased to wear the cloak of idiocy. But I am not deceived. You are far more proficient than you pretend. I shall report to the Commandant that you will be ready for examination in seven days' time."

"How's that again?" asked Leeming, putting on a baffled frown.

"You heard what I said and you understood me."

Slam went the door. Came the gruel and a jaundiced lump of something unchewable. Exercise time followed.

"They're going to put me through the mill a week hence."

"Don't let them scare you," advised the Rigellian. "They'd as soon kill you as spit in the sink. But one thing keeps them in check."

"What's that?"

"The Federation is holding prisoners, too."

"Yes, but what the Federation doesn't know it can't grieve over."

"There'll be more than grief for somebody if eventually the victor finds himself expected to exchange live prisoners for corpses.

"You've got a point there," agreed Leeming. "I could do with nine feet of rope to dangle suggestively in front of the Commandant."

"I could do with a very large bottle of *vitz* and a female to ruffle my hair," sighed the Rigellian.

The whistle again. More intensive study while daylight lasted. Another bowl of ersatz porridge. Darkness and four small stars peeping through the barred slot high up.

He lay on the bench and produced thoughts like bubbles from a fountain. No place, positively no place is absolutely impregnable. Given brawn and brains and enough time there's always a way in or out. Escapees shot down as they bolted had chosen the wrong time and wrong place, or the right time and wrong place, or the right place at the wrong time. Or they'd neglected brawn in favor of brains, a common fault of the impatient. Or they'd neglected brains in favor of brawn, a fault of the reckless.

With eyes closed he carefully reviewed the situation. He was in a cell with rock walls of granite hardness at least four feet thick. The only openings were a narrow gap blocked by five thick steel bars, also an armor-plated door in constant view of patrolling guards.

On his person he had no hacksaw, no lock pick, no implement of any sort, nothing but the clothes in which he lay. If he pulled the bench to pieces, and somehow succeeded in doing it unheard, he'd acquire several large lumps of wood, a dozen six-inch nails and a couple of steel bolts. None of that junk would serve to open the door or cut the window bars before morning. And there was no other material available.

Outside was a brilliantly illuminated gap fifty yards wide that must be crossed to gain freedom. Then a smooth stone wall, forty feet high, devoid of handholds.

Atop the wall an apex much too sharp to give grip to the feet while stepping over an alarm wire that would set the sirens going if touched or cut.

The wall completely encircled the entire prison. It was octagonal in shape and topped at each angle by a watchtower containing guards, machine guns, floodlights. To get out, the wall would have to be surmounted right under the noses of itchy-fingered watchers, in bright light, without touching the wire. That wouldn't be the end of it either; outside the wall was another illuminated fifty-yard area also to be crossed.

Yes, the whole set-up had the professional touch of those who knew what to do to keep them in for keeps. Escape over the wall was well-nigh impossible though not completely so. If somebody got out of his cell or dormitory armed with a fifty-foot rope and grapnel, and if he had a confederate who could break into the prison's power room and switch off everything at exactly the right moment, he might make it. Over the dead, unresponsive alarm wire in total darkness.

In a solitary cell there is no fifty-foot rope, no grapnel, nothing capable of being adapted as either. There is no desperate and trustworthy confederate.

If he considered once the most remote possibilities and took stock of the minimum resources needed, he considered them a hundred times. By two o'clock in the morning he'd been beating his brains sufficiently hard to make them come up with anything, including ideas that were slightly mad.

For example: he could pull a plastic button from his jacket, swallow it and hope the result would get him a transfer to the hospital. True, the hospital was within the prison's confines but it might offer better opportunity for escape. Then he thought a second time, decided that a plastic blockage would not guarantee his removal elsewhere. There was a chance that they might be content to force a powerful purgative down his neck and thus add to his present discomforts.

As dawn broke he arrived at a final conclusion. Thirty, forty or fifty Rigellians, working in a patient, determined group, might tunnel under the watched areas and the wall and get away. But he had one resource and one only. That was guile. There was nothing else he could employ.

He groaned to himself and complained, "So I'll have to use both my heads."

A couple of minutes later he sat up startled, gazed at the brightening sky and exclaimed, "Yes, sure, that's it! *Both* heads!"

By exercise time Leeming had decided that it would be helpful to have a gadget. A crucifix or a crystal ball provides psychological advantages. His gadget could be of any shape, size or design, made of any material, so long as it was obviously a contraption. Moreover, its potency would be greater if not made from items obtainable within his cell, such as parts of his clothing or pieces of the bench. Preferably it should be constructed of stuff from somewhere else.

He doubted whether the Rigellians could help. Six hours per day they slaved in the prison's workshops, a fate that he would share after he'd been questioned and his aptitudes defined. The Rigellians made military pants and jackets, harness and boots, a small range of engineering and electrical components. They detested producing for the enemy but their choice was a simple one: work or starve.

According to what he'd been told they had remote chance of smuggling out of the workshops anything really useful such as a knife, chisel, hammer or hacksaw blade. At the end of each work period the slaves were paraded and none allowed to break ranks until every machine had been checked, every loose tool accounted for and locked away.

The first fifteen minutes of the midday break he spent searching the yard for any loose item that might be turned to advantage. He wandered around with his gaze on the ground like a worried kid seeking a lost coin. The only things he found were a couple of pieces of wood four inches square by one inch thick. He slipped them into his pocket without having the vaguest notion of what he was going to do with them.

After that, he squatted by the wall, had a whispered chat with a couple of Rigellians. His mind wasn't on the conversation and the pair moved away when a patrolling guard came near. Later, another Rigellian mooched up.

"Earthman, you still going to get out of here?"

"You bet I am."

The Rigellian chuckled, scratched an ear, an action that his race used to express polite skepticism. "I think we've a better chance than you."

"Why?" Leeming shot him a sharp glance.

"There are more of us," evaded the other, as though realizing that he'd been on the point of saying too much. "What can one do on one's own?"

"Scoot like blazes first chance," said Leeming

His eyes suddenly noticed the ring on the other's ear-scratching finger and became fascinated by it. He'd seen the modest ornament before, and dozens like it. A number of Rigellians were wearing similar objects. So were some of the guards. The rings were neat affairs consisting of four or five turns of thin wire with the ends shaped and soldered to form the owner's initials.

"Where'd you dig up the jewelry?" he asked.

"The ring."

"Oh, that." The Rigellian lowered his hand, eyed the ring with satisfaction. "Make them ourselves in the workshops. It breaks the monotony."

"Mean to say the guards don't stop you?"

"They don't interfere. There's no harm in it. Anyway, we've made quite a number for the guards themselves. We've made them some automatic lighters as well. Could have turned out a few hundred for ourselves except that we've no use for them." He paused reflectively. "We think the guards have been selling rings and lighters outside. At least, we hope so."

"Why?"

"Maybe they'll build up a nice trade. Then, when they are comfortably settled in it, we'll cut supplies and demand a rake-off in the form of extra rations and a few unofficial privileges."

"That's smart of you," said Leeming. "It would help all concerned to have a salesman traveling around the planet. Put me down for that job."

The Rigellian gave a faint smile, went on, "Hand-made junk doesn't matter. But let the guards find that one small screwdriver is missing and there's hell to pay. Everyone is stripped naked on the spot and the culprit suffers."

"They wouldn't miss a small coil of that wire, would they?"

"I doubt it. They don't bother to check the stuff. What can anyone do with a piece of wire?"

"Heaven knows," admitted Leeming. "But I want some."

"You'll never pick a lock with it in a million moons," warned the other. "It's too thin and too soft."

"I want enough to make a set of Zulu bangles," Leeming told him. "I sort of fancy myself in Zulu bangles."

"You can steal some wire yourself in the near future. After you've been questioned they'll send you to the workshops."

"I want it before then. I want it just as soon as I can get it."

Going silent, the Rigellian thought it over, finally said, "If you've a plan in your mind, keep it to yourself. Don't give a hint of it to anyone. Let anything slip and somebody will try to beat you to it."

"Thanks for the advice, friend," said Leeming. "How about a bit of wire?"

"See you this time tomorrow."

The Rigellian left him, wandered into the crowd.

The wire proved to be a small pocket-sized coil of tinned copper. When unrolled in the darkness of the cell it measured his own length, namely, six feet.

Leeming doubled it, waggled it to and fro until it broke, hid one half under the bottom of the bench. Then he spent more than an hour worrying a loose nail out of the bench's end.

Finding one of the pieces of wood, he approximated its center, stamped the nail into it with his boot. Footsteps approached, he shoved the stuff out of sight, lay down just before the spyhole opened. The light flashed on, an eye looked in, somebody grunted. The light cut off, the spyhole shut.

Leeming resumed his task, twisting the nail one way and the other, pressing it with his boot from time to time, persevering until he had drilled a neat hole two-thirds of the way through the wood.

Next, he took his half-length of wire, broke it into two unequal parts, shaped the shorter piece to form a loop with two legs three or four inches long. He tried to make the circle as nearly perfect as possible. The longer piece of wire he wound tightly around the loop so that it formed a close-fitting coil with legs matching those of the loop.

Climbing the bench to the window, he examined his handiwork in the glow from outside floodlights, made a few minor adjustments and felt satisfied. After that, he used the nail to make on the edge of the bench two small nicks representing the exact diameter of the loop. He counted the number of turns the coil made around the loop. There were twenty-seven.

It was important to have these details because it was highly likely that he'd have to make a second gadget. If so, he must make it precisely the same. Once they noticed it, that very similarity might get the enemy bothered. When a plotter makes two things practically identical it's hard to resist the notion that he's up to something definite.

To complete his preparations, he chivvied the nail back into the place where it belonged. Sometime he'd need it again. He then forced the four legs of the coiled loop into the hole that he'd drilled, thus making the small piece of wood function as a stand. He now had a gadget, a doodad, a means to an end. He was the original inventor and sole owner of the Leeming Something-or-Other.

Certain chemical reactions take place only in the presence of a catalyst, like marriages legalized by the presence of a justice of the peace. Some equations can be solved only by the inclusion of an unknown quantity called X. If you haven't enough on the ball, you've got to add what's needed. If you require outside help that doesn't exist, you've got to invent it.

Whenever Man was unable to master his environment with his bare hands, thought Leeming, the said environment got bullied or coerced into submission by Man plus X. That had been so from the beginning of time—Man plus a tool or a weapon.

But X did not have to be anything concrete or solid, it did not have to be lethal or even visible. It could be a dream, an idea, an illusion, a bloody big thundering lie, just *anything.*

There was only one true test—whether it worked.

If it did, it was efficient.

Now to see.

There was no sense in using Terran except perhaps as an incantation when one was necessary. Nobody here understood it; to them it was just an alien gabble. Besides, his delaying tactic of pretending to be slow to learn was no longer effective. They now knew he could speak the local lingo almost as well as they could themselves.

Holding the loop assembly in his left hand, he went to the door, applied his ear to the closed spyhole, listened for the sound of patrolling feet. It was twenty minutes before he heard the approaching squeak of military boots.

"Are you there?" he called, not too loudly but enough to be heard. "Are you there?"

Backing off, he lay on his belly on the floor and stood the loop six inches in front of his face.

"Are you there?"

The spyhole clicked open, the light came on, a sour eye looked through.

Completely ignoring the watcher, and behaving with the air of one totally absorbed in his task, Leeming spoke through the coiled loop.

"Are you there?"

"What are you doing?" demanded the guard.

Leeming recognized the voice, decided that for once luck must be turning his way. This character, a chump named Marsin, knew enough to point a gun and fire it or, if unable to do so, yell for help. In all other matters he was not of the elite. In fact Marsin would have to think twice to pass muster as a half-wit.

"What are you doing there?" demanded Marsin, more loudly.

"Calling," said Leeming, apparently just waking up to the other's existence.

"Who are you calling?"

"Mind your own business," ordered Leeming, giving a nice display of impatience. He turned the loop another two degrees. "Are you there?"

"It is forbidden," insisted Marsin.

Leeming let go the loud sigh of one compelled to bear fools gladly. "What is forbidden?"

"To call."

"Don't be so flaming ignorant!" Leeming reproved. "My kind is *always* allowed to call. Where'd we be if we couldn't, eh?"

That got Marsin badly tangled. He knew nothing about Earthmen or what peculiar privileges they considered essential to life. Neither could he give a guess as to where they'd be without them.

Moreover, he dared not bust into the cell and put a stop to whatever was going on. An armed guard was prohibited from entering a cell by himself and that rule had been strict ever since a Rigellian had bopped one, snatched his gun and killed six while trying to make a break.

If he wanted to interfere, he'd have to go see the sergeant of the guard and demand that something be done to stop aliens making noises through loops. The sergeant was an unlovely character with a tendency to advertise personal histories all over the landscape. It was four o'clock in the morning, a time when the sergeant's liver malfunctioned most audibly. And lastly, he, Marsin, had proved himself a misbegotten faplap far too often.

"You will cease calling and go to sleep," said Marsin, with a touch of desperation, "or in the morning I shall report this matter to the officer of the day."

"Go ride a camel," Leeming invited. He turned the loop in the manner of one making careful adjustment. "Are you there?"

"I have warned you," Marsin persisted, his only visible eye popping at the loop.

"Fibble off!" roared Leeming.

Marsin shut the spyhole and fibbled off.

Leeming overslept as was inevitable after being up most of the night. His awakening was rude. The door opened with a crash, three guards plunged in followed by an officer.

Without ceremony the prisoner was jerked off the bench, stripped and shoved into the corridor stark naked. The guards hunted thoroughly through the clothing while the officer minced around them watching.

Finding nothing in the clothes they started searching the cell. Right off one of them found the loop assembly and gave it to the officer who held it gingerly as through it were a bouquet suspected of being a bomb.

Another guard found the second piece of wood with his boot, kicked it aside and ignored it. They tapped the floor and the walls, seeking hollow sounds. They dragged the bench from the wall and looked over the other side of it. Then they were about to turn the bench upside-down when Leeming decided that now was the time to take a walk. He started along the corridor, a picture of nonchalant nudity.

The officer let go an outraged howl and pointed. The guards erupted from the cell, bawled orders to halt. A fourth guard appeared at the bend of the corridor, aimed his gun and scowled. Leeming turned and ambled back.

He stopped as he reached the officer who was now outside the cell and fuming with temper. Striking a modest pose, he said, "Look, September Morn."

It meant nothing to the other who held the loop under his nose and yelled, "What is this thing?"

"My property," said Leeming with naked dignity.

"You are not supposed to possess it. As a prisoner of war you are not allowed to have anything."

"Who says so?"

"I say so!" declared the officer, somewhat violently.

"Who're you?" inquired Leeming.

"By the Sword of Lamissim," swore the other, "I'll show you who I am! Guards, take him inside and—"

"You' re not the boss," put in Leeming. impressively cocksure. "The Commandant is the boss here. I say so and he says so. If you want to dispute it, let's go ask him."

The guards hesitated, assumed expressions of chronic uncertainty. The officer was taken aback.

"Are you asserting that the Commandant has given permission for you to have this object?"

"I'm telling you he hasn't refused permission. Also that it isn't for you to give it or refuse it."

"I shall consult the Commandant about this," the officer decided, deflated and a little unsure of himself. He turned to the guards. "Put the prisoner back in the cell and give him his breakfast as usual."

"How about returning my property?" Leeming prompted.

"Not until I have seen the Commandant."

They hustled him into the cell. He got dressed. Breakfast came, the inevitable bowl of slop. He cussed the guards for not making it bacon and eggs. That was deliberate. A display of self-assurance and some aggressiveness was necessary to push the game along.

The tutor did not appear so he spent the morning furbishing his fluency with the aid of the books. At midday they let him into the yard and there was no evidence of an especial watch being kept upon him while there.

The Rigellian whispered, "I got the opportunity to swipe another coil. So I took it in case you wanted more." He slipped it across, saw it vanish into a pocket. "That's all I intend to take. Don't ask me again."

"What's up? Is it getting risky? Are they suspicious of you?"

"Everything is all right so far." He glanced warily around. "If some of the other prisoners get to know I'm taking it, they'll start grabbing it, too. They'll steal it in the hope of discovering what I'm going to use it for, so that they can use it for the same purpose. Everybody's always on the lookout for an advantage, real or imaginary, which he can share. This prison life brings out the worst as well as the best."

"I see."

"A couple of small coils will never be missed," the other went on. "But once the rush starts the stuff will evaporate in wholesale quantities. That's when all hell will break loose. I daren't chance starting anything like that."

"Meaning your fellows can't risk a detailed search just now?" suggested Leeming pointedly.

The Rigellian shied like a frightened horse. "I didn't say that."

"I can put two and two together same as anyone else." Leeming favored him with a reassuring wink. "I can also keep my trap shut."

He explored the yard seeking more pieces of wood but failed to find any. Oh, well, no matter. At a pinch he could do without. Come to that, he'd darned well have to do without.

The afternoon was given over to further studies. When light became too poor for that, and first faint flickers of starlight showed through the barred opening in the wall, he kicked the door until the sound of it thundered all over the block.

Feet came running and the spyhole opened. It was Marsin again.

"So it's you," greeted Leeming. He let go a snort. "You had to blab, of course. You had to curry favor by telling the officer." He drew himself up to full height. "Well, I am sorry for you. I'd fifty times rather be me than you."

"Sorry for me?" Marsin registered confusion. "Why?"

"You are going to suffer. Not yet, of course. It is necessary for you to undergo the normal period *of* horrid anticipation. But eventually you are going to suffer."

"It was my duty," explained Marsin, semiapologetically.

"That fact will be considered in mitigation," Leeming assured, "and your agonies will be modified in due proportion."

"I don't understand," said Marsin, developing a node of worry somewhere within the solid bone.

"You will—some dire day. So also will those four stinking faplaps who beat me up. You can inform them from me that their quota of pain is being arranged."

"I am not supposed to talk to you," said Marsin, dimly perceiving that the longer he stood there the bigger the fix he got into. He made to close the spyhole.

"All right. But I want something."

"What is it?"

"I want my bopamagilvie—that thing the officer took away."

"You cannot have it until the Commandant gives permission. He is absent today and will not return before tomorrow morning."

"That's no use. I want it now." He gave an airy wave of his hand. "Never mind. Forget it. I will summon another one."

"It is forbidden," reminded Marsin, very feebly.

"Ha-ha!" said Leeming, venting a hearty laugh.

Waiting for darkness to grow complete, he got the wire from under the bench and manufactured a second whatzit to all intents and purposes identical with the first one.

Twice he was interrupted but not caught.

That job finished, he upended the bench and climbed it. Taking the new coil of wire from his pocket, he tied one end tightly around the bottom of the middle bar, hung the coil outside the window gap.

With spit and dust he camouflaged the bright tin surface of the one visible strand, made sure it could not be seen at farther than nose-tip distance. He got down, replaced the bench. The window gap was so high that all of its ledge and the bottom three inches of its bar could not be viewed from below.

Going to the door, he listened and at the right time called, "Are you there?"

When the light came on and the spyhole was in use he got an instinctive feeling that there was a bunch of them clustered outside, also that the eye in the hole was not Marsin's.

Ignoring everything, he rotated the loop slowly and carefully, meanwhile calling, "Are you there?"

After traversing about forty degrees he paused, gave his voice a tone of intense satisfaction, said, "So you are there at last! Why the devil don't you keep within easy reach so's we can talk without me having to summon you with a loop?"

He went silent, put on the expression of one who listens intently. The eye in the hole widened, got shoved away, was replaced by another.

"Well," said Leeming, settling himself down for a cozy gossip, "I'll point them out to you first chance I get and leave you to deal with them as you think fit. Let's switch to our own language—there are too many big ears around for my liking." He took a long, deep breath, rattled off at top pace and without pause, "Out sprang the web and opened wide the mirror cracked from side to side the curse has come upon me cried the Lady of—"

Out sprang the door and opened wide and two guards almost fell headlong into the cell in their eagerness to make a quick snatch. Two more posed outside with the officer between them. Marsin mooned fearfully in the background.

A guard grabbed up the loop assembly, yelled, "I've got it!" and rushed out. His companion followed. Both seemed hysterical with excitement.

There was a ten seconds' pause before the door shut. Leeming exploited the fact. He stood up, pointed at the group by making horizontal stabbing motions with his two middle fingers. Giving 'em the Devil's Horns they'd called it when he was a kid. The classic gesture of donating the evil eye.

"Those," he declaimed dramatically, addressing what wasn't there, "are the scaly-skinned bums who've asked for trouble. See that they get plenty."

The whole bunch of them managed to look alarmed before the door cut them from sight with a vicious slam. He listened at the spyhole, heard them go away muttering steadily between themselves.

Within ten minutes he had broken a length off the coil hanging from the window bars, restored the spit and dust disguise of the holding strand. Half an hour later he had another bopamagilvie. Practice was making him an expert in the swift and accurate manufacture of these things.

Lacking wood for a stand, he used the loose nail to bore a hole in the dirt between the big stone slabs composing the floor of his cell. He rammed the legs of the loop into the hole, twisted the contraption this way and that to make ceremonial rotation easy.

When the right moment arrived he lay on his belly and commenced reciting through the loop the third paragraph of Rule 27, subsection B, of Space Regulations. He chose it because it was a gem of bureaucratic phraseology, a single sentence one thousand words long meaning something known only to God.

"Where refueling must be carried out as an emergency measure at a station not officially listed as a home station or definable for special purposes as a home station under Section A (5) amendment A (5) B the said station shall be treated as if it were definable as a home station under Section A (5) amendment A (5) B providing that the emergency falls within the authorized list of technical necessities as given in Section J (29.33) with addenda subsequent thereto as applicable to home stations where such are—"

The spyhole flipped open and shut. Somebody scooted away. A minute afterward the corridor shook to what sounded like a cavalry charge. The spyhole again opened and shut. The door crashed inward.

This time they reduced him to his bare pelt, searched his clothes, raked the cell from end to end. Their manner was that of those singularly lacking in brotherly love. They turned the bench upside-down, knocked it, tapped it, kicked it, did everything but run a large magnifying glass over it.

Watching this operation, Leeming encouraged them by giving a sinister snigger. Was a time when he could not have produced a sinister snigger even to win a fifty-credit bet. But he could do it now. The ways in which a man can rise to the occasion are without limit.

Giving him a look of sudden death and total destruction, a guard went out, brought back a ladder, mounted it, surveyed the window gap. It was a perfunctory glance, his mind being mostly concerned with the solidity of the bars. He grasped each bar with both hands, shook vigorously. Satisfied, he got down, took the ladder away.

They departed. Leeming dressed himself, listened at the spyhole. Just a very faint hiss of breath and occasional rustle of clothes nearby. He sat on the bench and waited. In short time the lights flashed and the spyhole opened. He stabbed two fingers toward the inlooking eye.

The hole closed. Feet moved away stamping much too loudly. He waited. After half an hour of complete silence the eye offered itself again and for its pains received another two-fingered hex. Five minutes later it had another bestowed upon it. If it was the same eye all the time, it was a glutton for punishment.

This game continued for three hours before the eye had had enough. Then he made another loop, gabbled through it in a loud voice and precipitated another raid. They did not strip him or search the cell this time. They contented themselves with confiscating the gadget. And they showed signs of being more than somewhat fed up.

There was just enough wire left for one more. He decided to keep that against a future need and get some sleep. Inadequate food and not enough slumber were combining to make inroads on his reserves.

He flopped on the bench and closed red-rimmed eyes. In due time he started snoring fit to saw through the bars. That caused a panic in the passage, brought the crowd along in yet another rush.

Waking up, he damned them to perdition. He lay down again. He was plain bone-tuckered—but so were they.

He slept solidly until midday without a break except for the usually lousy breakfast. Soon after awakening came the usual lousy dinner. At exercise time they kept him locked in. He hammered on the floor, demanded to know why he wasn't being allowed to walk in the yard. They took no notice.

So he sat on the bench and thought things over. Perhaps this denial of his only freedom was a form of retaliation for making them hop around like fleas in the middle of the night. Or perhaps the Rigellian was under suspicion and they'd decided to prevent contact.

Anyway, he'd got the enemy worried. He was bollixing them about, single-handed, far behind the lines. That was something. The fact that a combatant is a prisoner doesn't mean he's out of the battle. Even behind thick wire and high walls he can still harass the foe, absorbing his time and energy, undermining his morale, pinning down at least a few of his forces.

The next step, he decided, was to widen the hex. He must do it as comprehensively as possible. The more he spread it and the more ambiguous the terms in which he expressed it, the more plausibly he could grab the credit for any and every misfortune that was certain to occur sooner or later.

It was the same technique of the gypsy's warning. People tend to attach specific meanings to ambiguities when circumstances arise and suggest a given meaning. People don't have to be especially credulous, either. It is sufficient for them to he made expectant, with a tendency to wonder—after the event.

"In the near future a dark, tall man will cross your path."

After which any male above average height, and not a blond, fits the picture. And any time from five minutes to a full year is accepted as the near future.

"Mamma, when the insurance man called he really smiled at me. *D'you remember what the gypsy said?"*

Leeming grinned to himself as his brain assembled facts and theories and analyzed the possibilities. Somewhere not so far away a bunch of Rigellians—or several bunches for all he knew—were deep in the earth and burrowing slowly, without tools. A few pitiful handfuls at a time. Progress at the rate of a couple of pathetic inches per night. Dirt taken out in mere pocket-loads and sprinkled through the yard. A constant, never-ending risk of discovery, entrapment and perhaps some insane shooting. A year-long project that could be terminated by a shout and the chatter of guns.

But to get out of clink you don't have to escape. If sufficiently patient, determined, glib and cunning you can talk the foe into opening the doors and pushing you out. You can use the wits that God gave you.

By law of probability various things must happen in jail and out, and not all of them pleasing to the enemy. Some officer must get the galloping gripes right under his body-belt, or a guard must fall down a watchtower ladder and break a leg, somebody must lose a wad of money or his pants or his senses. Farther afield a bridge must collapse, or a train get derailed, or a spaceship crash at take-off, or there'd be an explosion in a munitions factory, or a military leader would drop dead.

He'd be playing a trump card if he could establish his claim to be the author of all misery. The essential thing was to stake it in such a way that they could not effectively combat it, neither could they exact retribution in a torture chamber.

The ideal strategy was to convince them of his malevolence in a manner that would equally convince them of their own impotence. If he succeeded, they'd come to the logical conclusion—that the only way to get rid of trouble was to get rid of Leeming, alive and in one piece.

It was a jumbo problem that would have appalled him way back home. But by now he'd had three months in which to incubate a solution—and the brain becomes stimulated by grim necessity. A good thing he had an idea in mind; he had a mere ten minutes before the time came to apply it.

The door opened, a trio of guards glowered at him and one of them rasped, "The Commandant wishes to see you at once. *Amash!*"

The Commandant squatted behind a desk with a lower-ranking officer on either side. He was a heavily built specimen. His horn-covered lidless eyes gave him a dead-pan look as he studied the prisoner.

Leeming calmly sat himself in a handy chair and the officer on the right immediately bawled, "Federation garbage! You will stand in the presence of the Commandant."

"Let him sit," contradicted the Commandant.

A concession at the start, thought Leeming. He eyed the pile of papers on the desk. Ten to one the Commandant had read a complete report of his misdeeds and decided to reserve judgment until he'd got to the bottom of whatever was going on.

That attitude was natural enough. The Federation knew nothing of this local life form. By the same token the inquisitors knew nothing of several Federation forms, those of Earth in particular. From their viewpoint they were about to cope with an unknown quantity.

Man, how right they were! A quantity doubled by plus X.

"I am given to understand that you now speak our language," began the Commandant.

"No use denying it," Leeming confessed.

"Very well. You will first give some information concerning yourself." He positioned an official form on his desk, held a pen in readiness. "Name of planet of origin?"

"Earth."

The other wrote it phonetically in his own script, continued, "Name of race?"

"Terran."

"Name of species?"

"Homo nosipaca," said Leeming keeping his face straight.

The Commandant wrote it down, looked doubtful, asked, "What does that mean?"

"Space-traversing Man," Leeming informed.

"Hm-m-m!" The other was impressed despite himself, inquired, "Your personal name?"

"John Leeming."

"John Leeming," repeated the Commandant, putting it down on the form.

"And Eustace Phenackertiban," added Leeming, airily.

That got written too, though the Commandant had some difficulty in finding hooks and curlicues to express Phenackertiban. Twice he asked Leeming to repeat it and that worthy obliged.

Studying the result, which resembled a Chinese recipe for rotten egg gumbo, the Commandant said, "It is your custom to have two names?"

"Most certainly," Leeming assured. "We can't avoid it seeing that there are two of us."

The listener twitched the eyebrows he lacked and showed mild surprise. "You mean that you are always conceived and born in pairs? Two identical males or females every time?"

"No, not at all." Leeming adopted the air of one about to state the obvious. "Whenever one of us is born he immediately acquires a Eustace."

"A Eustace?"

"Yes."

The Commandant frowned, picked his teeth, glanced at the other officers. They assumed the blank expressions of fellows who've come along merely to keep company.

"What," asked the Commandant at long last, "is a Eustace?"

Registering surprise at such ignorance, Leeming said, "An invisibility that is part of one's self."

Understanding dawned on the Commandant's scaly face. "Ah, you mean a soul? You give your soul a separate name?"

"Nothing of the sort," Leeming denied. "I have a soul and Eustace has a soul of his own." Then, as an afterthought, "At least, I hope we have."

The Commandant lay back and stared at him. There was quite a long silence. Finally, he admitted, "I do not understand."

"In that case," announced Leeming, irritatingly triumphant "it's evident that you have no alien equivalent of Eustaces yourselves. You're all on your own. Just singlelifers. That's your hard luck."

Slamming a hand on the desk, the Commandant gave his voice a bit more military whoof and demanded, "Exactly what is a Eustace? Explain to me as clearly as possible."

"I'm in poor position to refuse the information," Leeming conceded with hypocritical reluctance. "Not that it matters much. Even if you gain perfect understanding there is nothing you can do."

"We'll see about that," the Commandant promised. "Tell me all about these Eustaces.

"Every Earthling lives a double-life from birth to death," said Leeming. "He exists in association with an entity which always calls himself Eustace something-or-other. Mine happens to be Eustace Phenackertiban."

"You can *see* this entity?"

"No, never at any time. You cannot see him, smell him or feel him."

"Then how do you know that this is not a racial delusion?"

"Firstly, because every man can hear his own Eustace. I can hold long conversations with mine, providing that he happens to be within reach, and I can hear him speaking clearly and logically within the depths of my mind."

"You cannot hear him with the ears?"

"No, only with the mind." Leeming took a deep breath and went on. "Secondly, he has the power to do certain things after which there is visible evidence that such things have been done." His attention shifted to the absorbed officer on the left. "For example, if Eustace had a grudge against this officer and advised me of his intention to make him fall downstairs, and if before long the officer fell downstairs and broke his neck—"

"It could be mere coincidence," the Commandant suggested.

"It could," Leeming agreed, "but there can be far too many coincidences. When a Eustace says he's going to do twenty or fifty things in succession and all of them happen, he's either doing them as promised or he is a most astounding prophet. Eustaces don't claim to be prophets. I don't believe in them either. Nobody, visible or invisible, can read the future with such detailed accuracy."

"That is true enough," admitted the Commandant.

"Do you accept the fact that you have a father and mother?"

"Of course."

"You don't consider it strange or abnormal?"

"Certainly not. It is inconceivable that one should be born without parents."

"Similarly we accept the fact that we have Eustaces and we cannot conceive being without them."

The Commandant thought it over, said to the right-hand officer, "This smacks of mutual parasitism. It would be interesting to learn what benefit they derive from each other."

Leeming chipped in with, "I can't tell you what my Eustace gets out of me. I can't tell you because I don't know."

"You expect me to believe that?" asked the Commandant, making like nobody's fool. He showed his teeth. "On your own evidence you can talk with him. *Why have you never asked him?"*

"We got tired of asking long, long ago. The subject has been dropped and the situation accepted."

"Why?"

"The answer was always the same. Eustaces readily admit that we are essential to their existence but cannot explain how because there's no way of making us understand."

"That could be a self-preservative evasion," the Commandant offered. "They won't tell you because they don't *want* you to know."

"Well, what do you suggest we do about it?"

Evading that one, the Commandant went on, "What benefit do *you* get out of the association? What good is your Eustace to you?"

"He provides company, comfort, information, advice and—"

"And what?"

Bending forward, hands on knees, Leeming practically spat it at him. "If necessary, vengeance."

That shook them. The Commandant rocked back. The under-officers registered disciplined apprehension. It's a hell of a war when one can be chopped down by a ghost.

Pulling himself together, the Commandant forced a grim smile into his face. "You're a prisoner. You've been here a good many days. Your Eustace doesn't seem to have done much about it."

"That's what you think. He's been doing plenty. And he'll do plenty more, in his own time, in his own way."

"Such as what?"

"Wait and see," Leeming advised, formidably confident.

That did not fill them with delight, either.

"Nobody can imprison more than half a Terran," he went on. "The tangible half. The other half cannot be pinned down by any method whatsoever. It is beyond control. It wanders loose collecting information of military value, indulging a little sabotage, doing just as it pleases. You've created that situation and you're stuck with it."

"Not if we kill you," said the Commandant, in nasty tones.

Leeming gave a hearty laugh. "That would make matters fifty times worse."

"In what way?"

"The life span of a Eustace is longer than that of a Terran. When a man dies his Eustace takes five to ten years to disappear. We have an ancient song to the effect that old Eustaces never die, they only fade away. Our world holds thousands of lonely, disconnected Eustaces gradually fading."

"What of it?"

"Kill me and you'll isolate my Eustace on a hostile world with no man or other Eustace for company. His days are numbered and he knows it. He has nothing to lose, he is no longer restricted by considerations of my safety. He can eliminate me from his plans because I've gone for keeps." He eyed his listeners as he finished. "He'll run amok, indulging an orgy of destruction. Remember, you're an alien life form to him. He has no feelings and no compunctions with regard to you."

The Commandant reflected in silence. It was difficult to believe all this. But before space-conquest it had been even more difficult to believe things now accepted as commonplace. He could not dismiss it as nonsense. The stupid believe things because they are credulous. The intelligent do not blindly accept but, when aware of their own ignorance, neither do they reject. Right now the Commandant was acutely aware of general ignorance concerning this life form known as Terran.

"All this is not impossible," he said after a while, "but it appears to me somewhat improbable. There are twenty-seven life forms in alliance with us. I do not know of one that exists in natural co-partnership with another form."

"The Lathians do," Leeming told him, nonchalantly mentioning the leaders of the foe, the chief source of the opposition.

"You mean they have Eustaces, too?" The Commandant looked startled.

"No. Each Lathian is unconsciously controlled by a thing that calls itself Willy something-or-other. They don't know it and we wouldn't know it except that our Eustaces told us."

"And how did they learn it?"

"As you know, the biggest battles so far have been fought in the Lathian sector. Both sides have taken prisoners. Our Eustaces told us that each Lathian prisoner had a controlling Willy but was unaware of it." He grinned, added, "And a Eustace doesn't think much of a Willy. Apparently a Willy is a lower form of associated life."

The Commandant frowned, said, "This is something definite, something we should be able to check. But how're we going to do it if Lathian allies themselves are ignorant of the real state of affairs?"

"Easy as pie," Leeming offered. "They're holding a bunch of Terran prisoners. Get someone to ask those prisoners whether the Lathians have got the Willies."

"We'll do just that," approved the Commandant, in the manner of one about to call a bluff. He turned to the right-hand officer. "Bamashim, go beam a signal to our chief liaison officer at Lathian H.Q., and get him to question those prisoners."

"You can check further still," Leeming interjected, "just to make doubly sure. To us, anyone who shares his life with an invisible being is known as a Nut. Ask the prisoners whether the Lathians are all Nuts."

"Take note of that and have it asked as well," the Commandant ordered the officer. He returned attention to Leeming. "Since you could not anticipate your forced landing and capture, and since you've been closely confined, there is no possibility of collusion between you and Terran prisoners far away."

"That's right," Leeming agreed.

"Therefore I shall weigh your evidence in the light of what replies come to my signal." He stared hard at the other. "If those replies fail to confirm your statements, I will know that you are a liar in some respects and probably a liar in all respects. Here, we have special and very effective methods of dealing with liars."

"That's to be expected But if the replies do confirm me, you'll know I've told the truth, won't you?"

"No," snapped the Commandant.

It was Leeming's turn to be shocked. "Why not?"

Thinning his lips, the Commandant said, "Because I know full well that there cannot have been direct communication between you and the other Terran prisoners. However, that means nothing. There may have been collusion between your Eustace and their Eustaces."

Then he bent sidewise, jerked open a drawer, placed a loop assembly on the desk. Then another and another. A bunch of them.

"Well," he invited "what have you to say to that?"

Leeming beat his brains around fast. He could see what the other meant. He could talk to his Eustace. His Eustace could talk to other Eustaces. The other Eustaces could talk to their imprisoned partners.

Get yourself out of that!

They were waiting for him, watching his face, counting the seconds needed to produce an answer. The longer he took to find one the weaker it would be. The quicker he came up with something good the more plausible its effect.

He was inwardly frantic by the time he saw an opening and grabbed at it.

"You're wrong on two counts."

"State them."

"Firstly, one Eustace cannot communicate unaided with another over a distance so enormous. His mind won't reach that far. To do it he has to use a Terran who, in his turn, must have radio equipment available."

"We've only your word for it," the Commandant pointed out. "If a Eustace can communicate without limit, it would be your policy to try to conceal the fact."

"I can do no more than give you my word regardless of whether or not you credit it."

"I do not credit it—yet. Proceed to your second count. It had better be convincing."

"It is," Leeming assured. "On this one we don't have my word for it. We have yours."

"Nonsense!" exclaimed the Commandant. "I have made no statements concerning Eustaces."

"On the contrary, you have said that there could be collusion between them."

"What of it?"

"There can be collusion only if Eustaces genuinely exist, in which case my evidence is true. But if my evidence is false, then Eustaces do not exist and there cannot possibly be a conspiracy between nonexistent things."

The Commandant sat perfectly still while his face took on a faint shade of purple. He looked and felt like the trapper trapped. Left-hand officer wore the expression of one struggling hard to suppress a disrespectful snicker.

"If," continued Leeming, piling it on for good measure, "you don't believe in Eustaces then you cannot logically believe in conspiracy between them. Contrariwise, if you believe in the possibility of collusion then you've got to believe in Eustaces. That is, of course, if you're in bright green britches and your right mind."

"Guard!" roared the Commandant. He pointed an angry finger. "Take him back to the cell. They were hustling the prisoner through the door when he changed tactics and bawled, "Halt!" He snatched up a loop assembly, gesticulated with it at Leeming. "Where did you get the material to manufacture this?"

"Eustace brought it for me. Who else?"

"Get out of my sight!"

"Merse, faplap!" urged the guards, prodding with their guns. *"Amash! Amash!"*

He spent the rest of that day and all the next one sitting or lying on the bench reviewing what had happened, planning his next moves and, in lighter moments, admiring his own ability as a whacking great liar.

Now and again he wondered how his efforts to dig himself free with his tongue compared with Rigellian attempts to do it with bare hands. Who was making the most progress and—of the greatest importance—who, once out, would stay out? One thing was certain: his method was less tiring to the body though more exhausting to the nerves.

Another advantage was that for the time being he had sidetracked their intention of squeezing him for military information. Or had he? Possibly from their viewpoint his revelations concerning the dual nature of Terrans were infinitely more important than details of armaments, which data might be false anyway. Nevertheless he had dodged what otherwise might have been a rough and painful interrogation.

Next time the spyhole opened he got down on his knees and said in very loud tones, "Thank you, Eustace! Oh, thank you!" and left the jumpy Marsin to wonder who had arrived at the crossroads in time for some of Eustace's dirty work.

Near midnight, just before sleep came on, it occurred to him that there was no point in doing things by halves. Why rest content to smile knowingly whenever the enemy suffered a petty misfortune?

He could extend it farther than that. No form of life was secure from the vagaries of chance. Good fortune came along as well as bad. There was no reason why Eustace should not get credit for both, no reason why he, Leeming, should not take to himself the implied power to reward as well as to punish.

That wasn't the limit, either. Bad luck and good luck are positive phases. He could cross the neutral zone and confiscate the negative phases. Through Eustace he could assign to himself not only the credit for things done, good or bad, but also for things *not* done. He could exploit not only the things that happened but also those that did not happen.

The itch to make a start right now was irresistible. Rolling off the bench, he belted the door from top to bottom. The guard had just been changed, for the eye that peered in was that of Kolum, a character who had bestowed a kick in the ribs not so long ago. Kolum was a cut above Marsin, being able to count upon all twelve fingers if given time to concentrate.

"So it's you," said Leeming, showing vast relief. "I begged him to lay off you, to leave you alone at least a little while. He is impetuous and much too drastic. I can see you are more intelligent than the others and, therefore, able to change for the better. Nobody with brains is beyond hope."

"Huh?" said Kolum, half scared, half flattered.

"So he's left you alone," Leeming pointed out. "He's done nothing to you—yet." He increased the gratification. "I do hope I can continue to control him. Only the stupidly brutal deserve slow death."

"That is true," agreed Kolum, eagerly. "But what—?"

"Now," continued Leeming with firmness, "it is up to you to prove that my confidence is justified. All I want you to do is give a message to the Commandant."

"I dare not disturb him at this hour. It is impossible. The sergeant of the guard will not permit it. He will—"

"It is to be given to him personally when he awakes first thing in the morning."

"That is different," said Kolum, sweating slightly. "But if the Commandant disapproves of the message he will punish you and not me."

"Write," ordered Leeming.

Kolum leaned his gun against the opposite wall, dug pencil and paper out of a pocket.

"To the Most Exalted Lousy Screw," began Leeming.

"What does 'lousy screw' mean?" asked Kolum, struggling with the two Terran words.

"It's a title. It means 'your highness.' Boy, how high he is!" Leeming pinched his nose while the other pored over the paper. He continued to dictate. "The food is very poor and insufficient. I have lost much weight and my ribs are beginning to show. My Eustace does not like it. I cannot be held responsible for his actions. Therefore I beg Your Most Exalted Lousy Screwship to give serious consideration to this matter."

"There are many words," complained Kolum, martyred, "and I shall have to rewrite them more readably when I go off duty."

"I know. And I appreciate the trouble you're taking on my behalf." Leeming gave him a look of fraternal fondness. "That's why I feel sure that you'll live long enough to do it."

"I must live longer than that," insisted Kolum, bugging his eyes. "I have the right to live, haven't I?"

"That's exactly my own argument," said Leeming, in the manner of one who has striven all night to establish the irrefutable but cannot yet guarantee success.

He returned to the bench. The light went off, the spyhole shut. Four stars peeped through the window slot—and they were not unattainable.

In the morning breakfast came half an hour late but consisted of one full bowl of lukewarm pap, two thick slices of brown bread heavily smeared with grease, and a large cup of stuff vaguely resembling paralyzed coffee. He ate the lot with mounting triumph.

No interview that day or the next. No summons for a week. Evidently His Lousy Screwship was still awaiting a reply from the Lathian sector and didn't feel inclined to make another move before he got it. However, meals remained more substantial, a fact that Leeming viewed as positive evidence that someone was insuring himself against disaster.

Then one morning the Rigellians acted up. From the cell they could be heard but not seen. Every day at an hour after dawn the tramp of their two thousand pairs of feet sounded somewhere out of sight and died away toward the workshops.

This morning they came out singing, their voices holding a touch of defiance. Something about Asta Zangasta's a dirty old man, got fleas on his chest and sores on his pan. Guards yelled at them. Singing rose higher, the defiance increased. Leeming got below the window, listened intently, wondered who the blazes was this much-abused Asta Zangasta. Probably the local life form's largest cheese, the big boss of this world.

The bawling of two thousand voices rose crescendo. Guards shouted frenziedly and were drowned out. A warning shot was fired. Guards in the watchtowers edged their guns around.

Next came the sound of blows, shots, scuffling sounds, yells of fury. A bunch of twenty guards raced flatfooted past Leeming's window, heading for the fracas. The uproar continued for twenty minutes, died away. Resulting silence could almost be felt.

Exercise time, Leeming had the yard to himself. Not a soul there. He mooched around gloomily, found Marsin on yard patrol.

"What's happened?"

"They misbehaved. They are being kept in the workshops to make up loss of production. It is their own fault. They started work late to slow down output. We didn't even have time to count them."

Leeming grinned in his face. "And some guards were hurt. Not severely. Just enough to give them a taste of what's to come. Think it over."

"Eh?"

"But *you* were not hurt. Think that over, too!"

He ambled off, leaving Marsin bewildered. Then a thought struck him. *"We had not time even to count them."* He returned, said, "Tomorrow some of you will wish you'd never been born."

"You are threatening us?"

"No—I'm making a promise. Tell your officer. Tell the Commandant. It will help you escape the consequences."

"I will tell them," said Marsin, relieved and grateful.

His guess was dead on the beam. The Rigellians were too shrewd to invite thick ears and black eyes without good reason. It took the foe a full day to arrive at the same conclusion.

One hour after dawn the Rigellians were marched out dormitory by dormitory, in batches of fifty instead of the usual steady stream. They were counted in fifties, the easy way. This simple arithmetic got thrown out of kilter when one dormitory gave up only twelve prisoners, all of them sick, weak, wounded or otherwise handicapped.

Infuriated guards rushed indoors to drag out the nonattending thirty-eight. They weren't there. The door was firm and solid, the window bars intact. It took considerable galumphing around to detect a hollow spot in the floor, and under that a deep shaft from which ran a tunnel. The said tunnel was empty.

Sirens wailed, guards pounded all over the shop, officers shouted, the entire place began to resemble a madhouse. The Rigellians got it good and hard for spoiling the previous morning's count and thus giving the escapees an extra day's lead. Boots and gun butts were freely used, bodies dragged aside unconscious.

The surviving top-ranker of the offending dormitory, a lieutenant with a bad limp, was put against a wall and shot. Leeming could see nothing but heard the hoarse commands of, "Present . . . aim . . . fire!" and the following volley.

He prowled round and round his cell, clenching and unclenching his fists, swearing mightily to himself. The spyhole opened but hastily shut before he could spit right in somebody's eye.

The upset continued as inflamed guards searched all dormitories one by one, tested doors, bars, floors and walls. Officers screamed threats at groups of Rigellians who were slow to respond to orders.

At twilight outside forces brought in seven tired, bedraggled escapees caught on the run. "Present . . . aim . . . fire!" Leeming battered his door but the spyhole remained shut and none answered. Two hours later he'd made another coiled loop with the last of his wire. He spent half the night talking into it, menacingly, at the top of his voice. Nobody took the slightest notice.

A feeling of deep frustration had come over him by noon the next day. He estimated that the Rigellian escape must have taken at least a year to prepare. Result: eight dead, thirty-one still loose but planetbound and probably fated to ultimate recapture, most of two thousand getting it rough in consequence, his own efforts balled up. He did not resent the break, not one little bit. Good luck to them. But if only it had occurred a couple of months earlier or later.

Immediately after dinner four guards came for him. "The Commandant wants you at once." Their manner was surly, somewhat on edge. One wore a narrow bandage around his scaly pate, another had a badly swollen eye.

Just about the worst moment to choose, thought Leeming, gloomily. The Commandant would be in the mood to go up like a rocket. You cannot reason with a person who is in a purple rage. Emotion comes uppermost, words are disregarded, arguments are dismissed. He was going to have a tough job on his hands.

As before, the Commandant sat behind his desk but there were no accompanying officers. At his side posed an elderly civilian. The latter studied the prisoner curiously as he entered and took a seat.

"This is Pallam," introduced the Commandant, displaying unexpected amiability that dumfounded the hearer. "He has been sent along by no less a person than Zangasta himself."

"A mental specialist?" guessed Leeming, frowning at the oldster.

"Nothing like that," assured Pallam quietly. "I am particularly interested in all aspects of symbiosis."

Lemming's back hairs stirred. He didn't like the idea of being cross-examined by an expert. They had unmilitary minds and a pernicious habit of digging up contradictions in a story.

"Pallam wishes to ask you a few questions," informed the Commandant. "But those will come later." He leaned back, put on a self-satisfied expression. "For a start, let me say that I am indebted to you for the information you gave me last time you were here."

"You mean it has proved useful to you?" inquired Leeming, hardly believing his ears.

"Very much so. The guards responsible for Dormitory Fourteen are to be drafted to the battle areas where they will be stationed at space-ports liable to attack. That is their punishment for gross neglect of duty." He gazed thoughtfully at the other, went on, "The big escape would have made that my fate also had not Zangasta considered it a minor matter when compared with what I have discovered through you."

"But when I asked, you saw to it that I had better food. Surely you expected some reward?"

"Eh?" The Commandant registered surprise followed by slow understanding. "I did not think of that."

"So much the better," said Leeming, with hearty approval. "A good deed is doubly good when done with no ulterior motive. Eustace will take note of that."

"You mean," put in Pallam, "that his code of ethics is identical with your own?"

Why did that fellow have to put his spoke in? Be careful now!

"Similar in some respects but not identical."

"What is the most outstanding difference?"

"Well," said Leeming, playing for time, "it's hard to decide." He rubbed his brow while his mind whizzed dizzily. "I'd say in the matter of vengeance."

"Define the difference," invited Pallam, sniffing along the trail like a bloodhound.

"From my viewpoint," said Leeming, carefully, "he is unnecessarily sadistic."

There, that gave the needed coverage for any widespread claims it might be desirable to make later.

"In what way?" Pallam persisted.

"My instinct is to take prompt action, get things over and done with. His tendency is to prolong the agony."

"Explain further," pressed Pallam, making a thorough nuisance of himself.

"If you and I were deadly enemies, and I had a gun, I would shoot you and kill you. But if Eustace had you marked for death he'd make it slower, more gradual."

"Describe his method."

"First, he'd make you know that you were marked. Then he'd do nothing until at last you got the notion that nothing ever would be done. Then he'd remind you with a minor blow. When resulting alarm had worn off he'd strike a harder one. And so on and so on, with increasing intensity spread if necessary over months and years. That would continue until your doom became plain and too much to bear any longer." He thought again, added, "No Eustace has ever killed anyone. If anyone dies because of him, it is by his own hand."

"He drives a victim to suicide?"

"Yes."

"And there is no way of avoiding such a fate?"

"Yes there is," Leeming contradicted. "At any time the victim can gain freedom from fear by redressing the wrong he has done to that Eustace's partner."

"Such redress immediately terminates the vendetta?" pursued Pallam.

"That's right."

"Whether or not you approve personally?"

"Yes. If my grievance ceases to be real and becomes only imaginary, my Eustace refuses to recognize it or do anything about it."

"So what it boils down to," said Pallam, pointedly "is that his method provides motive and opportunity for repentance while yours does not?"

"I suppose so."

"Which means that he has a more balanced sense of justice?"

"He can be darned ruthless," said Leeming, momentarily unable to think of anything less feeble.

"That is beside the point." Pallam lapsed into meditative silence, then remarked to the Commandant, "It seems that the association is not between equals. The invisible component is also the superior one."

Cunning old hog, Leeming thought to himself. But if he was trying to tempt the prisoner into a complicated denial he was going to be disappointed.

So he sat and said nothing but carefully wore the hook of one whose status has been accurately weighed in the balance and found wanting. Coming to that, there's no shame in being defined as inferior to one's own mind.

Pallam took on an expression of sharpness as he continued, "I assume that when your Eustace takes upon himself the responsibility for wreaking vengeance he does so because circumstances prevent punishment being administered either by yourself or the community?"

"That's pretty well correct," admitted Leeming, warily.

"In other words, he functions only when both you and the law are impotent?"

"He takes over when need arises," informed Leeming, striving to give the point some ambiguity.

"That is substantially what I said," declared Pallam, a little coldly. He bent forward, watched the other keen-eyed and managed to make his attitude intimidating. "Now let us suppose your Eustace finds excellent reason to punish another Terran. *What does the victim's Eustace do about it?"*

Leeming's mouth opened and the words, "Not much," popped out of their own accord. For a mad moment he felt that Eustace had actually arrived and joined the party.

"Why not?"

"I have told you before and I am telling you again that no Eustace will concern himself for one moment with an imaginary grievance. A guilty Terran has no genuine cause for complaint. He brought vengeance on himself and the cure lies in his own hands. If he doesn't enjoy suffering, he need only get busy and undo whatever wrong he has done."

"Will his Eustace urge him or influence him to take action necessary to avoid punishment?"

"Never having been a victim myself," said Leeming, fairly oozing virtue, "I am unable to tell you. I suppose it would be near the truth to say that Terrans behave because association with Eustaces makes them behave. They've little choice about the matter."

"All that is acceptable," conceded Pallam, "because it is consistent—as far as it goes."

"What d'you mean?"

"Let's take it to the bitter end. I do not see any rational reason why any victim's Eustace should allow his partner to be driven to suicide. It is contrary to the basic law of survival."

"Nobody commits suicide until after he's gone off his rocker."

"What of it?"

"An insane person is of no avail to any Eustace. To a Eustace, he's already dead, no longer worth defending or protecting. Eustaces associate only with the sane."

Pouncing on that, Pallam exclaimed, "So the benefit they derive is rooted somewhere in Terran minds, it is a mental sustenance?"

"I don't know."

"Does your Eustace ever make you feel tired, exhausted, perhaps a little stupified?"

"Yes," said Leeming. And how, brother! Right now he could choke Eustace to death.

"I would much like to continue this for months," Pallam observed to the Commandant. "It is an absorbing subject. There are no records of symbiotic association in anything higher than plants and six species of the lower *elames.* To find it among sentient forms, and one of them intangible, is remarkable, truly remarkable!"

The Commandant looked awed.

"Give him your report," urged Pallam.

"Our liaison officer, Colonel Shomuth, has replied from the Lathian sector," the Commandant told Leeming. "He is fluent in Cosmoglotta and, therefore, was able to question many Terran prisoners. We sent him a little more information and the result is significant."

"What else did you expect?" asked Leeming.

Ignoring that, the Commandant went on, "He said that most of the prisoners refused to make comment or admit anything. That is understandable. Nothing could shake their belief that they were being tempted to surrender information of military value. So they remained silent." He glanced at his listener. "But some talked."

"There are always a few willing to blab," remarked Leeming, looking resigned.

"Certain officers talked, including Cruiser Captain Tompass . . . Tompus—"

"Thomas?"

"Yes, that's the word." Turning round in his chair the Commandant pressed a wall switch. "This is the beamed interview, unscrambled and recorded on tape."

A crackling hiss poured out of a perforated grid in the wall. It grew louder, died down to a background wash. Voices came out of the grid.

Shomuth: "Captain Thomas, I have been ordered to check certain information already in our possession. You have nothing to lose by giving answers, nothing to gain by refusing them. There are no Lathians present, only the two of us. You may speak freely and what you say will be treated in confidence."

Thomas: "What d'you want to know?"

Shomuth: "Whether our Lathian allies really are Nuts."

Thomas, after a pause: "You want the blunt truth?"

Shomuth: "We do."

Thomas: "All right, they are nuts."

Shomuth: "And they have the Willies?"

Thomas: "Where did you dig up this information?"

Shomuth: "That's our business. Please answer the question."

Thomas, belligerently: "Not only have they got the willies but they'll have a darned sight more of them before we're through."

Shomuth, puzzled: "How can that be? We have learned that each Lathian is unconsciously controlled by a Willy. Therefore the total number of Willies is limited. It cannot be increased except by birth of more Lathians."

Thomas, quickly: "You got me wrong. What I meant was that as Lathian casualties mount up the number of loose Willies will increase. There will be lots more of them in proportion to the number of Lathian survivors."

Shomuth: "Yes, I see what you mean. And it will create a psychic problem." Pause. "Now, Captain Thomas, have you any reason to suppose that many unattached Willies might be able to seize control of another and different life form? Such as my own species, for example?"

Thomas, with enough menace to deserve a space medal. "I wouldn't be surprised."

Shomuth: "You don't know for sure?"

Thomas: "No."

Shomuth: "It is true, is it not, that you are aware of the real Lathian nature only because you have been informed of it by your Eustace?"

Thomas, startled: "My *what?*"

Shomuth: "Your *Eustace.* Why should that surprise you?"

Thomas, recovering swiftly enough to earn a bar to the medal: "I thought you said Useless. Ha-ha! Silly of me. Yes, my Eustace, You're dead right there."

Shomuth, in lower tones: "There are four hundred twenty Terran prisoners here. That means four hundred twenty Eustaces wandering loose on this planet. Correct?"

Thomas: "I am unable to deny it."

Shomuth: "The Lathian heavy cruiser *Veder* crashed on landing and was a total loss. The Lathians attributed it to an error of judgment on the part of the crew. But that was just three days after you prisoners were brought here. Was it a mere coincidence?"

Thomas, oh, good, but good: "Work it out for yourself."

Shomuth: "All right. Here's something else. The biggest fuel dump in this part of the galaxy is located sixty miles south of here. A week ago it blew up to total destruction. The loss was very severe and will handicap our allied fleets for some time to come. Technicians theorize that a static spark caused one tank to explode and that set off the rest. We can always trust technicians to come up with a plausible explanation."

Thomas: "Well, what's wrong with it?"

Shomuth: "That dump has been there more than four years. There's been no static sparks during that time."

Thomas: "What are you getting at?"

Shomuth, pointedly: "You have admitted yourself that there are four hundred and twenty Eustaces free to do as they like."

Thomas, in tones of stern patriotism: "I am admitting nothing. I refuse to answer any more questions."

Shomuth: "Has your Eustace prompted you to say that?"

Silence.

Reversing the switch, the Commandant said, "There you are. Eight other Terran officers gave more or less the same evidence. Zangasta himself has listened to the records and is deeply concerned about the situation."

"Tell him he needn't bother nursing his pate," Leeming airily suggested. "It's all a lot of bunk, a put-up job. There was collusion between my Eustace and theirs."

Turning a faint purple, the Commandant retorted, "As you emphasized at our last meeting, there cannot be collusion without Eustaces. So it makes no difference either way."

"I'm glad you can see it at last."

"Let it pass," chipped in Pallam, impatiently. "It is of no consequence. The confirmatory evidence is adequate no matter how we look at it."

Thus prompted, the Commandant continued, "I have been doing some investigating myself. Eight of my guards earned your enmity by assaulting you. Of these, four are now in hospital badly injured, two more are to be drafted to the fighting front."

"The other two, said Leeming, "gained forgiveness. Nothing has happened to them."

"No. Nothing has happened."

"I cannot give the same guarantee with respect to the firing squad, the officer in charge of it, or the higher-up who issued the order that helpless prisoners be shot. It all depends on how my Eustace feels about it."

"Why should he care?" put in Pallam. "They were only Rigellians."

"They were allies. And allies are friends. I feel bad about the needless slaughtering of them. Eustace is sensitive to my emotions."

"But not necessarily obedient to them?"

"No."

"In fact," pressed Pallam, "if there is any question of one serving the other, it is *you* who obeys *him?"*

"Most times, anyway."

"Well, it confirms what you've already told us." He ventured a thin smile. "The chief difference between Terrans and Lathians is that you know you're controlled whereas the Lathians are ignorant of it."

"We are not controlled consciously or unconsciously," Leeming insisted. "We exist in mutual partnership, same as you do with your wife. It's mastery by neither party."

"I wouldn't know, never having been mated," said Pallam. He transferred his attention to one side. "Carry on, Commandant."

"You may as well be told that this has been set aside as a penal planet," informed the Commandant. "We are already holding a large number of prisoners, mostly Rigellians."

"What of it?" Leeming prompted.

"There are more to come. Two thousand Centaurians and six hundred Thetans are due to arrive and fill a new jail next week. Our allied forces will transfer more Federation life forms as soon as ships are available." He eyed the other speculatively. "It's only a matter of time before they start dumping Terrans upon us as well."

"Is it bothering you?"

"Zangasta has decided not to accept Terrans."

"That's up to him," said Leeming, blandly indifferent.

"Zangasta has a clever mind," the Commandant opined. "He is of the firm opinion that to assemble a formidable army of prisoners all on one planet, and then put some thousands of Terrans among them, is to create a potentially dangerous situation. He foresees trouble on a vaster scale than we could handle. Indeed, we might lose this world, strategically placed in the rear, and become subject to the violent attacks of our own allies."

"That's the angle he puts out for publication. He's got a private one too."

"Eh?"

Looking grim, Leeming continued, "Zangasta himself first gave orders that escaped prisoners were to be shot immediately after recapture. He must have done, otherwise nobody would dare shoot them. Now he's jumpy because of one Eustace. He thinks a few thousand Eustaces will be a greater menace to him. But he's wrong."

"Why is he wrong?" inquired the Commandant.

"Because it isn't only the repentant who have no cause to fear. The dead haven't either. He'd better countermand that order if he wants to keep on living."

"I shall inform him of your remarks. However, such cancellation of orders may not be necessary. As I have told you, he is clever. He has devised a subtle strategy that will put all your evidence to the final, conclusive test and at the same time may solve his problems."

Feeling vague alarm, Leeming asked, "Am I permitted to know what he intends to do?"

"He has given instructions that you be told. And he has started doing it." The Commandant waited for the sake of extra effect. "He has beamed the Federation a proposal to exchange prisoners."

Leeming fidgeted around in his seat. Holy smoke, the plot was thickening with a vengeance. His sole purpose from the beginning had been to talk himself out of jail and into some other situation from which he could scoot at top speed. Now they were taking up his story and plastering it all over the galaxy. Oh, what a tangled web we weave when first we practice to deceive.

"What's more," the Commandant went on, "the Federation has accepted providing only that we exchange rank for rank. That is to say, captains for captains, navigators for navigators and so forth."

"That's reasonable."

"Zangasta," said the Commandant, grinning like a wolf, "has agreed in his turn—providing that the Federation accepts all Terran prisoners first and makes exchange on a basis of two for one. He is now awaiting their reply."

"Two for one?" echoed Leeming. "You want them to surrender two prisoners for one Terran?"

"No, of course not." Leaning forward, he increased the grin and showed the roots of his teeth. "Two of ours for one Terran and his Eustace. That's fair enough, isn't it?"

"It's not for me to say. The Federation is the judge." Leeming swallowed hard.

"Until a reply arrives and the matter is settled, Zangasta wishes you to have better treatment. You will be transferred to the officers' quarters outside the walls and you will share their meals. Temporarily you'll be treated as a noncombatant and you'll be very comfortable. It is necessary that you give me your parole not to escape."

Ye gods, that was another stinker. The entire fiction was shaped toward ultimate escape. He couldn't abandon it now. Neither was he willing to give his word of honor with the cynical intention of breaking it.

"Parole refused," he said, firmly.

The Commandant registered incredulity. "You are not serious?"

"I am. I've no choice. Terran military law doesn't allow a prisoner to give such a promise."

"Why not?"

"Because no Terran can accept responsibility for his Eustace. How can we swear not to get out when all the time we're already half out?"

"Guard!" called the Commandant, visibly disappointed.

He mooched uneasily around the cell for a full week, occasionally chatting with Eustace night-times for the benefit of ears outside the door. The food remained better. The guards treated him with diffidence. Four more recaptured Rigellians were brought back but not shot. All the signs and portents were that he'd still got a grip on the foe.

Nevertheless, he was badly bothered. The Federation in general and Earth in particular knew nothing whatsoever about Eustaces and therefore were likely to view a two-for-one proposition with the contempt it deserved. A blank refusal on their part might cause him to be plied with awkward questions impossible to answer.

Sooner or later it would occur to them that they were afflicted with the biggest liar in cosmic history. They'd then devise tests of fiendish ingenuity. When he flunked them, the balloon would go up.

He wasn't inclined to give himself overmuch credit for kidding them along so far. The books he'd been reading had shown that the local religion was based upon reverence for ancestral spirits. They were also familiar with what are known as poltergeist phenomena. The ground had been prepared for him in advance. He'd merely plowed it and sown the crop. When a victim believes in two kinds of invisible beings it isn't too hard to make him swallow a third.

But when the Federation beamed a curt invitation to go jump, it was possible that the third type would be regurgitated with violence. Unless by fast talk he could cram it back down their gullets when it was already halfway out. How to do that?

He was still stewing it over and over when they came for him again. The Commandant was there but Pallam was not. Instead, a dozen civilians eyed him curiously. That made a total of thirteen, a very suitable number to pronounce him ready for the chopper.

Feeling as much the center of attention as a six-tailed wombat at the zoo, he sat down and four civilians started chivvying him at once, taking it in relays. They were interested in only one subject, namely, bopamagilvies. It seemed they'd been playing with them for hours and achieved nothing except some practice at acting daft.

On what principle did they work? Did they focus mental output into a narrow beam? At what distance did his Eustace get beyond straight conversation and need to be called with a loop? Why was it necessary to make directional search before getting a reply? How did he know how to make a loop in the first place?

"I can't explain. How does a bird know how to make a nest? The knowledge seems instinctive. I've known how to call Eustace ever since I was old enough to shape a piece of wire."

"Will any kind of wire do?"

"So long as it's nonferrous."

"Are all Terran loops of exactly the same construction and dimensions?"

"No. They vary with the individual."

Somehow he beat them off, feeling hot in the forehead and cold in the belly. Then the Commandant took over.

"The Federation has refused to accept Terran prisoners ahead of other species, or to exchange them two for one, or to discuss the matter any further. They accuse Zangasta of bad faith. What have you to say to that?"

Steeling himself, Leeming commented, "On your side there are twenty-seven life forms of which the Lathians and the Zebs are by far the most powerful. Now if the Federation wanted to give priority of exchange to one species, do you think the others would agree? If the favored species happened to be the Tansites, would the Lathians and Zebs vote for them to head the line-up?"

A civilian chipped in, a tall, authoritative specimen. "I am Daverd, personal aide to Zangasta. He is of your own opinion. He believes the Terrans have been outvoted. Therefore I am commanded to ask you one question."

"What is it?"

"Do your Federation allies know about your Eustaces?"

"No."

"You have succeeded in hiding the facts from them?"

"There's no question of hiding facts. With friends the facts just don't become apparent. Eustaces take action only against enemies and that's something that can't be concealed."

"Very well." Daverd came closer while the others looked on. "The Lathians started this war and the Zebs went with them by reason of military alliance. The rest of us got dragged in for one cause or another. The Lathians are powerful. But, as we now know, they're not responsible for their actions."

"What's this to me?"

"Separately, we numerically weaker life form cannot stand against the Lathians or the Zebs. But together we are strong enough to step out of the war and maintain our right to remain neutral. So Zangasta has consulted the others."

Jumping jimmy, what you can do with a few feet of copper wire!

"He has received their replies today," Daverd continued. "They are willing to make a common front and get out of the war providing that the Federation is equally willing to exchange prisoners and recognize neutrality."

"Such sudden unanimity among minors tells me something pretty good," observed Leeming, displaying satisfaction.

"It tells you what?"

"Federation forces have won a major battle lately. Somebody's been scalped."

Daverd refused to confirm or deny it. "At the moment you're the only Terran we hold on this planet. Zangasta thinks you could well be spared."

"Meaning what?"

"He has decided to send you to the Federation. It is your job to persuade them to agree to our plans. If you fail—a couple of hundred thousand hostages may suffer."

"For which the Federation may retaliate."

"They won't know. There'll be no Terrans or Eustaces here to inform them by any underhanded method. We're keeping Terrans out. The Federation cannot use knowledge it doesn't possess."

"No," agreed Leeming. "It's impossible to use what you haven't got."

They provided a light destroyer crewed by ten Zangastans and that took him to a servicing planet right on the fringe of the battle area. It was a Lathian outpost but those worthies showed no interest in what their smaller allies were up to. They got to work relining the destroyer's tubes while Leeming was transferred to a one-man Lathian scoutship. The ten Zangastans officiously saluted before they left him.

From that point he was strictly on his own. Take-off was a heller. The seat was awkwardly shaped and too big, the controls in the wrong places and too far apart. The little ship was fast and powerful but responded differently from his own. How he got up he never knew, but he made it.

After that, there was the constant risk of being tracked by Federation detecting devices and blown apart in full flight.

He arrowed straight for Terra. His sleeps were uneasy and restless. The tubes were not to be trusted despite that flight-duration would be only one-third of that done in his own vessel. The strange autopilot was not to be trusted merely because it was of alien design. The ship itself wasn't to be trusted for the same reason. The forces of his own side were not to be trusted because they'd tend to shoot first and ask questions afterward.

In due time he came in fast on Terra's night side and plonked it down in a field a couple of miles west of the main spaceport.

The moon was shining bright along the Wabash when he approached the front gate afoot and a sentry yelled, "Halt! Who goes there?"

"Lieutenant Leeming and Eustace Phenackertiban."

"Advance and be recognized."

He walked forward, thinking to himself that such an order was somewhat dunderheaded. Be recognized. The sentry had never seen him in his life and wouldn't know him from Myrtle McTurtle.

At the gate a powerful cone of light shot down upon him. Somebody with three chevrons on his sleeve emerged from a nearby hut bearing a scanner on the end of a black cable. The scanner got waved over the arrival from head to feet, concentrating mostly upon the face.

A loud-speaker in the hut said, "Bring him in to Intelligence."

They started walking.

The sentry let go an agitated yelp of, "Hey, where's the other guy?"

"What guy?" asked the escorting sergeant, looking around.

"He's nuts," Leeming confided.

"You gave me *two* names," asserted the sentry, slightly bellicose.

"Well, if you ask the sergeant nicely he'll give you two more," said Leeming. "Won't you, sarge?"

"Let's get going," suggested the sergeant, showing impatience.

They reached Intelligence H.Q. The duty officer was Colonel Farmer, a florid character Leeming had met many times before. Farmer gazed at him incredulously and said, "Well!" He said it seven times.

Without preamble, Leeming growled, "What's all this about us refusing to make a two-for-one swap for Terran prisoners?"

Farmer started visibly. "You know about it?"

"How could I ask if I didn't?"

"All right. Why should we accept such a cockeyed proposition?"

Bending over the desk, hands splayed upon it, Leeming said, "All we need do is agree—upon one condition."

"What condition?"

"That they make a similar agreement with respect to Lathians. Two Federation prisoners for one Lathian and one Willy."

"One *what?*"

"One Willy. The Lathians will take it like birds. They've been propaganding all over the shop that one Lathian is worth two of anything else. They're too conceited to refuse such an offer. They'll advertise it as proof that even an enemy knows how good they are."

"But—" began Farmer, a little dazed.

"Their allies will agree also, but from different motives that don't matter to us anyway. Try it for size. Two Federation prisoners for one Lathian and his Willy."

Farmer protruded his belly and roared, "What the blue blazes is a Willy?"

"You can easily find out," assured Leeming. "Consult your Eustace."

Showing alarm, Farmer lowered his tones to a soothing pitch and said as gently as possible, "You were reported missing and believed killed."

"I crash-landed and got taken prisoner in the back of beyond. They slung me in the jug."

"Yes, yes," said Colonel Farmer, making pacifying gestures. "But how on earth did you get away?"

"Farmer, I cannot tell a lie. I hexed them with my bopamagilvie."

"Huh?"

"So I left by rail," informed Leeming, "and there were ten faplaps carrying it."

Catching the other unaware he let go a vicious kick at the desk and made a spurt of ink leap across the blotter.

"Now let's see some of the intelligence they're supposed to have in Intelligence. Beam the offer. Two for a Lathian and a Willy Terwilliger." He stared wildly around. "And find me a bed. I'm dead beat."

Holding himself in enormous restraint, Farmer said, "Lieutenant, do you realize that you are talking to a colonel?"

Leeming used the word.

Study in Still Life

Astounding, January 1959

"What burns me up," said Purcell bitterly, "is the fact that one cannot get anything merely on grounds of dire necessity."

"Yeah," said Hancock, carrying on with his writing.

"If one gets it at all," continued Purcell, warming to his subject, "it is for a reason that has nothing whatever to do with need or urgency. One gets it because and only because one has carefully filled out the correct forms in the correct way, got them signed and countersigned by the proper fatheads and submitted them through the proper channels to the proper people on Terra."

"Yeah," said Hancock, the tip of his tongue moving in sympathy with his pen.

"Yeah, yeah, yeah," echoed Purcell in somewhat higher tones; "Can't you say anything but yeah?"

Hancock sighed, ceased writing, mopped his forehead with a sweaty handkerchief. "Look, let's do what we're paid for, shall we? Griping gets us nowhere."

"Well, what are we paid for?"

"Personally, I think that pilots grounded by injuries should be found employment elsewhere. They never settle down to routine work."

"That doesn't answer my question."

"We're here upon Alipan, in the newly settled system of B417," informed Hancock ponderously, "to coordinate the inflow of essential supplies, making the best use of cargo space available. We are also here to deal with internal demands for supplies and assign priorities to them."

"Priorities my foot," said Purcell. He snatched up a form and flourished it in midair. "What sort of priority should be given to twenty-four cases of gin?"

"If you bothered to look, you'd see," Hancock gave back. "Class B import. I stamped it myself and you initialed it."

"I must have been momentarily blind. Who says gin gets priority over high-pressure oxygen flasks, for instance?"

"Letheren." Hancock frowned, fiddled with his pen. "Mind you, I don't agree with it myself. I think it's an iniquity. But Letheren is a senior official. As a pilot you may have cocked many a snoot at senior officials and got away with it. But you're not a pilot now. You're just another desk-squatter. As such you'd better learn that it isn't wise to thwart senior officials. They get moved around and up as more senior ones die of fatty degeneration. In five, ten or fifteen years' time Letheren may be my boss. By then I'll be treading on his heels. I won't want him to turn around and kick me in the teeth."

"You really think that after all that time he'd hold it against you because you refused to bring in his gin?" asked Purcell incredulously.

"No, I don't. I'm bringing it in. He'll have no reason to gripe."

"What a system!" said Purcell. He glowered through the window at the B417 sun. Its greenish hue made him feel slightly sick. "I can see now what I suspected years ago; space is slowly but surely being conquered by a few crazy coots not because of Terra but in spite of Terra. It's being done by a small bunch of hotheads who like to zoom around in rocketships. They're getting results in the face of every handicap we can place upon them."

"Having been a pilot, you're prejudiced in their favor," said Hancock defensively. "After all, somebody has to do the paperwork."

"I'd agree if the paperwork was necessary and made sense."

"If there wasn't any paperwork, we'd both be out of a job."

"You've got something there. So on this planet there are two thousands of us sitting on our fundaments busily making work for each other. In due time there'll be five thousand, then ten thousand."

"I'm looking forward to it," commented Hancock, brightening. "It'll mean promotion. And the more subordinates we have the higher our own status."

"That may be so. I won't take it with an easy conscience but I'll take it just the same. Frail human flesh, that's me." Purcell scowled at his desk, went on, "Guess I'm not yet old enough and cynical enough to accept the general waste of time and effort. There are moments when I could go off with a very large bang. This is one of them."

Hancock, who had picked up his pen, put it down again and asked resignedly, "Exactly what irks your reformist spirit right now?"

"There's a fellow here, a bugologist—"

"An entomologist," Hancock corrected.

"You will kindly allow me to choose my own words," Purcell suggested. "This bugologist wants a cobalt-60 irradiation outfit. It weighs three-eighty pounds."

"What for?"

"To clear the Great Forest area of a disease-carrying fly."

"How's he going to do that?"

"According to section D7 of his application form under the heading of REASONS, he says that treated male flies will effectively sterilize all female flies with whom they mate. Also that if he traps, irradiates and frees enough males he can wipe out the species. Also that several centuries ago Terra got rid of screwworm, tsetse and other flies by precisely the same method. He claims that he can make the whole of the Great Forest area inhabitable, exploitable and save an unknown number of lives. Therefore he asks for top priority."

"That seems reasonable," Hancock conceded. "You would give his dingus top priority, eh?"

"Certainly. A Class A import."

"That is real nice to know," said Purcell. "I am heartened to find sweet reasonableness sitting behind a desk and wearing oilskin pants." He slung the form across to the other. "Some bead-brained four-eyes has stamped it Class L. So this bugologist won't get his fly-killer for at least another seven years."

"It wasn't me," protested Hancock, staring at it. "I remember this one now. I got it about four months ago and passed it to Rohm for his approval."

"Why?"

"Because he's in charge of forestry."

"Holy cow!" said Purcell. "What have flies got to do with forestry?"

"The Great Forest area is the responsibility of Rohm's department. Anything pertaining to it must be passed to him."

"And he's stamped it Class L. He must be off his head."

"We cannot assume inefficiency in another department," Hancock pointed out. "There may be a thousand and one things Rohm needs more urgently. Medical supplies for instance."

"Yes, to cure people of the staggers after being bitten by flies," Purcell riposted. "If space-scouts operated the way we work, they'd still be preparing photostats of their birth and marriage certificates in readiness for an attempt on the Moon." He took the form back, eyed it with distaste. "Letheren's gin aggravates me. I have always hated the stuff. It tastes the same way a dead dog smells. If he can wangle a dollop of booze, why can't we wangle a cobalt-60 irradiator?"

"You can't buck the system," declared Hancock. "Not until you're one of the top brass."

"I'm bucking it as from now," Purcell announced. He reached for a fresh form, started filling it in. "I'm making a top priority demand for a fly-killer for Nemo."

"Nemo?" Hancock looked stupefied. "What's that?"

Purcell waved a careless hand toward the window. "The newly discovered planet out there."

Shoving back his chair, Hancock waddled to the window and gazed through it a long time. He couldn't see anything. After a while he came back, puffed, mopped his forehead again, reached for the intercom phone.

Purcell snapped, "Put that down!"

Letting go as if it were red-hot, Hancock complained, "If they've started operations on a new planet, Collister's department should have notified us in the proper manner. I object to this sloppy method of passing news along by word of mouth during lunch-hour gossip. Essential information should be transmitted in writing and distributed to all the individuals concerned."

"Collister's crowd know nothing about Nemo."

"Don't they? Why not?"

"I just invented it," said Purcell evenly.

"You *invented* it?"

"That's what I said." Completing the form, Purcell smacked it with a huge red stamp bearing the letters TP, then with a smaller one reading *Consign via Alipan B417.* While Hancock goggled at him he signed it, shoved it into the pneumatic tube. Within four minutes the radio-facsimile would be flashed Earthward.

Hancock said, aghast, "You must be mad."

"Crazy like a fox," admitted Purcell, undisturbed.

"They won't accept a requisition for an unregistered planet without official advice of its discovery and notification of its coordinates."

"The demand is an advice and I included the coordinates."

"They'll check on this," warned Hancock.

"With whom? The department for Nemo?"

"There isn't one," said Hancock.

"Correct. They'll have to check with Yehudi."

"They'll find out sooner or later that, they've been taken. There will be trouble. I want you to know, Purcell, that I hereby disclaim all responsibility for this. Officially I know nothing whatever about it. It is solely and wholly your own pigeon."

"Don't worry. I'm willing to accept the full credit for a praiseworthy display of initiative. Anyway, by that time the bugologist will have got his equipment and all the flies will be dead."

Hancock simmered down for five minutes then took on a look of horror as a new thought struck him. "If they load three-eighty pounds of scientific hardware, it's highly likely that they won't load the gin."

"That's what I like about it."

"Letheren will run amok."

"Let him," said Purcell. "He thinks he's heap big. To me he's just a big heap."

"Purcell, I will accept no responsibility for this."

"So you said before." Then he added with some menace, "Always bear one thing in mind, Hancock—I don't look as daft as I am!"

At Terra the indent landed on Bonhoeffer's desk, he being in charge of the Incoming Mail (Pre-sorting) Department. Bonhoeffer was a real woman's man, big, handsome, muscular, stupid. He owed his eminence solely to the fact that while in ten years the incoming mail had increased by twelve per cent the number of his subordinates had gone up one hundred forty per cent. This was more or less in accordance with the rules laid down by Professor C. Northcote Parkinson.*

Bonhoeffer picked up the form with much reluctance. It was the only item on his desk. The slaves dealt with everything as a matter of daily routine and nothing was brought to his personal attention unless there was something awkward about it. This suited him topnotch; it gave him plenty of time not to think.

So he knew in advance that this particular form contained the subject of an administrative quibble and that he must demonstrate his intelligence by finding it alone and unaided. Slowly and carefully he read it from top to bottom four

* Parkinson's Law, *circa* 1958.

times. As far as he could see there was nothing wrong with it. This irritated him. It meant that he must summon the individual who had passed the invisible buck and do him the honor of asking his opinion.

He examined the form's top left corner to see who would be thus honored. The initials scrawled thereon were F. Y. That meant the buck-passer was Feodor Yok. He might have expected it. Yok was a clever bum, an office showoff. He looked like Rasputin with a crewcut. And he wore the knowing smirk of a successful ambulance chaser. Bonhoeffer would rather drop dead than ask Yok the time of day.

That made things difficult. He studied the requisition another four times and still it looked plenty good enough to pass any determined fault-finder, even Yok. Then it occurred to him that there was an escape from this predicament. He, too, could transfer the grief, preferably to an eager beaver. It was as easy as that.

Switching his desk-box, he ordered, "Send in Quayle."

Quayle arrived with his usual promptitude. He was built along the lines of a starving jackrabbit and tried to compensate for it with a sort of military obsequiousness. He wore a dedicated look and was the sort of creep who would salute an officer over the telephone.

"Ah, Quayle," began Bonhoeffer with lordly condescension. "I have been watching your progress with some interest."

"Really, sir?" said Quayle, toothy with delight.

"Yes, indeed. I keep a careful eye on everyone, though I doubt whether they realize it. The true test of managerial competence is the ability to depute responsibility. To do that one must know and understand the men under one. Naturally some are more competent than others. You gather my meaning, Quayle?"

"Yes, sir," agreed Quayle, straining to expand his halo.

"Yok has seen fit to bring this requisition form to my attention." Bonhoeffer handed it over. "I was about to transfer it for necessary action when it occurred to me that it would be useful to know whether the question it raises is as obvious to you as it was to Yok and myself, also whether you can be as quick to determine what should be done about it."

Quayle's halo faded from sight while his face took on the look of a cornered rat. In complete silence he studied the form from end to end, reading it several times.

Finally he ventured in uncertain tones, "I can find nothing wrong with it, sir, except that it is a demand for Nemo. I don't recall seeing that planet upon the supply list."

"Very good, Quayle, very good," praised Bonhoeffer. "And what do you think should be done about it?"

"Well, sir," continued Quayle, vastly encouraged but still weak at the knees, "since the requisition emanates from Alipan, which is on the list, I'd say that it is valid so far as our department is concerned. Therefore I would pass it to the scientific division for confirmation of the reasons given and the correctness of the specification."

"Excellent, Quayle. I may as well say that you have come up to my expectations."

"Thank you, sir."

"I am a great believer in giving encouragement where it is deserved." Bonhoeffer bestowed a lopsided smile upon the other. "Since you have the form in your hands you may as well deal with it. Yok brought it in but I prefer that you handle it in person."

"Thank you, sir," repeated Quayle, the halo bursting forth in dazzling glory. He went out.

Bonhoeffer lay back and gazed with satisfaction at the empty desk.

In due course—meaning about three weeks—the scientific division swore and deposed that there really was such an article as a cobalt-60 irradiator and that it could in fact cause flies to indulge in futile woo. Quayle therefore attached this slightly obscene certificate to the requisition and passed it to the purchasing department for immediate attention.

He felt fully justified in doing this despite that the mysterious Nemo was still absent from the official supply list. After all, he had been authorized by Bonhoeffer to take the necessary action and the scientific division had duly certified that there was something with which to act. He was covered both ways, coming and going. In effect, Quayle was fireproof, a much-to-be desired state of existence.

The form and attached certificate now got dumped on Stanisland, an irascible character generally viewed as the offspring of a canine mother. Stanisland read them to the accompaniment of a series of rising grunts, found himself in the usual quandary. The purchasing department was supposed to know the prime sources of everything from peanuts to synthetic hormones. To that end it had a reference library so large that a fully equipped expedition was needed to get anywhere beyond the letter F. The library was used almost solely to demonstrate frenzied overwork whenever a high-ranking senior happened around, the safest place being atop the ladder.

It was easier to ask the right questions in the right places than to go on safari through a mile of books. Moreover Stanisland could admit ignorance of nothing in a room full of comparative halfwits. So he adopted his favorite tactic. Scowling around to make sure nobody was watching, he stuffed the papers into a pocket, got up, hoarsely muttered something about the men's room and lumbered out.

Then he trudged along three corridors, reached a bank of private phone booths, entered one, dialed the scientific division and asked for Williams. He uttered this name with poor grace because in his opinion Williams had been designed by Nature specifically to occupy a padded cell.

When the other came on, he said, "Stanisland, purchasing department, here."

"How's the bile flowing?" greeted Williams, conscious that neither was senior to the other.

Ignoring that, Stanisland went on, "You have issued certificate D2794018 against a cobalt-60 irradiator on demand by Alipan."

"I don't take your word for it," said Williams. "Give me that number again and wait while I trace the copy."

Stanisland gave it and waited. He stood there about ten minutes knowing full well that Williams was taking one minute to find the copy and allowing him the other nine in which to grow a beard. But he was impotent to do anything about it. Finally Williams came back.

"My, are you still there?" he asked in mock surprise. "Things must be pretty quiet in your department."

"If we were as bone idle as other departments, we'd have no need to consult them," shouted Stanisland. "We'd have all the time in the world to dig up information for ourselves."

"Aha!" said Williams, nastily triumphant. "You don't know where to get an irradiator, eh?"

"It isn't a question of not knowing," Stanisland retorted. "It's a question of saving time finding out. If I search under C for cobalt, it won't be there. It won't be under I for irradiator either. Nor under S for sixty. In about a week's time I'll discover that it's under H because the correct technical name for it is a hyperdiddlic honey or something like that. Things would be a lot easier if you eggheads would make up your minds to call a spade a plain, ordinary spade and stick to it for keeps."

"Shame," said Williams.

"Furthermore," continued Stanisland with satisfying malice, "every alleged up-to-date supplement to the library comes to us seven years old. Why? Because your crowd keep 'em on file and won't part until they begin to stink."

"We need them to stay up-to-date ourselves," Williams pointed out. "The scientific division cannot afford to be behind the times."

"There you are then," said. Stanisland, winning his point. "I don't want to know who was making rudimentary irradiators way back when television was two-dimensional. I want to know who is making them *now.* And I don't want to put in to Abelson an official complaint about delayed data and willful obstruction."

"Are you threatening me, you baggy-eyed tub?" asked Williams.

Stanisland started shouting again. "I don't want to touch Abelson with a ten-foot pole. You know what he's like."

"Yeah, I know, I know." Williams let go a resigned sigh. "Hold on a piece." This time he was gone twelve minutes before he returned and recited a short list of names and addresses.

Reaching his desk, Stanisland rewrote the list more clearly, attached it to the form and certificate, passed the bunch to a junior.

In tones hearable all over the office, he said, "It's a lucky thing that I had the handling of this demand. It so happens that I know all the people who make such a rare piece of apparatus. Now you get their estimates as quickly as possible and submit them to me."

Then he glared happily around at all and sundry, enjoying their dead faces and knowing that they were hating him deep in their hearts. By hokey, he'd shown them who most deserved to be jacked up a grade.

Forman Atomics quoted the lowest price and quickest delivery. A month later they got a request for copy of their authorization as an approved supplier. They mailed it pronto. Three days afterward they were required to send a sworn affidavit that their employees included not less than ten per cent of disabled spacemen. They sent it. Two intelligence agents visited their head office and satisfied themselves that the flag flying from the masthead was a genuine Terran one in substance and in fact.

Meanwhile a subordinate from the Finance (Investigation) Department made search through the files of the Companies (Registered Statistics) Department, aided by two juniors belonging to that haven of rest. Between them they made sure that not one dollar of Forman stock was held or controlled by the representative of any foreign power, either in person or by nominee. Admittedly, there was no such thing in existence as a foreign power but that was beside the point.

By now the original requisition had attached to it the following:

1. The scientific division's certificate.

2. An interdepartmental slip signed by Quayle informing Stanisland that the requisition was passed to him for attention.

3. A similar slip signed by Bonhoeffer saying that he had ordered Quayle to do the passing.

4-11. Eight quotations for an irradiator, Forman's having been stamped: "Accepted subject to process."

12. A copy of Forman's supply authorization.

13. Forman's affidavit.

14. An intelligence report to the effect that whatever was wrong with Forman's could not be proved.

15. A finance department report saying the same thing in longer words.

Item twelve represented an old and completely hopeless attempt to buck the system. In the long, long ago somebody had made the mistake of hiring a fully paid-up member of Columbia University's Institute of Synergistic Statics. Being under the delusion that a line is the shortest distance between two points, the newcomer had invented a blanket system of governmental authorizations which he fondly imagined would do away with items thirteen, fourteen and fifteen.

This dastardly attempt to abolish three departments at one fell blow had gained its just reward; a new department had been set up to deal with item twelve while the others had been retained. For creating this extra work the author of it had been hastily promoted to somewhere in the region of Bootes.

Stanisland added the sixteenth item in the shape of his own interdepartmental slip informing Taylor, the head of the purchasing department, that to the best of his knowledge and belief there were no remaining questions to be raised and that it was now for him to place the order. Taylor, who had not been born yesterday, showed what he thought of this indecent haste. Throwing away the overstrained paper-clip, he added his own slip to the wad, secured it with a wide-jawed bulldog fastener and fired it back at Stanisland.

The slip said, "You are or should be well aware that a consignment of this description may not be within the capacity of the Testing (Instruments) Department. If it is not, we shall require a certificate of efficiency from the Bureau of Standards. Take the necessary action forthwith."

This resulted in Stanisland taking a fast walk around the corridors while the surplus steam blew out of his ears. He had never liked Taylor, who obviously enjoyed his seniority and would turn anyone base over apex for the sadistic pleasure of it. Besides, in his spare time the fellow lived the full life breeding piebald mice. With his beady eyes and twitching whiskers he bore close resemblance to his beloved vermin.

When pressure had dropped to the bearable, Stanisland returned to his desk, called a junior and gave him the wad plus a slip reading, "Can you test this thing?"

Within ten days all the papers came back accompanied by the reply. "For emission only. Not for functional purpose. To test for the latter we would require an adequate supply of the proposed subjects, namely and to wit, Nemo flies. Refer to Imports (Pest Control) Department."

So he phoned through to Chase who was sunbathing by a window and brought him back to his desk and Chase said with unnecessary surliness, "Importation forbidden."

"Can you quote authority for that?" asked Stanisland.

"Certainly," snapped Chase. "See the Bacteriological Defense Act, volume three titled Alien Insects, subsection fourteen under heading of Known Or Suspected Disease Carriers, I quote—"

"You needn't bother," said Stanisland hastily. "I've got to have it in writing anyway."

"All right. Give me those reference numbers again and I'll send you a documentary ban."

"I don't see how the testing department is going to cope in these circumstances."

"That's their worry, not yours," advised Chase. "Be your age!"

In due time—meaning another three weeks—Chase's prohibition arrived properly stamped, signed and countersigned. It got added to the growing bunch. Stanisland was now faced with the very serious question of whether a mere test for emission was adequate and in accordance with the rules. To resolve it one way or the other meant reaching A Decision. And that could be done only by an official in A Position Of Responsibility.

Yeah, Taylor.

At the prospect of consulting Taylor a great sorrow came upon him. It would imply that he, Stanisland, couldn't summon up the nerve. But the alternative was far worse, namely, to exceed his authority. He blanched at the thought of it.

For two days Stanisland let the papers lie around while he tried to think up some other way out. There was no other way. If he dumped the wad on Taylor's desk during his absence and then went sick, Taylor would hold the lot pending his return. If he transferred the file to the next department, it would be bounced back with malicious glee plus a note pointing to the lack of an order. Obviously, he had to see Taylor. He had nothing to fear but fear itself.

Finally he steeled himself, marched into Taylor's office, gave him the documents and pointed to the last two items.

"You will see, sir, that an adequate test cannot be performed because of an import restriction."

"Yes, my dear Stanisland," said Taylor, courteous in a thoroughly aggravating manner. "I suspected some such difficulty myself."

Stanisland said nothing.

"I am somewhat surprised that you failed to anticipate it," added Taylor pointedly.

"With all respect, sir, I have a lot of work to do and one cannot foresee everything."

"I am more impressed by efficiency than by apologies," commented Taylor in sugar-sweet tones. "And so far as I am concerned the test of efficiency is the ability to handle potentially controversial matters in such a manner that this department, when called upon to do so, can produce documentary justification for everything it has done. In other words, so long as there are no routine blunders within our own department it is not our concern what mistakes may be made in other departments. Do you understand me, my dear Stanisland?"

"Yes, sir," said Stanisland with bogus humility.

"Good!" Taylor lay back, hooked thumbs in armholes, eyed him, as if he were a piebald mouse. "Now, have you brought the order in readiness for my signature?"

Stanisland went purple, swallowed hard. "No, sir."

"Why haven't you?"

"It appeared to me, sir, that it would first be necessary to obtain your ruling on whether or not a test for emission is sufficient."

"My ruling?" Taylor raised his eyebrows in mock surprise. "Have you taken leave of your senses? I do not make decisions for other departments, surely you know that?"

"Yes, sir, but—"

"Anyone with the moral fortitude to look a fact in the face," interrupted Taylor, tapping the papers with a long, thin forefinger, "can see that here we have a written statement from the appropriate department to the effect that this piece of apparatus can be tested. That is all we require. The question of how it is tested or for what it is tested does not concern us in the least. We have enough responsibilities of our own without accepting those properly belonging to other departments."

"Yes, sir," agreed Stanisland, not inclined to argue the matter.

"Already there has been far too much delay in dealing with this requisition," Taylor went on. "The demand is now almost a year old. Disgraceful!"

"I assure you, sir, that it is not my—"

"Cut out the excuses and let me see some action."

"You wish me to write out the order at once, sir?"

"No, you need not bother. Go get your order book, give it to my secretary and tell her that I wish to deal with it personally."

"Very well, sir." Stanisland departed sweating a mixture of ire and relief.

Finding the order book, he took it to the secretary. She was a frozen-faced female who never lost an opportunity to admire his ignorance. She was named Hazel, after a nut.

On the face of it something had now been accomplished. A gadget had been demanded, the demand had been checked, counterchecked and approved, estimates had been obtained and the order placed. It remained for Forman Atomics to supply the irradiator, the Testing Department to test it, the Shipping (Outward) Department to authorize dispatch to Alipan and the Loading (Space Allocation) Department to put it aboard the right ship.

True, a dozen more departments had yet to handle the growing mass of papers which by now had attained the dignity of a box-file. Between them they'd fiddle around for another two years before the wad was reluctantly consigned to the morgue of the Records (Filing) Department. But all these were strictly post-shipment departments; the days, weeks and months they spent playing with documents did not matter once the consignment was on its way. Any irate hustle-up note from the top brass in Alipan could now be answered, curtly and effective, with the bald statement that Action Had Been Taken.

Stanisland therefore composed his soul in bilious peace, satisfied that he had hurdled an awkward obstacle to the accompaniment of no more than a few raspberries from Taylor. He gained some compensation for the latter by reminding everyone in the office that he was peculiarly qualified to advise on rare apparatus without first getting himself lost in the library. Having instilled that fact in their minds he carried on with routine work and began gradually to forget the subject. But he was not left in peace for long.

In more than due time—meaning at least twice three weeks—his telephone shrilled and a voice said, "This is Keith of Inspection Department."

"Yes?" responded Stanisland warily. He had never heard of Keith, much less met him.

"There's a difficulty here," continued Keith, smacking his lips. "I have been on to Loading about it and they've referred me to Shipping who've referred me to Testing who've referred me to Purchasing. I see by the papers that the order was placed by Taylor but that you did the processing."

"What's wrong?" asked Stanisland, immediately recognizing the swift passing of an unwanted buck.

"The manifest of the *Starfire* includes a thing called a cobalt-60 irradiator for delivery to Alipan. It has been supplied by Forman Atomics against your department's order number BZ12-l0127."

"What of it?"

"Testing Department has issued a guarantee that emission is satisfactory," Keith continued. "You know what that means."

Stanisland hadn't the remotest notion of what it meant but was not prepared to say so. He evaded the point by inquiring, "Well, what has it to do with this department?"

"It has got plenty to do with *some* department," Keith retorted. "They can't *all* disclaim responsibility."

Still feeling around in the dark, Stanisland said carefully, "I may have to take this to Taylor or even to Abelson. They will insist on me repeating your complaint in exact terms. Is there any reason why you can't send it round in writing?"

"Yes," said Keith. "There isn't time. The ship takes off this evening."

"All right. Exactly what do you want me to tell Taylor?"

Keith fell into the trap and informed, "This cobalt-60 contraption cannot have satisfactory emission without being radioactive. Therefore it comes under the heading of Noxious Cargo. It cannot be shipped by the *Starfire* unless we are supplied with a certificate to the effect that it is properly screened and will not contaminate adjacent cargo."

"Oh!" said Stanisland, feeling yet again that the only thing between him and the top of the ladder was the ladder.

"Such a certificate should have been supplied in the first place," added Keith, drowning his last spark of decency. "Somebody slipped up. I'm holding a wad three inches thick and everything's here but that."

Annoyed by this, Stanisland bawled, "I fail to see why the production of a non-contaminatory certificate should be considered the responsibility of this department."

"Testing Department say they offered to check for emission only and that you accepted this," Keith gave back. "The documents show that their statement is correct. I have them here before my very eyes."

"That is sheer evasion," maintained Stanisland. "It is your job to make them take back the apparatus and check it for screening."

"On the contrary," shot back Keith, "it is not, never has been and never will be my job to make good the shortcomings of other departments. The *Starfire* takes off at ten tonight. No certificate, no shipment. Sort it out for yourself." He cut off, effectively preventing further argument.

Stanisland brooded over the injustice of it before he went to see Taylor again, this time looking like hard luck on two feet. Taylor responded by meditating aloud about people who could not paint a floor without marooning themselves in one corner. Then he grabbed the phone and spent ten minutes swapping recriminations with Jurgensen of Testing Department. Jurgensen, a confirmed bachelor, flatly refused to hold the baby.

Giving the waiting Stanisland an evil stare, Taylor now tried to foist the problem onto the Scientific Division. All he got for his pains was a piece of Williams' mind, the piece with the hole in. Muttering to himself, he phoned Keith, who promptly gave him the merry ha-ha and repeated in sinister tones his remark about no certificate, no shipment.

Finally Taylor thrust the phone aside and said, "Well, my dear Stanisland, you have made a nice mess of this."

"Me?" said Stanisland, paralyzed by the perfidy of it.

"Yes, you."

This was too much. Stanisland burst out, "But you approved the order and tended to it yourself."

"I did so on the assumption that all routine aspects of the matter had been seen to with the efficiency that I expect from my subordinates. Evidently my faith was misplaced."

"That is hardly fair judgment, sir, because—"

"Shut up!" Taylor ostentatiously consulted his watch. "We have seven hours before the *Starfire* leaves. Neither the Testing Department nor the Scientific Division will issue the document Keith requires. We have no authority to provide one ourselves. But one must be got from somewhere. You realize that, don't you, Stanisland?"

"Yes, sir."

"Since you are directly responsible for this grave omission it is equally your responsibility to make it good. Now go away and exercise your imagination, if you have any. Come back to me when you have incubated a useful idea."

"I cannot forge a certificate, sir," Stanisland protested.

"It has not been suggested that you should," Taylor pointed out acidly. "The solution, if there is one, must be in accordance with regulations and not open to question by higher authority. It is for you to find it. And don't be too long about it."

Returning to his desk, Stanisland flopped into his chair and chased his brains around his skull. The only result was a boost to his desperation. He gnawed his fingers, thought furiously and always arrived at the same result: nobody, *but* nobody would produce anything in writing to cover up a blunder in another department.

After some time he went for a walk to the phone booths where he could talk in private, called the scientific division and asked for Williams.

"Williams," he said oilily, "I was there when Taylor baited you an hour ago. I didn't like his attitude."

"Neither did I," said Williams.

"You have been of great help to us on many occasions," praised Stanisland with an effort. "I'd like you to know that I genuinely appreciate it even if Taylor doesn't."

"It's most kind of you to say so," informed Williams, letting go a menacing chuckle. "But you still won't cajole from this department a document we are not authorized to give."

"I am not trying to do so," Stanisland assured. "I wouldn't dream of it."

"Taylor tried. He must think we're a bunch of suckers."

"I know," said Stanisland, gratefully seizing the opportunity thus presented. "To be frank, I wondered whether you'd be willing to help me give Taylor a smack in the eye."

"How?"

"By coming up with some suggestion about how I can get over this noxious cargo business."

"And why should that have the effect of twisting Taylor's arm?"

"He thinks he's got me where he wants me. I'd like to show him he hasn't. Some of these seniors need teaching a thing or two." He paused, added craftily, "Abelson for instance.

The effect of that name in the other's ears clinched the deal and Williams said without a moment's hesitation, "All right, I'll tell you something."

"What is it?" asked Stanisland eagerly.

"No reputable outfit such as Forman's would ship a radioactive apparatus inadequately screened. Probably seventy per cent of that irradiator's weight is attributable to screening. Ask Forman's and they'll tell you—in writing."

"Williams," said Stanisland delightedly, "I'll never forget this."

"You will," contradicted Williams. "But I won't."

Stanisland now phoned Forman's and explained the position in complete detail. Their response was prompt: they would prepare a written guarantee of safety and deliver it by special messenger to Keith within two hours. Stanisland sighed with heartfelt relief. Seemed there were times when the efficiency of private industry almost approached that of bureaucracy.

Over the next few days Stanisland waited with secret pleasure for a call from Taylor. It never came. Unknown to him, Taylor had phoned Keith to find out what had happened, if anything. Taylor then realized that an interview with Stanisland would permit that worthy a moment of petty triumph. It was unthinkable that a senior should permit a subordinate to gloat. He would summon Stanisland into his presence when and only when he had some pretext for throwing him to the crocodiles. So Stanisland went on waiting, first with growing disappointment, then with dull resignation, finally with forgetfulness.

The weeks rolled on while the wad of papers crawled through various offices and gained in mass at each desk. Then one day it reached the Documents (Final Checking) Department. It now weighed five pounds and was solid with words, figures, stamps, names and signatures.

From this mountain of evidence some assiduous toiler dug out the strange word Nemo. His nose started twitching. He made a few discreet inquiries and satisfied himself that (a) someone had blundered and (b) the cretin was not located within his own office. Then he steered the wad toward the Spatial Statistics Department.

Far away on Alipan a copy of the *Starfire*'s manifest landed on Hancock's desk. He scanned it carefully. Most of the stuff had been demanded three to four years ago. But he had a very good memory and the moment his eyes found an irradiator the alarm bells rang in his brain. He was swift to give the list to Purcell.

"You'd better deal with this."

"Me? Why? You got writer's cramp or something?"

"The ship is bringing an expensive present for a planet that doesn't exist. I don't handle consignments for imaginary worlds."

"Windy, eh?" said Purcell.

"Sane," said Hancock.

Examining the manifest, Purcell grumbled, "It's taken them long enough. Nobody broke his neck to get it here. If scout-pilots moved at the same pace, Lewis and Clark would still be pounding their dogs along the Oregon Trail."

"I am," announced Hancock, "sick and tired of the subject of scout-pilots."

"And where would you have been without them?"

"On Terra."

"Doing what?"

"Earning an honest living," said Hancock.

"Yeah—filling forms," said Purcell.

Hancock let it slide and pretended to be busy.

"Now this is where our right to determine priorities reaches its peak of usefulness," Purcell went on, flourishing the manifest as if it were the flag of freedom. "We issue an overriding priority in favor of our bugologist, his need being greater than Nemo's. The fly-killer will then be transferred to him without argument because nobody questions a proper form, properly filled, properly stamped and properly signed. Thus we shall have served humanity faithfully and well."

"You can cut out every 'we' and 'our,' " ordered Hancock. "I am having nothing to do with it." He put on another brief imitation of overwork, added as an afterthought, "I told you before, you can't buck the system."

"I have bucked it."

"Not yet," said Hancock positively.

Taking no notice, Purcell made out the priority, stamped it, signed it, studied it right way up and upside down, signed it again.

"I've forged your signature. Do you mind?"

"Yes," yelled Hancock.

"I am receiving you loud and clear." Purcell examined the forgery with unashamed satisfaction. "Too bad. It's done now. What's done can't be undone."

"I'd like you to know, Purcell, that in the event of that document being challenged I shall not hesitate to declare my signature false."

"Quite a good idea," enthused Purcell. "I'll swear mine is false also."

"You wouldn't dare," said Hancock, appalled.

"It'll take 'em at least ten years to figure who's the liar and even then they couldn't bet on it," continued Purcell with indecent gusto. "In the meantime I'll suggest that maybe every document of Alipan's and half of Terra's has phony signatures attributable to subordinates bypassing their seniors in order to avoid criticisms and conceal mistakes. The resulting chaos ought to create work for ten thousand checkers."

"You're off your head," declared Hancock.

"Well, you can keep me company," Purcell suggested. He exhibited the manifest at distance too far for the other to read. "I've got news for you."

"What is it?"

"No gin."

Hancock sat breathing heavily for quite a time, then said, "You're to blame for that."

"Nuts! I've no say in what Terra loads on or leaves off."

"But—"

"If you've told me once," Purcell went on remorselessly, "you've told me a hundred times that in no circumstances whatever will any department on Alipan accept responsibility for decisions made on Terra. Correct?"

"Correct," agreed Hancock as though surrendering a back tooth.

"All right. You ordered the gin and can prove it. You gave it high priority and can prove it. You're armor-plated front and back. All you need to do is go see Letheren and say, 'Sorry, no gin.' When he zooms and rotates you say, 'Terra!' and spit. It's so easy a talking poodle could do it."

"I can hardly wait to watch you get rid of Nemo the same way," said Hancock, making it sound sadistic.

"Nobody has said a word about Nemo. Nobody is the least bit curious about Nemo. Finally I, James Walter Armitage Purcell, could not care less about Nemo."

"You will," Hancock promised.

In due time—which on Alipan attained the magnitude of about three months—the intercom speaker squawked on the wall and a voice harshed, "Mr. Purcell of Requisitioning (Priorities) Department will present himself at Mr. Vogel's office at eleven hours."

Hancock glanced at his desk clock, smirked and said, "You've got exactly thirty-seven minutes."

"For what?"

"To prepare for death."

"Huh?"

"Vogel is a high-ranker with ninety-two subordinates. He controls four departments comprising the Terran Co-ordination Wing."

"What of it?"

"He makes a hobby of personally handling all gripes from Terra. Anyone summoned by Vogel is a gone goose unless he happens to be holding the actual documentary proof of his innocence in his hot little hands."

"Sounds quite a nice guy," Purcell commented, unperturbed.

"Vogel," informed Hancock, "is a former advertising man who got flatfooted toting his billboard around the block. But he's a natural for routine rigmarole. He's climbed high on the shoulders of a growing army of underlings and he's still climbing." He paused, added emphatically, "I don't like him."

"So it seems," said Purcell dryly.

"A lot of people don't like him. Letheren hates the sight of him."

"That so? I don't suppose he's choked with esteem for Letheren either, eh?"

"Vogel loves nothing but power—which in this racket means seniority."

"Hm-m-m!" Purcell thought a bit, went out, came back after twenty minutes, thought some more.

"Where've you been?" asked Hancock.

"Accounts Department."

"Getting your pay while the going is good?"

"No. I have merely satisfied myself that one hundred and five equals seventeen hundred."

"It wouldn't save you even if it made sense." Hancock continued to busy himself with nothing and kept one eye on the clock. When the moment arrived he said, "On your way. I hope you suffer."

"Thanks."

Opening his desk Purcell extracted an enormous roll of paper, tucked it under one arm. He tramped out, found his way to the rendezvous, entered the office. Vogel, dark-eyed, dark-haired and swarthy, studied him without expression.

"Sit down, Purcell," He bared long, sharp teeth and somehow managed to look like Red Riding Hood's grandmother. "Terra has brought to my attention a demand originating from a planet named Nemo."

"That, sir, is—"

Vogel waved an imperious hand. "Please be silent, Purcell, until I have finished. Your own remarks can come afterward." Again the teeth. "A lot of very valuable time has been spent checking on this. I like to have all the facts before interviewing the person concerned."

"Yes, sir," said Purcell, nursing his roll of paper and looking suitably impressed.

"I have found firstly that Terra's statement is quite correct; such a demand was in fact made and you processed it. Secondly, that the subject of the demand, an irradiator, was transferred by you to an address upon this planet. Thirdly, that no planet discovered before or since the date of this demand has been officially given the name of Nemo." He put hands together in an attitude of prayer. "One can well imagine the trouble and exasperation caused on Terra. I trust, Purcell, that you have a thoroughly satisfactory explanation to offer."

"I think I have, sir," assured Purcell glibly.

"I'll be glad to hear it."

"The whole bother is due to someone on Terra jumping to the erroneous and unjustifiable conclusion that Nemo is the name of a planet when in fact it is a code word used by my department to indicate a tentative priority as distinct from a definite one."

"A tentative priority?" echoed Vogel, raising sardonic eyebrows. "What nonsense is this? Don't you realize, Purcell, that all demands must be rated strictly in order of importance or urgency and that there is no room for indecision? How can anything have a *tentative* priority?"

"I find it rather difficult to tell you, sir," said Purcell, radiating self-righteousness.

"I insist upon an explanation," Vogel gave back.

Assuming just the right touch of pain and embarrassment, Purcell informed, "Since cargo space is severely limited the problem of granting priorities is a tough one. And when a senior official practically orders my department to assign to his demand a priority higher than it deserves it follows that, if we obey, something else of similar weight or bulk must accept lower priority than it deserves. But regulations do not permit me to reduce the status of a high-priority demand. Therefore I am compelled to give it a tentative priority, meaning that it will gain its proper loading-preference providing nobody chips in to stop it."

A gleam came into Vogel's eyes. "That is what happened in this case?"

"I'm afraid so, sir."

"In other words, you claim that you are suffering unwarranted interference with the work of your department?"

"That," said Purcell with becoming reluctance, "is putting it a little stronger than I'd care to do."

"Purcell, we must get to the bottom of this and now is not the time to mince words. Exactly what were you ordered to ship at high priority?"

"Gin, sir."

"Gin?" A mixture of horror and incredulity came into Vogel's face. But it swiftly faded to be replaced by a look of suppressed triumph. "*Who* ordered you to bring in gin?"

"I'd rather not say, sir."

"Was it Letheren?"

Purcell said nothing but assumed the expression of one who sorrows for Letheren's soul.

Gratified by this, Vogel purred. He rubbed his hands together, became positively amiable. "Well, Purcell, it appears to me that you have been guilty of no more than a small oversight. Should you find it necessary to employ code words as a matter of administrative convenience it is obvious that Terra should be notified through the proper channels. Without regular notification Terra would eventually find itself trying to cope with incomprehensible jargon. An impossible situation as doubtless you now appreciate, eh, Purcell?"

"Yes, sir," said Purcell, humble and grateful.

"But in the present circumstances it would not be wise to advise Terra of the true meaning of Nemo. To do so would be tantamount to admitting that our priority system is being messed up at anybody's whim. I hope you see my point, Purcell."

"I do, sir."

"Therefore I propose to inform Terra that the inclusion of this word was due to a departmental error born of overwork and lack of sufficient manpower." He exposed the teeth. "That will give them something to think about."

"I'm sure it will, sir."

"Purcell, I wish you to drop the use of all code words except with my knowledge and approval. Meanwhile I shall take the steps necessary to put a stop to any further interference with your department."

"Thank you, sir." Purcell stood up, fumbled with his roll of paper, looked hesitant.

"Is there something else?" asked Vogel.

"Yes, sir." Purcell registered doubt, reluctance, then let the words come out in a rush. "I thought this might be an opportune moment to bring to your attention a new form I have devised."

"A form?"

"Yes, sir." He unrolled it, put one in Vogel's hands. The other end reached almost to the wall. "This, sir, is a master-form to be filled up with the origin, purpose, details, progress and destination of every other form that has to be filled in. It is, so to speak, a form of forms."

"Really?" said Vogel, frowning.

"By means of this," continued Purcell greasily, "it will be possible to trace every form step by step, to identify omissions or contradictions and to name the individual responsible. Should a form get lost it will be equally possible to find at what point it disappeared and who lost it." He let that sink in, added, "From what I know of interdepartmental confusions, many of which are hidden from senior officials, I estimate that this form will save about twenty thousand man-hours per annum."

"Is that so?" said Vogel, little interested.

"There is one snag," Purcell went on. "In order to save all that work it will be necessary to employ more people. Since their work would be wholly coordinatory they would come under your jurisdiction, thus adding to your responsibilities."

"Ah!" said Vogel, perking up.

"In fact we'd have to create a new department to reduce the total of work done. However, I have studied the subject most carefully and I am confident that we could cope with a minimum of thirteen men."

"Thirteen?" echoed Vogel, counting on his fingers. He sat staring at the form while into his face crept a look of ill-concealed joy. "Purcell, I believe you have something here. Yes, I really do."

"Thank you, sir. I felt sure you would appreciate the potentialities. May I leave the form for your consideration?"

"By all means, Purcell." Vogel was now well-nigh jovial. Fondly he stroked the form, his fingers caressing it. "Yes, you must certainly leave it with me." He glanced up, beaming. "If anything is done about this, Purcell, I shall need someone to take charge of this new department. Someone who knows his job and in whom I have the fullest confidence. I cannot imagine a better candidate than yourself."

"It is kind of you to say so, sir," said Purcell with grave dignity.

He took his departure but as he left he turned in the doorway and for a moment their eyes met. A glance of mutual understanding sparked between them.

Back in his own office Purcell plonked himself in a chair and recited, "Whenever two soothsayers meet in the street they invariably smile at each other."

"What are you talking about?" demanded Hancock.

"I was quoting an ancient saying." He held up two fingers, tight together. "Vogel and I are just like that."

"You don't fool me," Hancock scoffed. "Your ears are still red."

"Vogel loves me and I love Vogel. I hit him right in his weak spot."

"He hasn't any weak spots, see?"

"All I did," said Purcell, "was point out to him that if the number of his subordinates should be increased from ninety-two to one hundred and five he'd be automatically jacked up from a Class 9 to a Class 8 official. That would gain him another seventeen hundred smackers per year plus extra privileges and, of course, a higher pension."

"Nobody has to tell Vogel that—he knows it better than anyone."

"All right. Let's say I merely reminded. In return he was good enough to remind me that a disabled hero bossing twelve underlings is far better off than one sharing an office with a surly bum."

"I neither ask nor expect the true story of your humiliation," growled Hancock. "So you don't have to cover up with a lot of crazy double-talk."

"Some day," offered Purcell, grinning, "it may dawn upon you that it is possible to buck a system, *any* system. All you need do is turn the handle the way it goes—only more so!"

"Shut up," said Hancock, "and talk when you can talk sense."

Tieline

Astounding, July 1955

He watched the needle of the output meter jump, wiggle and fall back. Thirty seconds later the same again, a rise, quiver and fall. Thirty seconds later the same again. It had been going on for weeks, months, years.

Outside the fused-stone building a lattice mast rose high into the air and pointed a huge cup at the stars. And from the cup, at half-minute intervals, there squirted a soundless, long-range voice.

"Bunda One. *Eep-eep-bop!* Bunda One. *Eep-eep-bop!*"

From eight synchronized repeater-stations on lonely islands around the planet's belly the same call went forth, radiating like the spokes of a wheel as slowly the world turned on its axis.

Out there, in the inter-nebular chasm where dark bodies lurked unaccompanied by revealing suns, an occasional ship would hear the voice, change course in its own horizontal or vertical plane and thunder steadily onward.

How often that happened, he'd no way of telling. He remained in awful solitude, pointing the way to those who never said, "Thanks!" Too small and fleeting ever to be seen, their flame-trails flickered briefly in the gap between star-whorls and then were gone. The ships that pass in the night.

Bunda One. A lighthouse of space. A world with Earthlike atmosphere but little land. A sphere of vast oceans dotted with craggy islands on which lived nothing that was company and comfort for anything in human form.

This very island was the largest solid foothold on a world of watery wastes. Twenty-two miles long by seven wide—a veritable continent in Bunda terms. No trees, no animals, no birds, no flowers. There were low, twisted shrubs, lichens and tiny fungi. There were fifty species of amphibious insects that maintained balance by warring upon each other. And nothing else.

Over all the planet lay a dreadful silence. That was the horror of it: the silence. The winds were gentle, consistent, never descending to a sigh or raising to a howl. The seas swelled lazily, crawled ten sluggish inches up the rocks, slid ten inches down without a thump, a splash, a rattle of flung spray. The insects were noiseless, without a chirp or squeak among the lot. The pale lichens and distorted shrubs stood unmoving, like bizarre entities paralyzed by eternal quiet.

Behind the building lay a garden. When the beacon constructors first set up the place they had desiccated half an acre of hard rock, turning it into cultivatable dirt, planting Earthborn roots and seeds therein. No flowers had come up but some vegetables flourished. Beets, spinach and broccoli —he had fifty rows of those. And he had onions the size of footballs.

At no time did he eat an onion. He detested the things. But he kept them along with the rest, tending them carefully for the sake of varying routine and for the pleasure of hearing the gritty thrust of a spade, the steady chink of a hoe.

The needle jumped, wiggled, fell back. If watched too often and too long it became hypnotic. There were times when he developed an insane desire to change its characteristic wiggle into something idiotic but refreshingly new, to tear out the great transmitter's key-code and substitute an imbecility that the cup would squirt at astounded stars.

"Wossop na bullwacka. *Bammer-bam-whop!* Wossop na bullwacka. *Bammer-bam-whop!*"

It had happened before and someday would happen again. Wasn't so long since a light cruiser had bolted to a Wolf-group station after its beacon had lapsed into incoherencies. One man's madness had endangered a liner bearing two thousand. Put out the light and there is stumbling in the dark.

To join the Beacon Service was to accept ten years of solitary confinement for very high pay and the satisfaction of fulfilling a public need. The prospect looked enticing when young, adaptable and still standing four-square upon good old Earth. The reality was grim, forbidding, and had proved too much for some. Man was not meant to live alone.

So you're from the Western Isles, eh? Just the sort of man we want! We've a station called Bunda One that's made to measure for you. You'll be able to tolerate it far better than most. City fellows aren't much use in a place like that; no matter how excellent their technical qualifications, sooner or later they tend to crack up from sheer lack of the bright lights. Yes, a man from the Western Isles is cut to size for Bunda One. You don't miss what you've never had. Bunda One's got all you're used to: rocky islands and great seas, just like home . . .

Just like home.

Home.

Down there on the waveless beach were pebbles and pretty shells and creeping things like tiny crabs. In the ocean swayed acres of seaweed through which darted vast shoals of fish, big and small, exactly like the fish of Earth. He knew, for he had cast lines from the shore, caught them, unhooked them and thrown them back to the freedom that he lacked.

But no worn stone jetty projected into the green waters, no rusty little steamers rolled across the bay, nobody on the beach busied themselves with tar-pots or mended nets. No barrels rolled and clattered from the cooperage, no shining blocks slithered out of the ice plant, no silver horde flopped and jerked under the hatches of full holds. And at eventide no voices in the chapel prayed for those in peril on the sea.

Back there on Earth the scientific big-brains were top notch when it came to dealing with purely technical problems. The Bunda One master-station was semi-automatic, its eight slave-beacons fully automatic, and they drew power from atomic generators that could run untended for a century or more. The strength of the warning voice was enough to boost it across a mighty chasm between clusters of uncountable suns. All that was needed to create one hundred percent efficiency was a watching eye backed by knowledge, ability and initiative, an emergency mechanism that would make the beacon a self-servicing unit. In other words, one man.

That's where their ingenuity fell short. One man. A man is not a gadget. He cannot be assessed as a gadget, be treated like one, be made to function like one.

Somewhat belatedly they'd recognized the fact after the third lunatic had been removed from his post. Three mental breakdowns in an organization numbering four hundred isolated stations is not a large proportion. Less than one percent. But it was three too many. And the number might grow larger as time caught up with those slower to break. They'd cogitated the problem. Ah, they'd exclaimed, preconditioning is the answer.

So the next candidates had been put through a scientifically designed mill, a formidable, long-term course calculated to break the breakable and leave a tough residue suitable for service. It hadn't worked out. The need for men was too great, the number of candidates too few, and they'd broken too many.

After that they'd tried half a dozen other theories with no better luck. Precept and practice don't always accord. The big-brains could have done with a taste of reality themselves.

Their latest fad was the tieline theory. Man, they asserted, is born of Earth and needs a tieline to Earth. Give him that and he's fastened to sanity. He can hang on through ten years of solitary confinement.

What's a tieline?

Cherchez la femme, suggested one, looking worldly-wise over his spectacles. They'd discussed it, dismissed it on a dozen counts. Imaginable complications ranged all the way from murder to babies. Besides, it would mean the periodic haul of supplies doubled in mass for the sake of a nontechnical entity.

A dog, then? All right for those few worlds on which a dog can fend for itself. But what about other worlds, such as Bunda? Space-loads are estimated in ounces, not tons, and the time is not yet for shipping dog-food around the cosmos for the benefit of single, widely-scattered mutts.

The first attempted tieline was makeshift and wholly mechanical and did have the virtue of countering the silence that was the curse of Bunda. The annual supply-ship dropped its load of food along with a recorder and a dozen tapes.

For the next month he had noise, not only words and music, but also characteristic Earth-sounds: the roar of holiday traffic along a turnpike, the rumble of trains, the chimes of Sunday morning bells, the high-pitched chatter of children pouring out of school. The aural evidence of life far, far away. At the first hearing he was delighted. At the twentieth he was bored. There was no thirtieth time.

The output needle jumped, wiggled, fell back. The recorder stood abandoned in a corner. Out there in the star-mists were his lonely brothers. He could not talk even to them, or listen to them. They were out of radio-reach and their worlds turned like his. He sat and watched the needle and felt Bunda's awful hush.

Eight months ago, Earth-time, the supply-ship had brought evidence that they were still fooling with the tieline theory. Along with the annual stores it had dropped a little box and a small book.

Detaching the box from its chute, he'd opened it, found himself confronted by a bug-eyed monster. The thing had turned its triangular head and stared at him with horrid coldness. Then it had moved long, awkward limbs to clamber out. He'd shut the box hurriedly and consulted the book.

This informed him that the new arrival's name was Jason, that it was a praying mantis, tame, harmless and fully capable of looking after itself on Bunda. Jason, they said, had been diet-tested on several species of Bunda insects and had eaten them avidly. In some parts of Earth the mantis was a pet of children.

That showed how their stubbornly objective minds worked. They'd now decided that the tieline must be a living creature, a natural-born Terran. Also that it must be capable of sustaining itself on an alien planet. But, being in armchairs and not lost in the starfield, they'd overlooked the essential quality of familiarity. They'd have done better to have sent him an alley cat. He didn't like cats and there was no milk, but at least the seas were full of fish. Moreover, cats make noises. They purr and yowl. The thing in the box was menacing and silent.

Who in the Western Isles had ever encountered a praying mantis? He'd never seen one in his life before. It resembled the nightmare idea of a Martian.

He never once handled it. He kept it in its box where it stood on long legs, eerily turning its head, watching him icy-eyed and never uttering a sound. The first day he gave it a Bunda hopper caught among the lichens, and was sickened by the way it bit off the victim's head and chewed. A couple of times he dreamed of a gigantic Jason towering over him, mouth opening like a big, hungry trap.

After a couple of weeks he'd had enough. Taking the box six miles to the north, he opened it, tilted it, watched Jason scuttle into the shrubs and lichens, It favored him with one basilisk stare before it disappeared. There were two Terrans on Bunda and they were lost to each other.

"Bunda One. *Eep-eep-bop!*"

Jump, wiggle, fall. No word of acknowledgment from an assisted ship fleeing through the distant dark. No sounds of life save those impressed on a magnetic tape. No reality within an alien reality daily growing more dreamlike and elusive.

Might be worth sabotaging the station for the sake of repairing it and getting it back into action, thus creating pretended justification for one's own existence. But a thousand lifeforms on one ship might pay for it with death. The price of monotony-busting amusement was too dear.

Or he could spend off-duty hours making a northward search for the tiny monster, calling, calling and hoping not to find it.

Jason! Jason!

And somewhere among the crags and crevices a pointed bulgy-eyed head turning toward his voice—and no reply coming back. If Jason had been capable of chirruping like a cricket, maybe he could have endured the creature, grown to love it, known that the squeaks were mantis-talk. But Jason was as grim and silent as the hushed, forbidding world of Bunda.

He made a final check of the transmitter, monitored its eight slaves calling in the distance, went to bed, lay there wondering for the thousandth time whether he would see the ten years through, or whether he was doomed to crack before the end.

If ever he did go nuts the scientists on Earth would promptly use him as a guinea pig, a test case for them to work on in their efforts to determine cause and cure. Yes, they were clever, very clever. But there were some things about which they weren't so smart. With that thought he fell into uneasy sleep.

Seeming stupidity sometimes proves to be cleverness compelled to take its time. All problems can be worked out given weeks, months or years instead of seconds or minutes. The time for this one was now.

The tramp-ship *Henderson* rolled out of the starfield, descended on wheezy antigravs, hung momentarily two thousand feet above the beacon. It lacked power reserves to land, take off and still make its appointed rounds. It merely paused, dropped the latest tieline thought up by the big-brains and beat it back into the dark. The cargo swirled down into the Bunda-night like a flurry of big gray snowflakes.

At dawn he awoke unconscious of the visit. The supply ship was not due for another four months. He glanced bleary-eyed at his clock, frowned with bafflement over what had caused him to wake so early. Something, a vague something that had intruded in his dreams.

What was it?

A sound.

A noise!

He sat up, listened. There again, outside, muffled by distance. The wail of an abandoned cat. No, not that. More like the cry of a lost baby.

Imagination. The cracking process must be starting already. He'd lasted four years. Some other hermit would put in the remaining six. He was hearing things and that a sure sign of mental unbalance.

Again the sound.

Getting out of bed, he dressed himself, examined himself in the mirror. It wasn't an idiot face that looked back at him. A little strained, perhaps, but otherwise normal. He went to the control room, studied the instrument board. Jump, wiggle, fall.

"Bunda One. *Eep-eep-bop!*"

Everything all right there. He returned to his own room, stretched his ears, listened. Somebody—some *thing*—was out there wailing in the dawnlight by the swelling waters. *What?* Unfastening the door with nervous fingers, he looked out.

The sound boosted, poured around him, all over him, flooded through his soul. He stood there a long time, trembling. Then gathering himself together he raced to the storeroom, stuffed his pockets with biscuits, filled both hands.

He stumbled with sheer speed as he bolted out the door. He ran headlong down to the shingly beach, loaded hands held out, his breath coming in glad gasps.

And there at the lazy ocean's edge he stood with shining eyes, arms held wide as seven-hundred sea gulls swirled around him, took biscuit from his fingers, strutted between his feet.

All the time they screamed the hymn of the islands, the song of the everlasting sea, the wild, wild music that was truly Earth's.

THE TIMID TIGER

Astounding, February 1947

Vast and tropical was the home of the timid tiger. There, the heat was oppressive, and moisture fell in great blobs, and only a fantastic light seeped past the mighty trees. The trunks of the trees were tremendous columns soaring up and into the ceiling of thick, ever-present mist, and between them the vari-colored grasses made a rich carpet along the jungle aisles.

In one of these aisles, as in the nave of a woody cathedral, dwarfed by vegetable immensity, Sam Gleeson knelt hip-deep in the carpet and poured a few more drops of ammoniated tincture of quinine between the lips of a prostrate Greenie. Four taller, lankier Greenies stood behind him watching gravely. The one he was ministering was female and below puberty. By Venusian standards, a moppet. Somebody's kid sister. He wondered whether she'd yet learned to write.

The patter of drops sounded constantly as the mist condensed and dripped down. The prostrate one licked her lips and shivered. The watching quartet leaned on their long blowpipes, their eyes intent, and the tiny green figure shivered again. She opened her eyes, revealing great, brilliant orbs like those of a cat. Her hand smoothed her grass skirt and she struggled to sit up.

"She'll be all right now," asserted Sam. He signed to one the natives. "Sit down with your back to hers to give her support. Let her rest thus for the period of one cigarette-smoke. Then give her this—all of it." He handed over a small phial. "It will do her good. When she has taken it, bear her home that she may sleep."

His knee joints creaked a little as he came erect. Closing his satchel, he hooked it on his cross-strap, swung it round behind him. Perspiration glossed his wizened face and beaded his white, goatee beard. Microscopic pearls of moisture shone in his bleached hair which had never known a hat.

One of the Greenies said, in his swift and liquid tongue, "For this, Earthman, you shall be the little one's father's father's father. The singing reeds shall tell of you to the trees."

"It is nothing," smiled Sam. "I become a great grandfather about once a month. Kids will be kids right across the Milky Way."

They made no reply to that. They had sudden taciturn moments that were disconcerting. Leaving them, he tramped along the glade, on through the welter of the rain forest. He was following an almost indiscernible path which, in an hour's walking, should bring him to his solitary cabin.

A shrill whistle sounded back in the glade now cut off from view by massive trunks. Without looking round he listened for an occasional swish of grass behind and to either side of him. Presently, it came, faint but persistent. He knew it would accompany him all the way home and he made a great pretense of being completely unaware of it. That pretense was proper. It was the polite thing for him to do—just as it was polite of them not to permit a friend to travel alone, without a bodyguard.

From the dark interior of his cabin he looked through his window hoping to catch a glimpse of his escort. It was their habit to circle his shack until his light went up. Once only he'd seen them, vague, shadowy figures gliding swiftly between trees. But he couldn't spot them this time. Sighing, he lit his kerosene lamp. Then he dug out his report book, made an entry in a clear, firm hand.

Again this afternoon I found one standing before my window. He was waiting with the solemn patience of a green statue. I cannot persuade them to knock on the door and come straight in—they remain convinced that that would be insolent. So they stand and wait some place where I'll see them. This one said that an hour to the north was a little girl with a curse in her belly. Of course, it was Raeder's Fever. I reached her in plenty of time and a stiff dose of quinine did the rest.

He stopped writing, gazed thoughtfully at the wall, stroked his goatee while murmuring to himself:

"No use mentioning that this is the seventh case in a child. It's not important, and it's already on the records. I still think Old Ma Nature has a remedy for everything and that somewhere on this planet is cinchona or a good Venusian substitute."

Putting away his book, he stood at the window and looked out again. The half-light that was day slowly faded to the luminous dark that was night. A mellow warbler began to flute five hundred feet up. There was a smell of trodden grass and of slumbering trees. He turned the lamp up a little more, went to his bookshelf, studied the small row of tomes. Howard Sax's *Medicinal Flora,* Professor Wentworthy's *Root Of All Good,* Gunnar Hjalmsen's *"Natural Drugs,"* Dr. Reilly's *Hahnemann's Theory* and a mere dozen more. He'd read them all, and again and again. Finally, he selected Walter Kayser's *How To Eat A Cannibal* and settled down with it.

> In dealing with primitive peoples it is essential to establish complete mastery from the start, to establish it firmly, without equivocation, and thereafter to maintain it by reacting sharply to anything which may be construed as a challenge. This means that while being fair, one must be firm; one must be harsh if circumstances so warrant, even brutal if necessary. The savage understands savagery if nothing else, and it is not for the club habitué in New York or Lon-

> don, but the administrator on the spot, with a heavy burden of responsibility upon him, to determine precisely how and when—

Sam frowned as he always did at this point. He had an intense admiration for Kayser, one of Earth's ablest men. This Kayser was now East Indies Controller of Native Peoples, an important post of high honor. It ill became one to disagree with a man of such eminence, but some of Kayser's views made him very fidgety.

> As for missionaries, they are good men oft made injudicious by their own enthusiasms. I like to see them—but not in lawless territory. One has only to consider the list of these brave men slaughtered by Dyaks in the Fly River area of Borneo alone to realize that they should time their arrivals a little later, when the country has settled down. Wild and bloody aborigines must be taught to fear God before they're invited to love Him.

Well, it was an old book, written when Kayser was young and somewhat fiery. Perhaps he'd changed now. Men usually changed with the passing years. Maybe he'd mellowed into gentler wisdom like Victor Hearn, the famous Consul of Luna, or Jabez Anderson, the equally great Consul of Mars. They were all very great men, able men, worthy pillars of the civilization which, having covered the Earth, had spread to the heavens.

With which concluding thought, Sam Gleeson went to bed.

All day he had plenty to occupy his mind and keep his hands busy. Besides the cooking of his own meals and various household chores there was the pressure of getting things ready in time for the next flight to Earth due in less than three weeks. When flights were timed as far apart as eight months, you just couldn't afford to miss one, and he'd a lot of stuff to consign to Terra.

Most of it was packed in readiness, some had still to be prepared. Those eight fine samples of *odontoglossum venusii* would have to be color-photographed, sketched, dried out and packed before they wilted. He had seventeen samples of bark and a report on one saying that natives distilled from it a crude exhilarant similar to cocaine. In his simple cabin were no facilities for doing fractional analyses and he wasn't a qualified chemist anyway. He was merely a field explorer for the National Botanical Institute and they'd do all the laboratory work.

His water-color sketches of the flowers were talented, but no collector would ever go searching for genuine Gleesons. Packing his sketches along with the spectochromes, he put the flowers deep in eight little fused-quartz bowls, sprinkled fine silver sand over them until they were covered, slid the bowls into a small oven. Leaving them to dry out, he went to the door and opened it. A Greenie was standing outside. The native posed a dozen feet from the door, his long blowpipe in one hand, an expression of ineffable patience on his sharp features.

"Well?" said Sam.

"Earthman, the Voice of my people would talk with you."

Sam looked around, stroked his beard worriedly. More natives waited between the trees. A bodyguard again.

"I am sorry, but I cannot come. I am extremely busy." He looked straight into the other's great cat-eyes. His voice was gentle. "I am very sorry." He went inside and closed the door.

The *odontoglossum venusii* dried out nicely and he repacked them and marked each sample box carefully. Sultriness had got him sweating again, and the beads of it collected in the myriad wrinkles at the corners of his eyes. Finishing the job, he ate, pondered awhile, then opened the door. Two hours had passed but the Greenie still stood there and his fellows still lurked in the background.

"I told you I could not come."

"Yes, Earthman."

Sam felt slightly confused. His mind was full of flowers and herbs and barks, not to mention the urgency of catching the coming flight.

"Why does the Voice want me?" he asked in an effort to clarify the situation.

"Lo, there is death over the mountains and six have died by each other's hands, three of our people and three of yours. Therefore the Voice has said that he must have word with the Gray Chanter or with you. 'Be ye fleet of foot,' he said, 'that I may speak with one.' "

"Hmph!" He stewed it over in his mind. Four years had he lived among the Greenies, but never had he met a Voice. Now was a mighty poor time to make up the deficiency. It would cost him a week. He could ill spare a week. "Did you speak with the Gray Chanter?" he asked.

"Earthman, we have seen him."

"And wouldn't he go?"

"He tried to. He came a little way. Then he struggled with his ghost and came a little further, but his feet were weary within a hundred paces."

"What, is he, too, cursed?" Sam was alarmed at the thought of Father Rooney sick in his solitude sixty miles to the south.

"He said, 'Alas, I am old and feeble, and my ancient bones refuse to be dragged. Seek the Wizened One and tell him my ghost is willing but my carcass mutinies.' "

"Wait," said Sam. He went inside, tidied up swiftly, got his satchel, saw that it held all he required. He'd no hat to put on and had never owned a gun. In all probability, he and Father Rooney were the only ones unarmed of the two thousand Terrestrials on Venus.

Before leaving, he took up an old letter, scanned it for the hundredth time. His beard bristled as he murmured its phrases. "You are employed for botanical and not for sociological research . . . expected to devote more time to flora and less to fauna . . . native welfare belongs to the proper department . . . last warning . . . your resignation—" He tore up the letter, stuffed its pieces into the embers beneath the oven, went out. His goatee was cocked defiantly as he emerged from the cabin.

A call good enough to arouse the aged priest was good enough to be answered by him. And besides—it was imperative that Terra should know the tiger, to walk in peace.

The native with whom he'd talked glided along in the lead and Sam followed at a steady, determined pace. The others shadowed silently behind. In single file they slipped through the half-light and the grasses while the mist swirled round the treetops and the dew dripped steadily down.

To reach a village they marched far into the night, with luminous herbs glowing pinkly in the growth through which they trod, and an occasional beacon tree shining like a giant specter between other darker trunks. Only one incident caused a momentary pause in their progress, this being when they found an immense constrictor lying across their path.

The reptile had a body three feet thick and its head and tail ran far away among the trees on either side. Its hide was an even dull-gray, and in the night time darkness that was never dark Sam could see the rise and fall of its sluggish breathing. It was asleep. They jumped it in rapid succession, then ran for a mile. So long as a man saw a constrictor before it saw him, he was safe—he could just outpace it.

A tiny village of lattice huts gave them food and shelter for the remainder of the night. They breakfasted on baked fish, *maro* roots and heavy bread washed down by genuine coffee. The latter had been the first discovery on Venus, and one regarded as sensational by Terrestrial botanists. This, together with the similarity between Venusians and Terrestrials, suggested parallel development of the two planets, producing many things of mutual resemblance, perhaps some identical. Sam was alone in thinking that parallelism somewhat askew. He knew the Greenies!

They were away before the first fishers set out to bait the roaring streams, before the first wild turkey could utter its eerie whistle to the dawn. Still in single file, they glided like phantoms through the rain forest which seemed never-ending, and late in the afternoon of the third day they slipped from a spur of immense trees and found themselves near to the mountains. One couldn't see the mountains, for they were deeply buried in the clouds, but one could see partway across a gradually rising plain which eventually met the mist at an elevation of more than a thousand feet—tree height.

Before them stood the village of the Voice, a large conglomeration of squat, rock-built houses. Their roofs were of pale slate, their windows of laminated quartz. The place stood in amazing contrast with the flimsy lattice hamlets deep in the forest. Around lay small, cultivated fields through which two narrow and noisy mountain streams pounded in liquid ecstasy. Sam had never seen anything like this, though he'd heard of it. The Greenies went up another notch in his estimation.

He found the Voice sitting on a stool in the main room of the central house. The chief proved to be a tall, slender native of well-preserved middle age. His green face was narrow and sharp and bore the peculiar pineapple marking of his kind. Like all Venusians, he was completely hairless and possessed great yellow eyes with slotted, catlike pupils.

Sam gave him a precious cigarette, lit it for him, sat on the stool facing him. There were no salutations among the Greenies. The chief stared at him imperturbably and dragged at his cigarette. After a while, he spoke.

"I am the Voice of my people."

Sam went through the polite routine of affecting dumbfounded surprise. Dipping into his satchel, he produced a full pack of cigarettes, gave them to the other. The chief accepted them graciously.

"You do not smoke?"

"I am awaiting your permission," said Sam.

The feline pupils widened as he studied Sam for a long time. The stare was unblinking.

"Smoke!" said the Voice.

Digging out a pellet, Sam lit up. No use hurrying the chief. He'd take his own time and, probably, there'd be the usual cross-examination before he got down to business.

"You speak with my mouth, as does the Gray Chanter," the chief remarked. "Other Earthmen do not, and content themselves with childish signs and gestures. Why?"

Sam fidgeted while he considered the matter. In the outlands, one had to be a diplomat among other things.

"My work," he explained carefully, "keeps me among your people. It is the same with the Gray Chanter. How can we acquire friends and neighbors if we speak not with their mouths? Would you that I sat among the trees and nursed a lonely ghost?" Sam paused inquiringly, but the chief said nothing, so he went on. "Therefore I learned so to speak, as the Gray Chanter."

"And what of the others?" asked the chief, his great orbs fixed and blinkless.

"Other men have other tasks. They work together and are not alone. Many work harder and longer hours than I do and they have not time to acquire other mouths. Some have not the ability because their virtues lie elsewhere. For me, it was easy. For the Gray Chanter it was not so easy. For others it may be hard."

The chief made no comment. He spurted a stream of smoke from between thin lips while his eyes did not shift a fraction. It didn't worry Sam. He'd got used to cat-eyes and to cat-stares, as one did after a while. Fifty months in the rain forest, and you began to understand Greenies—but only began! While he smoked and waited for the next question, he thought idly of Burrough's description of the first Venusian seen by a Terrestrial: physically four-fifths human and one-fifth heaven-knows-what; mentally four-fifths human and one-fifth cat. There was certainly a touch of cat behind their feline eyes; moments of drowsy thoughtfulness, moments of enigmatic stares. They had all the patience of cats, and often the same quiet dignity.

"I am what I am," said the chief suddenly, "and all my people are even thus. There are no differences, neither here, nor across the mountains, nor on the other side of our world. Yet you, an Earthman, have a countenance brown and wrinkled and moss-grown like the bark of an old *radus* tree, while the Gray Chanter, also an Earthman, is smooth and pale with the lightness of dawn."

"There is Cherokee in me," said Sam uninformatively. Then added, "There are men of many colors on Earth, some white, some red, some black, brown or yellow."

"Ah!" The chief was interested. "And any—green?"

"No, there aren't any green ones on Earth." His tongue got ahead of his mind as he commented, with a grin, "There are some said to be green." Then he frowned, put in hastily, "But they are not."

He wished it could have been unsaid even as the other pounced on it. He should have known the direct Venusian mind well enough not to have made such a slip.

"If they are not green," demanded the chief with perfect logic, "why call them green?"

The smile had vanished from Sam's face and the brilliant eyes were still upon him while his mind searched frantically for an explanation which would satisfy the literal-minded Venusian without hurting his feelings.

Finally, he said, "They are people who're honest, straightforward, without guile. Those are thought to be the virtues of green ghosts. Therefore they are said to be green."

The chief let it pass unchallenged, and still his eyes neither blinked nor shifted their steady gaze. The way they timed their silences added greatly to difficulties of conversation with Venusians, for you could never tell whether you'd convinced them or not. They had an embarrassing habit of asking pointed questions, and their usual response to an answer was another and more awkward question. This silence was a long one and outlasted the chief's cigarette.

In the end, the chief said, "I know many tales of you, Wizened One, for my mind does not miss the slide of a dewdrop down a leaf. I know that you are good." He paused a moment. "Some are good, some are not good. But of you and the Gray Chanter I know naught but good."

This, uttered in a level voice and accompanied by that hypnotic stare, made Sam feeble. He waved a hand in futile dismissal, sought words adequate to the occasion. A halo ill-became his grizzled pate and he'd feel better without it. From his viewpoint, he'd done nothing but lend an occasional helping hand and mind his own business. Back home in Neosho they called it being neighborly, and they spoke well of you for it, but handed out no diplomas. Before he could find anything to say, the chief went on.

"Now there is great trouble between your people and mine, and death stalks across the mountains. It is an evil thing, for it may spread as the waters spread when they break their bounds. I do not wish to see our forests sheltering only the hunters—and the hunted with no man daring to withhold death from the good lest the good prove bad."

Sam leaned forward, his leathery features intent, the crinkles deepening at the corners of his eyes. There had been trouble, mild trouble, between men and Greenies in the first months of settlement five years ago. Wisdom on both sides had abated it and there'd been no more since. But always it was feared. As Terrestrials gradually grew in numbers so also grew the risk that somebody might start something that couldn't be stopped. He didn't want that. Nobody in full possession of his senses wanted it.

"I am called Elran the Older," continued the chief. "Over the mountains are the people of Elran the Younger. He is my brother. And beyond his lands lie the pastures of the people of Mithra the Silent. My mate is Mithra's sister, and he is my brother-by-bond."

"So?"

"On Mithra's lands are Earthmen. They have been there nearly a year. They have been cutting into his land for some precious mineral, and Mithra approved because he had made a treaty with them. Now a difference has arisen. The Earthmen waxed arrogant and threatening. They brought out their fire weapons." His great eyes lidded for a fraction of a second. "They killed three of Mithra's people."

Sam sucked in his breath, then asked, "And what did Mithra do?"

"He took three for three. By patience and by craft he snared them. They bristled with darts as a tree bristles with leaves and they'd lost their ghosts before they hit the ground. With darts and cords he struck in the night and pulled down the wires that stretched across the roof of the Earthmen's far-speaking house, thus preventing them from summoning a blastship to their aid. Now the Earthmen are sitting in their house and have made it a fort. Mithra has surrounded it and awaits the decision of our kind—for the cry of evil is answered by the cry of good and our mind has got to tip the balance one way or the other."

"This," said Sam, "is bad."

"In the beginning, when Earthmen came to us out of the mist, there was death. But Vaxtre the Ancient and the Earthman we called Tall One came together in wisdom and made peace. Now I am of a mind, Wizened One, that perhaps you and Mithra can achieve the same before it is too late. If not—as Mithra does we shall all do, here and everywhere. A stifled scream is unheard in the glades."

"I shall see Mithra," promised Sam. "I shall go to him at once."

He was off again within the hour. Three days would bring him to the seat of the trouble: one day through the Great Valley and into the land of Elran the Younger, two more days to reach Mithra. That made a total of six days from the cabin to his destination and six days back. If he got stuck too long wherever he was going, his consignment would miss the ship. It required four days to transport it from the cabin to the spaceport. The margin was small.

His face was grim as he thought of that letter. "Native welfare belongs to the proper department." There wasn't a proper department on Venus. There wasn't even a Consul yet! There was only a spaceport still under construction and few Terrestrials outside of it; the majority clung together against the time when their numbers would be more. Those armchair warmers back on Earth ought to be exported and given a taste of forest life. They'd see things differently, after that. "Last warning . . . your resignation may be required." What did they think he was—a root-grubbing automaton?

The Greenies in front seemed to sense his urgency, for they loped along at top pace. The daylight, poor and inadequate by Terrestrial standards, didn't bother the native in the least, and neither did the fall of night. Daytime or night, it was all the same to these people. They could see equally well in either.

Ground rose up and the mist lowered. They were barely beneath the swirling canopy as they sped through the valley. It was a nuisance, that everlasting fog and, but for radar, would have made all spaceship landings impossibly dangerous. It hung over them like a perpetual shroud, and rays from the invisible sun struggled through so diffused that they threw no shadows.

Mid-afternoon of the second day brought them to the verge of the rain forest which encroached halfway across the lands of Elran the Younger. They plunged into it. That night they ate well, for an incautious turkey forgot to freeze in the gloom as they went past and a blown dart brought it down. The thing was featherless, reptile-skinned and bore no resemblance to a bird except that its cooked flesh was indistinguishable from that of roasted turkey.

Mithra's village was reached a couple of hours ahead of estimated time. It, too, proved to be stone-built, a little smaller than that of Elran the Older, and it was built upon a knoll from which the eternal forest had retreated in all directions. Within a radius of three miles the ground was clear of giant timber and well-tilled.

The Voice himself talked first with the escort, then summoned Sam. The latter found Mithra to be another middle-aged Greenie, shorter and stockier than Elran the Older, and with eyes of light amber.

"I am the Voice of my people," he said formally. Sam offered no reply, knowing that none was expected, but put on the usual surprise act. The chief came quickly to the point, showing himself more abrupt than his distant brother-by-bond. "I know of you as all know of you. Here, you are welcome—but I know not what you can do."

"What happened?" inquired Sam.

"An Earthman came when the life-tide was rising in the trees and stayed until it ebbed. He talked not with our mouth and spoke only by signs and picture writing. We gave him room and nourished his belly, for he was of our shape and alone. For many days he sought among the rocks, along the earthcracks and the chasms, until one day he came to me with his ghost a-dancing and said he'd found that which he'd been seeking. It was merely a vein of *rilla* metal which is of no use to man or beast."

"It hardens and toughens steel beyond belief," Sam told him. "There is none on Earth. We can use it in constructing spaceships."

"I made a treaty with him," the chief went on, "whereby he could dig up all the *rilla* metal within one hundred man-lengths of his discovery. He went away. A long time later, he came back with five others. My people helped them build a rock house. Over this house the Earthmen put a web of wires and through it they talked to a blastship and brought it down to them through the mist. Twenty more Earthmen came from the ship, with much machinery. The ship departed. Those left behind used the machinery to dig up and melt the *rilla* metal. They worked for almost a year and sent away much of it until there was no more." He hooded his eyes in thought while Sam waited for him to continue.

"Then they came and told me that there is a lot more *rilla* metal within this hill. They said they must have it, village or no village, and that I must make another treaty. I refused. They grew wroth and threatened to release my ghost. One of my people raised his blowpipe and they turned their weapons on him. We buried him in the dark. The Earthmen ran back to their house with many of my young men following in their tracks. We buried two of those also! The next night we trapped three Earthmen and appeased our dead. We also tore down the web of wires above the house and surrounded the place with warriors. Since then, they have not dared to come out and we have not dared to go in."

"May I speak with these Earthmen?" Sam asked.

The chief didn't hesitate, and said, "You shall be conducted to them whenever you wish."

"In the morning, then. I would first like to look around the village and the hill, also examine the place from which the *rilla* metal has been taken."

The building that had become a fort rested alongside another knoll a mile and a half to the south of Mithra's place. It squatted dull and menacing in the poor light of morning.

Countless Greenies prowled phantomlike in the nearest spurs of the rain forest. Some had huge, multi-mouthed blow-guns which needed the simultaneous impulse of six men but could throw heavy darts more than two hundred yards. Others bore accurate and vicious arbalests fitted with heavy metal springs and low-geared winders—a weapon Sam had never seen before. Although he did not come across any on his way to the fort, Sam knew that the Venusians also possessed flame throwers of alarming efficiency. The entire horde kept to the fringes of the forest, well out of range of the fort, and were content to wait. If you crouch by a water hole long enough, the trembling roebuck is bound to appear.

He tramped toward the house with his hands in his pockets, his goatee bristling, and an air of confident nonchalance which might serve to stay any itchy trigger-fingers behind those walls. In the bad illumination Earth-eyes couldn't distinguish friend from foe at any range greater than a voice could carry. The Greenies knew no such handicap. Folks back on Earth who blandly assumed that on any new world one automatically fitted in just couldn't realize the toughness of little things, such as being, by comparison, half-blind. It was always the little things that proved tough. Not the big ones. A bullet in the abdomen was only a little thing. His stomach jumped at the thought.

But no shot sounded. Within fifty yards of the house he passed a board crudely lettered:

TERRALOID
CORPORATION

That wasn't so good. Terraloid were big and powerful and not in business for the sake of their health. Their reputation wasn't evil, and they'd never been known to pull a deliberate swindle, but they were go-getters, efficient, impatient, unwilling to bide their time. Commercially, they were shortcut artists and more than once they'd fallen foul of consuls by their eagerness to march too far in advance of events.

A big, beefy man opened the door, growled, "How the blazes did you get here without masquerading as a pincushion? Don't you know there's plenty trouble hereabouts?"

"That's what I've come to discuss with you. Mithra sent me."

"Ho-hum, a dove of peace!" rumbled the other with a trace of sarcasm. He conducted Sam to an inner room in which were a dozen men, some cleaning and adjusting weapons, others busily completing a new web antenna. "Boys, here's a negotiator." They looked up disinterestedly. The big man sank into a chair which creaked under his weight, said to Sam, "I'm Clem Mason, manager of this outfit. Who're you, why did Mithra pick you out, what's he want to say, and what authority have you got—if any?"

"I'm Sam Gleeson. I'm merely a fieldman for the National Botanical Institute—for as long as that job lasts, which won't be long!" replied Sam evenly. "I've got as much authority as that gives me, which is none whatever. As for the reason why Mithra called me in, I guess it was because I speak his language and know his people." As an afterthought, he added, "And probably because Father Rooney couldn't come."

"Father Rooney!" Clem Mason scowled. "Never heard of him! But we don't want any priests interfering in this. They tell tales back home and the story loses nothing in the telling. Then boudoir warriors complain to the newscasts and the public tears its hair and the next thing you know we've got to say, 'Yes, sir,' and 'No, Sir,' and 'Thank you very much, sir,' to every stinking aborigine who comes our way. Why can't people leave us to do our own dickering?" He glared across at the well-oiled guns. "We know how!"

Sam smiled broadly and said, "Seems it's up to you and me to cool things down before Father Rooney comes along to make more trouble, eh?"

The other thought that one over, then growled begrudgingly, "Maybe you've got something!"

"I've heard Mithra's story about what happened," Sam pursued. "Let me hear yours. Then we'll see what we can do to straighten things out."

"It's simple. We worked out a *rilla* vein which we'd got under covenant with Mithra. It was a tentacle broken off from a mother lode some place. Our instruments found the lode far down under the northward knoll. There's tons of the stuff, and it's needed badly. Then we got all balled up because none of us knows a word of Venusian. We drew pictures and played snake-arms for hours trying to explain to Mithra that we'd found Aladdin's cave way down under his cellar and that we wanted another covenant to get it out. We offered him fair terms, were willing to play square, but the more we argued the tougher he got."

"Go on," Sam encouraged.

"I got riled by his stubbornness and cursed him for a skinny green nitwit. I knew he couldn't understand English anyway. After that, it was a case of one durned thing leading to another."

"In what way?"

"A young Greenie among Mithra's crowd lifted his blowpipe. Maybe he didn't like the way I'd said what I'd said. Or maybe he lifted it with nothing in mind. But Fargher was jumpy and taking no chances and popped him on the spot. We beat it back here with a splurge of angry Greenies slinking after us through the night, and we had to blow back at them to hold them a bit. I don't know whether we hurt any more."

"You killed two," Sam informed.

Mason made a negligent gesture and continued, "They were mighty swift to call it quits. They caught Fargher and Meakin and Wills out in the darkness and mauled them in ten seconds flat! They blew cord-carrying darts across the roof and lugged down our web. Since then, we've stuck to the house and tried to call base on our portable, but the range is too long and intervening mountains blot us out. So we're going to fix up a new web and they had better not try to get *that* down! We'll get a blastship here. After that, the fashionable attire for well-dressed Greenies will be sackcloth and ashes!"

"Trouble begets trouble," opined Sam. "I fear me that this is no petty skirmish with a local tribe. It isn't as simple as that. I've been getting the hang of some queer things about these Venusians. They've no tribes, no nations. They've no local patriotisms—but they're Venus-conscious! They've only one color, one language, and one something-else I've not yet been able to identify. But the divide and rule principal just won't work on this planet, for the woes of one are the woes of all."

"Never mind the lectures," put in Mason sourly. "Say what you've got to say and let's go digging."

"The point I'm trying to drive home is that you can't indulge in purely local shenanigans. Even Elran the Older, three days march away across the mountains, knows all that's going on and is ready to do exactly what Mithra does. The alternative to peace is an Earth-Venus war. For all our superior weapons there are only a couple of thousand of us on the planet. There are umpteen millions of Greenies, and we've got to seek them out, one at a time, every man jack of them, in the biggest jungle in the solar system. Fat lot of use our blastships and atomizers will prove in circumstances like that!" He mused a moment. "What's the use of the mightiest power if it can't be applied?"

"We can apply it all right," Mason asserted. "You've sat on your buttocks too long—you've forgotten the planet behind the two thousand!"

"Behind them for three weeks every eight months!" Sam retorted. "You know we're planet-raking before our time. We've not yet developed spaceships good enough to chase a world around its orbit. In another fifty years, maybe—but not yet. That shaves us down somewhat, doesn't it? Earth's in a poor position to conquer Venus by force."

"That's your—" Mason began, but Sam interrupted him.

"Let me go on. You want *rilla* metal. That's all you're here for. If you can get it by cajoling Mithra, it'll come a lot cheaper than by fighting him for it. If you're a shareholder, you should appreciate that. If you're not holding any of their stock, why should you do Terraloid's blood-letting?"

"He's dead to rights there, Clem," put in one of the listening men. "I came here to get on with a job of work and land home with a whole skin and plenty of moola. If there's any pushing around to be done, let 'em call in the marines!" Several others murmured agreement.

"O.K.," said Mason. He hooked big thumbs in the armholes of his vest, tilted backward in his chair. "So we soothe Mithra—how?"

"Can you get out that *rilla* without wrecking his village?"

"Sure we can. It's down deep. We can run inside shafts from the base of the knoll. It's dead easy!"

"Did you explain that to Mithra?"

"Goldarn it! That's what we tried to do," complained Mason, his voice rising, "but without his lingo we couldn't make him understand. He's seen what a mess we've made of the surface-vein here and thought there'd be the same upheaval there."

"Naturally?" prompted Sam.

Mason was reluctant, but after a while he gave in with, "Well, I guess so. It was natural. He's no miner or metallurgical engineer."

Sam leaned forward in his seat. "Now can I tell Mithra that the metal will be taken without disturbing one stone or slate within his village, and that after it is done you will leave him fine passages and underground rooms which his people can use for storage?"

"You bet!" The other became amiable suddenly. "We'd even trim up the walls for them."

"Good. I'll go and tell him. I think it'll satisfy him—in fact I'm sure of it."

"Let's hope so." Mason's chair came forward as he sat up. "But there's still one snag."

"What's that?"

"Three of my men died, and don't you forget it! What is Mithra going to do about that?"

Sam rose to his feet in readiness to leave. Now that his mission seemed to be getting some place, he felt tired, thoroughly tired and weary. Too much long distance marching and too little sleep. Six days to get back at the same hurried pace and the spaceship still to catch. This life was punishing to one's dogs.

"Mithra will send you the culprits and you may punish them as you wish."

"Like heck he will," said Mason. "Unless he's nuts."

"Oh, yes, he will—on one condition."

"What condition?"

"That you send him the three who killed his men and leave him to punish them."

"You got me there. It's even-Steven. They're dead, anyway."

"So are Mithra's men," said Sam.

Mithra made the peace, the prowling shadows vanished from the fringes near the fort, the arbalests and flame throwers were put away. No messenger went forth to bear the tidings, a fact Sam noted thoughtfully.

"I can't see what else we can call it but a miserable misunderstanding," said Sam to Mason as he made ready to leave the village. "It's not for me to place the blame, but I reckon it'd be wiser if you gave one of your guys time off to learn the language. When people on Earth can't always make themselves understood, what hopes have you got semaphoring at a Greenie?"

"I'll see what can be done," promised Mason. "And thanks a lot!" He frowned suddenly, and added, "If you meet that Father Rooney, stall him off for me, will you?"

"I will," agreed Sam, smiling. He hiked his satchel and left.

The same native who'd brought him was his guide on the way back, but the remainder of his bodyguard had increased in number from three to twelve. He was greatly honored, for this was the escort of a Voice. Politeness still demanded that he follow his guide and pretend not to notice the others.

Twelve protecting shadows stayed with him the full length of his journey home and duly circled his cabin before fading away into the heat-haze and the half-light. They'd been phantoms throughout the trip and like phantoms they disappeared.

It was good to be back in the shack, to see the old, familiar fragment of glade through the window, to hear the regular *put-put-put* of moisture falling onto the roof, to have books biding his perusal, a bed waiting for his body.

Morning found him frantically energetic. From Mithra's land he'd plucked a new herb which looked like heather but smelled and tasted like mint. It hadn't wilted during the journey. He sand-dried it, sketched it, photographed it, packed it in a box which he tagged: *erica mithrii.* There were four new roots with which to deal, in addition to the other roots and samples of bark still waiting attention. And a report to write about every one of them. He was still busy in the middle of it when a heavy metallic rattle and the deep roar of a Diesel engine brought him outside. He was just in time to see the caterpillar from Base rumble into the glade. There were four men aboard. The machine was two days early and much of his stuff wasn't ready for it; he stood and watched its approach with mixed feelings.

With a final burst of power that sent curls of thick blue smoke through the grasses and the herbs, the huge machine stopped before his door and its passengers climbed out. The treads had left two enormous weals across the glade to between the farther trees.

He recognized none of the four. The first of these, making no remark, handed him a bunch of mail and strolled into the cabin, the others following. Sam entered last shuffling his mail and feeling ireful.

Inside, he found the first entrant squatting on the edge of his bed; a beefy personage with a thick neck, a florid complexion, and an elusive touch of humor playing around his heavy jowls.

Without preamble, this one said, "Brother Gleeson, you're fired."

Sam tossed the mail unopened onto his bed, seated himself carefully on a sample box. "I've been expecting it."

"So have I," informed the other cheerfully. "I've been trying for months to persuade the Institute to shake you off."

"Indeed?" Sam wrinkled his eyes as he studied the speaker. "Why? What have I done to you?"

"You got me bothered by making me realize how much I've yet to learn." He jerked a brawny thumb to indicate the spectacled, apprehensive young man at his side. "Same with him. He's Jud Hancock, your successor, and he feels apologetic about it."

"All right," said Sam, listlessly. "Guess this is where I pack up and go home."

"Oh, no, you don't!" He leaned forward, rested thick arms on thicker knees. "Earth's decided that now's the time to appoint a Venusian Consul and get things better organized. I have been honored with the task, and I think it's a tough one. What I'm going to need, real bad, will be an adviser on native affairs. That's where you come in."

Sam said, quickly, "What makes you think that?"

"Your reports. I've read 'em all."

"Who are you?"

"Walt Kayser," answered the other.

A wave of embarrassment came over Sam, and he murmured, "You expect *me* to advise *you?*"

"Most certainly! Where the devil can I get advice except from the right people? Who understands Venusians better than you?" He looked up questioningly, his eyes keen and sharp. "For instance, what's all this stuff you've got about what you call 'Venusian auto-rapport?' "

"I don't quite know even now," Sam replied. His hair was standing up and his goatee lying down, and his mind was in a confused whirl. "All I've found out is that as long as things go smoothly for them the Greenies are individuals exactly as we are. But when involved in difficulties great enough to cause mental stress they appear to become part of a communal mind. Immediately a Greenie is in trouble the whole world of Greenies knows about it, discusses it, analyzes it, advises him what to do in some queer mental way, and, if necessary, comes to his aid."

"Telepathy?"

"No, it's definitely not that. It isn't deliberate. It's quite involuntary and automatic and operates only under strain. It's just a peculiar faculty unknown on Earth or Mars." Enthusiasm for his subject crept into his voice. "You know, it means we've got to be almighty careful in our dealings with them. Here, one sucker means a whole world warned. Venus is the wrong place for pulling fast ones. The only way in which we can let them know we're good is by being good all the time. We've got to maintain a code of ethics out of stern necessity."

"Or else?"

"Else they're likely to be tough—maybe too tough for us to handle. It's going to be a long, long time before we get the full measure of their capabilities!" His features grew reminiscent, thoughtful. "Sometimes I find myself quite unable to decide whether the Greenies are genuine individuals or merely independent fragments of some huge, incomprehensible, planet-covering Greenie entity. There are times when they show strange aspects of both. Occasionally I think of them not as a race, but as a being, a sort of timid tiger. It's polite and retiring—and it's wisest to let it stay that way."

"You see!" said Walter Kayser.

"See what?"

Kayser turned to his three companions and said, humorously, "He says, 'See what?' He can't hear himself talk!" He turned back to Sam. "The man who's playmate of a timid tiger is the man I need. What, in your opinion, is our most urgent requirement in creating wider and better contact with the Greenies?"

"Linguists," Sam told him emphatically. He stood up. "That's the only way in which I've gotten to know them."

"The only way?" queried Kayser, lifting an eyebrow.

"Sure!" Sam moved restlessly across the room, the others watching. The swift march of events was still a little too much for his orderly mind. What to do for the best? Wasn't Kayser weighing his friendship with natives a little too heavily? Darn it, all he'd done was learn to talk their own lingo. Any fool could do that if he took the trouble. His preoccupied gaze went through the window, saw a Greenie waiting patiently outside.

"Pardon me," he said to the quartet, opened the door, and went out.

The native leaned on his blowpipe, looked at Sam with great yellow eyes that were grave and brooding. "The Gray Chanter," he said.

"What of him? Is he sick?"

The other nodded. "They say he forbids us to summon you, but it is not good for him to struggle alone. He has spoken gently, saying that we are company enough. Alas, he cannot grasp the mind of his people."

Sam blinked and said, "Wait!"

Returning to the cabin, he snatched up his satchel, slung it over his shoulder. "Father Rooney is ill," he told his surprised visitors. "Unfortunately, you could never cross the ravines and rope bridges in that caterpillar. So this is where I go." With that, he was gone.

The dumbfounded four crowded the cabin door and watched him vanish through the trees behind his swiftly loping guide. The last branches rustled behind him, the leaves dripped down and all was silence. Then, suddenly, a dozen stealthy shapes, blowguns in hand, flitted from the trees and entered the invisible path Sam had taken.

"Hey, look at that!" breathed Hancock, grabbing Kayser's arm.

"His escort," murmured Kayser. He shrugged broad shoulders. "And I don't rate one better! Sixty miles—just like that!" He mused a lot, "There was a remark in one of his reports that caused effervescence in my thinkery. He said, 'They've been kind to me.' "

"Humph!" contributed Hancock, looking comforted.

"He didn't take up your offer," one of the others pointed out.

"He will, he will," asserted Kayser positively. "He's constitutionally incapable of refusing."

Top Secret

Astounding, August 1956

Ashmore said, with irritating phlegmaticism, "The Zengs have everything to gain and nothing to lose by remaining friendly with us. I'm not worried about them."

"But I am," rasped General Railton. "I'm paid to worry. It's my job. If the Zeng empire launches a treacherous attack upon ours and gains some initial successes, who'll get the blame? Who'll be accused of military unpreparedness?" He tapped his two rows of medal ribbons. "I will!"

"Understanding your position, I cannot share your alarm," maintained Ashmore, refusing to budge. "The Zeng empire is less than half the size of ours. The Zengs are an amiable and cooperative form of life and we've been on excellent terms with them since the first day of contact."

"I'll grant you all that." General Railton tugged furiously at his large and luxuriant mustache while he examined the great star-map that covered an entire wall. "But I have to consider things purely from the military viewpoint. It's my task to look to the future and expect the worst."

"Well, what's worrying you in particular?" Ashmore invited.

"Two things." Railton placed an authoritative finger on the star-map. "Right here we hold a fairly new planet called Motan. You can see where it is—out in the wilds, far beyond our long-established frontiers. It's located in the middle of a close-packed group of solar systems, a stellar array that represents an important junction in space."

"I know all that."

"At Motan we've got a foothold of immense strategic value. We're in ambush on the crossroads, so to speak. Twenty thousand Terrans are there, complete with two spaceports and twenty-four light cruisers." He glanced at the other. "And what happens?"

Ashmore offered no comment.

"The Zengs," said Railton, making a personal grievance of it, "move in and take over two nearby planets in the same group."

"With our agreement," Ashmore reminded. "We didn't need those two planets. The Zengs did want them. They put in a polite and correct request for permission to take over. Greenwood told them to help themselves."

"Greenwood," exploded Railton, "is someone I could describe in detail were it not for my oath of loyalty."

"Let it pass," suggested Ashmore, wearily. "If he blundered, he did so with the full approval of the World Council."

"The World Council," Railton snorted. "All they're interested in is exploration, discovery and trade. All they can think of is culture and cash. They're completely devoid of any sense of peril."

"Not being military officers," Ashmore pointed out, "they can hardly be expected to exist in a state of perpetual apprehension."

"Mine's not without cause." Railton had another go at uprooting his mustache. "The Zengs craftily position themselves adjacent to Motan." He swept spread fingers across the map in a wide arc. "And all over here are Zeng outposts mixed up with ours. No orderliness about it, no system. A mob, sir, a scattered mob."

"That's natural when two empires overlap," informed Ashmore. "And, after all, the mighty cosmos isn't a parade ground."

Ignoring that, Railton said pointedly, "Then a cipher book disappears."

"It was shipped back on the *Laura Lindsay.* She blew apart and was a total loss. You know that."

"I know only what they see fit to tell me. I don't know that the book was actually on the ship. If it was not where is it? Who's got it? What's he doing with it?" He waited for comment that did not come; finished, "So I had to move heaven and earth to get that cipher canceled and have copies of a new one sent out."

"Accidents happen," said Ashmore.

"Today," continued Railton, "I discover that Commander Hunter, on Motan, has been given the usual fat-headed emergency order. If war breaks out, he must fight a defensive action and hold the planet at all costs."

"What's wrong with that?"

Staring at him incredulously, Railton growled, "And him with twenty-four light cruisers. Not to mention two new battleships soon to follow."

"I don't quite understand."

"Wars," explained Railton, as one would to a child, "cannot be fought without armed ships. Ships cannot function usefully without instructions based on careful appraisal of tactical necessities. Somebody has to plan and give orders. The orders have to be received by those appointed to carry them out."

"So?"

"How can Zeng warships receive and obey orders if their planetary beam-stations have been destroyed?"

"You think that immediately war breaks out the forces on Motan should bomb every beam-station within reach?"

"Most certainly, man!" Railton looked pleased at long last. "The instant the Zengs attack we've got to retaliate against their beam-stations. That's tantamount to depriving them of their eyes and ears. Motan must be fully prepared to do its share. Commander Hunter's orders are out of date, behind the times, in fact plain stupid. The sooner they're rectified, the better."

"You're the boss," Ashmore reminded. "You've the authority to have them changed."

"That's exactly what I intend to do. I am sending Hunter appropriate instructions at once. And not by direct-beam either." He indicated the map again. "In this messy muddle there are fifty or more Zeng beam-stations lying on the straight line between here and there. How do we know how much stuff they're picking up and deciphering?"

"The only alternative is the tight-beam," Ashmore said. "And that takes ten times as long. It zigzags all over the star-field from one station to another."

"But it's a thousand times safer and surer," Railton retorted. "Motan's station has just been completed and now's the time to make use of the fact. I'll send new instructions by tight-beam, in straight language, and leave no room for misunderstanding."

He spent twenty minutes composing a suitable message, finally got it to his satisfaction. Ashmore read it, could suggest no improvements. In due course it flashed out to Centauri, the first staging-post across the galaxy.

In event of hostile action in your sector the war must be fought to outstretch and rive all enemy's chief lines of communication.

"That," said Railton, "expresses it broadly enough to show Hunter what's wanted but still leave him with some initiative."

At Centauri the message was unscrambled, read off in clear, read into another beam of different frequency, and boosted to the next nearest station. There it was sorted out, read off in clear, repeated into another beam and squirted onward.

It went leftward, rightward, upward, downward, and was dutifully recited eighteen times by voices ranging from Terran-American deep-South-suh to Bootean-Ansanite far-North-yezzah. But it got there just the same.

Yes, it got there.

Lounging behind his desk, Commander Hunter glanced idly at the Motan thirty-hour clock, gave a wide yawn, wondered for the hundredth time whether it was something in the alien atmosphere that gave him the gapes. A knock sounded on his office door.

"Come in!"

Tyler entered, red-nosed and sniffy as usual. He saluted, dumped a signal-form on the desk. "Message from Terra, sir." He saluted again and marched out, sniffing as he went.

Picking it up, Hunter yawned again as he looked at it. Then his month clapped shut with an audible crack of jaw-bones. He sat bolt upright, eyes popping, read it a second time.

Ex Terra Space Control. Tight-Beam, Straight. Top Secret. To Motan. An event of hospitality your section the foremost when forty-two ostriches arrive on any cheap line of communication.

Holding it in one hand he walked three times round the room, but it made no difference. The message still said what it said.

So he reseated himself, reached for the phone and bawled, "Maxwell? Is Maxwell there? Send him in at once!"

Maxwell appeared within a couple of minutes. He was a long, lean character who constantly maintained an expression of chronic disillusionment. Sighing deeply, he sat down.

"What's it this time, Felix?"

"Now," said Hunter, in the manner of a dentist about to reach for the big one at the back, "you're this planet's chief equipment officer. What you don't know about stores, supplies, and equipment isn't worth knowing, eh?"

"I wouldn't go so far as to say that. I—"

"You know *everything* about equipment," insisted Hunter, "else you've no right being here and taking money for it. You're skinning the Terran taxpayers by false pretenses."

"Calm down, Felix," urged Maxwell. "I've enough troubles of my own." His questing eyes found the paper in the other's hand. "I take it that something's been requisitioned of which you don't approve. What is it?"

"Forty-two ostriches," informed Hunter.

Maxwell gave a violent jerk, fell off his chair, regained it and said, "Ha-ha! That's good. Best I've heard in years.

"You can see the joke all right?" asked Hunter, with artificial pleasantness. "You think it a winner?"

"Sure," enthused Maxwell. "It's really rich." He added another ha-ha by way of support.

"Then," said Hunter, a trifle viciously, "maybe you'll explain it to me; I'm too dumb to get it on my own." He leaned forward, arms akimbo. "*Why* do we require forty-two ostriches, eh? Tell me that!"

"Are you serious?" asked Maxwell, a little dazed.

For answer, Hunter shoved the signal-form at him. Maxwell well read it, stood up, sat down, read it again, turned and carefully examined the blank back.

"Well?" prompted Hunter.

"I've had nothing to do with this," assured Maxwell, hurriedly. He handed back the signal-form as though anxious to be rid of it. "It's a Terran-authorized shipment made without demand from this end."

"My limited intelligence enabled me to deduce that much," said Hunter. "But as I have pointed out, you know all about equipment required for given conditions on any given world. All I want from you is information on why Motan needs forty-two ostriches—and what we're supposed to do with them when they come."

"I don't know," Maxwell admitted.

"You don't know?"

"No."

"That's a help." Hunter glowered at the signal. "A very big help."

"How about it being in code?" inquired Maxwell, desperate enough to fish around.

"It says here it's in straight."

"That could be an error."

"All right. We can soon check." Unlocking a big wall safe, Hunter extracted a brass-bound book, scrabbled through its pages. Then he gave it to Maxwell. "See if you can find a reference to ostriches or any reasonable resemblance thereto."

After five minutes Maxwell voiced a dismal, "No."

"Well," persisted Hunter, "have you sent a demand for forty-two of anything that might be misread as ostriches?"

"Not a thing." He meditated a bit, added glumly, "I did order a one-pint blow-torch."

Taking a tight grip on the rim of the desk, Hunter said, "What's that got to do with it?"

"Nothing. I was just thinking. That's what I ordered. You ought to see what I got." He gestured toward the door. "It's right out there in the yard. I had it dragged there for your benefit."

"Let's have a look at it."

Hunter followed him outside, inspected the object of the other's discontent. It had a body slightly bigger than a garbage can, and a nozzle five inches in diameter by three feet in length. Though empty, it was as much as the two could manage to lift it.

"What the deuce is it, anyway?" demanded Hunter. scowling.

"A one-pint blowtorch. The consignment note says so."

"Never seen anything like it. We'd better check the stores catalogue." Returning to the office, he dug the tome out of the safe, thumbed through it rapidly, found what he wanted somewhere among the middle pages.

19112. Blowtorch, butane, 1/2 pint capacity.

19112A. Blowtorch, butane, 1 pint capacity.

19112B Blowtorch (tar-boiler pattern), kerosene, 15 gallons capacity.

19112B(a). Portable trolley for 1912B.

"You've got B in lieu of A," Hunter diagnosed.

"That's right. I order A and I get B."

"Without the trolley?"

"Correct."

"Some moron is doing his best." He returned the catalogue to the safe. "You'll have to ship it back. It's a fat lot of use to us without the trolley even if we do find need to boil some tar."

"Oh, I don't know," Maxwell said. "We can handle it by sheer muscle when the two hundred left-legged men get here."

Hunter plonked himself in his chair, gave the other the hard eye. "Quit beating about the bush, What's on your mind?"

"The last ship," said Maxwell, moodily, "brought two hundred pairs of left-legged rubber thigh-boots."

"The next ship may bring two hundred pairs of right-legged ones to match up," said Hunter. "Plus forty-two ostriches. When that's done we'll be ready for anything. We can defy the cosmos." He suddenly went purple in the face, snatched up the phone and yelled. "Tyler! Tyler."

When that worthy appeared he said, "Blow your nose and tight-beam this message: *Why forty-two ostriches?"*

It went out, scrambled and unscrambled and rescrambled, upward, downward, rightward, leftward, recited in Sirian-Kham lowlands accents and Terran-Scottish highlands accents and many more. But it got there just the same.

Yes, it got there.

General Railton glanced up from a thick wad of documents and rapped impatiently. "What is it?"

"Top secret message from Motan, sir."

Taking it. Railton looked it over.

We've fought two ostriches.

"Ashmore!" he yelled. "Pennington! Whittaker!"

They came on the rim, lined up before his desk, assumed habitual expressions of innocence. He eyed them as though each was personally responsible for something dastardly.

"What," he demanded, "is the meaning of this?"

He tossed the signal-form at Pennington, who gave it the glassy eye and passed it to Whittaker, who examined it fearfully and got rid of it on Ashmore. The latter scanned it, dumped it back on the desk. Nobody said anything.

"Well," said Railton, "isn't there a useful thought among the three of you?"

Picking up courage, Pennington ventured, "It must be in code, sir."

"It is clearly and plainly captioned as being in straight."

"That may be so, sir. But it doesn't make sense in straight."

"Do you think I'd have summoned you here if it did?" Railton let go a snort that quivered his mustaches. "Bring me the current code-book. We'll see if we can get to the bottom of this."

They fetched him the volume then in use, the sixth of Series B. He sought through it at length. So did they, each in turn. No ostriches.

"Try the earlier books," Railton ordered. "Some fool on Motan may have picked up an obsolete issue."

So they staggered in with a stack of thirty volumes, worked back to BA. No ostriches. After that, they commenced on AZ and laboriously headed toward AA.

Pennington, thumbing through AK, let go a yelp of triumph. "Here it is, sir. An ostrich is a food supply and rationing code-word located in the quartermaster section."

"What does it mean?" inquired Railton, raising expectant eyebrows.

"One gross of fresh eggs," said Pennington, in the manner of one who sweeps aside the veil of mystery.

"Ah!" said Railton, in tones of exaggerated satisfaction. "So at last we know where we stand, don't we? Everything has become clear. On Motan they've beaten off an attack by three hundred fresh eggs, eh?"

Pennington looked crushed.

"Fresh eggs," echoed Ashmore. "That may be a clue!"

"What sort of clue?" demanded Railton, turning attention his way.

"In olden times," explained Ashmore, "the word fresh meant impudent, bold, brazen. And an egg was a person. Also, a hoodlum or thug was known as a hard egg or a tough egg."

"If you're right, that means Motan has resisted a raid by three hundred impertinent crooks."

"Offhand, I just can't think of any more plausible solution," Ashmore confessed.

"It's not credible," decided Railton. "There are no pirates out that way. The only potential menace is the Zengs. If a new and previously unsuspected lifeform has appeared out there, the message would have said so."

"Maybe they meant they've had trouble with Zengs," suggested Whittaker.

"I doubt it," Railton said, "In the first place, the Zengs would not be so dopey as to start a war by launching a futile attack with a force a mere three hundred strong. In the second place, if the culprits were Zengs the facts could have been stated. On the tight-beam system there's no need for Motan to be obscure."

"That's reasonable enough," Ashmore agreed.

Railton thought things over, said at last, "The message looks like a routine report. It doesn't call for aid or demand fast action. I think we'd better check back. Beam them asking which book they're quoting."

Out it went, up, down and around, via a mixture of voices.

Which code-book are you using?

Tyler sniffed, handed it over, saluted, sniffed again and ambled out, Commander Hunter picked it up.

Which goad-hook are you using?

"Maxwell! Maxwell!" When the other arrived, he said, "There'll never be an end to this. What's a goad-hook?"

"I'd have to look it up in the catalogue."

"Meaning that you don't know?"

"There's about fifty kinds of hooks," informed Maxwell defensively. "And for many of them there are technical names considerably different from space-navy names or even stores equipment names. A tension-hook, for instance, is better known as a tightener."

"Then let's consult the book." Getting it from the safe, Hunter opened it on the desk while Maxwell positioned himself to look over the other's shoulder. "What'll it be listed under?" Hunter asked. "Goad-hooks or hooks, goad? G or H?"

"Might be either."

They sought through both. After checking item by item over half a dozen pages, Maxwell stabbed a finger at a middle column.

"There it is."

Hunter looked closer. "That's *guard-hooks:* things for fixing wire fence to steel posts. Where's *goad*-hooks?"

"Doesn't seem to be any," Maxwell admitted. Suddenly suspicion flooded his features and he went on, "Say, do you suppose this has anything to do with those ostriches?"

"Darned if I know. But it's highly probable."

"Then," announced Maxwell, "I know what a goad-hook is. And you won't find it in that catalogue."

Slamming the book shut, Hunter said wearily, "All right. Proceed to enlighten me."

"I saw a couple of them in use," informed Maxwell. "Years ago, in the movies."

"The movies?"

"Yes. They were showing an ostrich farm in South Africa. When the farmer wanted to extract a particular bird from the flock, he used a pole about eight to ten feet long. It had a sort of metal prod on one end and a wide hook at the other. He'd use the sharp end to poke other birds out of the way, then use the hook end to snake the bird he wanted around the bottom of its neck and drag it out."

"Oh," said Hunter, staring at him.

"It's a thing like bishops carry for lugging sinners into the path of righteousness," Maxwell finished.

"Is it really?" said Hunter, blinking a couple of times. "Well, it checks up with that signal about the ostriches." He brooded a bit, went on, "But it implies that there is more than one kind of goad-hook. Also, that we are presumed to have one particular pattern in stores here. They want to know which one we've got. What are we going to tell them?"

"We haven't got any," Maxwell pointed out. "What do we need goad-hooks for?"

"Ostriches," said Hunter. "Forty-two of them."

Maxwell thought it over. "We've no goad-hooks, not one. But they think we have. What's the answer to that?"

"You tell me," Hunter invited.

"That first message warned us that the ostriches were coming on any cheap line of communication, obviously meaning a chartered tramp-ship. So they won't get here for quite a time. Meanwhile, somebody has realized that we'll need goad-hooks to handle them and shipped a consignment by fast service-boat. Then he's discovered that he can't remember which pattern he's sent us. He can't fill out the necessary forms until he knows. He's asking you to give with the information."

"If that's so," commented Hunter, "some folk have a nerve to tight-beam such a request and mark it top secret!"

"Back at Terran H.Q.," said Maxwell, "one is not shot at dawn for sabotage, treachery, assassination or any equally trifling misdeed. One is blindfolded and stood against the wall for not filling out forms, or for filling out the wrong ones, or for filling out the right ones with the wrong details."

"Nuts to that!" snapped Hunter, fed up. "I'm wasting no time getting a headquarters dope out of a jam. We're supposed to have a consignment of goad-hooks. We haven't got it. I'm going to say so—in plain language." He boosted his voice a few decibels. "Tyler! Tyler!"

Half an hour later the signal squirted out, brief, to the point, lacking only its original note of indignation.

No goad hyphen hooks. Motan.

Holding it near the light, Railton examined it right way up and upside down. His mustache jittered. His eyes squinted slightly. His complexion assumed a touch of magenta.

"Pennington!" he bellowed. "Saunders! Ashmore Whittaker!"

Lining up, they looked at the signal-form. They shifted edgily around, eyed each other, the floor, the ceiling, the walls. Finally they settled for the uninteresting scene outside the window.

Oh God how I hate mutton.

"Well?" prompted Railton, poking this beamed revelation around his desk.

Nobody responded.

"First," Railton pointed out, "they're fighting it out with a pair of ostriches. Now they've developed an aversion to mutton. If there's a connection, I fail to see it. There's got to be an explanation somewhere. What is it?"

Nobody knew.

"We might as well invite the Zengs to accept everything as a gift," said Railton. "It'll save a lot of bloodshed."

Stung by that, Whittaker protested, "Motan is trying to tell us something, sir. They must have cause to express themselves the way they are doing."

"Perhaps they have good reason to think that the tight-beam is no longer tight. Maybe a Zeng interceptor station has opened right on one of the lines. So Motan is hinting that it's time to stop beaming in straight."

"They could have said so in code, clearly and unmistakably. There's no need to afflict us with all this mysterious stuff about ostriches and mutton."

Up spoke Saunders, upon whom the gift of tongues had descended. "Isn't it possible, sir, that ostrich flesh is referred to as mutton by those who eat it? Or that, perhaps, it bears close resemblance to mutton?"

"Anything is possible," shouted Railton, "including the likelihood that everyone on Motan is a few cents short in his mental cash." He fumed a bit, added acidly, "Let us assume that ostrich flesh is identical with mutton. Where does that get us?"

"It could be, sir," persisted Saunders, temporarily drunk with words, "that they've discovered a new and valuable source of food supply in the form of some large, birdlike creature which they call ostriches. Its flesh tastes like mutton. So they've signaled us a broad hint that they're less dependent upon supplementary supplies from here. Maybe in a pinch they can feed themselves for months or years. That, in turn, means the Zengs can't starve them into submission by blasting all supply ships to Motan. So—"

"Shut up!" Railton bawled, slightly frenzied. He snorted hard enough to make the signal form float off his desk. Then he reached for the phone. "Get me the Zoological Department . . . Yes, that's what I said." He waited a while, growled into the mouthpiece, "Is ostrich flesh edible and, if so, what does it taste like?" Then he listened, slammed the phone down and glowered at his audience, "Leather," he said.

"That doesn't necessarily apply to the Motan breed," Saunders pointed out. *"You* can't judge an alien species by—"

"For the last time, keep quiet!" He shifted his glare to Ashmore. "We can't go any further until we know which code they're using out there."

"It should be the current one, sir. They had strict orders to destroy each preceding copy."

"I know what it *should* be. But is it? We've asked about this and they haven't replied. Ask them again, by *direct*-beam. I don't care if the Zengs do pick up the question and answer. They can't make use of the information. They've known for years that we use code as an elementary precaution."

"I'll have it beamed right away, sir."

"Do that. And let me have the reply the minute it arrives." Then, to the four of them, "Get out of my sight."

The signal shot straight to Motan without any juggling around.

Identify your code forthwith. Urgent.

Two days later the answer squirted back and got placed on Railton's desk pending his return from lunch. In due course he paraded along the corridor and into his office. His thoughts were actively occupied with the manpower crisis in the Sirian sector and nothing was further from his mind than the antics of Motan. Sitting at his desk, he glanced at the paper.

All it said was, *BF.*

He went straight up and came down hard.

"Ashmore!" he roared. "Pennington! Saunders! Whittaker!"

Ex Terra Space Control. Direct-Beam. Straight. To Motan. Commander Hunter recalled forthwith. Captain Maxwell succeeds with rank of commander as from date of receipt.

Putting on a broad grin of satisfaction, Hunter reached for the phone. "Send Maxwell here at once." When the other arrived, he announced, "A direct-beam recall has just come in. I'm going home."

"Oh," said Maxwell without enthusiasm. He looked more disillusioned than ever.

"I'm going back to H.Q. You know what that means."

"Yes," agreed Maxwell, a mite enviously. "A nice, soft job, better conditions, high pay, quicker promotion."

"Dead right. It is only proper that virtue should be rewarded." He eyed the other, holding back the rest of the news. "Well, aren't you happy about it?"

"No," said Maxwell flatly.

"Why not?"

"I've become hardened to you. Now I'll have to start all over again and adjust myself to some other nut."

"No you won't, chum. *You're* taking charge." He poked the signal form across the desk. "Congratulations. Commander!"

"Thanks," said Maxwell. "For nothing. Now I'll have to handle your grief. Ostriches. Forty-two of them."

At midnight Hunter stepped aboard the destroyer D10 and waved good-by. He did it with all the gratified assurance of one who's going to get what's coming to him. The prospect lay many weeks away but was worth waiting for.

The ship snored into the night until its flame trail faded out to the left of Motan's fourth moon. High above the opposite horizon glowed the Zeng's two planets of Korima and Koroma, one blue, the other green. Maxwell eyed the shining firmament, felt the weight of new responsibility pressing hard upon his shoulders.

He spent the next two weeks checking back on his predecessor s correspondence, familiarizing himself with all the various problems of planetary governorship. At the end of that time he was still baffled and bothered.

"Tyler!" Then when the other came in, "Man, can't you stop perpetually snuffling? Send this message out at once."

Taking it, Tyler asked, "Tight- or straight-beam, sir?"

"Don't send it direct-beam. It had better go by tight. The subject is tagged top secret by H.Q. and we've got to accept their definition."

"Very well, sir." Giving an unusually loud sniff, Tyler departed and squirted the query to the first repeater station.

Why are we getting ostriches?

It never reached Railton or any other brass hat. It fell into the hands of a new Terran operator who'd become the victim of three successive technical gags. He had no intention whatsoever of being made a chump a fourth time. So he read it with eyebrows waggling.

When are we getting ostriches?

With no hesitation he destroyed the signal and smacked back at the smarty on Motan.

Will emus do?

In due course Maxwell got it, read it twice, walked twice around the room with it and found himself right back where he'd started.

Will amuse you.

For the thirtieth time in four months Maxwell went to meet a ship at the spaceport. So far there had arrived not a goad-hook, not a feather, not even a caged parrot.

It was a distasteful task because every time he asked a captain whether he'd brought the ostriches, he got a look that pronounced him definitely tetched in the head.

Anyway, this one was not a tramp-boat. He recognized its type even before it sat down and cut power—a four-man Zeng scout. He also recognized the first Zeng to scramble down the ladder. It was Tormin, the chief military officer on Koroma.

"Ah, Mr. Maxwell," said Tormin, his yellow eyes worried. "I wish to see the commander at once."

"Hunter's gone home. I'm the commander now. What's your trouble?"

"Plenty," Tormin informed. "As you know, we placed ordinary settlers on Korima. But on the sister planet of Koroma we placed settlers and a large number of criminals. The criminals have broken out and seized arms. Civil war is raging on Koroma. We need help."

"Sorry, but I can't give it," said Maxwell. "We have orders that in no circumstances whatever may we interfere in Zeng affairs."

"I know, I know," Tormin gestured excitedly with long, skinny arms. "We do not ask for your ships and guns. We are only too willing to do our own dirty work. Besides, the matter is serious but not urgent. Even if the criminals conquer the planet they cannot escape from it. We have removed all ships to Korima."

"Then what do you want me to do?"

"Send a call for help. We can't do it—our beam-station is only half built."

"I am not permitted to make direct contact with the Zeng authorities," said Maxwell.

"You can tell your own H.Q. on Terra. They'll inform our ambassador there. He'll inform our nearest forces."

"That'll mean some delay."

"Right now there's no other way," urged Tormin. "Will you please oblige us? In the same circumstances we'd do as much for you."

"All right." agreed Maxwell, unable to resist this appeal. "The responsibility for getting action will rest with H.Q., anyway." Bolting to his office, he gave Tyler the message, adding, "Better send it tight-beam, just in case some Zeng stickler for regulations picks it up and accuses us of poking our noses in."

Out it went, to and fro, up and down, in one tone or another, this accent or that.

Civil war is taking place among local Zengs. They are asking for assistance.

It got there a few minutes behind Hunter, who walked into Railton's office, reached the desk, came smartly to attention.

"Commander Hunter, sir, reporting from Motan."

"About time, too," snapped Railton, obviously in no mood to give with a couple of medals. "As commander of Motan you accepted full responsibility for the text of all messages beamed therefrom, did you not?"

"Yes, sir," agreed Hunter, sensing a queer coldness in his back hairs.

Jerking open a drawer, Railton extracted a bunch of signal forms, slapped them on the desk.

"This," he informed, mustache quivering, "is the appalling twaddle with which I have been afflicted since Motan's station came into operation. I can find only one explanation for all this incoherent rubbish about ostriches and mutton, that being that you're overdue for mental treatment. After all, it is not unknown for men on alien planets to go off the rails."

"Permit me to say, sir—" began Hunter.

"I don't permit you," shouted Railton. "Wait until I have finished. And don't flare your nostrils at me. I have replaced you with Maxwell. The proof of your imbecility will be the nature of the next signals from Motan."

"But sir—"

"Shut up! I will let you see Maxwell's messages and compare them with your own irrational nonsense. If that doesn't convince—"

He ceased his tirade as Ashmore appeared and dumped the signal-form on his desk.

"Urgent message from Motan, sir."

Railton snatched it up and read it while Ashmore watched and Hunter fidgeted uneasily.

Sibyl Ward is making faces among local Zengs. They are asking for her sister.

The resulting explosion will remain a space legend for all time.

The Ultimate Invader

Planet Stories, January 1953

1.

The little ship, scarred and battered, sat on the plain and cooled its tubes and ignored the armed guard that had surrounded it at a safe distance. A large, bluish sun burned overhead, lit the edges of flat, waferlike clouds in brilliant purple. There were two tiny moons shining like pale specters low in the east, and a third was diving into the westward horizon.

To the north lay the great walled city whence the guard had erupted in irate haste. It was a squat, stark conglomeration of buildings in gray granite, devoid of tall towers, sitting four-square to the earth. An unbeautiful, strictly utilitarian place suitable for masses of the humble living in subservience to the harsh.

At considerable altitude above the granite mass roamed its aerial patrol, a number of tiny, almost invisible dots weaving a tangle of vapor-trails. The dots displayed the irritated restlessness of a swarm of disturbed gnats, for their pilots were uncomfortably aware of the strange invader now sitting on the plain. Indeed, they would have intercepted it had that been possible, which it wasn't. How can one block the path of an unexpected object moving with such stupendous rapidity that its trace registers as a mere flick on a screen some seconds after the source has passed?

Upon the ground the troops kept careful watch and awaited the arrival of someone who was permitted the initiative that they were denied. All of them had either four legs and two arms or four arms and two legs, according to the need of the moment. That is to say: the front pair of under-body limbs could be employed as feet or hands, like those of a baboon. Superior life does not establish itself by benefit of brains alone; manual dexterity is equally essential. The quasi-quadrupeds of this world had a barely adequate supply of the former compensated by more than enough of the latter.

Although it was not for them to decide what action to take against this sorry-looking object from the unknown, they had plenty of curiosity concerning it, and no little apprehension. Much of their noseyness was stimulated by the fact that the vessel was of no identifiable type despite that they could recognize all the seventy patterns common to the entire galaxy. The apprehension was created by the sheer nonchalance of the visitor's arrival. It had burst like a superswift bullet through the detector-screen that enveloped the entire planet, treated the sub-stratosphere patrols with disdain and sat itself down in clear view of the city.

Something drastic would have to be done about it, on that point one and all were agreed. But the correct tactics would be defined by authority, not by underlings. To make up his own mind one way or the other was a presumptuous task not one of them dared undertake. So they hung around in dips and behind rocks, and scratched and held their guns and hankered for the brass in the city to wake up and come running.

In much the same way that planetary defenses had been brought to naught by bland presentation of an accomplished fact, so were the guards now disturbed by being confronted with an event when none were present who were qualified to cope. Giving distant sluggards no time to make up their minds and spring into action, the ship's lock opened and a thing came out.

As a sample of unfamiliar life he was neither big nor fearsome. A biped with two arms, a pinkish face and close-fitting clothes, he was no taller than any of the onlookers and not more than one-third the weight. A peculiar creature in no way redoubtable. In fact he looked soft. One could jump on him with all four feet and squash him.

Nevertheless one could not hold him entirely in contempt. There were aspects that gave one to pause and think. In the first place, he was carrying no visible weapons and, moreover, doing it with the subtle assurance of one who has reason to view guns as so much useless lumber. In the second place, he was mooching airily around the ship, hands in pockets, inspecting the scarred shell for all the world as if this landing marked a boring call on tiresome relatives. Most of the time he had his back to the ring of troops, magnificently indifferent to whether or not anyone chose to blow him apart.

Apparently satisfied with his survey of the vessel, he suddenly turned and walked straight toward the hidden watchers. The ship's lock remained wide open in a manner suggesting either criminal carelessness or supreme confidence, more probably the latter. Completely at peace with a world in the midst of war, he ambled directly toward a section of guards, bringing the need for initiative nearer and nearer, making them sweat with anxiety and creating such a panic that they forgot to itch.

Rounding a rock, he came face to face with Yadiz, a common trooper momentarily paralyzed by sheer lack of an order to go forward, go backward, shoot the alien, shoot himself, or do something. He looked casually at Yadiz as if different life-forms in radically different shapes were more common than pebbles. Yadiz became so embarrassed by his own futility that he swapped his gun from hand to hand and back again.

"Surely it's not that heavy," remarked the alien with complete and surprising fluency. He eyed the gun and sniffed.

Yadiz dropped the gun which promptly went off with an ear-splitting crash and a piece of rock flew into shards and something whined shrilly into the sky. The alien turned and followed the whine with his eyes until finally it died out.

Then he said to Yadiz, "Wasn't that rather silly?"

There was no need to answer. It was a conclusion Yadiz already had reached about one second before the bang. He picked up the gun with a foot-hand, transferred it to a real hand, found it upside-down, turned it right way up, got the strap tangled around his fist, had to reverse it to get the limb free, turned it right way up again.

Some sort of answer seemed to be necessary but for the life of him Yadiz could not conceive one that was wholly satisfactory. Struck dumb, he posed there holding his weapon by the muzzle and at arm's length, like one who has recklessly grabbed a mamba and dares not let go. In all his years as a trooper, of which there were more than several, he couldn't recall a time when possession of a firearm had proved such a handicap. He was still searching in vain for a verbal means of salvaging his self-respect when another trooper arrived to break the spell.

A little breathless with haste, the newcomer looked askance at the biped, said to Yadiz, "Who gave you orders to shoot?"

"What business is it of yours?" asked the biped, coldly disapproving. "It's his own gun, isn't it?"

This interjection took the arrival aback. He had not expected another life-form to speak with the fluency of a native, much less treat this matter of wasting ammunition from the angle of personal ownership. The thought that a trooper might have proprietary rights in his weapon had never occurred to him. And now that he had captured the thought he did not know what to do with it. He stared at his own gun as if it had just miraculously appeared in his hand, changed it to another hand by way of ensuring its realness and solidity.

"Be careful," advised the biped. He nodded toward Yadiz. "That's the way *he* started."

Turning to Yadiz, the alien said in calm, matter-of-fact tones, "Take me to Markhamwit."

Yadiz couldn't be sure whether he actually dropped the gun again or whether it leaped clean out of his hands. Anyway, it did not go off.

2.

They met the high brass one-third of the way to the city. There was an assorted truckload ranging from two to five-comet rank. Bowling along the road on flexible tracks, the vehicle stopped almost level with them and two dozen faces peered at the alien. A paunchy individual struggled out from his seat beside the driver and confronted the ill-assorted pair. He had a red metal sun and four silver comets shining on his harness.

To Yadiz he snapped, "Who told you to desert the guard-ring and come this way?"

"Me," informed the alien, airily.

The officer jerked as if stuck with a pin, shrewdly eyed him up and down and said, "I did not expect that you could speak our language."

"I'm fully capable of speech," assured the biped. "I can read, too. In fact, without wishing to appear boastful, I'd like to mention that I can also write."

"That may be," agreed the officer, willing to concede a couple of petty aptitudes to the manifestly outlandish. He had another careful look. "Can't say that I'm familiar with your kind of life."

"Which doesn't surprise me," said the alien. "Lots of folk never get the chance to become familiar with us."

The other's color heightened. With a show of annoyance, he informed, "I don't know who you are or what you are, but you're under arrest."

"Sire," put in the aghast Yadiz, "he wishes to—"

"Did any one tell you to speak?" demanded the officer, burning him down with his eyes.

"No, sire. It was just that—"

"Shut up!"

Yadiz swallowed hard, took on the apprehensive expression of one unreasonably denied the right to point out that the barrel is full of powder and someone has lit the fuse.

"Why am I under arrest?" inquired the alien, not in the least disturbed.

"Because I say so," the officer retorted.

"Really? Do you treat all arrivals that way?"

"At present, yes. You may know it or you may not, but right now this system is at war with the system of Nilea. We're taking no chances."

"Neither are we," remarked the biped, enigmatically.

"What do you mean by that?"

"The same as you meant. We're playing safe."

"Ah!" The other licked satisfied lips. "So you are what I suspected from the first, namely, an ally the Nileans have dug up from some very minor system that we've overlooked."

"Your suspicions are ill-founded," the alien told him. "However, I would rather explain myself higher up."

"You will do just that," promised the officer. "And the explanation had better be satisfactory."

He did not care for the slow smile he got in reply. It irresistibly suggested that someone was being dogmatic and someone else knew better. Neither had he any difficulty in identifying the respective someones. The alien's apparently baseless show of quiet confidence unsettled him far more than he cared to reveal, especially with a dopey guard standing nearby and a truckload of brass looking on.

It would have been nice to attribute the two-legger's sang-froid to the usual imbecility of another life-form too dimwitted to know when its scalp was in danger. There were plenty of creatures like that: seemingly brave because unable to realize a predicament even when they were in it up to the neck. Many of the lower ranks of his own forces had that kind of guts. Nevertheless he could not shake off the uneasy feeling that this case was different. The alien looked too alert, too sharp-eyed to make like a cow.

Another and smaller truck came along the road. Waving it to a stop, he picked four two-comet officers to act as escort, shooed them into the new vehicle along with the biped who entered without comment or protest.

Through the side window he said to the officers, "I hold you personally responsible for his safe arrival at the interrogation center. Tell them I've gone on to the ship to see whether there's any more where he came from."

He stood watching on the verge while the truck reversed its direction, saw it roll rapidly toward the city. Then he clambered into his own vehicle which at once departed for the source of all the trouble.

Devoid of instructions to proceed toward town, return to the ship, stand on his head or do anything else, Yadiz leaned on his gun and patiently awaited the passing of somebody qualified to tell him.

The interrogation center viewed the alien's advent as less sensational than the arrival of a Joppelan five-eared munkster at the zoo. Data drawn from a galaxy was at the disposal of its large staff and the said information included descriptions of four hundred separate and distinct life-forms, a few of them so fantastic that the cogent material was more deductive than demonstrative. So far as they were concerned this sample brought the record up to four hundred and one. In another century's time it might be four hundred twenty-one or fifty-one. Listing the lesser lifes was so much routine.

Interviews were equally a matter of established rigmarole. They had created a standard technique involving questions to be answered, forms to be filled, conclusions to be drawn. Their ways of dealing with recalcitrants were, however, a good deal more flexible, demanding various alternative methods and a modicum of imagination. Some life-forms responded with pleasing alacrity to means of persuasion that other life-forms could not so much as sense. The only difficulty they could have with this specimen was that of thinking up an entirely new way of making him see reason.

So they directed him to a desk, giving him a chair with four armrests and six inches too high, and a bored official took his place opposite. The latter accepted in advance that the subject could already speak the local tongue or communicate in some other understandable manner. Nobody was sent to this place until educated sufficiently to give the required responses.

Switching his tiny desk-recorder, the interviewer started with, "What is your number, name, code, cipher or other verbal identification?"

"James Lawson."

"Sex, if any?"

"Male."

"Age?"

"None."

"There now," said the interviewer, scenting coming awkwardness. "You must have an age."

"Must I?"

"Everyone has an age."

"Have they?"

"Look," insisted the interviewer, very patient, "nobody can be ageless."

"Can't they?"

He gave it up, murmuring, "It's unimportant anyway. His time-units are meaningless until we get his planetary data." Glancing down at his question sheet, he carried on. "Purpose of visit?" His eyes came up as he waited for the usual boring response such as, "Normal exploration." He repeated, "Purpose of visit?"

"To see Markhamwit," responded James Lawson.

The interviewer yelped, *"What?"*, cut off the recorder and breathed heavily for a while. When he found voice again it was to ask, "You really mean you've come specially to see the Great Lord Markhamwit?"

"Yes."

He asked uncertainly, "By appointment?"

"No."

That did it. Recovering with great swiftness, the interviewer became aggressively officious and growled, "The Great Lord Markhamwit sees nobody without an appointment."

"Then kindly make one for me."

"I'll find out what can be done," promised the other, having no intention of doing anything whatsoever. Turning the recorder on again, he resumed with the next question.

"Rank?"

"None."

"Now look here—"

"I said *none!"* repeated Lawson.

"I heard you. We'll let it pass. It's a minor point that can be brought out later." With that slightly sinister comment he tried the next question. "Location of origin?"

"The Solarian Combine."

Flip went the switch as the unlucky desk instrument again got put out of action. Leaning backward, the interviewer rubbed his forehead. A passing official glanced at him, stopped.

"Having trouble, Dilmur?"

"Trouble?" he echoed bitterly. He mooned at his question sheet. "What a day! One thing after another! Now this!"

"What's the matter?"

He pointed an accusative finger at Lawson. "First he pretends to be ageless. Then he gives the motive behind his arrival as that of seeing the Great Lord without prior arrangement." His sigh was deep and heartfelt. "Finally, to top it all, he claims that he comes from the Solarian Combine."

"H'm! Another theological nut," diagnosed the passer-by. "Don't waste your time on him. Pass him along to the mental therapists." Giving the subject of the conversation a cold look of reproof he continued on his way.

"You heard that?" The interviewer felt for the recorder switch in readiness to resume operation. "Now do we get on with this job in a reasonable and sensible manner or must we resort to other, less pleasant methods of discovering the truth?"

"The way you put it implies that I am a liar," said Lawson, displaying no resentment.

"Not exactly. Perhaps you are a deliberate but rather stupid liar whose prevarications will gain him nothing. Perhaps you may have no more than a distorted sense of humor. Or you may be completely sincere because completely deluded. We have had visionaries here before. It takes all sorts to make a universe."

"Including Solarians," Lawson remarked.

"The Solarians are a myth," declared the interviewer with the positiveness of one stating a long-established fact.

"There are no myths. There are only gross distortions of half-remembered truths."

"So you still insist that you are a Solarian?"

"Certainly."

The other shoved the recorder aside, got up from his seat, "Then I can go no further with you." He summoned several attendants, pointed to the victim. "Take him to Kasine."

3.

The individual named Kasine suffered glandular maladjustment that made him grossly obese. He was just one great big bag of fat relieved only by a pair of deep-sunk but brilliantly glittering eyes.

Those optics looked at Lawson in much the same way that a cat stares at a cornered mouse. Completing the inspection, he operated his recorder, listened to a play-back of what had taken place during the previous interview.

Then a low, reverberating chuckle sounded in his huge belly and he commented, "Ho-ho, a Solarian! And lacking a pair of arms at that! Did you mislay them someplace?" Leaning forward with a manifest effort, he licked thick lips and added, "What a dreadful fix you'll be in if you lose the others also!"

Lawson gave a disdainful snort. "For an alleged mental therapist you're long overdue for treatment yourself."

It did not generate the fury that might well have been aroused in another. Kasine merely wheezed with amusement and looked self-satisfied.

"So you think I'm sadistic, eh?"

"Only at the time you made that remark. Other moments: other motivations."

"Ah!" grinned Kasine. "Whenever you open your mouth you tell me something useful."

"You could do with it," Lawson opined.

"And it seems to me," Kasine went on, refusing to be baited, "that you are not an idiot."

"Should I be?"

"You should! Every Solarian is an imbecile." He ruminated a moment, went on. "The last one we had here was a many-tendriled octoped from Quamis. The authorities on his home planet wanted him for causing an end-of-the-world panic. His illusion of Solarianism was strong enough to make the credulous believe it. But we aren't foolish octopeds here. We cured him in the end."

"How?"

Kasine thought again, informed, "If I remember aright, we fed him a coated pellet of sodium and followed it with a jar of water. Whereupon he surrendered his stupidities with much fuss and shouting. He confessed his purely Quamistic origin shortly before his insides exploded." Kasine wagged his head in patronizing regret. "Unfortunately, he died. Very noisily, too."

"Bet you enjoyed every instant of it," said Lawson.

"I was not there. I dislike a mess."

"It will be worse when it's your turn," observed Lawson, eyeing the enormous body.

"Is that so? Well, let me tell—" He stopped as a little gong sounded in the depths of his desk. Feeling under the rim, he pulled out a small plug at the end of a line, inserted it in an ear and listened. After a while he put it back, stared at the other. "Two officers tried to enter your ship."

"That was foolish."

Kasine said heavily, "They are now lying on the ground outside, completely paralyzed."

"What did I tell you?" commented Lawson, rubbing it in.

Smacking a fat hand on the desk, Kasine made his voice loud. "What caused it?"

"Like all your kind, they are allergic to formic acid," Lawson informed. "It's a fact I had ascertained in advance." He gave a careless shrug. "A shot of diluted ammonia will cure them and they'll never have rheumatics as long as they live."

"I want no abstruse technicalities," harshed Kasine. "I want to know what caused it."

"Probably Freddy," thought Lawson, little interested. "Or maybe it was Lou. Or possibly Buzwuz."

"Buzwuz?" Kasine's eyes came up a bit from their fatty depths. He wheezed a while before he said, "The message informs that both were stabbed in the back of the neck by something tiny, orange-colored and winged. What was it?"

"A Solarian."

His self-control beginning to slip, Kasine became louder. "If you are a Solarian, which you are not, this other thing cannot be a Solarian too."

"Why not?"

"Because it is totally different. It has not the slightest resemblance to you in any one respect."

"Afraid you're wrong there."

"Why?"

"It is intelligent." Lawson examined the other as though curious about an elephant with a trunk at both ends. "Let me tell you that intelligence has nothing whatever to do with shape, form or size."

"Do you call it intelligent to stab someone in the neck?" asked Kasine, pointedly.

"In the circumstances, yes. Besides, the resulting condition is harmless and easily curable. That's more than you can say for an exploded belly."

"We'll do something about this." Kasine was openly irritated.

"It won't be easy. Take Buzwuz, for instance. Though he's small even for a bumblebee from Callisto, he can lay out six horses in a row before he has to squat down someplace and generate more acid."

"Bumblebee?" Kasine's brows tried to draw together over thick rolls of flesh. "Horses?"

"Forget them," advised Lawson. "You know nothing of either."

"Maybe not, but I do know this: they won't like it when we fill the ship with a lethal gas."

"They'll laugh themselves silly. And it won't pay you to make my vessel uninhabitable."

"No?"

"No! Because those already out of it will have to stay out. Most of the others will get out fast in spite of anything you can do to prevent their escape. After that, they'll have no choice but to settle down and live here. I would not like that if I were you: I wouldn't care for it one little bit."

"Wouldn't you?"

"Not if I were you which, fortunately, I am not. A world soon becomes mighty uncomfortable when you've got to share it with hard-to-catch enemies steadily breeding a thousand to your one."

Kasine jerked and queried with some apprehension, "Mean to say they'll actually remain here and increase that fast?"

"What else would you expect them to do once you've taken away their sanctuary? Go jump in the lake just to please you? They're intelligent, I tell you. They will survive even if they have to paralyze every one of your kind in sight and make it permanent."

The gong clanged again. Inserting the ear-plug, Kasine listened, scowled, shoved it back into its place. For a short time he sat glowering across the desk. When he did speak it was irefully.

"Two more," he said. "Flat out."

Registering a thin smile, Lawson suggested, "Why not leave my ship alone and let me see Markhamwit?"

"Get this into your head," retorted Kasine. "If any and every crackpot who chose to land on this planet could walk straight in to see the Great Lord there would have been trouble long ago. The Great Lord would have been assassinated ten times over."

"He must be popular!"

"You are impertinent. You do not appear to realize the peril of your own position." Leaning forward with a grunt of discomfort, Kasine hushed his tones in sheer awe of himself. "Outside that door are those empowered merely to ask questions. Here, within this room, it is different. Here, I make decisions."

"Takes you a long time to get to them," said Lawson, unimpressed.

Ignoring it, the other went on, "I can decide whether or not your mouth gives forth facts. If I deem you a liar, I can decide whether or not it is worth turning to less tender means of obtaining the real truth. If I think you too petty to make even your truths worth having, I can decide when, where and how we shall dispose of you." He slowed down by way extra emphasis. "All this means that I can order your immediate death."

"The right to blunder isn't much to boast about," Lawson told him.

"I do not think your effective removal would be an error," Kasine countered. "Those creatures in your ship are impotent so far as this room is concerned. What is to prevent me from having you destroyed?"

"Nothing."

"Ah!" Slightly surprised by this frank admission, the fat face became gratified. "You agree that you are helpless to save yourself?"

"In one way, yes. In another, no."

"Meaning?"

"You can have me slaughtered if you wish. It will be a little triumph for you if you like that sort of thing." Lawson's eyes came up, looked levelly at the other's. "It would be wisest if you enjoyed the triumph to the full and made the very most of it, for it won't last long."

"Won't it?"

"Pleasure is for today. Regrets are for tomorrow. After the feast, the reckoning."

"Oho? And who will present the bill?"

"The Solarian Combine."

"There you go again!" Kasine rubbed his forehead wearily. "The Solarian Combine. I am sick and tired of it. Forty time have I faced so-called Solarians all of whom proved to be maniacs escaped or expelled from some not too faraway planet. But I'll give you your due for one thing: you're the coolest and most collected of the lot.

"I suspect that it is going to be rather difficult to bring you to your senses. We may have to concoct an entirely new technique to deal with you."

"Too bad," said Lawson, sympathetically.

"Therefore I—" Kasine broke off as the door opened and a five-comet officer entered in a hurry.

"Message from the Great Lord," announced the newcomer. He shot an uneasy glance at Lawson before he went on. "Regardless of any conclusion to which you may have come, you are to preserve this arrival intact, unharmed."

"That's taking things out of my hands," grumbled Kasine. "Am I not supposed to know the reasons?"

Hesitating a moment, the officer said, "I was not told to keep them from you."

"Then what are they?"

"This example of other-life must be kept in fit condition to talk. Reports have now come in from the defense department and elsewhere. We want to know how his ship slipped through the planetary detector-screen, how it got past the aerial patrols. We want to know why the vessel differs from all known types in the galaxy, where it comes from, what gives it such tremendous velocity. In particular, we must find out the capabilities and military potential of those who built the boat."

Kasine blinked at this recital. Each of these questions, he felt, was fully loaded and liable to go bang. The mind behind his ample features worked overtime. For all his gross bulk he was not without mental agility. And one thing he'd always been good at sniffing was the smell of danger.

Words and phrases whirled through his calculating brain: slipped past, origin, type of ship, tremendous velocity, bumblebees, the coolest and most collected. His brilliant and sunken eyes examined Lawson again. In the light of what the officer had brought he could now see more clearly the feature of this strange biped that inwardly had worried him most. It was a somewhat appalling certitude!

He felt impelled to take a gamble. If it did not come off he had nothing serious to lose.

If it did he would get the credit for great perspicacity.

Very slowly, Kasine said, "I think I can answer those questions in part. This creature claims that he is a Solarian. I consider it remotely possible that he may be!"

"May be! A Solarian!" The officer stuttered a bit, backed toward the door. "The Great Lord must know of this. I will tell him your decision at once."

"It is not a decision," warned Kasine, hastily ensuring himself against future wrath. "It is no more than a modest opinion."

He watched the other go out. Already he was beginning to wonder whether he had adopted the correct tactics or whether there was some other as yet unperceived but safer play.

His gaze turned toward the subject of his thoughts.

Lawson said, very comfortingly, "You've just saved your fat neck."

4.

Markhamwit went through the data for the fourth time, pushed the papers aside, walked restlessly up and down the room.

"I don't like this incident. I view it with the greatest suspicion. We may be victims of a Nilean trick."

"That is possible, my lord," endorsed Minister Ganne.

"Let's suppose they've invented an entirely new type of vessel they've reason to think invincible. The obvious step is to test it as conclusively as can be done. They must try it out before they adopt it in large numbers. If it can penetrate our defenses, land here and get out again, it's a success."

"Quite, my lord." Ganne had built his present status on a firm foundation of consistent agreement.

"But it would be a giveaway if it arrived with a Nilean crew aboard," Markhamwit went on, looking sour. "So they hunt for and obtain a non-Nilean life-form as ally. He comes here hiding himself behind a myth." He smacked one pair of hands together, then the other pair. "All this is well within the limits of probability. Yet, as Kasine thinks, the arrival's story may be true."

Ganne doubted it but refrained from saying so. Now and again the million-to-one chance turned up to the confusion of all who had brashly denied its possibility.

"Get me Zigstrom," decided Markhamwit suddenly. When the connection had been made he fitted the earplug, spoke into the thin tube, "Zigstrom, we have many authorities on the Solarian Myth. I have heard it said there are one or two who believe it to have a real basis. Who is the chief of these?"

He listened a bit, growled, "Don't hedge with me. I want his name. He has nothing to fear." A pause followed by, "Alemph? Find him for me. I must have him here without delay."

The required expert turned up in due course, sweaty with haste, disheveled and ill at ease. He came hesitantly into the room, bowing low at every second step.

"My lord, if Zigstrom has given you the impression that I am a leader of one of these foolish cults, I must assure you that—"

"Don't be so jittery," Markhamwit snapped. "I wish to pick your mind, not deprive you of your bowels." Taking a chair, he rested his four arms on its rests, fixed authoritative eyes upon the other. "You believe that the Solarian Myth is something more than a frontier legend. I want to know why."

"The story has repetitive aspects that are too much for mere coincidence," said Alemph. "And there are other and later items I consider significant."

"I have no more than perfunctory knowledge of the tale," Markhamwit informed. "In my position I've neither time nor inclination to study the folklore of our galaxy's outskirts. Be more explicit. You have been brought here to talk, not to suffer."

Alemph plucked up courage. "At one edge of our galaxy are eight populated solar systems fairly close together and arranged in a semicircle. They have a total of thirty-nine planets. At what would be the center of their circle lies a ninth system with seven inhabitable planets devoid of any life higher than the animals."

"I am aware of that much," commented Markhamwit. "Carry on."

"The eight populated systems have never developed space travel even to the present day. Yet when we first visited them we found they knew many things about each other impossible to learn by astronomical observation. They had a strange story to account for this knowledge. They said that at some unspecified time in the very far past they'd had repeated visits from the ships of the Elmones, a life-form occupying this ninth and now deserted system. All eight believe that the Elmones ultimately intended to master them by ruthless use of superior techniques. They were to be subdued and could do nothing effective to prevent it."

"But they weren't," Markhamwit observed.

"No, my lord. It is at this point that the myth really begins. All eight systems tell the same story. That is an important thing to remember. That is what I call too much for coincidence."

"Get on with it," ordered the Great Lord, showing a touch of impatience.

Continuing hurriedly, Alemph said, "Just at this time a strange vessel emerged from the mighty gulf between our galaxy and the next one, made its landing on the Elmones' system as the most highly developed in that area. It carried a crew of two small bipeds. They claimed the seemingly impossible feat of having crossed the gulf. They called themselves Solarians. There was only one piece of evidence to support their amazing claim: their vessel had so tremendous a turn of speed that while in flight it could neither be seen nor detected."

"And then?"

"The Elmones were by nature incurably brutal and ambitious. They slaughtered the Solarians and pulled the ship to pieces in an effort to discover its secret. They failed absolutely. Many, many years later a second Solarian vessel plunged out of the enormous void. It came in search of the first and it soon suffered the same fate. Again its secret remained inviolable."

"I can credit that much," said Markhamwit. "Alien techniques are elusive when one cannot even imagine the basis from which they've started. Why, the Nileans have been trying—" He changed his mind about going on, snapped, "Continue with your story."

"It would seem from what occurred later that this second ship had borne some means of sending out a warning signal for, many years afterward, a third and far larger vessel appeared but made no landing. It merely circled each Elmone planet, dropped thousands of messages saying that where death is concerned it is better to give than receive. Maybe it also bathed each planet in an unknown ray, or momentarily embedded it in a force-field such as we cannot conceive, or dropped minute bacteria along with the messages. Nobody knows. The vessel disappeared into the dark chasm whence it came and to the present day the cause of what followed has remained a matter for speculation."

"And what did follow?"

"Nothing immediately. The Elmones made a hundred crude jokes about the messages which soon became known to the other eight systems. The Elmones proceeded with preparations to enslave their neighbors. A year later the blow fell, or it would be better to say began to fall. It dawned upon them that their females were bearing no young. Ten years later they were frantic. In fifty years they were numerically weak and utterly desperate. In one hundred years they had disappeared forever from the scheme of things. The Solarians had killed nobody, injured nobody, shed not a single drop of blood. They had contented themselves with denying existence to the unborn. The Elmones had been eliminated with a ruthlessness equal to their own but without their brutality. They have gone. There are now no Elmones in our galaxy or anywhere in Creation."

"A redoubtable tale ready-made for the numerous charlatans who have tried to exploit it," said Markhamwit. "The credulous are always with us. I am not easily to be taken in by tall tales of long ago. Is this all your evidence?"

"Begging your pardon, my lord," offered Alemph. "There are the seven inhabitable but deserted worlds still in existence. There is precisely the same story told by eight other systems who remained out of touch until we arrived. And, finally, there are these constant rumors."

"What rumors?"

"Of small, biped-operated and quite uncatchable ships occasionally visiting the smallest systems and loneliest planets in our galaxy."

"Bah!" Markhamwit made a gesture of derision. "We receive such a report every hundredth day. Our vessels repeatedly have investigated and found nothing. The lonely and the isolated will concoct any fanciful incident likely to entice company. The Nileans probably invent a few themselves, hoping to draw our ships away from some other locality. Why, we blew apart their battleship *Narsan* when it went to Dhurg to look into a story we'd permitted to reach their stupid ears."

"Perhaps so, my lord." Having gone so far, Alemph was not to be put off. "But permit me to point out that well as we may know our own galaxy, we know nothing of others."

Markhamwit eyed Minister Ganne. "Do you consider it possible for an intergalactic chasm to be crossed?"

"It seems incredible, my lord," said Ganne, more than anxious not to commit himself. "Not being an astronautical expert I am hardly qualified to give an opinion."

"A characteristic ministerial evasion," scoffed Markhamwit. Resorting to his earplug and voice tube again, he asked for Sector Commander Yielm, demanded, "Regardless of the practical aspect, do you think it theoretically possible for anyone to reach us from the next galaxy?" Silence while he listened, then, "Why not?" He listened again, cut off, turned to the others. "That's his reason: nobody lives for ten thousand years.

"How does he know, my lord?" asked Alemph.

Half a dozen guards conducted James Lawson to the august presence. They formed themselves into a stiff, expressionless row outside the door while he went into the room.

His approach from the entrance to the middle of the floor was imperturbable. Nothing in his manner betrayed slightest consciousness that he was very far from home and among a strange kind. Indeed, he mooched in casually as if sent on a minor errand to buy a pound of crackers.

Indicating a chair, Markhamwit spent most of a minute weighing up the visitor, then voiced his skepticism. "So you are a Solarian?"

"I am."

"You come from another galaxy?"

"That is correct."

Markhamwit shot a now-watch-this glance at Minister Ganne before he asked, "Is it not remarkable that you can speak our language?"

"Not when you consider that I was chosen for that very reason," replied Lawson.

"Chosen? By whom?"

"By the Combine, of course."

"For what purpose?" Markhamwit insisted. "To come here and have a talk with you."

"About what?"

"This war you're having with the Nileans."

"I knew it!" Folding his top arms, Markhamwit looked self-satisfied. "I knew the Nileans would come into this somewhere." His chuckle was harsh. "They are amateurish in their schemings. The least they could have done for you was to think up a protective device better than a mere myth."

"I am little interested in protective devices," said Lawson, carelessly. "Theirs or yours."

Markhamwit frowned. "Why not?"

"I am a Solarian."

"Is that so?" He showed his teeth, thin, white and pointed. "In that case our war with Nilea is none of your business."

"Agreed. We view it with splendid indifference."

"Then why come to talk about it?"

"Because we object to one of its consequences."

"To which one do you refer?" inquired Markhamwit, no more than mildly curious.

"Both sides are roaming the spaceways in armed vessels and looking for trouble."

"What of it?"

Lawson said, "The spaceways are free. They belong to everyone. No matter what rights a planet or a system may claim for its own earthly territory, the void between worlds is common property."

"Who says so?" demanded Markhamwit, scowling.

"We say so."

"Really?" Taken aback by the sheer impudence of it, the Great Lord invited a further display by asking, "And what makes Solarians think they can lay down the law?"

"We have only one reason," Lawson told him. His eyes took on a certain coldness. "We have the power to enforce it."

The other rocked back, glanced at Minister Ganne, found that worthy studiously examining the ceiling.

"The law we have established and intend to maintain," Lawson went on, "is that every space-going vessel shall have the right of unobstructed passage between worlds. What happens after it lands does not concern us unless it happens to be one of our own." He paused a moment, still cold-eyed, added, "Then it does concern us very much."

Markhamwit did not like that. He didn't like it one little bit. It smacked of an open threat and his natural instinct was to react with a counter-threat. But the interview with Alemph was still fresh in his mind and he could not rid his thoughts of certain phrases that kept running around and around like a dire warning.

"Fifty years later they were weak and desperate. In a hundred years they were gone—forever!"

He found himself wondering whether even now the ship in which this biped had arrived was ready to broadcast or radiate an invisible, unshieldable power designed to bring about the same result. It was a horrid thought. As a method of coping with incurably antagonist life-forms it was so perfect because so permanent. It smacked of the appalling technique of Nature herself, who never hesitated to exterminate a biological error.

One tended to think that this biped was talking out of the back of his neck. The tendency was born of hope that it was nothing but a tremendous bluff waiting to be called. One could call it all too easily by removing the bluffer's headpiece and tearing his ship apart.

As the Elmones were said to have done.

What Elmones? There were none!

Suppose that it was not bluff?

5.

Much as he hated to admit it even to himself, the situation had unexpectedly shaped up into a tough one. If in fact it was a cunning Nilean subterfuge it was becoming good enough to prove mighty awkward.

A ship had been dumped on this world, the governmental center of a powerful system at war. On the strength of an ancient fable and its pilot's glib tongue it claimed the ability to sterilize the entire planet. Therefore it was in effect either a mock-bomb or a real one. The only way in which to ascertain its real nature was to hammer on its detonator and try to make it explode.

Could he dare?

Playing for time, Markhamwit pointed out, "War is a two-sided affair. Our battleships are not the only ones patrolling in space."

"We know it," Lawson informed. "The Nileans are also being dealt with."

"You mean you've another ship there?"

"Yes." Lawson registered a faint grin. "The Nileans are stuck with the same problem, and doubtless are handicapped by the dark suspicion that it's another of your tricks."

The Great Lord perked up. It gave him malicious satisfaction to think of the enemy in a jam and cursing him for it. Then his mind suddenly perceived a way of at least partially checking the truth of the other's statements. He turned to Ganne.

"That neutral world of Vaile still has contact with both sides. Go beam it a call. Ask if the Nileans have a vessel claiming to be of Solarian origin."

Ganne went out. The answer could not be expected before nightfall yet he was back with it in a few moments.

Shaken and nervous, he reported, "The operators say Vaile called a short time ago. A similar question was put to us at the request of the Nileans."

"Hah!" Markhamwit found himself being unwillingly pushed toward Alemph's way of looking at the matter. Folklore, he decided, might possibly be founded on fact. Indeed, it was more likely to have a positive basis than not. Long-term effects had to have faraway causes.

Then just as he was nearing the conclusion that Solarians actually do exist it struck him with awful force that if this were a crafty stunt pulled by the Nileans they could be depended upon to back up their stooge in every foreseeable manner. The call through Vaile could he nothing more than a carefully planned byplay designed to lend verisimilitude to their deception. If so, it meant that he was correct in his first assumption: that the Solarian Myth was rubbish.

These two violently opposed aspects of the matter got him in a quandary. His irritation mounted because one used to making swift and final decisions cannot bear to squat on the horns of a dilemma. And he was so squatting.

Obviously riled, he growled at Lawson, "The right to unobstructed passage covers our vessels as much as anyone else's."

"It covers no warship bearing instructions to intercept, question, search or detain any other spaceship it considers suspicious," declared the other. "Violators of the law are not entitled to claim protection of the law."

"Can you tell me how to conduct a war between systems without sending armed ships through space?" asked Markhamwit, bitterly sarcastic.

Lawson waved an indifferent hand. "We aren't the least bit interested in that problem. It is your own worry."

"It cannot be done," Markhamwit shouted.

"That's most unfortunate," remarked Lawson, full of false sympathy. "It creates an awful state of no-war."

"Are you trying to be funny?"

"Is peace funny?"

"War is a serious matter," bawled Markhamwit, striving to retain a grip on his temper. "It cannot be ended with a mere flick of the finger."

"The fact should be borne in mind by those who so nonchalantly start them," advised Lawson, quite unmoved by the Great Lord's ire.

"The Nileans started it."

"They say that you did."

"They are incorrigible liars."

"That's their opinion of you, too."

A menacing expression on his face, Markhamwit said, "Do you believe them?"

"We never believe opinions."

"You are evading my question. Somebody has to be a liar. Who do you think it is?"

"We haven't looked into the root-causes of your dispute. It is not our woe. So without any data to go upon we can only hazard a guess."

"Go ahead and do some hazarding then," Markhamwit invited. He licked expectant lips.

"Probably both sides have little regard for the truth," opined Lawson, undeterred by the other's attitude. "It is the usual setup. When war breaks out the unmitigated liar comes into his own. His heyday lasts for the duration. After that, the victorious liars hang the vanquished ones."

Had this viewpoint been one-sided Markhamwit could have taken it up with suitable fury. A two-sided opinion is disconcerting. It's slippery. One cannot get an effective grip on it.

So he changed his angle of attack by asking, "Let's suppose I reject your law and have you shot forthwith. What happens then?"

"You'll be sorry."

"I have only your word for that."

"If you want proof you know how to get it," Lawson pointed out.

It was an impasse over which the Great Lord brooded with the maximum of disgust. He was realizing for the first time that by great daring one creature could defy a world of others. It had pregnant possibilities of which he had never previously thought. Some ingenious use could have been made of it, to the great discomfort of the enemy—assuming that the enemy had not thought of it first and were now using it against him.

There was the real crux of the matter, he decided. Somehow, anyhow, he had to find out whether the Nileans had a hand in this affair. If they had they would make every effort to conceal the fact. If they had not they would be only too willing to show him that his troubles were also theirs.

But then again, how deep was their cunning? Was it more than equal to his own perceptive abilities? Might they not be ready and willing to hide the truth behind a smoke screen of pathetically eager cooperation?

If this new ship actually was a secret Nilean production it followed that those who could build one could equally well build two. Also, the unknown allied world that had provided a biped stooge plus some winged, stinging creatures could provide a second set of pseudo-Solarians.

So even now another fake extra-galactic vessel and crew might be grounded on Nilean territory waiting the inspection of his own or some neutral deputation; everything prepared to convince him that fiction is fact and thereby persuade him to recall all warships from the spaceways. That would leave the foe a clear field for long enough to enable them to grasp victory. He and his kind would know that they had been taken for a ride only when it was too late. About the sole crumb of comfort he could find was the thought that if this were not an impudent hoax, if all this Solarianism were genuine and true, then the Nileans themselves were being tormented by exactly the same processes of reasoning. At this very moment they might be viewing with serious misgivings the very outfit that was causing all his bother, wondering whether or not the ship was supporting evidence born of the Great Lord's limitless foresight.

This picture of the Nileans' predicament served to soothe his liver sufficiently to let him ask, "In what way do you expect me to acknowledge this law of yours?"

Lawson said, "By ordering the immediate return of all armed vessels to their planetary bases."

"They'll be a fat lot of use to us just sitting on their home stations."

"I don't agree. They will still be in fighting trim and ready to oppose any attack. We deny nobody the right to defend themselves."

"That's exactly what we're doing right now," declared Markhamwit. "Defending ourselves."

"The Nileans say the same."

"I have already told you that they are determined and persistent liars."

"I know, I know." Lawson brushed it aside like a subject already worn thin. "So far as we are concerned you can smother every one of your own worlds under an immense load of warships ready to annihilate the first attacker. But if they fight at all it must be in defense of their territory. They must not roam around wherever they please and carry the war someplace else."

"But—"

"Moreover," Lawson went on, "you can have a million ships roaming freely through space if you wish. Their numbers, routes or destinations would be nobody's business, not even ours. We won't object so long as each and every one of them is a peaceful trader going about its lawful business and in no way interfering with other people's ships."

"You won't object?" echoed Markhamwit, his temper again tried by the other's airy self-confidence. "That is most gracious of you!"

Lawson eyed him coolly. "The strong can afford to be gracious."

"Are you insinuating that we are not strong?"

"Reasonableness is strength. Irrationality is weakness."

Banging a hand on a chair arm, Markhamwit declaimed, "There are many things I may be, but there is on thing I am not: I am not irrational."

"It remains to be seen," said Lawson significantly.

"And it will be seen! I have not become the ruler of a great system by benefit of nothing. My people do not serve under a leader whose sole qualification is imbecility. Given time for thought and the loyal support of those beneath me, I can cope with this situation or any other that may come along."

"I hope so," offered Lawson in pious tones. "For your own sake."

Markhamwit leaned forward, exposed his teeth once more and spoke slowly. "No matter what decision I may come to or what consequences may follow, the skin in danger is not mine. It is yours!" He straightened up, made a motion of dismissal. "I will give my answer in the morning. Until then, do plenty of worrying about yourself."

"A Solarian deeply concerned about his own fate," Lawson informed, his hand on the door, "would be rather like one of your hairs bothered about falling out." Opening the door, he stared hard at the Great Lord and added, "The hair goes and is lost and becomes at one with the dust, but the body remains."

"Meaning—?"

"You're not dealing with me as an individual. You are dealing with my kind."

6.

The guard was alerted and accompanied Lawson to the interrogation center, left him at the precise spot where they had first picked him up. Going through the door, he closed it behind him, thus cutting himself off from their view. In leisurely manner he ambled past desks where examiners looked up from their eternal piles of forms to watch him uncertainly. He had reached the main exit before anyone saw fit to dispute his progress.

An incoming three-comet officer barred his way and asked, "Where are you going?"

"Back to my ship."

The other showed vague surprise. "You have seen the Great Lord?"

"Of course. I have just left him." Then with a confiding air, "We had a most interesting conversation. He wishes to consult with me again first thing in the morning."

"Does he?" The officer's eyes hugely magnified Lawson's importance. It did not take him a split second to conceive a simple piece of logic: to look after Markhamwit's guest would be to please Markhamwit himself. So with praiseworthy opportunism he said, "I will get a truck and run you back."

"That is very considerate of you," assured Lawson, looking at the three comets as if they were six.

It lent zip to the other's eagerness. The truck was forthcoming in double-quick time, rolled away before Ganne or Kasine or anyone else could intervene to question the propriety of letting the biped run loose. Its speed was high, its driver inclined to be garrulous.

"The Great Lord is a most exceptional person," he offered, hoping it might be repeated in his favor on the morrow. Privately he thought Markhamwit a pompous stinker. "We are most fortunate to have such a leader in these trying times."

"You could have one worse," agreed Lawson, blandly damning Markhamwit with faint praise.

"I remember once—" The other broke off, brought the vehicle to an abrupt stop, scowled toward the side of the road. In a rasping voice he demanded of the new object of his attention, "Who gave you orders to stand there?"

"Nobody," admitted Yadiz, dolefully.

"Then why are you there?"

"He cannot be somewhere else," remarked Lawson.

The officer blinked, studied the windshield in complete silence for a while, then twisted to face his passenger.

"Why can't he?"

"Because wherever he happens to be *is* there. Obviously he cannot be where he isn't." Lawson sought confirmation of Yadiz. "Can you?"

Something snapped, for the other promptly abandoned all further discussion, flung open the truck's door with a resounding crash and snarled at Yadiz, "Get inside, you gaping idiot!"

Yadiz got in, handling his weapon as if it could bite him at both ends. The truck moved forward. For the remainder of the trip its driver hunched over the wheel, chewed steadily at his bottom lip and said not a word. Now and again his eyebrows knotted with the strain of thought as he made vain attempts to sort out the unsortable.

At the guard-ring the paunchy individual who had first consigned the arrival to the interrogation center watched the truck jerk to a stop and the trio get out. He came up frowning.

"So they have let him go?"

"Yes," said the driver, knowing no better.

"Whom did he see?"

"The Great Lord himself."

The other gave a little jump, viewed Lawson with embarrassed respect and took some of the authority out of his tones,

"They didn't say what is to be done about these four casualties we've suffered?"

"Made no mention of them," the driver answered. "Maybe they—"

Lawson chipped in, "I'll tend to them. Where are they?"

"Over there." He indicated a dip to his left. "We couldn't shift them pending instructions."

"It wouldn't have mattered. They'd have recovered by this time tomorrow, anyway."

"It isn't fatal then?"

"Not at all," Lawson assured. "I'll go get them a shot of stuff that will bring them to life in two ticks."

He went toward the ship. The driver climbed moodily into his truck and headed back to town.

The creature perched on the rim of the little controlroom's observation-port was the size of Lawson's fist. Long extinct Terran bees would have thought it a giant among their kind. Modern Callistrian ones might have regarded the Terran variety as backward pygmies had there been any real consciousness of Callistrianism or Terranism or any other form of planetary parochialism.

But at this far advanced stage of development of an entire solar system there had ceased to be an acute awareness of worldly origin, shape or species. A once essential datum in the environment had been discarded and no longer entered into the computations of anyone. The biped was not mentally biased by his own bipedal form; the insect not obsessed by its insectual condition. They knew themselves for what they were, namely, Solarians and two aspects of one colossal entity that had a thousand other facets elsewhere.

Indeed, the close-knit relationship between life-forms far apart in shape and size but sharing a titanic oneness in psyche had developed to the point where they could and did hold mental intercourse in a manner not truly telepathic. It was "self-thinking," the natural communion between parts of an enormous whole.

So Lawson had no difficulty in conversing with a creature that had no aural sense adequately attuned to the range of his voice, no tongue with which to speak. The communication came easier than any vocal method, was clear and accurate, left no room for linguistic or semantic boobytraps, no need to explain the meaning of meaning.

He flopped into the pilot's seat, gazed meditatively through the port and opined, "I'm not sanguine about them being reasonable."

"It does not matter," commented the other. "The end will be the same."

"True, Buzwuz, but unreasonableness means time and trouble."

"Time is endless; trouble another name for fun," declared Buzwuz, being profound. He employed his hind legs to clean the rear part of his velvet jacket.

Lawson said nothing. His attention shifted to a curiously three-dimensional picture fastened to the side wall. It depicted four bipeds, one of whom was a swart dwarf, also one dog wearing sun-glasses, six huge bees, a hawk-like bird, a tusked monster vaguely resembling a prick-eared elephant, something else like a land-crab with long-fingered hands in lieu of claws, three peculiarly shapeless entities whose radiations had fogged part of the sensitive plate, and finally a spider-like creature jauntily adorned with a feathered hat.

This characteristically Solarian bunch was facing the lens the stiff, formal attitudes favored by a bygone age and so obviously were waiting for the birdie that they were unconsciously comical. He treasured this scene for its element of whimsy, also because there was immense significance in the amusing similarity of pose among creatures so manifestly unconscious of their differences. It was a picture of unity that is strength; unity born of a handful of planets and a double-handful of satellites circling a common sun.

Another bee-mind as insidious as part of his own came from somewhere outside the ship, saying, "Want us back yet?"

"No hurry."

"We're zooming around far beyond the city," it went on. "We've shown ourselves within reach of a few of them. They swiped at us without hesitation. And they meant it!" A pause, followed by, "They have instinctive fear of the unfamiliar. Reaction-time about one-tenth second. Choice of reaction: that which is swiftest rather than that which is most effective. Grade eight mentalities lacking unity other than that imposed upon them from above."

"I know." Lawson squirmed out of his seat as a heavy hammering sounded on the ship's shell somewhere near the air-lock. "Don't go too far away, though. You may have to come back in a rush."

Going to the lock, he stood in its rim and looked down at a five-comet officer. The caller had an air of irateness tempered by apprehension. His eyes kept surveying the area above his head or straining to see past the biped's legs lest something else spring out to the attack.

"You're not supposed to be here," he informed Lawson.

"Aren't I? Why not?"

"Nobody gave you permission to return."

"I don't need permission," Lawson told him.

"You cannot come back without it," the other contradicted.

Registering an expression of mock-bafflement, Lawson said, 'Then how the deuce did I get here?"

"I don't know. Someone blundered. That's his worry and not mine."

"Well, what *are* you worrying about?" Lawson invited.

"I've just had a message from the city ordering me to check on whether you are actually here because, if so, you shouldn't be. You ought to be at the interrogation center."

"Doing what?"

"Awaiting their final decisions."

"But they aren't going to make any," said Lawson, with devastating positiveness. "It is we who will make the final ones."

The other didn't like the sound of that. He scowled, watched the sky, kept a wary eye on what little he could see of the ship's interior.

"I've been instructed to send you to the city at once."

"By whom?"

"Military headquarters."

"Tell them I'm not going before morning."

"You've got to go now," insisted the officer.

"All right. Invite your superiors at headquarters to come and fetch me."

"They can't do that."

"I'll say they can't!" agreed Lawson, with hearty emphasis.

This was even less to the visitor's taste. He said, "If you won't go voluntarily you'll have to be taken by force."

"Try it."

"My troops will receive orders to attack."

"That's all right with me. You go shoo them along. Orders are orders, aren't they?"

"Yes, but—"

"And," Lawson continued firmly, "it's the order-givers and not the order-carry-outers who'll get all the blame, isn't it?"

"The blame for what?" inquired the officer, very leerily.

"You'll find out!"

The other stewed it a bit. What would be found out, he decided, was anyone's guess, but his own estimate was that it could well be something mighty unpleasant. The biped's attitude amounted to a guarantee of that much.

"I think I'll get in touch again, tell them you refuse to leave this vessel and ask for further instructions," he decided rather lamely.

"That's the boy," endorsed Lawson, showing hearty approval. "You look after yourself and yourself will look after you."

7.

The Great Lord Markhamwit paced up and down the room in the restless manner of one burdened by an unsolvable problem. Every now and again he made a vicious slap at his harness, a sure sign that he was considerably exercised in mind and that his liver was feeling the strain.

"Well," he snapped at Minister Ganne, "have *you* been able to devise a satisfactory way out?"

"No, my lord," admitted Ganne, ruefully.

"Doubtless you retired and enjoyed a good night's sleep without giving it another thought?"

"Indeed, no, I—"

"Never mind the lies. I am well aware that everything is left to me." Going to his desk he employed its plug and tube, asked, "Has the biped started out yet?" Getting a response, he resumed his pacing. "At last he condescends to come and see me. He will be here in half a time-unit."

"He refused to return yesterday," remarked Ganne, treating disobedience as something completely outside all experience. "He viewed all threats with open disdain and practically invited us to attack his ship."

"I know. I know." Markhamwit dismissed it with an irritated wave of the hand. "If he is a bare-faced bluffer it can be said to his credit that he is a perfect one. There is the real source of all the trouble."

"In what way, my lord?"

"Look, we are a powerful life-form, so much so that after we have defeated the Nileans we shall be complete masters of our entire galaxy. Our resources are great, our resourcefulness equally great. We are highly scientific. We have spaceships and formidable weapons of war. To all intents and purposes we have conquered the elements and bent them to our will. That makes us strong, does it not?"

"Yes, my lord, very strong."

"It also makes us weak," growled Markhamwit. "This problem dumped in our laps proves that we are weak in one respect, namely, we have become so conditioned in dealing with concrete things that we don't know how to cope with intangibles. We match rival ships with better ships, enemy guns with bigger guns. But we are stalled immediately when a foe abandons all recognized methods of warfare and resorts to what may be no more than a piece of sheer, unparalleled impudence."

"Surely there must be some positive way of checking the truth and—"

"I can think of fifty ways." Markhamwit ceased his trudging and glared at Ganne as if that worthy were personally responsible for the predicament. "And the beauty of them all is that not one is genuinely workable."

"No, my lord?"

"No! We could check on whether Solarians actually do exist in the next galaxy if our ships could get there, which they can't. And neither can any other ship, according to Yielm. We could make direct contact with the Nileans, call off the war and arrange mutual action against Solarian interlopers, but if the whole affair is a Nilean trick they will continue to deceive us to our ultimate downfall. Or we could seize this biped, strap him to an operating table and cut the truth out of him with a scalpel."

"That ought to be the best way," ventured Ganne, seeing nothing against it.

"Undoubtedly, if his story is a lot of bluff. But what if it is not?"

"Ah!" said Ganne, feeling for an itch and pinching deep into his hide.

"The whole position is fantastic," declared Markhamwit. "This two-armed creature comes here without any weapons identifiable as such. Not a gun, not a bomb, not a ray-projector. So far as we know there isn't so much as a bow and arrow on his boat. His kind have killed nobody, injured nobody, shed not a drop of blood either now or in our past, yet he claims powers of a kind we hesitate to test."

"Do you suppose that we are already sterilized and therefore doomed, like the Elmones?" Ganne asked, plainly uneasy.

"No, certainly not. If he had done such a thing he would have blasted off during the night because there would be no point in dickering with us any longer."

"Yes, that's true." Ganne felt vastly relieved without knowing why.

Markhamwit continued, "Anyway, he's said nothing whatever about such methods of dealing with us. We know of them only fictionally, as part of the Solarian Myth. The sole threats he has made are that if we destroy him we shall then have to cope with those winged creatures who will remain here to outbreed us, and that if by some means we succeed in destroying them also, we shall still have to face whatever the Combine may bring against us later on. I cannot imagine the true nature of that particular menace except that by our standards it will be unorthodox."

"Their methods may represent the normal ways of warfare in their own galaxy," Ganne pointed out. "Perhaps they never got around to inventing guns and high explosives."

"Or perhaps they discarded them a million years ago in favor of techniques less costly and more effective." Markhamwit cast an impatient glance at the time recorder whirring on the wall. "Trickery or not, I have learned a valuable lesson from this incident. I have learned that tactics are more important than instruments, wits are better than warheads. If we had used our brains a bit more we might have persuaded the Nileans to knock themselves out and save us a lot of bother. All that was needed was a completely original approach."

"Yes, my lord," agreed Ganne, privately praying that he would not be commanded to suggest one or two original approaches.

"What I want to know," Markhamwit went on, bitterly, "and what I must know is whether the Nileans have thought of it first and are egging us on to knock ourselves out. So when this self-professed Solarian arrives I'm going to—"

He ceased as a knock sounded, the door opened and the captain of the guard showed himself, bowing low.

"My lord, the alien is here."

"Show him in."

Plumping heavily into a chair, Markhamwit tapped restless fingers on four armrests and glowered at the door.

Entering blithely, Lawson took a seat, smiled at the waiting pair and asked, "Well, does civilization come to these parts or not?"

It riled the Great Lord, but he ignored the question, controlled his temper and said heavily, "Yesterday you returned to your vessel contrary to my wishes."

"Today your warships are still messing around in free space contrary to ours." Lawson heaved a sigh of resignation. "If wishes were fishes we'd never want for food."

"You appear to forget," informed Markhamwit, "that in this part of the cosmos it is my desires that are fulfilled and not yours!"

"But you've just complained about yours being ignored," remarked Lawson, pretending surprise.

Markhamwit licked sharp teeth. "It won't happen again. Certain individuals made the mistake of letting you go unopposed, without question. They will pay for that. We have a way with fools."

"So have we!"

"That is something of which I require proof. You are going to provide it." His voice had an authoritative note. "And what is more, you are going to provide it in the way I direct, to my complete satisfaction."

"How?" inquired Lawson.

"By bringing the Nilean high command here to discuss this matter face to face."

"They won't come."

"I guessed you'd say that. It was such a certainty that I could have said it for you." Markhamwit displayed satisfaction with his own foresight. "They've thought up an impudent bluff. Now they're called upon to support it in person by chancing their precious hides. That is too much. That is taking things too far. So they won't do it." He threw a glance at Minister Ganne. "What did I tell you?"

"I don't see how the Nileans or anyone else can bolster a non-existent trick," offered Lawson, mildly.

"They could appear before me to argue the problem. That would be convincing so far as I'm concerned."

"Precisely!"

Markhamwit frowned. "What d'you mean, precisely?"

"If it's a stunt of their own contriving why shouldn't they back it to the limit and risk a few lives on it? The war is on and they've got to suffer casualties anyway. If they can dig up volunteers for one dangerous mission they can find them for another."

"So?"

"But they won't gamble one life on a setup they suspect to be of your making. There's no percentage in it."

"It is not of my making. You know that."

"The Nileans don't," said Lawson.

"You claim to have another ship on their world. What's it there for if not to persuade them?"

"You're getting your ideas mixed."

"Am I?" Markhamwit's grip was tight on the arms of his chair. He'd almost had enough of this biped. "In what way?"

"The vessel is there solely to tell the Nileans to cease cluttering the space lanes—or else! We're not interested in your meetings, discussions or wars. You can kiss and be friends or fight to the death and it makes not the slightest difference to us one way or the other. All that we're concerned about is that space remains free, preferably by negotiation and mutual agreement. If not, by compulsion."

"Compulsion?" snapped Markhamwit. "I would give a great deal to learn exactly how much power your kind really does possess. Perhaps little more than iron nerves and wagging tongues."

"Perhaps," admitted Lawson, irritatingly indifferent.

"I'll tell you something you don't know," Markhamwit leaned forward, staring at him. "Our first, second, third and fourth battle fleets have dispersed. Temporarily I've taken them out of the war. It's a risk, but worth it."

"Doesn't alter the situation if they're still chasing around here, there and everywhere."

"On the contrary it may alter the situation very considerably if we have a fair measure of luck," contradicted Markhamwit, watching him closely. "They have been redirected into colossal hunt. I now have a total of seventeen thousand vessels scouting all cosmic sectors recently settled or explored by Nileans. Know what they are looking for?"

"I can guess."

"They're seeking a minor, unimportant, previously unnoticed planet populated by pink-skinned bipeds with hard faces and gabby mouths. If they find it"—he swept an arm in a wide, expressive arc—"we'll blow them clean out of existence and the Solarian Myth along with them."

"How nice."

"We shall also deal with you in suitable manner. And we'll settle with the Nileans once and for all."

"Dear me," offered Lawson, meditatively. "Do you really expect us to sit around forever while you play hunt the slipper?"

For the umpteenth time thwarted by the other's appalling nonchalance, Markhamwit lay back without replying. For a wild moment he toyed with the notion that perhaps the Nileans were infinitely more ingenious than he'd first supposed and were taking him for a sucker by manning their ship with remotely controlled robots. That would account for this biped's unnatural impassivity. If he were nothing more than the terminal instrument of some highly complicated array of electronic apparatus operated by Nilean science from afar, it would account for his attitude. A talking-machine has no emotions.

But it just wasn't possible. Months ago, before the war started, a radio-beamed message to the nearest fringe of Nilean's petty empire had to be relayed from planet to planet, system to system, took a long time to get there, an equally long time for a reply to come back. It was completely beyond the power of any science, real or imaginary, so to control an automaton across many light years that it could respond conversationally with no time lag whatsoever.

Lawson, he decided uneasily, was robotic in some ways but definitely not a robot. Rather was he a life-form possessed of real individuality plus a queer something else impossible to describe. A creature to whom an unknown quantity or quality has been added and therefore unlike anything formerly encountered.

Emerging from his meditations, he growled, "You'll sit around because you'll have no choice about the matter. I have ordered that you be detained pending my further decision."

"That doesn't answer my question," Lawson pointed out.

"Why doesn't it?"

"I asked whether you expect *us* to sit around. What you see fit to do with this portion can have no effect upon the remainder."

"This portion," echoed Markhamwit, his air that of one not sure whether he has heard aright. "I have got *all* of you!" He pressed a stud on his desk.

Lawson stood up as the guards came in, smiled thinly and said, "I can tell you a fable of the future. There was once an idiot who picked a grain of sand from a mountain, cupped it in the palm of his hand and said, 'Look, I am holding a mountain!' "

"Take him away," bawled Markhamwit at the escort. "Keep him behind bars until I want him again."

Watching them file out, and the door close, he fumed a bit. "Creating cock-eyed problems for others is a game at which two can play. In this existence one has to use one's wits."

"Undoubtedly, my lord," indorsed Minister Ganne, dutifully admiring him.

8.

James Lawson carefully surveyed his cell. Large and fairly comfortable, with a queer-shaped bed, a thick, straw-stuffed mattress, the inevitable four-armed chair, a long, narrow table. A generous basket of fruit stood on the middle of the latter, also some brownish objects resembling wholemeal cakes.

He was as amused by the sight of the food as he had been by the rough courtesy with which the guard had conducted him here. Evidently Markhamwit had been specific in his instructions. Put him in the jug. Don't harm him, don't starve him, but put him in the jug.

Markhamwit wanted it both coming and going. The Great Lord was establishing a claim to kindness as a form of insurance against whatever might befall while, at the same time, keeping the victim just where he wanted him until thoroughly satisfied that nothing dreadful could or would befall.

There was a small barred window twenty feet up, more for ventilation than for light. The only other opening was the big grille across the entrance. A guard sat on a stool the other side of the bars boredly reading a narrow but thick cylindrical scroll which he unwound slowly as his gaze followed the print down.

Tilting back in the chair and resting his heels on the end rim of the bed, Lawson had a look at his ship. This was fully as easy as staring at the blank walls of the cell. All that was necessary was to readjust his mind and look through other eyes elsewhere. It can be done, indeed it becomes second nature when the mind behind the other eyes is to all intents and purposes a part of one's own.

He got a multiple picture because he was looking through multiple lenses, but he was accustomed to that. Meeting and knowing other shapes and forms is as nothing compared with the experience of actually sharing them, even those employing organs stranger than eyes.

The ship was resting exactly as he'd left it. Its lock still stood wide open but nobody was entering or attempting to do so. The guards maintained their ring, watched the vessel in the perfunctory manner of those already sick of the sight of it.

As he studied the scene the swiftly moving eyes swung low, dived toward an officer who loomed enormously with sheer closeness. The officer made a wild swipe at the eyes with a short sword curved two ways like a double sickle. Involuntarily Lawson blinked, for it came like a slash at his own head. His neck went taut as the shining blade whistled through the space occupied by his gullet had he been there in person.

"Someday, Lou," he thought, "I'll do as much for you. I'll give you a horrible nightmare."

The bee-mind came back. "Ever looked through somebody landbound, trying to escape danger on legs and without wings? That *is* a nightmare!" A pause as what could be seen through his optics showed him to be zooming skyward. "Want out yet?"

"No hurry," Lawson answered.

Withdrawing from that individual he reangled his mind and let it reach outward, tremendously outward. This, too, was relatively easy. The velocity of light is sluggish, creeping when compared with near-instantaneous contact between mental components of a psychic whole. Thought is energy, light is energy, matter is energy, but the greatest of these is thought.

Some day his enormously advanced multikind might prove a thesis long evolved: that energy, light and matter are creations of super-thought. They were getting mightily near to it already: just one or perhaps two more steps to godhood when they'd have finally established the mastery of mind over matter by using the former to create the latter according to their needs.

So there was no time lag in his reaching for the central world of Nilea, nor would there have been one of any handicapping duration had he reached across the galaxy and over the gulf into the next. He merely thought "at" his objective and was there, seeing through eyes exactly like his own at the interior of a ship exactly like his own except in one respect: it harbored no big bees.

This other vessel's crew consisted of one biped named Edward Reeder and four of those fuzzy, shapeless entities who had fogged his souvenir picture. A quartet of Rheans, these, from a moon of the ringed planet. Rheans in name only; Solarians in long-established fact.

Callistrian bees wouldn't be of much avail in coping with Nileans who were likely to hang around inviting hearty stings for the sheer pleasure of resulting intoxication. Their peculiar make-up enabled them to get roaring drunk on any acid other than hydrofluoric, and even that corrosive stuff was viewed as a liquid substitute for scoot berries.

But the Nileans were south-eyed, scanning a band of the spectrum that ran well into the ultra violet. And one has to be decidedly north-eyed to see a Rhean with real clarity. So far as local life-forms were concerned this Solarian vessel was crewed by one impertinent biped and several near-ghosts. Like most creatures suffering optical limitations, the Nileans suspected, disliked—aye, feared—living things never more than half visible.

It might have been the same with other Solarians in their attitude toward peculiar fellows from a moon of the ringed planet but for one thing: that which cannot be examined visually can be appreciated and understood mentally. The collective Rhean mind was as much intimate part of the greater Solarian mass-mentality as was any other part. The bipeds and the bees had phantom brothers.

* * * * * * * *

Reeder was thinking "at" him, "I've just returned from the third successive interview with their War Board, which is bossed by a hairy bully named Glastrom. He's completely obsessed by the notion that your Markhamwit is trying to outsmart him."

"Similar reaction at this end. I've been stuck in clink while Markhamwit waits for destiny to intervene in his favor."

"They've come near trying the same tactic with me," informed Reeder's mind, showing strange disinterest in whether or not the other was being made to suffer during his incarceration. "Chief item that has made them hesitate is the problem of what do about the rest of us." His gaze shifted a moment to the shadowy, shapeless quartet posing nearby. "The boys put over a mild demonstration of what can be done by wraiths with the fidgets. They switched off the city's light and power and so forth while crosseyed guards fired at the minor moon. The Nileans didn't like it."

"Can't say they're overfond of our crowd here, either." Lawson paused thoughtfully, went on, "Chronic distrust on both sides is preventing conformity with our demands and seems likely to go on doing so until the crack of doom. Markhamwit is in a mental jam and his only solution is to play for time."

"Same way with Glastrom and the War Board."

"Limit their time," interjected four laconic but penetrating thought-forms from the shapeless ones.

"Limit their time," simultaneously endorsed several bee-minds from a source much nearer.

"Give them one time-unit," confirmed a small and varied number of entities scattered through the galaxy.

"Give them one time-unit," decided an enormous composite mentality far across the gulf.

"Better warn them right away." Reeder's eyes showed him to be making for the open lock. His mind held no thought of personal peril that might arise from this ultimatum. He was as ageless as that of which he was part, and as deathless because, whether whole or destroyed, he was part of that which can never die. Like Lawson, he was man plus men plus other creatures. The first might disappear into eternal nothingness, but the plus-quantities remained for ever and ever and ever.

For the same reasons Lawson followed the same course in much the same way. The intangible thread of his thought-stream snapped back from faraway places and the eyes he now looked through were entirely his own. Taking his heels off the bed, he stood up, yawned, stretched himself, went to the grille.

"I've got to speak to Markhamwit at once."

Putting down the scroll, the guard registered the disillusioned expression of one who hopes everlastingly for peace and invariably hopes in vain.

"The Great Lord will send for you in due course," he informed. "Meanwhile you could rest and have a sleep."

"I do not sleep."

"Everybody sleeps sometimes or other," asserted the guard, unconsciously dogmatic. "They have to."

"Speak for yourself," advised Lawson. "I've never slept in my life and don't intend to start now."

"Even the Great Lord sleeps," mentioned the guard with the air of one producing incontrovertible evidence.

"You're telling me?" Lawson inquired.

The other gaped at him, sniffed around as if seeking the odor of a dimly suspected insult. "My orders are to keep watch upon you until the Great Lord wishes to see you again."

"Well, then, ask him if he so wishes."

"I dare not."

"All right, ask someone who does dare."

"I'll call the captain of the guard," decided the other with sudden alacrity.

He went along the passage, came back in short time with a larger and surlier specimen who glowered at the prisoner and demanded, "Now, what's all this rubbish?"

Eyeing him with exaggerated incredulity, Lawson said, "Do you really dare to define the Great Lord's personal affairs as rubbish?"

The captain's pomposity promptly hissed out of him like gas from a pricked balloon. He appeared to shrink in size and went two shades paler in the face. The guard edged away from him like one fearful of being contaminated by open sedition.

"I did not mean it that way."

"I sincerely hope not," declared Lawson, displaying impressive piety.

Recovering with an effort, the captain asked, "About what do you want to speak to the Great Lord?"

"I'll tell you after you've shown me your certificate."

"Certificate?" The captain was mystified. "Which certificate?"

"The document proving that you have been appointed the censor of the Great Lord's conversations."

The captain said hurriedly, "I will go and consult the garrison commander."

He went away with the pained expression of one who has put his foot in it and must find somewhere to scrape it off. The guard resumed his seat on the stool, mooned at Lawson, killed a cootie.

"I'll give him a hundred milliparts," Lawson remarked. "If he's not back by then, I'm coming out."

The guard stood up, hand on gun, face showing alarm. "You can't do that."

"Why not?"

"You are locked in."

"Hah!" said Lawson as if enjoying a secret joke.

"Besides, I am here."

"That's unfortunate for you," Lawson sympathized. "Either you'll shoot me or you won't. If you don't, I'll walk and Markhamwit will be most annoyed. If you do, I'll be dead and he'll be infuriated." He shook his head slowly. "Tsk-tsk! I would not care to be you!"

His alarm mounting to a near-unbearable point, the guard tried to watch the grille and the end of the passage at the same time. His relief was intense when the captain reappeared and ordered him to unlock.

The officer said to Lawson, "The commander passed on your request. You will be permitted to talk over the line to Minister Ganne. The rest is up to him."

Leading the way, with the guard in the rear, he conducted the prisoner to a small office, signed to a plug and tube. Taking them up, Lawson held the plug to his ear, it being too big to fit in the locally accepted manner. At the same time his mind sent out a soundless call shipwards.

"This is as good a time as any."

Then he listened to the plug and heard Ganne saying, "What you want to tell the Great Lord can be told to me."

"Pass him the news that he's got seven-eighths of a time-unit," Lawson suggested. "They've wasted the other eighth at this end."

Out one corner of his eye he noted the listening captain registering surly displeasure. His gaze lifted, observed that the door and two windows were half open. Lou, Buzwuz and the others would have no trouble, no trouble at all.

"He's got seven-eighths of a time-unit?" echoed Ganne, his voice rising a fraction. "To do what?"

"Beam his orders for recall."

"Recall?"

Lawson said with tired patience, "You're only wasting valuable moments repeating the end of each sentence. You know what I meant. You were there all the time, listening to our talk. You're not hard of hearing, are you?"

Ganne snapped, "I'll stand for no gross impertinence from you. I want to know precisely what you mean by saying that the Great Lord has seven-eighths of a time-unit."

"It's more like thirteen-sixteenths now. He has got to take action by then."

"Has he?" sneered Ganne. "Well, suppose he doesn't?"

"We'll take it."

"That comes well from you. You're in no—" His voice broke off as another one sounded authoritatively in the background. More dimly he could be heard saying, "Yes, my lord. It's the biped, my lord."

Behind him in the little office Lawson could also hear something else: a low drone coming nearer, nearer, through the door, through the window. There were exclamations from the other pair, a few scuffling, jumping noises, two thin yelps, two dull thumps and silence.

Markhamwit came on the line, spoke in harsh tones. "If you hope to precipitate the issue by further bluff, you are very much mistaken." Then with added menace, "Reports from my fleets have now started to come in. Sooner or later I'll get the one for which I am waiting. I shall then deal with you rather drastically."

"You've now got approximately three-quarters of a time-unit," Lawson gave back. "At the end of that period we shall take the initiative, do whatever we consider to be for the best. It won't be drastic because we shed no blood, take no lives. All the same, it will be quite effective."

"Will it?" Markhamwit emitted sardonic chuckles. "In that case I will do part of that which you require of me. In other words, I will institute action at the exact moment you have nominated. But it will be the action I deem best fitted to the circumstances."

"Time's marching on," remarked Lawson. The drone had left the room but could still be heard faintly from somewhere outside. He could see the soles of a pair of recumbent jack-boots lying near his own feet.

"You cannot get to your ship, neither can you communicate with it," Markhamwit went on, highly pleased with the situation. "And in precisely three-quarters of a time-unit there will be no ship to which you can return. The aerial patrol will have blasted it clean out of existence while it sits there, a steady target that cannot be missed."

"Can't it?"

"The sterilizing apparatus, if there is one, will be vaporized with it before it can be brought into action. Any winged things left flying around will be wiped out one by one as and when opportunity occurs. Since you've seen fit to push this matter to a sudden conclusion I am prepared to take a chance on anything the Solarian Combine may do." Finally, with sarcasm, "*If* there is a Solarian Combine and *if* it can do anything worth a moment's worry."

He must have flung down the plug and tube at his end, for his voice went less distinct as he said to Ganne, "Get Yielm for me. I'm going to show those Nileans that hoodwinking is a poor substitute for bombs and bullets."

Dumping his own end of the line, Lawson turned, stepped over two bodies unable to do more than curse him with their eyes. Going outside, he found himself in a large yard.

He crossed this diagonally under the direct gaze of half a dozen guards patrolling the wall top. Curiosity was their only reason for watching him, the interesting spectacle of a life-form not listed among the many with which they were familiar. It was his manifest confidence that fooled them, his unmistakable air of having every right to be going wherever he was going. Nobody thought to question it, not a momentary notion of escape crossed their minds.

Indeed, one of them obliged by operating the lever that opened the end gate, and lived to damn the day when he permitted himself to be misled by appearances. Not to be out-done, another whistled a passing truck which stopped for the fugitive. And the driver, too, found later reason to deplore the pick-up.

Lawson said to the driver, "Can you take me to that ship on the plain?"

"I'm not going that far."

"It's a matter of major importance. I've just been speaking to Minister Ganne about it."

"Oh, what did he say?"

"He put me on to the Great Lord who told me I've got little more than half a time-unit to spare."

"The Great Lord," breathed the other, with becoming reverence. He revved up, sent the truck racing onward. "I'll get you there in plenty of time."

There was no need to burst through the guard-ring; it no longer existed. Troops had been withdrawn to a safe distance, assembled in a solid bunch, and were leaning on their arms like an audience awaiting a rare spectacle. A couple of officers danced and gestured as the truck swept alongside the ship, but they were far off, well beyond calling distance, and the driver failed to notice them.

"Thanks!" Lawson tumbled out of the cab. "One good turn deserves another, so I'm telling you to get out faster than you came."

The other blinked at him. "Why?"

"Because in about one-fifth of a time-unit a dollop of bombs will land right here. You'll make it with plenty to spare provided you don't sit there gaping."

Though puzzled and incredulous, the driver saw clearly that this was a poor time to probe further into the matter. Taking the offered advice, he got out fast, his vehicle rocking with sheer speed.

Lawson entered the lock, closed it behind him. He did not bother to inquire whether all his crew were aboard. He knew that they were there in the same way that they had known of his impending return and intended take-off.

Dumping himself into the pilot's seat he fingered the controls, eyed the ship's chronometer thoughtfully. He'd got just seventy-two milliparts in which to beat the big bang. So he shifted a tiny lever one notch and went out from under.

The vacuum created by the vessel's departure sucked most of the troops' hats from their heads. High above, the aerial patrol swooped and swirled, held on to its missiles and sought in vain for the target.

9.

The world was a wanderer, a planet torn loose from its parent sun by some catastrophe far back in the tremendous past. At an equally distant time in the future it would be captured by some other star and either join the new family or be destroyed. Meanwhile it curved aimlessly through space, orphan of a bygone storm.

It wasn't cold, it wasn't dark. Internal fires kept it warm. Eternal stars limned it in pale, ethereal light. It had tiny, pastel-shaded flowers and thin, delicate trees that pushed their feet toward the warmth and kept their faces to the stars. It also held sentient life, though not of its own creation.

There were fourteen ships on this uncharted sphere. Eleven were Solarian. One was Nilean. Two belonged to the Great Lord Markhamwit. The Solarian vessels were grouped together in a gentle valley in one hemisphere. The remainder were on the opposite side of the planet, the Nileans separated from their foes by a couple of hundred miles, each combatant unaware of the other's existence.

The situation of these last two groups was a curious one. Each of their three ships had detected the gypsy-sphere at times a few days apart and landed upon it in the hope of discovering bipeds or, at least, gaining some clue to their whereabouts. Each crew had promptly suffered an attack of mental aberration verging upon craziness, exploded the armory, wrecked the vessel and thus marooned themselves. Each crew now sat around stupified by their own idiocy and thoroughly convinced that not another spaceship existed within a billion miles.

The secret of this state of affairs reposed with two of the eleven Solarian vessels. These had on board a number of homarachnids, spiderish quasi-humans from a place unknown to the galaxy, a hot, moist world called Venus. It happened that this world circled around an equally unknown sun called Sol. Which meant that the homarachnids were Solarians along with the bipeds and bees and semivisible fuzzies.

From the purely military viewpoint there was nothing redoubtable about homarachnids. They were unsoldierly, knew nothing of weapons and cared nothing either. They were singularly lacking in technical skills, viewed even a screwdriver as a cumbersome, patience-straining device. Outwardly, their most noticeable feature was an incurable penchant for wearing the most incongruous feathered hats that the milliners of Venus could devise. In some respects they were the most child-like of the Solarian medley. In one way they were the most deeply to be feared, for they had refractive minds.

With the absolute ease of those to whom it comes naturally any homarachnid could concentrate the great Solarian mass-mentality, projecting it and focusing it where required. The burning point of an immense magnifying glass was as nothing to the effect caused when a non-Solarian mind became the focal point of an attentive homarachnid's brain. The result was temporary but absolute mental mastery.

It *had* to be temporary. The Solarian ethic denied the right to bring any mind into permanent subjection, for that would amount to slavery of the soul. But for this, any pair of homarachnids could have compelled antagonistic warlords to "see reason" in a mere couple of milliparts. But mentally imposed agreement is worth nothing if it disappears the moment the cause is removed. The final aim must be to persuade Markhamwit and Glastrom to cooperate from motives of expediency and for keeps. The same ethic insisted that this goal be reached without spilling of life fluids if possible or else at cost of blood only to the high and mighty.

Nobody knew better than Solarians that wars are not caused, declared or willingly fought by nations, planetary peoples or shape-groups, for these consist in the main of plain, ordinary folk who crave nothing more than to be left alone. The real culprits are power-drunken cliques of near-maniacs who by dint of one means or another have coerced the rest. These were the ones to provide the blood if any was going to be shed at all.

Lawson and Reeder and the rest knew the operations of the Solarian mass-mind as well as they knew their own, for it was composed in part of their own. They were sharers in an intellectual common property. Therefore no issuing of detailed orders was necessary to get them to do whatever might be needed. Decisions reached them in identically the same form as if thought out by their independent selves.

As others had found to their cost and would do so again and again, the Solarians had an immense advantage in being able to give highly organized battle without benefit of complicated signaling and communications systems. So far as Solarians were concerned, lack of such antiquated technical adjuncts was lack of something susceptible to error, something to go wrong. There would be no mistaken charge of a light brigade in their history.

Lawson's ship was one of the assembled eleven. Reeder's was another. Seven more had come in from lonelier parts of the galaxy for the same purpose: to rendezvous with the remaining two and add a few homarachnids to their crews. Had the enemy been of different nature they might have been reinforced by a different shape, perhaps, elephantine creatures from Europa or dark dwarfs from Mars. The physical instruments were chosen to suit the particular task, and the hat-models of Venus would do fine for this one.

Two of them, gray-skinned and bristly-haired of body, six-legged and with compound eyes, scuttled aboard Lawson's vessel, sniffed suspiciously through organs that were not noses, looked at one another.

"I smell bugs," announced the one adorned with a purple toque around which a fluffy plume was tastefully coiled.

"This can needs delousing," agreed the other who wore a glaring red fez with a long, thin crimson ribbon protruding vertically from its top.

"If you prefer," offered Lawson, "you can go on Reeder's boat."

"What, with that gang of spooks?" He cocked the toque sidewise. "I'd sooner suffer the bugs."

"Me too," agreed Red Fez.

"That is most sociable of you," sneered the mind-form of Buzwuz, chipping in suddenly. He zoomed out of the navigation-room and into the passage, an orange ball on flashing wings. "I think we can manage to—" He broke off as he caught sight of the arrivals, let out a mental screech of agony, whirled round in circles. "Oh, look at them! Just *look!*"

"What's the matter?" aggressively demanded he in the purple toque whose name this year was Nfam. Next year it would be Nfim. And the year after, Nfom.

"The vile headgear," complained Buzwuz, shuddering visibly. "Especially that red thing."

The owner of the fez, whose current name was Jlath, waxed indignant. "I'd have you know this is an original creation by the famous Oroni and—"

Frowning at all and sundry, Lawson interrupted, "When you mutual monstrosities have finished swapping compliments maybe you'll make ready for take-off. The fact that we're inertialess doesn't mean you can clutter up the passage." He slammed the door of the lock, fastened it, went to the pilot's cabin and moved the little lever.

That left ten ships. Reeder's departed soon afterward. Then the others, one by one. And that left nothing but three ruined cylinders and three ruminative crews unable to do anything but mourn their own inexplicable madness.

10.

First contact was one of the Great Lord's heavy battle cruisers, a long, black cylinder well-armed with large caliber guns and remotely controlled torpedoes. It was heading at fast pace for Kalambar, a blue-white sun with a small system of planets located on the rim of what the Nileans regarded as their sphere of interest. Those aboard it had in mind that the Kalambar group was believed to be habitable but little else was known about it; therefore it was a likely hiding-place of Nilean allies, two-legged or winged.

Lawson knew of this cruiser's existence and intent long before it loomed large enough to obscure a noticeable portion of the starfield and even before sensitive detectors started clicking to mark the presence of something metallic, swift-moving and emitting heat. He knew of it simply because the exotically-hatted pair probed forth as twin channels of a far-away supermind, had no difficulty in picking up the foe's group-thoughts or determining the direction, course and distance of the source. All he had to do was take the ship where they indicated, knowing in precise detail what he'd find when he got there.

Even at the tremendous velocities commonplace only to another galaxy the catching-up took time. But they made it in due course, burst out of the starfield with such suddenness that they were bulleting at equal pace and on parallel course before the other's alarm system had time to give warning.

By the time the bells did set up their clamor it was too late. With remarkable unanimity the crew had conceived several strange notions and were unable to sense the strangeness simply because all were thinking alike. Firstly, the alarm was about to sound and that must be the signal for action. Secondly, it was sheer waste of precious lifetime to mess around in empty space when one could put in some real existence on good, solid earth. Thirdly, there was a suitable haven shining through the dark four points to starboard and much nearer than Kalambar. Fourthly, to place the ship completely out of action on landing would be the most certain way of ensuring a long period of rest and relaxation.

These ideas ran contrary to their military conditioning, were directly opposed to duty and discipline, but they accorded with inward instincts, secret desires, and moreover were imposed with suggestive power too great to resist.

So the alarm system duly operated and the battle cruiser at once turned four points to starboard. With the Solarian boat following unheeded it sped straight for the adjacent system, made its landing on a world owned by backward, neutral and embarrassed Dirkins who were greatly relieved when a loud bang marked the vessel's disabling and its crew proceeded to lounge around like beachcombers. Only thing the Dirkins could not understand was why this party of intended lotus-eaters suddenly became afflicted with vain regrets coincidentally with the disappearance of that second ship from the sky.

In short order twenty-seven more vessels went the same way, turning off route, dumping themselves on the habitable sphere and sabotaging themselves clean out war. Seventeen of these belonged to the Great Lord Markhamwit; ten to the Nileans. Not one resisted. Not one fired a gun, launched a torpedo or so much as took evasive action. The partway products of science are pitifully ineffectual when suddenly confronted with the superb end-product, namely, superiority of the brain over all material things.

Nevertheless, ancient ingenuity did try to strike a telling blow at the ultramodern when Lawson came across ship number twenty-nine. The manner in which this one was discovered told in advance of something abnormal about it. The detectors reported it while Jlath and Nfam were mentally feeling through the dark and getting no evidence of anything so near. The reason: the homarachnids were seeking enemy thought-forms and this ship held no thoughts, not one.

Orbiting around a lesser moon, the mystery vessel's design and markings showed it to be an auxiliary warship or armed freighter of Nilean origin. An old and battered rocket-job long overdue for scrapping, it appeared to have been pressed into further service for the duration of the war. It had a medium gun in its bow, fixed torpedo tubes to port and starboard and could aim its missiles only by laboriously positioning itself with respect to the target. A sorry object fit for nothing but escort duty on short runs in a quiet sector, it seemed hardly worth the bother of putting down to ground.

But Lawson and his crew were curious about it. An old but quite intact spaceship totally devoid of evidence of thinking mentalities was somewhat of a phenomenon. It could mean several unusual things all equally worth discovering. No matter how extremely remote the likelihood of anyone developing a screen that homarachnids could not penetrate in search of mind-forms lurking behind, the theoretical possibility could not be ruled out. Nothing is finally and completely impossible.

Alternately there was the million to one chance that the vessel was crewed by a nonthinking, purely reactive and robotic life-form allied to the Nileans. Or, more plausibly, that one of Markhamwit's warships was employing a new weapon capable of slaughtering crews without so much as scratching their vessels, and this particular vessel was a victim. Or, lastly and likeliest, that it had been abandoned and left crewless but carefully parked in a balanced orbit for some reason known only to the deserters.

As the Solarian boat swooped toward the point marked by its detectors, Nfam and Jlath strode hurriedly to probe the nearby moon for any minds holding the secret of the silent objective. There wasn't time. They whirled high above the target, automatically recorded its nature, type and markings, and in the next breath had been carried leagues beyond it. The Solarian ship commenced to turn into a wide curve that would bring it back for another once-over. They did not get a second look.

Designed to cope with objects moving considerably slower, the instruments aboard the silent freighter registered the presence of another vessel just a little too late. In less than a millipart, vacuum tubes flashed, relays snapped over and the freighter exploded. It was vivid and violent blast guaranteed to disable and possibly destroy any battleship that came within distance. It failed in intent solely because the prospective recipient of the thump already was far outpacing the flying fragments, of which there were plenty.

"Booby trap," said Lawson. "We'd have been handed a beautiful wallop if our maximum velocity was down to the crawl that local types regard as conventional."

"Yes," responded a bee-mind from somewhere nearer the tail. "And did those two mad hatters warn you of it? Did you hear them screaming, 'Don't go near! Oh, please don't go near!' and feel them pawing at your arm?"

"It seems to me," remarked Nfam to Jlath, "that I detect the sharp, grating voice of jealousy, the bitter whine of a lesser life-form incapable of and unsuitable for self-adornment."

"We don't need it," retorted the critic back. "We don't have to return to artificial devices as a means of lending false color to pale, insipid personalities. We have—"

"No hands," put in Nfam, with great dexterity.

"And they fight with their rear ends," added Jlath for good measure.

"Now see here, Frog-food, we—"

"Shut up!" roared Lawson with sudden violence

They went silent. The ship bulleted onward in search of target number thirty.

The next encounter provided an orgy that served to illustrate the superiority of mass-mind efficiency as compared with artificial methods of communication and coordination. Far off across the wheel of light that formed the galaxy a Solarian named Ellis pursued a multitude of bellicose thought-forms traced by his homarachnids and discovered two fleets assembling for battle. The news flashed out to all and sundry even as he snatched a super-dreadnaught lumbering toward the scene and planted it where it would stay put.

Lawson immediately altered course, boosted his vessel to detector-defeating velocity. There was a long way to go according to this galaxy's estimates of distances but a relative jaunt from the Solarian viewpoint. Unseen and unsuspected, the vessel scudded over a host of worlds, most of them uninhabitable, sterile, deserted.

At one point Nfam's questioning mind found a convoy of ten ships huddled together and heading for the system of a binary, determined them to be neutral traders hoping to make port without interference by one or the other belligerents. Farther on, nearer the twin suns, a pair of Markhamwit's light destroyers hung in space ready to halt and search the convoy for whatever they saw fit to declare illegal transport of strategic war materials. The Solarian vessel promptly cut its speed, herded these two wolves into a suitable cage, raced onward. The convoy continued to plug along innocent of the obstruction so arbitrarily removed from its path.

By the time Lawson got there the scene of intended conflict already had lost some of its orderliness and was dissolving toward eventual chaos. A Nilean force of many hundreds had disposed itself in a huge hemisphere protecting a close-packed group of seven solar systems that were not worth a hoot. Markhamwit's fleet commanders accordingly reasoned that such strength would be marshaled only to defend a sector vital to the enemy's war economy and that therefore these seven systems must be captured and scoured regardless of cost. Which was what the Nileans wanted them to think, for, being slightly the weaker party, they knew the value of diverting attention from genuinely critical points by offering the foe a glittering but valueless prize elsewhere. So both sides beamed frantic orders to and fro, strove to get ready to rend the heavens for the sake of what neither could use. The trouble was that preparations refused to work out as they should have done according to the book.

Established tactics of space warfare seemed to be becoming disestablished. Orthodox methods of squaring up to the enemy were not producing orthodox results. The recognized moves of placing light forces here and heavy ones there, a spearhead thus and a defensive screen so, a powerful reserve in that place and a follow-up force in this place, were making a fine mess of the whole issue. Bewilderment among commanders on both sides resembled that of an expert who finds that a certain experiment produces the same results nine hundred ninety-nine times but not the thousandth.

Introduction of a new and yet unidentified factor was the cause of all this. The time lag in their communications beam systems, with coded messages flashed from repeater station to repeater station, was so great that none in this sector knew what had happened to the impudent visitors on their home worlds or that Solarians had turned from argument to action. True, some ships were overdue in this area and presumed lost, but that was inevitable. Losses must be expected in time of war and there was nothing to be gained by investigating the fate of the missing or by trying to ascertain the cause of their disappearance.

So deeply embedded were these notions that for quite a time both sides remained blindly unaware of what was happening right under their noses. And the emotions of opposing commanders remained those of extreme irritation rather than real alarm. Inside their military minds conditioning masqueraded as logic and stated that a fight was trying to get going, that any fight is between two parties with nobody else present except maybe one or two mere lookers-on. Such pseudo-reasoning automatically prevented swift realization of intervention by a third party. Whoever heard of a three-sided battle?

Mutually bedevilled, both belligerents postponed their onslaughts while they continued to try and get ready, meanwhile blundering around like a pair of once-eager boxers temporarily diverted from their original purpose by the sudden appearance of numerous ants in the pants.

And the ants kept them on the hop. Lawson's vessel plummeted unseen and undetected right into the middle of the Nilean hemisphere, picked up three boats thundering along under orders to patrol off a certain planet, put them down on said planet for keeps. So far as the Nilean order-giver was concerned, three of his vessels had commenced to move in obedience to commands, had continuously signaled progress, then cut off without warning as if snatched out of Creation. He sent a light fast scout to discover what had occurred. That one radiated messages until within viewing distance of the appointed post and went silent. He sent another. Same result. It was like dropping pennies down the drain. He gave up, reported the mystery to battle headquarters, sought under his back-strap for a persistent nibbler that had been pestering him all day.

The causes of all this cussedness would have been identified more quickly and easily had one crew been able to beam a warning that they were about to come under the mental mastery of those in a strange vessel of unknown origin. But none were ever aware of what was about to happen. None were aware that it had happened until the cause had gone elsewhere, the influence had been removed and they found themselves sitting on solid earth and dumbfoundedly contemplating a vessel converted to so much scrap.

It was like stealing lollipops from the inmates of a babies' home except that there always lurked an element of danger due to lining up of fortuitous circumstances that none could anticipate. Ellis and his ship and crew went out of existence in a brilliant flash of light when they dived down upon what appeared to be a Nilean flotilla moving at sedate pace toward the hemisphere's rim and discovered one millipart too late that it consisted of a heavy cruiser shepherding under remote control a group of unmanned booby traps.

Every Solarian in the tremendous area knew of this counterblow the instant the stroke took place. Everyone sensed it as a sudden cessation of life that has been a small part of one's own. It was like the complete vanishing from one's mind of a long-held and favorite thought. None brooded. None felt a pang of regret. They were not inclined to such sentiment because sorrow can never remove its own cause. A few hairs had fallen from an immense corporate whole, but the body remained.

Half a time-unit afterward James Lawson and his crew exacted sweet revenge, not with that motive, but purely as a tactic. They did it by making opportune use of the enemy's organizational setup which like many sources of great strength was also a source of great weakness. Weld men and materials into a mighty machine and they are thereby converted into something capable of mighty collapse the moment the right nut or bolt is removed.

A formidable Nilean battle squadron of one hundred forty assorted ships was running out of the hemisphere in a great, curving course that eventually would position them slightly behind the extreme wing of Markhamwit's assembly. This was the strictly orthodox move of trying to place a flanking party strong enough to endanger any main thrust at the center. If Markhamwit's scouts spotted this threat, his array would have to divert a force able to meet and beat it. It was all so easy for those who sat in opposing battle headquarters, planning and counterplanning, directing vessels here and there, operating the great combat machines.

And just because the machines were machines, Lawson had no difficulty in pulling out an essential bolt. He took over the entire squadron lock, stock and barrel. All that was necessary was for Nfam and Jlath to gain mental mastery of those aboard the admiral's vessel commanding the rest. One ship! The others did exactly as this enslaved vessel ordered, moving through space like a flock of sheep.

The big squadron turned into a new course, built up to top velocity because the admiral's boat so ordered. They ignored the now visible Solarian stranger in their midst because the admiral unquestioningly accepted its presence. They pushed for their faraway home world as fast as they could drive because The Boss so commanded.

Lawson stayed with them to the halfway point and long after he'd left they continued on course, made no attempt to return. The Boss was not going to admit to an entire fleet that he was afflicted with mental confusion, could not remember receiving or transmitting an order to head for home. Obviously he must have had such instructions, or why were they here, making for where they were going? Best to keep straight on and hide the fact that he was subject to spasms of dopiness. So on they went, one hundred forty vessels bamboozled right out of the fray.

In short time Reeder's vessel performed a similar service for the Great Lord. A reserve force of eighty-eight ships, mostly heavy cruisers, pushed homeward with closed signal channels in accordance with orders from their own commanding officer. Soon informed of this unauthorized departure, the top brass at battle headquarters foamed at the mouth, switched switches, levered levers and stabbed buttons, filled the ether with contra-commands, threats and bloodthirsty promises while still the reserve continued to blunder through the starfield with all receivers sealed and no mutinous ears burning.

Bombs and bullets are of little avail without intelligence to direct them. Take away the intelligence, if only for a little while, and the entire warmaking appurtenances of a major power become so much junk. The Solarian attack was irresistibly formidable because it was concentrated on the very root-cause of all action, the very motivating force behind all instruments great or small. Solarian logic argued that gun-plus-mind is a weapon whereas gun-without-mind is a mere article no matter how inherently efficient.

The Nilean booby traps were no exception, neither was any other robotic arm, for in effect they were delayed action weapons from which minds had gone into hiding by removing themselves in space and time. The minds originating each booby trap were difficult to trace, hence the fate suffered by Ellis and his crew. But in the long run they were being dealt with as ship after ship became grounded, squadrons, flotillas and convoys departed for someplace else and chaos threatened to become complete. In proof of which the jumpy Nilean high command twice made serious errors by diverting ships that sprang their own traps and thus added a pleasing note to the general confusion.

By the fiftieth time-unit the Solarians had an imposing array of statistics to consider. Fourteen ships destroyed by accident, including one of their own. Eight hundred fifty-one vessels nailed down to various inhabitable planets and satellites. One thousand two hundred sixty-six shiploads of the mentally deceived hellbent for other places, mostly home. Increasing evidence of demoralization in the battle headquarters of both belligerents. Truly the long term chivvying of weaker neutrals was being paid for, heavily, with compound interest. It might be sufficient to convince stubborn minds that a myth can be a very real thing when dragged out of the past and dumped into the present day.

They conferred among themselves and across a galactic gap while their ships continued to flash to and fro. If the opposing parties' battle headquarters were taken under mental control the entire war parade could be scattered through the heavens at a few imposed words of command. They were reluctant to take matters as far as that. It would come much too near a demonstration of near-godlike dictatorship over all lesser creatures.

The basic Solarian idea was to create respect for an essential law by creating respect for those behind it. To overdo the job by just a little too much would be to establish wholesale fear of themselves throughout the galaxy. Some dread here and there could not be avoided when dealing with less developed minds inclined to superstition, but they were deeply anxious not to create ineradicable fear as a substitute for enlightened tolerance. Since they were trying to cope with two kinds of alien minds not identically the same, it was a touchy matter judging exactly how far they must go in order to achieve the desired result while avoiding the other. How many times should a candidate for baptism be dunked to give him salvation without pneumonia?

By mutual consent they carried on for another time-unit, at the end of which the movements of vessels still controlled by the top brass showed that Nilean forces were striving to regroup in readiness for withdrawal. Their answer to that was to cease all blows at Nileans and concentrate exclusively on Markhamwit's equally confused but more mulish armada. Though slower to make up their minds, the Great Lord's commanders were swifter to act once they'd reached a decision. In due time they saw without difficulty that this was an inauspicious date for victory and they'd do better to bide next Friday week. Which means that they started to pull out, fast.

"Enough!"

It flashed from mind to mind, and Lawson said with approval, "Good work, boys."

"Our work invariably is first class," assured Nfam. Removing his toque, he blew imaginary dust from it, smoothed its feather, put it on at a rakish angle. "I have earned myself a new bonnet."

"Treat yourself to a new head while you're at it," advised the thought-form of Buzwuz from his haunt nearer the stern.

"Petty spitefulness characteristic of the child-like," commented Jlath, nodding his fez until its crimson ribbon waggled. "I have long been intrigued by a phenomenon that someday must be investigated."

"Such as?" prompted Nfam.

"The nearer they are to Sol, the higher in intelligence. The farther out, the lower."

Buzwuz shrilled back, "Let me tell you, Spider-shape, that outside the Asteroid Belt they're—"

"Shut up!" bellowed Lawson, thus staking a biped claim in this scramble for superiority.

They went quiet, not because they were overawed by him, not because they considered him any better or worse than themselves, but solely because it was notorious that his two-legged kind could argue the tail off an alligator and cast grave doubts upon its parentage while doing so. If the Solarian mass-mind had a special compartment reserved for flights of vocal fancy duly embellished with pointed witticisms it was without doubt located on a dump called Terra.

So they held their peace while he boosted the speed and headed for the gypsy planet on which two ships already were waiting to collect the various homarachnids and take them nearer home. There was no need to consult star maps and seek the highly erratic course of the wandering sphere. He could have chased it across half the galaxy and hit it dead center with his eyes shut. All that was needed was to steer straight along the thought-stream emanating from the pair of Solarian vessels waiting there.

It was as easy as that.

11.

The follow-up process was delayed. Held back deliberately and of malice aforethought. The sluggish communications systems of warring life-forms had been greatly to the advantage of Solarians, but now time must be allowed for those same systems to deliver data to Markhamwit and Glastrom. No use Lawson and Reeder taking them the news in person. They would not be believed until confirmation arrived in large dollops.

And after the warlords had gained a clear picture of recent events further time must be given for the complete digestion thereof. Since the Nileans were by nature a little more impulsive and a little less stubborn than their opponents it was likely that they would be the first to agree that it is unprofitable to play hob with common property such as the free space between worlds.

Markhamwit would be the last to give in. He would have a soul-searing period of balancing loss of face against the growing pile of awkward facts. He must have time to work out for himself that it is better to drop an autocratic obsession than ultimately drop at the end of a rope. Being what he was—a prominent member of his own kind—he'd have no illusions about the fate of one who insists on leading his people to total defeat.

A couple of days before the Nileans were due to become mentally ripe, Reeder burst through the defense screen of their home world, dropped a packet in Glastrom's palace yard, back into the eternal starfield before guards or aerial patrols fully realized what had taken place.

Ten time-units later—making carefully estimated allowance for Markhamwit's more reluctant character—Lawson obliged with a similar bundle that crowned the fat Kasine as he waddled across the area outside the interrogation center. The thump on that worthy's dome was not intentional. Nobody could go by at such pace and achieve such perfection of aim. It was wholly accidental, but to the end of his days Kasine would never believe it.

Struggling to his feet, Kasine addressed a few well-chosen words to the sky, took the bundle indoors, gave it to the captain of the guard who gave it to the garrison commander who gave it to the chief of intelligence. That official immediately recalled the fate of a predecessor who hurriedly burst open a parcel from someone who was not a friend. So with the minimum of delay he passed it to Minister Ganne who with equal alacrity handed it to the addressee, the Great Lord Markhamwit, and found an excuse to get out of the room.

Viewing the unwanted gift with much disfavor, Markhamwit found his plug and tube, called the chief of intelligence, ordered him to provide an expendable warrior to come lean out the window and open the thing. The chief of intelligence told the garrison commander who told the captain of the guard who duly pushed along a loyal thickhead of low rank and no importance.

The task performed without dire result, Markhamwit found himself with a thick wad of star maps. Spreading them over his desk he stared at them irefully. All bore liberal markings, with certain worlds and satellites clearly numbered. On the reverse side of each was a list of ships stalled on the appropriate spheres, plus roughly estimated strength of crews thus marooned and a further estimate of how long each group could survive unaided.

The longer he studied this collection the more riled he felt. Approximately one-fifth of his total forces had been put out of action according to this data. One-fifth of his battle-wagons were scrap metal scattered far across the light years. Assuming that it would be asking for further trouble to employ armed vessels, it would require full use of his gunless merchant-fleet to rescue and bring home the crews languishing on a couple of hundred worlds. And if he made no attempt to save them there would be trouble aplenty on this world.

He did not know it, but he had another twenty time-units which to think things over.

At the end of that period Lawson returned.

The second arrival was exactly like the first. At one moment the plain stood empty, with the city gray and grim in the north, the bluish sun burning above and the smallest of the three moons going down in the east. Next moment the ship was there, a thin streak of dust settling behind its tail as if to show that there had been motion even though unseen.

Overhead the aerial patrol circled and swirled as before. This time there was some risk that they might bomb without waiting for orders. A slick trick creates greater fury when repeated and sometimes becomes too much to bear.

"If a man does thee once it's his fault; if he does thee twice it's thy fault!"

But again the Solarian visitor's behavior was that of one completely unconscious of such dangers or completely indifferent to them. It lay on the plain, a clear target. The patrol dropped nothing but did scream the news to the city's chief communications center.

Consequence was that a couple of truck-loads of troops raced onto the plain even as Lawson emerged from the lock. He came out breathing deeply, enjoying the fresh air, the feel of solid earth underfoot. Several winged shapes buzzed ecstatically out of the lock, zoomed into the sky, chased after each other and put over a bee-version of sailors in port.

Disregarding the oncomers from the city, the bee-minds were swapping thoughts intended mainly for the benefit of the biped. They deplored his lack of wings. They questioned the wisdom of Nature in putting sentient life upon two inadequate feet. Ah, the pity of it all!

So far as Lawson and his crew were concerned the truck-loads making toward them contained an armed company of mental moppets of no particular shape or form. And Markhamwit himself would have been appalled to learn that his own status was that of the muscular bully of grade one.

The trucks pulled up and the troops tumbled out. Though Lawson did not know it, his attitude and expression had been perfectly duplicated in the dawn of history by a gentleman named Casey who wore a cap and badge. The corner cop watching the kids come out of school. The lesson learned was the same now as then, produced the same results: the unruly members of this crowd had had to be taught respect for Casey.

They'd learned it all right; it was evident from what they did. There was no hostile surrounding of the ship, guns and held ready. Instead they formed up in two ranks, apart like a guard of honor. A three-comet officer marched forward, saluted ceremoniously.

"Sire, you have returned to see the Great Lord?"

"I have." Lawson blinked, looked him over. "Why the 'sire'? I do not have any military rank."

"You are the ship's commander," said the other, signing toward the vessel.

"I am its pilot," Lawson corrected. "Nobody commands it." With a touch of desperation, the officer ended the disconcerting talk by motioning toward a truck. "This way, sire."

Grinning to himself, Lawson climbed into the cab, was driven citywards. He kept silence during the journey. The officer did likewise, inwardly feeling that this was one of those days when one can be tempted to say too much.

The Great Lord Markhamwit was sitting in his chair with his four arms lying negligently on its rests, his features smooth and composed. Many days ago he had been in a choleric frenzy of activity as he strove to organize a war that refused to jell. A few days back he'd been in a blind fury, pacing the room, hammering the table, volleying oaths and threats as a volcano spews lava. A few time-units ago reaction had set in as he contemplated an enormous mass of frustrating data topped by the star maps that had bounced off Kasine. Now he was resigned, fatalistic. It was the calm after the storm. He was nearly ripe for reason.

This was to be expected. Solarian tactics did not accord paramount importance to the question of *what* must be done to achieve a given end. It was of equal and occasionally of greater importance to determine precisely *when* it must be begun, how long it must be maintained and *when* it should be ended. Words like *how* or *what* did not dominate a word like *when* in Solarian thinking.

Circumstances were radically altered when Lawson ambled into the room for his third interview. His manner was the same as before, but now Markhamwit and Ganne studied him with wary curiosity rather than bellicose irritation.

Seating himself, Lawson crossed his legs, smiled at the Great Lord rather as one would at an obstreperous child after a domestic scene.

"Well?"

Markhamwit said slowly and evenly, "I have been in touch with Glastrom. We are recalling all ships."

"That's being sensible. More's the pity that it's had to be paid for by many of your crews languishing on lonely worlds."

"We have agreed to cooperate in bringing them home. Nileans pick up and deliver any of our people they find. We do the same for them."

"Much nicer than cutting each other's throats, isn't it?"

Markhamwit countered, "You told me you didn't care."

"Neither do we. It's when innocent bystanders get pushed around that we see fit to chip in."

Lawson made to get up as if at his stage his task was finished because Solarian aims had been gained. Nothing daunted, the Great Lord spoke hurriedly.

"Before you go I'd like answers to three questions."

"What are they?"

"In honest fact do you come from a galaxy other than this one?"

"Most certainly."

Frowning at a secret thought, Markhamwit went on, "Have you sterilized any world belonging to us or the Nileans?"

"Sterilized?" Lawson registered puzzlement.

"As you are said to have done to the Elmones"

"Oh, that!" He dismissed it in the manner of something never contemplated even for a moment. "You're referring to an incident of long, long ago. We used weapons in those days. We have outgrown them now. We harm nobody."

"I beg to differ," Markhamwit pointed to the star maps piled up on one side. "On your own showing eight of my ships have been destroyed, crews and all."

"Plus five Nilean vessels and one of our own," Lawson said. "All by accidents over which we had no control. For example, two of your cruisers collided head-on. Our presence had nothing to do with it."

Accepting this without dispute, Markhamwit leaned forward, put his last question. "You have established a law that free space shall be completely free to all. We have recognized it. We have given in. I think that entitles us to know why you are so interested in the space ethics of a galaxy not your own."

Standing up, Lawson met him eye for eye. "Behind that query lurks the agreement you have just made with Glastrom, namely, that you drop all your differences in the face of common peril from outside. You have secretly agreed to conform to the common law until such time as you have developed ships as good as or better than our own. Then, when you feel strong enough, you will join together and shave us down to whatever you regard as proper size."

"That does not answer my questions," Markhamwit pointed out, not bothering to confirm or deny this accusation.

"The answer is one you'll fail to see."

"Let me be the judge of that."

"Well, it's like this," Lawson explained. "Solarians are not a shape or form. They're a multikind destined ultimately to lose identity in a combine still greater and wider. They are the beginning of a growth of associated minds designed to conquer universal matter. The free, unhampered use of space is the basic essential of such growth."

"Why?"

"Because the next contributions to a cosmos-wide supermind will come from this galaxy. That's where the laugh is on you."

"On me?" The Great Lord was baffled.

"On your particular life-form. You overlook the question of time. And time is all-important."

"What do you mean?"

"By the time either you or the Nileans have created techniques advanced enough to challenge us even remotely, both you and they will be more than ready for assimilation."

"I don't understand."

Lawson went to the door. "Someday both you and the Nileans will be inseparable parts of each other and, like us, components of a mightier whole. You will come to it rather late but you'll get there just the same. Meanwhile we will not allow those in front to be held back by those behind. Each comes in his own natural turn, delayed by no pernickety neighbors."

He smiled. Then he departed.

"My lord, did you understand what he meant?" Minister Ganne said.

"I have a glimmering." Markhamwit was thoughtful. "He was talking about events not due until five, ten or twenty thousand years after we two are dead."

"How did he get to know our arrangement with Glastrom?"

"He doesn't know since nobody could have told him. He made a shrewd guess, and he was absolutely correct as we are aware." Markhamwit brooded a bit, added, "It makes me wonder how close he'll get with his longer shot."

"Which one, my lord?"

"That by the time we're big enough to dare try beat up what he calls his multikind it will be too late, for we shall be part of that multikind."

"I can't imagine it," admitted Ganne.

"I can't imagine people crossing an intergalactic chasm. Neither can Yielm or any of our experts," Markhamwit said. "I can't imagine anyone successfully waging a major war without any weapons whatsoever." His tone became slightly peevish as he finished. "And that supports the very one of his points that I dislike the most: that our brains are not yet adequate. We suffer from limited imaginations."

"Yes, my lord," agreed Ganne.

"Speak for yourself," snapped Markhamwit. "I can stir up mine a bit even if others can't. I'm going to see Glastrom in person. Maybe we can get together and, by persuasion rather than by force, so reorganize the galaxy that it becomes too big and strong and united to be absorbed by any menagerie from elsewhere. It's well worth a try." He stopped, stared at Ganne, demanded, "Why do you look like a bilious skouniss?"

"You have reminded me of something he said," explained Ganne unhappily. "He said, 'Someday both you and the Nileans will be inseparable parts of each other and, like us, components of a mightier whole.' If you go to see Glastrom it means we're heading exactly that way—already!"

Markhamwit flopped back in his chair, gnawed the nails on four hands in turn. He hated to admit it but Ganne was right. The only satisfactory method of trying to catch up on Solarian competition was to toil along the same cooperative path to the same communal end that could not and would not remain compartmented in one galaxy. Not to try was to accept defeat and sink into dark obscurity that ultimately would cover them for all time, making them like the Elmones, a name, a memory, a rumor.

There were only two ways to go: forward or backward. Forward to the inevitable. Or backward to the inevitable. And it had to be forward.

Lawson returned to the ship and he knew that his crew already were aboard and eager to go. Getting out of the truck, he thanked the driver, walked toward the lock, stopped when nearby and carefully examined the sentry posted outside it.

"I think we have met before," he offered pleasantly.

Yadiz refused the bait. He kept tight hold on his gun, ignored the voice, ignored a couple of persistent itches. One learns by experience he had decided, and when in the presence of a Solarian the safest thing is to play statues.

"Oh, well, if that's the way you feel about it." Lawson shrugged, climbed into the lock, looked down from the rim and advised, "We're taking off. There'll be some suction. If you don't want a sudden rise in the world you'd better take shelter behind that rock."

Thinking it over, Yadiz decided to take the suggestion. He marched toward the indicated point, still saying nothing.

Lawson sat in the pilot's seat, fingered the little lever. Far out at the edge of the galaxy, lost to view in the great spray of stardust, were a pair of life-forms developing a kindred spirit. Near to them was a third form, more numerous, arrogant and ready to fill the power vacuum left by Glastrom and Markhamwit. Far out there among the stars the stage was set for interference. Something must be done about it. A few knuckles must be rapped. He moved the lever.

The Undecided

Astounding, April 1949

Peter the Pilot made his crash landing with skill deserving of all the huzzahs he did not get. It is no small feat to dump a four-hundred tonner after a flying brick has loused up the antigrav and left nothing dependable but the pipes.

The way he used those tubes verged on the superhuman. They roared and thrust and braked and flared and balanced so that ultimately the vessel hit with no more than a mildly unpleasant thump that added nothing to the damage. For the time being the ship and its eight man crew was safe. Or, to be more precise, its crew of seven men and one woman were safe—if there is any safety in an unknown and possibly hostile world.

While the others telepathed their congratulations which modestly he shrugged off, Peter the Pilot remained in his seat, locked in the control cabin, and studied what was visible of this strange planet. The armorglass window mirrored a ghostly reflection of his blue, thoughtful eyes which were set in a face queerly suggestive of youth preserved to great age. Even his hair showed the silky whiteness of the very old, yet somehow remained lush and strong. Making no attempt to get out, he sat there and thought because it was his duty to think. Subconsciously he was aware that three of his crew already had left the vessel and that the others were retaining mental contact with them.

They were eight Terrans temporarily marooned far off the beaten tracks. He wasn't unduly worried about that because the ship was repairable and they had enough fuel for return. Moreover, the fact that three had gone out showed that this world could be endured. It would permit life; a point already suggested by its superficial resemblance to Terra as seen through the armorglass. No, the worry was not an immediate one. So far, so good. Sufficient unto the day is the evil thereof. The trouble which most encouraged him to ponder was that repairs take time, a long time, and menacing complications not present today can arrive tomorrow or next week.

The prospective threat he had in mind was that other lifeform of shape and powers unknown. They had ships, slow, cumbersome, too short-ranged to overlap the Terran sphere of influence, but still ships. Manifestly they had intelligence of a high order.

For twelve centuries this other-form had chased in fruitless pursuit of every Terran vessel straying within their range and had enjoyed the doubtful pleasure of seeing each one's rapidly diminishing rear end. It is galling to have one's curiosity repeatedly stimulated and left unsatisfied, even more galling to know that the interest is not reciprocated. Peter the Pilot had no notion of what bizarre form this other-life might take but he was willing to gamble that they had no teeth—having ground them away long ago.

Now there was excellent chance of a snoopover and much expressing of resentment if the ship remained pinned by its pants, for misfortune had dumped it right in the other's bailiwick. Not even a Sirian Wotzit, he decided, would resist a sitting duck. Hitching his shoulders fatalistically, he opened his mind to the mental voices of his crew.

Rippy the Ranger was saying, "Found a stream. The water is drinkable."

"*You* found it?" harshed Sammy the Sharpeye. "How do you discover something to which you've been directed like a small child?"

"I went the way you told me and I found it," came back Rippy. "Does that satisfy you? Why don't you trim your nails and take a pill?"

Peter sent out a call, "What do you see, Sammy?"

"Trees and trees and trees. You sure picked a hideout—if it will do you any good." Silence, followed by, "I can also see a strange, repulsive, nightmarish shape lurking by the stream. It is guzzling the water because there's no charge. Now it is scowling horribly and—"

"Leave Rippy alone," ordered Peter. "Where's Kim?"

"Don't know," admitted Sammy the Sharpeye indifferently. "He got out fast and vanished some place. You'll hear Hector swearing pretty soon."

"Oh, no you won't," interjected Hector the Hasher, his mental impulses strong because of his nearness within the ship. "I had ten locks on the galley, see? I've made landings before, and with a load of gutsies at that!"

"Kim!" called Peter.

Silence.

"When will that guy learn to keep his mind open and respond," Peter complained.

"When he's hungry," offered Hector morbidly.

A new tone chipped in, hooting with irritation. "Let . . . me . . . *sleep,* willya? I gotta catch up . . . somehow!"

"Nilda the Nightwatcher," sighed Hector. "Nilda the Nuisance I call her. What makes her that way?" He paused, then his thought-form boosted with sudden outrage. "Clobo, take your mitt outa that can! By the—"

Peter cut them off while he writhed out of his seat, had a closer look through the armorglass. He was surveying a tiny portion of a world which itself was small part of an alien system and a corresponding fragment of the great unknown. As a representative of a nearby empire firmly founded upon swiftness and sureness of personal decision, he stood ready with the rest to face decisively whatever might befall. Apprehension was not within him, nor the elements of fear. There was only estimation, calculation, and preparedness to decide.

After one million years of Terran growth and mutual acceptance of the consequence of growth, nobody thought of themselves as peculiarly undecided.

Sector Marshal Bvandt slurged in caterpillarish manner across the floor and vibrated his extensibles and closed two of the eight eyes around his serrated crown and did all the other things necessary to demonstrate an appropriate mixture of joy, satisfaction and triumph.

"One is down." He smacked his lips. "At last. After all these years."

"One what?" inquired Commander Vteish.

"A mystery ship. A sample of those ultra-fast cylinders we've never been able to catch."

"No?" Vteish was astounded.

"Yes! It had an accident, or something went bust. The message had just come in but does not give details of what forced it to land. Zwilther was following it in the *CX66,* and losing distance as usual, when he saw it go off-curve. It chopped around a bit, still at high clip, then made for Lanta."

"Lanta," echoed Commander Vteish. "Why, that is in our sector."

"A most remarkable coincidence," observed Bvandt sarcastically, "seeing that any emergency message is automatically directed to the marshal in charge of the sector it concerns."

"Of course, of course," agreed Vteish hurriedly. "I overlooked that much in the excitement of the moment." Dutifully he slurged, vibrated and performed the eye-shutting to remind his superior that they were two hearts beating as one. "Now what?"

"Lanta is sparsely settled. Its people are simple scrabblers in the dirt. I have sent an order warning them not to interfere with this alien cylinder, to keep clear of it. We cannot permit a gang of hicks to handle a case of this magnitude. Too much depends upon it and such an opportunity may never occur again. Our best brains are needed to make the most of it."

"Definitely," endorsed Vtish. "Undoubtedly."

"Therefore I am going to deal with them myself," announced Bvandt.

"Ah!" said Vteish, carefully using his speaking-mouth. He had two mouths, one on each side. The penultimate insult was to make eating motions with the speaking-mouth. The ultimate:—to make garbled speech-noise with the eating-mouth. For a moment he had been sorely tempted.

"And you are coming with me," Bvandt went on. "Also Captain Gordd and Captain Hixl! We'll take two ships. We'd take fifty if they were immediately available, but they aren't. However, these two are of our latest, most powerful pattern."

"Couldn't some of the other vessels be summoned?"

"They have been called already, but it will take them some time to reach Lanta. We cannot wait for them, we dare not wait. At any time this alien contraption may be away faster than zip. We have got to deal with it before it becomes too late."

"Yes, marshal," admitted Vteish.

"What luck! What a gift!" If Bvandt had possessed hands, he would have smacked them together with the acme of delight. So he jiggled his extensibles in the nearest equivalent. "Now is our chance to get the measure of this other-life while leaving it ignorant concerning ourselves. After preliminary study of them we will test their defenses by a light attack. Finally, we'll seize their vessel, dig out the secret of its speed and maneuverability. All that knowledge, my dear commander, will give us our biggest boost in twenty lifetimes."

"A boost in one lifetime is enough for me," said Vteish with unashamed cynicism. "I was peculiarly disinterested before I was hatched and expect to be strangely indifferent after I'm burned." He humped toward the coolness of the wall, leaned against it and mused. "Do you suppose that this other-life might be . . . might be . . . like us?"

"I see no reason why not," declared Bvandt, after some thought. "We are by far the highest form in the known cosmos, therefore any other high form must be similar."

"The logic of that is not evident." Vteish drew a crude sketch on the wall. "They might be like this, for example."

"Don't be stupid. Why should they resemble anything so fantastic?"

"Why not?"

Bvandt said severely: "You are too fond of those dreamplays at the festivals. You have leanings toward mental extravagance. Your brain spends half its time conjuring crazy visions for lack of anything better to do." His rearward pair of eyes examined the time-meter on the wall. "Your cure is at hand—you can get busy right now. The ships will be ready within the hour and I shall tolerate no delay on anyone's part. See that you are packed and on board in good time."

"Yes, marshal. Most certainly, marshal," promised Vteish, again carefully using his speaking-mouth.

From the eastward rise over which the trees marched in solid ranks the Terran vessel could be seen as if lying in a hollow.

Like a big, fat slug, Bvandt stuck sucker-footed to the bole of a tree while he applied a powerful monocular to one eye and closed the others. The field of vision did not shift or tremble, for under the monocular his extensibles were braced together and formed a fulcrum much steadier than Terran hands.

Adjusting his instrument's focus, Bvandt got a clear, sharp view of Peter the Pilot sitting on the bottom rung of his vessel's landing ladder and smoking a pipe. He almost fell from the tree.

"By the egg that held me!" Detaching his optic from the eyepiece, he bugged the others, stared around "Do you see this thing?"

"Yes," said Vteish calmly. "It has only two legs, longer and skinnier than ours. Only two eyes. Its upper limbs bend always in the same place as if they are hard-cored and jointed."

"I see it, too," put in Captain Gordd, who was high on an adjacent tree. He spoke with a kind of incredulous hush. "It resembles nothing on any of our twenty-four planets."

"The question is," said Bvandt, "how many more of these creatures are inside that ship."

Gordd pondered it, guessed: "Any number between ten and twenty. Possibly thirty, though I doubt it."

Having another long, careful look, Bvandt pocketed his monocular inched down the trunk, gained the ground. "Hurry up with that pictograph."

One of the men descended from his vantage point, did things to the boxlike instrument he was carrying, eventually produced from it a large photo of Peter complete with pipe.

"Well, we've a record of how they look," grunted Bvandt, studying the picture closely. "I would never have believed it if I hadn't seen for myself. Fancy thousands of things like this!"

"Millions," corrected Vteish joining him.

"Yes, millions, all like this." He handed back the photograph, saying: "Prepare copies for transmission to all sector headquarters." Then to Vteish, "Now we'll find out what they've got." He called a nearby trooper. "Get as near as you can and shoot."

"To kill?" asked the trooper.

"To kill," Bvandt confirmed.

"Is that necessary?" Vteish chipped in, greatly daring.

"It is essential that we have a demonstration of their strongest, most desperate reaction," Bvandt said stiffly. He eyed the trooper. "Well, why do you wait? You have your orders!"

The other shuffled off between the trees and into the undergrowth toward the alien ship. The sound of his passage ceased as he dropped to a cautious creep. Beneath the trees the rest waited for the shot and the resulting uproar. Twelve were high in the trees ready to observe and record the other-life's method of defense.

Sitting mild-eyed and sucking his pipe, Peter the Pilot listened, listened, not with his ears but with his mind. Sammy the Sharpeye's tones were coming to him coolly, without emotion.

"They are in the trees a mile to your front. I've been near enough to make certain that they're still there. Boy, what a gang of slooperoos! They sloop and slurp this way and that. They've eight eyes apiece, all on top, but swiveling independently. They've refused to see me so often that I wonder if I'm getting transparent."

"Not with what you're full of !" cracked Rippy's thought-form.

"Shut up!" ordered Peter. "This is a poor time for crosstalk."

"The trees are the trouble," went on Sammy. "They hide too much. Clobo ought to be able to tell you more than I can."

"So at last it is admitted that Clobo has his uses," interjected that worthy. "Clobo comes into his own—during his bedtime. No sleep for the wicked!" He managed to put over a deep mental sigh. "And tomorrow all will be forgotten."

"What do you see, Clobo?" asked Peter, projecting sympathy.

"They are conferring with ugly mouth-noises. It is evident that they are in no way telepathic."

"If they were they'd have overheard us long ago," Sammy pointed out.

"They appear to have reached some sort of decision and have sent away one who bears an object suspiciously like a weapon," Clobo went on. "This one is edging cautiously toward the ship. Now he sinks low and creeps. I have a strange feeling."

"Of what?" demanded Sammy.

"That he does not desire to blow kisses."

"Ho-hum," said Peter knocking the dottle from his pipe. "I do not think it wise to take action myself until I know for certain whether or not his intentions are honorable."

"If you ask me, I wouldn't trust him with Hector's can opener," opined Clobo.

"Listen who's talking!" invited Hector.

"Now he has paused by a suitable gap and is pointing his weapon forward. If I could see into his alien mind, I'd find it bloated with mayhem. He is about to fire at you, I think. Rippy is hidden in the grass ten yards to his front."

"I shall now reveal myself," announced Rippy.

"Mind you don't get a slug in your bean," warned Peter. He screwed up his eyes as he tried to spot Rippy amid the vegetation more than half a mile away. Nothing could be seen; the growths were too thick.

Clobo's impulses now became a rapid series of high-pitched mental squeaks as he chattered at top pace like an excited commentator at a champ contest. One got the impression that he was jigging up and down as he broadcast.

"Rippy gets to his feet and stares this guy straight in the pan. The sniper lets out a startled hiss and drops his weapon. Rippy doesn't move. The other recovers. Keeping all eight eyes and the whole of his attention on Rippy, he feels for his gun, finds it, picks it up. What's the use of having eyes all around if you don't use them? He's just leveled the gun as Kim arrives from where he isn't looking and jumps on his back. Whoo! Socko! Kim is tearing off lumps and giving them to the frogs. The other has rolled onto his back, making noises with both mouths. and waving his legs in all directions. Kim is now extracting his plumbing and draping it tastefully over the bushes. There's a funny sort of blue goo all—"

Closing his mind, Peter opened his ears. There were faint threshing sounds mingled with queer, unidentifiable noises deep in the far vegetation. He eyed the sky as if searching for something now at too great an altitude to be seen. Pulling out his tobacco pouch, he refilled his pipe, tamped it, sucked it unlit.

" . . . leaving only a rank and unappetizing mess," finished Clobo, worn out.

"Soup's ready," announced Hector, unimaginatively choosing the worst of moments.

The three troopers sneaked back with their eyes wary on all sides and especially to the rear. Two told their story while the third worked at his box and gave the resulting pictograph to Bvandt.

"Torn to pieces?" said Bvandt incredulously. They made nervous assent. He stared at the pictograph as it was placed in his gripping extensibles. He was appalled. "By the great, red, incubating sun!"

"Let me see." Vteish had a look over the other's ropey limb. His first, second and third stomachs turned over one by one. "Sliced apart with a thousand knives!"

"They must have been lying in ambush," decided Bvandt, not bothering to wonder how the ambushers had known where to place themselves. "Several of them. They attacked with the utmost ferocity. He never had a chance even to use his weapon." He turned to the silent troopers. "That reminds me—where is his gun? Did you retrieve it?"

"It was not there. It had gone."

"So!" Bvandt became bitter. "Now they have a gun. One of our guns."

"Only a common hand-gun," soothed Vteish. "We have others bigger and better. They don't know about those."

"What do *we* know?" Bvandt snapped. "Nothing—except that they have knives."

"Super-fast ships and ordinary knives," Vteish commented thoughtfully. "The two items just don't go together. They seem incongruous to me."

"To eternal blackness with the incongruity!" swore Bvandt. "Their sharp blades have proved superior to our guns. They have made a kill while we have not. I cannot tolerate that!"

"What do you suggest?"

"We'll try again in the dark." Bvandt slurged to and fro, his voice irritable. "I do not expect to catch them asleep—if they do sleep—for they will keep watch now they know we're around. But if by any chance they are less accustomed to darkness it will give us some slight—"

He stopped as metallic clangings sounded from the distant ship and one of his treetop observers called urgently. Mounting the bole, he used his spyglass.

Something had emerged from the Terran vessel. It was a bright, new and entirely strange shape bearing no resemblance to the two-legged creature previously observed.

This one was rhomboidal in sideview and shone beneath the sun. It possessed no legs and appeared to move upon rotating but unseeable bands, or perhaps on hidden rollers. Many limbs projected from it at the oddest angles, some multiple-jointed, some tentacular. Trailing behind it a long, thick cable which ran back into the ship, this weird object trundled partway toward the tail end bearing in two of its limbs a large, curved metal plate.

While Bvandt watched pop-eyed, the newcomer turned its back on far-off observers, held the curved plate to the ship, applied something to one edge. An intense and flickering light bloomed at the end of its extended limb and crawled slowly up the plate's side.

"Welding!" offered Vteish unnecessarily.

Bvandt scowled, glanced higher up his tree, said to the pictograph operator above him, "Are you recording this?"

"Yes."

"Make several records while you're at it." He looked downward upon half a dozen fidgeting troopers. "You six go a quarter circle round while remaining within gun-range of that vessel. Keep together. Don't separate no matter what happens.

Find a good aiming-stand no nearer than you can help and give that legless nightmare a volley. See that you hit it—I'll flay the one who misses!"

They moved off obediently but without eagerness. Bvandt went a little higher up the tree, squatted in a crotch, kept his glass centered upon the shining alien which continued to concentrate upon its task as if it had not an enemy in the whole of creation. Vteish, Gordd and Hixl all had their monoculars aimed at it. The pictograph operator maintained it in his screen.

Slowly, uneasily, the troopers crawled round, their senses alert, jumpy, yet unconscious of other eyes watching, other minds talking.

To the waiting Bvandt the execution squad seemed to take an interminable time. He was toying with the morbid notion that already they had met a silent but terrible end when the hard cracks of six guns made him jerk in his seat. The brief swish of the missiles could be heard distinctly, and even louder were the fierce clunks with which they struck their target.

The brilliant welding light snuffed out. Its shining operator slid three feet noseward, stood still. Tense seconds went by. Then calmly he applied his limb to the opposite seam, the light spurted afresh and the weld-line crept upward.

There was a word so rarely used that some had never heard it in a lifetime. Bvandt not only employed it, but distorted it with his eating-mouth. Vteish was shocked, Gordd astounded, Hixl filed it for further reference.

Then while they watched, the two-legged, two-eyed thing appeared. It came out of the ship, pipe in mouth, a tiny gadget in its hand. The most that their monoculars could determine was that the strange instrument had a hand-grip topped by a small platform on which a little tube of pencil-like proportions pointed upward at a high angle. The two-legger squeezed the handle, the tiny tube spat fire, sprang from its platform and speeded into invisibility. A thin arc of vapor hung high to mark its passage.

Enough silence followed to make this performance seem pointless. It ended with a gigantic thunderclap and a distinct quiver in the ground. Over to the right, where the hidden squad lay low, a great tree sprang five or six hundred feet into the air with a ton of earth stiff sticking to its roots. Other trees leaned sidewise and toppled as if to provide room for it to fall back.

Of the six troopers there was not even a bluish smear.

Climbing tiredly onto his bunk, Peter the Pilot wound the chronometer set in the wall, looked through the tiny three-inch port at the darkness outside, lay back and closed his eyes. Something weightily nonchalant and stone-deep trundled noisily through the ship, made many clatterings and clinkings.

Hector's thought-form came through with a touch of exasperation. "Good as he may be, I maintain there's plenty of room for improvement. Why can't he be telepathic? If they'd found some way to make him telepathic, I could put over some choice remarks about juggling hardware in our sleeping hours."

"Anyone who can respond to anxiety about mechanical matters, and jump to the job, is a marvel in my opinion," offered Peter. "Be thankful that he's got a one-track mind and sleeps only when there is nothing to do."

"That's just when *I* want to sleep," complained Hector. "When a lot of bellies aren't hanging around me rumbling for chow." A raucous rattle like that of a pneumatic hammer came from near the tail, and Hector yelped: "Get a load of that! Aren't I entitled to some shut-eye?"

"I don't remember you screaming about my rights when I was fooling around in my bedtime," Clobo's mind put in.

"Bedtime!" scoffed Hector. "Any guy who says daytime is bedtime is too daffy to have any rights."

"The trouble with this ship," interjected Sammy, "is too many incurable yaps. My patience is running out fast. Pretty soon I'm going to give up all pursuit of sweet dreams and go around cutting myself a few throats."

"Bah!" said Hector feebly.

Clank whirr! Nobody took further notice. Closing his eyes again, Peter drifted slowly away. As usual, his astral body beat it back to Terra where—on an average of once a week—it roamed its dream-town and—perhaps once a month—joined its dream-blonde.

This proved to be one of the times when the said blonde was among those present. She was facing him across a table, looking bright-eyed at him over a vase of flowers, when suddenly her conversation made a switch.

"But, dear, if we buy this planetoid just for ourselves, you'll have to leave the service because it doesn't make sense for you to run off and—" She paused, then said sharply, "Peter, you are dreaming! *Wake up!*"

He sat up wide awake, still feeling the shock of it.

"All right, Dozey," came the mental impulses of Nilda the Nightwatcher. "Fun's a coming!"

"I'll say!" endorsed Clobo, with relish.

"What do you see, Nilda?"

"A big gun. They've brought it from one of their ships and are now hauling it up the other side of the rise. Reckon it will take them about an hour to reach the crest."

"Do you think it might be powerful enough to damage our plates?"

"For all I can tell it might be able to splash us over the landscape. It is no toy. It takes about sixty of them to drag it along. The trees are impeding them more than somewhat." She was quiet for a time, gave several little indistinguishable mutterings, then finished: "You're the official think-box. What do you want me to do about this?"

"If you gave me the precise range and angle with reference to this ship, I could donate a hoister," he mused. "But that would tell them something about our heavy armament. The light stuff doesn't matter. I'd rather not use the heavy if it can be avoided. Besides, it might shake us to pieces while we're grounded."

"So what?" invited Nilda.

"So I'll leave you a medium disruptor at the bottom of the ladder. You can plant it where it will be most disconcerting."

"All right," agreed Nilda with lack of emotion strange in a female.

Clobo promptly screamed: "Give me time to get clear, you bug-eyed assassin! I'm right in the trees and almost over them!"

"Are *you* calling *me* bug-eyed?" demanded Nilda. "Why, you spook-faced runt, I've half a mind—"

"That's just it—you've half a mind," said Clobo. "Lemme out before it does me damage."

"Give him time to duck out," ordered Peter. "I'll check whether any of the others are roaming around in the dark." Grabbing his torch, he entered the passage, went from cubicle to cubicle. The remainder of his crew were there, all asleep but Rippy who was stirring in semiwakefulness. Dodging the rhomboidal object which trundled busily along the passage, he reached the armory, selected a small one-pound disruptor, placed it at the bottom of the ladder. Then he returned to his bunk, broadcast, "All set, Nilda," closed his eyes and tried to get back to the blonde.

Sleep refused to come. He found himself listening for Nilda coming to pick up the bomb though he knew he would not hear her. Although the three-inch port was on the blind side of the ship with respect to the distant gun, he felt impelled to glance through it every now and again. There were no more comments from Nilda or Clobo, and the others were deep in their slumbers. Silence lay over the outer world; there were no noises inside the ship apart from a steady hum and occasional clinks at its rear end.

After half an hour the trees facing the port lit up briefly in vivid crimson. The entire vessel gave a jolt. A terrible roar followed. The crew came awake with language more fluent than seemly.

"That was tricky," remarked Nilda. "I had to move faster than the drop."

Four mental voices choroused sardonically: "Or you'd have ruined your make-up."

"Yes," agreed Nilda calmly. "Someone has to look decent."

Hector alone had the ability to make the answering noise telepathically.

Gloomily posing by the edge of the crater, and secretly impressed by its size as seen in the light of the new day, Sector Marshal Bvandt said to a land-force captain, "O.K., what's your story?"

"We stood guard in a ring, two body-lengths apart, all through the night. The whole of the ground between us remained under such close observation that nothing could possibly have slipped through unseen."

"So it appears," commented Bvandt nastily. He scuffed some dirt with three of his feet, watched it slide down the great hole.

"Nothing passed," insisted the captain. "We had constant watch on every inch of ground around the ring. We maintained that watch even after the explosion and right up to dawn."

"Yet this disaster occurred behind you. You were between it and the ship. Something must have caused it—some *thing!*"

"I cannot explain it. I can only say that no alien passed through the ring of guards." He was very positive about it.

"Humph!" Openly dissatisfied, Bvandt turned his attention to a wounded trooper waiting nearby. "Well?"

"They had got the gun and its ammunition-trailer this far." Four of his eight eyes bent to stare into the crater. "I was following at short distance. All was dark and quiet. There was nothing unusual that I could see or hear, no noise, no warning. Then all of a sudden this happened." He used a shaky extensible to point at the hole. "I was lifted off my feet and flung against a tree."

"Nobody knows anything," spat Bvandt, kicking more dirt. "A gun, a trailer, two captains and sixty men go to blazes in one midnight blast—and nobody knows anything." He scowled at the land-forces captain. "Did the alien vessel remain silent, undisturbed, all through this?"

"No." The captain fidgeted.

"Come on then, you fool, speak the rest! I am able to understand speech!"

"Immediately after darkness had fallen we heard the vessel's door open and close as if something had emerged, but there were no noises on the ladder, and in the darkness we could see nothing—if anything did come out. In any case, no attempt was made to penetrate our ring or even to approach it. Then toward midnight, and shortly before the explosion, the door opened and shut again. There were faint sounds up and down the ladder as if what was making them had come out and gone in almost without pause."

"That," declared Bvandt with much ire, "is too revealing for words. It tells me practically everything I wish to know."

"I am glad of that," assured the captain, stupidly pleased.

"Get out of my sight!" Bvandt waved furious extensibles at him.

"We have scanners," remarked Vteish thoughtfully. "We have apparatus that can scan mechanically by night and day. What a pity we don't utilize it here."

"You are not ahead of me," Bvandt snapped. "You are several days behind. I considered the matter en route. Scanning equipment cannot be extracted from the ships, neither can it be operated without power supplied by the ships, neither can we bring the ships any nearer than they are."

"I seem to have heard of self-contained transportables," ventured Vteish, glancing at him. "Small ones with their own generators."

"You talk like an imbecile. Firstly, I cannot produce by magic a transportable we do not possess. A couple of sets are being brought by ships not due for many days. It is beyond even my power to accelerate them."

"Of course."

"Secondly," he continued testily, "I doubt the usefulness of these scanners when they do arrive. Whatever can blow up a big gun obviously can blow up a transportable viewer. Thirdly, it is evident that this alien cylinder has some sort of unimaginable scanning apparatus superior to ours."

"In what way?"

"In what way?" echoed Bvandt, pointing all his eyes in dire appeal to the indifferent skies. "He asks me, 'In what way?' See here, Commander Vteish, we are upon the slope of a rise. The enemy vessel is over the other side. We cannot see it from here. It is out of sight because we are unable to view it through some thousands of tons of intervening dirt. No scanner we possess, no scanner we can conceive is capable of seeing straight through a hill." He nudged the other in emphasis—"Apparently *they* can see through a hill. How else could they know of the gun and strike at its precise position?"

"Possibly they have a contraption which employs sky-reflection in a manner similar to our electro-communicators," suggested Vteish, striving to look profound. "In which case hills and mountains would be no obstacles."

"Bunk! *Kaminnif!* You are back in your dream-plays! Even if hills and mountains could be visually surmounted there would be nothing to see but treetops. How is it possible to devise anything so selective that it can dissolve the concealing foliage to reveal what is beneath?"

"I would not venture to argue the possibility," said Vteish. "I am content only to point." He pointed to the crater. "There is the incontrovertible evidence that despite every technical difficulty they can see and do see, through hills or through foliage, by night as well as day."

"That's what I've been telling you all along," exploded Bvandt. "You have argued right around in a circle. Do you talk for the pleasure of your own voice?"

He was still fuming when a courier arrived, handed him a message-cylinder which he unscrewed impatiently. Extracting the missive, he read it aloud.

"Have received your pictograph of biped other-life. Good work!" Crumpling the paper, he tossed it into the crater. "Headquarters calls it good work. For lack of their support it has been mighty bad work so far."

"There is another," said the courier, offering a second cylinder.

Bvandt grabbed it, read, "Have now received pictograph of skew-shaped, multi-limbed, legless other-life, and cannot reconcile this with record previously delivered. What is relationship? Clarify without delay." He glared at the courier who edged away self-consciously. "Clarify without delay. Do they think I am omnipotent?"

"I am only the courier," reminded the other.

A pictograph operator arrived before Bvandt could find another avenue for expression. He had his box in one bunch of extensibles, several glossy sheets in another. His expression was slightly befuddled.

"Well?" demanded Bvandt, glowering at him.

The operator gabbled nervously: "Last night we set boxes in trees on the order of Captain Hixl. They had back flashes and snare-lines attached. As expected, we get several records of tree-lizards." He held out the sheets. "We also got these. We might have got more if some boxes had not been destroyed by this explosion."

Snatching the sheets, Bvandt gave them the eight-eyed stare. Both his mouths worked around and his body humped with shock.

Three of the sheets showed different aspects of the same fantastic thing. It was sitting on a branch as if out to enjoy the air. It bore a perfunctory resemblance to the two-legged pipe-smoking creature first observed, for it had two legs, two jointed arms and somewhat similar form. But it was far smaller and, moreover, possessed a single tentacle which was curled around the branch on which it sat. Its tiny, impish face held a pair of tremendous eyes which stared from the picture like twin moons.

"By space!" swore Vteish, breathing close. "What an object!"

His breath jerked out in a sharp hiss as Bvandt shuffled the sheets to show the others. These depicted another, differently shaped but equally nightmarish thing also on a branch. It had a pair of three-fingered hands in lieu of legs, and no visible arms, tentacles or extensibles. Apart from the hands which gripped the branch it appeared limbless. Its body made one smooth curve on each side and the outlines of it were peculiarly fuzzy.

What got them most was the face, the awful face. Flat-topped, with demoniac horns at the sides, it had a great, menacing nose jutting between a couple of huge, glowing eyes still larger than those of the thing on the other sheets. Even in picture form those enormous optics fascinated them with the hypnotic quality of their cold, haughty, all-observing stare.

"Now we have *four* forms," mourned Bvandt, unable to tear his gaze away from those immense eyes. "You can see what is going to happen. I will transmit these to headquarters. In due time they will send acknowledgment." His voice changed to a mocking imitation of the stiff, officious tones beloved of bureaucrats. "Have received your pictographs of two more other-life forms. Reply without delay stating which of these is the master-type and define the relationship of the others."

"I do not know what answer can be given," Vteish confessed.

"No answer can be given—yet." Bvandt made an irritated gesture in the general direction of the alien vessel. "In the name of the eternal cosmos, why can't they make up their minds what shape and form they're going to take? In the name of the red sun, blue sun or any other sun, why can't they decide on one particular identity and stick to that?"

"Possibly their nature does not permit a decision," theorized Vteish after exercising his mind. "It is thinkable by me that they are all of the same type but, under some alien compulsion with which we are not familiar, are impelled to change shape from time to time. They may be creatures who can't help altering at certain moments, in response to certain impulses."

"Anything is thinkable by you," scoffed Bvandt. "Sometimes I wonder why you don't leave the service and become a constructor of dream-plays." He stared again at the great eyes of Clobo, the greater ones of Nilda. "We must solve this problem forthwith."

"How?"

"We have two choices. For one, we can make an assault in full strength from every direction, using every trooper and the ship's crews."

"That may cost us many lives," Vteish pointed out. "And if we fail there will be no replacements for at least four days. It will take us that long to conscript a force of local settlers; longer if we wait for the other ships."

"I have considered that," said Bvandt. "I prefer the alternative plan, though it is risky. We can take up a ship and use its armament to wreck the alien vessel or, at least, damage it sufficiently to ground it for keeps."

"By space!" exclaimed Vteish. "I wouldn't care to try that! The minimum velocity at which a ship is controllable means that you'd have to shoot in less than one-hundredth the blink of an eye. And hit the target. And fire while in a dive. And pull out in time to avoid plunging into the earth."

"I know, I know."

"Low level bombardment by spaceships is not possible because of the tremendous speeds involved."

"Many an impossibility has been achieved in a pinch," declared Bvandt.

Vteish said, "An ordinary air machine would be better."

"I agree. The idea is excellent, my dear commander. I congratulate you upon it. Please bring me an air machine."

"Perhaps the settlers—?"

"There are no air machines anywhere in the vicinity, none owned by any of the dirt-scrabblers. Do you expect all the amenities of civilization on this outpost world?" He sniffed his contempt. "There will not be one solitary air machine available until the main fleet arrives—and that will be several weeks behind the first comers." He sniffed again. "We must make do with what we've got precisely as these aliens are making do with what they've got. We'll bring a ship into action and hope for the best. When that fails, *if* it fails, I'll consider risking an assault and take a chance on losses."

"How about flying a bomb-carrying kite with an automatic release?" asked Vteish, picturing himself among the casualties to come.

Bvandt responded generously. "I will give the bomb if you will provide the kite and the necessary mechanism and clear away ten thousand infernal trees." Glancing upward, he added in different tones, "It has just occurred to me—what outlandish thing may be sitting up there now, hidden by the leaves, listening to us, glaring at us goggle-eyed?"

"Eh?" Startled, Vteish followed his gaze. So did several troopers. With a coldness upon them they ignored the many sky-gaps and studied the silent trees.

Their mistake lay in not looking higher, much higher.

Sammy the Sharpeye's mind cut through the ether saying: "One of their vessels is warming its main propulsors."

"I guessed it," answered Peter. "I can hear the dull roar of them from here." He paused while he thought it over. "Are there any of these eight-footed uglies hanging around me?"

"A ring of watchers," came Rippy's thought-form. "They're keeping at good distance, up in the trees, as if they're sort of nervous."

"Do you think they saw you boys go out?"

"A jump from a hole straight into deep brush doesn't tell much. You see something, you know it's something, but you don't know what. So you stick to the trees and say your prayers. Anyway they've not seen me since. Kim neither." Rippy sounded contemptuous.

"Kim!" called Peter.

No reply.

"What's the matter with Kim?"

"He's laconic," said Rippy. "Aren't you, Kim?"

"Speechless," corrected Hector, "with snitched food."

"There are times," snarled a menacing thought-form, heard for the first time in days, "when I am tempted to change my diet." Then, more sharply, "There's a dope on the ground, Rippy! Crawling toward you, dragging a box. Do you want him, or shall I take him?"

"This one's on me," said Rippy.

Sammy chipped in again with: "They are now closing all vents and trimming ship for a take-off, leaving troops on the ground. The bow armament turrets are projected. Looks like they've a notion to blow off somebody's britches."

"I'll check," said Peter calmly. Going to the control cabin, he switched the space-radio, sent out a call, listened. He repeated several times without result. "No Terran in this sector," he told Sammy. "So that means there's nobody to shoot up but us. Heck, that's going to be a chancy business with a spaceship, even one so slow as theirs are."

"Reckon they're going to risk it, all the same," replied Sammy. "I'm nicely set to copy Nilda's tactics, but a one-pounder won't get me much. These ships need something more."

"We'll give them more," decided Peter. "Get me the range and bearings."

Knowing that this would take Sammy a minute or two, he used the interval to broadcast a wordless but definite anxiety, and aching concern about a mechanical matter. The thing now listed by the pictographs as superior life-form number two promptly dropped what it was doing, clanked and buzzed along the passage, helped him load a robot bomb and slide it out upon its launching-rack. That done, the noisy one returned to his task.

"Relative to your longitudinal axis, I make it forty-seven degrees leftward, exit side," Sammy informed. "Range: slightly over six miles—say six point two."

"I hate to do this because it tells too much," observed Peter. "So long as we remain in this jam we can't stop them learning something, but I don't feel like giving them more information than is necessary."

"You've about two minutes in which to relent, think up something better and bring it into action," Sammy commented. "The propulsors are reddening. They'll be boosting pretty soon."

"Ah, well, this is going to hurt them more than it hurts me." Shrugging resignedly, he tripped the trigger.

Twin rockets blasted, forced the winged projectile up to two thousand feet before their castings fell away. The intermittent jet-engine took over and the bomb speeded high above the treetops. Steadily it hammered into the distance with a noise like that of an asthmatic motorcycle.

Sitting on the empty launching-rack, Peter swung his legs idly to and fro while his fingers rested on the key of the little transmitter standing nearby. The staccato noise of the jet had now died away in the distance. Even the trees seemed to be waiting, waiting.

"Now!" rasped Sammy.

Peter pressed the key, held it down. Resulting sound took a long time to come; when it did arrive it was muffled by mileage and trees to no more than a dull thump. Later, a thin, dark column of smoke snaked out of the landscape partway to the horizon.

"That," Sammy was saying, with grim satisfaction, "is what I call a number one big-time smiffelpitzer! Bang on the button! I could feel it even from here."

Nilda's tones hooted irritably: "Aren't you guys *ever* going to let me *sleep?"*

"Shut up!" ordered Sammy. "They were lying nose to tail about four hundred yards apart. The one which was warming up lost most of what it was warming. Nobody has come out of it, either. Maybe you've laid them for keeps."

"What of the other vessel?" Peter prompted.

"That's without a chunk of its bow; it could be repaired—in a month or two."

"It can't take off?"

"Definitely not," assured Sammy.

"Sle-e-eep!" wailed Clobo. "Ain't me and Nilda allowed any?"

"No more than I get when you two gabble all through the night," Sammy retorted.

"Lay off!" ordered Peter. "Let 'em have some peace and quiet for a while. Don't call me unless it's urgent."

He listened now. Sammy and the others remained obediently silent. With typical consideration he decided against winding in the launching-rack, a process much lacking in slumbersome music. He felt a bit anxious about leaving it extended, for perforce the exit-trap had to remain open. But no matter.

Superior life-form number two responded to his momentary thought by clanking uproariously along the passage and winding in the rack. He did it right under Peter's nose, with great gusto, the maximum of noise, and complete indifference to the resulting flood of telepathic insults.

And that was that!

The most pungent portions of Sector Marshal Bvandt's speech were uttered with his eating-mouth. Moreover, he garbled the words and made simultaneous eating motions with his speaking-mouth. His whole performance set a new low in uninhibited vulgarity but was excusable on the grounds of sheer exasperation.

Having reached the end of his impressively extensive vocabulary, which included a description of the aliens as a cosmically misbegotten shower of *nifts,* he snarled at Vteish, "Now count 'em."

Vteish went around adding them up, came back, said: "One ship's crew intact, plus three survivors from the other. Also five land-force captains and four hundred six troopers."

"So!" said Bvandt. "So!" He jiggled his extensibles, humped himself and fumed. "So!"

"So what?" inquired Vteish, blundering badly.

That started Bvandt off again. He went a second time through his long list of choice vituperations, this time taking care to emphasize their especial application to supporting officers in general and one dream-play addict named Vteish in particular.

Yes," agreed Vteish, when he had finished. He looked abashed.

"Now," continued Bvandt, gaining control of himself with an effort, "I have noticed one peculiar feature of the enemy's tactics." He fixed three cold, contemptuous eyes on Vteish while the other five watched the trees. "I do not suppose that you have observed it."

"To what feature do you refer?"

"The enemy keeps to a one-blow technique." Bvandt carried on to explain it further. "There was one blow at our sniper, one at our six marksmen, one at the gun, one at these ships. Each succeeded because it was perfectly aimed and timed—but each was only one blow devised to suit a specific occasion. They have not yet demonstrated their ability to deliver two blows simultaneously, or three, or six." He stared meaningly at the other. "Perhaps because they are not able to."

"Ah!" said Vteish.

"Being alien, they have alien minds," Bvandt went on. "It is remotely possibly that they lack the ability to concentrate on more than one thing at one time. A confrontation with several simultaneous threats might prove too much for them."

"Might," said Vteish dubiously.

"Do you hold the view that we should withdraw—and accept the consequences back at headquarters?" demanded Bvandt, quick to seize upon his skepticism.

"Oh, no, not at all," Vteish denied hurriedly.

"Then be good enough to display a visible measure of co-operation and enthusiasm. Remember that you are an officer. As such, you must set an inspiring example." He shifted his feet to strike an attitude more important. "As I do!"

"Yes."

"All right! For a start you can supervise the salvaging of the sideguns. Get them out of the ships, attach their ammunition-trailers and position them in a semicircle barely within range of the alien vessel."

"A semicircle?"

"Of course, you idiot! If we place them in a complete circle, we'll have them firing upon each other."

"What," persisted Vteish, "when the alien ship—which is the center of the circle—is barely within range?"

"I take no risk of range estimates and overshooting," Bvandt shouted. "We may have casualties enough." He gave himself time to cool down before he added: "The important thing is to spread the guns immediately they are out, and to keep them spread while making the approach. See that they are hauled to their stands while widely dispersed; they cannot then be put out of action with one selective blow." Glowering at the other, he snapped, "Get going!"

"Very well."

Bvandt turned to Captain Hixl. "You will remain here with the surviving crew. Take your orders from Commander Vteish and see that the crew digs out those guns in double-quick time." Then to Gordd. "You will command the land-force captains and their troops. Deploy them and make careful approach to the alien ship. Keep no closer together than is necessary to maintain contact. Select and guard a semicircle of sites for the guns which Vteish will bring. Hold them until he arrives. Beat off any attacks as best you can, and be careful to watch the trees."

He got eight times an eyeful of the nearest tall growths before he repeated, "Watch the trees!"

"As you order." And with an air of ill-concealed foreboding, Gordd departed with his small army. Bvandt roamed irritably around, watching the trees and ignoring the sky-gaps. Now and again he chivvied the crew as they sweated and strained to get out the guns.

One by one the heavy weapons were extracted, and lugged among the trees. There were twelve altogether. Bvandt would much have preferred to use the still larger and heavier bow-rifles, but these were fixtures impossible to remove without dockyard facilities. He had to be content with the two batteries of mobile side-guns.

The job was completed as dusk began to fall. Nothing untoward happened—except the death of Gordd. A trooper brought the news. Encouraged by the aliens' seeming indifference, Gordd had attempted to get nearer their ship. He had crept cautiously forward, covered by two nervous troopers. He had been attacked in the deep brush by something swift and black and manifestly spawned of a ferocious world. The assailant had made violent, non-speech noises as it took Gordd apart.

"And what of the troopers covering him?" asked Bvandt stabbing the messenger with his eight-eyed glare. "What did they do—sit around and chew leaves?"

"The black thing darted out too suddenly to permit a shot," explained the trooper. "It was upon Captain Gordd in a flash, became mixed up with him. Before the escort could intervene to separate them, they also were attacked."

"By what?"

"Another and different creature. It had a few points of resemblance to the black one but was not the same. It was more slender, more agile, and yellow-colored with curious markings. Its face was blunter, more terrible. It made no noises, and fought with an awful silence." He permitted himself a reminiscent shudder. "This yellow horror was faster moving than the black one, much faster. Indeed, it made motions so confusingly swift that the escort was ripped to pieces under our eyes, and even the pictograph operators did not succeed in making a clear record of it."

"These creatures, the black one and the yellow one, did not correspond with other aliens already recorded?"

"No."

"Then that makes *six* types," observed Bvandt. He spoke to Vteish as the latter came up. "We have now discovered two more alien shapes. They've just slaughtered Gordd." He flourished his extensibles irefully. "How many more forms do they take? In the name of a thousand blue comets, why can't they make up their minds?"

Vteish pondered it before he suggested: "Might not their kind of life be shapeless?"

"What do you mean by that?"

"Now and again we hatch malformations," Vteish pointed out. "Some examples have been weird in the extreme, so much that we have destroyed them on sight. But they were weird only in our estimation, not in their own! If malformations occurred frequently enough, they would become the norm. Infinite variety would be accepted as the natural course of events. The process would be self-sustaining, variations breeding further variations. No parents could forecast the shape and form of their offspring or expect those offspring to resemble themselves."

"Kaminnif!" snapped Bvandt. "We have other forms of life on our own worlds, tree lizards and water reptiles and insects. I can stretch my imagination far enough to conceive some nonexistent life-form able to progress through the air without engines, perhaps an ultra-light form with tremendously enlarged fins of a fish. But I just cannot accept the notion of different forms mating to produce other and more different forms, haphazardly, without law or order."

"Then how do you explain their great variety?" challenged Vteish. "So far, we have found no two alike."

"There is only one solution—they represent the inhabitants of several worlds. Each shape is the master-type of its own planet."

"If that were true it would mean that we're opposed not by one world but by an empire," protested Vteish.

"Why not? We have an empire. We cover twenty-four worlds. I see no reason why this mob of repulsive *nifts* should be confined to one. We do not know whether this vessel is small or large by their standards. If small, what do they call a big one? How many more outlandish shapes might be on *that*? How many worlds do they control—a thousand?"

"Not a thousand, surely!" said Vteish, finding this too much.

"We don't know." He slurged again, discontent rivaling anger. "We don't know anything of real importance. We have suffered losses and gained nothing worthy of the sacrifice. What makes their vessels so fast? How far through the cosmos do they spread? What is their power relative to ours? How many other strange entities have they got and what form do they take?" He made a spitting sound. "We are as ignorant as at the start."

"But we'll soon find out," Vteish promised.

"We better had! It will go ill with us if we fail. Are those guns positioned yet?"

"Almost."

"Then why do you hang around here? Go to them. Hustle them along. See that they open fire immediately they're ready. Maintain the bombardment until you are satisfied that the target is grounded forever—but don't wreck it completely. We want to learn things from it, valuable things."

"I will go at once." Suiting the action to the word, Vteish hastened between the trees.

Bvandt stared officiously at the trooper who had brought the news of Gordd. "Well, have you taken root like a vegetable? Or has someone granted you leave of absence?"

"No." Sullenly the trooper made off in the wake of Vteish.

Already it was dark. A few stars shone in the sky-gaps. The trees rustled in the cool night air. Something floated low over the trees, obscuring the stars in its passage and silently on. It was like a wide-eyed ghost. Bvandt failed to notice it.

Humping across to the least damaged ship, Bvandt squatted within the shelter of its main port and waited for the fire works. Hixl joined him. Together they brooded and waited—and watched the half-visible trees.

In due time the guns thundered raggedly. The whistle of their shells could be heard through the dark. Nearby trees quivered in response to the bursts. There was a long pause, then a second uproaring barrage. Shells screamed toward their mutual aiming point. The blasts caused a bright crimson flickering in the distance.

With much satisfaction, Bvandt said: "I guess that settles that!"

Hixl said nothing.

The penetrating thought-form of Sammy the Sharpeye came through with, "Their newest stunt is to extract their side-shooting mediums and drag 'em into the woods. They don't appear to be bothering with the bow heavies."

"Bringing them thisaways?" Peter asked. He was in the control cabin, rubbing his chin and listening, listening.

"Yes, of course."

"How many?"

"Ten so far. Wait a bit." He was quiet for a while, then said: "Plus two more. That's twelve. We should have mailed them another hoister."

"It's too late now," observed Peter. He grabbed the sides of his pilot-seat and hung on as the whole vessel suddenly floated a few feet upward and come down with a wallop. "Youps!"

"What's that for?" demanded Sammy.

"Results. We soared a yard."

"About time too," contributed Rippy's mind. "I get pretty sick of dumps like—" He broke off for a moment, returned excitedly. "Jeepers! Here's one of them practically crawling into my mouth. There are two more on his tail, holding handguns, and somewhat jumpy. How about it, Kim?"

"I'll take the two," Kim replied.

"Greedy!" defined Rippy. "All right, here goes!"

Both went silent, and Sammy came in again saying, "That pair of landbound lugs get fed too much. They don't know what to do with their surplus zip."

"Boys will be boys," Peter reminded. "What do you see now?"

"The guns have been dragged away, with plenty of ammo. I get occasional glimpses of them through the trees and they're spread over a couple of miles. The light is getting lousy—reckon it's time Nilda took over."

"Coming right now," Nilda chipped in.

"Three slurpers have lost interest," announced Rippy suddenly. "Pfaugh! What a mess they make." Pause. "Nice work, Kim."

Kim did not reply.

The boat floated again, remained poised ten feet from the ground. A shrill shriek like that of a whirling grinder-wheel came from the rear. It ceased abruptly. Someone started bouncing ball bearings on a pile of empty cans. The vessel remained steady at its new elevation.

"We are now in a state of suspense," Peter informed all and sundry.

"I know it," retorted Hector. "I've four full pans, two double boilers, one percolator and one pressure cooker all waiting for the drop."

The ship promptly dropped, not too hard, but hard enough.

Hector bawled: "There, what did I tellya?"

Leaving the control cabin, Peter went along the passage, had a look in the antigrav chamber. All within was quiet and peaceful. There was no sign of the rhomboidal object.

Hopefully, he tried the fourth cubical along the passage, shoved open its door, had a glance through. Superior lifeform number two was standing impassively in a corner, his various limbs folded or retracted, his air that of one patiently prepared to wait the crack of doom.

"Mechano has finished!" Peter transmitted the news like a mental yelp. He did a little dance. "Back in the ship, all of you. Make it snappy!"

Clobo complained, "Just as I was going out. Oh, well—"

Regaining the control cabin, Peter fastened himself into the pilot-seat, fingered the familiar gadgets, stared anxiously through the armorglass and into the pall of darkness. He was not unduly worried about the hidden guns. He had the choice of six effective methods of dealing with those now that they were no longer shielded over the rise of land, the simplest being to cause a gentle but not soothing vibration in the molecules of their ammunition. The result would be drastic. He could arrange it right now if necessary, but was not sure of the necessity. Peter's tendency was to slaughter only in minimum terms suitable to the circumstances.

At the moment his only anxiety was for the missing members of the crew, and since they were strictly nonmechanical the noisiest *nift* reposed in his cabin and refused to do anything about the woe.

"Rippy in," suddenly reported that worthy.

"Sammy in," followed right after the other.

"They're ranging and aiming the guns but haven't yet loaded," informed Nilda, blandly ignoring the order to return. "We'll just about make it."

"Kim!" called Peter urgently. Bending forward in his seat, he stared hard into the dark. Nothing could be seen other than a faint haze of starlight over distant trees.

"Coming!" answered a harsh tone presently. Then, half a minute later, "Kim in."

"Now they've loaded!" screeched Nilda from somewhere far off in the gloom. "Take her up! Leave the lock open for me!"

Automatically, Peter shifted the antigrav control. The ship did a sharp, sickening rise to five hundred feet, hung there. An instant later great throbs of fire spurted in a half-circle from the trees. Unseen things whined shrilly through the night. A dozen gouts of crimson sprang from the ground immediately beneath.

"Nilda!"

"Keep your hair on—I'm coming."

He lifted two hundred feet higher, waited, fingers ready at the controls, eyes gazing expectantly through the armorglass. He did not see her approach but shortly she said: "Nilda in."

More fire spurted below. The closer sound of the missiles and spread of resultant bursts showed that the hidden guns had been elevated. With a brief, *"Tsk-tsk!"*

he gave the anti-grav full play. An hour later he cut them off, switched in the rockets. The world shrank behind.

The advance guard of four oncoming alien vessels sighted him half a million miles out, reangled in pursuit. He did not bother to change course. Shifting the propulsor controls to the end notch, he watched the others gradually slide off his side-screen, reappear on his tail-screen and slowly diminish. By the time they had shrunk to barely discernible dots they had given up and turned back.

Setting a new course, he locked the automatic pilot onto it, checked its operation, unstrapped from his seat, stretched and yawned.

Hector's thought-form complained: "I've told you ten times that chow's ready. Dontcha want any?"

"Yes, sir! Give me a minute."

He watched the autopilot a little while before he left the cabin. There was laughter-impulses coming from the combined galley and messroom toward the tail. It was an easy guess that Clobo was putting on one of his ever-popular acts, probably his famous impression of Fleet Admiral Dickson going pop-eyed over his food. A good guy, Clobo, whose value lay mostly in his ability to entertain, to beat off space-boredom and maintain morale.

The same old wonder came to Peter as he closed the control cabin door, the marvel of a million long, long years, the frequently recurring realization that the hugeness of space is matched by the immensity of time.

For all had passed through the many eons. Some had leaped ahead, some lagged behind. But several of the laggers had put on last-moment spurts—because of late functioning of natural laws—and the impact upon their various kinds of the one kind called Man.

Until they had breasted the tape together.

For the hundredth or two-hundredth time he paused on his way to the galley and studied the inscribed plate set in the wall. It read:

Patrol Boat *Letitia Reed.*

(Presented to the Associated Species by Waldo Reed.)

Crew.	Kind.
Peter the Pilot.	Terraman.
Sammy the Sharpeye.	White-crested Eagle.
Hector the Hasher.	Venusape.
Rippy the Ranger.	Terradog.
Kim the Killer.	Hunting Cheetah.
Mechano the Mender.	Automaton.
Clobo the Clown.	Spectral Tarsier.
Nilda the Nightwatcher.	Great Horned Owl.

Grinning, Peter carefully left his mind wide open while he thought to himself, "Boy, what a bunch of bums we've got!" Then just as carefully he closed his mind while he added, "But I'd sooner lose my legs than any one of 'em!"

"For the eleventh time, you bum—" howled Hector.

"Coming!" He took his eyes off the plate and hurried to chow.

U-Turn

Astounding, April 1950

He came slow-footed from the spaceport's ramp with one thought recurrent in his mind: *We are scientific and highly civilized—-therefore I am going to die.*

Nearby officials gave him no more than the usual cursory glances as he wandered across the landing area toward the exit gates. Outside he stood at the verge of the city street and surveyed it with eyes half-blinded by thought.

We are scientific and highly civilized—therefore I am going to die. His teeth chewed around lightly with the tip of his tongue. *It will be easy. They will make it easy for me. Afterward I shall neither know nor care. I have been nonexistent before. I was dead before I was born and my nonexistence didn't bother me then.*

His gaze shifted to the overcast sky, the dull gray Earth sky so different from that of Mars. Rain was falling in a steady torrent but none touched him, not a drop. The great plastic roof above the street caught it and bore it all away. The street remained warm, dry, dustless, dirtless, germless. It was a street of the sanitary age, designed for cleanliness, comfort and total independence of the elements.

An electro-taxi hummed smoothly along the road, the silver balls of its antenna spinning almost to invisibility as it sucked at power broadcast from far away. He waved to it, his hand moving as though stubborn determination had overcome his own inherent unwillingness. The cab sighed as it stopped. Its driver regarded him impassively.

"Where to, mister?"

Climbing in, he said, "Life Terminal Building."

Lips parted in readiness to repeat the instructions, the cabbie changed his mind, firmed his mouth, said nothing. Switching power, he started off, covering ground at little better than a crawl while he brooded solemnly over the wheel. He did not like passengers for Life Terminal. They reminded him too much that man has little way to go and little time in which to do it.

His passenger endured the snail's pace without reproof and exhibited the fatalistic patience of one whose mind is made up and who has never been known to unmake it. Several sleek electro-sportsters flashed past at speed that made air-blasts rock the creeping vehicle but failed to shake the driver from his morbid mood.

Reaching the great marble entrance to Life Terminal, the passenger watched the machine depart at swifter pace. He had another look at the sky, the street, the even, architectural line of high roofs between the two. Then he mounted the forty steps leading to the crystal doors, starting off with a reluctant right foot, followed by a reluctant left, gradually overcoming the pedal inertia and increasing his pace until he arrived at the top practically at a run.

Beyond the doors lay a circular floor flowered in mosaics from the center of which arose a gigantic hand of sparkling granite five or six times the height of a man. One mighty forefinger was raised in warning. Imprisoned within the hand was a vibratory command which resounded in the depths of his brain like a telepathic cry.

"Stop! Think! What have you left unfinished?"

He walked steadily around the hand toward the far counter, his rubberoid feet-pads moving silently. Behind the counter a young, sweet-faced girl in white uniform came erect as he neared. Her full lips parted.

"Can I help you, sir?"

He gave her a wry smile. "I'm afraid you can."

"Oh!" Her clear blue eyes registered understanding. "You are not here for information? You wish to . . . to—?"

"Yes," he said. It echoed hollowly around the hall and made a solemn sound in the overhead cupola. "Yes."

The granite hand vibrated. *"Stop! Think! What have you left unfinished?"*

"Third door on the right," she whispered.

"Thank you!"

She watched him all the way to the door, watched him as he shoved it open and passed through. Even after he had gone she continued to survey the door as if she wanted no part of it whatever.

The man occupying the room behind the third door bore no resemblance to an official executioner. He was plump, jovial, quick to rise at his visitor's entrance, swift to shake his hand and offer him a seat. Resuming his own chair, he slid a bunch of forms into convenient position on his own desk, held his pen poised in readiness, eyed the other enquiringly.

"Your name?"

"Douglas Mason."

He wrote it down, said, "Resident on Terra?"

"Mars."

"Mars, h'm! What is your age?"

"Two hundred and eighty-seven."

"Ah, then you will have had your third rejuvenation?"

"Yes." Mason fidgeted. "Do we have to fill up forms even for this?"

"Not at all." The official studied him carefully, found him tall, slender, gray-suited, tired-eyed. "A civilized state makes no claim upon the life of any individual citizen. Anyone has the unalienable right to end his life for any reason he considers adequate or for no reason at all, even at the merest whim, providing that the method of accomplishing the said ending does not cause danger, discomfort or distress to fellow citizens."

"I know my rights," assured Mason.

"Therefore," the official went on in the manner of one reciting an oft-repeated rite, "we must accept your choice regardless of whether or not you see fit to co-operate in this matter of form-filling. If you do not care to answer our questions it will not make the slightest difference—but the data we need is very useful and we would appreciate your help. It isn't much to ask when as far as you're concerned there is little left to be asked."

"Help?" echoed Mason, rubbing his chin. He gave the same wry smile as he had bestowed upon the girl outside. "I am under the impression that I can no longer be of help to anyone."

"Many have that idea. Usually they are wrong. In fact," continued the plump man, waxing still more jovial, "I have officiated here for twenty years and have yet to meet the individual who is completely useless."

Mason said, "I suspect you of trying to talk me out of this." His tones became hard. "My mind is made up!"

"Would you care to tell me on what grounds?"

"There's no reason why I should. If a person decides to die he has reasons that seem good and sufficient to himself. But for the sake of informing you I'll say that my best reason is that I do not fear death."

"Nor life?" put in the official. His fat face suddenly seemed not so fat. It had taken on a deep shrewdness.

"Nor life," confirmed Mason without hesitation. He carried on, "When all one's plans have been accomplished, all one's purposes achieved, all one's ambitions realized, all one's friends long departed, and one has to retire for sheer lack of anything further to do, life ceases to be life. It becomes mere existence, a waiting-time. I can stand only so much of that."

The official shrugged resigned shoulders. "It is not for me to argue your motives much as I would like to." He indicated the forms. "May I fill these up now or do you refuse to oblige?"

"Oh, go ahead with the rigmarole," said Mason.

The other took up his pen. "Married?"

"Never found the time, much of it as I've had."

"Really?" He noted it with a faint air of incredulity. "No children then?"

"What d'you mean by that?"

"You have never functioned as a donor?"

Mason snapped, "I disapprove of such practices even if they are embodied in our civilization."

"They are necessary because they are helpful to someone," the other retorted. "The driving-force behind our present-day science is the need to help people. Would you rather have it as it was in the barbaric ages when science was prostituted and knowledge was misapplied?"

"I'm not so sure I wouldn't. Things were messier but a damnsight livelier."

"You prefer them lively?"

"At this stage, yes." Mason continued as if he were pondering aloud rather than talking. "I have an alabaster villa with a forty-acre cactus garden on Mars. It represents the *ne plus ultra* of something or other. In many ways it is also a mausoleum. Within it I can suffer the nagging pain of acute boredom in absolute comfort. What little real work has still to be done is reserved for younger ones, the first and second rejuvenations. Earth is civilized. Venus is civilized. So is Mars. So is the Moon underneath its various domes. Everywhere is civilized, orderly, regulated, under control."

"Everywhere?" queried the official, raising his eyebrows.

"Even the jungles are artificial ones, designed for the edification of the curious and the coddled," Mason went on, a hint of contempt in his voice. "Full of carefully cultivated plants and cunningly doctored animals. The lion at last lies down with the lamb. Pah!"

"You don't like that?" said the official.

Mason gave back, "For centuries the Chinese used an ancient curse: 'May you live in interesting times!' It isn't a curse any more. It's a blessing. We're scientific and civilized. We've got so many rights and liberties and freedoms that one can yearn for chains for the sheer pleasure of having something to fight against and break. I reckon life would be more interesting if there were any chains left to bust."

"I doubt that," the official asserted. "People are very happy until eventually the frustration of idleness overcomes them. With most folk it's a long, long time before that occurs." He pointed his pen at his papers. "On your own showing it has taken you nearly three centuries to reach this stage."

"Yes," admitted Mason, "because I had a good spell of plenty to do. Now I've got nothing. Eventually I'll be due for yet another rejuvenation. What will be the use of it? A man can hang around too long." He leaned forward, hands on knees, face taut. "Know, what I think? I think science has overdone it."

"Not necessarily."

"It has," Mason insisted, "I'm telling you that science has us all trapped between its accomplishments and its failures. It has got us all the way out to Venus and Mars. It can get us no farther. The outer planets are completely beyond reach of any human being in any human-built spaceship. No rocket-fuel concoctable and no propulsive system designable can cope with a gap like that. It's been admitted time and time again. Science has taken us right up to the last frontier—and I've got a press-button, fully automatic alabaster villa on that frontier. Science can go no farther, so it has turned inward and civilized what it's got. Result is we're pinched and confined in absolute freedom and made so darned happy that we could burst into tears."

The official pulled a face expressive of polite but unvoiced disagreement remarked pointedly, "Isn't it rather incongruous that one so condemnatory of science should seek its aid in escaping from it?"

"In finding my way out I conform to the conventions," Mason retorted. "Besides, I readily admit that science has its uses. But I don't consider it above criticism."

"You may have something there," conceded the other, enigmatically. "I often wonder where it'll stop."

"It has stopped to all intents and purposes. Anything that fails to expand has stopped."

"That is an opinion to which you as a citizen are fully entitled." The official's manner made his own opinion clear. Shuffling his forms, he selected one. "Having made the finality of your decision most obvious, I have no choice but to sign your warrant."

"Ye Gods, so I must have a warrant!" Mason bent forward, took it after it had been signed, waved it around like a white flag. "What do I do with this?"

Nodding toward the door, the official said, "Take it through there and give it to the attendant arranger. He will consult you about the manner of your passing."

"You put it so prettily," said Mason. He waved the flag again. "Well, thanks for everything. See you in the next world."

"The meeting will take place only when my constitution can stand no further rejuvenations," promised the other.

The arranger proved to be tall, thin, bald and taciturn. He took the warrant and scanned it with care.

"Do you prefer it swiftly or slowly?"

"Holy smoke, what a question! Who on earth would want to die slowly?"

In funereal tones the arranger said, "I am not talking about the process of expiring but about the condition of death. Do you wish it to occur soon or after an interval?"

"Better make it soon, with minimum delay." Mason added, with grim humor, "Otherwise I might weaken and change my mind."

"That has happened."

"So?"

"Often," confirmed the arranger

"That's news to me," Mason confessed. "I've never heard of anyone getting this far and living to tell the tale."

"Nobody tells the tale. Silence is the price of freedom."

"In that case I can change my mind at my time up to the final moment and walk straight out provided I swear to say nothing?"

"You don't have to swear."

"Why not?"

"You would not care to advertise your moral cowardice."

"How right you are!" said Mason.

The other looked him over. "Somehow I don't think you will change your mind. Unless your reactions are extremely fast you're likely to be one of the many who've put off their mind-changing until it becomes too late."

"I get you. Let me tell you I've already weakened six times in the last two years. I'm not going to soften a seventh time." He examined the room. Except for a desk and hanging calendar, it was bare. "Mind telling me how it will hit?"

"Unawares."

"I know that much, but how?"

The arranger said, "The method is adapted to suit the individual case."

"I'm only curious."

"You won't be—afterward," promised the other. He went on, "The procedure is that you go through that door over there and take the automatic elevator to the Life Terminal hotel where you can select any room you please. They are all most comfortable and—"

"Take the elevator to *where?*" asked Mason loudly.

"The hotel," repeated the arranger. "You will reside there, well-served, entertained, happy in the company of others, until the culmination which will occur only when you are completely off guard and thoroughly at ease. That may mean hours or days before the end, according to the psychology of the subject but as a method it is merciful."

"So, I'll just sit around and wait for it?"

"There are adequate diversions. Nobody broods, nobody mopes. Indeed, there is no cause for apprehension since the subject either weakens and changes his mind or stubbornly sees it through."

"You can't tell me my more than that?"

"Right now I cannot imagine you caring very much."

"Which I don't," Mason assured. "Not a hoot. Do I get on with the job or are there further indispensable bureaucratic preliminaries?"

The other winced. "There are two forms I'm supposed to fill. If you're in such a hurry I'll let them go blank." He pointed to the nearer of the two internal doors. "You can take your choice. That is the way out." He indicated the other. "That also is the way out."

Mason went boldly to the first, opened it and looked through. Beyond lay the mosaic-floored hall with its great granite hand.

"Stop! Think! What have you left unfinished?"

He tried the other door. Behind stood the elevator, bare, metal-lined, with a red button in one wall.

Stepping inside, he peered out and said with a touch of ghastliness, "Going down?" Then he closed the door and rammed his thumb on the red button and instantly realized that this was it!

The button sank under his thumb while he stared at it fascinatedly and lacked the power to release his pressure. It appeared to sink in with an awful slowness born of a time-sense distorted by peril. The approach to death is difficult, the contact tremendously breath-taking. His pores were wide open, his body tense, his heart thudding, his mind whirling when the button closed a circuit and the mock-elevator performed its designed function.

There was only a pale blue luminescence in the air and a split second of immense agony during which his body seemed to be torn into a million pieces and further dispersed to its last molecule.

Voices murmured deep in a blank, colorless haze. Slow mouthing voices that advanced upon him and receded and came back again. They sounded close to his ears and whispered away through illimitable distances and returned. There was a peculiar rhythm to this vocal coming and going, like the steady swing of a sonic wave-form through positive and negative amplitudes enormously stretched in terms of time. It was quite a while before he could distinguish comprehensible words.

"Three in succession. That plays hob with the odds."

"Oh, I don't know. The odds take account of rare runs. You're holding too short a view."

"Or maybe they're improving at the other end?"

"I'd like to think so but I can't see it yet."

Mason sat up and held his head. The voices ran away, ran back. "Give him a shot . . . yes, just there." Someone stuck a pin in him.

He opened his eyes, snapped at a gray-bearded man, "Go easy, will you? I've got a fat nut."

"You're lucky," commented a second heavily built man standing close by his side. "Some get through with only half a nut, others none at all."

"Some never use more than half anyway," said Mason. He ceased nursing his head, braced his hands on the floor and helped himself upright. The room whirled wildly awhile before it steadied.

The graybeard eyed him speculatively, hitched a blued-steel, long-snouted gun more comfortably over one hip, went behind a rough wood desk. Sitting down, he pawed a printed form into position, licked the end of a primitive pencil, looked at Mason again. "Name?"

Mason teetered, felt the bulky man's hand steadying him, protested hoarsely, "Holy smoke! Do we have to go through that again?"

"What we want," informed the greybeard, "are three items: your name, your remaining rejuvenation-run and your qualifications."

"Douglas Mason, twenty-four, suicide," Mason gave succinctly.

The bulky man chipped in with, "Hah-hah!" When Mason turned to look at him, he added, "You've been foxed."

"Shut up, Corlett." The greybeard registered mild annoyance. "I have told you repeatedly that arrivals must be cushioned against mental shock." He showed white teeth and his beard waggled as he concluded, "You're no cushion."

"And I'm no hothouse flower," Mason said. "Neither of you need be afraid of me wilting."

Corlett again said, "Hah!" and added, "Hear that, Dexter? He doesn't want cushioning."

The greybeard named Dexter leaned over his desk, spoke sharply to Mason. "Just what do you mean?"

"It was like this," explained Mason, "I'd got nothing left to do but sit around and think. For a while I thought of all sorts of things, most of them futile. I had become a useless cog in a big, complicated machine and all I could do was wait until my time to be discarded."

"I know," assured Dexter. "I've had some of that myself."

"Then one day a lecturer on the video sent me off on a new tack. He'd been praising our civilization, its scientific exactitude, its perfection. It worked so wonderfully, he said, because every man had his place and every place its man. All the cogs interlocked, the big and the small, mutually necessary. His speech was a supposed morale-lifter, the old it-all-depends-on-you technique."

"Well?" prompted Dexter.

"Then he blundered. He opined that our inability to reach the outer planets was a blessing in disguise. He said our world-wide civilization was so intricate and highly organized that a sudden rush of cogs elsewhere might make it fall apart. There could he chaos. The machine of super-civilization could not run effectively if losing its parts faster than they could be replaced."

"That makes sense," contributed Corlett. "But what of it?"

"I stewed it over in my alabaster villa on Mars." Mason glanced enquiringly at Corlett. "Do you know that there is no alabaster on Mars?"

"No."

"Well, there isn't. Not an ounce, not a grain. It set me back a small fortune to transport the lot from Earth more than a century ago. And it wasn't ship-borne. It was shot across space by vibro-transference. In loads of two thousand pounds which, at that time, represented the limit per boost over that distance. They had to send a good deal more than was needed because three-quarters of it reintegrated wrongly at the focal point and ceased to be alabaster. That's the big, big trouble with vibro-transference. As a process it is ultra-swift, but darned temperamental."

"Go on!" urged Dexter, watching him.

"Human beings make the Earth-Mars run by rocketship. It's slow but certain. They get across alive, in one piece, and still in human shape." Mason paused and rubbed his head which still contained a faint but persistent fizzing. "Just for the hell of it I spent four years working out the odds on a human being getting himself dumped alive and kicking on an outer planet by means of vibro-transference. I found the load-limit per boost would be something over two hundred pounds."

"Two-eighty-four," corrected Dexter.

"And I calculated that the odds were appallingly low. No more than three chances in a thousand."

"Seven," said Dexter.

"As good as that? Efficiency must have improved."

"It has. There is improvement all the time no matter how gradual it may be."

"Anyway," Mason went on, "the odds against success stood so murderously high that obviously it was a technique to be reserved exclusively for lunatics or would-be suicides. Or, in other words, *for the few cogs who became superfluous on their own showing.*"

"Of which you were one?" said Dexter. He stroked his beard, cast a thoughtful look at Corlett returned his gaze to Mason.

Mason nodded agreement "There'd be a big scramble for new frontiers if everyone knew they were available and within reach. There is no similar enthusiasm, for the death-house. The self-confessed superfluous can be handled where the downright adventurous cannot; their numbers are small and they don't matter much."

"So you put two and two together?"

"And made it four. I thought of the basic rights of individuals craftily established by law, of occasional puffs of publicity for Life Terminal's facilities, and of the fact that as far as further rocket efforts are concerned the experts don't seem to be really trying. Yet scientists are notorious fidgets even in their sleep. Why should they give up trying? Answer: becaue they've got there!"

Dexter gave a brief chuckle. "There's one flaw in your complaint about scientific secrecy. If you can think this out all on your ownsome, why shouldn't a million others do likewise—and start the dreaded rush?"

"Because the conclusion can be no more than a suspicion until one obtains positive proof." Mason looked lugubrious. "That is where the powers-that-be did have me foxed. I put over my best act from the moment I left Mars and stepped on Earth, I bet my life on those seven chances in a thousand and I got through pure, white and uncontaminated. I was born lucky. I got the proof I wanted."

"And now you're stuck with it," Corlett interjected. "There are eight hundred of us here. At the rate that newcomers reintegrate in living and recognizable form, it will be a long, long time before we're eighty thousand much less eight millions. So right now we haven't got much. No airplanes, no rocketships, no video, no rejuvenation-plant, no dream-gardens, no alabaster villas, no vibro-boosters. You cannot go back. You cannot return from the dead triumphantly waving your evidence."

"I know it." Mason pursed his lips, made a sucking sound. He let his eyes linger on the blue sheen of Dexter's gun. "The big brains have created a tricky setup, a very neat play. This is life after death and nobody can return to say that it isn't. The stunt cannot be exposed or busied until we have grown big enough and powerful enough to build a civilization of our own."

"You said it!" agreed Corlett, with special emphasis.

"But it doesn't worry me. I wanted proof for my own satisfaction alone. I've done a u-turn. I've turned right round and gone back to where I started—at the bottom with a shovel in my hands."

"You'll need more than that," promised Dexter. He patted the weapon at which Mason was still looking. "This planet isn't as amiable as it might be."

"So much the better. Chains were made to be broken. There will be no more rejuvenation in my time and I haven't got long. Give me a gun and a shovel and let me get started."

They found both for him, took him outside. He leaned on the shovel, sniffed the heavy air, looked at a small group of crude stone houses standing nearby. His gaze swung from there, studied the great red spot on the monstrous thing hanging in the heavens. His feet shuffled around in queer purple grass.

He said, "As one Callistrian to a couple of others, that's a mighty fine sight!"

The Waitabits

Astounding, July 1955

He strode toward the Assignment Office with quiet confidence born of long service, much experience and high rank. Once upon a time a peremptory call to this department had made him slightly edgy, exactly as it unnerved the fresh-faced juniors today. But that had been long, long ago. He was gray-haired now, with wrinkles around the corners of his eyes, silver oak-leaves on his epaulettes. He had heard enough, seen enough and learned enough to have lost the capacity for surprise.

Markham was going to hand him a tough one. That was Markham's job: to rake through a mess of laconic, garbled, distorted or eccentric reports, pick out the obvious problems and dump them squarely in the laps of whoever happened to be hanging around and was considered suitable to solve them. One thing could be said in favor of this technique: its victims often were bothered, bedeviled or busted, but at least they were never bored. The problems were not commonplace, the solutions sometimes fantastic.

The door detected his body-heat as he approached, swung open with silent efficiency. He went through, took a chair, gazed phlegmatically at the heavy man behind the desk.

"Ah, Commodore Leigh," said Markham pleasantly. He shuffled some papers, got them in order, surveyed the top one. "I am informed that the *Thunderer's* overhaul is complete, the crew has been recalled and everything is ready for flight."

"That is correct."

"Well now, I have a task for you." Markham put on the sinister smile that invariably accompanied such an announcement. After years of reading what had followed in due course, he had conceived the notion that all tasks were funny except when they involved a massacre. "You are ready and eager for another trip, I trust?"

"I am always ready," said Commodore Leigh. He had outgrown the eagerness two decades back.

"I have here the latest consignment of scout reports," Markham went on. He made a disparaging gesture. "You know what they're like. Condensed to the minimum and in some instances slightly mad. Happy the day when we receive a report detailed with scientific thoroughness."

"You'll get that only from a trained mind," Leigh commented. "Scouts are not scientists. They are oddities who like roaming the loneliest reaches of space with no company but their own. Pilot-trained hobos willing to wander at large, take brief looks and tell what they've seen. Such men are useful and necessary. Their shortcomings can be made up by those who follow them."

"Precisely," agreed Markham with suspicions promptness. "So this is where we want you to do some following."

"What is it this time?"

"We have Boydell's latest report beamed through several relay-stations. He is way out in the wilds." Markham tapped the paper irritably. "This particular scout is known as Gabby Boydell because he is anything but that. He uses words as if they cost him fifty dollars apiece."

"Meaning he hasn't said enough?" asked Leigh, smiling.

"Enough? He's told us next to nothing!" He let go an emphatic snort, "Eighteen planets scattered all over the shop and not a dozen words about each. He discovers a grand total of eighteen planets in seven previously unexplored systems and the result doesn't occupy half a page."

"Going at that speed, he wouldn't have time for much more," Leigh ventured. "You can't write a book about a world without taking up residence for a while."

"That may be. But these crackpot scouts could do better and it's time they were told as much." He pointed an accusing finger. "Look at this item. The eleventh planet he visited. He has named it Pulok for some reason that is probably crazy. His report employs exactly four words: 'Take it and welcome.' What do you make of that?"

Leigh thought it over carefully. "It is inhabitable by humankind. There is no native opposition, nothing to prevent us grabbing it. But in his opinion it isn't worth possessing."

"Why, man, why?"

"I don't know, not having been there."

"Boydell knows the reason." Markham fumed a bit and went on, "And he ought to state it in precise, understandable terms. He shouldn't leave a mystery hanging in mid-air like a bad smell from nowhere."

"Won't he explain it when he returns to his sector headquarters?"

"That may be months hence, perhaps years, especially if he manages to pick up fuel and replacement tubes from distant outposts. Those scouts keep to no schedule. They get there when they arrive, return when they come back. Galactic gypsies, that's how they like to think of themselves."

"They've chosen freedom," Leigh offered.

Ignoring that remark, Markham continued, "Anyway, the problem of Pulok is a relatively minor one to be handled by somebody else. I'll give it to one of the juniors; it will do something for his education. The more complicated and possibly dangerous tangles are for older ones such as yourself "

"Tell me the worst."

"Planet fourteen on Boydell's list. He has given it the name of Eterna, and don't ask me why. The code formula he's registered against it reads O-1.1-D.7. That means we can live on it without special equipment, it's an Earth-type planet of one-tenth greater mass, and it's inhabited by an intelligent lifeform of different but theoretically equal mental power. He calls this lifeform the Waitabits. Apparently he tags everything and everybody with the first name that pops into his mind."

"What information does he offer concerning them?"

"Hah!" said Markham, pulling a face. "One word. Just one word." He paused, then voiced it. "Unconquerable."

"Eh?"

"Unconquerable," repeated Markham. "A word that should not exist in scout-language." At that point he became riled, jerked open a drawer, extracted a notebook and consulted it. "Up to last survey, four hundred twenty-one planets had been discovered, charted, recorded. One hundred thirty-seven found suitable for human life and large or small groups of settlers placed thereon. Sixty-two alien lifeforms mastered during the process." He shoved the book back. "And out there in the dark a wandering tramp picks a word like unconquerable."

"I can think of only one reason that makes sense," suggested Leigh.

"What is that?"

"Perhaps they really are unconquerable."

Markham refused to credit his ears. "If that's a joke, Commodore, it's in bad taste. Some might think it seditious."

"Well, can you think up a better reason?"

"I don't have to. I'm sending you there to find out. The Grand Council asked specifically that you be given this task. They feel that if any unknown aliens have enough to put the wind up one of our own scouts, then we must learn more about them. And the sooner the better."

"There's nothing to show that they actually frightened Boydell. If they had done so he'd have said more, much more. A genuine first-class menace is the one thing that would make him talk his head off."

"That's purely hypothetical," said Markham. "We don't want guesses. We want facts."

"All right."

"Consider a few other facts," Markham added. "So far, no other lifeform has been able to resist us. I don't see how any can. Any creatures with an atom of sense soon see on which side their bread is buttered—*if* they eat bread and like butter. If we step in and provide the brains while they furnish the labor, with mutual benefit to both parties, the aliens are soon doing too well for themselves to complain. If a bunch of Sirian Wimpots slave all day in our mines, then fly in their own helicopters back to homes such as their forefathers never owned, what have they got to cry about?"

"I fail to see the purpose of the lecture," said Leigh, dryly.

"I'm emphasizing that by force, ruthlessness, argument, persuasion, precept and example, appeal to common sense or any other tactic appropriate to the circumstances, we can master and exploit any lifeform in the cosmos. That's the theory we've been using for a thousand years—and it works. We've proved that it works. We've *made* it work. The first time we let go of it and admit defeat, we're finished. We go down and disappear along with all the other vanished hordes." He swept his papers to one side. "A scout has admitted defeat. He must be a lunatic. But lunatics can create alarm. The Grand Council is alarmed."

"So I am required to seek soothing syrup?"

"Yes. See Parrish in the charting department. He'll give you the coordinates of this Eterna dump." Standing up, he offered a plump hand. "A smooth trip and a safe landing, Commodore."

"Thanks."

The *Thunderer* hung in a balanced orbit while its officers examined the new world floating below. This was Eterna, second planet of a sun very much like Sol. Altogether there were four planets in this particular family, but only the second harbored life in any detectable form.

Eterna was a pretty sight, a great blue-green ball shining in the blaze of full day. Its land-masses were larger than Earth's, its oceans smaller. No vast mountain ranges were visible, no snow-caps either, yet lakes and rivers were numerous. Watersheds lay in heavily forested hills that crinkled much of the surface and left few flat areas. Cloud-banks lay over the land like scatterings of cotton-wool, widely dispersed but thick, heavy and great in number.

Through powerful glasses, towns and villages could be seen, most of them placed in clearings around which armies of trees marched down to the rivers. There were also narrow, winding roads and thin, spidery bridges. Between the larger towns ran vague lines that might be railroad tracks but lacked sufficient detail at such a distance to reveal their true purpose.

Pascoe, the sociologist, put down his binoculars and said, "Assuming that the night side is very similar, I estimate their total strength at no more than one hundred millions. I base that on other planetary surveys. When you've counted the number of peas per bottle in a large and varied collection, you develop the ability to make reasonably accurate guesses. One hundred millions at most."

"That's low for a planet of this size and fertility, isn't it?" asked Commodore Leigh.

"Not necessarily. There were no more of us in the far past. Look at us now."

"The implication is that these Waitabits are a comparatively young species?"

"Could be. On the other hand, they may be old and senile and dying out fast. Or perhaps they're slow breeders and their natural increase isn't much."

"I don't go for the dying out theory," put in Walterson, the geophysicist. "If once they were far bigger than they are today, the planet should still show signs of it. A huge inheritance leaves its mark for centuries. Remember that city-site we found on Hercules? Even the natives didn't know of it, the markings being visible only from a considerable altitude."

They used their glasses again, sought for faint lines of orderliness in wide tracts of forest. There were none to be seen.

"Short in history or slow to breed," declared Pascoe. "That's my opinion for what it's worth."

Frowning down at the blue-green ball, Leigh said heavily, "By our space-experienced standards a world of one hundred millions is weak. It's certainly not sufficiently formidable to turn a hair on a minor bureaucrat, much less worry the Council itself." He turned, lifted a questioning eyebrow as a signals-runner came up to him. "Well?"

"Relay from Sector Nine, sir."

Unfolding the message, he found it duly decoded, read it aloud:

" 'Nineteen-twelve, ex Terra. Defense H.Q. to C.O. battleship *Thunderer*. Light cruiser *Flame*, Lt. Mallory commanding, assigned your area for Pulok check. Twentieth heavier cruiser squadron readied Arlington port, Sector Nine. This authorizes you to call upon and assume command of said forces in emergency only. Rathbone. Com. Op. Dep. D.H.Q. Terra.' "

He filed the message, shrugged and said, "Seems they're taking few chances."

"Yes," agreed Pascoe, a trifle sardonically. "So they've assembled reinforcements near enough to be summoned but too far away to do us any good. The *Flame* could not get here in less than seven weeks. The ships at Arlington couldn't make it in under nineteen or twenty weeks even at superdrive. By then we could be cooked, eaten, burped and forgotten."

"I don't see what all this jumpiness is about," complained Walterson. "That scout, Boydell, went in and came out without losing his edible parts, didn't he? Where one can go a million can follow."

Pascoe regarded him with pity. "A solitary invader rarely frightens anyone. That's where scouts have an advantage. Consider Remy II. Fellow name of James finds it, lands, makes friends, becomes a blood brother, finally takes off amid a burst of fond farewells. Next, down come three shiploads of men, uniforms and guns. That's too much for the locals to stomach. In Remitan psychology the number represents critical mass. Result: the Remy war, which—if you remember your history—was long, costly and bitter."

"I remember history well enough to recall that in those primitive days they used blockheaded space-troopers and no specially trained contact-men," Walterson retorted.

"Nevertheless, what has happened before can happen again."

"That's my problem right now," Leigh interjected. "Will the sight of a battleship a mile in length cause them to start something that can't be finished without considerable slaughter? Had I better risk the crew of a lifeboat in effort to smooth the introduction? I wish Boydell had been a little more informative." He chewed his bottom lip with vexation, picked up the intercom phone, flipped the signals-room switch, "Any word from Boydell yet?"

"No, Commodore," responded a voice. "Sector Nine doesn't think there will be any, either. They've just contacted us to say he doesn't answer their calls. They believe he's now out of range. Last trace they got of him showed him to be running beyond effective communication limits."

"All right." He dumped the phone, gazed through the port "Seven hours we've waited. Nothing has come up to take a look at us. We can detect no signs of excitement down there. Therefore it's a safe bet that they have no ships, perhaps not even rudimentary aircraft. Neither do they keep organized watch on the sky. They're not advanced in our sense of the term."

"But they may be in some other sense," Pascoe observed.

"That is what I implied." Leigh made an impatient gesture. "We've hung within telescopic view long enough. If they are capable of formidable reaction we should be grimly aware of it by now. I don't feel inclined to test the Waitabits at the expense of a few men in an unarmed lifeboat. We'll take the *Thunderer* itself down and hope they're sane enough not to go nuts."

Hastening forward to the main control-cabin he issued the necessary orders.

The landing place was atop a treeless bluff nine miles south of a large town. It was as good a site as any that could have been chosen. The settling of great tonnage over a mile-long area damaged nobody's property or crops, the ground was solid enough not to furrow under the ship's weight, the slight elevation gave a strategic advantage to the *Thunderer's* guns.

Despite its nearness the town was out of sight, being hidden by intervening hills. A narrow road ran through the valley but nothing moved thereon. Between the road and the base of the bluff lay double railroad tracks of about twenty-inch gauge with flat-topped rails of silvery metal. The rails had no splices or ties and appeared to be held firmly in position by being sunk into long, unbroken ridges of concrete or some similar rock-like substance.

The *Thunderer* reposed, a long, black, ominous shape with all locks closed and gun-turrets open, while Leigh stared speculatively at the railroad and waited for the usual call from the metering lab. It came within short time. The intercom buzzed, he answered it, heard Shallom speaking

"The air is breathable, Commodore."

"We knew that in advance. A scout sniffed it without dropping dead."

"Yes, Commodore," agreed Shallom, patiently. "But you asked for an analysis."

"Of course. We don't know how long Boydell was here—perhaps a day, perhaps a week. Whatever it was, it wasn't enough. He might have curled up his toes after a month or two. In his brief visit he'd have avoided any long-term accumulative effect. What we want to know is whether this atmosphere is safe for keeps."

"Quite safe, Commodore. It's rather rich in ozone and argon, but otherwise much like Earth's."

"Good. We'll open up and let the men stretch their legs."

"There's something else of interest," Shallom went on. "Preliminary observation time occupied seven hours and twenty-two minutes. Over that period the longitudinal shift of a selected equatorial point amounted to approximately three-tenths of a degree. That means this planet's period of axial rotation is roughly equivalent to an Earth-year. Its days and nights are each about six months long."

"Thanks, Shallom." He cut off without surprise, switched the intercom, gave orders to Bentley in the main engine-room to operate the power-locks. Then he switched again to Lieutenant Harding, officer commanding ground forces, gave permission for one quarter of his men to be let out for exercise, providing they bore arms and did not stray beyond direct cover of the ship's guns.

That done, he swiveled his pneumatic chair to face the port, put his feet up with heels resting on a wall-ridge, and quietly contemplated the alien landscape. Walterson and Pascoe mooched around the room in the restless manner of men waiting for a burning fuse to reach a gunpowder barrel.

Shallom phoned again, recited gravitational and magnetic-field readings, went off. A few minutes later he came through once more with details of atmospheric humidity, barometric variations and radioactivity. Apparently he cared nothing for what might be brewing beyond the hills, as long as it failed to register on his meters and screens. To his mind, no real danger could exist without advertising itself through a needle waggling or a fluourescent blip.

Outside, two hundred men scrambled noisily down the edge of the bluff, reached soft green sward that was not grass but something resembling short, heavily matted clover. There they kicked a ball around, wrestled, or were just content to lie full length on the turf, look at the sky, enjoy the sun. A small group strolled half a mile to the silent railroad, inspected it, trod precariously along its rails with extended arms jerking and swaying in imitation of tightrope walkers.

Four of Shallom's staff went down, two of them carrying buckets and spades like kids making for the seashore. A third bore a bug-trap. The fourth had a scintilloscope. The first pair dug clover and dirt, hauled it up to the ship for analysis and bacteria-count. Bug-trap dumped his box, went to sleep beside it. Scintilloscope marched in a careful zigzag around the base of the bluff.

After two hours Harding's whistle recalled the outside lotus-eaters who responded with reluctance. They slouched back into the gigantic bottle that already had contained them so long. Another two hundred went out, played all the same tricks, including the tightrope act on the rails.

By the time that gang had enjoyed its ration of liberty, the mess-bells announced the main meal. The crew ate, after which Number One Watch took to its berths and the deepest sleep within memory. A third freedom party cavorted on the turf. The indefatigable Shalom passed along the news that nine varieties of flea-sized bugs were awaiting introduction to Garside, the entomologist, whenever that worthy deigned to crawl out of bed.

By the time the fourth and last section of the crew turned from its two-hour spree, Pascoe had had enough. He was baggy-eyed from lack of slumber, disappointed with having curiosity left unsatisfied.

"More than seven hours waiting in the sky," he complained to Leigh, "and another eight down here. That's over fifteen hours all told. Where has it got us?"

"It has given the men a badly needed break," Leigh reproved. "The first rule of captaincy is to consider the men before considering an exterior problem. There is no real solution to any predicament unless there is also the means to apply it. The men are the means, and more so than the ship or any part of it. Men can build ships, but ships cannot manufacture men."

"All right. They've had their outing. They are refreshed and their morale is boosted, all in accordance with the best psychological advice. What next?"

"If nothing turns up it will enable them to catch up on their sleep. The first watch is snoring its collective head off right now. The other two watches are entitled to their turn.'"

"But that means sitting on our idle behinds for another eighteen hours," Pascoe protested.

"Not necessarily. The Waitabits may arrive at any time, in unguessable number, with unknown intentions and with unknown means of enforcing them. If so, everyone will have a rude awakening and you may get enough action to last you a lifetime." Leigh jerked a thumb toward the door. "Meanwhile, go to bed while the going is good. If trouble starts it's likely to be days before you get another chance. Exhausted men are crippled men in a situation such as this."

"What about you?"

"I intend to slump into sweet dreams myself as soon as Harding is ready to take over."

Pascoe snorted with impatience, glanced at Walterson, gained no support from that quarter. Walterson was dozing on his feet at mere mention of bed. Pascoe snorted again, more loudly this time, departed with the other following.

They returned within ten hours, found Leigh freshly shaved and spruced. A look through the port revealed the same landscape as before. Some two dozen of the crew were fooling around outside, beneath a sun that had not visibly changed position in the sky. The road still wound through the valley and over the hills without a soul upon it. The railroad track still reposed with all the impassive silence of a long-abandoned spur.

Pascoe said, thoughtfully, "This is a good example of how one can deduce something from nothing."

"Meaning what?" inquired Leigh, showing interest.

"The town is nine miles away. We could walk there in about two hours. They've had several times that long in which to sound the alarm, summon the troops, launch an assault." He gestured toward the peaceful scene. "Where are they?"

"You tell us," Walterson prompted.

"Any lifeform capable of constructing roads and rails obviously must have eyes and brains. Therefore it is pretty certain that they've seen us either hanging above or coming down. I don't believe that they remain unaware of our existence." He studied his listeners, went on, "They haven't shown up because they're deliberately keeping away from us. That means they're afraid of us. And that in turn means they consider themselves far weaker, either as a result of what they've seen of us so far or maybe as a result of what they learned from contact with Boydell."

"I don't agree with that last bit," opined Leigh.

"Why not?"

"If they saw us either up above or coming down, what did they actually see? A ship and nothing more. They observed nothing to indicate that we are of Boydell's own kind, though it would be reasonable to assume it. Factually, we're still a bunch of unknowns to them."

"That doesn't make hay of my reasoning."

"It spoils it on two counts," Leigh insisted. "Firstly, not having weighed and measured us, how can they tell they're weaker? Secondly, Boydell himself called them unconquerable. That suggests strength. And strength of a redoubtable order."

"Look," said Pascoe. "It doesn't really matter whether they're stronger or weaker in their own estimation. In the long run they can't buck the power of the human race. The cogent point right now is that of whether they are friendly or antagonistic."

"Well?"

"If friendly, they'd have been around dickering with us hours ago. There's no sign of them, not a spit or a button. Ergo, they don't like us. They've crawled into a hole because they lack the muscle to do something effective. They've ducked under cover hoping we'll go away and play some place else."

"An alternative theory," put in Walterson, "is that they're tough and formidable just as Boydell implied. They've kept their distance because they're wise enough to fight on ground of their own choosing and not on ours. If they refuse to come here, we've got to go there or accept stalemate. So they're making ready for us to walk into their parlor, after which"—he wiped a forefinger across his throat—*"skzzt!"*

"Bunk!" said Pascoe.

"We'll soon learn where we stand one way or the other." Leigh stated. "I've ordered Williams to get the helicopter out. The Waitabits can't avoid seeing that thing whooshing around. We'll learn plenty if they don't shoot it down."

"And if they do shoot it down?" inquired Pascoe.

"That question will be answered if and when it arises," Leigh assured. "You know as well as I do the law that hostility must not be accepted until demonstrated."

He went to the port, gazed across the scene to the tree-swathed hills beyond. After a while he reached for his binoculars, focused them upon the mid-distance.

"Holy smoke!" he said.

Pascoe ran to his side. "What's the matter?"

"Something's coming at last. And it's a train, no less." He handed over the glasses. "Take a look for yourself."

A dozen crewmen were on the track, industriously filing from a rail sufficient metallic powder to be analyzed in the lab. They straightened up as the line conducted sounds of the newcomers approach. Shading their eyes, they stood like men paralyzed while they gaped toward the east.

A couple of miles away the streamlined express came tearing around the base of a hill at nothing less than one and a half miles per hour. The men remained staring incredulously for ten minutes during which time the phenomenon covered a full quarter mile.

The *Thunderer*'s siren wailed a warning, the sample-takers recovered their wits and without undue exertion made more speed up the forty degree bluff than the possible menace was doing on the flat. The last of them had sufficient presence of mind to bring with him an ounce of dust that Shalom later defined as titanium alloy.

Monstrous and imposing, the *Thunderer* sat waiting for first official contact. Every port held at least three expectant faces watching the track and the train. Every mind took it for granted that the oncoming machine would halt at the base of the bluff and things weird in shape emerge therefrom in readiness to parley. Nobody thought for a moment that it might pass on.

It did pass on.

The train consisted of four linked metal coaches and no locomotive, the source of power not being evident. The tiny cars, less than the height of a man, rolled by holding a score of crimson-faced, owl-eyed creatures, some of whom were looking absently at the floor, some at each other, anywhere but directly at the great invader atop the bluff.

From the time the train was first observed until realization dawned that it was not going to stop occupied precisely one hour and twenty four minutes. That was its speed record from the eastward hill to the bluff.

Lowering his binoculars, Commodore Leigh said in baffled tones to Pascoe, "Did you get a clear, sharp view of them?"

"Yes. Red-faced with beak noses and blinkless eyes. One had his hand resting on a window ledge and I noticed it was five-fingered like ours but with thinner digits."

"Far less than walking pace," commented Leigh. "That's what it's doing. I can amble faster even with corns on both feet." He had another puzzled look outside. The train had gained forty yards in the interval. "I wonder whether the power Boydell attributed to them is based on some obscure form of cunning."

"How do you mean?"

"If they can't cope with us while we hold the ship in force, they've got to entice us out of it."

"Well, we aren't out of it, are we?" Pascoe countered. "Nobody has developed a mad desire to catch that train. And if anybody did he'd overtake it so fast he'd get wherever its going before he had time to pull up. I don't see how they can bait us into being foolhardy merely by crawling around."

"The tactic would be according to their own logic, not ours," Leigh pointed out. "Perhaps on this world to crawl is to invite attack. A wild-dog pack reacts that way: the animal that limps gets torn to pieces." He thought it over, continued, "I'm suspicious of this episode. I don't like the ostentatious way in which they all kept their eyes fixed on something else as they went past. It isn't natural."

"Hah!" said Pascoe, prepared to argue.

Leigh waved him down. "I know it's a childish blunder to judge any species by the standards of our own. But I still say it isn't natural to have eyes and not use them."

"On Terra," Walterson chipped in seriously, "some folks have arms, legs, eyes and even brains that they don't use. That's because they have the misfortune to be incurably afflicted, as you know." He went on, encouraged by the others' silence.

"What if this track is a connecting link between town and a sanatorium or hospital? Maybe its sole purpose is to carry sick people."

"We'll soon find out." Leigh resorted to the intercom. "Williams, is the 'copter ready yet?"

"Assembled and now being fueled, Commodore. It can take off in ten minutes' time."

"Who is duty pilot?"

"Ogilvy."

"Tell him to fly ahead of that train and report what's at the other end of the tracks. He's to do that before taking a look at the town." Turning to the others, he added, "Shallom has some aerial shots that were taken before we landed, but Ogilvy will be able to provide us with more details."

Pascoe, again standing at the port, asked, "How much slower is slower?"

"What?"

"When a thing is already creeping as though next year will do, how can you tell that it has decided to apply the brakes?" He elucidated further, "It may be my imagination but I fancy that train has reduced velocity by a few yards per hour. I hope none of its passengers suffered injury by being slung from one end to the other."

Leigh had a look. The train had now gone something less than half a mile from his observation point. The tedious speed and slight foreshortening made it impossible to decide whether or not Pascoe was correct. He had to keep watch a full fifteen minutes before he too agreed that the train was slowing down.

During that time the helicopter took off with a superfast *whoosh-whoosh* from whirling vanes. Soaring over the track, it fled ahead of the train, shrank into the hills until its plastic-egg cabin resembled a dewdrop dangling from a spinning sycamore seed.

Contacting the signals-room, Leigh said, "Put Ogilvy's reports through the speaker here." He returned to the port, continued watching the train. All the crew not asleep or on duty were similarly watching.

"Village six miles along line," blared the speaker. "A second four miles farther on. A third five miles beyond that. Eight thousand feet. Climbing."

Five minutes later, "Six-coach train on tracks, headed eastward. Appears stalled from this height but may be moving."

"Coming the other way and at a similar crawl," remarked Pascoe, glancing at Walterson. "Bang goes your sick theory if that one also holds a bunch of zombies."

"Altitude twelve thousand," announced the loudspeaker "Terminal city visible beyond hills. Distance from base twenty-seven miles. Will investigate unless recalled."

Leigh made no move to summon him back. There followed a long silence. By now the train was still less than a mile away and had cut progress down to about one yard per minute. Finally it stopped, remained motionless for a quarter of an hour, began to back up so gradually that it had inched twenty yards before watchers became certain that it had reversed direction. Leigh leveled powerful glasses upon it. Definitely it was returning to the base of the bluff.

"Funny thing here," bawled Ogilvy from the wall. "Streets full of people all struck stiff. It was the same in those villages now that I come to think of it. I went over them too fast for the fact to register."

"That's crazy," said Pascoe. "How can he tell from that height?"

"I'm hovering right over the main stem, a tree-lined avenue with crowded sidewalks," Ogilvy continued. "If anyone is moving I can't detect it. Request permission to examine from five hundred."

Using the auxiliary mike linked through the signals-room, Leigh asked, "Is there any evidence of opposition such as aircraft, gun emplacements or rocket-pits?"

"No, Commodore, not that I can see."

"Then you can go down but don't drop too fast. Sheer out immediately if fired upon."

There was silence during which Leigh had another look outside. The train was continuing to come back at velocity definable as chronic. He estimated that it would take most of an hour to reach the nearest point.

"Now at five hundred," the loud-speaker declared. "Great Jupiter, I've never seen anything like it. They're moving all right. But they're so sluggish I have to look twice to make sure they really are alive and in action." A pause, then, "Believe it or not, there's a sort of street-car system in operation. A baby could toddle after one of those vehicles and catch it."

"Come back," Leigh ordered sharply. "Come back and report on the nearby town."

"As you wish, Commodore," Ogilvy sounded as if he were obeying with reluctance.

"Where's the point of withdrawing him from there?" asked Pascoe, irritated by this abrupt cutting-off of data. "He's in no great danger. What will he learn from one place that he can't get from another?"

"He can confirm or deny the one thing that is all-important namely, that conditions are the same elsewhere and are not restricted to one locale. When he's had a look at the town I'll send him a thousand miles away for a third and final check." His gray eyes were thoughtful as he went on, "In olden times a Martian visitor could have made a major blunder if he'd judged Earth by one of its last remaining leper colonies. Today we'd make precisely the same mistake if this happens to be a quarantined area full of native paralytics."

"Don't say it," put in Walterson, displaying some nervousness. "If we've sat down in a reservation for the diseased, we'd better get out mighty fast. I don't want to be smitten by any alien plague to which I've no natural resistance. I had a narrow enough escape when I missed that Hermes expedition six years ago. Remember it? Within three days of landing the entire complement was dead, their bodies growing bundles of stinking strings later defined as a fungus."

"We'll see what Ogilvy says," Leigh decided. "If he reports what we consider more normal conditions elsewhere, we'll move there. If they prove the same, we'll stay."

"Stay," echoed Pascoe, his features expressing disgust. "Something tells me you picked the right word—*stay*," He gestured toward the port beyond which the train was a long time coming. "If what we've seen and what we've heard has any meaning at all, it means we're in a prize fix."

"Such as what?" prompted Walterson. "We can stay a million years or go back home. For once in our triumphant history we're well and truly thwarted. We'll gain nothing whatever from this world for a good and undefeatable reason, namely, life's too short."

"I'm jumping to no hasty conclusions," said Leigh. "We'll wait for Ogilvy."

In short time the loud-speaker informed with incredulity, "This town is full of creepers, too. And trolleys making the same speed, if you can call it speed. Want me to go down and tell you more?"

"No," said Leigh into the mike. "Make a full-range sweep eastward. Loop out as far as you can go with safety. Watch especially for any radical variation in phenomena and, if you find it, report at once." He racked the microphone, turned to the others. "All we can do now is wait a bit."

"You said it!" observed Pascoe pointedly. "I'll lay odds of a thousand to one that Boydell did no more than sit futilely around picking his teeth until he got tired of it."

Walterson let go a sudden laugh that startled them.

"What's the matter with you?" demanded Pascoe, staring at him.

"One develops the strangest ideas sometimes," said Walterson apologetically. "It just occurred to me that if horses were snails they'd never be compelled to wear harness. There's a moral somewhere but I can't be bothered with digging it out."

"City forty-two miles eastward from base," called Ogilvy "Same as before. Two speeds: dead slow and slower than dead."

Pascoe glanced through the port. "That train is doing less than bug-rate. I reckon it intends to stop when it gets here." He thought a while, finished, "If so, we know one thing in advance: they aren't frightened of us."

Making up his mind, Leigh phoned through to Shallom. "We're going outside. Make a record of Ogilvy's remarks while we're gone. Sound a brief yelp on the alarm if he reports rapid movement any place." Then he switched to Nolan, Hoffnagle and Romero, the three communications experts. "Bring your Keen charts along in readiness for contact."

"It's conventional," reminded Pascoe, "for the ship's commander to remain in control of his vessel until contact has been made and the aliens found friendly or, at least, not hostile."

"This is where convention gets dumped overboard for once," Leigh snapped. "I'm going to check on the load in that train. It's high time we made some progress. Please yourselves whether or not you come along."

"Fourteen villages so far," chipped in Ogilvy from far away over the hills. "Everyone in them hustling around at the pace that kills—with boredom. Am heading for city visible on horizon."

The communicators arrived bearing sheafs of colored charts. They were unarmed, being the only personnel forbidden to wear guns. The theory behind this edict was that obvious helplessness established confidence. In most circumstances the notion proved correct and communicators survived. Once in a while it flopped and the victims gained no more than decent burial.

"What about us?" inquired Walterson, eyeing the newcomers. "Do we take weapons or don't we?"

"We'll chance it without any," Leigh decided. "A lifeform sufficiently intelligent to ride around in trains should be plenty smart enough to guess what will happen if they try to take us. They'll be right under the ship's guns while we're parleying."

"I've no faith in their ability to see reason as we understand it," Pascoe put in. "For all their civilized veneer they may be the most treacherous characters this side of Sirius." Then he grinned and added, "But I've faith in my legs. By the time these aliens got into action, I'd be a small cloud of dust in the sunset."

Leigh smiled, led them through the main lock. Every port was filled with watching faces as they made their way to the track.

Gun-teams stood ready in their turrets, grimly aware that they could not beat off an attempted snatch except at risk of killing friends along with foes. But if necessary they could thwart it by wrecking the rails behind and ahead of the train, isolating it in readiness for further treatment. For the time being their role was the static one of intimidation. Despite this world's apparent lack of danger, there was a certain amount of apprehension among the older hands in the ship. A pacific atmosphere had fooled humans before and they were wary of it.

The six reached the railroad a couple of hundred yards in advance of the train, walked toward it. They could see the driver sitting behind a glass-like panel in front. His big yellow-eyes were staring straight ahead, his crimson face was without expression. Both his hands rested on knobbed levers and the sight of half a dozen other-worlders on the lines did not make him so much as twitch a finger.

Leigh was first to reach the cab door and stretch out a hand to grasp incurable difficulty number one. He took hold of the handle, swung the door open, put a pleasant smile upon his face and uttered a cordial, "Hello!"

The driver did not answer. Instead, his eyeballs edge around sidewise while the train continued to pelt along at such a rate that it started pulling away from Leigh's hand. Perforce, Leigh had to take a step to keep level. The eyes reached their corners by which time Leigh was compelled to take another step.

Then the driver's head started turning. Leigh took a step. More turn. Another step. Behind Leigh his five companions strove to stay with him. It wasn't easy. In fact it was tough going. They could not stand still and let the train creep away. They could not walk without getting ahead of it. The result was a ludicrous march based on a hop-pause rhythm, with the hops short and the pauses long.

By the time the driver's head was halfway around, the long fingers of his right hand had started uncurling from the knob it was holding. At the same overstretched instant the knob commenced to rise on its lever. He was doing something no doubt of that. He was bursting into action to meet a sudden emergency.

Still gripping the door, Leigh edged along with it. The others went hop-pause in unison. Pascoe wore the pained reverence of one attending the tedious funeral of a rich uncle who has just cut him out of his will. Imagination told Leigh what ribald remarks were being tossed around among the audience in the ship.

He solved the problem, of reclaiming official dignity by simple process of stepping into the cab. That wasn't much better, though. He had avoided the limping procession but now had the choice of standing half-bent or kneeling on the floor.

Now the driver's head was right around, his eyes looking straight at the visitor. The knob had projected to its limit. Something that made hissing noises under the floor went silent and the train's progress was only that of its forward momentum against the brakes, A creep measurable in inches or fractions of an inch.

"Hello!" repeated Leigh, feeling that he had never voiced a sillier word.

The driver's mouth opened to a pink oval, revealed long, narrow teeth but no tongue. He shaped the mouth and by the time he'd got it to his satisfaction the listener could have smoked half a cigarette. Leigh perked his ears for the expected greeting. Nothing came out, not a sound, a note, a decibel. He waited awhile, hoping that the first word might emerge before next Thursday. The mouth made a couple of slight changes in form while pink palps at the back of it writhed like nearly dead worms. And that was all.

Walterson ceased his hop-pause routine and called, "It has stopped, Commodore,"

Stepping backward from the cab, Leigh shoved his hands deep into his pockets and gazed defeatedly at the driver whose formerly blank face was now acquiring an expression of surprised interest. He could watch the features registering with all the lackadaisical air of a chameleon changing color and at about the same rate.

"This is a hell of a note," complained Pascoe, nudging Leigh. He pointed at the row of door-handles projecting from the four cars. Most of them had tilted out of the horizontal and were moving a degree at a time toward the vertical. "They're falling all over themselves to get out."

"Open up for them," Leigh suggested.

Hoffnagle, who happened to be standing right by an exit, obligingly twisted a handle and lugged the door. Out it swung, complete with a clinging passenger who hadn't been able to let go. Dropping his contact-charts, Hoffnagle dexterously caught the victim, planted him on his feet. It took forty-eight seconds by Romero's watch for this one to register facial reaction which was that of bafflement.

After this, doors had to be opened with all the caution of a tax collector coping with a mysterious parcel that ticks. Pascoe, impatient as usual, hastened the dismounting process by lifting aliens from open doorways and standing them on the green sward, The quickest witted one among the lot required a mere twenty-eight seconds to start mulling the problem of how he had passed from one point to another without crossing intervening space. He would solve that puzzle—given time.

With the train empty there were twenty-three Waitabits hanging around. None exceeded four feet in height or sixty pounds Eterna-weight. All were well-clothed in a manner that gave no clue to sex. Presumably all were adults, there being no tiny specimens among them. Not one bore anything remotely resembling a weapon.

Looking them over, Leigh readily conceded that no matter how sluggish they might be they were not dopy. Their outlandishly colored features held intelligence of a fairly high order. That was already self-evident from the tools they made and used, such as this train, but it showed on their faces, too.

The Grand Council, he decided, had good cause for alarm—although for a reason not yet thought of by its members. If the bunch standing before him were truly representative of their planet, then they were completely innocuous. They embodied no danger whatsoever to Terran interests anywhere in the cosmos. Yet, at the same time, they implied a major menace of which he hated to think.

With their easily comprehensive charts laid out on the ground, the three communicators prepared to explain their origin, presence and purposes by an effective sign-and-gesture technique basic for all first contacts. The fidgety Pascoe speeded up the job by arranging the Waitabits in a circle around the charts, picking them up like so many lethargic dolls and placing them in position.

Leigh and Walterson went to have a look at the train. If any of its owners objected to this inspection they didn't have enough minutes in which to do something about it.

The roofs of all four cars were of pale yellow, transparent plastic extending down the sides to a line flush with the door tops. Beneath the plastic lay countless numbers of carefully arranged silicon wafers, Inside the cars, beneath plates forming the center aisles, were arrays of tiny cylinders rather like nickel-alloy cells. The motors could not be seen; they were hidden beneath small driving-cabs of which there was one to each car.

"Sun power," said Leigh. "The prime motive force is derived from those solar batteries built into the roofs." He paced out the length of a car, made an estimate. "Four feet by twenty apiece. Including the side-strips, that's six-forty square feet of pickup area."

"Nothing marvelous about it," ventured Walterson, unimpressed. "They use better ones in the tropical zones of Earth and have similar gadgets on Dramonia and Werth."

"I know. But here the nighttime lasts six months. What sort of storage batteries will last that long without draining? How do they manage to get around on the night-side? Or does all transportation cease while they snore in bed?"

"Pascoe could make a better guess at their boudoir habits. For what it's worth, I'd say they sleep, six months being to them no more than a night is to us. Anyway, why should we speculate on the matter? We'll be exploring the night-side sooner or later, won't we?"

"Yes, sure. But I'd like to know whether this contraption is more advanced than anything we've got, in any single respect."

"To discover that much we'd have to pull it to pieces," Walterson objected. "Putting Shallom and his boys on job would be a lousy way of fending off hostility. The Waitabits won't like it even if they can't stop us."

"I'm not that ham-handed," Leigh reproved. "Apart from the fact that destruction of property belonging to non-hostile aliens could get me a court-martial, why should I invite trouble when we can get the information from them in exchange for other data? Did you ever hear of an intelligent lifeform that refused to swap knowledge?"

"No," said Walterson. "And neither did I ever hear of one that took five years to pay for what it got in five minutes." He grinned with malicious satisfaction, added, "We're finding out what Boydell discovered, namely, you've got to give in order to receive—and in order to receive you've got to wait a bit."

"I won't argue with you because something inside of me insists that you're dead right." Leigh made a gesture of dismissal. "Anyway, that's the Council's worry. Let's get back to the ship. We can do no more until the contact men have made their report."

They mounted the bluff. Seeing them go, Pascoe hastened after them, leaving the trio of communicators to play with Keen charts and make snakes of their arms.

"How's it going?" Leigh inquired as they went through the lock.

"Not so good," said Pascoe. "You ought to try it yourself. It would drive you crazy."

"What's the trouble?"

"How can you synchronize two values when one of them is unknown? How can you make rhythm to a prolonged and completely silent beat? Every time Hoffnagle uses the orbit-sign he is merely demonstrating that the quickness of the hand deceives the eye, so far as the audience is concerned. So he slows, does it again and it still fools them. He slows more," Pascoe sniffed with disgust. "It's going to take those three luckless characters all of today and maybe most of a week to find, practice, and perfect the quickest gestures that register effectively. They aren't teaching anybody anything—they're learning themselves. It's time-and-motion study with a vengeance."

"It has to be done," Leigh remarked. "Even if it takes a lifetime."

"*Whose* lifetime?" asked Pascoe, pointedly.

Leigh winced, sought a satisfactory retort, failed to find one.

At the corner of the passageway Garside met them. He was a small, excitable man whose eyes looked huge behind thick lenses. The great love of his life was bugs, any size, shape, color or origin, as long as they were bugs.

"Ah, Commodore," he exclaimed, bubbling with enthusiasm. "A most remarkable discovery, most remarkable! Nine species of insect life, none really extraordinary in structure, but all afflicted with an amazing lassitude. If this phenomenon is common to all native insects, it would appear that local metabolism is—"

"Write it down for the record," advised Leigh, patting him on the shoulder. He hastened to the signals-room. "Anything special from Ogilvy?"

"No, Commodore, All his messages have been repeats of his first ones. He is now most of the way back and due in about an hour."

"Send him to me as soon as he returns."

"As you order, sir."

Ogilvy appeared in the promised time. He was a lanky, lean-faced individual given to irritating grins. Entering the room he held his hands behind his back, hung his head and spoke with mock shame.

"Commodore, I have a confession to make."

"So I see from the act you're putting on. What is it?"

"I landed, without permission, right in the main square of the biggest city I could find."

Leigh raised his eyebrows. "And what happened?"

"They gathered around and stared at me."

"Is that all?"

"Well, sir, it took them twenty minutes to see me and assemble, by which time the ones farther away were still coming. I couldn't wait any longer to discover what they'd do next. I estimated that if they fetched some rope and tied down my landing-gear, they'd have the job finished about a year next Christmas."

"Humph! Were things the same everywhere else?"

"Yes, sir, I passed over more than two hundred towns and villages, reached extreme range of twelve-fifty miles. Conditions remained consistent." He gave his grin, continued, "I noticed a couple of items that might interest you."

"What were those?"

"The Waitabits converse with their mouths but make no detectable noises. The 'copter has a supersonic converter known as bat-ears which is used for blind flying. I tuned its receiver across its full range while I was in the middle of that crowd, but it didn't pick up a squeak. So they're not talking high above us. I don't see how they can be subsonic, either. It must be something else."

"I've had a one-sided conversation with them myself," Leigh informed. "It may be that we're overlooking the obvious while seeking the obscure."

Ogilvy blinked and asked, "How do you mean, sir?"

"They're not necessarily employing some unique facility such as we cannot imagine. It is quite possible that they communicate visually. They gaze into each others' gullets and read the waggling palps. Something like you semaphoring with your tonsils." He dismissed the subject with a wave of his hand. "And what's your other item?"

"No birds," replied Ogilvy. "You'd think that where insects exist there would also be birds or at least things somewhat birdlike. The only airborne creature I saw was a kind of membrane-winged lizard that flaps just enough to launch itself, then glides to wherever it's going. On Earth it couldn't catch a weary gnat."

"Did you make a record of it?"

"No, sir. The last roll of film was in the camera and I didn't want to waste any of it. I didn't know what else more important might turn up."

"All right."

Leigh watched the other depart, picked up the intercom, said to Shallom, "If those 'copter reels prove sharp enough for long-range beaming, you'd better run off an extra copy for the signals-room. Have them boost it to Sector Nine for relay to Earth."

As he put down the phone Roman entered, looking desperate. "Commodore, could you get the instrument mechs to concoct a phenakistoscope with a revolution-counter attached?"

"We can make anything, positively anything," chimed Pascoe from near the port. "Given enough centuries in which to do it."

Ignoring the interruption, Leigh asked, "What do you want it for?"

"Hoffnagle and Nolan think we could use it to measure the precise optical register of those sluggards outside. If we can find out at what minimum speed they see pictures merge into motion, it would be a great help."

"Wouldn't the ship's movie projector serve the same purpose?"

"It isn't sufficiently variable," Romero objected. "Besides, we can't operate it independently of our own power supply. A phenakistoscope can be carried and cranked by hand."

"This becomes more fascinating every moment," Pascoe interjected. "It can be cranked. Add a few more details and I'll start to get a hazy idea of what the darned thing is."

Taking no notice of that either, Leigh got through to Shallom again, put the matter to him.

"Holy Moses!" ejaculated Shalom. "The things we get requests for! Who thought up that one?" A pause, followed by, "It will take two days."

"Two days," Leigh repeated to Romero.

The other looked aghast.

"What's eating you?" asked Pascoe. "Two days to get started on measuring visual retention is mighty fast in this world, You're on Eterna now. Adapt, boy, adapt!"

Leigh eyed Pascoe carefully and said, "Becoming rather snappy this last hour or two, aren't you?"

"Not yet. I have several dregs of patience left. When the last of them has trickled away you can lock me in the brig, because I'll be nuts."

"Don't worry. We're about to have some action."

"Ha-ha!" said Pascoe disrespectfully.

"We'll drag out the patrol wagon, go to town and have a look around in the middle of them."

"About time, too," Pascoe endorsed.

The armored, eight-seater car rumbled down the ramp on heavy caterpillars, squatted in the clover. Only a short, flared nozzle in its bonnet and another in its tail revealed the presence of button-controlled snort-guns. The boxed lens on its roof belonged to an automatic camera. The metal whip atop the box was a radio antenna.

They could have used the helicopter, which was capable of carrying four men with equipment, but, once landed, that machine would have been of little good for touring the streets.

Leigh shared the front seat with Lieutenant Harding and the duty driver. Behind him were two of Harding's troop and Pascoe. At back sat the radio operator and the snort-gunner. Walterson, Garside and all the other specialists remained with the ship.

Rolling forward, they passed the circle of Waitabits, who were now sitting cross-legged in the turf and staring at a Keen chart which Nolan was exhibiting with an air of complete frustration. Nearby, Hoffnagle was chewing his nails while trying to decide how much of the lesson was being absorbed and how much missed. Not one of this bunch show the slightest surprise when the car charged down the steep bluff and clattered by them.

With jerks and heaves the car crossed the lines behind the stalled train, gained the road. Here the surface proved excellent, the running smooth. The artery would have done justice to a Terran race-track, Before they had gone five miles they encountered an alien using it for exactly that.

This one half-sat, half-reclined in a long, narrow, low-slung single-seater that had 'hot-rod' written all over it. He came along like a maniac, face strained, eyes popping, hands clinging firmly to the wheel. According to the photoelectric telltale on the patrol wagon's instrument board, he roared past them at fifty-two and a quarter miles per hour. Since the speedometer on the same board recorded precisely fifty, it meant that the other was going all out at a harrowing two and a quarter.

Twisting his head to gaze through the rear window, Pascoe said, "As a sociologist I'll tell you something: some of this crowd are downright reckless. If that lunatic is headed for the city thirty miles away, he'll make it in as little as twelve hours." Then he frowned, became serious as he added, "Seeing that their reactions are in keeping with their motions, one being as tedious as the other, it wouldn't surprise me if they have traffic problems comparable with those of any other world."

Nobody got a chance to comment on that. The entire eight bowed in unison as the brakes went on. They were entering the suburbs with pedestrians, cars and trolleys littering the streets. After that it was strictly bottom-gear work; the driver had to learn a completely new technique and it wasn't easy.

Crimson-faced people in the same sexless attire ambled across the roads in a manner suggesting that for two pins they'd lie down and go to sleep. Some moved faster than others, but the most nimble ones among the lot were an obstacle for an inordinate while. Not one halted and gaped at the invading vehicle as it trundled by, but most of them stopped and took on a baffled expression by the time they'd been left a mile behind.

To Leigh and his companions there was a strong temptation to correlate slowness with stupidity. They resisted it. Evidence to the contrary was strong enough not to be denied.

The streets were level, straight and well-made, complete with sidewalks, gullies and drains. No buildings rose higher than sixty feet, but all were solidly built and far from primitive. Cars were not numerous by Terran standards, but those that were in evidence had the appearance of engineering jobs of no mean order. The street-trolleys were small, sun-powered, languidly efficient, and bore two-dozen passengers apiece.

For a few minutes they halted near a building in the process of construction, maintained attention upon a worker laying a brick, estimated that the job required twenty minutes. Three bricks per hour.

Doing some fast figuring, Leigh said, "Taking their days and nights as six months apiece and assuming they put in the equivalent of an eight-hour day, that fellow is laying something over a thousand bricks per hour." He pursed his lips, gave a brief whistle. "I know of no lifeform capable of building half as fast. Even on Earth it would take a robot to equal it."

The others considered that aspect of the matter in silence. The patrol wagon moved on, reached a square in which was a civic car-park containing some forty machines. The sight was irresistible. Driving straight in past two uniformed attendants they lined their vehicle neatly at the end of a row. The attendants' eyeballs started edging around.

Leigh spoke to the driver, radioman and gunner. "You three stay here. If anyone interferes, pick him up, put him down a hundred yards away and leave him to try all over again. If they show signs of getting organized to blow you sky-high, just move the wagon to the other end of the park. When they catch up with you, move back here."

"Where are you going?" inquired Harding.

"Over there." He pointed toward an official-looking building. "To save time I'd like you, your men and Pascoe to try the other places. Take one apiece, go inside, see if you learn anything worth picking up." He glanced at his watch. "Be back promptly at three. No dallying. The laggard will be left to take a nine-mile walk."

Starting off, he found an attendant twenty yards away and moving toward him with owl-eyes wide. Going boldly up to him, he took the book of tickets from an unresisting hand, tore one off, pressed the book back into crimson fingers, added a silver coin by way of payment and passed on. He derived amused satisfaction from that honest gesture. By the time he'd crossed the square and entered the building the recipient had got around to examining the coin.

At three they returned to find chaos in the square and no sign of the patrol wagon in the park. A series of brief wails on its siren drew them to a side street where it was waiting by the curb.

"Slow as they may be, they can get places given long enough," said the driver, "They started creeping around us in such numbers that it seemed like we were being hemmed in for keeps. We wouldn't have been able to get out without running over fifty of them. I beat it while there was still a gap to drive through." He pointed through the windshield, "Now they're making for here. The tortoise chasing the hare."

One of Harding's men, a grizzled veteran of several space-campaigns, remarked, "It's easier when you're up against guppies that are hostile and fighting mad. You just shoot your way out." He grunted a few times. "Here, if you sit around too long you've got to let yourself be trapped or else run over them in cold blood. That's not my idea of how to do things." Another grunt. "Hell of a planet. The fellow who found it ought to be made to live here."

"Find anything in your building?" Leigh asked him.

"Yes, a dozen cops."

"What?"

"Cops," repeated the other. "It was a police station. I could tell because they all had the same uniforms, all carried duralumin bludgeons. And there were faces on the wall with queer printing beneath. I can't recognize one face from another—they are all alike to me. But something told me those features hadn't been stuck to the wall to commemorate saintliness."

"Did they show any antagonism toward you?"

"They didn't get the chance," he said with open contempt. "I just kept shifting around looking at things and that had them foxed. If any of those poor slouches had reached for me; I could have got behind him and jerked down his pants before his arm was halfway out."

"My building was a honey," informed Pascoe. "A telephone exchange."

Leigh twisted around to stare at him. "So they are supersonic speakers after all?"

"No. They use scanners and three-inch visiscreens. If I've looked down one squirming gizzard, I've looked down twenty. What's more, a speaker sometimes removes his palps from the screen and substitutes a sort of slow-motion display of deaf-and-dumb talk with his fingers. I have a vague idea that some of those digital acrobatics represented vitriolic cussing."

The driver put in nervously, "If we squat here much longer the road will be blocked at both ends."

"Then let's get out while there's time."

"Back to the ship, sir?"

"Not yet. Wander around and see if you can find an industrial area."

The car rolled forward, went cautiously past a bunch of oncoming pedestrians, avoided the crowded square by trundling down another side street.

Lying back in comfort, Pascoe clasped his hands together over his stomach and inquired interestedly, "I suppose none of you happened to find himself in a fire station?"

Nobody had.

"That's what I'd give a thousand credits to see," he said. "A couple of pumps and a hook-and-ladder squad bursting out to deal with a conflagration a mile away. The speed of combustion is no less on this world than on our own. It's a wonder to me the town hasn't burned down a dozen times."

"Perhaps it has," offered Harding. "Perhaps they're used to it. You can get accustomed to anything in the long run."

"In the long run," agreed Pascoe. "Here it's long enough to vanish into the mists of time. And it's anything but a run." He glanced at Leigh. "What did you walk into?"

"A public library."

"That's the place to dig up information. How much did you get?"

"One item only," Leigh admitted with reluctance. "Their printed language is ideographic and employs at least three thousand characters."

"There's a big help," said Pascoe, casting an appealing glance heavenward, "Any competent linguist or trained communicator should be able to learn it from them.

Put Hoffnagle on the job. He's the youngest among us and all he needs is a couple of thousand years."

The radio burped, winked its red eye, and the operator switched it on. Shallom's voice came through.

"Commodore, an important-looking specimen has just arrived in what he probably thinks of as a racing car. It may he that he's a bigwig appointed to make contact with us. That's only our guess, but we're trying to get confirmation of it. I thought you'd like to know."

"How's progress with him?"

"No better than with the others. Possibly he's the smartest boy in college. Nevertheless, Nolan estimates it will take most of a month to convince him that Mary had a little lamb."

"Well, keep trying. We'll be returning shortly." The receiver cut off and Leigh added to the others, "Sounds like the road-hog we passed on the way here." He nudged the driver, pointed leftward. "That looks like a sizable factory. Stop outside while I inspect it."

He entered unopposed, came out after a few minutes, told them, "It's a combined flour-mill, processing and packaging plant. They're grinding up a mountain of nut-kernels, probably from surrounding forests. They've a pair of big engines down in the basement that beat me. Never seen anything like them. I think I'll get Bentley to come and look them over. He's the expert on power supplies."

"Big place for a mill, isn't it?" ventured Harding.

"They're converting the flour into about twenty forms. I sampled some of it."

"What did it taste like?"

"Paste." He nudged the driver again. "There's another joint." Then to Harding. "You come with me."

Five minutes later they returned and said, "Boots, shoes and slippers. And they're making them fast."

"Fast?" echoed Pascoe, twitching his eyebrows.

"Faster than they can follow the process themselves. The whole layout is fully automatic and self-arresting if anything goes wrong. Not quite as good as we've got on Earth, but not so far behind, either." Leigh sat with pursed lips, musing as he gazed through the windshield. "I'm going back to the ship. You fellows can come for further exploration if you wish."

None of them registered enthusiasm.

There was a signal waiting on the desk, decoded and typed.

C.O. FLAME to *C.O.* THUNDERER. *Atmosphere Pulok analyzed good, in fact healthy. So instruments insist. Noses say has abominable stench beyond bearing. Should be named Puke. Proceeding Arlington Port 88.137 unless summoned by you. Mallory.*

Reading it over Leigh's shoulder, Pascoe commented. "That Boydell character has a flair for picking ugly ones right out of the sky. Why doesn't someone choke him to death?"

"Four hundred twenty-one recorded in there," reminded Leigh, tapping his big chart-book. "And about two-thirds of them come under the heading of ugly ones."

"It would save a lot of grief if the scouts ignored those and reported only the dumps worth having."

"Grief is the price of progress, you know that." Leigh hurriedly left his desk, went to the port as something whirred outside. He picked up the phone. "Where's the 'copter going?"

"Taking Garside and Walterson some place," replied a voice. "The former wants more bugs and the latter wants rock samples."

"All right. Has that film been finished yet?"

"Yes, Commodore. It came out good and clear. Want me to set it up in the projection room?"

"You might as well. I'll be there right away. Have somebody get to work on the magazine in the patrol wagon. About half of it has been exposed."

"As you order, sir."

Summoning the rest of the specialist staff, of whom there were more than sixty, he accompanied them to the projection room, studied the record of Ogilvy's survey. When it had finished the audience sat in glum silence. Nobody had anything to say. No comment was adequate.

"A nice mess," griped Pascoe, after they had returned to the main cabin. "In the last one thousand years the human race has become wholly technological. Even the lowest ranking space-marine is considered a technician, especially by standards of olden times."

"I know." Leigh frowned futilely at the wall.

"We are the brains," Pascoe went on, determined to rub salt into the wounds. "And because we're the brains we naturally dislike providing the muscle as well. We're a cut above the mere hewing of wood and drawing of water."

"You're telling me nothing."

Determined to tell it anyway, Pascoe continued, "So we've planted settlers on umpteen planets. And what sort of settlers are they? Bosses, overseers, boys who inform, advise, and order while the less advanced do the doing."

Leigh offered no remark.

"Suppose Walterson and the others find this lousy world rich in the things we need," he persisted. "How are we going to get at the stuff short of excavating it ourselves? The Waitabits form a big and probably willing labor force, but what's the use of them if the most rudimentary job gets completed ten, twenty or fifty years hence? Who's going to settle here and become a beast of burden as the only way of getting things done in jig time?"

"Ogilvy went over a big dam and what looked like a hydroelectric plant," observed Leigh, thoughtfully. "On earth the entire project might have cost two years at most. How long it required here is anyone's guess. Two hundred years perhaps. Or four hundred. Or more." He tapped fidgety fingers on his desk. "It worries me."

"We're not worried; we're frustrated. It's not the same."

"I tell you I'm worried. This planet is like a lighted fuse long ignored but now noticed. I don't know where it leads or how big a bang is waiting at the other end."

"That's frustration," insisted Pascoe, completely missing the point because he hadn't thought of it yet. "We're thwarted and don't like it. We're the irresistible force at long last meeting the immovable object. The bang is within our own minds. No *real* explosion big enough to shake us can ever come from this world's lifeform. They're too slow to catch cold."

"I'm not bothered about them in that respect. They worry me by their very existence."

"There always have been sluggards, even in our own world."

"Precisely!" endorsed Leigh with emphasis. "And that's what's raising my hackles right now."

The loudspeaker interrupted with a polite cough and said, "Ogilvy here, sir. We've picked up granite chippings, quartz samples and other stuff. At the moment I'm at sixteen-thousand feet and can see the ship in the distance. I don't like the looks of things."

"What's the matter?"

"The town is emptying itself. So are nearby villages. They've taken to the road in huge numbers and started heading your way. The vanguard should reach you in about three hours." A brief silence, then, "There's nothing to indicate hostile intentions, no sign of an organized advance. Just a rabble motivated by plain curiosity as far as I can tell. But if you get that mob gaping around the ship you won't be able to move without incinerating thousands of them."

Leigh though it over. The ship was a mile long. Its lifting blasts caromed half a mile on each side and its tail blast was equally long. He needed about two square miles of clear ground from which to take off without injury to others.

There were eleven-hundred men aboard the *Thunderer*. Six hundred were needed to attend the boost. That left five hundred to stay grounded and keep the mob at bay around the perimeter of two square miles. And they'd have to be transferred by 'copter, a few at a time, to the new landing place. Could it be done? It could—but it was hopelessly inefficient.

"We'll move a hundred miles before they get here," he informed Ogilvy. "That should hold them for a couple of days."

"Want me to come in, sir?"

"Please yourself."

"The passengers aren't satisfied and want to add to their collections. So I'll stay out. If you drop out of sight, I'll home on your beacon."

"Very well." Leigh turned to the intercom. "Sound the siren and bring in those yaps outside. Check crew all present and correct. Prepare to lift."

"Rule Seven," said Pascoe, smirking. "Any action causing unnecessary suffering to non-hostile life will be deemed a major offense under the Contact Code." He made a derisive gesture. "So they amble toward us like a great army of sloths and we have to tuck in our tails and run."

"Any better solution?" Leigh asked irritably.

"No. Not one. That's the devil of it."

The siren yowled. Soon afterward the *Thunderer* began a faint but steady shuddering as combustion chambers and venturis warmed up. Hoffnagle rushed into the cabin. He had a roll of crumpled Keen charts in one fist and a wild look in his eyes.

"What's the idea?" he shouted, flourishing the charts and forgetting to say 'sir.' "Two successive watches we've spent on this, given up our off-duty time into the bargain, and have just got one of them to make the orbit-sign. Then you recall us." He waited, fuming.

"We're moving."

"Moving?" He looked as if he'd never heard of such a thing. "Where?"

"A hundred miles off."

Hoffnagle stared incredulously, swallowed hard, opened his mouth, closed it, opened it once more. "But that means we'll have to start over again with some other bunch."

"I'm afraid so," agreed Leigh. "The ones you've been trying to talk to could come with us, but it would take far too long to make them understand what's wanted. There's nothing for it but to make a new start."

"No!" bawled Hoffnagle, becoming frenzied. "Oh, no! Anything but that!"

Behind him, Romero barged in and said, "Anything but what?" He was breathing heavily and near the end of his tether.

Trying to tell him the evil news, Hoffnagle found himself lost for words, managed no more than a few feeble gestures.

"A communicator unable to communicate with another communicator," observed Pascoe, showing academic interest.

"They're shifting the ship," Hoffnagle got out with considerable effort. He made it sound dastardly.

Releasing a violent, *"What?"* Romero went two shades redder than the Waitabits. In fact, for a moment he looked like one as he stood there pop-eyed and half-paralyzed.

"Get out," snapped Leigh. "Get out before Nolan comes in and makes it three to two. Go some place where you can cool down. Remember, you're not the only ones caught in this fix."

"No, maybe we aren't," said Hoffnagle, bitterly. "But we're the only ones carrying the entire onus of—"

"Everybody's carrying onuses of one sort or another," Leigh retorted. "And everybody's well and truly bollixed by them. Beat it before I lose my own temper and summon an escort for you."

They departed with unconcealed bad grace. Leigh sat at his desk, chewed his bottom lip while he tended to official papers. Twenty minutes went by. Finally, he glanced at the wall chronometer, switched the intercom, spoke to Bentley.

"What's holding us up?"

"No signal from the control room, sir."

He re-switched to the control room. "What are we waiting for?"

"That bunch from the train is still lounging within burning distance, Commodore. Either nobody's told them to go back or, if they have been told, they haven't got around to it yet."

Leigh seldom swore but he did it this time, one potent word uttered with vigor. He switched a third time, got Harding.

"Lieutenant, rush out two platoons of your men. They are to return all those alien passengers to their train. Pick them up, carry them there, tuck them into it and return as quickly as possible."

He resumed his paperwork while Pascoe sat in a corner nibbling his fingers and grinning to himself. After half an hour Leigh voiced the word again and resorted to the intercom.

"What is it now?"

"Still no signal, Commodore," said Bentley in tones of complete resignation.

On to the control room. "I gave the order to lift immediately there's clearance. Why haven't we done so?"

"One alien is still within the danger area, sir."

Next to Harding, "Didn't I tell you to get those aliens onto their train?"

"Yes, sir, you did. All passengers were restored to their seats fifteen minutes ago."

"Nonsense, man! They've left one of them hanging around and he's holding up the entire vessel."

"That one is not from the train, sir," said Harding, patiently. "He arrived in a car. You gave no order concerning him."

Leigh used both hands to scrabble the desk, then roared, "Get him the heck out of here. Plant him in his contraption and shove it down the road. At once." Then he lay back in his chair and muttered to himself.

"How'd you like to resign and buy a farm?" Pascoe asked.

The new landing-point was along the crest of the only bald hill for miles around. Charred stumps provided evidence of a bygone forest fire which had started on the top, spread down the sides until halted, probably by heavy rain.

Thickly wooded hills rolled away in every direction. No railroad tracks ran nearby, but there was a road in the valley and a winding river beyond it. Two villages were visible within four miles distance and a medium-sized town lay eleven miles to the north.

Experience with local conditions enabled a considerable speed-up in investigation. Earnshaw, the relief pilot, took out the 'copter with Walterson and four other experts crowded inside. The patrol wagon set off for town bearing a load of specialists, including Pascoe. Three botanists and an arboriculturalist took to the woods accompanied by a dozen of Harding's men who were to bear their spoils.

Hoffnagle, Romero and Nolan traipsed cross-country to the nearest village, spread their explanatory charts in the small square, and prayed for a rural genius able to grasp the true meaning of a basic gesture in less than a week. A bunch of ship's engineers set forth to examine lines strung on lattice masts across hills to the west and south. A piscatorial expert, said to have been conditioned from birth by the cognomen of Fish, sat for hours on the river bank dangling his lines without knowing what bait to use, what he might catch, or whether it could be caught in less than a lifetime.

Leigh stayed by the ship during this brief orgy of data gathering. He had a gloomy foreboding concerning the shape of things to come. Time proved him right. Within thirty hours Earnshaw had handed the 'copter over to Ogilvy twice and was flying for the third time, He was at fifteen-thousand above the *Thunderer* when he called.

"Commodore, I hate to tell you this, but they're coming again. They seem to have caught on quicker. Maybe they were warned over that visiscreen system they've got."

"How long do you give them?"

"The villages will take about two hours. The mob from the town need five or six. I can see the patrol wagon heading back in front of them."

"You'd better bring in whoever you're carrying and go fetch those three communicators right away," said Leigh. "Then pick up anyone else on the loose."

"All right, sir."

The siren moaned eerily across the valleys. Over in the village Hoffnagle suddenly ceased his slow-motion gesturing and launched into an impassioned tirade that astonished the Waitabits two days later. Down in the woods the arboriculturalist fell out of a tree and flattened a marine who also become vocal.

It was like the ripple effect of a stone cast into a pond. Somebody pressed an alarm-stud and a resulting wave of adjectives spread halfway to the horizon.

They moved yet again, this time to within short range of the terminator. At least it served to shift the sun which had hung stubbornly in mid-sky and changed position by no more than one degree per Earth-day.

The third watch took to bed, dog-tired. Data hunters went out feeling that, paradoxically, time was proving all too short on a planet with far too much of it. Ogilvy whined away for first look at the night-side, discovered half a world buried in deep sleep with nothing stirring, not a soul, not a vehicle.

This situation lasted twenty-one hours, at the end of which all natives for miles around had set out for the circus. Once more the siren stimulated enrichment of Earth-language. The *Thunderer* went up, came down four hundred miles within the night-side.

That tactic, decided Leigh, represented a right smart piece of figuring. Aroused aliens on the day-side would now require about twelve days to reach them. And they'd make it only if some insomniac had spotted and phoned the ship's present location. Such betrayal was likely enough because the *Thunderer'* s long rows of ports poured a brilliant blaze into darkness, and caused a great glow in the sky.

It wasn't long before he gained assurance that there little danger of a giveaway. Nolan entered the cabin and stood with fingers twitching as if he yearned to strangle someone very, very slowly, much as a Waitabit would do it. His attitude was accentuated by possession of unfortunate features. Nobody aboard the *Thunderer* better resembled the popular notion of a murderer.

"You will appreciate, Commodore," he began, speaking with great restraint, "the extreme difficulty involved in making contact with creatures that think in hours rather than split-seconds."

"I know it's tough going," Leigh sympathized. He eyed the other carefully. "What's on your mind?"

"What is on my mind," informed Nolan in rising tones, "is the fact that there's one thing to be said in favor of previous subjects." He worked the fingers around. "At least they were awake."

"That is why we had to move," Leigh pointed out. "They're no nuisance to us while dead abed."

"Then," Nolan burst forth, "how the blue blazes do you expect us to make contact with them?"

"I don't. I've given it up. If you wish to continue trying that's your affair. But you're under no compulsion to do so." Crossing the room, he said more gently, "I've sent a long signal to Earth giving full details of what we're against. The next move is up to them. Their reply should come in a few days' time. Meanwhile, we'll sit tight, dig out whatever information we can, leave what we can't."

Nolan said morbidly, "Hoff and I went to a hamlet far down the road. Not only is everyone asleep but they can't be wakened. They can be handled like dolls without stirring in their dreams. The medics came and had a look at them after we'd told them about this wholesale catalepsy."

"What did they say?"

"They're of the opinion that the Waitabits are active only under stimulous of sunlight. When the sun goes down they go down with it." He scowled at his predicament, suggested hopefully, "But if you could run us a power-line out there and lend us a couple of sunray lamps, we could rouse a few of them and get to work."

"It isn't worth it," said Leigh.

"Why not?"

"Chances are that we'll be ordered home before you can show any real progress."

"Look, sir," pleaded Nolan, making a final effort. "Everyone else is raking in results. Measurements, meterings, and so forth. They've got bugs, nuts, fruits, plants, barks, timber sections, rocks, pebbles, soil samples, photographs—everything but shrunken heads. The communicators are the only ones asked to accept defeat, and that's because we've not had a fair chance."

"All right," Leigh said, taking up the challenge. "You fellows are in the best position to make an accurate estimate. So tell me: how *long* would a fair chance be?"

That had him stomped. He shuffled around, glowered at the wall, examined his fingers.

"Five years?" prompted Leigh.

No answer.

"Ten maybe?"

No reply.

"Perhaps twenty?"

Nolan growled, "You win," and walked out. His face still hankered to create a corpse.

You win, thought Leigh. Like heck he did. The winners were the Waitabits. They had a formidable weapon in the simple, incontrovertible fact that life can be too short.

Four days later Sector Nine relayed the message from Earth.

37.14 ex Terra. Defense H.Q. to C.O. battleship THUNDERER-. *Return route D9 calling Sector Four H.Q. Leave ambassador if suitable candidate available. Position in perpetuity. Rathbone. Com. Op. Dep. D.H.Q. Terra.*

He called a conference in the long room amidships. Considerable time was spent coordinating data ranging from Walterson's findings on radioactive life to Mr. Fish's remarks about creeping shrimps. In the end three conclusions stood out clearly.

Eterna was very old as compared with Earth. Its people were equally old as compared with humankind, estimates of life-duration ranging from eight hundred to twelve hundred for the average Waitabit. Despite their chronic sluggishness, the Waitabits were intelligent, progressive, and had advanced to about the same stage as humankind had reached a century before the first jump into space.

There was considerable argument about whether the Waitabits would ever be capable of a short rocket-flight, even with the aid of automatic, fast-functioning controls. Majority opinion was against it, but all agreed that in any event none would live to see it.

Then Leigh announced, "An Earth ambassador is to be left here if anyone wants the job." He looked them over, seeking signs of interest.

"There's little point in planting anybody on this planet," someone objected.

"Like most alien people, the Waitabits have not developed along paths identical with our own," Leigh explained. "We're way ahead of them, know thousands of things that they don't including many they'll never learn. By the same token they've picked up a few secrets we've missed. For instance, they have types of engines and batteries we'd like to know more about. They may have further items not apparent in this first superficial look-over. And there's no telling what they've worked out theoretically. If there's one lesson we've learned in the cosmos, it's that of never despising an alien culture. A species too big to learn soon goes small."

"So?"

"So somebody's got to take on the formidable task of systematically milking them of everything worth a hoot. That's why we are where we are: the knowledge of creation is all around and we get it and apply it."

"It's been done time and again on other worlds," agreed the objector. "But this is Eterna, a zombie-inhabited sphere where the clock ticks about once an hour. Any Earthman marooned in this place wouldn't have enough time if he lived to be a hundred."

"You're right," Leigh told him. "Therefore this ambassadorial post will be strictly a hereditary one. Whoever takes it will have to import a bride, marry, raise kids, hand the grief to them upon his deathbed. It may last through six generations or more. There is no other way." He let them stew over that awhile before he asked, "Any takers?"

Silence.

"You'll be lonely except for company provided by occasional ships, but contact will be maintained and the power and strength of Terra will be behind you. Speak up! The first applicant gets it."

Nobody responded.

Leigh consulted his watch. "I'll give you two hours to think it over. After that, we blow. Any candidate will find me in the cabin."

At zero-hour the *Thunderer* flamed free leaving no representative on the world. Someday there would be one, no doubt of that. Someday a willing hermit would take up residence for keeps. Among the men of Terra, an oddity or a martyr could always be found.

But the time wasn't yet.

On Eterna the time never was quite yet.

The pale pink planet that held Sector Four H.Q. had grown to a large disc before Pascoe saw fit to remark on Leigh's meditative attitude.

"Seven weeks along the return run and you're still brooding. Anyone would think you hated to leave that lousy place. What's the matter with you?"

"I told you before. They make me feel apprehensive."

"That's illogical," Pascoe declared. "Admittedly, we can't handle the slowest crawlers in existence. But what of it? All we need do is drop them and forget them."

"We can drop them, as you say. Forgetting them is something else. They have a special meaning that I don't like."

"Be more explicit," Pascoe suggested.

"All right, I will. Earth has had dozens of major wars in the far past. Some were caused by greed, ambition, fear, envy, desire to save face, or downright stupidity. But there were some caused by sheer altruism."

"Huh?"

"Some," Leigh went doggedly on, "were brought about by the unhappy fact that the road to hell is paved with good intentions. Big, fast-moving nations tried to lug slower moving ones up to their own superior pace. Sometimes the slow-movers couldn't make it, resented being forced to try, started shooting to defend their right to mooch. See what I mean?"

"I see the lesson but not the point of it," said Pascoe. "The Waitabits couldn't kill a lame dog. Besides, nobody is bothering them."

"I'm not considering that aspect at all."

"Which one then?"

"Earth had a problem never properly recognized. If it had been recognized, it wouldn't have caused wars."

"What problem?"

"That of pace-rate," said Leigh. "Previously it has never loomed large enough for us to see it as it really is. The difference between fast and slow was always sufficient to escape us." He pointed through the port at the reef of stars lying like sparkling dust against the darkness. "And now we know that out there is the same thing enormously magnified. We know that included among the numberless and everlasting problems of the cosmos is that of pace-rate boosted to formidable proportions."

Pascoe thought it over. "I'll give you that. I couldn't argue it because it has become self-evident. Sooner or later we'll encounter it again and again. It's bound to happen somewhere else eventually."

"Hence my heebies," said Leigh.

"You scare yourself to your heart's content," Pascoe advised. "I'm not worrying. It's no hair off my chest. Why should I care if some loony scout discovers lifeforms even slower than the Waitabits? They mean nothing whatever in my young life."

"Does he have to find them slower?" Leigh inquired.

Pascoe stared at him. "What are you getting at?"

"There's a pace-rate problem, as you've agreed. Turn it upside down and take another look at it. What's going to happen if we come up against a lifeform twenty times faster than ourselves? A lifeform that views us much as we viewed the Waitabits?"

Giving it a couple of minutes, Pascoe wiped his forehead and said, unconvincingly, "Impossible!"

"Is it? Why?"

"Because we'd have met them long before now. They'd have got to us first."

"What if they've a hundred times farther to come? Or if they're a young species one-tenth our age but already nearly level with us?"

"Look here," said Pascoe, taking on the same expression as the other had worn for weeks, "there are troubles enough without you going out of your way to invent more."

Nevertheless, when the ship landed he was still mulling every possible aspect of the matter and liking it less every minute.

A Sector Four official entered the cabin bearing a wad of documents. He was a plump specimen exuding artificial cordiality.

"Lieutenant Vaughan, at your service, Commodore" he enthused. "I trust you have had a pleasant and profitable run."

"It could have been worse," Leigh responded.

Radiating good will, Vaughan went on, "We've had a signal from Markham at Assignment Office on Terra. He wants you to check equipment, refuel and go take a look at Binty. I've brought the coordinates with me."

"What name?" interjected Pascoe.

"Binty."

"Heaven preserve us! Binty!" He sat down hard, stared at the wall. "Binty!" He played with his fingers, voiced it a third time. For some reason best known to himself he was hypnotized by Binty. Then in tones of deep suspicion he asked, "Who reported it?"

"Really, I don't know. But it ought to be here." Vaughan obligingly sought through his papers. "Yes, it does say. Fellow named Archibald Boydell."

"I knew it," yelped Pascoe. "I resign. I resign forthwith."

"You've resigned forthwith at least twenty times in the last eight years," Leigh reminded him. "It's getting monotonous."

"I mean it this time."

"You've said that, too." Leigh sighed, added, "And if you run true to form, you'll soon invite me to go to hell."

Pascoe waved his hands around. "Now try to calm yourself and look at this sensibly. What space-outfit which is sane would take off for a dump with a name like Binty?"

"We would," said Leigh. He waited for blood pressure to lower, then finished, "Wouldn't we?"

Slumping into his seat Pascoe glowered at him for five minutes before he said, "I suppose so. God help me, I must be weak." A little glassy-eyed, he shifted his attention to Vaughan. "Name it again in case I didn't hear right."

"Binty," said Vaughan, unctuously apologetic. "He has coded it 0-0.9-E5 which indicates the presence of an intelligent but backward lifeform."

"Does he make any remark about the place?"

"One word," informed Vaughan, consulting the papers again. "Ugh!"

Pascoe shuddered from head to feet.

The Man Who (Almost) Never Was

by Mike Resnick

He should have been a contender.

I mean, hell, he wrote *Sinister Barrier* and *Wasp* and the Jay Score stories, and he won a Hugo, and he was a major talent.

But he was a major talent who seems to have all but vanished from history

Take Tom Disch's 1998 critical look of the field, *The Dreams Our Stuff Is Made Of.* Check the index. You won't find a single mention of Eric Frank Russell.

Try Alex Panshin's 1990 Hugo winner, *The World Beyond the Hill.* It's probably the ultimate analysis of John Campbell's influence on the field—and Campbell was Russell's primary editor. 650 pages. One lone mention. Look at Dave Hartwell's brilliant *Age of Wonders,* which came out in 1984. Russell's name never appears. Or Don Wollheim's 1971 survey of the field, *The Universe Makers.* No mention of Russell. Let's go back to 1953, and L. Sprague de Camp's *Science-Fiction Handbook.* Two mentions and a footnote.

Okay, so much for the historians. Let's try the critics. And to make sure we're not choosing loaded examples, let's try the two major critics who were his contemporaries, Damon Knight and James Blish.

In Knight's *In Search of Wonder* (3rd edition, just under 400 pages), there are three mentions of Russell's name. In Blish's *The Issue at Hand,* there are two mentions and a footnote. In his *More Issues at Hand,* three more mentions. No mention at all in *The Tale That Wags the God.*

But these books were all by Americans. What about his own countrymen?

In Brian Aldiss's *Billion Year Spree,* Russell gets four brief mentions and a footnote.

What the hell is going on here? Are we misremembering the man's career? Wasn't he one of the giants—maybe not as tall as Heinlein and Clarke and Asimov and Bradbury, but a giant nonetheless?

Let's see if we can figure out what happened.

1. He wrote his best book for the wrong audience.

The book, of course, was *Wasp*. It is a brilliantly-conceived interstellar espionage novel, based on a perfectly valid premise: a car carrying four grown men, each physically robust, goes off the road, killing them all. Why? Because a tiny wasp was in the car, and it either stung or otherwise distracted the driver enough to take his attention off his driving.

The hero's assignment? Go to the enemy planet, where he happens to speak the language like a native, disguise himself (or, better still, prepare a number of disguises), and become a wasp. Distract them. Make entire regiments that could be fighting against the Good Guys search for him instead.

So what was wrong with that? Nothing. But he wrote it for a science fiction audience, which then numbered perhaps one thousand buyers of hardcovers.

Set that same story, scene for scene, action for action, in Nazi Germany, and he'd have had an international bestseller and been acclaimed the next Eric Ambler.

Okay. So what else happened?

2. He won his Hugo for the wrong story.

Russell won the Hugo in 1955, the second year it was presented. It didn't have quite the clout and cachet then as it does now—in fact, it had so little that they didn't even give the Hugos out in 1954—and the winning story, "Allamagoosa", while a delightful piece of fluff, is unquestionably the slightest story ever to win a Hugo.

No, it's not Russell's fault, and surely no one would have expected him to turn it down—but because Hugo winners tend to get noticed and anthologized, and because Isaac Asimov edited the first book of Hugo winners (which remained in print for years), "Allamagoosa" has become Russell's most famous story, dwarfing such stellar pieces as "Dear Devil" and "Late Night Final". People tend to take one look and conclude: "Lightweight."

3. His most famous book is his clumsiest.

Everybody knows the story of *Sinister Barrier*. It crossed John Campbell's desk, he loved it, wanted to buy it, but realized that it didn't fit the format he had created for *Astounding*, so he created *Unknown*, arguably the greatest fantasy magazine of all time, just to accommodate Russell's novel.

Not true, of course, but enough people believe it (including a number of the field's historians) that *Sinister Barrier* has become Russell's most famous novel, always mentioned in the same breath with the fabled *Unknown*. It's a pity, too, because Russell was just learning how to write novels at the time, and *Sinister Barrier*, though oft-reprinted, simply doesn't hold up today. The writing is amateurish and clumsy, but this is the novel people go to when they want to find out what Eric Frank Russell is all about. Another example of science fiction being judged by its worst examples, as Theodore Sturgeon was wont to say.

4. He quit his most popular character after only one book.

This is the era of the series. A generation of readers raised on television craves the comfort of meeting the same unchanging characters book after book, in generic adventure after generic adventure. Once in a while an author of genius can come up with a truly unique and quality-laden trilogy or tetralogy—Kim Stanley Robinson's Mars trilogy, Gene Wolfe's *Book of the New Sun*, and George Alec Effinger's Marid novels come immediately to mind—but brilliant or mundane, what today's reader wants is a continuing hero in a continuing story.

Russell's only continuing hero is Jay Score, the robot. And he stars in four pretty good stories. But each story is a novelette, and together they form only one novel. Just about the time the series-loving reader—who, alas, represents the science fiction readership today—is ready to read more Jay Score books, there's aren't any.

And it's not enough to say that series have only become popular lately—not when Edgar Rice Burroughs paved the way with ten Martian novels, and contemporaries such as Isaac Asimov and Fritz Leiber were turning out the Foundation trilogy and the Gray Mouser tales at the same time Russell was creating Jay Score.

5. He can't stay in print.

According to *Locus*, there are about 1,700 science fiction and related books published every year. The dead author who stays in print with the mass market publishers must be one whose reputation can turn over his readership every three or four years, always producing new ones to take the departing ones' places.

Who stays in print? Authors as varied as Robert A. Heinlein and Edgar Rice Burroughs. What they have in common, of course, is that they were both more popular than Russell in life, and are still more popular than him now that all three are dead.

6. No specialty publisher has fallen in love with him—prior to this book, anyway.

If you are not going to be a mass market superstar, then the only way to remain constantly in print and available to readers is to be adopted by a science fiction specialty publisher. Take a look at what Underwood-Miller did for Jack Vance, or what a handful of small publishers are doing for R. A. Lafferty.

Russell, to remain in print in this day and age, needs a dedicated specialty publisher. Unfortunately, no specialty house has yet stepped forward.

7. He's wrong about what's important.

In an introduction Alan Dean Foster wrote for another book by Russell, he quotes him as saying that it was getting harder and harder to come by really good, saleable ideas, but that most of the stuff he'd picked lately up was about people rather than ideas—and that left him cold. He was not happy the way several practitioners of science fiction dwelt on character rather than ideas.

He was wrong, of course. Most of the rules for general fiction, evolved over the centuries, make it clear that if the reader doesn't feel something, doesn't react with a sense of empathy or sympathy, the writer has either lost his audience or soon will.

There are no Ahabs or Hamlets in Russell's work, no Zorbas or Yossarians. His most memorable characters are a robot (Jay Score) and an alien (Dear Devil), just as Asimov's are a robot (R. Daneel Olivaw) and a mutant (the Mule). That Asimov is more popular than Russell is perhaps a quirk of fate, aided by seamless if not always soaring prose; that both of them would have been better (and Russell more popular) had they created truly memorable, three-dimensional characters is no longer even arguable.

So where *does* Russell stand in the ranks of science fiction?

A cut below the top rank, but far higher than his prolonged absence from the stands and the stores would lead you to believe.

Acknowledgments

The following people helped produce this book. The list is long. *Dirac Angestun Gesept.*

Technical help was provided by Mark L. Olson, Tony Lewis, Tim Szczesuil, Deb Geisler, Mike Benveniste, Mark Hertel, Ted Atwood, Dave Anderson, and Alice Lewis.

Proofreading was done by Ann Broomhead, Tim Szczesuil, Dave Anderson, Tony Lewis, Bonnie Atwood, Joe Rico, Mark Hertel, Michael A. Burstein, Nomi Burstein, Gay Ellen Dennett, George Flynn, Pam Fremon, Lisa Hertel, Suford Lewis, Mark L. Olson, Priscilla Olson, Kelly S. Persons, and Sharon Sbarsky.

The dust jacket design was created by Alice Lewis.

Copy editing was done by Sara Schwager.

The book was set in Adobe Garamond using Adobe Pagemaker and printed by Sheridan Books of Ann Arbor, Michigan, on acid-free paper.

Rick Katze
July, 2000